An
Elm Creek Quilts Sampler

The First Three Novels in the Popular Series

Jennifer Chiaverini

Simon & Schuster
NEW YORK LONDON TORONTO SYDNEY

Simon & Schuster
Rockefeller Center
1230 Avenue of the Americas
New York, NY 10020

First Simon & Schuster edition 2003

SIMON & SCHUSTER and colophon are registered trademarks
of Simon & Schuster, Inc.

For information regarding special discounts for bulk purchases,
please contact Simon & Schuster Special Sales at 1-800-456-6798 or
business@simonandschuster.com

Manufactured in the United States of America

10 9

Library of Congress Cataloging-in-Publication Data
Chiaverini, Jennifer.
An Elm Creek quilts sampler : the first three novels in the popular series /
Jennifer Chiaverini.
p.cm.
Contents: The quilter's apprentice—Round robin—The cross-country
quilters.
1. Domestic fiction, American. 2. Compson, Sylvia (Fictitious character)—
Fiction. 3. Female friendship—Fiction. 4. Quiltmakers—Fiction. 5.
Quilting—Fiction. I. Chiaverini, Jennifer. Quilter's apprentice. II. Chiaverini,
Jennifer. Round robin. III. Chiaverini, Jennifer. Cross-country quilters.
IV. Title.
PS3553.H473A6 2003   813'.54—dc22   2003059192
ISBN-13: 978-0-7432-6018-3
ISBN-10:   0-7432-6018-X

These titles were originally published individually by Simon & Schuster, Inc.

Plan of Elm Creek Manor by Nic Neidenbach

Contents

Elm Creek Manor

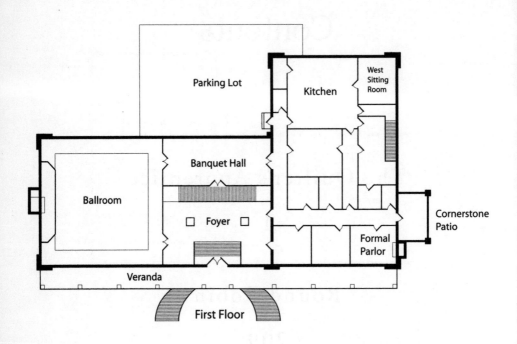

First Floor

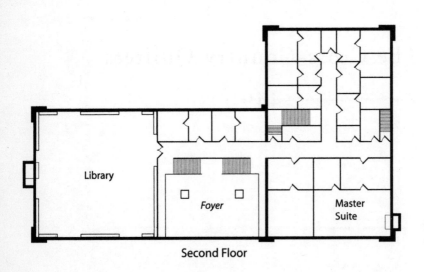

Second Floor

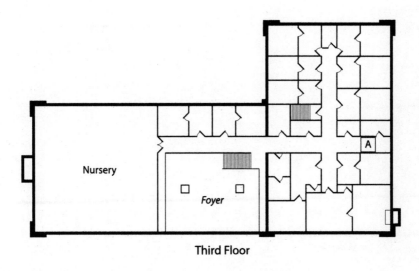

Nursery

Foyer

Third Floor

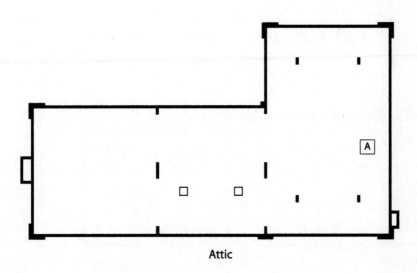

A

Attic

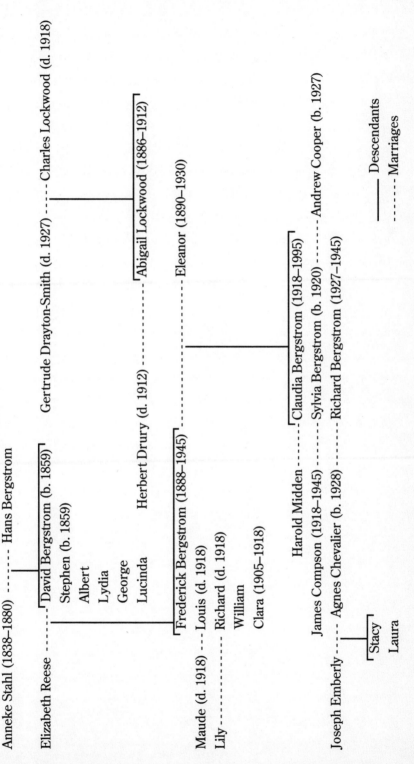

Gerda Bergstrom (b. 1831)
other unnamed siblings ------- Hans Bergstrom

Anneke Stahl (1838–1880) ------- Hans Bergstrom

Elizabeth Reese ------- David Bergstrom (b. 1859)

Gertrude Drayton-Smith (d. 1927) ----- Charles Lockwood (d. 1918)

Stephen (b. 1859)
Albert
Lydia
George
Lucinda

Herbert Drury (d. 1912) ------- Abigail Lockwood (1886–1912)

Eleanor (1890–1930)

Frederick Bergstrom (1888–1945)

Claudia Bergstrom (1918–1995) ------- Andrew Cooper (b. 1927)

Harold Midden ------- Sylvia Bergstrom (b. 1920)

Maude (d. 1918) --- Louis (d. 1918)

James Compson (1918–1945) ------- Richard Bergstrom (1927–1945)

Lily ------- Richard (d. 1918)

Joseph Emberly ----- Agnes Chevalier (b. 1928)

William

Clara (1905–1918)

Stacy
Laura

———— Descendants
- - - - Marriages

THE
Quilter's
Apprentice

ACKNOWLEDGMENTS

I am deeply grateful to the many people who have made this book possible:

My editor, Laurie Chittenden, for opening her heart to this story and helping to make it even better; and my agent, Maria Massie, for her help and advice.

The members of QuiltNet, for their friendship and generosity.

My teachers, especially Percival Everett and James Walton, who told me I could do this.

The members of the Internet Writing Workshop, especially Lani Kraus, list owner, who supervises a wonderful forum for aspiring writers; Dave Swinford, administrator of the novels list and one of the nicest people on the net; Jody Ewing, for her kindness; and Candace Byers, Warren Richardson, and Lesli Richardson for their critiques.

My friend Christine Johnson, who read every chapter and never failed to encourage me when I needed it most.

Geraldine, Nic, and Heather Neidenbach; Virginia and Edward Riechman; and Leonard and Marlene Chiaverini, for their love and support.

And most of all, to my husband, Marty, for everything.

For Geraldine Neidenbach
and Martin Chiaverini
with all my love

One

Sarah leaned against the brick wall and tried to look comfortable, hoping no one walking by would notice her or wonder why she was standing around in a suit on such a hot day. She shaded her eyes with her hand and scanned the street for Matt's truck—their truck—but she didn't expect to see it. He wasn't late; she was early. This interview had been her shortest one yet.

A drop of perspiration trickled down between her shoulder blades to the small of her back where her silk blouse was tucked into her navy skirt. She removed her suit jacket and folded it over her arm, but she knew she wouldn't feel comfortable until she was back in her customary T-shirt and shorts. A barrette held her hair away from her face, and the back of her neck sweltered beneath the thick, brown waves. The people who slowly passed on their way to jobs, shopping, or summer classes at nearby Waterford College looked as uncomfortable and as drained by the humidity as Sarah felt. In a few months, she knew, she'd be griping about the snow like everyone else in central Pennsylvania, but today she longed for autumn.

The handle of her briefcase began to dig into her palm. As she shifted it to her other hand, she glanced at the revolving door half a block away. With her luck, some of the interviewers would leave early for lunch and spot her lingering there. They'd probably urge her to wait inside in the air-conditioning, and then she'd have to figure out some polite way to refuse. That, or slink back inside like a reprimanded child. The thought of it made her shrink back against the wall.

Two staccato beeps of the horn sounded before Sarah saw the red truck pull up and park along the opposite curb. She pushed herself away from the wall and hurried across the street.

"How'd it go?" Matt asked as she slid into the passenger's seat.

"Don't ask."

Though she had tried to keep her voice light, Matt's face fell. He started the truck, then reached over and patted her knee. "I guess you already know how sorry I am about all this."

"Sorry about what? You're early."

"You know what. Don't pretend you didn't understand. If not for me and my job, we never would've moved here."

"It's not like you dragged me here by my hair." Sarah closed her eyes and sank back into her seat. "It's not your fault I don't have a clue how to make it through a job interview without sounding like an idiot."

"You're not an idiot."

"And you're not responsible for my unemployment."

"Well, I feel bad anyway," he responded as he pulled into traffic. "I mean it, Sarah. I'm really sorry."

Of course he felt sorry. So did she, but feeling sorry didn't make her any less unemployed. Apparently, neither did working her tail off to graduate with a great GPA and sacrificing every other available moment to part-time jobs and internships to gain work experience. Even the years she had invested in her last job apparently did her more harm than good. Potential employers took one look at her résumé, noted all the accounting experience, and refused to consider her for any other kind of work.

Sometimes Sarah thought back to those first years after college and wondered how she and Matt ever could have been so hopeful, so optimistic. Of course, their prospects had seemed brighter then, colored by newlywed joy and professional naïveté. Then the newness faded from her job as a cost accountant for a local convenience store chain, and the days began to follow each other in an unrelenting cycle of tedium. Matt enjoyed his job working on the Penn State campus, but just after he had been promoted to shift supervisor, the state legislature slashed the university's budget. College officials decided that they could do without new landscaping more easily than library books and faculty salaries, so Matt and many of his coworkers found themselves out of work.

They soon learned that open positions were hard to come by in a medium-sized college town in the middle of Pennsylvania. Matt couldn't find anything permanent, only occasional landscaping jobs for some of his former agricultural science professors. One by one, his former coworkers found jobs in other towns, sometimes in other states. But Matt was determined to find something in State College, the town where he and Sarah had met, where they had married, and where one day they hoped to raise children.

Eventually even Matt's natural optimism waned, and he grew more discouraged every month. Soon Sarah found herself slinking off to work every morning, wondering if she should be doing something more to help him find a job and fearing that if she did get more involved he'd think she doubted his ability to find a job on his own.

As time passed, the sharpness of her worries dulled, but they never completely faded. Matt made the best of the part-time work he managed to find, and Sarah was proud of him for it. She watched him persevere and tried not to complain too much about the drudgery of her own job. Instead, year after year, she put in her hours and collected her paychecks, and thanked her boss for her annual bonuses. She knew she should be grateful, but in her heart she felt something was missing.

One December, as she and Matt decorated their Christmas tree, Sarah counted the number of Christmases they had spent in that apartment.

"Has it been that many?" Matt asked. His eyes grew sad. "I thought we'd have a house of our own by now."

Sarah placed another ornament on a high branch and thought quickly. "Lots of people wait much longer than this before they buy a house. Besides, I like it here."

"So many years in this apartment, and too much of that time without steady work."

"So many years of bean counting. It's amazing my brain hasn't melted into mush."

Matt tried to grin. "Maybe we're just having a midlife crisis."

"Speak for yourself. I don't think I've hit midlife just yet."

"You know what I mean. Wouldn't it be nice to get a fresh start, knowing now what we didn't know then?"

She reached out for his hand and squeezed it to show him she understood.

A few weeks later, a group of their friends gathered at their tiny apartment on College Avenue to welcome the New Year. They spent the day watching bowl games and proclaiming the superiority of the Nittany Lions, and in the last half hour before midnight they watched the ball drop in Times Square on television and took turns announcing their New Year's resolutions. Everyone burst out laughing when Sarah resolved to take the CPA exam so she could go into business for herself. They quite rightly noted that a CPA's life wasn't much of a departure from the work she already knew and despised. She saw their point, but any change, however slight, would be a relief.

Then Matt stood up and announced his resolution: to find a permanent job even if it meant leaving State College.

Sarah raised her eyebrows at him, a silent message he immediately understood. He quickly added, "As long as that's okay with you, honey. As long as you don't mind moving."

"I'd rather not, if you want to know the truth."

"But we both want a fresh start. You've said so."

"I think it's time to cut you off." She smiled to soften her words as she took the beer can from his hand. It wasn't his resolution that troubled her so much as the way he had presented it, springing something that big on her so unexpectedly—and in front of an audience. Matt was methodical and patient, never one for surprises. It wasn't like him to make decisions that affected them both without talking to her first.

She waited until the guests had left and the mess from the party had been cleared away. Then she cornered him in the bathroom as he brushed his teeth. "Do you think you could warn me next time before you make major life decisions for us, especially if you're going to do it in front of all our friends?"

Matt spat out his toothpaste. "I'm sorry, Sarah. I spoke without think-ing." He rinsed his mouth and spat again. "Actually, that's not entirely true. I've been thinking about this a lot."

"About moving?"

"About getting a fresh start somewhere else. Come on, Sarah. You hate your job; I can't find one. It couldn't be any worse in a new place, and I'm willing to risk that it would be even better." He studied her for a moment. "Are you willing to risk that?"

Sarah watched him, and thought about how long he had been looking for permanent employment, how he sometimes scraped together a full day's work out of a few odd jobs, and how her own career bored her so senseless that she hated to get up in the morning.

"I'll sleep on it," she said.

In the morning she told him she was ready to risk it, too.

A few weeks later, Matt finally landed a job—a job in a town more than two hours' drive away. Sarah celebrated with him and tried not to be too dis-mayed when he described Waterford, an even smaller college town in an even more remote location in Pennsylvania with an even tighter job market than State College. But how could she refuse when Matt was so elated at the chance to work again? And how could she not side with Matt after her mother had shrieked into the phone, "You mean you're giving up your pro-fessional job to go with that—that—that gardener?"

Sarah had curtly reminded her mother that "that gardener" was her hus-band and that he had a bachelor of science degree in landscape architecture, and added that if her mother didn't approve Sarah wouldn't bother to leave a forwarding address. Her mother had never understood about Matt, had never tried to understand. She just set her mouth in a prim line and refused to see what Sarah saw, that Matt was an intelligent, thoughtful, caring man with a good heart and a love for earth and rain and all growing things. If

Sarah's mother wailed and moaned to think that her daughter was yoking herself to a country bumpkin, she had it all wrong.

Sarah reached over and stroked Matt's curly hair. From April through October he had sun-streaked blond hair and a perpetually sunburned nose. "It's only been eight weeks. I didn't expect to find something as soon as we rode into town. That's not realistic."

Matt glanced at her before returning his gaze to the road. "I know you said not to ask, but how did it go?"

"Same old thing," Sarah grumbled. "The more I talked, the more his eyes glazed over. And then he said, 'Frankly, we're looking for someone who conforms better to our company persona.' And then a smile and a handshake and he was showing me the door."

"What's a 'company persona'?"

"I think he meant I wouldn't fit in."

"They usually at least think about it for a day or two before rejecting someone."

"Thanks, sweetheart. Now, which part of that remark was supposed to make me feel better?"

"You know what I mean." Matt gave her an apologetic look. "Did you tell them that you don't want to work in accounting anymore?"

"Yeah, but that didn't help. I feel like I've been typecast."

"Well, don't give up, honey. Something will come along."

"Yeah." Sarah didn't allow herself to say anything more because she wasn't sure she'd be able to keep the sarcasm out of her voice. Something will come along. That's what she had told Matt at least once a week while he was unemployed, and he'd never believed it. But now that he was the one repeating the refrain, it took on the status of gospel. She loved Matt, but sometimes he drove her nuts.

Matt signaled for a left turn and pulled off the main street onto a gravel road. "I hope you don't mind a detour."

"Where are we going?" Sarah asked as the truck jolted unsteadily down the narrow road, leaving a cloud of dust behind it.

"A new client stopped by the office yesterday to set up a contract. She brought a few photos of her house, but I need to take a look at the grounds myself before Tony can finalize the agreement. It's just a little place, just some lady's little cottage. I thought maybe you could help me find it."

"Fine by me. I'm not in any hurry." It wasn't as if she had anywhere to go. She looked around but saw no houses, only farmers' fields already knee-high with pale green cornstalks, and beyond them the darker green of rolling hills covered with trees.

The road forked ahead, and Matt turned the truck onto an even narrower road that arced sharply to the left into a thick forest. "See that road?" Matt asked, jerking a thumb over his shoulder at the fork they had not taken. "That leads right up to the front of the house, or it would if the bridge over Elm Creek wasn't out. The lady who owns the place warned us to use the back way. She said she's tired of having people complain about having to hike into town to call a tow truck."

Sarah smiled weakly and clutched at her seat as the truck bounded jerkily up a gradual incline. Pennsylvania roads were infamous for their potholes, but this drive seemed worse than most. As the grade became steeper, Sarah hoped that no one was approaching them from the opposite direction. She doubted that both cars could stay on the road without one of them scraping a side on a tree. Or worse.

Suddenly the forest gave way to a clearing. Before them stood a two-story red barn built into the side of a hill. The road, now little more than two dirt trails an axle's width apart surrounded by overgrown grass, climbed away from them up the hill and disappeared behind the barn. Matt shifted gears and followed.

Just beyond the barn, the path crossed a low bridge and then widened into a tree-lined gravel road. "Elms," Matt noted. "They look healthy, but I'll have to check. The house should be around here somewhere."

Sarah glimpsed something through the trees. "There. I see it." And then, as they approached and she was able to see more, her eyes widened. Matt's description hadn't prepared her for anything this grand. The gray stone mansion was three stories tall and L-shaped, with Tudor woodwork along the eaves and black shutters bordering each of the many windows. The shorter branch of the L pointed west, toward them, and the other wing stretched to the south. Where the two wings met there were four stone stairs leading to a door.

"You call this 'some lady's little cottage,' Matt?"

The truck slowed as they pulled into a gravel driveway encircling two enormous elm trees. Matt stopped the truck and grinned at Sarah as he put on the parking brake. "What do you think? Pretty impressive, huh?"

"That's an understatement." Sarah left the car and shut the door behind her without taking her eyes from the mansion. A twinge of envy pricked her conscience, and she hastily buried it.

"I thought you'd like it." He came around the truck to join her. "Tony was lucky to get her as a client. I can't wait to get a look at the rest of the grounds."

They climbed the steps and knocked on the door. Sarah closed her eyes and savored the breeze while they waited. Despite the bright afternoon sun, it felt at least ten degrees cooler there than in town.

After a few moments Matt knocked again. "Maybe nobody's home."

"Did they know you were coming?"

"Tony told me he made an appointment for today. I usually call to confirm, but they don't have a phone here." He raised his hand to knock a third time.

Suddenly the door swung open. Hastily, Matt dropped his hand to his side as a woman who looked to be in her mid-seventies wearing a light blue dress appeared in the doorway. She was taller than Sarah, and more slender, with silver-gray hair parted on the right and blunt cut a few inches below her chin. The only softness to her face was in the gentle sagging of skin along her jaw and in the feathery lines etched around her eyes and mouth. Something in her bearing suggested that she was used to being obeyed, and for a moment Sarah wondered if she ought to curtsy. Whoever the old woman was, she fit the proud old manor as surely as Matt fit his sturdy, reliable pickup, as surely as Sarah herself fit—what? She couldn't think of any way to finish the thought, and she wished she could.

The woman put on a pair of glasses that hung around her neck on a fine silver chain. "Yes?" she asked, frowning as if she wasn't sure she liked what she saw.

"How do you do, ma'am. I'm Matt McClure from Exterior Architects. I have an appointment to photograph the grounds for the restoration you requested."

"Hmph." The suspicious gaze shifted to Sarah. "And who are you?"

"Oh, I'm—uh, Sarah. I'm Matt's wife. I'm just here with Matt." She gave the woman a quick smile and extended her hand.

The woman paused a moment, then shook her hand. "Well, you probably know that I'm Sylvia Compson. You may call me Mrs. Compson." She looked Matt up and down and frowned. "I expected you earlier." She turned and walked into the foyer. "Well, come on, Matt and 'Uh, Sarah.' Come on inside. Shut the door behind you."

Sarah and Matt exchanged a quick look, then followed Mrs. Compson inside. She entered a doorway on the left and led them into a spacious kitchen. The left wall was lined with cupboards and appliances, and there was a window over the sink. A microwave oven rested incongruously on a counter next to a rickety old stove directly across from them. There was an open doorway on the other side of the stove, and a closed door on the adjacent wall. A long wooden table took up the center of the room. Mrs. Compson eased herself onto a low bench next to the table and regarded them for a moment. "Would you like a glass of lemonade, or perhaps some iced tea?" she finally asked, directing the question to Matt.

"No thank you, ma'am. I just need you to show me the grounds so I can take a few pictures, and then we'll be on our way."

Her eyes still on Matt, Mrs. Compson jerked her head in Sarah's direction. "What about her? Maybe she wants something."

"A glass of lemonade would be wonderful," Sarah said. "Thank you. I've been standing outside downtown and—"

"There are glasses in the cupboard and a pitcher of lemonade in the icebox. Don't expect me to wait on you."

Sarah blinked. "Thanks. I'll just help myself." She gave the woman a tight smile and walked around the table toward the cupboard.

"And now I suppose we'll all have to wait around while you sip your beverage, even though you've come here later than your appointment and you've already kept me from my work long enough."

Sarah stiffened. "If it's that much trouble—"

"Mrs. Compson," Matt broke in, shooting Sarah a helpless look over the old woman's shoulder. "Tony made the appointment for two. We're five minutes early."

"Hmph. Ten minutes early is 'on time' and fifteen minutes is 'early,' if one cares about one's first impression. Now, is she going to get on with that drink or will she stand there gaping at me until she puts down roots?"

"Mrs. Compson—"

"Don't worry about it, Matt," Sarah interrupted, hoping she was meeting Mrs. Compson's stern gaze with one equally strong. "I'll wait for you here." A beautiful estate to explore, and to keep Matt's client happy Sarah would see no more of it than this one room. Still, she'd rather have a glass of lemonade than another moment of Mrs. Compson's company.

Mrs. Compson nodded, satisfied. "Come on," she said to Matt, rising stiffly from the bench. "I'll show you the front grounds." She left the kitchen without a backward glance.

Astonished, Sarah caught Matt's sleeve as he turned to go. "What did I do?" she asked, whispering so that the old woman wouldn't overhear.

"You didn't do anything wrong. I don't know what her problem is." He glanced at the doorway and shook his head in exasperation. "Look, why don't I take you home? I can come back for the pictures another time."

"No, that's okay. That would just make things worse. I don't want you to get in trouble."

"I won't get in trouble."

"It's all right. I don't mind waiting here. Really."

"Well, if you're sure . . ." Matt still looked doubtful, but he nodded. "Okay. But I'll be as quick as I can so we can get out of here." He gave her a quick kiss and a reassuring smile before hurrying out of the kitchen after Mrs. Compson.

Sarah watched him go, then sighed and opened the cupboard doors in search of the glasses. She wondered why the woman had even offered the drink in the first place, if it were so much trouble. She found a glass, and as she shut the cupboard, she glanced out the window and spotted the truck. She considered waiting there until Matt finished, but then the old woman might think she'd scared her off, and Sarah wasn't about to give her the satisfaction.

The refrigerator stood next to the closed door. After pouring herself some lemonade and returning the pitcher, Sarah sat down on the bench and rested her elbows on the table. She sipped the cool, sweet liquid and looked around the room. Matt might not finish for an hour, maybe more. Her gaze rested on the closed door next to the refrigerator.

Curious, Sarah rose and shifted the glass to her left hand. She wiped the condensation off her right hand and tested the doorknob. Finding it unlocked, she opened the door and peered inside to find a tiny room. It was a pantry, apparently, judging by the shelves filled with canned fruits and vegetables and cloth sacks whose contents she could not determine. She closed the door and, after a quick glance in the direction the old woman had taken, stepped through the open doorway to the left.

She found herself in a sunny, pleasant sitting room, larger and wider than the kitchen, with overstuffed furniture arranged by the windows and the fireplace. Cheerful watercolors hung on the walls, and a small sewing machine sat on a nearby table. A chair stood nearby as if someone had been sitting there recently. Two pillows and a small stack of neatly folded sheets rested on the largest sofa, right next to—

Sarah caught her breath and walked over for a better look. She unfolded the blanket with one hand and draped it over the sofa. *Not a blanket, a quilt,* she corrected herself, stroking the fabric. Small diamonds of all shades of blue, purple, and green formed eight-pointed stars on a soft ivory background. Tiny stitches formed smaller diamonds within each colorful piece, and the lighter fabric was covered with a flowing, feathery pattern, all made from unbelievably small, even stitches. A narrow vine of deep emerald-green meandered around the edges. "How lovely," Sarah whispered, lifting an edge up to the light to better examine it.

"If you spill lemonade on that quilt I promise you you'll wish you hadn't," a voice snapped behind her. With a gasp Sarah dropped the quilt and spun around. Mrs. Compson stood scowling in the doorway, her hands on her hips.

"Mrs. Compson—I thought you were with Matt—"

"I don't remember inviting you in here," the older woman interrupted. Sarah jumped aside as Mrs. Compson strode to the fallen quilt and slowly bent to pick it up. She straightened with an effort, folded the quilt carefully, and returned it to the sofa. "You may wait for your husband outside," she said over her shoulder. "That is, if you can be trusted to find your way to the back door without wandering about?"

Wordlessly, Sarah nodded. She left her glass in the kitchen sink and hurried across the hall. *Idiot,* she berated herself as she pushed open the back door. Flying down the back steps, she walked as quickly as her heels would allow to the pickup. She climbed into the passenger seat, rested her elbow on the open window, and chewed on her thumbnail. Was Mrs. Compson angry enough to cancel the contract? If Matt lost his new job because Sarah had offended one of his company's clients, she'd never forgive herself.

Thirty minutes later Matt appeared from around the south wing. Sarah watched as he walked over to the back door and knocked. The door swung open almost immediately, but from the truck Sarah could not see inside the house. She fidgeted in her seat as Matt and the unseen old woman conversed. Finally, Matt nodded and raised his hand in farewell. The door closed, and Matt walked down the steps, back to the truck.

Sarah tried to read his expression as he climbed into the cab. "I thought you were going to wait inside, honey. What are you doing out here?" he asked with a cheerful grin, then continued without waiting for an answer. "You should've seen the grounds."

"I wanted to," Sarah mumbled.

If Matt heard, he was too caught up in his enthusiasm to think of a response. Instead, as they drove back to town he described the sweeping front lawn, the gardens gone wild, the orchard, and the creek that ran through the estate grounds. Ordinarily, Sarah would have been intrigued, but now she was too worried about what he would say when she told him she had been snooping about in his client's home.

She waited until after dinner, when the anxiety finally became too much. "Matt," she ventured as she stacked plates in the dishwasher. "What were you and Mrs. Compson talking about right before we left?"

Matt rinsed their knives and forks and turned off the tap. "Nothing important," he said, placing the utensils in the silverware basket. "She wanted to know what I thought of the north gardens, and she said she'd see me tomorrow."

"So she didn't cancel the contract?"

"No. Why would she do that?"

Sarah hesitated. "Well, actually, I was kind of poking around her house and she caught me."

He looked wary. "Poking around?"

"It's not as bad as it sounds. I went into her sitting room and touched a quilt. She got all mad about it." Sarah couldn't look at him. "I was afraid she'd switch to another landscaper."

Matt chuckled and turned on the dishwasher. "You worry too much. She didn't cancel the contract." He held out his arms for her.

She slipped into his embrace and sighed with relief. "I guess I should've stayed in the kitchen, but I was bored. I wanted to see something of the house, since I didn't get to see the grounds."

"I'll be there all summer. I'll show you around some other time."

"As long as Mrs. Compson doesn't find out." Sarah was in no hurry to see her again. "Tell me, Matt, how come this rude old lady gets a beautiful mansion and the lovely quilt and the gardens while a nice couple like us only gets half of a run-down duplex? It's not fair."

Matt pulled away and studied her expression. "I can't tell if you're joking or not. Would you really want to be like her, living all alone in that big place with no family or even a dog to keep you company?"

"Of course not. Obviously the place hasn't made her happy. I'd rather be with you in a tiny little shack than alone in the biggest mansion in the world. You know that."

"That's what I thought." He held her tightly.

Sarah hugged him—and wanted to kick herself. How much longer would it be before she learned to consider her words before blurting them out? The same habit hurt her in job interviews, and if she didn't overcome it soon, that hypothetical little shack might be their next address.

Two

The next morning Sarah sat at the breakfast table leafing through the newspaper and wishing that, like Matt, she needed to get ready for work. She heard him moving about upstairs, and from the noises coming through the wall she knew that some of the six undergraduates who rented the other half of the duplex were also preparing for the day. Each morning it seemed as if everyone but Sarah had a place to go, a place with people who needed them.

"So instead you'll sit here and whine. That'll help," she muttered. She sipped her coffee and turned the page, though she hadn't read a word on it. Someone next door turned on the stereo, loud enough for the bass line to throb annoyingly at the edges of her perception but not so loud that Sarah could justify pounding on the wall. She knew from experience that the low drone would go on hiatus at noon, then resume somewhere between six-thirty and seven in the evening and persist until midnight. Sometimes the pattern varied on weekends, but not by much.

The noise probably wouldn't have bothered her if she weren't already in such a foul mood. Unemployment had stopped feeling like a vacation more than a month earlier, ever since she realized that few of the *Waterford Register's* Help Wanted ads even remotely applied to her. And after eight weeks of unemployment, four unremarkable interviews, and more unanswered application letters than she could stomach, Sarah half feared she'd never work again.

Matt bounded down the stairs and into the room. He paused behind her chair to squeeze her shoulder before continuing on into the kitchen. "Anything?" he called over the sound of coffee pouring into his travel mug.

"I don't know. I haven't looked through the classifieds yet."

"You used to read that section first."

"I know. It's just that I found this really interesting article about—" She glanced at the largest headline on the page. "The Dairy Princess. They just picked a new one."

Matt appeared in the doorway and grinned. "You expect me to believe you're so interested in the new Dairy Queen that you forgot to look at the classifieds?"

"Not Dairy Queen, Dairy Princess." She folded the newspaper, rested her elbows on the table, and rubbed her eyes. "Dairy Queen's an ice cream parlor. A Dairy Princess is . . . well, I guess I don't know what a Dairy Princess is."

"Maybe you should call Her Majesty and see if she's hiring any account- ants to help her count cows."

"Gee, you're just bursting with humor today, aren't you?"

"Yep, that's me. Matt McClure, comedian." He reached over to stroke her shoulder. "Come on, Sarah. You know that if you keep looking, you'll definitely find a job you like. I'm not saying it'll be easy or quick, but it will happen."

"Maybe." Sarah wished she could be so sure.

Matt glanced at his watch. "Listen, I don't want to leave when you're feel- ing so bad—"

"Don't be silly." Sarah stood up and pushed in her chair. "I'm fine. If you took off work every time I got a little down pretty soon you'd be as unem- ployed as I am."

She followed him to the door and kissed him good-bye, watching through the screen until he drove away. Then she ordered herself to return to the table and the prematurely discarded newspaper. After fifteen minutes of scrutinizing the pages, she felt some hope rekindling. Two new ads announced positions requiring a bachelor's degree in a business or sales field. She carried the newspaper and a fresh cup of coffee upstairs to the small sec- ond bedroom they used as an office. Maybe she should adopt Matt's philos- ophy. Maybe all it took was hard work and a bit of luck. If she stuck with it, she'd surely find a good job sometime before she reached retirement age.

Her Job Hunt disk sat next to the computer, where she had left it the last time she worked on her résumé. She made a few revisions, printed out a cou- ple of copies, then showered and dressed. Within an hour she was waiting at the bus stop for a ride downtown.

Waterford, Pennsylvania, was a town of about 35,000 people, except when Waterford College was in session and the population rose by 15,000 young adults. The downtown bordered the campus, and, aside from a few city government offices, consisted mainly of bars, faddish restaurants, and shops catering to the students. The local residents knew they owed their livelihoods to the transient student population, and although they were grateful for the income, many resented the dependence. Sometimes the town's collective resentment erupted in a flurry of housing and noise ordinances, and the students would strike back with boycotts and sarcastic editorials in the school newspaper. Sarah wasn't sure which group she sided with. The students treated her like a suspicious member of the establishment, and the locals assumed she was a despicable student. She tried to compensate by being polite to everyone, even their rowdy neighbors and the occasional shopkeeper who eyed her as if she might make off with half of the inventory, but it didn't seem to help.

She got off at the stop closest to the post office, carrying her job application materials in her backpack. The day was humid and overcast. She scanned the gray clouds and quickened her pace. In the past few weeks she had learned the hard way that summer rainstorms in her new hometown were as brief and drenching as they were sudden. She would have to hurry if she wanted to stop at the market and catch the bus home without getting soaked.

The errand at the post office took only a few minutes, and after picking up some groceries, Sarah still had ten minutes until the next bus would arrive. She strolled down the street to the bus stop, window-shopping and listening for thunder.

When a patch of bright colors caught her eye, she stopped for a closer look. Her eyes widened in admiration as she studied the red-and-green quilt hanging in the shop window. Eight identical diamonds, each composed of sixteen smaller diamonds, formed a large, eight-pointed star. The arrangement of colors created the illusion that the star radiated outward from its center. Between the points of the star, tiny stitches created intricate wreaths in the background fabric. Something about the quilt seemed familiar, and then she remembered why; its pattern was similar to the quilt she had seen the day before in Mrs. Compson's sitting room.

Studying it, Sarah wished she knew how to make something so beautiful. She had always loved quilts, loved the feel of the fabric and the way a quilt could make color blossom over a bed or on a wall. She couldn't see a quilt without thinking of her grandmother and without feeling a painful blend of love and loss. When Sarah was a child, her family made the long drive to Grandma's small house in Michigan's Upper Peninsula only twice a year, once in summer and once at Christmas. The winter visits were best. They would bundle up on the sofa under two or three of Grandma's old quilts, munch cookies, sip hot chocolate, and watch through the window as snow blanketed the earth. Some of Grandma's creations still decorated Sarah's childhood home, but Sarah couldn't remember ever seeing her mother so much as touch a needle. If quiltmaking was a skill handed down from mother to daughter, her mother must have been the weak link in the chain. Grandma surely would have taught her if she had wanted to learn.

Sarah looked overhead for the sign bearing the shop's name, and laughed in surprise when she saw the words GRANDMA'S ATTIC printed in gold letters on a red background. She checked her watch, gave the bus stop one last quick glance, and entered the shop.

Shelves stacked high with bolts of fabric, thread, notions, and other gadgets lined the walls and covered most of the floor. Celtic folk music played in the background. In the middle of the room, several women stood chatting and laughing around a large cutting table. One looked up from the conversation to smile at her, and Sarah smiled back. She made her way around the checkout counter to the front window and discovered that the quilt was even more beautiful up close. She tried to estimate how the quilt would fit their bed.

"I see our Lone Star charmed another new visitor inside," a pleasant voice broke in on her thoughts. Sarah turned and found the woman who had smiled at her standing at her elbow. She looked to be in her mid-fifties, with dark, close-cropped hair, ruddy skin, and a friendly expression.

"Is that what it's called, a Lone Star? It's beautiful."

The woman casually brushed pieces of thread from her sleeve as she joined Sarah in admiring the quilt. "Oh, yes, it's lovely, isn't it? Wish I could take the credit, but one of our local quilt artists made it. It's queen-sized, entirely hand-quilted."

"How much do you want for it?"

"Seven hundred and fifty dollars."

"Thanks anyway," Sarah said, not entirely able to keep the disappointment out of her voice.

The woman smiled in sympathy. "I know—it's a lot, isn't it? Actually, though, if you took that price and calculated an hourly wage from it, you'd see that it's a bargain."

"I can believe that. It must've taken years to make."

"Most people stop by, hear the price, then head straight to some discount store for a cheap knockoff." The woman sighed and shook her head. "People who don't know quilts can't detect the obvious differences in quality of materials and workmanship. Mrs. Compson's lucky to get what she can for those she displays here."

"Mrs. Compson?"

"Yes, Sylvia Compson. She's been staying up at Elm Creek Manor since her sister died two months ago. Temperamental as hell—I had to install an awning outside before she'd agree to display her quilts in the window. She's right, of course. I'd hate to have one of her pieces fade from the sunlight. She has two quilts in the American Quilter's Society's permanent collection in Paducah."

"That's good, right?"

"Good? I'd be glad just to have something accepted in the AQS annual show." The woman chuckled. "I thought every quilter around here knew about Sylvia Compson."

"I've met Mrs. Compson, but I'm not a quilter. I do love quilts, though."

"Is that so? You should learn how to quilt, then."

"Watch out, everyone, Bonnie's about to make another convert," one of the women called out from the cutting table.

"Run for it, honey," another warned, and they all burst out laughing.

Bonnie joined in. "Okay, I admit I have a vested interest. Satisfied?" She pretended to glower at the others before turning back to Sarah. "We do offer lessons, um . . . ?"

"Sarah. Are you the Grandma from the sign?"

"Oh, no," Bonnie said, laughing. "Not yet at least, thank God, although I do get asked that a lot. There's no Grandma. There's no attic, either. I just liked the name. Kind of homey, don't you think? As you already heard, my name's Bonnie, and these are some of my friends, the Tangled Web Quilters. We're sort of a renegade group separate from the local Waterford Quilting Guild. We take our quilting—and ourselves—very seriously." Her tone suggested that the remark was only half true. She handed Sarah a photocopied calendar. "Here's a schedule if you're interested in the lessons. Is there anything else I can help you with?"

Sarah shook her head.

"Well, thanks for stopping by. Come back anytime. Now, if you'll excuse me, I need to get back to that crowd before Diane hides my rotary cutter again." She smiled and returned to the cutting table.

"Thanks," Sarah answered, folding up the paper and tucking it into her backpack. She left the store, ran half a block to the bus stop, and climbed on the bus just as heavy drops of rain began to pelt the sidewalk.

Three

S arah's heart leaped when she returned home to find the answering machine's light blinking. A message. Maybe Waterford College had called about that admissions counselor job. She let her packages fall to the floor and scrambled for the button. Or maybe it was from Penn-Cellular Corporation. That would be even better.

"Hi, Sarah. It's me."

Matt.

"I'm calling from the office, but I was up at Elm Creek Manor this morning, and—well, I guess it can wait until I get home. Hope you don't have any plans for tomorrow. See you tonight. Love you."

As the tape rewound, Sarah left her backpack on the hallway floor and brought the groceries into the kitchen. What was it that could wait until he got home? She considered phoning Matt to see what was going on, but decided not to interrupt his work. Instead she put away the groceries and went into the living room. She opened the sliding door just enough to allow a breeze to circulate through the duplex, then stretched out on the sofa and listened to the rain.

What should she do now? She'd done the laundry the day before and wouldn't have to start dinner for a while. Maybe she could call one of her friends from school. No, at this time of day they would all be working or busy with their graduate school classes and research.

Funny how things had turned out. In college she had been the one with clear goals and direction, taking all the right classes and participating in all the right extracurricular activities and summer internships. Her friends had often remarked that their own career plans seemed vague or nonexistent in comparison. And now they were going places while she sat around the house with nothing to do.

She rolled over on her side and stared at the blank television screen.

Nothing would be on now—nothing good, anyway. She almost wished she had some homework to do. If only she had picked a different major—marketing, or management, maybe. Something in the sciences would have been even better. But in high school Sarah's guidance counselor had told her that there would always be jobs for accountants, and she had taken those words to heart. She had been the only freshman in her dorm who knew from the first day of classes what major she was going to declare at the end of the year. It had seemed so self-indulgent to ask herself if she enjoyed accounting, if she thought she would find it a fulfilling career. If only she had listened to her heart instead of her guidance counselor. Ultimately, though, she knew she had no one but herself to blame now that she had no marketable job skills beyond bean counting.

Suddenly exasperated with herself, she shoved the whining voices from her mind. True, she didn't have a job, but she didn't have to mope and complain like the voice of doom. That was what her mother would do. What Sarah needed was something to keep herself occupied until a job came along. Moving into the duplex had kept her too busy to worry for a couple of weeks; maybe she could join a book club or take a course up at Waterford College.

Then her thoughts returned to the quilt she had seen in the shop window earlier that day. She jumped up from the sofa and retrieved her backpack from the hallway. The quilt shop's class schedule was still there, a bit damp from her rainy walk home from the bus stop. Sarah unfolded it and smoothed out the creases, studying the course names, dates, times, and prices.

Her heart sank. The costs seemed reasonable, but even reasonable expenses were too much when she hadn't seen a paycheck in more than two months. Like so many other things, quilting lessons would to have to wait until the McClures were a dual-income family. But the more Sarah thought about it, the more she liked the idea. A quilt class would give her a chance to meet people, and a handmade quilt might make the duplex seem more like a home. She would talk to Matt about it. Maybe they could come up with the money somehow.

She decided to bring it up over supper that evening. "Matt," she began. "There's something I've been thinking about all day."

Matt took a second helping of corn and grinned. "You mean my phone message? I'm surprised you didn't ask about it sooner. Usually you hate it when I keep you in suspense."

Sarah paused. She had forgotten all about it. "That's right. You said you had to talk to me about something."

"First, though, do you have any plans for tomorrow?"

Something in his tone made her wary. "Why?"

"Yes or no?"

"I'm afraid to answer until I know why you're asking."

"Sheesh. So suspicious." But he put down his fork and hesitated a moment. "I spent the day up at Elm Creek Manor inspecting the trees. Not a trace of Dutch elm disease anywhere. I don't know how they managed it."

"I hope you didn't get caught in the rain."

"Actually, as soon as the thunder started, Mrs. Compson made me come inside. She even fixed me lunch."

"You're kidding. She didn't make you cook it yourself?"

"No." He chuckled. "She's a pretty good cook, too. While I was eating, we kind of got to talking. She wants you to come see her tomorrow."

"What? What for? Why would she want to see me?"

"She didn't say exactly. She said she wanted to tell you in person."

"I'm not going. Tell her I can't come. Tell her I'm busy."

Matt's face assumed the expression it always did when he knew he was about to get in trouble. "I can't. I already told her you'd come in with me tomorrow morning."

"Why'd you do that? Call her and tell her—tell her something. Say I have a dentist appointment."

"I can't. She doesn't have a phone, remember?"

"Matt—"

"Think of it this way. It's a lot cooler out there than in town, right? You could get out of this heat for a while."

"I'd rather stay home and turn on the air-conditioning."

"Oh, come on, honey, what would it hurt?" He put on his most effective beseeching expression. "She's an important client. Please?"

Sarah frowned at him, exasperated.

"Please?"

She rolled her eyes. "Oh, all right. Just, please, next time, ask me before you commit me to something."

"Okay. Promise."

Sarah shook her head and sighed. She knew better.

The next morning was sunny and clear, not nearly as humid as it had been before yesterday's rainstorm. "Why would she want to see me?" Sarah asked again as Matt drove them to Mrs. Compson's home.

"For the fourth time, Sarah, I don't know. You'll find out when we get there."

"She's probably going to demand an apology for snooping around her house." Sarah tried to remember the exchange in the sewing room. She'd apologized when Mrs. Compson caught her, hadn't she? "I don't think I actually said I was sorry. I think I was too surprised. She probably dragged me out here to give me a lecture on manners."

Her stomach twisted into a nervous knot that tightened as the truck pulled into the gravel driveway behind the manor.

"You could apologize before she asks you to," Matt said as he parked the truck. "Old people like apologies and polite stuff like that."

"Yeah. I hear they also love being referred to as 'old people,'" Sarah muttered. She climbed out of the truck and slammed the door. But maybe Matt had a point. She trailed behind him as he led the way to the back door.

Mrs. Compson opened it on the first knock. "So, you're here. Both of you. Well, come on in." She left the door open and they followed her into the hall.

"Mrs. Compson," Matt called after her as she walked ahead of them down a wide, dimly lit hallway. "I was planning to work in the orchard today. Is there anything else you'd like me to do first?"

She stopped and turned around. "No, the orchard is fine. Sarah may remain here with me." Matt and Sarah exchanged a puzzled glance. "Oh, don't worry. I won't work her too hard this morning. She'll see you at lunchtime."

Matt turned to Sarah, uncertain. "Sound okay to you?"

Sarah shrugged and nodded. She'd assumed that Mrs. Compson would want her to come in, make her apology, and leave, but if the woman wanted to drag things out . . . Sarah steeled herself. Well, Mrs. Compson *was* an important client.

With one last, uncertain smile, Matt turned and left the way they came. Sarah watched him go, then faced the old woman squarely. "Mrs. Compson," she said firmly, trying to sound regretful but not nervous, "I wanted to apologize for going into your sitting room with my lemonade and touching your quilt without permission. I shouldn't have done it and I'm sorry."

Mrs. Compson gave her a bemused stare. "Apology accepted." She turned and motioned for Sarah to follow.

Confused, Sarah trailed behind her as they reached the far end of the hall and turned right through a doorway. Wasn't that enough of an apology for her? What else was Sarah supposed to say?

The hallway opened into a large foyer, and Sarah slowly took in a breath. Even with the floor-to-ceiling windows covered by heavy draperies, she could tell how splendid the entryway could be if it were properly cared for. The floor was made of black marble, and to Sarah's left were marble steps leading down to twelve-foot-tall heavy wooden double doors. Oil paintings and mirrors in intricately carved frames lined the walls. Across the room was a smaller set of double doors, and a third set was on the wall to their right. In the corner between them a wooden staircase began; the first five steps were semicircular and led to a wedge-shaped landing from which a staircase climbed to the second-story balcony encircling the room. Looking up, Sarah could see another staircase continuing in a similar fashion to the third floor, and an enormous crystal chandelier hanging from the frescoed ceiling far above.

Mrs. Compson crossed the floor, carefully descended the marble steps, and waving off Sarah's efforts to assist, slowly pushed open one of the heavy doors.

Sarah followed her outside and tried not to gawk like a tourist. They stood on a wide stone veranda that ran the entire length of the front of the mansion. White columns supported a roof far overhead. Two stone staircases began at the center of the veranda, gracefully arcing away from each other and forming a half circle as they descended to the ground. The driveway encircled a large sculpture of a rearing horse; a second look told Sarah that it was a fountain choked with leaves and rainwater. Only that and the road leading from the driveway interrupted the green lawn that flowed from the manor to the distant trees.

Mrs. Compson eyed Sarah as she took all this in. "Impressed? Hmph." She stepped inside and reappeared with a broom, which she handed to Sarah. "Of course you are. Everyone is, the first time they see the place. At least they used to be, when we used to have visitors, before the estate went to pieces."

Sarah stood there uncertainly, looking from the broom to Mrs. Compson and back.

"At least you came dressed for work, not like last time." Mrs. Compson gestured, first waving her arm to the north end of the veranda and then to the south. "Take care of the whole thing, and do a thorough job. Don't neglect the dead leaves in the corners. I'll be back later." She moved toward the open doorway.

"Wait," Sarah called after her. "I think there's been a mistake. I can't sweep your porch."

Mrs. Compson turned and frowned at her. "A girl your age doesn't know how to sweep?"

"It's not that. I know how to sweep, but I—"

"Afraid of a bit of hard work, are you?"

"No, it's just that I think there's been a misunderstanding. You seem to think I work for Matt's company, but I don't."

"Oh. So they fired you, did they?"

"Of course not. They didn't fire me. I've never worked for Matt's company."

"If that's so, why did you accompany him that first time?"

"It was on the way. He was driving me home from a job interview."

"Hmph. Very well, then. Sweep the veranda anyway. If you're looking for work, I'd say you've found some. Just be glad I didn't ask you to mow the lawn."

Sarah gaped at her. "You know, you're really something." She threw down the broom and thrust her fists onto her hips. "I tried to apologize, tried to be polite, but you're just the rudest, the—the—if you had asked nicely I might have swept your porch as a favor to you, and to Matt, but—"

Mrs. Compson was grinning at her.

"What's so funny? You think being rude is funny?"

The old woman shrugged, clearly amused, which only irritated Sarah more. "I was beginning to wonder if you had any backbone at all."

"Believe me, I do," Sarah said through clenched teeth. She spun around and stormed down the nearest staircase.

"Wait," Mrs. Compson called. "Sarah, please, just a moment."

Sarah thought of Matt's contract, sighed, and stopped on the bottom step. She turned around to find Mrs. Compson preparing to come down the stairs after her. Sarah then realized there was no handrail, and the stone wall was worn too smooth for a secure grip. Mrs. Compson stumbled, and instinctively Sarah put out her arms as if to steady her, though she was too far away to make any difference if Mrs. Compson fell.

"All right," Sarah said. "I'm not going anywhere. You don't have to chase me."

Mrs. Compson shook her head and came down the stairs anyway. "I really could use some more help around here," she said, breathing heavily from exertion. "I'll pay you, of course."

"I'm looking for a real job. I went to college. I have a degree."

"Of course you do. Of course you do. But you could work for me until you find a better job. I won't mind if you need to leave early sometimes for job interviews."

She paused for a reply, but Sarah just looked at her, stone-faced.

"I don't know anybody else, you see," Mrs. Compson continued, and to Sarah's astonishment, her voice faltered. "I'm planning to sell the estate, and I need someone to help me collect my late sister's personal belongings and take an inventory of the manor's contents for auction. There are so many rooms, and I can't even imagine what could be in the attic, and I have trouble with stairs."

"You're going to sell the estate?"

The old woman shook her head. "A home so big and empty would be a burden. I have a place of my own, in Sewickley." Her lips twisted until they resembled a wry smile, but it looked as if she were out of practice. "I know what you're thinking. 'Work for this crotchety old thing? Never in a million years.'"

Sarah tried to compose her features so that her expression wouldn't give anything else away.

"I know I can be difficult sometimes, but I can try to be—" Mrs. Compson pursed her lips and glanced away as if searching for the proper adjective. "More congenial. What would it take to persuade you?"

Sarah studied her, then shook her head. "I'll need some time to think about it."

"Very well. You may remain here or in the kitchen if you like, or feel free to explore the grounds. The orchards are to the west, beyond the barn, and the gardens—what remains of them—are to the north. When you've decided, you may join me in the west sitting room. I believe you already know where that is." With that, she turned and made her way up the stairs and into the manor.

Sarah shook her head in disbelief as she watched Mrs. Compson go. When she said she needed some time to think about the offer, she'd meant a few days, not a few minutes. Then again, she had already made up her mind. Wait until Matt heard about this. As soon as he stopped laughing Sarah would get him to take her home, and with any luck she'd never have to see that strange old woman again.

Her eyes scanned the front of the manor. Mrs. Compson was right; she was impressed with the place. Who wouldn't be? But she doubted she could tolerate an employer like Mrs. Compson in order to work there. She was impressed, not masochistic. She walked around the tree-lined north side of the building and the west wing. She walked briskly, but it still took her ten minutes to reach the barn and another five to reach the orchard, where she found Matt retrieving some tools from the back of the pickup.

"You aren't going to believe this," she greeted him. "Mrs. Compson needs someone to help her get the manor ready for sale and she wants to hire me."

But Matt didn't burst into laughter as she had expected. Instead he set down his tool kit and leaned against the tailgate. "That's great, honey. When do you start?"

For a moment Sarah was too surprised to do anything but blink at him. "When do I start?"

"You're going to help her, aren't you?"

"I wasn't planning to," she managed to say.

"Why not? Why wouldn't you want the job?"

"It should be obvious. She hasn't been exactly nice to me, as you very well know."

"Don't you feel sorry for her?"

"Of course I feel sorry for her, but that doesn't mean I want to spend every day working with her."

"That's got to be better than moping around the house all day, right?"

"Not necessarily. If I'm sweeping porches around here, I won't be sending out résumés and going on interviews."

"I'm sure you could work something out."

"Matt, you don't get it. I've invested years in my career. I think I'm a little overqualified for cleaning up a house."

"I thought the whole idea was to start fresh."

"There's starting fresh and then there's starting over at the very bottom. There are limits."

Matt shrugged. "I don't see any. Honest work is honest work."

Sarah stared at him, perplexed. He had always been the first to point out that her career was her business, but now here he was practically pressuring her into a job that didn't even require a high school diploma. "Matt, if I take this job, my mother will have a fit."

"Why does it matter what your mother thinks? Besides, she wouldn't care. If anything, she'd be glad you're helping out an old lady."

Sarah started to reply, then held back the words and shook her head. If he only knew. She could almost hear that familiar chorus of shrill "I told you so"s already. If she took this job, she'd prove that her mother had been right all along when she'd insisted that leaving State College for Matt's sake would send Sarah's career into an inevitable spiral of downward mobility.

Then suspicion crept into her thoughts. "Matt, what's going on?"

"Nothing's going on. What do you mean?"

"First you brought me out here after my interview. Then, without checking with me first, you promised her that I'd come see her. You didn't look at all surprised when I told you she offered me a job, and now you're pushing me to take it. You knew she was going to offer me this job, didn't you?"

"I didn't know for sure. I mean, she hinted, but she didn't come right out and say it." He looked at the ground. "I guess I like the idea better than you do."

Exasperated, Sarah struggled for something to say. "Why?"

"It would be nice if we worked at the same place. We'd get to see more of each other."

"That might be part of it, but what else?"

Matt sighed, took off his cap, and ran his fingers through his curly hair until it looked even more unruly than usual. "You're going to think I'm being silly."

Silly was more benign than the adjectives Sarah considered using. "Maybe, but tell me anyway."

"Okay, but don't laugh." He tried to smile, but his eyes were sad. "Mrs. Compson, well, she reminds me of my mom. Same mannerisms, same way of dressing; she even looks kind of the same. Except her age, of course. I mean, I know she's probably old enough to be our grandmother . . ."

"Oh, Matt."

"It's just that, well, my mom's probably out there all alone somewhere, and I'd like to think that if some young couple had a chance to look out for her they'd take it."

If your mother's out there alone, it's her own fault for running out on you and your dad, Sarah thought, pressing her lips together to hold back the automatic response. She went to him and hugged him tightly. How could Matt remember his mother's mannerisms? Mrs. McClure had left when he was only five years old, and although Sarah would never say so, she suspected Matt knew his mother only from photographs.

Matt stroked her hair. "I'm sorry if I was being pushy. I didn't mean it. I should've come right out and told you what I was thinking."

"Yes, you should have."

"I'm sorry. Really. I won't do it again."

Sarah almost retorted that she wouldn't give him the chance, that she'd be on her guard for the rest of their marriage, but he looked so remorseful that she changed her mind. "Okay," she said instead. "Let's just forget it. Besides, you're right. It would be nice if we worked at the same place."

"We might not run into each other much during the day, but at least we can have lunch together."

Sarah nodded, thinking. She'd wanted the chance to do something different with her career, and this job was certainly different. Besides, it would only be for a few months at most. It would help fill up the days and take her mind off her unsuccessful job search.

Then she remembered the quilt she'd seen on her first visit to the manor, and found another reason to take the job.

"So what do you say?" Matt asked.

"The house is gorgeous, and it's so much cooler out here, too, like you said." Sarah took Matt's hand and squeezed it. "I'm going to go back there right now and tell her I'll take the job, okay?" She turned and started back for the manor.

"Okay," Matt called after her. "See you at noon."

As she walked, Sarah decided that the situation had enough advantages to outweigh Mrs. Compson's eccentricities. She could always quit if things didn't work out. Besides, she knew the perfect way Mrs. Compson could pay her. She hurried up the back steps and knocked on the door.

Immediately, Mrs. Compson opened it. "Have you decided?" She pursed her lips as if she expected bad news.

"I'll take the job, on one condition."

Mrs. Compson raised an eyebrow. "I already planned to feed you."

"Thank you, but that's not it."

"What, then?"

"Teach me how to quilt."

"I beg your pardon?"

"Teach me how to quilt. Teach me how to make a quilt and I'll help you with your work."

"Surely you don't mean it. There are several fine teachers in Waterford. I could give you some names."

Sarah shook her head. "No. That's the deal. You teach me how to quilt, and I'll help you take inventory and prepare the manor for sale. I've seen your quilts, and—" Sarah tried to remember what Bonnie had said. "And you're in the QAS permanently. You ought to be able to teach me how to quilt."

"You mean AQS, but that's not the point. Of course I could teach you. It's not a question of my ability." The old woman eyed her as if she found her quite inscrutable, then shrugged and extended a hand. "Very well. Agreed. In addition to your wages, I'll teach you how to quilt."

Sarah pulled her hand away an instant before she would have been grasping Mrs. Compson's. "No, that's not what I meant. The lessons are my wages."

"Goodness, child, have you no bills to pay?" Mrs. Compson sighed and looked to the heavens. "Don't let these somewhat dilapidated conditions deceive you. My family may not be what it once was, but we aren't ready to accept charity quite yet."

"I didn't mean to imply that."

"Yes, yes. Of course you didn't. But I simply must insist on some sort of payment. My conscience wouldn't give me a moment's peace otherwise."

Sarah thought about it. "Okay. Something fair." She wasn't about to take advantage of someone who was obviously lonely, no matter how rude she was.

They settled on a wage, but Sarah still felt that she was receiving the best part of the bargain. When they shook on it, Mrs. Compson's eyes lit up with triumph. "I think you would have held out for more if you knew how much work there is to be done."

"I'm hoping that I'll have a real job before long."

Mrs. Compson smiled. "Forgive me if I hope not." She held open the door, and Sarah went inside. "Would you really have swept the veranda for free if I had asked you nicely?"

"Yes." Sarah thought for a moment and decided to be honest. "Maybe. I'm not sure. I'll do it now, though, since I'm on the payroll."

"Let me know when you're ready for lunch," Mrs. Compson said, as Sarah continued down the hallway toward the front entrance.

Four

A s she had promised, Sarah swept the veranda. When every dead leaf had been gathered up and even the corners were surely neat enough to win Mrs. Compson's approval, most of the morning still stretched ahead of her. She decided to move on to the staircases, and swept twigs and leaves and crumbling fragments of mortar to the ground as she descended each curving step. Often she had to stoop over and pull up weeds and tufts of grass that had grown in the spaces between the gray stones. She hadn't noticed the cracks and the scrawny pale shoots earlier, and she reminded herself to tell Matt about them. From the looks of things, he might need to replace some of the mortar, maybe even some of the stones on the lower steps.

As she worked, the manor's shade and a gentle southwest breeze kept the worst of the sun's heat from troubling her. And as noon approached, she felt her thoughts unsnarling until she realized with a start that she was enjoying herself. If her mother could see her now. Sarah pictured her mother's reaction when she learned the truth about her daughter's new career, and had to smile.

At lunchtime, Sarah returned to the kitchen to find Matt setting the table and Mrs. Compson stirring a bowl of tuna salad. While they ate, Mrs. Compson quizzed them on their morning's accomplishments, nodding in satisfaction at their replies. When Matt tried to show Mrs. Compson some preliminary sketches of the north gardens, though, she gave them only the barest of glances, nodded, and abruptly rose from her seat.

Matt and Sarah exchanged a puzzled look. Did that nod mean she liked Matt's ideas or not? "Here, we'll help clean up," Sarah said, standing.

Matt jumped to his feet and began collecting the dirty plates. "No, you two go on. I'll take care of it."

Mrs. Compson stared at him. "You'll take care of it?"

"Sure." He grinned and carried the dishes to the sink. "Don't worry. I won't drop anything."

"I should hope not." Mrs. Compson turned to Sarah. "Well, I suppose this would give us more time to talk about quilts later. But first, Sarah, come with me."

Sarah kissed Matt good-bye and followed Mrs. Compson out of the room. Mrs. Compson stopped at a small closet on the right and retrieved a bundle of dust rags, which she deposited in Sarah's arms before moving on down the long hallway.

"We'll start upstairs," Mrs. Compson announced as they turned right in the front foyer. "Or rather, you'll start upstairs."

Sarah trailed after her. "Where do these doors lead?"

Without breaking her stride, Mrs. Compson pointed to the double doors on the right. "Banquet hall. No mere dining room for Elm Creek Manor." She pointed to the other set of doors, directly in front of them and to the left of the wedge-shaped steps leading into the corner. "Ballroom. At one time the entire first floor of this wing was devoted almost exclusively to entertaining." She reached the staircase, grasped the railing, and led Sarah upstairs. "We'll begin in the library. It's directly above the ballroom."

"What's above that?"

"The nursery. Oh, I know what you're thinking. Why on earth would any family need a nursery so large? Well, I agree. It's much larger than necessary."

Sarah nodded, wondering what an acceptable size for a nursery would be. As they continued up the stairs, she considered offering the older woman her arm. She suspected she'd be reprimanded for the attempt, though, and decided not to risk it.

Halfway to the second floor, Mrs. Compson paused on the step, breathing heavily. "As for the rest of it," she said, waving a hand in no particular direction. "Bedrooms, each with its own sitting room."

"Why so many?"

"This was supposed to be a family house—several generations, aunts, uncles, and cousins, all living together happily under one roof. Hmph."

"Which room's yours?"

Mrs. Compson glanced at her sharply, then continued her climb. "I have my sitting room downstairs."

"You mean you sleep on the sofa? Aren't the bedrooms furnished?"

Mrs. Compson said nothing. Sarah bit the inside of her upper lip in a belated attempt to restrain the question. When they reached the top step, Mrs. Compson let out a relieved sigh and turned left down another hallway. "My sister saved everything," she finally said as they passed two closed doors on the right. When the hallway widened and dead-ended at another set of double doors, Mrs. Compson stopped. "And I do mean everything. Old magazines, newspapers, paperbacks. I want you to help me sort the rubbish from anything salvageable."

With her lips firmly pursed, Mrs. Compson swung open both doors, and they entered the library. The musty, cluttered room spanned the width of the south wing's far end. Dust specks floated lazily in the dim light that leaked in through tall windows on the south-, east-, and west-facing walls. Oak book-cases, their shelves stacked with books, knickknacks, and loose papers, stood between the windows. Two sofas faced each other in the center of the room, dusty lamps resting on end tables on either side of both, a low coffee table turned upside down between them. More books and papers were scattered on the floor near the large oak desk on the east side of the room. Two high-backed, overstuffed chairs stood near a fireplace in the center of the south wall, and a third chair was toppled over onto its side nearby.

Sarah sneezed.

"God bless you." Mrs. Compson smiled. "Let's open these windows and see if we can clear out some of the dust with some fresh air, shall we?"

Sarah set the dust rags on the desk and helped her carefully swing open the windows, which were made of small diamond-shaped pieces of glass joined with lead solder. Some of the panes were clear, but others were cloudy with age and weathering. Sarah leaned her head and shoulders out of one of the south windows. She could see the roof of the barn through the trees.

She smiled and turned back to her new employer, who was trying to set the overturned chair onto its feet. "Where do you want me to begin?" she asked, hastening to help.

"Begin wherever you like. Just see that you get the job done." Mrs. Compson brushed the dust from her hands. "Separate all of the old news-papers into a pile for recycling, and do the same for the magazines. Loose papers may be recycled—or discarded, if you think it best. Gather the old paperbacks somewhere. Later we can box them and donate them to the public library, if they're in suitable condition. I'd like to keep the hardcover books, at least for now. Those you may dust off and return to the shelves."

"Waterford Library may have to open up a new branch for all of this," Sarah remarked, scanning the shelves. "Your sister must've liked reading."

The older woman gave a harsh laugh that sounded more like a strangled cough. "My sister liked reading junk—the cheapest romances, the most triv-ial tabloid magazines. In her later years she saved newspapers, too, but I don't think she actually read them. No, she just piled them up here, creating a fire hazard, leaving them for someone else to clean up later." She shook her head. "The finer books were my father's. And mine."

Sarah felt her cheeks grow warm. Apparently it was time to stop bringing up Mrs. Compson's family. "Well, I guess I'll get started, then," she said.

Mrs. Compson gave her a brisk nod. "You may work until four, then meet me in the sitting room and we'll discuss your quilting lessons."

Sarah breathed a quick sigh when Mrs. Compson left the library, relieved to have escaped another scolding. Mrs. Compson didn't seem to think very much of her sister. Or maybe she was so grief-stricken that she couldn't bear to think about her and that was why she seemed so abrupt. Sarah stooped over to pick up some scattered newspaper pages, vowing to keep her mouth shut more often.

Even with the windows open, the library was a dusty, stuffy place to work. As Sarah sorted through the clutter, she found several fine leather-bound volumes which she carefully dusted and returned to the cleaned shelves. When she found the piles of yellowed newspaper taking up an entire bookcase in the northeast corner of the room, she leafed through them eagerly. Newspaper clippings from the manor's earlier and happier years would tell her more about the people who used to live there. To her disappointment, however, Sarah soon realized that none of the papers dated from earlier than the mid-1980s. As she continued to work, she began to believe that Mrs. Compson's dismissive critique of her late sister's reading habits had been accurate.

At four o'clock Sarah heard Mrs. Compson calling her from the bottom of the stairs. She arched her back, stretched, and wiped her brow on a clean corner of a dust cloth. There was still a lot of work to be done, but even Mrs. Compson would have to agree that Sarah had made a noticeable dent in it.

She hurried downstairs, where Mrs. Compson greeted her with an amused look. "There seems to be more dust on you than there was in the entire library."

Sarah hastily wiped her palms on her shorts and tucked in her blouse. "No, don't worry. There's plenty more dust up there for anyone who wants it."

Mrs. Compson chuckled and motioned for Sarah to follow her down the hallway. "How much did you accomplish today?"

"I took care of everything that was on the floor and finished the bookcases on the north and west walls. I closed the windows, too, in case it rains tonight. Do you want to look through anything before it's recycled?"

"Did you follow my instructions? Were you careful?"

"I think I was, but it's your stuff. I'd hate to throw out anything you might miss later. Maybe you should look through the piles just the same."

They entered the kitchen. "No need for that. Anything I ever wanted from this place isn't here for the taking." Mrs. Compson gestured to the sink.

"When you've cleaned yourself up a bit, join me in the sitting room."

Sarah washed her hands and face, then hesitated in the sitting room doorway. Mrs. Compson was pulling some quilts from a cedar chest and draping them on the sofa. Open books were piled on an end table. Mrs. Compson turned and spotted her. "Well, are you coming in or aren't you? It's all right. You've been invited this time, not like that first day."

"I was kind of hoping you'd forgotten about that."

"I never forget."

Sarah figured the older woman probably never forgave, either. She entered the room and walked over to the quilts. The fabric seemed worn and faded, even faintly stained in some places, but the quilting stitches and the arrangements of tiny pieces of cloth were as lovely as the newer quilts she had recently seen. Gingerly she traced the pattern of a red-and-white quilt with a fingertip. "Did you make these?"

"All of them. They're old."

"They're beautiful."

"Hmph. Young lady, if you keep saying things like that I might just have to keep you around." Mrs. Compson closed the cedar chest and spread one last quilt on the sofa. "They shouldn't be stored in there. Contact with wood can damage them. But Claudia was too scatterbrained to remember such simple things." She sighed and eased herself onto a chair beside the end table. "Not that it really matters. These quilts were made to be used, and to be used up. I thought they might at least give you some ideas, a place to start."

Claudia—she must be her sister, Sarah thought as she pulled a chair closer to Mrs. Compson's.

"The last time I taught someone to quilt—why, it must have been fifty years ago," Mrs. Compson said, as if thinking aloud. "Of course, she never truly wanted to learn. I'm sure you'll do much better."

"Oh, I really do want to learn. My grandmother quilted, but she died before I was old enough for her to teach me."

Mrs. Compson raised an eyebrow. "I learned when I was five years old." She put on her glasses and peered at one of the books. "I thought you could best learn by making a sampler. Mind you, I plan to teach you the traditional way, hand piecing and hand quilting. You shouldn't expect to finish your quilt this week or even this year."

"I know it'll take time. I don't mind."

"There are many other perfectly acceptable modern techniques that make quilting faster and easier." She indicated the sewing machine with a jerk of her head. "I use some of them myself. But for now, hand piecing will do."

Sarah looked at the small machine in disbelief. "You can sew on that toy sewing machine?"

Matt had an expression very much like the one Mrs. Compson wore then, one he usually assumed when Sarah called an amaryllis a lily or when she called everything from mulch to peat moss dirt. "That's no toy. That model isn't manufactured anymore, but it's one of the finest sewing machines a quilter can own. You shouldn't judge things by their size, or by their age."

Chastened, Sarah changed the subject. "You said I should make a sampler?"

Mrs. Compson nodded. "How big do you want the finished quilt to be?"

"Big enough for our bed. It's queen-size."

"Then you'll need about twelve different blocks, if we use a straight setting with sashing and borders instead of setting the blocks on point. Then we'll attach wide strips of your background fabric between the blocks and your outer border so you have plenty of space to practice your hand quilting stitches." Mrs. Compson handed Sarah one of the books. "Pick twelve different blocks you'd like to try. There are more patterns in these other books. I'll help you find a good balance."

With Mrs. Compson's guidance, Sarah selected twelve blocks from the hundreds of patterns in the books. Mrs. Compson explained the difference between pieced blocks, ones that were made from seaming the block's pieces together, and appliquéd blocks, which were made by sewing figures onto background fabric. Mrs. Compson encouraged her to choose some of each style for her sampler. The time spent choosing, reconsidering, and rejecting blocks passed quickly, and before Sarah knew it, it was half past five. She had selected twelve blocks that varied in style, appearance, and difficulty, and Matt was standing in the sitting room doorway smiling at her.

"How's quilt school going?" he asked, crossing the room and giving Sarah a hug.

Sarah smiled up at him. "I'm getting my homework assignment as we speak."

"Yes, Sarah has decided to become a student again," Mrs. Compson said as she jotted down some notes on a pad. She tore off the top sheet and handed it to Sarah. "This is a list of the fabrics and other tools you'll need to complete the quilt top. We'll worry about the other materials later. Do you know the quilt shop downtown?"

"I've been there once."

"Ask someone there to help you select the items from this list. Bonnie Markham is the owner. A very pleasant woman. She'll know what to do."

Sarah nodded, remembering the friendly, dark-haired woman. She scanned the list, then folded the paper and placed it in her pocket. "I'll see you on Monday, then."

Mrs. Compson escorted them to the door, and Sarah and Matt drove home.

The answering machine's light blinked a welcome when they entered the duplex. Sarah's stomach flip-flopped as she ducked around Matt and reached for the playback button.

"This is Brian Turnbull from PennCellular Corporation."

Sarah closed her eyes and suppressed a groan.

"I'm trying to reach Sarah McClure regarding the résumé you sent us. If you're still interested in the position, give me a call today before five so we can set up an interview."

Sarah glanced at the clock in dismay. It was already almost six.

"If you can't reach me before then, I'll be back in the office first thing Monday morning." He quickly recited his telephone number and hung up.

"Doesn't that just figure?" Sarah muttered, snatching up the phone. "The only day I'm not around, and that's the day he calls."

"He might still be there. You could try."

Sarah was already dialing the number. She reached an answering machine and hung up without leaving a message. "If only I'd been here. What if he thinks I'm not interested? By now he could have offered the job to someone else."

"Hey, relax," Matt said, rubbing her shoulders. "He said you could call on Monday, right? Why would he say that if he wasn't interested?"

Sarah shook her head. "This is a sign."

"It's not a sign."

"It is, too. It's a very bad sign."

"Sarah, you're overreacting. You shouldn't—" Matt broke off and sighed, shaking his head and furrowing his brow in exaggerated helplessness. "I'll tell you what. First, we make supper. I'm starved."

Sarah's anxiety began to wane. "And then what?"

"Then we clean up."

"Then what?"

"Then," he said, dropping his hands to her waist and pulling her into a hug. "You forget all about work for a while." He kissed her and smiled, his eyes twinkling with mischief.

Sarah smiled back. "Why wait until after supper?"

Five

Over breakfast on Saturday morning, Sarah approached the Help Wanted ads with more confidence than she had felt in weeks. Now that she could count on her job with Mrs. Compson for a regular paycheck, she didn't need to find the perfect career right away. Besides, she'd rather spend the summer exploring Elm Creek Manor than crunching numbers in some climate-controlled office cubicle.

Sarah found three new ads for accounting positions, and she took them as a sign that her luck had changed at last. Usually she struggled to choose the perfect words for her cover letters, but today her fingers flew over the keyboard. On a whim she changed the typeface on her résumé from Helvetica to New Century Schoolbook, since it looked more optimistic and might make a better impression. At ten o'clock she and Matt drove downtown to the post office, where she sent her résumés on their hopeful journeys. Then, while Matt drove off to complete some errands of his own, Sarah hurried down the sidewalk to Grandma's Attic.

The store was more crowded than it had been on her first visit. Several customers browsed through the aisles, studiously comparing different bolts of fabric or leafing through the books and quilt patterns near the front entrance. Sarah spotted Bonnie standing with five other women around the far end of the long cutting table. She was about to approach them when they erupted in peals of laughter. Feeling awkward, she hung back. They didn't seem standoffish, but their friendship was so tangible that Sarah felt like an unwanted eavesdropper. She waved discreetly instead, trying to catch the shop owner's eye without interrupting the lively conversation.

The youngest woman in the group looked her way, smiled, and left the table. She had long, straight auburn hair that was parted in the middle and reached halfway down her back. "May I help you?" she asked as she approached. She seemed several years younger than Sarah, perhaps in her late teens or early twenties.

Bonnie followed close behind. "So, Sarah, you've decided to take the plunge?"

Sarah pulled Mrs. Compson's list from her pocket. "Yes, and I'm supposed to get a bunch of supplies. But I'm not really sure . . . well, like this. I'm supposed to get 'three yards of a medium print.' Does that mean medium as in medium-size?"

"Dark, medium, and light refer to a fabric's value," the auburn-haired girl explained.

"You mean, how much it costs?"

The girl's smile deepened, and a dimple appeared in her right cheek. "Not that, either. Let me start over. Value refers to how dark or light a color is, how much black or white has been added to a hue. You need to have contrasting values in a quilt so the block pattern shows up. It's like if you track dark brown mud all over a light beige carpet. The mud and the carpet have very different values so the footprints really show up. But if you track dark brown mud on a dark blue carpet, you can't see the footprints as much. And if your mom's anything like mine, she won't even notice the stains."

"I heard that, kiddo," one of the women called out from the cutting table. "You know you're not supposed to air my housekeeping foibles in public." She, too, was auburn-haired, but more sturdily built than her slender daughter. She wore a long flowing skirt and several beaded necklaces.

"She isn't telling us anything we don't already know, Gwen," the woman at her side drawled. She was strikingly pretty, tall, thin, and tan, and she wore her short blond hair in curls.

"Besides, Mom, it was for a good cause. I was helping a new quilter."

Gwen shrugged. "Oh. In that case, go right ahead."

The others burst into laughter again. Sarah felt a smile twitching in the corners of her mouth as she watched them.

"It looks like Summer has everything under control, so why don't I leave you in her capable hands?" Bonnie suggested. "She knows as much about quilts as anyone here."

"Not exactly. I'm still learning, too," Summer replied, but she looked pleased as she motioned for Sarah to follow her to the closest aisle of fabric bolts.

After searching through cotton prints of every imaginable pattern and color, Sarah found a medium value print she liked, a paisley pattern in shades of red, blue, cream, and brown. Then Summer showed her how to match other fabrics to the colors in the first print. At first Sarah selected all floral designs, but Summer explained that different prints—some large,

some airy, some geometric, some tone-on-tone, and others multicolored—
would give the finished quilt a more interesting texture.

"There's so much to think about," Sarah said, overwhelmed. "I didn't
think making a quilt would be easy, but if the shopping's this difficult, I can't
imagine what the sewing will be like."

"It gets easier, but I know what you mean," Summer confided, lowering
her voice. "When my mom first started teaching me how to quilt, I felt the
same way. But don't tell her I said so. She's convinced I was a child prodigy,
and I'd hate to ruin my image."

Sarah laughed and agreed. It felt good to have a friendly person to talk to
again. With a pang, she suddenly realized how much she missed her friends
from State College. They used to talk and laugh and have a good time no
matter where they were or what they were doing. Even trips to the Laundro-
mat could be fun with them, and no terrible workday or argument with her
mother could withstand their power to commiserate and comfort. Bonnie
and the other women around the table acted as if they had a friendship like
that. As Summer helped her find the other items on Mrs. Compson's list,
Sarah wished that she and Summer were friends and that Summer would
take her over there and introduce her to the other women. They all looked so
cheerful, so comfortable together.

"Are you taking one of Bonnie's classes?" Summer asked as they carried
the bolts to the other end of the cutting table. She unrolled the first bolt and
began to cut the fabric.

"No, Sylvia Compson is going to teach me."

Summer stared at her, scissors frozen in mid-cut. "Sylvia Compson is
your quilt teacher? No way."

At that, the conversation at the other end of the table broke off, and the
women looked their way. Their expressions varied from mild surprise to outright astonishment. A woman of Asian heritage broke the silence. "She
always quilts alone—at least, that's what they say." She held a baby in a carrier on her back, and as she spoke she absentmindedly removed a lock of her
black hair from the child's fist.

The oldest woman, petite and white-haired, shook her head. "I believe
Judy's right." Her blue eyes were wide with amazement behind pink-tinted
glasses. "She doesn't teach anymore, and hasn't for a very long time, as far as
I know."

"Looks like you've got yourself some competition, Bonnie," the blond
woman beside Gwen added.

"I'm glad for it," Bonnie protested. "She's so talented. It's wonderful that
she's passing along that gift."

"It's about time she stopped being so stuck up," the blond woman muttered. "She'll take all the ribbons all right, but she won't join a guild."

"Knock it off, Diane." Gwen elbowed her in the side. Diane's mouth opened in protest, but she said nothing else.

"Not everyone's a joiner," Judy said. "Besides, she hasn't been back in town very long, only since Claudia passed away. Who knows? Maybe she belonged to a guild back in—wherever she was."

"Sewickley," Sarah said.

Six pairs of eyes fixed on her.

"Are you from Sewickley, too?" the oldest woman asked. "Are you a friend of hers? Can you tell us how she's doing? I'm Mrs. Emberly. Mrs. Compson wouldn't mind if you told me—in fact, I suppose she'd expect me to ask. Are you a relation?"

"Well, no, I mean, I'm not a relation. I work for Mrs. Compson. But I'm not from Sewickley. I'm from State College." Sarah tried not to fidget. "I don't really know Mrs. Compson all that well—"

"Ah, yes. State College." Gwen grinned. "Of course, that means you must be a Penn State grad."

"That's right. I just moved to town."

"Have you signed with a team yet or are you still a free agent?"

Sarah's brow furrowed in puzzlement.

Summer came to her rescue. "What Mom's trying to ask is, did you already join the Waterford Quilting Guild or are you still looking for a bee?"

"I guess I'm still a free agent, not by choice, but—"

"Then you can join our group," Summer exclaimed. "I mean, if you want to. If you're not too busy."

"I'd love to. But I'm just a beginner. Is that okay?"

"We were all beginners once," Gwen assured her. She introduced the other women, who smiled at Sarah as Gwen went around the circle.

Gwen explained that the 100-member Waterford Quilting Guild met once a month on the college campus to discuss guild business and activities, and broke up into smaller groups for weekly quilting bees. "The Tangled Web Quilters started out as one of those bees, but eventually we stopped going to the guild's monthly meetings. I for one got tired of all the bureaucracy, electing officers for this, selecting a committee for that . . . all that nonsense takes up valuable quilting time. You're more than welcome to join us if you like, if your Thursday evenings are free."

"You'll enjoy yourself, Sarah," Bonnie said. "Bring something to quilt and be prepared to tell us your life story."

Diane grinned. "Or, as we usually say, 'Stitch and Bitch.'"

They all laughed.

"Don't tell her that," Mrs. Emberly said, struggling to hide a smile. "She'll think we're horribly rude."

"No, not at all," Sarah assured her. The Tangled Web Quilters were more like her State College friends than she ever could have suspected.

Summer finished cutting Sarah's fabric while Gwen wrote down some information about the next week's quilting bee. Sarah paid for her supplies, said good-bye to her new friends, and left the store. Swinging her shopping bag cheerfully, she walked up the street to the coffee shop where Matt was going to meet her for lunch. For the first time since they'd moved to Waterford, the downtown seemed the warm, friendly place their real estate agent had promised.

"This Diane sounds like she's jealous of Mrs. Compson," Matt said after Sarah told him about her morning.

"Oh, I'm sure she's nice enough. They all seemed very nice." Sarah regarded him closely and tried to suppress a grin. He looked ready to leap to Mrs. Compson's defense if he heard another word against her.

"While you were at the quilt shop I picked up a car phone from work," Matt went on. "I thought we could use one since we're going to be spending a lot of time out at Elm Creek Manor."

"That's a good idea."

"Maybe we should try to talk Mrs. Compson into having a phone installed. Not for us, for her, in case she has an accident or something. I can't figure why she wouldn't have one already." Suddenly he frowned and looked puzzled. "What? Do I have crumbs on my face or something? What are you grinning at?"

"You," Sarah teased. "You're so cute, the way you're so concerned about Mrs. Compson. It's like you've adopted her or something."

Matt looked embarrassed. "You make me sound like a Boy Scout."

"I think you're sweet." She reached across the table and squeezed his hand affectionately. "You're right about the phone, too. I wonder what she could do in an emergency. I don't think anyone would hear her if she shouted for help."

"I doubt it. The main road's too far from the house, and not many people use it. Elm Creek Manor's pretty isolated, especially if you don't drive."

"Doesn't she?"

"Think about it. Did you ever see any cars behind the manor? Except for ours, I mean?"

Sarah tried to remember. "No, I don't think so, and she'd probably park as close to the back door as possible, since she has some trouble walking." That thought troubled her. No phone, probably no car, and no one else in the house except when Sarah was working. How did Mrs. Compson get groceries? What if she had an accident?

"No wonder she wants to sell the place and move back to Sewickley." Matt shook his head. "It's too bad. When we finish our work that place is going to be awesome, and she won't be able to enjoy it."

"Yeah. It's a shame." Sarah frowned and tapped her fingers on her coffee cup.

Six

Before Sarah and Matt left for Elm Creek Manor on Monday morning, Sarah gathered her courage and called Mr. Turnbull at PennCellular Corporation. "Why don't you go upstairs or something?" she said to Matt as she dialed the kitchen phone. "You'll distract me."

"Okay," Matt agreed, but he lingered in the doorway.

After a few rings a receptionist answered and promptly put Sarah on hold. As she waited, she began to feel her throat tightening.

"Don't be nervous," Matt whispered.

Sarah waved him away, but he only took one step out of the kitchen.

"Turnbull here," a gruff voice suddenly barked in her ear.

"Good morning, Mr. Turnbull," Sarah said. She forced some confidence into her voice. "This is Sarah McClure. I'm returning your phone call about—"

"Oh, yes, right. Sarah McClure." Papers shuffled in the background. "You applied for a job in our public relations office, correct? Quite a nice résumé you sent in."

"Thank you."

"I'm a Penn State grad myself, you know. 'Course, that was before your time. I see you took advanced auditing. Is Professor Clarke still teaching it?"

"Yes. I mean, as far as I know she is. I had her years ago."

"Liked her lectures, hated her exams." Mr. Turnbull chuckled. "Well, let's see here. I've been going over your background, and you know something, Sarah? You really seem more suited for a job in our accounting department."

Sarah's heart sank. She tried to think of an appropriate response.

"Now, it just so happens we have an entry-level opening there, too," Mr. Turnbull went on. "It hasn't even been advertised yet. What do you say? Interested?"

"Well, sure, but I'm also very interested in the other—"

"Good. Then some of the folks in the accounting department want to meet you and talk about it. How about some time this week?"

"That would be great, thanks."

"How about tomorrow, say, about one o'clock?"

So soon? "That sounds fine." Sarah knew she ought to say something else, something impressive, something brilliant, but the words eluded her.

Mr. Turnbull raced through directions to his office as Sarah scrambled to write them down. "See you tomorrow, then."

"Thank you, Mr. Turnbull. I'm looking forward to meeting with you. I'll see you tomorrow. Thanks again."

Matt had been studying her expression throughout the conversation, and he stepped back into the kitchen when Sarah hung up the phone. She groaned, closed her eyes, and slumped against the kitchen wall. "It couldn't have been that bad," Matt said, incredulous. "You weren't on the phone long enough to do that much damage."

"I should've practiced what I was going to say. God, won't I ever get this right?" She thumped her head against the wall.

"Well, hitting your head on the wall isn't going to help."

"He's not considering me for the PR job."

"What do you mean? Didn't you just schedule an interview?"

"For an accounting job. Every time I tried to talk about the PR job, he steered the conversation back to accounting."

"You're meeting with him tomorrow, right? Talk about it then."

"No, I blew it. Talk about terrible first impressions. Maybe I should call him and cancel."

Matt laughed. "Oh, sure. That'll make an even better impression." He crossed the room and put his hands on her shoulders. "Give yourself a break, Sarah. So you were a little nervous. That doesn't mean you blew it. I bet everyone he talks to gets nervous, probably more than you did. He must've liked how you sounded or he wouldn't have offered you the interview, right?" He stooped down until his eyes were level with hers, and gave her a playful grin. "Am I right? Tell me I'm right."

Sarah managed the barest hint of a smile in return. "Okay, maybe you're right. I guess he could've hung up on me. And he's Penn State alumni. He had Professor Clarke."

"Well, there you go. Turnbull likes Professor Clarke, and Professor Clarke likes you, right? You're a shoo-in."

"I don't think it's that simple, Matt."

"You never know." He gave her a quick kiss, then picked up his wallet and keys from the counter. "Come on, let's get going. Mrs. Compson might not be too thrilled if we're late."

Sarah snatched up her bag of quilting supplies, threw on her raincoat, and hurried after him to the truck. By the time he dropped her off behind Elm Creek Manor, she was about fifteen minutes late. She tried to avoid the biggest puddles as she ran from the gravel driveway to the back steps.

Mrs. Compson was waiting in the foyer. "You're late," she said before Sarah had a chance to say hello. "I didn't think you were coming."

"I'm sorry, Mrs. Compson." She took off her raincoat and shook the rain from her hair. "I had to make an important phone call, and their office didn't open until eight."

"At eight you were supposed to be here working, not at home making phone calls."

"I said I'm sorry. It won't happen again."

"Hmph." Mrs. Compson sniffed, relenting a little. "I suppose you forgot to buy your quilting materials."

"Everything's right here." Sarah showed her the bag.

"Did you wash and press the fabric?"

"Just as you told me."

"Hmph. Well, I suppose you might as well continue with the library this morning until lunchtime." Mrs. Compson took the bag and turned toward the kitchen. "Leave your shoes here. It won't do to have you tracking mud everywhere."

Sarah made an exasperated face at Mrs. Compson's back. That woman had a real gift for overreacting. She knew that Sarah's search for a real job had to be her first priority. If Mrs. Compson had a phone like normal people, Sarah could have come to work on time and called from there. She jerked off her shoes, and the chill from the cold tile floor crept into her toes. Muttering complaints under her breath, she pulled up her socks and followed her employer into the kitchen.

"Was my quilt still in the window of Grandma's Attic?" Mrs. Compson asked as Sarah entered the kitchen. She was sitting at the table, peering through her glasses at a newspaper.

"It was still there Saturday morning."

Mrs. Compson frowned and shook her head. "Maybe it's time for them to take it down. I doubt if anyone will buy it. I should just stick it in the cedar chest with the others."

"Oh, no, they should leave it up. It's so pretty. Someone will buy it soon, I'm sure."

Mrs. Compson looked up then, her face uncertain. "Do you really think so?"

"I'd buy it, if I could."

"You're a sweet girl to say so, but I have my doubts. It just seems like people don't care about things like quilters anymore."

Sarah thought about Bonnie, Summer, and the other Tangled Web Quilters. "I don't know. I think a lot of people care about quilts."

Mrs. Compson smiled halfheartedly. "That's not what I said." She sighed and returned to her newspaper.

Sarah watched her for a moment, then turned and went upstairs to the library. She didn't feel like a sweet girl. She wished she could be more like Matt—always accepting people, never making snap judgments, giving people the benefit of the doubt instead of getting angry over the least little thing. Maybe Mrs. Compson had overreacted, but Sarah had been late for work, if only by a few minutes. She felt a tiny prick of guilt on her conscience, more for her angry reaction to Mrs. Compson's behavior than for her tardiness.

Mrs. Compson had left three empty cartons, a ball of twine, a can of furniture polish, and a pile of clean rags on the floor next to the desk. Since the wind was blowing from the south, Sarah opened the windows on only the east wall so she could get some fresh air without soaking the hardwood floor or the Persian carpet that covered its center. Then she began her day's work by filling the cartons with Claudia's old paperbacks and tying up bundles of newspaper with the twine. The library was pleasantly cool that morning, and Sarah hummed cheerfully as she worked, listening to the rain outside. Sometimes a low peal of thunder would toll far off in the distance, making the windows tremble and the lights flicker.

At noon she heard Mrs. Compson's slow step from the top of the stairs. Sarah set down her dust rag and hurried to open the library door. Mrs. Compson stood there with a tray loaded with sandwiches, fruit salad, and a pitcher of iced tea.

"You didn't need to come all the way up here." Sarah took the tray and carried it to the coffee table. "I would've come downstairs."

"I thought I might like to see how you're coming along up here instead." Mrs. Compson looked around, nodding in satisfaction as she joined Sarah in the center of the room. "Yes, you're doing a fine job. This place looks almost as I remember it." She gingerly lowered herself onto the sofa, and a cloud of dust rose.

Sarah made a mental note to beat the cushions after lunch. She sat on the floor on the other side of the table and poured herself a glass of iced tea.

"I thought I'd join you for lunch," Mrs. Compson said. "If you don't mind the intrusion."

"It's no intrusion. I'd like the company." Sarah poured a second glass and handed it to her employer. She took a sandwich from the top of the pile and placed it on the delicate china plate Mrs. Compson set before her. The plate was almost translucent, with scalloped edges trimmed in gold and a rearing stallion etched in the center. "You know, I've noticed this horse emblem all over the place," Sarah mused, forgetting her earlier vow to resist prying into Mrs. Compson's life. "There's the fountain in the front of the manor, and the same horse is etched on the china, and it's embossed in gold on the desk—"

"Compson is my married name." Mrs. Compson sipped her iced tea. "Oh, yes, of course. You're new to Waterford. You haven't heard, I suppose, of Hans Bergstrom? Or of Bergstrom Thoroughbreds?"

Sarah shook her head.

"What do you know of horses?"

"Not much."

"Hans Bergstrom was my great-grandfather." Mrs. Compson rose and went over to the desk. She ran a hand over the emblem of the rearing stallion. "In his time he raised the finest horses in the country. I never knew him, except from my parents' stories, but he must have been a remarkable man. All Bergstrom men were remarkable men."

❧

I remember one story in particular. Out of all the stories this house holds, it's my very favorite.

My great-grandfather was the youngest son of a rather well-to-do family in Germany from a small city near Baden-Baden. I say the family was from Baden-Baden, but that's not entirely true. Hans's grandfather moved there from Stockholm when he married a German girl. And you'd think that would be enough moving about for one family, but you'd be wrong.

I suppose Hans Bergstrom was a lot like his grandfather—never one to stay in one place. His parents wanted him to go into the clergy, but he would have none of that. He wanted to seek adventure and fortune in America. When he was a young man, perhaps only a few years younger than you, he boarded a ship and emigrated without his parents' permission, without even informing them of his journey. Only his eldest sister knew, and she told no one until his ship was a week at sea.

Before long he made his way to Pennsylvania and began to use his knowledge of horse breeding and raising in other men's employ, saving every spare cent he could. He had a plan, you see, to establish his own stables someday and to breed the finest horses anywhere, new world and old alike.

When he was ready, he found this land and built a small house on the western edge of the property, where the orchard grows today. Such a confident man he was, brash even, so certain he was of his future success. He wrote to his family back in Germany to urge them to join him here, but only his eldest sister, Gerda, agreed to make the journey. She was unmarried, and very sensible, but not afraid to take a few risks.

When Gerda's ship was scheduled to arrive, Hans traveled to New York City to meet her. And this is the part of the story I like best. When he arrived at Immigration, he found a small knot of men talking excitedly and waving their arms about and carrying on as men always do when they argue. Never one to keep his nose in his own business, Hans nudged one man and asked him what was going on.

"They've got a girl there," the man told him. "Folks say she's been loitering here for three days now."

"I heard a week," another man interjected.

The first man shrugged. "Either way, they want her gone. They're trying to figure out what to do with her."

Intrigued, Hans pushed his way to the center of the crowd, and there he discovered the prettiest girl he had ever seen. Oh, she looked exhausted, to be sure, but with her green eyes and brown hair—well, I've seen her portrait, and I tell you she must have been a vision. She sat on top of a shining new treadle sewing machine cabinet, ankles crossed, hands folded primly in her lap, brave chin up, for all the world as if she were sitting on a throne. A couple of steamer trunks rested on the floor beneath her feet, and beside her three men in uniforms debated her future as if she had no say in the matter—which, I suppose, she probably didn't. She ignored them with all the dignity she could muster.

After questioning some others in the crowd, Hans learned that this young woman was from Berlin and that she was supposed to have been met there three days before by the man who had promised to marry her. She had spent her life savings on her passage to America and on the sewing machine with which she hoped to earn her keep, had gambled everything on that scoundrel's promise. The officials did not know what to do with her. She had no other family in the country, spoke no English, and had no one to sponsor her now that her good-for-nothing fiancé had betrayed her. Most of the men were all for bundling her back on board the next ship for Germany, but she refused to budge. She wouldn't disobey them, but she wouldn't allow herself to be meekly driven away, either.

Now, if I had been that young woman, I would have planted my feet, looked those men straight in the eye, and dared them to try to put me on board a ship when I didn't want to go, but times were different then. I suppose my day was as different from hers as yours is from mine.

Then one of the officials threw up his hands in exasperation. "Well, unless one of you lot wants to marry her, I'm all for tossing her on the next ship east, sewing machine and all!"

"I'll marry her," my great-grandfather said, stepping forth from the crowd. He turned to the beautiful girl sitting on top of her sewing machine and greeted her in German.

She blinked in astonishment at the sound of her own language coming from an American. She became even more surprised when he translated what he had told the men.

"I'd marry you today and consider myself a lucky man," Hans said in German. "But it would be wrong for me to expect you to decide under these circumstances. Besides, I'd like to think that my bride chose me for myself and not because her only other option was deportation."

The beautiful girl smiled at that.

"We'll tell these men that you're my bride," Hans continued. "What they don't know won't hurt them. You can live with my sister and me as long as you want. Maybe in a year or two, you'll tell me that you truly will be my bride. Or maybe you'll find another fellow. I hope you'll choose me, but I want you to know what you're getting before you say yes."

She smiled and gave him her hand. "Perhaps you'll give me your name first, and we can discuss marriage later. In a year or two."

It turned out that she needed only six months to make up her mind. They fell in love, and that speeded her decision. Sometimes I wonder if she fell in love first with Hans's dream, with its hopes and challenges, and then with the man himself. Or perhaps her love for the man grew into love for his dream. I suppose I'll never know.

Well, I suppose you've figured out by now that the beautiful girl was my great-grandmother, Anneke. She and my great-grandfather were married eight months after they met, and Gerda was the maid of honor. As the years passed they established Elm Creek Manor and spent their lives working tirelessly until Bergstrom Thoroughbreds were recognized everywhere as the pinnacle of excellence. Even today the world's finest horses can be traced back to this land.

My great-grandparents raised their children here, and when the children married, their spouses lived here as well with their children. Some moved away, but when my father married he brought my mother here. I remember having fourteen young playmates close at hand when I was a child. It was a wonderful, happy time.

⚜

"Then what happened?" Sarah prompted. Why had Mrs. Compson sounded so sad at the end? And what had happen to change everything? The manor was all but abandoned now, unrecognizable as the happy place Mrs. Compson had described.

"The manor thrived. My father continued the tradition my great-grand-father had begun, as did my husband and I, for a time." Mrs. Compson sighed and went to an east-facing window. She gazed outside. "But that was all a very long time ago, and things are much different now. Much of the land we once held has been sold off, and all that is left of Great-Grandfather Bergstrom's dream is this house, a handful of acres, beautiful horses scattered around the world—" Mrs. Compson's voice caught in her throat. "And memories. But I suppose that will have to be enough. Sometimes it's too much."

Sarah wanted to say something but could only watch as Mrs. Compson stared outside at the rain. In the tightness of the older woman's shoulders and in the bowing of her head, Sarah thought she could see the surface of a grief she could not understand.

Mrs. Compson turned and crossed the room. "Bring the tray down with you at three, will you?"

"Aren't you going to finish your lunch?"

"No, thank you, dear. I'm not hungry after all. I'll see you downstairs this afternoon." She left the room, shutting the library door behind her.

Frowning, Sarah started to finish her lunch. Then she set down her sandwich and pushed the plate away. What could have happened to the Bergstrom family to make Mrs. Compson so unhappy?

Sarah went to the window where Mrs. Compson had been looking out at the storm. If there were answers in the rain-drenched lawn, the distant trees tossing their green boughs in the wind, and the pool of the rearing horse fountain rapidly filling with rainwater, Sarah couldn't see them.

Seven

At three o'clock Sarah carried the tray downstairs to the kitchen and joined Mrs. Compson in the sitting room. The well-lit room was snug and cheerful in spite of the storm outside. Mrs. Compson had draped Sarah's fabric over the sofa and was studying it when Sarah greeted her.

"You have a good eye for color, Sarah."

"One of Bonnie's employees helped me match things up." Sarah picked up one of the quilting books and flipped through the pages. "Are we going to start quilting today?"

"If you mean quilting as in the whole process of making a quilt, yes. If you mean quilting as in sewing through the three layers of the quilt, no." Mrs. Compson pushed her sewing machine against the wall and beckoned Sarah to join her at the table. "We'll begin by making templates for your first block, the Sawtooth Star."

"Templates?"

Mrs. Compson found the block's diagram in a quilt book. "We transfer the pieces of the block from the drawing to this clear plastic. Then we cut out the template, place it on the wrong side of our fabric, and draw around it. Cut a quarter of an inch around the drawn line, and you have your first quilt piece."

"Why don't we cut on the line?"

"The drawn line is your sewing line. The extra quarter inch is the seam allowance."

"Oh." Sarah wasn't sure she understood, but she sat down and took the sheet of plastic Mrs. Compson handed her. A grid of fine red lines covered it. "Should I just trace it out of the book? It looks too small."

"That's quite correct," Mrs. Compson said. "If you simply traced the pieces, your finished block would be six inches square, only half the size we need. Many books and magazines provide actual-size drawings, but we will need to enlarge this one."

She showed Sarah how to use the author's half-scale diagram and the grid on the plastic sheet to create a template of the correct size. With Mrs. Compson's help, Sarah soon created four templates: a small square, a larger square, a small isosceles right triangle, and a larger isosceles right triangle.

As Sarah worked, a memory tickled in the back of her mind. Whenever she looked at the Sawtooth Star diagram, she felt as if she were missing something obvious, something important, something she ought to see but didn't. She tried to shake the feeling, but it lingered.

"Now for the tracing." Mrs. Compson selected Sarah's medium blue print and her cream background fabric from the pile on the sofa. She instructed Sarah to cut one larger square and eight smaller triangles from the blue, and to cut four small squares and four larger triangles from the cream. When Sarah had finished, Mrs. Compson arranged the pieces on the table so that the different shapes formed a star.

The persistent sense of familiarity tugged at Sarah as she studied the pieces. "I've seen this before."

"Of course you have. You chose this block yourself."

"No, that's not it." Sarah thought hard, and then it was as if a blurry image suddenly shifted into focus. "I had a quilt like this once." As she said the words, she could almost see the pink-and-white quilt her grandmother had made for her eighth birthday.

She could still remember the way her mother's mouth had tightened when Sarah unwrapped the present. "Good Lord, Mother," her mother had said. "You didn't need to do that. I just bought her a new bedspread two months ago."

"A granddaughter deserves a handmade quilt. It was a joy to make."

"She'll just spill something on it and ruin it."

"No, I won't. I promise," Sarah had said, running her small hand over the quilt.

"Don't you like the bedspread we picked out together?"

Sarah had looked up then, startled by the warning tone in her mother's voice. "Y-yes." She hesitated. "But I like the quilt, too."

"Which one do you like better?"

"Don't ask her that," Grandmother had murmured.

"No, no. Don't worry about offending me, Mother. I want to know. Come on, Sarah. The truth."

"I like—" Sarah remembered looking from her mother's hard eyes to her grandmother's sad ones. "I like the quilt best."

"Figures." Her mother stood up. "I guess that's what you hoped to hear, right, Mother?"

"It isn't a contest."

"Easy for you to say. You won." Her mother took the quilt and stuffed it back into the box. "Sarah will take good care of it, won't you, Sarah?" She carried the box away without another word.

Grandmother held out her arms then, and Sarah climbed into her lap. She squeezed her eyes shut against the tears, but they fell anyway.

Even now, so many years later, resentment washed over her. She pushed the memory away. "My grandmother made me a Sawtooth Star quilt when I turned eight."

"Is that so?"

"Uh huh." Sarah stared at the quilt block. "I wasn't allowed to use it, though. My mother said it was too fancy for every day, so she kept it in a box in her closet. I was only allowed to use it when Grandmother came to visit."

"I see." Mrs. Compson gave her a knowing look. "So your mother was the fussy type, with plastic on the furniture and all that, hmm?"

"No." Sarah moved two of the block pieces closer together and studied them. "She wasn't like that about anything except this quilt." She wondered where it was now. Still on the floor of her mother's closet, probably. "I had forgotten all about it. Funny, isn't it, that out of all of those blocks you showed me, I would pick this one?"

"Not necessarily. Perhaps you chose this block because some part of you never forgot your grandmother's quilt and never stopped missing it."

"Do you think so?"

"Or perhaps the gift wasn't a Sawtooth Star quilt but a Dove in the Window or a Sunbonnet Sue. Or maybe it wasn't a quilt at all, but a doll or a pretty dress. Memory can be a tricky thing sometimes."

The thought made Sarah uneasy. "So you think I'm remembering something that never happened?" That didn't make sense. She could picture herself holding that quilt, running her hand over its softness and delighting in the bright colors.

"Certainly not. Something happened, some conflict with your mother, some tension between her and her own mother. But whether it was over a Sawtooth Star quilt or something else entirely, I couldn't say."

Sarah frowned. Mrs. Compson's explanation was no comfort. She rearranged some of the block pieces and glowered at them. "These corners— they don't match up right."

Mrs. Compson tapped her wrist. "Stop fiddling with the pieces. You're forgetting about the seam allowances again. Once the pieces are sewn together, everything will match up just fine and you'll see how pretty the block will be." She opened a small tin container full of pins. "Now you'll learn how to hand piece."

Sarah knew how to sew on a button but nothing more complicated than that, so she listened carefully as Mrs. Compson explained what to do. Following Mrs. Compson's directions, she picked up a cream triangle and a blue triangle, placed the right sides facing each other, and pinned them together along the sewing line. Then she took the threaded needle Mrs. Compson handed her, tied a small knot at the end of the thread, and sewed a running stitch from the beginning to the end of the line, removing the pins as she came to them. After tying a second knot and trimming the extra thread, she creased the seam flat with a fingernail.

"Now, if you do that several thousand times, you'll have a quilt top," Mrs. Compson remarked.

Sarah continued to work, with Mrs. Compson looking over her shoulder and giving advice. When Sarah had finished all the straight seams and had joined several units into rows, Mrs. Compson explained how to sew through seams when joining rows together. Although Sarah's piecing became faster and more accurate with every seam, Matt arrived before she was able to finish the block. She put the pieces and her sewing tools into her backpack so that she could continue sewing at home.

The rain had stopped, and the usual heat and humidity had returned. On the drive home, Sarah told Matt the little Mrs. Compson had revealed about her family and the history of Elm Creek Manor.

"I wonder what went on here to ruin everything," Matt said when she finished.

"Me, too. For a moment I thought she was about to tell me, but just when she opened up, she got all upset and left. I can't figure it out. From what she said, they had everything. Literally. A family, a home, enough money to take care of everything. Why would someone want to leave all that?"

"You're asking the wrong guy."

Sarah barely heard him. "I wonder," she mused. "Claudia or someone must have done something terribly wrong to Mrs. Compson for her to break off all ties with her family."

"Sometimes people break off all ties even when the family does everything right."

Sarah started in realization. "Matt, honey, I didn't mean—"

"Can we drop it, please?"

"But I didn't mean that your mother left because you—"

"I said, can we drop it?"

Sarah watched him as he stared grimly out at the road in front of them. A long moment passed in silence.

"Matt?"

"What."

"Mrs. Compson came back to Elm Creek Manor. You never know, maybe—"

"No, I do know. If my mother was coming back, she would have done it a long time ago. Don't treat me like I'm five, okay?"

Stung, Sarah sat back in her seat and stared out the window. When they reached their duplex she jumped out of the truck and ran inside. She hurried upstairs and took a long shower, rinsing her stinging eyes again and again. She finished reluctantly and lingered in the steam, not knowing how to avoid her husband in such a small home.

When she finally pulled on her robe and went to the bedroom, Matt was sitting cross-legged on the bed, looking miserable.

Sarah tried to ignore him as she put on a T-shirt and cotton shorts.

"Sweetheart, I'm sorry I snapped at you."

Sarah didn't answer. She found some socks in her drawer and sat down on the bed to pull them on.

"Sarah, I'm really sorry."

"I didn't mean anything," she muttered, looking at the floor. "I was only trying to make you feel better."

"I know." He touched her gently on the shoulder.

"I always make things worse."

"No, you don't."

"Yes, I do. I don't mean to, but I do. I always say the exact wrong thing at the worst possible time."

"That has nothing to do with it. I just don't like talking about my mother."

"Okay." Sarah thought for a moment. "But in the truck I wasn't talking about your mother. I was talking about Mrs. Compson's sister."

"You were talking about people going away."

"Oh, right." Sarah turned to face him and gave him a small smile. "So let me make sure I have this straight. I shouldn't talk about families, or people going away, or mothers—"

"We can talk about your mother if you want."

"Please, no. Anything but that." Sarah flopped onto her back on the bed and closed her eyes.

"You know, you really ought to give your mother a break."

Sarah groaned and threw an arm over her face. "Please don't start." They'd had this discussion many times before, and neither one ever altered the other's opinion. Ever since Sarah's mother had started dating again, three months after Sarah's father died, every conversation between Sarah and her mother had turned into an argument. Sarah's solution was to avoid contact as much as possible, even though it was obvious how much this disappointed

Matt. He probably thought that if not for Sarah's attitude, they could all be one big happy family. If he only knew what Sarah's mother said about him when he wasn't there to hear.

Sarah sighed. "I won't talk about your mother anymore tonight if you don't talk about mine."

Matt chuckled. "Okay. Deal."

Sarah reached out for his hand and pulled him down beside her. She rested her head on his shoulder and breathed in his scent of grass and earth and sunlight.

Her family, Matt's, Mrs. Compson's—none had lasted. She searched her memory and concluded that she knew only a few families that weren't obviously screwed up. And those few probably just hid it better.

She held Matt closer. He was her family now. They would make their own family, one that didn't hurt.

Eight

As she worked in the library the next morning, Sarah tried to concentrate on reorganizing the bookshelves instead of worrying about her upcoming job interview with PennCellular. After sorting the last pile of books, papers, and loose pages, she carried the newspaper bundles downstairs. Later she and Matt could load them into the truck and leave them in the recycling bin near their duplex.

With most of the clutter removed, the library took on a more dignified air. Sarah looked around, satisfied with her work. If she and Matt ever bought a house, she would love to have a room just like this one, full of books, with comfortable sofas to curl up on and a cheery fire in the fireplace in the winter. Before they could buy a house, though, Sarah would have to have a job. A real job.

Sarah sighed and gave up. It was no use; every random thought led her back to the job interview no matter how hard she tried to keep busy. Working at Elm Creek Manor was fine for now, but she had to find something with a future. If only she had a relative or a friend of the family who could help her get her foot in the door somewhere. But she had no such connections, and it wasn't likely that she'd make any in Middle of Nowhere, Pennsylvania.

At noon Sarah changed into her interview suit and went to the sewing room to tell Mrs. Compson she was about to leave. The older woman set her quilt aside and scrutinized Sarah's outfit. "Stand up straight," she admonished. "You want them to think you have confidence, don't you? They won't want to hire someone who slouches."

Sarah wished all she had to worry about was her posture.

Matt dropped her off a good fifteen minutes early, which she thought was just about right: early enough to make a good impression but not so early that she seemed desperate. "Maybe you are desperate, but Brian Turnbull doesn't need to know that," Sarah muttered to her reflection as she pulled open the glass door.

A receptionist near the entrance greeted her and directed her to a small waiting room. Some of the men sitting there glanced up as she entered, then returned to their newspapers and magazines.

She took the last empty seat and tried to get a look at the other applicants without being too obvious. They were all men, which was odd enough in itself, but they were also in their late forties to mid-fifties, surely too experienced for the kind of work Sarah was qualified to do. They wore expensive and expertly made suits. Dismayed, Sarah fingered the hem of her off-the-rack suit jacket and felt her cheeks starting to burn. She could have sworn Turnbull had said the position was entry-level. This interview was going to be a nightmare.

The man in the next chair turned to her and smiled. "Are you here for the cost accounting interview?"

Sarah nodded. "Yes."

"We all are." The man shifted in his seat and rubbed his palms on his fine pinstriped slacks. The large rings on the fourth finger of each hand glistened as he gestured to the occupied chairs. "Look at all these folks, and the opening hasn't even hit the papers yet."

"I guess a lot of people want to work here."

"A lot of people want to work, period." He leaned back and rested his right ankle on his left knee. His hair and mustache were thick and dark, sprinkled heavily with gray throughout. "Did you just graduate from college?"

Sarah smiled. "I'll take that as a compliment. Actually, it's been a while."

"Oh. You look younger." He let out a heavy sigh. "An accounting major?"

"That's right."

"There sure are a lot of you out there, aren't there?"

Sarah looked him squarely in the eye. "I'm not sure I know what you mean."

"Nothing. I don't mean anything." His smile appeared forced. "Just . . . there seem to be more accounting majors every year."

Sarah shrugged, wishing she could find a polite way to get out of the conversation. "I guess so. It's an interesting field, I guess, and it's a pretty stable career choice—"

"Stable?" a stocky man seated across from them interrupted. "Haven't you ever heard of downsizing?"

"Bill, is that necessary?" the dark-haired man asked. He turned back to Sarah. "Don't mind him. He gets cranky if he has to go five minutes without a cigarette."

The stocky man glowered and raised his newspaper to block their view of him.

"Sounds like you know him," Sarah murmured.

"We worked a temp job together during tax season. Bill smokes like a chimney, all right. I quit six months ago, myself. Did you know that corporate insurance rates are higher for smokers than for nonsmokers?"

Sarah shook her head.

"Well, it's true. That's why I quit. Why hire a smoker when you can save money by hiring a nonsmoker?"

"Can they really do that? Isn't that discrimination?"

"Strictly speaking, they probably aren't allowed to, but they can always find some other excuse to write down. 'You're overqualified.' Or 'The new owners like to hire their own teams.' Some such nonsense." He sighed. "The point is, why risk it?"

"I see what you mean."

"I worked for the largest corporate insurance company in Pittsburgh for twenty years, and I know what I'm talking about."

Everyone looked up as a tall woman in an elegant tailored dress appeared at the door. "Thomas Wilson?" she announced.

The dark-haired man picked up his leather briefcase and stood. "Nice talking with you. Good luck." He extended his hand.

Sarah shook it. "Thanks. Good luck to you, too." He followed the woman out of the room.

Her nervousness suddenly returned in full force. She selected a magazine from the pile on a nearby table and tried to concentrate on an article about HMOs. Occasionally the elegant woman would return and call out the name of another applicant, who would rise and follow her out of the room.

Finally, it was Sarah's turn.

When they left the waiting room, the woman greeted Sarah with a firm handshake and a pleasant smile. "It's good to meet you, Sarah. I'm Marcia Welsh, Director of Personnel."

"It's nice to meet you, too." Sarah was surprised to hear that her voice sounded far more confident than she felt.

Marcia stopped at a door bearing a sign that read CONFERENCE ROOM. She opened the door and let Sarah enter before her.

The conference room was roughly the same size as the waiting room, but it was almost completely filled by a large table. The four men and the woman sitting on the other side wore conservative business attire and stern expressions. Marcia closed the door and took a seat between two of the men. She gestured to a lone chair on Sarah's side of the table. As Sarah sat down, the man closest to her poured a glass of water from a crystal pitcher and pushed it across the table to her.

"Thank you," Sarah said. He ignored her.

"Well, let's get started," the man in the center began. "I'm Brian Turnbull, owner and CEO of PennCellular Corporation." He reeled off the others' names and titles so quickly that Sarah had no hope of catching them. She did get the impression that the group included the company's top executives and representatives from the accounting department, but no one, it seemed, from public relations.

"It's nice to meet you." Sarah stood and tried to reach across the table to shake their hands, but she couldn't quite make it. Embarrassed, she quickly sat down. Marcia smiled understandingly, but the others showed no reaction.

Brian Turnbull began by asking her the same questions she always heard at these interviews: what made her decide to go to Penn State, what she had accomplished at her last job, what did she think her strengths and weaknesses were, and so on. She recited the answers she had prepared in advance, taking care to make eye contact with everyone around the table. They seemed satisfied with her answers, so Sarah's anxiety began to ebb.

Then the man who had poured the water set down his pen and pushed his pad away. "Enough of this beating around the bush. How are your math and reasoning skills?"

Sarah started, not because the question was difficult but because until then no one but Mr. Turnbull had addressed her. And Mr. Turnbull had been much nicer. "I feel that they're quite good," she replied, trying to look confident. "As you can see from my résumé, I have a three-point-nine GPA in my accounting courses and experience in—"

"Yes, yes, I can see the résumé. That doesn't answer my question."

Sarah hesitated. Why did he look so annoyed? "Well—"

"Can you, for example, tell me how many grocery stores there are in the United States of America?"

"How—how many grocery stores?"

"Yes. How many grocery stores. You can include convenience stores if you need to water it down."

Sarah stared at him. "Grocery stores. Sure." She decided to take a drink to buy some time. She watched as her hand lifted the glass in slow motion to her lips. It trembled dangerously, and for an instant she imagined it sending a shower of water in all directions. She tried to smile as she carefully returned the glass to the safety of the tabletop. "I was probably sick the day they taught that."

No one smiled.

Okay, wrong answer. "I guess I could try to figure it out."

"Try." The man on the end shoved his pen and pad at her.

"Okay, well, the population of the United States is about a quarter of a billion, right?"

No response.

"Okay, a quarter of a billion." She scribbled the number on the pad, her heart sinking when she realized they weren't going to give her a single hint. The interviewers' silence made her nervous, so she described the steps in the problem aloud as she worked through them on paper. First she estimated the number of aisles in a typical grocery store, then the amount of time an average customer spent in line. As she used those numbers to calculate the number of customers per store per day, she knew her figures could be off by several thousand or by several hundred thousand, but there was nothing she could do to verify them.

She plowed on doggedly, since she had no other choice. As she worked, her nervousness hardened into anger. It was an unfair question, one with no relevance to the job she sought, one she had no chance of answering accurately. She had researched PennCellular, she knew everything there was to know about the latest trends in the profession—but none of that made any difference. All they cared about was this ridiculous grocery store tally.

The man on the end rolled his eyes and shook his head when Sarah had to double back to correct a mistake; she had been working with the number of people in the country rather than the number of families, which was a more appropriate figure since usually one person did the shopping for their household. She tried not to let the man's disdain bother her, but she felt her cheeks growing hot and she wished she had never come. She raced through the last calculations. The sooner she finished, the sooner she could leave.

"Okay," Sarah said at last. "If we have sixty-two million five hundred thousand shoppers—"

"That's a pretty big 'if,' " the man on the end muttered.

Sarah took a deep breath, fighting to keep the tremor out of her voice. "If that's how many shoppers we have, we would need, um . . . four thousand, one hundred thirty-three and a half grocery stores. Except there wouldn't be a half of a grocery store, so let's say four thousand, one hundred and thirty five." She stared at the figure. "That doesn't sound right. It seems like there should be more than that." She bit her lip and looked at the man on the end. "Is that right?"

He straightened in his seat, indignant. "How should I know?"

Sarah gaped at him. "But—"

"Well, I guess that should pretty much do it," Turnbull said. "Do you have any questions?"

"Huh?" Her eyes were still fixed on the man on the end.

"Do you have any questions about PennCellular or the job?"

Questions—she had to ask some questions about the job. Frantically she searched her memory for the list she had prepared. Where was it? "Cell phones," she blurted out. "You sell cell phones?" It sounded like a tongue twister. You sell cell phones by the sell shore.

Turnbull looked puzzled. "Yes, of course we do. I thought you knew that."

"Oh, I did. I was just checking. Maybe you sell something else, too."

"No, just cell phones." He paused and studied her. "Anything else?"

"No—no, I don't think so."

"Well, then, we're all set." Turnbull rose and the others jumped to their feet. Sarah stood, her legs trembling. He reached across the table and shook her hand. "You'll be hearing from us either way in a few weeks. Thanks for coming. Ms. Welsh will show you out."

Sarah nodded. "Thank you." She felt numb. Marcia led her to the exit and bid her good-bye.

Sarah spotted the truck in the parking lot and almost ran to it. "Thank God you're here." She took her seat and leaned back, closing her eyes.

Matt started the truck. "I've been here a while. They sure kept you long enough."

"I spent most of that time in the waiting room. That was the most bizarre interview I've ever had." She told him what had happened, not omitting a single strange or embarrassing detail.

When she finished, Matt shrugged. "Sounds to me like you handled everything just fine."

"'Just fine'? I sounded like I never made it past high school algebra." Then she thought of something else and slapped a palm to her forehead. "Oh, no."

"What?"

"I calculated how many grocery stores there need to be, not how many there are."

Matt glanced away from the road to look at her. "That doesn't really matter, though, right?"

"What do you mean? Of course it matters. It's a completely different issue."

"Maybe he's interested in how you tackled the problem, not in whether you got the right number. It's not like he could check your answer, right? Maybe he was also trying to see how you respond to pressure."

"Do you really think so?"

"Well, sure."

"Then it's worse than I thought."

"Oh, Sarah." He chuckled and shook his head. "I'm sure you did as well as anyone else they talked to. Probably better."

"Think so? You didn't see the waiting room. All those older men, with all that experience. How am I suppose to compete with them?"

"They probably wonder how they're supposed to compete with someone younger who won't expect as much money and won't be thinking about retirement in five or ten years."

Sarah looked out the window and said nothing. True, she did wonder why anyone with their experience would be interested in an entry-level job and why they would be out of work in the first place. But those men surely wouldn't be out of work for long, not with their backgrounds. Everyone else who passed through that waiting room that day would probably have another job before she even had another interview.

Nine

Two days later, Sarah finished her work in the library and was ready to move on to the next cleaning and inventory assignment. But not right away. First, she wanted to continue her quilting lessons. She took the stairs two at time and hurried to the sitting room.

"Fine work," Mrs. Compson remarked, studying Sarah's finished Sawtooth Star block with a critical eye. "These stitches are a bit crooked here, but not so bad that you need to rip them out. Fine work for a beginner."

"What's next?"

"You'll need to make templates for your next block, the Double Nine Patch. This block is still rather simple since it has no curved seams or set-in pieces, but it can be tricky. Some of the pieces are small and there are many places where the seams must match up perfectly or the design will be ruined." As Sarah took a seat, Mrs. Compson handed her the template drafting supplies.

The Double Nine Patch block, Mrs. Compson explained, was one of many quilt blocks based on a three-by-three grid; they were called nine patches because a single large square was divided by the grid into nine smaller squares. In the Double Nine Patch, the smaller squares in the corners and in the center were further divided into nine even smaller squares.

This time Sarah made two square templates, one large and one small. She cut four of the bigger squares from the cream background fabric, then used the smaller template to make twenty-five little squares from the dark red fabric and twenty from the cream.

"The first quilt I ever made was a Nine Patch," Mrs. Compson remarked, picking up some quilting of her own to work on while monitoring Sarah's progress. "Not a Double Nine Patch, a Nine Patch. It looked like a checkerboard in all different colors."

Sarah looked up from pinning two of the tiny squares together at the corners. "Did someone give you lessons like you're giving me?"

"Hmph. My sister and I learned together, and our lessons were hardly this pleasant. Nothing ever went smoothly when Claudia and I were in the same room. See now, I think that's where my mother went wrong. Instead of teaching us at the same time she should have taught Claudia first, a few years earlier, when I would have been too young to care." She shook her head and sighed. "Perhaps that would have made a difference."

"What happened? Will you tell me about it?"

Mrs. Compson hesitated. "If you'll get me a glass of water first."

Sarah jumped up and quickly returned with the glass. Mrs. Compson took a deep drink, then set the glass aside. "Well, then, I'll tell you," she said. "But don't get so distracted that you don't pay attention to your quilting. If your stitches aren't good enough I'll make you take them out."

My sister, Claudia, was two years older than I, but since I was just as smart and almost as big as she was, people treated us as if we were the same age. Claudia was the pretty one; she had our mother's thick brown hair rippling in shining waves down her back, while at that age my darker hair was always dull and wildly unkempt from running around outdoors. All the grown-ups said Claudia was the very image of Great-Grandmother Anneke, but they respected our ancestors too much to hold any of them responsible for my appearance. I did better with my lessons, but the teachers always liked Claudia best. Everyone did. She was always friendly and cheerful, while I was sulky and sensitive. I imagine it must have been a terrible disappointment to our mother, to have a child like me after doing so well the first time.

The winter when I was five and Claudia was seven, we had a blizzard. It snowed so terribly that we couldn't go to school. Claudia was relieved; she had not learned her lessons for that day and dreaded to disappoint our pretty young teacher, Miss Turner, whom everyone liked. I, on the other hand, fretted for hours, glaring out of the nursery windows and stomping about. What if the other children learned something and I missed it? My mother assured me that none of the other children would be going to school that day, either, but I was not consoled until she promised to teach us something new that day. "But not reading or math," she said, to my surprise. "It's time you two girls learned to quilt."

We had watched Mother sew before, but this was the first time we would be allowed to quilt, like our aunts and Mother's grown-up lady friends. They used to quilt all the time. Some of their quilts may still be around here someplace—up in the attic, perhaps.

So Mother showed us how to quilt, very much as I have shown you, except with scraps from her sewing basket. We scarcely wanted to stop for lunch, we were having so much fun. We carefully selected the prettiest scraps, cut our pieces, and sewed them together. By late afternoon we had each finished several small blocks.

I counted the blocks in my pile, and then those on the floor by Claudia's side. "I have four in my pile, and you only have three," I said.

"Maybe, but I'm almost finished with this one," she told me. She held the unfinished block close to her eye and struggled to tie a knot at the end of a seam.

"But I'm almost done with this one, too. That means I'll have five and you'll have four."

Claudia merely shrugged and yanked on the knot.

"That means I should get to use the quilt first."

At that she finally looked at me. "I'll get to use it first because I'm oldest and that means I'm first."

"I'll get to use it first if I do more of the work."

"Well, maybe you won't do more of the work."

"Well, maybe I will."

"Girls, girls," Mother broke in helplessly. "There's no need to argue. You'll share the work and the quilt equally."

But we paid no attention. As soon as Mother left the room, the race was on. We both scrambled for fabric, fought for the scissors, pieced our blocks with the biggest stitches you've ever seen. Our piles grew, but although I blazed through my sewing, growing angrier and more determined with each seam, Claudia began to grow tired. She rubbed at her eyes and struggled over and over again to poke the same end of thread through the needle's eye. Sometimes she had to take out stitches after sewing the wrong side of one piece to the right side of the other. She began to mutter a little under her breath, and let out a frustrated whine every now and then, but I paid her no mind. My pile of Nine Patches was growing and growing, and I was going to win.

Suddenly she flung down her block and burst into tears. "It's not fair," she sobbed. "You always do everything best. You always beat me. I hate you!" She ran out of the room.

I didn't look up. I kept sewing, but more slowly now. I counted the blocks Claudia had scattered as she ran away. There were six. I had nine, including the one I was still working on.

Mother must have heard my sister's outburst, because moments later, she entered the room. "Sylvia, what's going on here?"

"Nothing, Mother. I'm just sewing, like you told us to." The picture of innocence and obedience, I was.

Mother shook her head, troubled. "Claudia's in her bedroom, crying. Why is that?"

I shrugged, not lifting my eyes from my sewing.

Mother sighed and sat down on the floor beside me. "Sylvia, my little girl, what am I going to do with you?"

I shrugged again. My eyes began to fill with tears.

"I want you to go and tell your sister you're sorry, and I want you to play nice from now on."

"But I didn't do anything," I protested. All I had done was sew faster and better than Claudia had done. I hadn't called her any names or hit her or pulled her hair. Was I supposed to sew slowly just because Claudia did? That wasn't right.

Mother frowned at me, a sad and disappointed frown. I felt simply awful. She never looked at Claudia that way.

I trotted down the hallway to Claudia's bedroom. She lay facedown on the bed, her sobs muffled by a pillow.

"Claudia?"

"Go away."

"Mother said to say I'm sorry, so . . . I'm sorry I sewed faster than you."

"Go away." She sat up and wiped her nose on her sleeve. "You're just a mean, awful brat. Go away."

Then I started to cry, and I hated crying in front of other people. "I said I was sorry. Claudia?" But she'd flung herself onto the bed again. I backed out of the room and softly closed the door.

She didn't come out for supper, and I could hardly swallow a bite myself. All through the meal my parents and my aunts and uncles—and even Grandpa—frowned sternly at me as if I were the worst little girl in the world. My cousins just stared at me wide-eyed and wondering, whispering to each other.

Claudia didn't speak to me for the remaining two days we were snowed in. When school resumed, she finally forgave me and let me help her with her spelling.

She never touched those Nine Patch blocks again. I put hers with mine and finished the quilt a few months later. I offered it to Claudia, but when she said sleeping under it would give her nightmares, I gave it to my cousin, who had just turned four and had dark, unruly hair like mine.

"Claudia did finally learn how to quilt, of course," Mrs. Compson said. "She made a somewhat acceptable green-and-white Irish Chain quilt for Grandpa when she was eight."

"Whatever happened to the Nine Patch quilt?"

"I don't know. I imagine it's long gone. A four-year-old can quite literally love a quilt to pieces."

"Did you and Claudia ever quilt together again?"

"Hmph." Mrs. Compson stood up and walked to the window. "Of course we did. But not for a long time. Maybe I'll tell you about that another day."

Sarah certainly hoped so. If Mrs. Compson told her more about her life at Elm Creek Manor, Sarah might learn why she had left and what had happened to her family.

"Matthew is here." Just as Mrs. Compson spoke, Sarah heard the truck pull up behind the manor. She set her quilt block aside and they went to meet him in the kitchen, where he gratefully accepted the glass of lemonade Mrs. Compson offered.

"The orchards are in much better shape than I expected," he told Mrs. Compson after taking a deep drink and wiping his brow. "From what you first told me, I thought the trees hadn't been tended for years."

"They haven't been tended *well* for years," Mrs. Compson corrected. "But my sister did manage to hire help and make a bit of a harvest every year, as far as I know."

"With some care, you should be able to get a good harvest this year, too. I can't do the work alone, though. I'll need you to sign off on the additional expense."

"Certainly. That should be no trouble."

Matt finished his drink and set the glass in the sink. "I don't think Waterford College has an agriculture program. It's too bad we aren't closer to Penn State. Ag majors would manage this place for you as interns, pretty cheap, to get the experience and to run tests. You know, new organic fertilizers, cultivation methods, things like that."

"That's a great idea," Sarah said. "We aren't too far away. You had to travel farther than this for your internship, and I took a whole semester off for mine."

Mrs. Compson nodded. "It may indeed be something the new owners should consider."

Sarah's heart sank. Just for that moment, she had forgotten that Elm Creek Manor was going to be sold.

"Dear, is anything wrong?"

"No—no, Mrs. Compson. I just remembered that—I forgot my quilting stuff." Sarah returned to the sitting room and collected her sewing tools and quilt block pieces. Matt was watching her worriedly when she came back, so she gave him a bright smile to reassure him.

On the way home Sarah thought about the library she had worked so hard to restore. Somebody else would probably come along and change everything, putting wall-to-wall carpet on the beautiful hardwood floor, covering up the fireplace with ugly wallpaper, and doing other things, worse things that would give any decorator with taste nightmares. Sarah frowned and stared out of the truck window. Maybe Mrs. Compson wouldn't find a buyer. How many people in Waterford had that kind of money anyway?

Then Sarah felt a stab of guilt. If Mrs. Compson wanted to sell her home, it wasn't right for Sarah to hope she'd fail. But she couldn't ignore the fact that Mrs. Compson's success meant no more visits to Elm Creek Manor, no more job, no more quilting lessons, and no more interesting stories about Claudia and the Bergstroms. The best she could hope for was that buyers wouldn't appear for a long time and that the new owners would appreciate Elm Creek Manor as much as the Bergstroms once had.

The day's mail did nothing to improve her mood. She received two rejection letters, both from jobs she'd thought she had a reasonable chance of getting. And there was a postcard. The photograph showed an enormous cruise ship anchored in a serene tropical bay. "Having a wonderful time, Darling," her mother had written on the back. "Uncle Henry sends his love."

Uncle Henry. Unbelievable. If she were a child, Sarah might have tolerated calling her mother's many boyfriends Uncle, but not now. Even the title boyfriend seemed inappropriate.

Sarah crumpled up the postcard and threw it away before Matt noticed.

Ten

Since the library was finished, the next morning Mrs. Compson and Sarah began working on a bedroom suite near the library. "We'll keep the furniture in the rooms until the auction," Mrs. Compson said. "We'll probably discard nearly everything else, though."

The furniture in these rooms, Mrs. Compson explained, was from Lancaster and had been handmade by Amish craftsmen. Sarah ran her hand over the dresser's smooth wooden surface. A blue-and-rose Lone Star quilt, faded but still lovely, was draped over the bed. Net curtains hung across a thin metal rod over the large window in the east wall. A door on the left led to a dressing room, where she spotted a dusty overstuffed sofa with wood armrests carved to resemble a swan's profile, and a small vanity with a cracked mirror.

"These were my Aunt Clara's rooms," Mrs. Compson said. She removed the quilt from the bed, gave it a quick shake, and folded it carefully. "She died of influenza when she was only thirteen."

"I'm sorry."

"Oh, don't be. It was a very long time ago. I never knew her. Almost everyone I've ever known is dead now, and you can't feel sorry all day long." Mrs. Compson placed the quilt on the floor. "Let's start a 'save' pile and a 'throw away' pile, shall we?"

"I hope that's the 'save' pile," Sarah said, indicating the quilt. "You wouldn't throw it away after spending so much time on it, would you?"

"Of course not! But I didn't make this quilt. Claudia did." She bent over and unfolded a corner so that the pattern was visible. "See how the corners of these four diamonds don't meet? That's a sure sign of Claudia's piecing every time."

"I take it this isn't a quilt you two worked on together?"

"Certainly not." Mrs. Compson sniffed indignantly. "I would've made her take out those stitches and do them over, and if you match your points as poorly, I'll do the same to you."

Sarah grinned. "Don't worry. I know better."

"As indeed you should." Mrs. Compson opened a closet and began to sort through the clutter. "See if there is anything worth saving in the dresser. This room should be easy to finish. It hasn't been used in a long time."

Sarah pulled open two empty drawers before she found one half full of worn handkerchiefs, scarves, and a few pieces of costume jewelry. "When did you and Claudia finally start quilting together again?"

"Oh, let's see." Mrs. Compson tapped her chin with a finger. "Why, it must have been to make the baby quilt. Yes, that's right."

⚓

Before we worked together on that project we both still quilted, just not together. The summer after the Nine Patch fiasco we both had quilts in the state fair, and we both won blue ribbons in the girls' competition. The following summer I won a blue ribbon and Claudia took second. My, she was furious. She told me, when Mother and Father couldn't overhear, that the judges gave me the ribbon only because I was younger. I stuck my tongue out at her, which, naturally, Mother saw. At first she said I would not be allowed to ride, as a punishment, but Father was so proud of my riding so well at such a young age that he convinced Mother to relent. I won a ribbon in riding, too, my first ever. That probably made Claudia even angrier. She was afraid of horses, and Father teased her about it.

When I was seven and Claudia was nine, Mother and Father had such wonderful news. We were going to have a new baby brother or sister—

⚓

"You never mentioned another brother or sister."

"You never asked."

"I thought it was just you and Claudia."

"Well, now you know differently. Are you planning to interrupt anymore, or may I continue?"

"Sorry. No more interruptions. Please go on."

"Very well."

⚓

As I was about to explain, when I was seven and Claudia was nine, Mother and Father told us they were going to have another child. We were thrilled. Claudia couldn't wait to help Mother take care of the new baby, and I was looking forward to having a new playmate. We were busy preparing for many months. One of the rooms was made over for the baby, and of course, the baby would need a quilt.

Claudia said that she should be in charge of making the baby's quilt because she was the oldest. I said I should get to be in charge because I was the better quilter. "If that's the way you're going to be, I'll make the quilt all by myself," Claudia announced.

Naturally, I piped up that I would make my own quilt for the baby, too. Then we began to argue over whose quilt the baby would use first, and Claudia said hers, since she was the oldest. My, how that argument infuriated me. Claudia would always be the oldest, and there was nothing I could do about that, so she would always use age to justify everything, from who had to help Cook with the dishes to who got the best scraps from Mother's basket.

"I know," I suggested. "How about this: the baby will use first the quilt that's finished first?"

Well, that just made her angry. I thought it might, which is why I suggested it.

As the argument escalated, Mother decided we should both work on the quilt together. We pouted, but with Mother watching, we had to agree. We decided that I would pick out the block pattern and Claudia could pick out the colors. I selected the Bear's Paw; there would be many triangle points to match, but since there were no curved seams or set-in pieces, Claudia couldn't mess it up too badly. And then it was Claudia's turn.

"Pink and white, with a little bit of green."

I screwed up my nose. "What if it's a boy?"

Claudia folded her arms. "I like pink, white, and green, and I get to choose, remember?"

"But what if it's a boy?"

"It's a baby. It won't care."

"If he's a boy he'll care. Let's pick something else."

"You picked the pattern. I get to pick the colors. You can't pick everything."

"Compromise, girls." That was Mother. She shook her head and gave me that disappointed smile again. In all those years I don't think Claudia ever received one of those looks.

I looked away. "Okay," I said to my sister. "Then you pick the pattern and I'll pick the colors."

Claudia beamed at Mother. "Then I pick Turkey Tracks."

Just for a moment, my heart seemed to beat more quickly, and I gasped. "I don't think that's a very good idea."

"What's wrong now?"

"Yes, Sylvia, what's wrong?" Mother looked surprised. "You've made blocks like it before."

"She doesn't think I can make it, that's what's wrong." Claudia glared at me. "But I can, as good as you, too."

"Sylvia, is that so?" Mother asked.

I shook my head no.

"What is it, then?"

"Turkey Tracks." My voice held a fearful tremor as I said the name. "It's also called Wandering Foot, remember? Remember what Grandma used to say?"

Mother and Claudia stared at me. Then Claudia began to giggle. "That's just a silly superstition, silly."

Even Mother smiled. "Sylvia, you shouldn't let Grandma's old stories worry you so. I think it's a lovely pattern."

I bit my lip. I didn't like being laughed at, and I didn't like being called silly, but I still knew it wasn't a good idea. It would have been better to make a pink quilt and hope Mother had a girl than to do this.

"How about if we make the Bear's Paw instead?" I said. "We can use pink if you want."

Claudia shook her head. "No, I like this idea better."

"Come now, what colors would you like?" Mother beckoned me over to her scrap basket.

I took all the blue and yellow pieces from the overflowing basket. If we had to make a Wandering Foot quilt, and I didn't see any way out of it, then at the very least I was going to make it from my lucky colors.

I think it was about two months later when we finished the quilt. It was very pretty, but I still had misgivings. And a few months after that, in January, Mother had a baby boy. Father named him Richard after his brother who died in the Great War, and we all adored him.

⚜

Mrs. Compson finished cleaning out the closet and stood, rubbing her lower back. For a moment Sarah only watched her, puzzled. "I don't understand," she finally said.

"Don't understand what?"

"The quilt pattern. What was wrong with Turkey Tracks?"

"Oh." Mrs. Compson sat on the bed, her thin figure barely compressing the mattress. "Some people think that by changing a block's name you get rid of the bad luck, but I know that bad luck isn't so easily fooled. Turkey Tracks is the same pattern as Wandering Foot. If you give a boy a Wandering

Foot quilt, he will never be content to stay in one place. He'll always be restless, roaming around, running off from home to who knows where—and I can't even begin to tell you what that pattern will do to a girl." She shook her head. "What a silly choice. Claudia should have known better."

Sarah nodded, but secretly she sympathized with Mrs. Compson's mother. She wouldn't have pegged Mrs. Compson as the superstitious type, especially over something like a quilt.

Mrs. Compson studied Sarah's expression and frowned. "Now, I'm not superstitious, mind, but why take unnecessary chances? Life will give you plenty of necessary ones on its own. And I was right, too, as it turned out. But that's no consolation. I would have preferred for Claudia to be right this time."

"What do you mean? The superstition came true?"

Just then she heard voices downstairs.

"My hearing isn't what it used to be, but that sounds like Matthew. Let's go see if I'm right." Mrs. Compson rose and left the room.

Sarah followed, wishing Mrs. Compson had answered her question. But it was a stupid question anyway. A quilt pattern couldn't bring bad luck, unless . . . Annoyed and exasperated with herself, Sarah shook her head as if to clear it of such illogical thoughts.

Eleven

M att and another man Sarah recognized from Exterior Architects were waiting just outside the front entrance. "We didn't want to track mud all over the place," Matt explained as his friend gestured sheepishly at their muddy work boots. "We're going to head on in to town to grab some lunch. Is there anything you need us to do for you while we're there?"

"You needn't go into town. I'll make lunch for you."

"There're six of us, ma'am," the other man said. Joe, that was his name. "We don't want you to go to any trouble."

"Even so. What a poor hostess your friends will think me."

"Not at all." Matt grinned. "Besides, for what our boss charges you, we should be making *you* lunch."

"Is that so? Very well, then. In that case, I won't insist. As for your offer to run errands for me, thank you, but no. The grocery store delivers weekly and I don't need anything else right now."

"If you ever do, just ask." Matt gave Sarah a quick kiss, and he and Joe left.

Mrs. Compson turned to Sarah. "Perhaps we should be thinking about lunch ourselves."

"Do you want me to finish upstairs first?"

"Leave it until tomorrow. I'd prefer to work on our quilts for a while. In fact, I believe I feel like seeing the old gardens. Would you like to take our lunch and our quilting outside?"

"Oh, I'd love to. I haven't seen the gardens yet."

"Don't expect much. I doubt if they've been tended for a long time. I should have been to see them before now, if only to tell Matthew what to do there."

They went to the kitchen and packed a small wooden basket with sandwiches, fruit, and a plastic jug of iced tea. Mrs. Compson fetched an old quilt and a wide-brimmed hat from the hall closet while Sarah collected the quilt blocks and the tackle box Mrs. Compson used to store her sewing tools. Then Mrs. Compson led her down the hallway toward the front foyer, but instead of turning right toward the front entrance, they turned left. Several doors lined the hallway until it ended at an outside door at the corner of the L-shaped manor. The door opened onto a gray stone patio surrounded by lilac bushes and evergreens. At the edge of the patio, a stone path continued north into the bushes.

Mrs. Compson paused in the center of the patio. "Out of all the lovely places on the estate, this was my mother's favorite. In fair weather, she would have her afternoon tea out here. It was so pleasant in springtime when the lilacs were flowering. She called this place the cornerstone patio."

"Why did she call it that?"

"You wouldn't need to ask if these bushes were properly pruned. Here, help me with this." She went to where the edge of the patio met the north-west corner of the manor and struggled to push the branches aside. Sarah hurried to help her.

"See there?" Mrs. Compson pointed to a large engraved stone at the base of the building.

Sarah pushed through the branches and kneeled on the stone patio so that she could read the carved letters. " 'Bergstrom 1858.' Was that when the manor was built?"

"Yes, but only the west wing, of course. Hans, Anneke, and Gerda laid that cornerstone with their own hands. My grandfather was only a toddler then, and my great-aunt was not yet born." Mrs. Compson sighed. "Some-times I picture them, so young and hopeful and brave, laying the foundation of Elm Creek Manor, and of the Bergstrom family itself. Do you suppose they ever dreamed they would accomplish so much?"

Sarah thought for a moment. "From what you've told me about them, I think they probably did. They sound like the sort of people who dreamed big and had the fortitude to match."

Mrs. Compson looked thoughtful. "Yes, I believe you're right." Then her gaze swept around the patio, taking in the tangled bushes, the weeds growing up between the stones, and the peeling paint on the door. "I suppose they never thought their heirs would neglect what they had worked so hard to build."

Sarah rose and brushed off her knees. "I think they'd understand." She let the branches fall back into place in front of the cornerstone.

"Hmph. That's kind of you, dear, but I don't even understand, and I'm one of those neglectful heirs myself. Come along, now." She continued across the patio to the stone path, which disappeared into the surrounding bushes. In another moment, the foliage hid her from view.

Sarah pushed after her, only to find herself standing on the lawn on the north side of the building. She spun around, but could not see the patio or the door through the thick brush. The other day when she had passed this side of the manor while mulling over Mrs. Compson's job offer, she had not even suspected an entrance was there.

"What's keeping you?" Mrs. Compson called. She had already crossed the lawn and was waiting where the stone pathway continued into the woods. Sarah followed her down the shaded, meandering path until it broadened and opened into an oval clearing surfaced with the same gray stone. In the foreground were four round planters, each about fifteen feet in diameter and three feet high; the lower halves of their walls were two feet thicker than at the top, forming smooth, polished seats where visitors could rest. The planters, which now held only rocky soil, some dry branches that might once have been roses, and weeds, were spaced evenly around a black marble fountain of a mare prancing with two foals. Beyond them was a large wooden gazebo, paint peeling and gingerbread molding sagging dejectedly. Through the wooden slats Sarah could see terraces cut into the slope of a gentle hill on the other side, but their supporting stones had long since fallen away, allowing the beds to erode. As Sarah watched, a bird flew from inside the roof of the gazebo, alighted on the mare's head, then flitted away.

Mrs. Compson draped the quilt over the nearest planter's seat and sat down. "It used to look much nicer than this," she said dryly. Sarah nodded, thinking that her employer had a gift for understatement. They unpacked the basket and ate their lunches in silence. As usual, Mrs. Compson only nibbled at hers. Most of the time she sat with her hands clasped in her lap as she looked around the garden. Occasionally her lips would part as if she were about to speak, but then she would sigh and press them together again, shaking her head in regret and disappointment.

"You should have seen it when I was a girl," she finally said as Sarah packed up their leftovers and trash. "The planters were full of roses and ivy, the fountain would sparkle, the terraces held bulbs that bloomed with every variety of lovely blossom. What a shame. What a shame."

Sarah touched her arm. "Matt can restore it. You'll see."

"It never should have been allowed to fall into such disrepair in the first place. Claudia could have easily afforded a gardener—a whole staff of gardeners. She should have had better sense."

"Mrs. Compson, why do you want to sell the manor? I know it needs some fixing up, but it could be such a wonderful place again, and Matt and I will help."

"I could never be happy here. Even if it were as beautiful as it once was, it could never be what it was supposed to be. You couldn't possibly under-stand, a child your age."

She frowned so gloomily that Sarah looked away. Certainly the garden needed a lot of work, but Matt had restored places in even worse disrepair. If Mrs. Compson just gave him a chance—

"Besides, I already have a buyer."

Sarah whirled on her. "You what?"

Mrs. Compson studied the stone bench beside her. "A local real estate company has already expressed a great deal of enthusiasm. A gentleman from University Realty visited me Tuesday afternoon, while you were at your interview. Of course, we haven't agreed to any terms yet, but I'm sure we'll strike a fair bargain." Mrs. Compson surveyed the garden with a critical eye. "That's why I'm investing so much in the restoration, to increase the estate's value."

"I see."

"Now, don't sound so dejected, Sarah. I'll be here all summer. That's plenty of time to teach you how to quilt."

"But what will you do after that?"

"Sell the manor, auction off the contents, and return to my house in Sewickley. Don't look so surprised. You do recall why you were hired, don't you?" Abruptly, she rose. "If you're finished eating, I have something else to show you."

Sarah followed her to the gazebo. The steps creaked tiredly, as if they would have collapsed except it required too much effort. Wood benches resembling rectangular wooden crates lined the walls of the octagon-shaped structure.

Mrs. Compson pointed to the top of each bench in turn, and cocked her head to one side. "What do you think?"

Sarah peered closer. Inlaid in the middle of each seat was a pattern of interlocking multicolored wood rectangles fitted around a small center square. Some benches had a yellow center square—yellow pine, perhaps—while the rest had a red center square. The colors might have been vivid once but were now weathered and faded. Sarah traced one of the blocks with a fin-ger. "This pattern looks familiar, but I can't place it."

"It's a quilt pattern called Log Cabin. Supposedly it was invented to honor Abraham Lincoln, but that might just be a myth. According to tradition, the quilter should always put a red square in the middle, to sym-bolize the hearth, or a yellow square, to represent a light in the cabin window."

"It's pretty."

"That's true, but there's more. Look carefully."

Sarah carefully examined each bench in turn, not sure what she should be looking for. Then she saw it. "This one," she said, pointing. "Its center square is different. It's black."

"Good girl." Mrs. Compson nodded. "Lift up the bench."

"It lifts up?" Sarah grasped the edge of the bench. She saw no hinges, nothing to distinguish it from the other benches.

"Carefully, now. Lift up the edge and slide it back."

The wooden seat creaked in protest and stuck, but Sarah jimmied it lose. As she eased it away from her, the wooden slats folded into a hidden recess beneath the bench, almost like a rolltop desk. "What in the world—" The seat had covered some kind of opening. Sarah saw narrow boards nailed in a column, like a ladder leading down from a child's treehouse.

"In the Civil War era, Elm Creek Manor was a stop on the Underground Railroad," Mrs. Compson explained in a conspiratorial tone. "A Log Cabin quilt with a black center square was a signal. If an escaped slave saw a log cabin quilt with black center squares hanging on the washline, he knew it was safe to knock on the door."

"But wouldn't bounty hunters or whatever see the quilt, too?"

Mrs. Compson regarded her with mock astonishment. "Why, who pays attention to women's work? Laundry, hanging on the line? Sorry, we can't be bothered. We're out doing important man things."

Sarah bent forward, trying to make out the ground below in the darkness. "So people would see this design on the bench and know it was a hiding place. This is amazing. Does it go underground?"

"Just deep enough so that one can stand comfortably beneath the gazebo. My grandmother told me that every evening someone would come out to check if anyone was in the hiding place and see to their needs. Then when it was safe, they could be brought inside the manor."

"I'm going to check it out." Sarah sat on the adjacent bench and swung her legs through the opening.

Mrs. Compson placed a hand on her elbow. "I wouldn't if I were you. Who knows what could be down there now—snakes, rabid squirrels—better let Matthew take care of it."

Quickly, Sarah withdrew her legs, then pulled the seat back to cover the opening. If a rabid squirrel had made the hiding place its home, she didn't want Matt to go down there, either. She rose and dusted off her hands, "You can't tell me there's anything this interesting in some house in Sewickley."

"How would you know? You've never been there," Mrs. Compson replied, but then she sighed. "Very well, I won't pretend to think Elm Creek Manor is any less wonderful than I know it truly is. But Sarah, my dear, don't wish for excitement. Interesting doesn't always mean good. Sometimes the most ordinary things are the ones we learn to miss the most." Mrs. Compson sighed again more deeply, placed her hands on the gazebo rail, and looked out over the garden. "Why don't you fetch our things, and we'll quilt for a while until it's time for you to go."

Twelve

That evening Sarah went to her first Tangled Web Quilters' meeting. As she drove downtown, she realized that this was the first time she had gone out in the evening without Matt since they moved to Waterford. Driving without him made her feel strange, as if she had forgotten something at home but couldn't remember what.

She found a parking spot across the street from Grandma's Attic, picked up the white cardboard box of chocolate chip cookies she had baked after work, and left the truck. She was halfway across the street before she remembered her quilting supplies. Exasperated, she went back for them. She'd been less nervous going to PennCellular the other day. The Tangled Web Quilters had already invited her to join their group, and since they hadn't said anything about a trial membership, she had no reason to be so anxious. Just because they were the only people in Waterford who wanted to be her friends . . .

Her thoughts went to Mrs. Compson as she walked down the alley between the building that held Grandma's Attic and a similar three-story building next door. Didn't Mrs. Compson have any friends? She never spoke of any, and no one ever came to visit her while Sarah was there. The last time Sarah had been at Grandma's Attic, Diane had hinted at some kind of conflict. Maybe tonight Sarah could get her to explain more. Diane would probably enjoy talking about it—if Gwen let her.

She found the back door; it was unlocked, as Bonnie had promised. Just inside the door there was a steep, narrow staircase, which Sarah climbed to the second-story landing while balancing her bag of quilting supplies on top of the box. She knocked on the only door.

It swung open on the second knock, and Bonnie stuck her head into the hallway. "Welcome, new member," she cried, and her eyes widened when she spotted the box in Sarah's arms. "Ooh, what did you bring?"

"Chocolate chip cookies. I can't supply much in the way of quilting advice, but at least I can bring snacks."

"And we love you for it. You can never have too many snacks, not with this crowd." Bonnie took the box out of Sarah's arms and led her into the house. "Hey, everybody, Sarah's here."

Mrs. Emberly, Gwen, Judy, and Diane greeted her from their places around a kitchen counter covered with goodies. Judy was holding her baby.

"I guess that means we're just waiting for the kid," Gwen said, helping herself to a brownie.

Judy put on a puzzled frown and looked from her baby to Gwen. "You mean Emily?"

"No, you nut. I mean my kid."

"I bet she loves it when you call her that," Diane said.

"She doesn't mind."

Mrs. Emberly smiled. "I hope when I'm not around you don't call me 'the old lady.' "

"No, we call you Lady Emberly of the Perfect Stitches."

"What do you call me?" Diane asked.

"You don't want to know."

The door slammed, and Summer rushed in, breathless. "Sorry I'm late," she said. "I had to finish typing a paper."

"It's nice of you to join us at all, instead of going to the bars like all the other students," Diane said.

Summer rolled her eyes. "Not all students live and die for beer." She put an arm around Sarah's shoulders. "I'm glad you're here. If we bring down the average age of the group, they won't be able to treat me like the baby anymore."

"You'll always be my baby," Gwen said.

"That's different. That, I expect."

Everyone laughed.

"You're not the youngest, anyway," Judy reminded her, giving Emily a little pat on her diapered bottom and carrying her into the other room to her playpen.

Sarah picked up a red plastic plate from the counter and joined the others in selecting treats. Carrying her plate and the bag of quilting supplies in one hand and a cup of diet soda in the other, she followed Summer into the living room.

A breeze came in through the two large windows along the north wall, carrying with it the sounds of cars passing and people laughing on the street below. The Markham home seemed like an extension of Grandma's Attic; a rose-and-hunter-green quilt hung above the sofa on the wall opposite the windows, and there was an old treadle sewing machine near the doorway. Sarah wished she could see the other rooms. She had expected a home above a store to be—well, she wasn't exactly sure what she had expected, but she hadn't expected a regular middle-class home.

She found a seat in an armchair next to an upright piano at the far end of the room. Gwen and Summer sat side by side on a loveseat to her left, between the windows. Bonnie carried a rocking chair in from another room and placed it in the corner between Gwen and Sarah.

When Mrs. Emberly entered, Judy jumped up from her place on the sofa beside Diane. "Here, take my seat."

"No, no, that's all right," Mrs. Emberly said, settling beside her in an armchair identical to Sarah's. "This is comfortable. And I like being next to Emily."

Emily looked up and smiled when her name was spoken. She shook a plastic ring of keys at the older woman and squealed.

"I guess Emily wants you there, too," Judy said, laughing.

"Just think, Judy," Diane said. "Fifteen more years and she'll want real keys, and a car to go with them."

Judy pretended to shudder. "Don't remind me. I have enough to think about between now and then." She reached into a tote bag and brought out a small quilt in primary colors.

From across the room, Bonnie looked on in interest. "How's that coming?"

"Not bad, though I wish I had more time to work on it. At this rate it won't be done until Emily's in first grade."

"So I guess you won't be entering it in the Waterford Summer Quilt Festival after all," Summer said.

"No, but I don't mind. My Log Cabin will be there."

Mrs. Emberly reached over to stroke the quilt. "Didn't I tell you the Jacob's Ladder would be prettier than a Wandering Foot?"

Sarah almost dropped her block. "You shouldn't make a Wandering Foot quilt for Emily."

The others looked at her and smiled.

"I'm only teasing her, honey," Mrs. Emberly said. "How did you learn about that old superstition? I thought only senior ladies like me believed them anymore."

Sarah felt her cheeks growing warm. "I don't believe it, exactly. Mrs. Compson told me about it."

Everyone's hands froze over their work. The room went quiet.

After a moment Mrs. Emberly resumed sewing. "Oh. Of course."

The others exchanged glances and continued quilting.

Summer met Sarah's gaze for the briefest instant before turning to Mrs. Emberly. "What's that you're working on? Is it something new?"

"No, just another Whig Rose block, same as last time."

"Can I see it?"

Mrs. Emberly smiled as Summer came over and sat down on the floor by her feet. She took the block from the older woman and held it up for the others to see.

Gwen shook her head in admiration. "Beautiful. How are you going to set them?"

"Oh, I haven't decided yet. I have to make six more blocks first. Maybe I'll use a Garden Maze setting."

"What's that?" Sarah asked.

"You sew dark strips around each block, and then you sew the blocks to each other, separated by light strips."

Sarah tried to picture it and couldn't.

Mrs. Emberly smiled. "I'll bring a photo next time."

"That's at my place," Diane told Sarah. "I'll draw you a map if you want."

"Sure, thanks."

"Won't you guys be too tired from quilt camp to have a bee that night?" Summer asked.

Gwen rolled her eyes. "Right, kid. We'd better just sit around in our rocking chairs recuperating."

"What's quilt camp?" Sarah asked.

"Next week a few quilt instructors are running a three-day session of workshops and seminars in the Poconos," Bonnie said. "It's a fun way to get together with lots of other quilters, learn some new techniques, stuff like that."

"That sounds like fun."

"Everyone's going but you, me, and Bonnie," Summer said. "And Emily. I have classes."

"I wish I could go," Bonnie said. "But someone has to run the store. Besides, Craig and I are trying to watch the money, what with all three of the kids in college."

Sarah figured that if Bonnie couldn't afford it, she certainly couldn't either.

"You guys'll have to take good notes and share them with us when you get back," Summer said.

"It'll cost you." Diane nudged Summer with her foot. "Hey, you're on the wrong side of the room."

"Huh?" Summer rose and returned the appliqué block to Mrs. Emberly.

"This is where the real quilters sit. You belong over there with the machine people."

Gwen turned to Bonnie and Sarah, shaking her head in sorrow. "Her mind has finally gone."

"No, look," Diane said. "Mrs. Emberly, Judy, and I always sit on this side of the room, and you, Bonnie, and Summer always sit over there."

"I sit here because I want to be near Emily's playpen," Judy said.

"And I sit here because it's next to the lamp and away from the window," Mrs. Emberly added.

Gwen grinned. "So much for your theory."

"And excuse me, but I resent that comment about real quilters." Summer made a face and returned to her seat beside her mother.

"Oh, come on," Diane protested. She looked to Mrs. Emberly and Judy for support. "We all know that true quilts are made entirely by hand."

Bonnie sighed. "Here we go again."

"That's tradition. Hand piecing, hand quilting. It's not that machine quilts aren't pretty, but they aren't true quilts. Even if you hand quilt a machine-pieced top, it's not the same."

Gwen set her sketch pad and colored pencils aside. "Diane, I do believe that's the most ridiculous thing I've ever heard you say."

"You only think that because you're a machine person. Come on. I know I'm not the only one who feels this way. Judy?"

"Don't drag me into this."

"Back me up here."

"I would if I agreed with you, but I don't. The only reason I hand piece and hand quilt is because I work with computers and lab equipment all day. The last thing I need is another machine in my life."

Diane groaned. "You're no help."

"Sorry."

"Looks like you're outnumbered," Gwen said.

Diane looked around the room, glaring. "You all know I'm right." She stood, snatched up her plate, and stomped out of the room.

Shocked, Sarah watched her go. The others were smiling and shaking their heads. As Mrs. Emberly and Judy struck up a conversation on the other side of the room, Sarah turned to Gwen. "Should we go after her?"

"Why would we do that?"

"Because . . . because she feels bad."

"Oh, it's all right," Gwen said. "This happens at least twice a month."

"Really?" Sarah craned her neck and tried to see into the kitchen.

"Sure. You'll get used to it."

"I thought you guys were friends."

"We are friends."

"But—"

"We are friends. All of us. We accept each other the way we are. Friends don't demand that you overhaul your entire personality. They know your faults and love you anyway. That means we tolerate Diane's moods—and my tendency to make speeches."

Sarah smiled. "I think I'm catching on."

"Good." Gwen picked up her sketch pad and resumed coloring a quilt pattern. "Hmm . . . I wonder what we're going to have to tolerate about you?"

Sarah laughed.

"So what are you working on, Sarah?" Bonnie asked.

"I'm working on a Double Nine Patch block now." She took the Sawtooth Star block out of her bag and held it up. "I finished this one on Tuesday."

"How pretty," Summer said.

Gwen motioned for Sarah to hand her the block. "Time for inspection." Sarah passed it over, and Gwen scrutinized the seams. "Not bad." She passed it to Summer. As the block went around the circle, each person complimented Sarah on her piecing skills.

"Your first quilt block ever," Mrs. Emberly said when it was her turn. "This is quite an occasion. I must say this looks much better than my first block did."

"Mine, too," Diane said as she came back into the room. "I chopped off all the tips of my triangles and the block buckled in the middle." She sat down and gave Sarah a searching look. "So I guess the lessons are going well?"

Everyone looked at Sarah, and from their expressions she could tell that each had been wondering the same thing. "They're going great. Mrs. Compson is a really good teacher."

"See, ladies, I told you it would be all right," Mrs. Emberly admonished them. She turned to Sarah. "She taught me how to quilt—or tried to, rather. I wasn't the best student back then and our lessons didn't go well. That was years ago, though, and I've learned a trick or two since."

"Of course you have," Bonnie said. "Your appliqué is the best of everyone here."

The others chimed in their agreement.

Sarah told them about her lessons, but she mentioned nothing about Claudia or the other Bergstroms she had come to know through Mrs. Compson's stories because it would have been like divulging a secret. She also told them about the Wandering Foot superstition and the meaning of the Log Cabin pattern with a black center square, but here, too, she omitted the personal details about Elm Creek Manor.

"I've heard those stories before," Gwen said. "I came across them in my research when I was planning the syllabus for my history of American folk art course." She hesitated for a moment. "Sarah, are you and Mrs. Compson friends?"

"I think so. At least, I think we're getting there."

"Do you think Mrs. Compson would be interested in visiting my class sometime as a guest lecturer?"

"I don't know. She likes to talk about quilts, but—"

"Sylvia is a teacher—or, rather, she was," Mrs. Emberly broke in. "She has a degree in art from Carnegie Mellon. Perhaps she'd enjoy talking to students again."

Gwen turned to Sarah. "What do you think?"

"I can ask," Sarah said. "The worst she can do is say no, right?"

Mrs. Emberly sighed. "No, she can do far worse than that."

"What do you mean?" Sarah asked, surprised.

"Nothing," Bonnie said quickly. "So, what are you all going to enter in the Waterford Quilting Guild's Summer Quilt Festival?"

"There's no need to change the subject," Mrs. Emberly told her, then turned to Sarah. "Sylvia and I had a falling out a long time ago."

"She's had a falling out with most of the quilters around here," Diane muttered.

Mrs. Emberly silenced Diane by patting her wrist. "I won't pretend it doesn't still trouble me, but I don't like to talk about it."

Sarah nodded, uncomfortable. She was growing fond of Mrs. Compson, but knew how abrasive the older woman could be sometimes.

"I do miss Elm Creek Manor, though. It was so lovely once."

"She's going to sell it," Sarah responded automatically, immediately regretting it when she saw Mrs. Emberly's shocked expression.

"What do you mean?" Judy asked.

Sarah shrugged, wishing she could just drop it. Maybe Mrs. Compson didn't want anyone to know. "She said University Realty may buy the estate."

Summer and Gwen exchanged a quick look.

"University Realty manages my apartment building," Summer said.

Her mother nodded. "All of their holdings are student apartments. That's what they do. They're in property management, not home sales."

"You don't think—" Mrs. Emberly looked around the circle. "You don't think they'd take that lovely manor and turn it into a student apartment building, do you?"

"If they do, I'm going to enroll next semester," Diane said.

"Now, don't you worry about anything." Bonnie shot Diane an exasperated look before turning back to Mrs. Emberly. "We don't know that she'll sell it to them—or to anyone, for that matter. And think about how impractical it would be to turn Elm Creek Manor into an apartment building. They'd have to spend a fortune."

"I suppose." But Mrs. Emberly still looked doubtful.

"I probably heard her wrong," Sarah said. "She probably meant some other company."

Mrs. Emberly tried to smile, then busied herself with her appliqué.

Gwen quickly changed the subject, and before long the earlier spirit of the gathering returned. Mrs. Emberly remained quiet, however, and Sarah noticed her deep frown of concern. She looked as worried as Sarah felt. Sarah understood that the students had to live somewhere, but did they have to live in Elm Creek Manor?

Thirteen

Mrs. Compson spent the next morning sorting through documents in the library while Sarah worked alone in Aunt Clara's suite. It took all the self-discipline she had to keep from dashing down the hallway and confronting Mrs. Compson with her worries about the future of Elm Creek Manor. She knew, though, that if she burst out with her questions, the older woman would just purse her lips and walk away.

Not long after lunch Sarah finished the suite, which gave her the perfect excuse to join Mrs. Compson in the library. The older woman was sitting at the desk behind a stack of yellowing papers, one hand resting on the arm of her chair, the other holding up a water-stained document.

When Sarah lingered in the doorway Mrs. Compson looked up and peered at her over her glasses. "Finished already?"

Sarah nodded. "What should I work on next?"

"Leave the work for now. I'll finish up here and then we can have a quilt lesson." Her gaze returned to the paper.

"What's that?" Sarah asked, pointing at the paper and walking over for a closer look.

"Don't point, dear. It's nothing of your concern, just the family accounts. Claudia was never a good bookkeeper, and she became even more careless after her husband passed." She shook her head and pushed the chair away from the desk. "She and Harold made a mess of things, though it's not their fault alone."

"Maybe I could help. I know something about accounting."

"That's right. You do indeed, don't you?" Mrs. Compson rose and returned the document to the top of the pile. "How is your search for a *real* job going, by the way?"

Only Sarah's faint blush showed that she realized Mrs. Compson's emphasis was a teasing imitation of her own. "I have another interview Monday morning. I meant to tell you about it. It's in the morning so I won't be in until after lunch, if that's okay."

"You don't sound particularly enthusiastic."

Sarah shrugged.

Mrs. Compson smiled. "Well, don't get discouraged. You need to be confident. Show them what you've got. Something will come along."

"Sometimes I wonder."

"Now, none of that. You'll have plenty of time for self-pity when you're old and gray, like me."

"You're not old."

"Oh, I'm not, then? How very interesting. I'll have to remember that." She patted Sarah's arm. "Now, dear, I'm only teasing you. Surely you must be used to that by now."

"Not as used to it as I'm going to be, I bet."

Mrs. Compson laughed and motioned for Sarah to follow her out of the library. "How are you coming with the Double Nine Patch?"

Sarah followed her down the hallway and to the stairs. "I finished it last night. There's a group called the Tangled Web Quilters, some people I met at Grandma's Attic. They get together and quilt once a week, and they asked me to join them."

"How nice."

"You could come next week, too. It would be fun."

Mrs. Compson shook her head. "They didn't invite me."

"But I'm a member now. They invited me, and I'm inviting you."

"That's not the same thing and you know it. I used to belong to the local guild—Claudia, too. We started going to meetings with my mother when we were young girls and sometimes held quilting bees here. We would set up several quilt frames in the ballroom and everyone would come over, and we would have such a grand time." Mrs. Compson paused on the bottom step, her eyes distant. Then she sighed and continued across the marble floor and down the hallway leading to the west wing. "But we left the guild when the other women showed us we weren't welcome."

"What did they do?"

"Hmph. Their feelings were obvious, believe me. Even Claudia noticed."

"When was this?"

"Oh, I don't know. Fifty years ago, give or take."

"Fifty years? But—well, don't you think it's time to give it another chance, maybe? The Tangled Web Quilters are really nice. You'd have a good time. Besides, they're a different group, not the Waterford Quilting Guild."

"Now, dear." Mrs. Compson stopped outside the kitchen and placed a hand on Sarah's arm. "No more of this. The local quilters made it clear I was not welcome, and until they let me know they've changed their minds, I must assume their feelings haven't altered. I'd rather quilt with you or alone than with a group of strangers who don't want me among them in the first place. Now, are we agreed?"

Sarah opened her mouth to protest, but Mrs. Compson's expression silenced her. She nodded instead, reluctantly.

They went to the sitting room, where Sarah was struck by the feeling that something was different about the room. She looked around for a moment before realizing that the neatly folded pile of sheets and pillows Mrs. Compson usually kept on the sofa was gone.

Mrs. Compson noticed her staring at the sofa. "I decided to move back into my old room, if you must know," she said crisply, before Sarah even spoke a word.

Mrs. Compson leafed through a pattern book and found Sarah's third quilt block, Little Red Schoolhouse. For this block Sarah needed to make templates for several rectangles in different sizes, a parallelogram, and another four-sided figure. When she had cut pieces using all but the last template, Mrs. Compson showed her how to "reverse a template" by tracing around it to make one piece, then flipping the template over and tracing around it again to make its mirror image.

When Sarah had finished piecing some of the straight seams, Mrs. Compson showed her how to set in pieces, sewing a third piece of fabric to two others that met at an angle. Sarah attached the new piece to the first by sewing a straight seam into the angle where the three pieces would meet. Then she pivoted the new piece around her needle until the next edge was aligned with the edge of the second piece, and continued her running stitch to join them. She hoped Mrs. Compson was right and that setting in pieces would become easier each time she did it.

Once satisfied that Sarah could manage on her own, Mrs. Compson began to work on one of her own quilts. "Richard used to call this block the Little Red Playhouse," she remarked, smiling as she worked her needle in tiny stitches through the smooth layers held snugly in her quilting hoop.

"Why did he call it that?"

"Probably because Father once built him a little playhouse painted red, near the gardens, where the stables and exercise rings were. Richard loved to watch Father work with the horses, and this way Father could keep him near enough to watch without fearing for his safety."

"Where was it? Near the gazebo?"

"Oh, no. Near the edge of the old gardens, on land that was sold off a long time ago to build the state road." Mrs. Compson rested the quilt hoop in her lap. "My, how we all doted on that child. We had to, of course, to try to make up for losing Mother."

"You lost your mother? Did she—was it when she had Richard?"

"No, thank God. Not until a few years later, when I was ten and Richard was three. At least he had that little time with her."

"I'm sorry." The words sounded hopelessly inadequate.

Mrs. Compson slipped the silver thimble from her finger and handed it to Sarah. "This was Mother's. She gave it to me when she became ill the last time. She gave Claudia another just like it. I suppose she must have known, somehow, that she would be leaving us."

⁜

Although the way I remember it Mother was a spirited woman, she tired easily. We children knew to keep quiet when she went about the manor pressing her fingers to the side of her head, almost blind from headaches that could last for days. Father worried about her and often sent an older cousin running for the doctor. Mother tolerated the doctor's orders for bed rest and limited activity only reluctantly; as soon as the headaches passed she would be playing dolls with us on the nursery floor, planning a ball with Father, or exercising the horses. He would protest that she should not work herself so hard, but she would pretend not to hear him, and he would pretend she was fine.

She was not supposed to have any more children, but there it was, and she was so happy that none of the aunts could scold her. I did not know that until much later. At the time, Claudia and I and the cousins were only happy about the news.

The pregnancy was difficult, and Richard arrived almost a month early. We other children were not allowed to see him until he was nearly five weeks old. I overheard some of the older cousins whispering that it was because the grown-ups thought he would die, and that it would be easier for us if we had not seen him. I had such terrible nightmares after hearing that.

But the baby grew stronger, and Mother seemed to be well again. Father was so thrilled to have a son. Not that he didn't love Claudia and me, mind you, but I think a man just feels something different, something special, about a son. At least at first—then the son gets older and the father and son fight like a mother and daughter or a mother and son never would. It happens all the time that way, and I don't know if anyone really knows why.

As I was saying, the baby grew stronger, and Mother seemed healthy for a while, but as Richard learned to walk and talk and play, Mother seemed to weaken, almost to fade away. First she stopped riding, then even quilting became too much for her, and then one morning the rest of us woke but Mother did not.

How dark and lonely Elm Creek Manor became then. I don't like to think about it, when I can help it.

We all went on, as people always have to, but it was difficult. Mother's passing left an enormous emptiness in our lives. Claudia and I tried to take Mother's place raising Richard—with our aunts' help, of course. How he managed to become such a dear boy instead of a spoiled brat . . . well, I surely don't know. Between the two of us, Claudia and I made sure he never wanted for anything. What a pair of young mother hens we were.

Father, too, indulged him, just as he had always indulged Mother, I suppose. When Richard demanded to be allowed to ride alone when he was barely tall enough to bump his head if he walked under the horse, Father would hold him on the back of a tired old mare and walk them slowly around the grounds. Richard had little patience for school as he grew older, and when I tried to tutor him he would dash off to explore the barn, or run away to the orchard to see if the apple trees were blossoming.

Such a headstrong, mischievous boy. But he had such a kind heart, that one. Once, when he was in his third or fourth year of school, a new boy came to his class. I would see him every morning when Claudia and I dropped Richard off before walking down the block to our school. It was heartbreaking, really. The boy's clothes looked as if they had not been washed, his eyes looked tired and hungry, and sometimes he would have such awful bruises on his arms. Most of the children avoided him, but Richard became his friend.

Once, at dinner, Richard asked Father if the boy could come and live with us, because his mommy and daddy were mean. Father and Uncle William exchanged looks—you know the kind of looks I mean, the ones they think the children don't see. After dinner they took Richard aside and questioned him. They went out that evening and would not tell the rest of us where they were going.

Later I overheard them talking to my aunts. Very well, if you must know, I crept out of bed and pressed my ear against the library door. Father and Uncle William told my aunts that they had gone to the little boy's house to speak with his father. Father wanted to see the boy, but when his daddy went to check his bed, the little boy wasn't there. His sister spoke up then and said that her brother hadn't been home for two days.

Father grew so angry that Uncle William had to hold him back or he might have hit the man. "How can a man not know whether his eight-year-old son is under his own roof?" he had shouted. They stormed out of the house and went straight to the police, who went back and took the little sister away from those horrible people. But no one knew what had happened to the little boy. He had disappeared.

"Did he run away?" I asked Richard the next morning.

He hesitated, then shrugged. "He didn't tell me he was going anywhere."

I didn't know what to think. The rumors raced around school like wildfire. Some said the little boy had been murdered by his own parents. Others said he had run off to the city. I couldn't bear to believe the former, but I knew he was too young for the latter.

A week later, I woke early and heard someone walking in the hallway past my bedroom. It was not yet dawn. I crept from the bed, tiptoed across the room, and opened the door.

Richard's back was just disappearing around the corner. I crept after him, downstairs to the kitchen, out the side door and down the stone path to the garden. It was a clear evening in early autumn, and my bare toes were chilly as I trailed Richard beyond the gardens to his playhouse. He ducked inside, and I heard soft voices murmuring.

I followed, only to find Richard and the little boy sharing a loaf of bread and a paper sack of apples. They looked up in fright when I entered. The little boy jumped up and tried to run for the door, but I was blocking his way and caught him around the waist. He shrieked and tried to punch me with his fists, but Richard grabbed his wrists.

"No, Andrew, it's Sylvia. She's my sister. Everything's okay now," he said, his voice sounding so much like Father's when soothing a jittery colt. He repeated the refrain until Andrew went limp in our arms.

Our two dogs had started barking when Andrew cried out, and soon all the grown-ups were awake. Fine guard dogs, indeed, to be silent until then. Before long we were inside the warm kitchen with quilts wrapped around us, sipping warm milk. I didn't know why they gave me warm milk, since I had not been hiding in a playhouse or sneaking outside every night to care for a friend, but never mind.

Richard later tried to convince me that he hadn't lied to me, not exactly. "I said Andrew didn't tell me he was going anywhere," he argued. "That's true. Andrew didn't tell me that because I already knew."

I told him he intended to deceive me, and that was as bad as a lie. He was quite abashed and said he would never lie to me again.

But that tells you what kind of boy Richard was: good intentioned but so very impulsive. His instinct was to help his friend the only way he knew how. It never occurred to him that the grown-ups could help Andrew more than Richard himself could.

Who knows what might have happened if I had not found them in the playhouse that night. As usual, Richard's luck rescued him in the end.

※

"What happened to Andrew?" It was Matt, leaning against the wall near the sitting room doorway. Sarah had not heard him arrive.

"The police came for him. He and his sister were taken to live with an aunt in Philadelphia. Richard saw him again, but not until they were young men. His parents moved away, and I don't know what became of them. Good riddance." She sighed and stood up, making a tsking sound with her tongue when she saw how little piecing Sarah had finished. "No more stories. It distracts you from your quilting."

"No, don't say that. I can sew and listen at the same time. Really."

"Hmph." Mrs. Compson shook her head, but a slow smile crept across her face. "One more chance. I'll be watching carefully next time, mind you." She rose and left the room, returning with a brown leather purse. She took out a checkbook and a pen and filled out one of the checks. "Here," she said, tearing the check from the book and giving it to Sarah. "Your wages. I'll see you Monday."

Sarah was about to put the check away when she noticed something odd. "This can't be right."

"Not enough for you? Hmph."

"No, that's not it." In her head Sarah calculated her wages for the number of hours she had worked. "Mrs. Compson, you overpaid me. I think you accidentally paid me for the hours we spent quilting, too, not just the hours I worked."

"Accident has nothing to do with it." Mrs. Compson zipped her purse shut and folded her arms.

"But that's not fair to you. That's not what we agreed." Sarah tried to return the check, but Mrs. Compson shook her head and refused to listen. Instead she guided Matt and Sarah out the back door. As they drove away, they spotted her on the back porch, watching them go.

Fourteen

arah had all weekend to finish the Little Red Schoolhouse block, and—despite Matt's attempts to distract her—to worry about her upcoming job interview. This time, she resolved, she was going to be perfect. She would answer every question with intelligence and charm. Sure, it had been years since she'd attended those job interview seminars at Penn State, but she remembered the most important tips. And hadn't her professors told her that with each interview she would improve?

Several of them had, and every so often she felt like giving them a call and asking them when she could expect this improvement to kick in.

"How do you feel?" Matt asked as she finished her breakfast on Monday morning.

"Not bad, considering that I've done this about a million times. Now I'm really an expert at interviewing." She was also becoming all too familiar with the variety of ways employers delivered rejection.

Hopkins and Steele was a small public accounting firm two blocks away from Grandma's Attic. The secretary greeted her and led her down a carpeted hallway. "The nine-o'clock was a no-show," she confided in a whisper. They stopped in front of a windowless door, and the secretary gestured for Sarah to sit in a nearby armchair. "They'll come out for you when they're ready."

About five minutes after the secretary left, the door opened. "Sarah?" a tall, balding man asked. He shook her hand and led her into the office, where another man sat at a round table. The first man pulled out a chair for Sarah, then took his own seat.

The interview was more casual than Sarah had anticipated. Mr. Hopkins and Mr. Steele were good-humored and friendly, and Sarah felt she responded to their questions well. She even remembered to ask a few questions to demonstrate her interest in the position. By the time the interview ended, Sarah felt she had made her best showing yet.

Afterward, Mr. Hopkins offered to show Sarah out. When they opened the door and stepped into the hallway, they saw a man waiting in the armchair.

"Guess we're running behind," Mr. Hopkins said. "Sarah, do you mind finding your own way out?"

"No, not at all."

"Follow this hall all the way down to the receptionist's desk and you'll see the exit. You'll be hearing from us." He smiled, then turned to the man in the armchair. "If you'll give us a minute to regroup, we'll be right with you."

"Thank you," Sarah said. Mr. Hopkins nodded and shut the door, and she turned to leave.

"Well, hello again," the man in the armchair said.

Sarah looked at him closely. Where had she seen him before? "Oh . . . hi."

"Tom Wilson. From the PennCellular waiting room? Hey, we really have to stop meeting like this. Although I guess it had to happen, so many accountants and so few jobs, and all."

"Yes, of course. How are you?"

He shrugged. "Oh, you know. Same old, same old." He grimaced and jerked his head toward the closed office door. "How was it in there?"

"Oh, fine. Very nice people."

"Good, good. You must have done really well for them to keep you late like that. That's a good sign. You must have impressed them."

"Really? Do you think so?"

"Well, sure. My appointment was for ten, and here it is quarter after. They wouldn't run overtime for just anybody."

Sarah felt a small spark of hope. "You know, I think it went well, too. They really seemed interested in me. I almost wish—" She bit her lip.

"Wish what?"

"Nothing."

"Come on, what?"

"It's just—" She glanced at the office door to assure herself that it was still closed. She lowered her voice. "It's just that I was hoping to find something outside of accounting. I mean, I know that's where all my experience is, and I know I can do the work, but—" She searched for the words.

"But what?"

"I don't know. I guess I just wanted to try something different, something, well, more interesting. No offense." He was an accountant himself, after all.

He chuckled. "None taken. But why are you applying for jobs you don't want?"

"It's not that I don't want them. I need a job, and I'll be grateful for whatever I get. I just wanted to try something else, maybe something I would enjoy more. You know, explore my options. Except I don't seem to have any options. Like with PennCellular? I really wanted to apply for the opening in their PR department, but they wouldn't even give me a chance. One look at my accounting degree and that was that."

He shrugged. "At least you're getting the interviews. And you're still young. You have plenty of time to switch careers if you want. Me, on the other hand—well, like they say, you can't teach an old dog new tricks. They call us displaced workers. There's so many of us we even have our own buzz-word. Can you believe that?"

Sarah couldn't decide what to say, so she shook her head.

"Besides," he continued, "who's going to hire a guy like me who wants to be paid what he's worth and knows more about the boss's job than the boss does? Not like some green college kid who—" Suddenly his gaze shifted over her left shoulder.

Sarah heard the door open behind her and Mr. Hopkins speaking to Mr. Steele. "I'd better go," she said. Tom raised his hand in farewell, and she hurried down the hallway to the exit.

She met Matt at the square, a small downtown park near Waterford's busiest intersection. They stopped home for a quick lunch, where Sarah told him about the interview. It had been a long time since she'd had good news to share about her job search, and even longer since she'd left an interview thinking she had a good chance of landing the job.

When she finished, Matt placed his elbows on the table and frowned. "I don't know if it was such a good idea to tell that Tom guy how you felt about the job."

Sarah's smile faded. "Why? I made sure the door was shut first."

"Maybe the interviewers didn't overhear you, but that doesn't mean they won't find out."

"What do you mean? You think he went in there and told them what I said?"

"No, I don't think that, but—"

"Then what do you think?"

"I think you ought to be more careful, that's all. If you want to get a job, you have to be smarter. You can't keep screwing up your chances like this."

"So you think I don't have a job yet because I'm not smart enough or I'm messing up on purpose?"

"That's not exactly how I put it."

"It's pretty close. God, Matt, that was the best interview I've had since we moved here, and all you can do is criticize me."

"You're overreacting. I'm not criticizing you." Matt shoved his chair back from the table and stood. "But if you didn't want my advice, then why tell me about it?"

"I am not overreacting." She hated it when he said that. "I told you about the interview because I thought you might be interested in what goes on in my life, not because I want to be criticized every time I do something."

"How do you expect to improve if you don't get any feedback?"

"I don't see how you know any more about the interviewing process than I do. I managed to find myself a job in State College, remember?"

"Fine. It's my fault you don't have that job anymore, and it's my fault if you can't find a new one. Satisfied?"

"I didn't say it was your fault. Now who's overreacting?"

"I'll be waiting in the truck." Matt grabbed his lunch dishes and stormed into the kitchen. Sarah heard them clatter in the sink, and then the front door slammed. Red-faced and fuming, she raced after him.

They drove out to Elm Creek Manor in silence. When the truck pulled up behind the manor, Sarah jumped out and slammed the door without a word. The truck sped away, its tires kicking up a shower of dirt and gravel.

Sarah went inside and paused in the back hallway, fuming. He was right, and she knew it. She shouldn't have confided in Tom Wilson. But the other things he'd said were so wrong. He had no right to criticize her for not finding anything yet. Hadn't she left her job in State College for his sake? Matt's new job didn't pay any more than Sarah's old one had, so they weren't any better off financially. Matt was better off—at least, he seemed happier—but what had Sarah gained?

"We should've stayed in State College," Sarah said aloud.

The manor's silence absorbed her words.

She closed her eyes and leaned back against the wall, her stomach tightening. Moving to Waterford had been a mistake. They should have stuck it out in State College a little while longer; surely Matt would have found something. He was more likely to find a job in State College than Sarah was to find something in Waterford.

She knew this as certainly as she knew that she could never tell Matt how she felt.

It was too late, anyway. She'd made her choice and she had to live with it. It would be a lot easier to live with, though, if Matt appreciated her sacrifice. Sometimes she thought he didn't even realize she'd made one.

She took slow, deep breaths until most of her irritation subsided. She felt the manor surrounding her, comforting and quiet, more like home than the duplex would ever be.

Another quiet minute passed before Sarah opened her eyes and went upstairs.

She found Mrs. Compson in the suite next to Aunt Clara's. She was sitting on the floor on top of a folded quilt and removing faded clothing from the bottom drawer of a bureau.

"I'm here," Sarah said as she came into the room.

"So I see." Mrs. Compson eyed her. "Should I not ask how it went, then?"

"Hmm? Oh. The interview. No, the interview was fine."

"Of course. That explains why you're so cheerful this afternoon."

Sarah almost smiled.

Mrs. Compson set aside a flannel work shirt. "Well, then, since you clearly aren't in the mood for working today, why don't we have a quilt lesson instead?"

"But I haven't done any work yet today."

"True, but I've been working all morning."

Sarah shrugged. "Okay. You're the boss."

"Indeed I am," Mrs. Compson said. She motioned for Sarah to help her to her feet. "You'll be starting a new block today, the Contrary Wife."

Sarah snorted. "Got one called the Contrary Husband instead?"

Mrs. Compson raised an eyebrow. "Do I detect a note of discord? That can't be, not with the two lovebirds."

"Matt was being a pain today. I told him about my interview, and all he could do was pick apart everything I said."

"That doesn't sound like him."

"And I didn't even do anything wrong." Sarah explained what had happened.

Mrs. Compson drew in a breath and grimaced. "I'm afraid I have to agree with Matthew." She raised a hand when Sarah opened her mouth to protest. "With what he said, not with how he said it. He should have been more tactful. But I think he's right to caution you against speaking too freely with others who are competing for the same jobs."

Sarah plopped down on the bed. "I knew you'd take his side."

"Oh, is that what I'm doing? I thought I was merely offering my opinion." Mrs. Compson sat down beside her. "If I am taking his side, it's because he's right. This Tom Wilson didn't need to know how you feel about your profession."

Sarah sighed. Maybe Mrs. Compson and Matt were right. She'd really blown it this time.

"I don't think this Tom Wilson will divulge your secret, however," Mrs. Compson said.

"I hope not, but why wouldn't he?"

"Because he'll seem terribly unprofessional if he does. Why should they believe him, anyway, someone spreading rumors about another applicant?"

"That's probably true."

"However, I do hope you've learned a lesson. Be careful to whom you divulge your secrets. You never know—" Mrs. Compson paused, smiling to herself.

"What? What's so funny?"

"Oh, nothing." Mrs. Compson's smile grew. "I was just thinking about how I met my husband."

"You met him at a job interview?"

"No, no." Mrs. Compson laughed. "But the day we met, he was even less discreet than you were today, much to his later embarrassment."

⚜

I told you before how every year at the state fair Claudia and I would show our quilts, and how I would compete in the riding events. Father would show his prize horses and spend hours debating the merits of various breeding and training practices with the other gentlemen. Richard hung on every word; he wanted to be ready for the day he would take over Bergstrom Thoroughbreds. He spent nearly every moment with Father and the horses. Despite my efforts, however, he did not have the same diligence for his schoolwork. I suppose that isn't unusual for a nine-year-old boy.

I was sixteen, and I loved the fair. And I loved to ride. I must have annoyed some of the other girls, since I took first place in every competition I entered. But I didn't care as much about the ribbons and trophies as they thought I did. What I loved was flying like the wind, feeling the horse gather all its strength before soaring over a jump, the delicate power of the flashing hooves and flowing manes—oh, it was wonderful. Seeing the pride in Father's eyes when I won on his horses—well, that was wonderful, too.

One morning I was riding Dresden Rose in the practice ring when I noticed a young man leaning against the fence, watching us exercise, just as he had for the past two mornings of the fair. After returning his greeting with a nod I pretended to ignore him, but it was difficult not to watch him out of the corner of my eye as I rode. It was also rather annoying to have him there again. I had my first competition coming up and needed to concentrate, and I couldn't do so very well with someone staring.

Afterward in the stable, I was brushing Dresden Rose, checking her feed, and murmuring to her encouragingly to build up her confidence for the afternoon's events. Then I heard the stall door open behind me.

I whirled around, startling Rose. The young man from the practice ring stood there grinning at me.

"Beautiful animal," he said.

"Yes, she is," I replied, my voice tinged with irritation. I stroked Rose's neck and spoke soothingly to calm her.

The man reached over to stroke her muzzle. "A Bergstrom?"

"Yes." Then I realized he meant Rose, not me. "Yes, she is."

His admiring gaze turned to me. "You're a fine rider."

My cheeks flushed, although I willed them not to. He was quite handsome, tall and strong with dark eyes and dark, curly hair. I was very aware that there was no one else around, and how I probably looked to him. I was never the beauty Claudia was, but in my own way I was quite pretty back then, or at least he seemed to think so.

"Thank you," I finally managed, half hoping that Richard or Father would suddenly appear, and half afraid that they would.

He moved along Rose's side, and I stepped back involuntarily even though the horse was between us. "Don't worry," he murmured to Dresden Rose as he stroked her neck. "I don't mean you any harm." He ran a hand along her flank, looking her over with a practiced eye. "Do you get to ride Bergstroms often?"

I looked at him in disbelief. "Of course."

"They're supposed to be the finest horses around."

"A lot of people think so."

He grinned at me. "I know I shouldn't admit this, but the best of my family's stable can't match the worst of old Bergstrom's."

"Oh, really?" I was so surprised I almost laughed. "Well, I suppose 'old Bergstrom' would be delighted to hear that."

"I bet he already knows." He had continued around Rose's hindquarters and was now on my side of the stall. "My father has plans, though. He thinks he'll catch up to Bergstrom in a generation."

"Those must be some plans." My voice trembled as he drew closer, and I busied myself with Rose's mane. "Will they work?"

He shook his head. "Not a chance. His ideas are a good start, but they don't go far enough. And you can't get anywhere in this life without taking a few chances."

"My father would agree."

"No, no one will catch Bergstrom for a while yet. But someday I'm going to breed horses that will rival his. Maybe even surpass them."

I raised my eyebrows in surprise and challenge. "Do you really think you can?"

"Oh, sure. Not soon, but someday. I have some ideas." He stepped closer and took the brush from my hand. "May I?" I nodded, and he continued Rose's grooming. "Hard to imagine there could ever be a finer horse than you, though, isn't it?" he murmured in Rose's ear. She nuzzled his face.

"Her name is Dresden Rose."

"And what's yours?"

I paused for a moment. "Sylvia."

He smiled, his eyes crinkling in the corners. "Sylvia. Lovely name."

"Thank you."

"I'm James Compson."

I took in a breath. "One of Robert Compson's sons?" Robert Compson raised horses in Maryland. He was my father's nearest rival.

His smile turned wry. "The youngest of many."

"I see." I reached out for the brush.

He dropped the brush and took my hand in both of his. Startled, I moved as if to pull away.

"Please, don't run off," he said, stepping closer. "It's taken me two days just to get up the courage to speak to you."

"My father will be here soon." My voice shook and I felt very strange, but I didn't back away.

A hurt look flashed in his eyes, and he released my hand. "Do you want me to leave?"

I shook my head, and then I nodded, and then I just looked at him in dismay. I wanted him to take my hand again, and I wanted him to be gone.

"I'm sorry. This was foolish of me." He opened the stall door and left.

By the time I finished caring for Dresden Rose, my hands had stopped shaking. By the time Father, Claudia, and Richard arrived to help me prepare for the competition, I was able to appear calm. I didn't fool Claudia, though; she knew something had happened, but she wouldn't press me to explain, not with Father and Richard there.

The competition began, and soon it would be my turn. I spotted my family cheering in the spectators' seats, and I grinned as I waved back, my confidence bolstered.

Then, as I looked away from my family and into another part of the stands, my eyes met James's. My stomach flip-flopped. His gaze was so steady and intense, and it so unsettled me, that I sawed on Rose's reins. She whinnied in protest, jolting me back to alertness.

Then it was my turn. "Our fifth competitor," the announcer's voice rang out so that all could hear. "Sylvia Bergstrom."

There was just enough time before I trotted into the ring for me to see James's jaw drop.

❧

"You see, he didn't know who I was."

"Yes, I figured that out," Sarah managed to say through her laughter. "But when he asked for your name, why didn't you say Sylvia Bergstrom instead of just Sylvia?"

Mrs. Compson looked abashed. "I was having too much fun at his expense, I'm afraid." She laughed. "My goodness, how embarrassed he must have been. Can you imagine?"

"But everything worked out fine in the end, didn't it?" Sarah teased. "I mean, you did marry him, right?"

Mrs. Compson smiled. "Yes, I did. So maybe everything will work out just fine for you, too, but I do hope you'll be more cautious."

"I will."

They went downstairs to the sewing room, where Mrs. Compson helped Sarah draft her new templates. As they worked, Sarah realized that most of her anger had faded, but Matt's criticism still stung. Was it because she knew he had been right—not just about divulging secrets but about everything? Was she subconsciously screwing up her search for a real job?

Sarah thought about it and decided that it couldn't be true. Why would she want to do that, subconsciously or otherwise?

She concentrated on her quilting—and on figuring out a way to get Matt to apologize before she confessed that he'd been right.

Fifteen

That week Sarah and Mrs. Compson finished the second suite and started a third, working on the manor in the mornings and quilting in the afternoons. On Thursday, Sarah completed the Contrary Wife block and began another, which Mrs. Compson called the LeMoyne Star. Mrs. Compson must have liked the pattern herself, since it appeared in several of the quilts she had taken from the cedar chest.

Thursday was also the day Sarah remembered Gwen's request. "You know that group of quilters I told you about?" she asked as she traced a figure onto the template plastic.

Mrs. Compson kept her eyes on her quilting. "No, I've never made their acquaintance."

"Actually, you do know one of them, Bonnie Markham. But you know what I mean. Do you remember them?"

"How could I remember them if I've never met them?"

Sarah decided to start over. "Last week when I went to the Tangled Web Quilters' meeting, I met a woman named Gwen Sullivan. She's a professor at Waterford College."

"How very nice for her."

"She's teaching a course on the history of American folk art, and she wondered if you might be willing to be a guest speaker."

"Really." Mrs. Compson set down her quilt hoop. "Does she want me to teach the class how to quilt or to teach them about quilt history?"

"I think she wants you to talk about quilt history and folklore and stuff."

"If Gwen is a quilter herself, why does she need me?"

Sarah hesitated. "Well, sometimes it's more fun for the students to listen to someone other than the professor. And you tell good stories."

Mrs. Compson smiled. "Very well, then. You may tell your friend it would be my pleasure to speak to her class."

"Great. Gwen will be glad to hear that." Sarah paused. "You could come to the Tangled Web Quilters' meeting with me tonight and tell her yourself."

"I don't think that will be necessary. I'm sure you're responsible enough to carry the message."

"Of course I am, but—"

"Then it's settled."

Sarah gave up.

They worked without talking for a few minutes until Mrs. Compson broke the silence with a chuckle. "So I tell good stories, do I?"

"Of course you do. It's too bad you don't like to tell them."

Mrs. Compson looked astonished. "Why, what on earth do you mean?"

"Getting information out of you is like pulling teeth, or—or like setting in pieces."

"That's not so."

"It is too. You started to tell me about James on Monday, and here it is Thursday already and you still haven't explained how you ended up together. I've been wondering about it all week, but you haven't said a word."

"My, all week," Mrs. Compson teased. "If you think that's long, I have to wonder if you have the diligence and perseverance it takes to finish a quilt."

"It's not the same thing and you know it."

"Very well, then. If only to prove that I'm not as reticent as you think."

James avoided me for the rest of the fair that summer. I know, because I looked for him everywhere, but I saw neither hide nor hair of him the rest of the week. I supposed he must have been terribly embarrassed, and perhaps he thought I had been making fun of him by not telling him who I was. And perhaps he felt that he had insulted me by suggesting he could one day challenge Father's business. I wasn't insulted, however; I just knew he was wrong. The very idea—to surpass Bergstrom Thoroughbreds.

In autumn Father was invited to teach a course in the agricultural school at your alma mater, though it was called Pennsylvania State College then. Richard begged and pleaded to be allowed to accompany him. Oh, how Richard wanted to see the world, even at that age. Father refused, saying that he would not have time to care for a young boy and that Richard could not miss school. But he refused so reluctantly—he hated to be away from his son—that Richard must have thought there was still a chance.

He came running out to the garden, where Claudia and I were having a party with some of our friends. It was a picnic of sorts, to say a sad good-bye to the summer and welcome in the new school year. One fellow was especially fond of Claudia, though he was too shy to even look her in the eye, much less speak to her. I used to tease her about him mercilessly, of course. She was not the only one who interested the boys, either. I had two young men who adored me, too, although I was indifferent to them both and had told them so. They still insisted on courting me, though, which I found highly irritating—did they think I didn't know my own mind? Honestly. Since they were determined to pine away rather than heed my words, well, I decided to let them. I used to enjoy watching them glower at each other when I would seem to prefer one more than the other, and would pretend not to notice when they fought for the next dance or the empty seat by my side.

One of the young men was telling a joke when Richard burst into the party. "Sylvia, Sylvia," he cried, tugging at my hand.

"What is it, darling? Are you hurt?"

"No, no." He glared, impatient. I had forgotten that he had made me promise not to call him "darling" in front of the older boys anymore. "I figured out how to get Father to take me with him."

I pulled him onto the gazebo seat by my side. "I thought Father already told you no."

"But we can change his mind. If you come, too, Sylvia, you can look after me. Then Father has to say I can go."

"But what about school?"

"I won't mind missing school."

I laughed. "I realize that, but you have to go to school if you want to run Bergstrom Thoroughbreds someday. And I have to go to school, too, if I want to go to college."

Claudia had been listening in. "Have you forgotten something?" she asked, approaching us from across the gazebo. She stood behind Richard and placed her hands on his shoulders. "I've graduated already, so I wouldn't miss any school. I could look after you."

"But Sylvia and I would have fun." Richard's face assumed its familiar stubborn frown. Claudia pursed her lips, and I shot my brother a look of warning. "We would, too, Claudia, but Elm Creek Manor couldn't get along without you for so long."

You charmer, I thought, as he tried to hide a grin. Good thing Claudia couldn't see his face. "Since Claudia is needed here, and I can't leave school—I'm sorry, Richard, but it doesn't sound feasible."

Richard looked down at the gazebo's wooden floor, crestfallen. "I know you want to go to college, Sylvia. I'm sorry—I didn't think about you missing school. But just think of it—the chance to go somewhere."

I was thinking about it, and as much as I loved my home, I too wanted to see some of the world before I returned to Elm Creek Manor to settle down. "I'm sorry, sweetheart. Maybe when you're older."

"When I'm older. That's what Father said. Everything's when I'm older."

Claudia sighed. "I'm sure they have schools near the college. You could both probably transfer easily enough. It's only for a semester, after all."

Richard brightened. "Do you think so?"

"I don't see why not, if Father agrees. And if Sylvia wants to transfer."

"Of course I want to," I exclaimed. "It would almost be like going away to college myself. Think of all the new things to see and people to meet."

My two young men frowned uneasily at that.

Richard crowed triumphantly and hopped down from the seat. He grabbed my hand and began to run from the gazebo toward the house, pulling me after him.

We spoke to Father, and without too much wheedling on our part, he agreed. Before long all the arrangements were made. We were to live in a faculty house on campus, and Richard would be able to attend a nearby elementary school. But the best part was that I would be allowed to continue my studies at the college.

My, how I enjoyed those days! I made many new friends, and Richard and I had a grand time exploring the campus. My classes were challenging, but not nearly as difficult as I had thought they would be. I was very proud that I could hold my own with the older students.

Our faculty home, while it could not be compared to Elm Creek Manor, was cozy and snug. Sometimes Father would bring home some of his students or other faculty members for supper, and they would banter and debate every conceivable topic late into the night. Often they discussed the news from Europe, sometimes in hushed tones that I had to strain to hear from the kitchen, sometimes in angry shouts that would make the china rattle in the cupboards. I would usually make some excuse so that I would not have to stay and listen. Even though we Bergstroms had considered ourselves thoroughly American since Great-Grandfather's time, and if we still had any distant relatives in Germany we did not know of them, the stories about Hitler and his politics always filled me with dread. Richard would eavesdrop if I could not find his hiding place and shoo him off to bed first.

One evening, Father came home joking merrily with two students. "Sylvia!" he called. "Come meet our guests for dinner."

In the kitchen, I sighed. I never knew when Father would bring company home until they stood on the doorstep. Wiping my hands on my apron, I hurried to the foyer, where Father and his guests were removing their coats and Richard was peppering them with questions. Then I froze in my tracks.

One of the young men was James Compson.

Father made the introductions. "James says he knows you, Sylvia," he said, bemused. "But I can't imagine how that's possible."

I gave James a sidelong glance. "We met at the fair, Father, last summer. He watched me ride."

"And a fine rider you are." James's eyes crinkled when he smiled, and I found myself smiling back.

I served supper, using a few tricks I had picked up from Cook to stretch the food for three into a meal for five. Throughout the meal, every time I looked up, James would be gazing steadily at me. His eyes were so intense that I could hardly bear to return his looks, but I could bear less turning away from him. I tried to keep my voice steady during the polite conversation, but I admit I was nervous.

"I'm surprised to find you here, Sylvia," James finally said when we were finished eating.

"I'm surprised to find you here as well."

"He won't be here for long," Father said. "He has big plans for himself, don't you, young man?"

"That's right, sir," James said. "I could stay with my family's operation, but with my older brothers in charge, there isn't a lot of room for me. Or for any new ideas."

"You could come work for Father," Richard chimed in. "Couldn't he, Father?"

Everyone laughed. It was clear that Richard admired his new friend very much.

"Perhaps he could." Father chuckled.

"What do you think of that, Sylvia?" James's eyes twinkled with amusement.

"I couldn't possibly say one way or the other. Why on Earth would you consult me about your plans?"

"James always wonders what pretty girls think about him," the other student joked. "It's one of his few redeeming qualities."

"Thanks for nothing," James protested with a grin, elbowing his friend in the side. "I was doing badly enough on my own without your help."

I eyed Father surreptitiously, but his expression suggested nothing. We might have been discussing horse feed for all he seemed to care. I had expected a more outraged response to the obvious flirtation with his daughter being conducted under his very nose. It was indeed puzzling.

After I had cleared away the dishes and had attempted unsuccessfully to put Richard to bed, I went into the other room while the men drank coffee and talked by the fire. I was pretending to study, but in truth I was eavesdropping. I wouldn't have, except I wanted to hear what James would say, and if he would say anything about me.

The conversation quickly turned to politics, and their voices became heated.

"I cannot believe it, not even of that little man," Father's voice boomed from the other room.

"He's right, James. Be reasonable. Think of the Olympic Games," the other student added.

"Berlin was whitewashed for the games. You know it as well as I." James's voice was low, but steady and emphatic. "It was a disgrace. A sham put on for an audience of people who want to be deluded, because we fear another war."

My heart seemed to skip a beat. Another war? I clutched my mathematics textbook with cold and trembling hands. That could not be. Germany was so far away, and no one wanted to get involved in another war so soon, if ever.

"But twelve thousand Jews died for Germany in the Great War," Father protested. "Surely that will count for something."

"I wish I could believe that, sir," James replied. "But I doubt it. Think of the Nuremberg laws. They aren't even a year old and look at what's happened already."

"It's strictly an economic problem," the other student said. "You tell him, Mr. Bergstrom. When their economy improves, the Nazi influence will waver again. Hitler can't last. With all his crazy talk about the Jews—why, surely he can only stay in power so long spouting nonsensical rubbish like that. He talks like an insane man."

"An insane man that an entire country listens to with enthusiasm," James said. "Haven't you read his writings?"

"God forbid you should fill your minds with such filth," Father broke in.

"Point taken, sir, but a man should know his enemies. I've read them, and it's clear that he fully intends to take over the world, if he can, and this alliance with Italy is only the beginning. There won't be a Jew left in Europe, or the world, if he isn't stopped. And if he isn't stopped soon, now, as his power is still growing, I shudder to think what it will take to stop him later."

A fist pounded on the table, and I jumped. "Germany will not follow Hitler like a newborn colt does its mother," Father shouted. "We are a logical people. We will not so blindly follow a madman."

There was silence.

Then the other student spoke up. "It's a European problem, anyway. It won't affect us here." I could almost see Father nodding. He had said as much before.

"The Great War affected us here," James reminded them.

I set down my book and crept away, my thoughts in turmoil. Was another war like the Great War truly possible? What would this mean for my friends—for James? They were old enough to go to war now, if there were to be a war. I thanked God that Richard was such a young child still. If the worst happened, he would at least be safe. I prayed he would remain so.

The disobedient subject of my prayers was crouched outside the door, listening to every word. I scolded him in a whisper and marched him upstairs.

"Did you hear, Sylvia?" His eyes were shining as I tucked him into bed. "Maybe I could be a soldier like Uncle Richard."

"Yes, and get yourself killed like Uncle Richard." My voice was harsh. I pulled the blankets up to his chin, blinking back tears.

But here I've been going on and on about one evening when you wanted to know how James and I fell in love and married. Well, that was the first of many evenings he spent at our residence that semester. When we returned to Waterford, James wrote me at least once a week, and two years later he asked me to marry him. I made him wait two years more while I attended Waterford College to study art. I fancied myself an artist and wanted to be an art teacher someday, but I left college before receiving my degree. When I was twenty and James was twenty-two, we were married, and James joined our family at Elm Creek Manor.

⚓

"Claudia had not yet married," Mrs. Compson added. "My aunts said I should let her marry first since she was the eldest sister, but Father quickly silenced them. He was almost as fond of James as I was, and was eager for him to join the family."

"Was Claudia jealous?"

"No, at least, not always. She would have preferred to be the first to marry, but she rarely complained. Besides, the shy young man from the party—Harold—had found his tongue, and so we all thought her own wedding wouldn't be far behind."

Sixteen

After work Sarah baked brownies to take to the meeting of the Tangled Web Quilters. She followed Diane's map a few blocks south of campus to a neighborhood populated by Waterford College professors and administrators. The gray stone houses with their sloped roofs and Tudor woodwork looked like scaled-down versions of Elm Creek Manor. Their carefully landscaped front yards heightened the similarity, except that oak trees rather than elms lined the street.

As she parked the truck behind Judy's minivan, Sarah figured that few landscape architects and personal assistants to wealthy recluses lived nearby.

A walkway of red bricks in a herringbone pattern led from the driveway to the front porch. Sarah went up to the house and rapped on the front door with the brass knocker.

The door opened enough for a boy about thirteen years old to look out and study her. "Yeah?" He wore jeans several sizes too big for his slender frame and a baseball cap turned backward. His black T-shirt bore a grinning skull with fire streaming from the eye sockets.

"Hi," Sarah said. She heard the Tangled Web Quilters laughing somewhere inside. "I'm here to see your mom."

He sighed and looked over his shoulder. "Ma!" he bellowed.

Sarah winced and tried not to cover her ears.

The boy turned back to Sarah. "Summer with you?"

"No."

Disappointment crossed his face.

Sarah hid a smile. "She'll be here soon, probably."

He shrugged. "Whatever."

Just then Diane appeared behind him. "Leave her standing on the porch, why don't you," she grumbled to the boy, who rolled his eyes and shuffled away. Diane turned to Sarah and opened the door wider. "I see you've met the pride and joy."

Sarah smiled and went inside. "Just barely. I didn't catch his name."

"Michael. Except these days he prefers to go by Mikey J." Diane led her along a carpeted hallway and downstairs to the basement. "He's okay, if you ignore the flaming skulls."

"I didn't know you had a son."

"Two, actually. The other's eleven, so he's still relatively normal."

In the finished half of the basement, the Tangled Web Quilters were gathered around a card table covered with snacks. Sarah added her plate of brownies to the lot. "How come every time I see you guys you're always standing next to the food?" she teased, by way of a greeting.

"You better hurry or there won't be anything left for you," Judy retorted. "Serves you right."

A few minutes later Summer burst into the room carrying a large plastic trash bag. "Hi, everybody. Sorry—"

"We know," Diane said. "Sorry you're late."

"I was here on time, but I was upstairs. Mike wanted to show me his new zip drive."

Gwen grinned. "Oh, so that's what the kids call it these days."

"You're sick, Mom. Mike's just a baby."

"Don't tell him that," Diane said. "You'll break his heart."

When everyone had sampled enough treats, they sat down in the sofas and chairs Diane had arranged. Sarah showed the others her new finished blocks, and they praised her progress.

Then Bonnie took a sheet of paper out of her sewing basket. "The president of the Waterford Quilting Guild dropped off a flyer at Grandma's Attic the other day. They're asking for volunteers to help set up for the Waterford Summer Quilt Festival."

"Can't they get their own people to do it?" Diane asked.

"I guess they need more help. Waterford College won't let them set up until the evening before the festival because there's some other display in the library atrium."

Summer shrugged and looked around the circle. "I'll go if some of you go."

"I can help," Sarah said.

"I'll go if it will help me win a ribbon," Diane said.

Everyone chuckled.

"You can have one of mine," Gwen offered.

"Thanks, but I'd rather earn my own, if I live that long."

Summer brushed some cookie crumbs off her lap and unfastened a twist-tie on the garbage bag. "While you guys were off having fun at quilt camp, I was getting some work done." She reached into the bag and pulled out a folded bundle.

"Oh, you finished piecing the Bear's Paw," Mrs. Emberly exclaimed. "Let's have a look at it."

Summer and Gwen each took two corners of the quilt top and held it open between them. Sarah could see where the pattern had earned its name, as it did resemble a bear's footprints. Summer had selected a different solid fabric for each of the twelve blocks, and the vivid colors stood out from the black background fabric. There were three rows of four blocks each, and a border of small isosceles right triangles surrounded them.

"Nice work," Diane said. "You can hardly tell it's machine pieced."

Summer rolled her eyes. "Gee, thanks." Then she turned a hopeful gaze on them all. "I thought maybe since we're all here, you could help me baste it?"

"Baste it?" Sarah asked. "You mean like a turkey?"

The others burst into laughter.

Sarah looked around in surprise. "What? What did I say?"

"I'm so glad you joined the Tangled Web Quilters, Sarah," Gwen said, wiping her eyes.

"Now, stop teasing the poor girl," Mrs. Emberly admonished. "We were all new quilters once. Sarah, basting stitches are large stitches that hold something in place temporarily."

"You might baste an appliqué to the background fabric so that it stays put while you blind stitch it down," Judy said.

"But in this case, basting means sewing big stitches through the quilt top, batting, and backing fabric so that the three layers don't shift around while you're quilting them," Summer said. "Basting's actually kind of boring."

"A true quilter enjoys all stages of the quilting process," Diane said, and earned herself a chorus of groans.

Gwen shook her head. "You should've been a philosopher, you're so concerned with what's true."

"Well, who says I'm not? Maybe I'm a quilt philosopher."

Diane led them to a Ping-Pong table in another corner of the basement. After removing the net and the dust, Summer and Gwen placed a large piece of black fabric right side down on the table. Summer unrolled a sheet of thin cotton batting on the fabric, enlisting the group's help to smooth out the wrinkles. Sarah then helped her place the quilt top right side up on the batting.

"This is what we call a quilt sandwich," Gwen told Sarah.

Summer showed Sarah how to sew large, zigzag stitches through all three layers of the quilt. "I won't take out the basting until I finish quilting," she explained. "If you don't keep the layers smooth your quilt will be all wrinkly and puckered on the back."

Each of them threaded a needle and began basting a section of the quilt sandwich.

"How was quilt camp?" Bonnie asked.

Summer smiled. "Yeah, tell us all about it and make us jealous."

"Oh, it was even nicer than last year," Mrs. Emberly said.

Gwen, Diane, and Judy joined her in describing quilt camp: the classes they had taken, which nationally famous quilters had turned out to be equally skilled as teachers and which had not, and all the new quilts they were now inspired to make.

"It would have been more fun if you three had been able to come, too," Judy added.

Diane sighed. "It was such a treat to be able to spend the whole weekend quilting, without having to worry about getting somebody's dinner or cleaning house or doing the laundry—"

"Or checking papers or dealing with undergraduates or taking care of the kids," Gwen said. "No offense, Summer."

"None taken, Mom."

"Life is too short to worry about chores when there's important quilting to be done," Mrs. Emberly said, smiling. "Most people I know don't see it that way, though."

Gwen stopped basting and rested her elbows on the table. "Why do you suppose that is?"

Mrs. Emberly shrugged. "A sense of duty, I suppose."

"Or guilt," Bonnie said. "Sometimes people look critically at a woman who spends time on her hobbies when the carpet needs to be vacuumed."

"Yes, but think about it." Gwen rested her chin in her palm. "Who would criticize a male artist who spent the day painting or sculpting instead of mowing the lawn? Nobody, I bet. 'He's an artist; he must paint.' Or sculpt. Whatever. That's what they'd say."

"I think most people don't consider quilting to be art," Sarah said.

The others groaned in protest.

"Heresy," Gwen cried, laughing.

Diane frowned. "Of course it's art."

"I didn't say I feel that way, just that other people might."

"And why is that?" Gwen mused. "Consider that even today there are far more female quilters than male. Is quilting not considered art, then, because it's something women do, or are women allowed to quilt because it isn't considered art? Quilting does have a practical purpose, after all, so it could be said that the women are not creating art but are instead remaining within their acceptable domestic sphere—"

"All right, Professor," Diane broke in. "We aren't in one of your classes."

Sarah wondered how Mrs. Compson would respond to this discussion. "Of course it's art; what a question," she'd probably declare, and then stare down anyone who dared to disagree.

"Well," Bonnie sighed, tying a knot in her basting thread, "as far as I'm concerned, women need art at least as much as men do, even if no one sees their work but themselves. We all need to give ourselves that time and try to ignore other people's criticism if it comes."

"And we need to give ourselves that space," Judy said. "One of the nicest things about quilt camp was that we all had so much room to ourselves, to spread out our fabric and our templates and things without worrying about getting in someone else's way or having a baby crawl on a rotary cutter or needles."

"Time, space, and lots of friends—that's what you need to be a successful quilter," Summer said. She surveyed their work as Mrs. Emberly put the last basting stitch in the quilt sandwich, tied a knot, and cut the thread. "This would have taken me hours, but now it's all done. Thanks, everybody."

For the rest of the evening they worked on their own projects, and Sarah was able to finish the LeMoyne Star block. Gwen took a piece of paper out of her bag and gave it to Sarah. "This will tell Mrs. Compson everything she needs to know about the lecture," she said. "When, where, how long, all that. If she has any questions, though, she can give me a call."

"Thanks," Sarah said, tucking the note into her bag of quilting supplies. She knew Mrs. Compson couldn't and wouldn't call, but Sarah could carry messages if necessary.

Mrs. Emberly had looked up when Gwen mentioned Mrs. Compson. "Sarah, dear, is there any news about the sale of Elm Creek Manor?"

"Nothing as far as I know. Sorry, Mrs. Emberly."

"Oh, that's all right. Perhaps no news is good news. Perhaps she's decided not to sell after all."

"I wish she wouldn't," Sarah confided. "I tried to get her to join the Tangled Web Quilters, but—"

"You did what?" Diane demanded.

Startled, Sarah looked around at the others. Their expressions were guarded. "I—I'm sorry," Sarah said. She felt her face growing warm. "I thought that since I was a member I was allowed to invite others to join. I—I'm really sorry. I should have checked first."

"Please tell me she said no," Diane said.

"Well—yes. I mean, yes, she did say no."

"What a relief."

Mrs. Emberly drew herself up and gave Diane a sharp look. "I disagree. Have some compassion. She just lost her sister, and she's already lost so much in her life. I for one would welcome her into our group, and who here has more cause to exclude her than I?"

Abashed, Diane looked at the floor.

"She's right," Bonnie said. "I'll never forget how you all rallied around me when Craig was in the hospital last year. Whom does Sylvia Compson have?"

"Well, she must have someone," Diane muttered.

"Maybe she does and maybe she doesn't," Gwen said. She turned to Sarah. "You go ahead and ask anyone you want to join. Sylvia Compson or anyone."

The others nodded and murmured their agreement.

Sarah nodded, but felt herself withdrawing from the circle of friends, suspended in the middle between the Tangled Web Quilters and Mrs. Compson. She wanted Mrs. Compson to make friends in Waterford so that the friendships would encourage her to stay at Elm Creek Manor. But Diane— well, Diane seemed to enjoy having a recognizable enemy, a clear boundary between those who were good enough to get in and those who would be excluded. Mrs. Emberly was another mystery. Could she have been one of those Waterford girls who had been jealous of Mrs. Compson's quilting and riding awards so many years ago?

Sarah sighed to herself. She wouldn't give up. The others seemed willing to welcome Mrs. Compson into the group, though it might be awkward at first. As for Diane, she would just have to get used to the idea.

If Mrs. Compson would agree to join. And if she wouldn't sell Elm Creek Manor and move away.

Seventeen

The next morning, Sarah and Matt arrived at Elm Creek Manor to find a dark blue luxury car parked in their usual spot.

"Was Mrs. Compson expecting someone today?" Matt asked as they went up the back steps and into the manor.

"She didn't say anything to me. I hope nothing's wrong."

They hurried inside, calling Mrs. Compson's name. Her voice returned an unintelligible reply from somewhere in the west wing. To their relief, they found her seated on an upholstered armchair in the formal parlor, sipping coffee. A thin, dark-haired man in a black pinstriped suit was with her.

Mrs. Compson smiled warmly when she spotted them in the doorway. "Ah. There they are. Matthew and Sarah, come meet Mr. Gregory Krolich from University Realty."

Matt and Sarah exchanged a quick look as the man stood to greet them.

"How do you do," he said, smiling. His ring bit into Sarah's hand when he shook it. "Mrs. Compson has been telling me how much you two have been helping her lately."

"Oh, yes indeed. We'll have this place looking wonderful in no time," Mrs. Compson said. "They're both such good workers."

"I'm sure they are. I've heard a lot of good things about Exterior Architects." He smiled ruefully at Matt. "I guess I can't enlist your help, then."

Matt looked puzzled. "My help for what?"

"I'm trying to convince Mrs. Compson that the restoration isn't necessary."

"And I find his argument contrary to everything I've ever heard about selling a home," Mrs. Compson said.

Matt smiled. "Sorry, Mr. Krolich. I'm afraid I have to side with Mrs. Compson on this one. I'm not about to bite the hand that feeds me."

"Please, call me Greg," Krolich urged. "Just my luck. It's three against one. Unless . . . ?" He turned to Sarah. "You're an accountant, right? Help me explain the economics of the situation to your friend here."

His tone wasn't patronizing, not exactly, but it irritated her just the same. "Economics? Well, I'm not in real estate, but I guess you could offer Mrs. Compson less if the manor isn't yet fully restored, right?"

Mrs. Compson turned to Krolich. "Is that what's behind all this?"

He chuckled and held up his palms in defense. "Mrs. Compson, I assure you, I know how much Elm Creek Manor is worth. I'd be a fool to insult you by offering anything less than a fair price. I just hate to see you invest money in restoration when you're planning to sell the place. Save your money for your new home."

"Hmph." Mrs. Compson eyed him. "I think that's my decision, to dispose of my money how I see fit."

"You're right, you're right." He smiled agreeably. "I shouldn't butt in. Especially when you have such ardent defenders." He turned his smile on Sarah. "You have to admire someone who wants the best for her friends. That's the kind of business instinct you'll need in Waterford. You don't get far in a small town like this by making enemies."

"Thank you," Sarah replied. Then she thought about his words and wondered if he really had complimented her.

"What are your career plans for after the manor sells?" Krolich asked Sarah.

"Now, don't you get any ideas," Mrs. Compson warned. "You'll have to be patient. I plan to keep Sarah very busy for the next few months."

"I'll wait my turn." Krolich chuckled. He reached into his breast pocket and retrieved a business card, which he handed to Sarah. "Give me a call when you're available, will you?"

Sarah fingered the card without looking at it. "I don't know anything about real estate."

"I wasn't thinking of my department. We'll try to find something for you in accounting."

"Okay. Thank you." Then she thought of something. "Could you tell me more about your company? University Realty manages student rental properties, right?"

He blinked, but his smile never wavered. "Why, yes. We do run many student properties."

"All of your properties are student rentals, right?"

"Currently, they are." His voice took on a slight edge.

Mrs. Compson looked from Krolich to Sarah and back. "What does this mean? Are you planning to turn Elm Creek Manor into some kind of frat house?"

"Certainly not. Nothing of the sort. We screen all our potential student renters very carefully. We get references, parents' addresses, all that."

Mrs. Compson drew in a sharp breath and shook her head. "I realize the number of bedrooms and baths might seem to lend itself towards that sort of thing, but you see, I couldn't bear to think of drunken undergraduates swinging from the chandeliers or performing hazing rituals in the gardens—"

"I assure you, that will never happen."

"How can you guarantee that?" Sarah asked. "Are you planning to move in and baby-sit?"

Krolich focused two steely eyes on her. "You're not long out of college yourself, are you? Would you have been swinging from the chandeliers if you'd been able to live in a place like this?"

"Of course not, but I appreciate—"

"Well, there you have it." He turned back to Mrs. Compson. "And most college students are as pleasant as your friend Sarah here. It's not fair to stereotype." He glanced at Sarah over his shoulder. "We mustn't alarm people unnecessarily."

"No one's getting alarmed as far as I can see," Matt said. "We're just asking a few questions. Mrs. Compson doesn't have to sell to you if she doesn't think you'll take care of the place."

Krolich looked wounded. "I don't know where all of this is coming from. I assure you, University Realty has an outstanding reputation in this community."

Mrs. Compson waved her hand impatiently. "Yes, yes, of course you do. No one is questioning your character or your company's willingness to properly care for a historic building."

I am, Sarah thought as she studied him.

His eyes told her he had noted her gaze, but his expression remained amiable. "Thank you for the coffee, Mrs. Compson, but I must be going. Please look over those papers, and we'll discuss them soon. No, no, I'll show myself out," he hastened to add as Mrs. Compson began to rise from her seat. He shook her hand and picked up his attaché case. He gave Sarah one last smile as he left the room. "Think about that job, will you?"

When he had gone, Mrs. Compson sighed and leaned back in her chair. A troubled frown lingered on her face, and her eyes were tired. "It's not that I want to see Elm Creek Manor become student apartments," she told them. "That certainly wasn't what I had in mind. I thought—well, a nice family, perhaps, with children . . ."

"You don't have to decide right now," Sarah said after Mrs. Compson's voice trailed off.

"I have to decide soon." Mrs. Compson stood and briskly smoothed her skirt. "They've made a reasonable offer, one I'd be foolish to simply disregard."

"What should I do about the outdoor restoration?" Matt asked.

Mrs. Compson thought for a moment. "Continue. He may use the unfinished work as an excuse to reduce his offer later, regardless of what he says now."

So Mrs. Compson didn't trust Krolich either, at least not completely. Sarah picked up the two coffee cups and carried them into the kitchen, then joined Mrs. Compson in the front foyer. Matt kissed Sarah good-bye and left for the north gardens.

As they worked upstairs, Sarah and Mrs. Compson made only a few half-hearted attempts at conversation. Sometimes, out of the corner of her eye, Sarah would see Mrs. Compson's hands drop from her work as she stared unseeing at some corner of the room.

Sarah watched and wished she could think of the right words to convince Mrs. Compson not to sell her home.

At noon Matt joined them for lunch. Sarah longed to take him aside and get his opinion about Krolich when Mrs. Compson couldn't overhear, but she didn't get an opportunity. During the meal no one mentioned the real estate agent or the manor's impending sale, and to Sarah it seemed as if the others were ignoring the morning's events. She couldn't decide if that made her disappointed or relieved.

After Matt left, Sarah remembered Gwen's notes. Mrs. Compson spread them out on the kitchen table and looked them over, nodding. "Everything seems to be arranged," she remarked. "On Gwen's end, at least. I still need to work on my own presentation if I am to be ready by the ninth. That's a Tuesday, I think."

"I didn't know it was going to be so soon."

"Soon? We have more than a week. We'll be ready. Don't worry." Mrs. Compson smiled reassuringly. "Perhaps that's what we should work on today. That may shake off our gloom."

Sarah nodded. Gregory Krolich sure knew how to ruin a perfectly good summer day. Knowing Elm Creek Manor was going to be sold was bad, and knowing it was going to be turned into student apartments was worse. But there was something else, something Krolich wasn't telling them. Or maybe it was all in Sarah's mind. Maybe she was just looking for reasons to dislike him.

"So. You don't care for our Mr. Krolich," Mrs. Compson suddenly said.

Sarah looked up, surprised.

"Oh, don't worry, dear. You haven't said anything, and I appreciate that, but your feelings are as clear as could be."

"I don't fully trust him," Sarah admitted. "But I don't know if I could like anyone who took Elm Creek Manor away from you."

"Away from you, you mean."

"That's silly. Elm Creek Manor isn't mine to begin with."

"Of course it is." Mrs. Compson reached across the table and patted Sarah's arm. "You've worked here, quilted here, heard the stories of its former occupants—though not all of its former occupants, and not all of its stories. That makes Elm Creek Manor partly yours, too."

"If Elm Creek Manor is partly mine, then I'm not selling my part."

Mrs. Compson chuckled. "I know how you feel. I don't want to sell my part, either."

"Then why are you talking to a real estate agent? If you don't want to sell, don't."

"It's not that simple." Mrs. Compson clasped her hands, fingers interlaced, and rested them on the table. "At first, I thought I wanted to sell. I admit that much. But since I've spent more time here, with you and Matthew, I've found that this is indeed my home and that I've missed it very much."

Sarah jumped to her feet. "Then let's get this settled," she exclaimed. "Matt has a car phone. I'll run out to the orchard and call this Krolich guy and tell him to forget it. I'm so glad you decided to stay, I—"

Mrs. Compson was shaking her head.

"What? What is it?"

Mrs. Compson motioned for Sarah to sit down. "It's not that I want to sell Elm Creek Manor; I have to sell it."

"Have to? Why? Is it—"

"No, it's not the money, and let's leave it at that."

"I can't leave it at that. You know how much I want you to stay. Can't you at least explain why you won't?"

"Not won't, can't," Mrs. Compson said. "You're a very demanding young woman, aren't you?"

"When I have to be."

"Oh, very well. Though I doubt if my explanation will satisfy you, here it is. Elm Creek Manor was great once. The Bergstroms made it great. But now—" She sighed and looked around the room. "Well, you see what it is now. Emptiness. Disrepair. And I am responsible for its decline."

"How can you blame yourself?" Sarah asked. "Claudia's the one who let things go. You weren't even here."

"Precisely. I should have been here. Bergstrom Thoroughbreds was my responsibility and I abandoned it. Oh, I didn't see it that way at the time, and I didn't know Claudia would fare so poorly. But that's no excuse. Elm

Creek Manor will never be what it once was, and I can't bear to live here, reminded every day of what has been lost."

Sarah reached across the table and took Mrs. Compson's hand. "That's not true. You, me, and Matt—together we're going to make this place as beautiful as ever. You'll see."

"Hmph." Mrs. Compson gave her a fond, wistful look. "We can restore its beauty but not its greatness. Perhaps you're too young to understand the difference."

She squeezed Sarah's hand, then let go. "The only right action is for me to pass the estate to another family who will make the place live again. I have no direct descendants, only second and third cousins scattered who knows where around the country. I'm the only Bergstrom left, and I can't bring Elm Creek Manor back to life by myself. I'm not strong enough, and I don't have enough time left to reverse the effects of years."

Mrs. Compson paused. "Perhaps it would be best to let Krolich hand it over to the students. A bunch of young people certainly would liven up the place, and that's what I said I wanted, didn't I? What do you suppose old Great-Grandfather Hans would think of that?" She laughed quietly.

Sarah couldn't join in. "If Elm Creek Manor does comes back to life, don't you want to be here for it?"

Mrs. Compson said nothing.

"I think you're being too hard on yourself."

"I could never be too hard on myself in this matter." Her voice was crisp. "That's enough of this. Let's go to the library and take care of my lecture materials. I have several boxes of slides to sort through. When we're finished, we can have a quilt lesson. I believe you said you're ready to start a new block?"

Sarah saw that the confidences were over, for now. "I finished the LeMoyne Star last night."

"Good. Good." Mrs. Compson rose and left the kitchen.

Sarah followed her upstairs, thoughts racing and worries growing.

Eighteen

The several boxes of slides turned out to be four large cartons of slides, photographs, and newspaper clippings. Mrs. Compson explained that for over thirty years she had photographed every quilt she had made.

"Gwen's lucky you brought all this with you from Sewickley," Sarah said.

"Luck has nothing to do with it. I still have some of these quilts, but most of them have been sold or given away. I'd no sooner leave this record of my life's work unattended than I'd sleep outside in a snowstorm."

As Mrs. Compson opened the first box of slides, Sarah unfolded one of the newspaper clippings. The headline announced WATERFORD QUILTING GUILD TO RAFFLE 'VICTORY QUILT.' Beneath it was a photo of several women holding up a quilt pieced from small hexagons.

"Are you in this picture?" Sarah asked.

"What do you have there?" Mrs. Compson took the clipping. "Oh, goodness. Wasn't that a long time ago." She pointed to one of the women. "That's me, holding on to the corner."

Sarah looked closely at the slender young woman in the photo. She was holding her chin up and looking straight into the camera, a determined expression on her face. "What's a Victory Quilt?"

"It's not a particular block pattern, if that's what you mean. That's a Grandmother's Flower Garden quilt."

"It looks like a honeycomb."

Mrs. Compson laughed. "I suppose it does. The small pieces were well suited to using up scraps, though, and with the war on, not even the Bergstroms could afford to waste a single thread. We ladies made this quilt and raffled it off to raise money for the war effort. You can't see it in this picture, but each of the light-colored hexagons was embroidered with the name of a local boy in the service. We stitched a gold star near his name if he had given up his life for his country." She sighed and handed back the clipping. "We embroidered so many gold stars that summer."

Sarah studied the picture a little while longer before returning it to the box.

"Let's see, now," Mrs. Compson said as she took a slide and held it up to the light. "Yes, this is a good one. Sarah, take that slide projector wheel out of that box and dust it off, would you? This slide should be the first."

Two hours passed as Mrs. Compson examined slides, considered them, and either rejected them or told Sarah where to place them in the slide projector wheel. Mrs. Compson explained that she planned to discuss the history of quilting. The slides would show Gwen's students how quilting had changed over time and how it had stayed the same.

"Are you going to tell them the Wandering Foot story?"

"Yes, and perhaps a few others like it, if there's time." Then Mrs. Compson sighed and pushed the last carton away. "That's all the slides I'll need. I'll prepare my lecture notes another day, but now it's time for another quilt lesson."

They put away the cartons and returned to the sewing room, where Sarah got out her template-making supplies.

"This time I'll show you how to make the Bachelor's Puzzle block," Mrs. Compson said, a smile flickering in the corners of her mouth.

"What's so funny?" Sarah asked, wondering if there was a superstition attached to this block, too. Next thing she knew, Mrs. Compson would be telling her that a quilt with a Bachelor's Puzzle block in it would doom the maker to eternal unemployment.

Mrs. Compson's smile broadened. "It's nothing, really. An inside joke between Claudia and me. Not a very nice joke, I'm ashamed to say."

"Don't keep me in suspense. What's the joke?"

"I did say you didn't know all of the manor's stories or all of its occupants," Mrs. Compson murmured as if thinking aloud. "And she was a very important person here once." She sighed and focused on Sarah again, her cheeks slightly pink, her expression almost embarrassed. "Very well, I'll explain while we work on this new block. But I'll warn you, this story puts me in a rather bad light. I admit I was not always kind when I was younger."

"Gee, that's hard to believe," Sarah replied in a dry tone rivaling Mrs. Compson's own.

✺

As I told you before, Richard was not fond of school. If Father had not repeatedly told him that he must have a proper education if he wished to run Bergstrom Thoroughbreds someday, he probably wouldn't have gone at all. Our semester at the Pennsylvania State College had not satisfied his thirst for travel and adventure, either. Richard often complained to me that Waterford High School was stifling him, the teachers were horrendous, the town was dull, et cetera, et cetera. When Richard turned sixteen, he and Father reached a compromise: if Richard kept his marks up, he would be allowed to attend school in Philadelphia.

"If you blame this on that baby quilt," my sister told me when we heard the news, "I'll never forgive you."

"Why, Claudia, I haven't said a word," I replied, all innocence. My amusement lasted only a moment, however. The thought of Richard's absence left me feeling hollow inside. I tried my best to feel happy for him, but I could never be so, not entirely.

So Richard went to Philadelphia to continue his education. Father had friends in the city who agreed to take him in while he was in school, so my worrying about him was really quite unwarranted. He wrote to me often, and when I read his letters aloud to Claudia and the rest of the family, it eased our hearts but made us miss him all the more.

Fortunately, James was there to brighten my spirits. He and Father were two of a kind—kindhearted, virtuous, determined men. With James's help, Bergstrom Thoroughbreds was better than it had ever been. James handled many of the more dangerous tasks that were now becoming more difficult for Father.

We had been married three years, each day happier than the last. What carefree times we had then. But of course you know what I mean, being newly married yourself, and to such a fine young man as Matthew. We were eager for children, and even after three years we weren't worried. James would always stroke my head and tell me that we had all the time in the world, that we had forever. Young brides still like to hear that sort of thing, I suppose.

So, as much as Richard's departure made my heart ache, I knew he would return when his education was complete. Maybe he would even be an uncle by then, I would think to myself, hiding a smile so that Claudia wouldn't pester me to share my thoughts. Remember, too, that it was the autumn of 1943. With so many families losing brothers and sons every day, I had no right to complain when my brother was merely away at school.

After what seemed like the longest time, the Christmas holidays finally approached. You can imagine the bustle and excitement around here then. Christmas at Elm Creek Manor was always such a lovely time, but now we had the added joy of Richard's homecoming. We had to be more creative than ever with our celebrations, due to rationing and shortages and all that, but we pushed troubling thoughts from our minds for a while. Richard was coming home at last.

On the day of his arrival, the family's impatience and expectation seemed to fill the house. All day I paced around, taking care of last-minute preparations and moving from window to window, looking out through the falling snow for him. Suddenly one of the cousins ran downstairs from the nursery shouting that a car was coming up the drive.

It seemed as if everyone was in the front entry at once, laughing and arguing over who would get to open the door for him, who would get to take his coat, who would get to sit next to him at dinner. Father reached the door first, with me at his elbow. Father swung open the door, and there he was.

"Richard," I cried, leaping forward to embrace him. And then I froze.

A small figure peeked out from behind him. The biggest blue eyes I had ever seen peered up at me from beneath a white fur hood, the rest of the small face hidden behind a thick woolen muffler.

"Well, sis? Are you going to let us in or keep us standing out here in the snow?" Richard demanded, grinning at me as I stood there gaping. He took the bundled-up figure by the elbow and guided her into the house, giving me a quick peck on the cheek as he passed.

I followed them inside, still dumbfounded. Everyone tried to hug Richard at once, and their welcomes created quite a din. The bundled figure stood apart, looking anxiously from one strange face to the next.

Then Richard broke free from the crowd and turned to his companion. "Still bundled up, are you?" he teased gently, and the eyes seemed to smile over the muffler. Mittened hands fumbled clumsily with the hood and the coat buttons. Richard shrugged off his own coat and began to help.

The family fell silent. Even the little cousins watched them expectantly. Richard turned to face us, draping their wraps over his arm. "Everyone, I'd like you to meet my—I'd like you to meet Agnes Chevalier." He said her name just like that—Ahn-YES instead of the normal way, AG-nes.

"Hello," Agnes said, her smile trembling a little. I already told you she had the biggest blue eyes I had ever seen. She also had the longest, darkest hair I had ever seen, longer than mine, even. Her skin was so fair, except where the cold had brought roses to her cheeks, and she was so small that the top of her head barely reached my shoulder. I remember thinking she looked just like a little porcelain doll.

"Welcome to Elm Creek Manor, Agnes," Claudia said, stepping forward to take their things. She handed them to a cousin with instructions that they were to be hung someplace where they would dry. Then she turned to Richard and Agnes, placing an arm around the tiny girl's shoulders. "Let's get you two by a nice warm fire, shall we?" As she guided Agnes down the hallway toward the parlor, two cousins seized Richard's hands and pulled him after them.

Father and I trailed along behind the crowd. We exchanged a quick glance, enough to confirm that the other had not known about Richard's traveling companion either.

As they warmed themselves with hot tea and warm quilts, Richard told us that Agnes was the sister of a classmate, and they had met when he went to his friend's home for dinner two months before. Her father was a successful attorney and her mother was from an enormously wealthy and prominent political family—although Richard put it more politely than I have done. They had been distressed to learn that they would not be spending the holidays with their only daughter, but they sent the Bergstroms their warmest holiday wishes.

"Maybe Agnes should be put back on the next train to Philadelphia to spend Christmas with her own family," I whispered to Claudia. I said the girl's name AG-nes, without the affected French pronunciation.

Claudia sighed. "We'll get to the bottom of this soon enough, but in the meantime, you mustn't be rude." She turned away from me and smiled brightly across the room at our unexpected guest.

It wasn't until the next afternoon that I was able to pull Richard aside for a private chat. "Isn't she just wonderful, Sylvia?" he exclaimed, his eyes dazzled. "She's just the best girl I ever met. I couldn't wait for you to meet her."

"Why didn't you say anything in any of your letters?"

Richard looked abashed. "I knew you'd tell Claudia and Father, and I didn't want them to think I was neglecting my studies. I haven't been," he hastily added, probably seeing my eyebrows rise in inquiry. "My marks are good, and I'm learning a lot, I think." He hesitated. "She's only fifteen. I know she's just a kid, but she's really special, and—"

"And you're just sixteen yourself, too young to be serious about a girl. What were her parents thinking, letting her travel across the state unchaperoned like that?"

Richard scowled. "You know me better than that. I'd never take advantage of a girl."

"Hmph. Maybe she'd take advantage of you." He bristled, and I held up a hand in apology. "Sorry. That was uncalled for. But goodness, Richard, couldn't you have given us some kind of warning?"

He grinned, and looked over his shoulder as footsteps approached. "I know you'll love her, too, once you get to know her," he whispered, giving my hand a squeeze before sauntering down the hall.

You can imagine how I felt about that. "You'll love her, too," he'd said, which meant that he loved her, or at least he thought he did. I squared my shoulders and returned to the rest of the family, hoping for the best.

Before long, I determined that just as surely as Agnes was the prettiest girl

I had ever seen, she was also the silliest, most spoiled, and most childish creature ever to step foot into Elm Creek Manor.

She pouted if her tea was too cold, then batted her eyelashes at Richard until he leaped up to fetch her a fresh cup, only to send him racing back to the kitchen again because he had added too much sugar. We gave her the finest guest room, only to hear that it was "unbearably cold, not like in Philadelphia." She picked at her food, remarking that one could not expect to find Philadelphia's fine cookery so far out here in the country. She would try to participate in dinner conversation, prefacing each inane chirping remark with "Papa says . . ." And the way Richard treated her, as if she were made of priceless, delicate china, giving her the best seat nearest the fire, carrying everything for her, taking her arm as she went upstairs, hanging on to her every word as if it fell from the lips of Shakespeare himself—my, it was tiresome.

I was not the only one who found her insufferable. We adults would exchange amazed looks at each new piece of foolishness, and even the children screwed up their faces in bewilderment as they looked from their favorite cousin to this strange creature from the apparently heavenly land of Philadelphia. We all pondered the same question: yes, she's lovely to look at, but what on earth does our dear Richard see in her?

James warned me that I had better get used to her, just in case Agnes became a permanent addition to the family. Oh, I tried to like her, and I vowed to keep my feelings hidden for Richard's sake. Surely, I told myself, once we knew Agnes better, we would come to see her as Richard did.

One afternoon Claudia and I invited her to join us as we quilted. "How charming," she exclaimed, fingering the edge of my latest quilt. Do you remember the pictures of the Baltimore Album style quilts I showed you? Well, that's what I was working on then. I much prefer piecing to the intricate appliqué required for that style, but one of my closest school friends was planning to be married in the spring. This style was not quite as fashionable as others then, but it was my friend's favorite. The quilt was going to be a surprise, you see. Her husband-to-be was fighting in Europe, and they were to be wed as soon as he came home.

But as I was saying, Agnes fingered the edge of my quilt and exclaimed, "How charming." Then she added, "In Philadelphia we can buy our own blankets, but I don't suppose you can do that out here in the country, can you?"

I removed the edge of the quilt from her tiny, grasping hand. "Quite right. There isn't a single store within a hundred miles of here. I hope you remembered to pack everything."

"Sylvia." Claudia's voice held a note of warning.

"Really?" Agnes's mouth fell open in a way that made her look quite foolish. "Not a single store?"

"Not a one," I replied. "In fact, I had never even heard of a store until Richard described them to me in one of his letters. At first I thought he was just making them up, but Father told me he was telling the truth. To me it sounded like the stuff of fairy tales, but then, I've never been to Philadelphia." I picked up my needle and continued sewing.

Out of the corner of my eye I could see Agnes staring at me in confusion, her cheeks growing pink. Then she turned on her heel and flounced out of the room.

"Sylvia, that wasn't very nice."

"After that remark, she's lucky I didn't say worse. Why make a quilt when you can just buy a blanket? Honestly."

"I agree she could be more tactful, but even so—"

"What does Richard see in her?"

"I don't know. It's a puzzle."

"She's the puzzle," I retorted, and that's how it started. From that time on, whenever Claudia or I referred to Agnes, we called her Bachelor's Puzzle. Sometimes we called her BP, or the Puzzle, as in "I wonder if Richard will bring the Puzzle home for spring break?" or "Richard writes that he and BP are going to the Winter Ball." Or "Dear me, I hope Bachelor's Puzzle can remember her own name today, indeed I do."

We never said it to her, or when anyone else other than Claudia and I could hear. But we said it all the same, and it wasn't very nice, and I'll never forgive myself for giving her that dreadful nickname.

※

"Sounds to me like she deserved it," Sarah said, laughing.

"Oh, no, not you, too," Mrs. Compson protested, joining in. "It isn't nice to laugh at other people, even if they are silly, foolish creatures. Especially not then." She wiped tears from the corners of her eyes.

"What did Richard say when Agnes told him about it?"

Mrs. Compson stopped laughing. "He never said anything, so I assume she didn't tell him." She fixed Sarah with a studious gaze. "And now, young lady, it's your turn."

"My turn for what?"

"I'm tired of doing all the talking around here. Now it's your turn to answer some questions."

Sarah shifted in her seat. "What kind of questions?"

"Let's start with your family. What about your parents? Any brothers or sisters?"

"No, I'm an only child. So's Matt. My father died years ago." Sarah paused. "Your stories are much more interesting than anything I could tell. I don't see why you'd be interested—"

"Indulge me. Did your mother ever remarry?"

"No, but she's probably set a world record for the number of boyfriends held in a single lifetime. Does that count?"

"Ah. I see I've struck a nerve." Mrs. Compson leaned forward. "Why does that bother you?"

"It doesn't bother me. She can date whomever she likes as far as I'm concerned. It doesn't affect me or my life."

"Quite right. Of course not." Mrs. Compson cocked her head to one side and smiled knowingly.

Sarah tried not to fidget. "You know, Matt and I were talking—"

"About why you're angry with your mother?"

"No. I mean, of course not. I'm not angry with her. What makes you say that?"

"Tell me about her."

"Well . . . she's a nurse, and she kind of looks like me except she has shorter hair, and she and my dad met at a bowling alley, and now she likes to take expensive trips that her boyfriends pay for. Really, there's not much to say."

"Sarah?"

"What?"

"Your storytelling abilities leave much to be desired."

"Thanks."

"Perhaps you might as well tell me what you and Matthew were discussing instead."

Sarah paused for a moment, wondering if Mrs. Compson really did intend to let her off the hook that easily. "Matt and I were wondering if you'd like to celebrate the Fourth of July with us. Bonnie Markham says there's going to be a parade downtown, an outdoor concert on the square, and a quilt show on campus. We'd like to go, and we thought you'd like to join us, maybe?"

"I think I'd like that very much." Mrs. Compson looked pleased. "And since I entered a quilt in that show myself, I suppose I ought to see how it fared."

Nineteen

Early the next week Sarah finished cleaning two more suites in the south wing and started a new block, Posies Round the Square. Mrs. Compson warned her that this block would be the most difficult by far since it required two new piecing techniques: sewing curved seams and appliqué.

Forewarned though she was, Sarah still found herself becoming frustrated. As she gritted her teeth and attempted for the third time to join the same convex blue piece to the same concave background piece without stretching the bias edges out of place, Sarah decided that sewing a straight seam was to sewing a curved seam as brushing her teeth was to having emergency root canal. Her skills improved by the time she finished the block, however, so she admitted that curved seams were pretty, and they did create many new design possibilities. Still, she didn't want to sew any more curved seams anytime soon.

She found appliqué easier. Mrs. Compson instructed her to cut the leaf-shaped piece from the darkest fabric, but to add a seam allowance of only an eighth of an inch this time. Sarah basted the appliqué in place on the background fabric, and after securing the thread with a knot, she used the tip of her needle to tuck the raw edge of the appliqué under as she sewed it down. Sarah was pleased to see that her stiches were virtually invisible from the front of the block, and that the curves of the leaf were smooth and the two points were sharp. Before long she added a second leaf and two concentric circles resembling a flower to the design.

Sarah finished the Posies Round the Square and started a new appliqué block called Lancaster Rose on Wednesday, the same day she planned to meet the Tangled Web Quilters after work to help set up for the Waterford Summer Quilt Festival.

After sharing a quick supper with Matt, Sarah drove to the Waterford College campus, hoping she'd be able to find a parking space on the main street near the front gates, where she planned to meet Summer. To her dismay she

found most of the streets adjacent to campus blocked off by blaze-orange saw-
horses as city workers assembled refreshment stands and bleachers along the
parade route. Finally she found an empty spot designed for a compact car and
somehow managed to maneuver the pickup into it. By the time she locked
the truck and ran to the meeting place, Summer was already there.

"Hi, Sarah," Summer called when she came into view, jumping up from
the bench where she had been waiting. Her long auburn hair swung lightly
around her shoulders.

"I'm really sorry I'm late," Sarah said, catching her breath. "Will the
quilting guild still let us in?"

Summer laughed. "You're only a few minutes late. Don't worry so much.
They wouldn't make us sit outside when there's so much work to do. The rest
of the Tangled Webbers are already there."

The two young women hurried up the hill to the library. Sarah had never
been there, but Summer claimed to have spent the equivalent of one third of
her life within its walls. A security guard waved them through the turnstile
when Summer flashed her student ID and explained their errand.

Once inside, Summer led Sarah around a corner and through a set of
glass double doors into a long, spacious gallery. Four skylights down the center of the high ceiling left squares of light on the gleaming parquet floor. On
the long wall to their left hung several portraits of library benefactors, while
the opposite wall was covered almost entirely by rectangular, mirrored-glass
windows separated by thin steel frames. Sarah could see the grassy hill crisscrossed by sidewalks sloping toward the main street, but the students outside
would see only their own reflections. The dark tint would allow enough sunlight in to brighten the room without fading the colors of the quilts that
would soon be displayed there.

Fifty or more women of all ages had gathered in several scattered groups
throughout the gallery, their conversations creating a sonorous hum occasionally punctuated by bursts of laughter. At the far end of the room several
women were setting up folding tables and covering them with colorful print
fabric. In the middle of the room, armchairs and loveseats had been pushed
aside to make room for what looked like stacks of lumber. In a group of
helpers near one of the piles, Sarah and Summer easily spotted Gwen's red
hair standing out among the blonds, browns, blacks, and grays of the Tangled Web Quilters surrounding her.

They joined their friends. Summer greeted her mother with a hug and a
kiss on the cheek. As Gwen laughed and brushed her daughter's hair out of
her eyes, Sarah felt a pang of envy. She wondered what it would be like to
have a mother who was also a friend. Summer and Gwen were always doing
things together, but Sarah couldn't spend more than fifteen minutes with her

mother without feeling exhausted and strained, as if every detail of her life had been dissected and denounced.

She realized she was grinding her back molars just thinking about it, and made herself relax.

The others were poking through the nearest stack of boards and chatting, and Sarah pretended she had been listening all along. She noticed that the boards were cut to specific lengths, and some of the pieces had notches carved into their ends.

"The first thing you need to do is take one of these long poles," Bonnie was saying as she pulled a long piece of wood from the pile. "Attach four of these feet so that the pole will stand up."

"I'll sort out the pile while you younger girls take care of the lifting," Mrs. Emberly said.

"Then you assemble another pole and put the crossbar across the top," Bonnie continued. "It should fit into the notches."

"Will we drape the quilts over the crossbars?" Sarah asked.

"Each quilt will have a hanging sleeve, a tube of fabric sewn on the back," Judy said. "We'll take down the crossbar, slide it into the hanging sleeve, and then put the bar back up."

"It's kind of like hanging curtains with a curtain rod, only heavier," Summer added.

The Tangled Web Quilters got to work. When they had finished three quilt stands, a tall woman wearing her dark brown hair in a pageboy cut waved to them from across the room.

"Get ready for inspection," Gwen said as the woman approached.

"Just ignore her and maybe she'll go away," Diane hissed.

"Be nice," Bonnie said. "It isn't easy to run a quilt show."

Sarah didn't have time to ask who the woman was before she reached them. "We're so glad you could make it," she exclaimed. She squinted at their quilt stands. "How are things going over here?"

"Just fine, Mary Beth," Bonnie said.

Mary Beth grasped the nearest pole and shook it. "Seems sturdy enough. Maybe a little wobbly."

Diane frowned. "No one will be grabbing the poles like that during the show, so we're probably safe."

"Oh, you'd be surprised. You wouldn't believe some of the things we've seen at these shows. Someone could trip and fall, bump into a pole and knock it on someone's head, and then it's lawsuit city."

"We'll be sure they're safe before you put the quilts on them," Judy said.

"That's all we ask," Mary Beth said. "When you're done, we'll double-check them just to be sure." She smiled and hurried across the room to inspect another group.

"Must she refer to herself as 'we'?" Diane grumbled.

Gwen grinned. "You're just annoyed because she's been guild president six years in a row." She turned to Sarah. "After her first two years, Diane offered to take over—"

"I thought she might want a break from it, that's all. It's a lot of work."

"—but Mary Beth took it the wrong way."

"She acted like Diane was plotting a military overthrow," Judy said.

"That's because it looked like I was going to win."

Mrs. Emberly sighed. "It was quite unpleasant. At the meeting before the election, Mary Beth stood up in the front of the room and asked us if we'd feel comfortable putting the guild and the Waterford Summer Quilt Festival in the hands of someone who had never won a ribbon."

"How mean," Sarah exclaimed. "What did you do?"

"You won't believe this," Gwen said. "Diane just laughed it off."

"Until after the meeting, that is," Summer said. "Then she totally blew up. I'd tell you what she said, but Mom covered up my ears for most of it."

"I did not."

"Soon after that, and not coincidentally, our bee seceded from the Waterford Quilting Guild," Judy explained. "We still enter our quilts in the shows and help out with various projects, but for weekly meetings, we prefer our own little group."

"Most guilds aren't so political," Bonnie said. "And not everyone in the Waterford Quilting Guild is like Mary Beth. You'll find that out when you get to know them."

That evening, though, Sarah was too busy to meet anyone new. Several hours passed as she and the other Tangled Web Quilters assembled the large wooden stands and moved them into rows. The wooden pieces were heavy, and after a while Sarah began to grow weary.

When the last stands were in place, Mary Beth went to the front of the room and waved her arms in the air to get everyone's attention. "Thanks again for all your help," she called out. "We'll see you tomorrow at the quilt show. Now we have to ask everyone who isn't on the Festival Committee to leave, please. Thanks again."

The helpers began to move toward the doors.

Even though it was almost midnight, Sarah was dismayed. "But I wanted to see the quilts," she protested as the Tangled Web Quilters went outside. They headed down the hill to the main street where Sarah and Gwen had parked their cars; the others lived close enough to campus to walk home.

"Only members of the Festival Committee are allowed to see the quilts before the show opens tomorrow," Summer explained. "They'll hang the quilts and get them ready for the judges."

"How will they decide who gets a ribbon?"

"There are six categories according to style and size, with ribbons for first, second, and third place in each category. Then there's Best of Show, which means exactly that: the best quilt out of all categories. Each of the four judges also gets to pick a Judge's Choice, and then there's Viewers' Choice. If you get to the show early enough you get to vote for your favorite quilt."

"How early?" Sarah asked, thinking about Mrs. Compson's entry.

"Before ten. My mom won one of those a few years ago, and she said it was the highest honor any one of her quilts had ever received."

"That's because judges' methods are utterly inscrutable," Gwen said. "You might make an absolutely stunning quilt, but a judge might disregard it if you quilted it by machine rather than by hand, or for some other reason whose grounds are wholly personal."

Bonnie sighed. "Now Gwen, be fair."

"Who's not being fair? I didn't mean to suggest that judges make arbitrary choices, just that matters of personal taste strongly influence how we evaluate art. That being the case, I'd prefer the appreciation of a broad range of people, quilters and nonquilters alike, rather than the stamp of approval from a few select so-called experts."

"Mom's had some conflict with judges in the past," Summer explained to Sarah in an undertone.

"I never would've guessed."

"Then again," Gwen mused, "the Viewers' Choice ribbon poses problems of its own. Does one pander to the opinions of the general public or does one pursue one's own artistic vision? What if those two paths cannot coincide? And then there's that whole problem of pitting artists against each other. Talk about stifling artistic cooperation. What should one do then?"

"Stop entering your stuff in quilt shows, I suppose," Diane said. "I could do without your competition, especially if you're going to fret about it so much."

Everyone laughed.

"Fine," Gwen said, pretending to be wounded. "I'll just continue to wrestle with these important moral issues myself, thank you very much."

They reached Sarah's truck. "I'll see you all tomorrow at the celebration," she called, unlocking the truck and climbing inside. They waved good-bye, and she drove home.

Twenty

When Matt and Sarah pulled up behind the manor the next morning, Mrs. Compson was waiting on the back steps wearing a red-and-white-striped dress, white tennis shoes, and a wide-brimmed blue hat decorated with red and white flowers. Sarah opened the passenger door and slid over to the middle of the seat.

"Good morning, you two. Are you ready for some fun?" Mrs. Compson said.

"We're always ready," Matt assured her.

Since the parade route had been closed to traffic, they parked in a municipal lot near the edge of campus and joined the hundreds of people already milling through the streets. Dixieland music floated through the warm and hazy air. "What should we do first?" Sarah asked. "Do you want to go to the quilt show?"

"Let's see what there is to see downtown first," Mrs. Compson replied, smiling as a juggler in clown makeup passed unsteadily on a unicycle, an impromptu parade of delighted children close behind.

The next few hours passed quickly as they strolled around the downtown enjoying the street performers. Musicians entertained the crowds from small stages in the intersections. A magician's bewildering display of sleight-of-hand sparked a hot debate between Mrs. Compson and Matt regarding who was and who wasn't watching carefully enough to figure out how the tricks worked. Children seemed to be everywhere, shouting and laughing, darting in and out of the crowd, balloons tethered to their wrists. Parents gathered in friendly groups wherever a storefront window or a tree offered shade, laughing and chatting as they kept one eye on their friends and the other on their rambunctious offspring. The delicious fragrance of popcorn and broiling chicken and spicy beef drifted through the streets.

Matt must have noticed it, too, for he glanced at his watch. "It's almost noon."

"Already? I can't believe it," Mrs. Compson exclaimed. "Is anyone else ready for lunch?"

They all were, so they approached the closest food vendor and ordered three Cajun-style blackened chicken sandwiches with curly fries and lemonade. Mrs. Compson insisted on treating them. Matt carried Mrs. Compson's lunch for her as they made their way through the ever-increasing crowd to the square, where a ten-piece band was belting out dance tunes from the forties. They managed to find a seat on a tree-shaded bench for Mrs. Compson, and Sarah and Matt sprawled out on the grass nearby. Mrs. Compson tapped her foot in time with the music as they ate and talked.

Sarah noticed that people were starting to gather along the sidewalks, some sitting in folding chairs facing the street. "The parade must be about to start," she guessed, just as the band wrapped up its final set.

"I'll grab us a spot," Matt called over his shoulder as he dashed into the crowd, his curly head bobbing above those surrounding him. Sarah and Mrs. Compson disposed of their trash and followed more slowly, joining him in a clear space right next to the street, the perfect spot to view the parade as it approached the judges.

Several parade officials wearing red, white, and blue sashes passed, motioning the last stragglers off the street and onto the curbs. A cheerful woman in colonial dress handed them each a small flag. In the distance they heard a marching band and cheers from spectators lining earlier stages of the parade route. Soon the first float came into view, and the crowd responded with appreciative cheers and flag-waving. Sarah told the others what Summer had told her the night before, that each Waterford College fraternity and sorority entered a float into the competition. Between the floats came marching bands from each of the local junior and senior high schools. The mayor, the police chief, and the Dairy Princess, all clad in eighteenth-century costume, were driven by in an old Model T. Behind them marched Betsy Ross, George Washington, and Ben Franklin, waving and throwing candy to the audience.

Betsy Ross passed within a yard of their spot. "Hi, Sarah," she called, beaming.

Sarah stared at her. "Diane?" But by then she was gone.

Then a murmuring chorus of adoring parents signaled the highlight of the event: the Children's Bike Parade. First came cautious five-year-olds on tricycles, followed by older children on two-wheelers with training wheels, and lastly by sixth graders on fifteen-speeds and off-road bikes. Each bike was festooned with red, white, and blue crepe paper streamers and balloons. There would be prizes, Sarah overheard, for the best decorated bike in each age group.

As the last child passed and the next float drove slowly by, Sarah turned to Mrs. Compson with a grin. "What do you think?"

"Oh, it's delightful. The children are so charming."

A group of sequin-clad teenage girls whirled by, batons flashing in the sunlight. After the next float the crowd suddenly quieted, and then there began a sprinkling of applause that grew louder each moment. Sarah heard a lone snare drum beating out a measured march. Mrs. Compson placed a hand over her heart and gave Matt a quick elbow in the ribs. He hastily snatched off his baseball cap.

A color guard marched slowly past, holding the flag high. Behind them in two open convertibles sat seven elderly men, their lined faces stern and proud. "World War One," Matt said, nodding to their uniforms. Behind them twenty other men clad in uniforms from the Second World War stiffly marched in four rows. Some wore medals; some also wore empty jacket sleeves rolled up and pinned at the shoulder. Other veterans, men and women who had fought in later wars, followed, some smiling and waving to the crowd, others staring straight ahead, faces grim. One long-haired man in his forties held his flag clenched in his teeth because his hands were occupied with propelling his wheelchair along.

Mrs. Compson sighed. "I think I'd like to sit down now."

Sarah nodded and took her elbow. Matt cleared a path for them through the crowd, and they made their way back to the square and the shady bench. The lawn was now empty except for discarded sandwich wrappers and cups. Mrs. Compson eased herself onto the seat. They heard the Waterford College marching band approaching, playing a stirring Sousa march that soon had the spectators clapping along.

"Quite a patriotic town you have here," Matt remarked, stretching out on his back on the grass and resting his head in his hands.

"Patriotic? Hmph. I suppose they would call it that."

Matt's brow furrowed slightly. "Wouldn't you?"

Mrs. Compson shrugged and looked away. "This might sound petty, but it's hard for me to see their frenetic flag-waving in an entirely positive light."

"Frenetic?" Sarah laughed. "Don't you think that's a little harsh?"

"I'm entitled to my point of view. This town wasn't very friendly to the Bergstroms when I was a young woman because of their so-called patriotism."

"I don't understand. Your family immigrated to America a long time ago, right? I thought you said they've been here since your great-grandfather's time."

"I did."

Matt and Sarah exchanged bewildered looks.

Mrs. Compson noted them, and gave a wry smile. "I'll tell you what happened. Maybe then you'll see why I have mixed feelings about this town."

†

Matthew, I assume that Sarah has told you most of what I have already said about my family and Elm Creek Manor, but if you get lost, stop me and I'll explain.

It was March of 1944, and I was twenty-four years old. Father's declining health had put me and James all but entirely in charge of Bergstrom Thoroughbreds by this time, and Richard was still away at school in Philadelphia. Our family business, which had grown so much since my great-grandfather's time and had survived the Depression and the Great War, was now struggling. It seemed selfish then to worry about our own fortunes when so many were suffering, so we did what we could to maintain the business until the war ended and we could properly invest in it again.

In Waterford, everyone's thoughts were on the war effort. Claudia's young man, Harold, was the assistant air raid warden for our area. Although James assured me we were safe, the whole town picked up the habit of nervously scanning the skies for German bombers who might mistake us for Pittsburgh or Ambridge, to the west. It was a difficult time, but we made the best of it.

Richard's letters did little to put me at ease. He wrote about his friends who were going off to war and how he envied them the grand adventures they would have. Oh, and remember his childhood friend Andrew, from the playhouse? Richard had looked him up in Philadelphia and they were two peas in a pod again. When Richard wrote and reminded me that both he and Andrew were seventeen and men now, I felt my heart quake, but I tried to put it out of my mind.

For Claudia and me, our weekly quilting guild meeting was our escape. Every member saved scraps of fabric to make raffle quilts to raise money for the war effort, like that Grandmother's Flower Garden quilt in the picture you saw, Sarah. That was our first Victory Quilt. We'd made it the previous summer, when I was guild president, when I thought the war couldn't possibly last much longer.

But the following March it seemed that we had always been at war, and hanging blackout curtains, and rationing everything. We worked on new Victory Quilts and talked in hushed tones about husbands, brothers, and sons overseas. When one of us experienced the worst sort of loss, the others would do what we could to comfort and console her.

One evening our meeting was held in the high school cafeteria, and I was sitting at a quilt frame with Claudia and four other women as the other quilters worked in smaller groups on other projects. I mentioned that in two weeks Richard would be coming home for spring break.

"The rich little German schoolboy's coming home. Not like my boy," a voice muttered behind me.

I spun around. "And what exactly is that supposed to mean?" I demanded, only to be met by stony silence.

I looked around the quilt frame. Only Claudia's eyes, wide with shock, met mine.

"Better not to have those Krauts fighting with our boys, anyway," a different voice hissed.

"Not unless you want to wake up with a knife in your back," said a third.

"Must be nice to have enough money to buy your way out of the service."

Claudia flushed, and her eyes brimmed with tears. She opened her mouth as if to speak, then scrambled to her feet, snatched her sewing basket, and fled.

"If any one of you has anything to say to me or my family, say it now." Inside I felt as if I were trembling to pieces, but my voice sounded like stone.

No one said a word.

"Very well, then," I said, turning an icy gaze on each of them in turn. "You can apologize to my sister next week." I spun on my heel, grabbed my sewing basket, and marched out the same door Claudia had taken.

Even though it was early March, it was still bitter cold. I found Claudia walking toward home, her shoulders shaking. I ran to catch up with her. "Claudia?"

She was crying into her handkerchief. "For months it's been like this, at the grocery store, the library, everywhere, but this is too much. How could they? How could my own friends be so hateful?"

I put my arm around her. "Don't mind them, Claudia. They're just upset. Everyone is. It's the war, that's all. They don't mean it. Everything will be fine next week."

"I have to wonder." She sniffled. We walked the rest of the way home in silence.

Claudia had always been so popular with the local girls, and so their comments wounded her much more than they did me. Their behavior confused her. There were so many German families in Waterford, and some who taunted us were of even more recent German origin than we. Remember, too, that our name and a significant portion of our heritage were Swedish. We were hardly just off the boat from Berlin. Why had we been singled out?

I understood well enough.

Although Father and our uncles had fought in the Great War, we were one of the few families in town who did not have someone currently in the military. James was already twenty-six, though there were plenty of men even older who had enlisted. Richard was still too young, and the only cousins of suitable age were girls. What's more, our wealth had always made us the target of envious remarks. They weren't shunning us because we were German but because we were fortunate.

I tried to explain this to Claudia, but I don't think she ever really understood. You'd think that of all people Claudia would recognize jealousy when she saw it, but in this matter that wasn't so.

The next week's guild meeting was even worse. I could feel their accusing glares boring into the back of my head, their hateful whispers burning in my ears. Claudia and I sat close together and looked at no one, trying to pretend we didn't notice.

At the end of the evening, the guild president, Gloria Schaeffer, drew us aside. She didn't even apologize as she politely suggested that we leave the guild for the duration. Can you imagine? For the duration. Honestly. And from Gloria *Schaeffer,* of all people.

I clamped my mouth shut before I let loose with exactly what I thought of her and her petty little friends. I gathered up our things, took Claudia by the elbow, and steered her out of there before she could burst into tears. If we had to leave, best to leave with as much dignity as we could muster.

Sarah, you've wondered why I won't join the Waterford guild, and now you know. Yes, I realize most of the people there that night aren't around anymore, but it's the principle of the thing. They didn't want us then, fine. I don't want them now.

We tried to forget the guild and how our so-called friends had treated us by throwing ourselves into preparing for Richard's homecoming. How wonderful it would be to see him again.

His first dinner home, he talked endlessly about Andrew, his friends away in Europe, and of course, the Puzzle. Father beamed at him adoringly. I suppose we all did, though I could have done without all that talk about the war.

"No one at school is cruel to you because of your ancestry, are they, Richard?" Claudia asked suddenly.

James gave her a sharp look, and I kicked her, none too gently, under the table. She let out a squeak and glared at me.

Richard set down his fork. "No, of course not. Everyone who knows me knows how I feel about Hitler. Why do you ask?" Claudia swallowed and glanced at me. I gave her a warning stare, which Richard immediately recognized. "Come on, Claud, don't let Sylvia shut you up. What's going on?"

Hesitantly, Claudia told him how the residents of Waterford had been treating us lately. As she continued, Richard's jaw clenched ever tighter and his eyes narrowed into icy blue slits.

Father looked around the table in bewilderment. "Sylvia, James? You've been keeping all this from me? Why?" His voice was troubled and hurt, and we couldn't bear to meet his gaze. "I cannot understand their behavior, when we Bergstroms have done so much for this town. No one has ever questioned our family's patriotism. I fought in the Great War and lost two brothers to it. What further proof do they require?"

Grimly, Richard resumed eating, his white-knuckled fists trembling with rage. His expression filled me with fear.

When everyone else had gone to bed, Richard drew me and James aside. "Whatever happens, I want you to promise me you'll look after Agnes."

My eyes widened. "What do you mean, whatever happens?"

"You explain it to her," Richard said to James over my head.

"I'm standing right here. Talk to me." My voice broke, and I clutched at Richard's sleeve. My baby brother was now taller than I by several inches, but he was still only a boy of seventeen. "What are you planning? You need to finish school, and then you're needed here."

James placed an arm around me and pulled me away. "We'll talk about it in the morning. In the morning, Richard," he emphasized. "I'll expect you to be here."

Richard nodded. He watched us climb the stairs and disappear around the corner.

Somehow I managed to sleep that night, but I woke the next morning with an uneasy knot in the pit of my stomach. I shook James awake. "Something's wrong," I whispered, my voice an anxious hiss between my teeth.

We hurried into our clothes and downstairs, where Claudia was bustling about the kitchen, humming cheerfully as she helped Cook prepare breakfast. Richard was an early riser, and by all rights he should have been there before us, charming Cook out of a scarce pastry made with carefully conserved sugar rations. Claudia's bright smile faded when she saw our faces.

A quick search of the manor and the grounds established that Richard and his suitcase were gone. He wouldn't have left without saying good-bye, I was certain, or at least without leaving a note. The house was in an uproar, with James at the center trying to calm the storm. My thoughts were in a whirl, when suddenly I remembered the playhouse.

I ran as fast as I could to the dilapidated old structure near the stables. The door had long since fallen from its hinges, and I ducked past it, my eyes searching the musty room.

Then I spotted it—a folded edge of paper sticking out from beneath a rusted coffee tin in the middle of the floor, where Richard had known I would find it right away. I unfolded the paper with shaking hands.

"Dear Sylvia," he had written. "I'm sorry to go off like this, but I know you'll forgive me. I figured you'd find this note soon, but not soon enough to stop me. Andrew and I have been thinking, and what Claudia said tonight clinches it. We're going to enlist, and whip those Germans until they know they're licked. No one is going to say Bergstroms are chicken, or question our loyalties, not as long as I can do something to prove otherwise. Remember what I asked you to promise me. Don't worry. I'll be fine."

I fled back to the manor clutching the note to my heart. The others had not even noticed my absence, and they broke off their argument when I rushed in. I held out the paper and sank into a chair. James hurried over and held my hand as he read the note, grim-faced.

He crumpled it in a fist. "I'll get Harold and we'll catch the next train to Philadelphia."

"How do you even know he's heading for Philadelphia? He could enlist here just as easily."

"That's where Andrew is, and from the sound of Richard's note, they're signing up together." His voice was calm for everyone else's benefit, but his eyes told me the truth. He didn't know if Richard had returned to Philadelphia, but it seemed a reasonable conclusion. For all our sakes, it had to be the correct one.

"James, if anything happens to him—"

James gripped my shoulders with both hands. "Don't worry. I'll take care of it." He kissed me, quickly, then hurried off to pack his bag.

He and Harold wired us two days later with dreadful news.

They had found Richard at school, packing his things. He and Andrew had already enlisted in the army and were to report in less than two weeks. With the Chevaliers' reluctant blessing, Richard and Agnes had married. They would be bringing her back to Elm Creek Manor on the next train.

When they finally returned, James and Harold looked resigned, the Puzzle was tearful, and Richard could barely contain his excitement. I hugged him so hard he had to gasp for breath. "What have you done?" I cried, not expecting or receiving an answer.

That night, when James and I were alone, he took me in his arms. His face wore the strangest expression—regret, love, concern, I don't know. I assumed he thought I was angry, or thought he had failed.

"James, I know you did the best you could," I said, trying to comfort him. "I know you tried to stop him. It's in God's hands now."

"Sylvia, I'm going, too."

I stared at him. "What?"

"It was the only way. Sylvia, it was the only way. He had already joined up, and if I signed up right away, we would be placed in the same unit. Harold signed up, too, although I'm not sure why. It was clear he didn't want to."

"My God." I pressed a hand to my lips and sank down upon the bed. The room spun about me.

"I'll look after him. I promise you that. I promise we'll all come home safe to you. Sylvia, you have my word. I'll always come home to you."

What could I say to him then? What more could he say to me?

The next morning we learned that Harold had asked Claudia to marry him and that she had accepted. I tried to be happy for her sake.

After the shortest week of my life, James, Richard, and Harold left us. Around the same time I realized I was pregnant, they were sent to the Pacific to fight the Japanese.

⚓

The parade had ended, and revelers filled the square as a jazz quartet began to play in the concert shell. Mrs. Compson, Sarah, and Matt listened without speaking for a time.

Then Mrs. Compson rose. "I think I'd like to see that quilt show now, wouldn't you?" Her smile was forced. "Perhaps I've taken a ribbon or two."

Sarah nodded, and Matt attempted a smile. They walked along the parade route toward the campus.

Twenty-One

Two women at the library entrance took their admission fees and offered them programs. Sarah was disappointed to learn they had arrived too late to vote for the Viewers' Choice award.

"Come on, you two," Mrs. Compson urged them. "You'll miss everything if you poke around like that all day."

The library concourse was full of enthusiastic quilt lovers of all ages, and the stands Sarah had helped assemble were now displaying the quilters' handiwork. They viewed each quilt in turn, reading the program for the artists' names and thoughts on their work. Guild members wearing white gloves mingled through the crowd, ready to turn over an edge so a quilt's backing could be examined.

Mrs. Compson knew so much about block patterns, design elements, and construction techniques that Sarah and Matt felt as if they were enjoying a museum tour with an expert guide. Often Sarah noticed that other spectators were listening in on Mrs. Compson's analyses of the pieces, nodding occasionally in agreement.

Sarah was pleased to find that even with a beginner's eye she could study an unfamiliar block and figure out how the quilt had been constructed. She was able to see how subtle variations in color and contrast made a traditional quilt sparkle, and how other quilts used the traditional as a starting point for devising something truly innovative. Soon the show became a dizzying and enthralling display of color and pattern, inspiring in that she saw so many possibilities, and humbling in that her own handful of simple pieced blocks couldn't begin to compare.

"I'll never be able to make a quilt like this," she said, gazing at a particularly stunning Dresden Plate variation whose wheel-shaped blocks had pieced "spokes" intensifying in hue as they radiated outward. A pieced border resembling a twisted ribbon spiraled along the outside edges. The quilting stitches were too tiny to be believed.

"You shouldn't make a quilt like this. You should make your own quilt," Mrs. Compson chided.

"What I meant was I'll never make a quilt as good as this one."

"Not with that attitude you won't," Matt said, grinning.

"My thoughts exactly." Mrs. Compson gave Sarah a pointed look. "This particular quilter has been working on her skills since before you left high school. If you've already decided you'll never make a quilt so fine, then you never will, and my lessons will be wasted on you. If, however, you're willing to stick to it and keep in mind that few if any first quilts are as lovely as this one, well, then, perhaps there's still hope for you." She turned and moved on to the next quilt.

"See? Just like I've been telling you all along: think positive," Matt said over his shoulder as he followed her.

Sarah sighed and went after them.

The Tangled Web Quilters had done well. Bonnie's blue-and-gold Celtic knotwork quilt had taken first place in the appliqué/large bed quilt division, and Judy's log cabin variation had also won a blue ribbon in the pieced/small bed quilt category. Together Gwen and Summer had claimed a second place in the innovative division for a family tree quilt that blended piecing, appliqué, and photo transfer techniques. When Sarah came across Diane's floral appliqué wall hanging, she was delighted to see a third-place ribbon hanging by its side. Sarah admired Diane's first ribbon and promised herself that next year she would enter a quilt, too.

Matt, eager to see how Mrs. Compson's entry had fared, went on ahead to find it.

"Mrs. Compson, do you think I'll be able to finish my quilt in time for my anniversary?" Sarah asked as soon as he was out of earshot.

"Well, that depends. When is it?"

"August fifth. I'd like to have my quilt done by then so I can give it to Matt for a present. It'll be our first anniversary spent in Waterford, so I want to give him something special. What could be more special than my first quilt? I'd like to use a garden maze setting, too, and maybe a pieced border."

Mrs. Compson held up her hands, chuckling. "Slow down. You still have a few blocks to go. August fifth, hmm? Even if I help you with the quilting, that might be pushing things a bit." She thought for a moment. "Perhaps it's time to teach you how to machine piece. I suppose I could let you use my sewing machine."

"Really?"

"If you promise to be careful."

"Of course I'll be careful." They rounded the corner and found Matt standing in front of Mrs. Compson's quilt, grinning from ear to ear. "But don't say anything to Matt. I want the quilt to be a surprise."

Mrs. Compson nodded and wove her way through the onlookers to see her quilt, with Sarah following close behind. She recognized the blue, purple, green, and ivory eight-pointed star quilt immediately. It was the same one she had seen on the sofa the first time she'd visited Elm Creek Manor.

Beside the quilt hung a blue ribbon for first place in the pieced/large bed quilt category, a purple Judge's Choice ribbon, another purple ribbon for Best Hand Quilting, and a gold ribbon for Best of Show.

"You won more ribbons than anyone else here," Sarah exclaimed.

Mrs. Compson bent forward to examine the ribbons herself. "Hmph. No Viewers' Choice?" Her voice sounded amused, but Sarah detected how pleased she was.

"Congratulations, Mrs. Compson." Matt tipped his baseball cap in her direction.

"Why thank you, Matthew." Other viewers who had overheard offered their congratulations, which she graciously accepted.

"Sarah?" someone called out.

Sarah spun around and caught a glimpse of red hair in the throng of people behind them. "Oh, hi, you guys. I was hoping I'd run into you. There's someone I'd like you to meet." She beckoned to Mrs. Compson, and they made their way back through the crowd. "Gwen, Bonnie, and Summer, I'd like you to meet Mrs. Compson. Mrs. Compson, this is Gwen, Bonnie, and Summer, a few of the Tangled Web Quilters."

"We've met," Bonnie said.

Mrs. Compson nodded pleasantly to the others, then turned to Gwen. "Professor, it's a pleasure to meet you. I'm looking forward to meeting your students next week."

"And they're looking forward to meeting you, too. They'll be impressed when they hear about this." Gwen indicated Mrs. Compson's awards.

"Ooh, how did you do?" Summer asked, stepping through the crowd for a closer look. Mrs. Compson went with her, responding to Summer's stream of eager questions as rapidly as they came.

Gwen caught Bonnie by the elbow before she could follow. "Where's Mrs. Emberly?" she whispered, looking around anxiously.

"She left earlier, with Judy and Emily." Bonnie turned to Sarah. "Judy raised a stink when they told her she couldn't bring Emily's stroller in here. Diane would've been proud."

Gwen released Bonnie's arm. "Thank goodness. That was a narrow miss."

Sarah's brow furrowed. "What do you mean? What's wrong?"

Gwen and Bonnie exchanged a look. "Mrs. Compson and Mrs. Emberly don't exactly—" Bonnie hesitated. "Well, you know Mrs. Emberly said they had a falling out, but it's worse than that. It would be very awkward if they happened to run into each other here."

"Rumor has it they've been feuding for more than fifty years," Gwen added. "They could just ignore each other while they weren't living in the same town, but it's been more difficult ever since Mrs. Compson returned to Waterford."

Sarah thought back. "Was Mrs. Emberly one of the people who kicked Mrs. Compson out of the Waterford Quilting Guild?"

Gwen's eyes widened and she exchanged a surprised look with Bonnie. "She got kicked out? That's news to me. We never even knew she had been a member."

"That's not it, though," Bonnie said. "It's a family quarrel. Mrs. Emberly and Mrs. Compson are sisters-in-law."

Sisters-in-law? "Oh, my God. Mrs. Emberly is the Puzzle."

"The what?"

"Nothing—I mean, her first name is Agnes, right? She married Mrs. Compson's brother, Richard?"

Gwen nodded. "That's right."

"Those two." Bonnie shook her head in exasperation. "It's such a shame, what with most of the family gone. Honestly—to have to dodge your own sister-in-law at a quilt show, rather than speak to her."

"Maybe we should stop running interference for them," Gwen mused. "Maybe if they're forced to speak to each other they'll achieve some sort of reconciliation."

Bonnie looked dubious. "I don't know. From what I've seen, Sylvia Compson's temper is as flammable as her quilts."

"I think you mean volatile," Gwen said. "But I know what you mean. What do you think, Sarah? You know Mrs. Compson pretty well."

"Apparently there's still a lot I don't know." Sarah's thoughts were in a whirl. If Mrs. Emberly was the Puzzle, then shouldn't her name be Agnes Chevalier instead of Agnes Emberly? But no, that wasn't right, either; her name should be Agnes Bergstrom.

Just as Sarah was about to press Bonnie and Gwen for more details, Mrs. Compson and Summer returned. "Are you ready to go on and see the rest of the show?" Mrs. Compson asked.

Sarah nodded. The Tangled Web Quilters joined them as they viewed the remaining quilts. Mrs. Compson chatted pleasantly with the group, especially with Summer, but Sarah barely listened to the conversation. She should have guessed from Mrs. Emberly's remarks that there was more to her relationship with Elm Creek Manor than she had mentioned.

After the show, Sarah, Matt, and Mrs. Compson had dinner at an outdoor restaurant, then went to the Waterford College stadium for the fireworks display. As Matt and Mrs. Compson gazed at the brilliant spectacle overhead and let out murmurs of awe and cheers of delight, Sarah watched in silence. When Mrs. Compson eyed her and remarked that she was being rather quiet, Sarah made an effort to seem cheerful and relaxed. Mrs. Compson seemed to accept that, but inside Sarah was troubled. The quiet, pleasant woman she had come to know through the Tangled Web Quilters seemed nothing like the foolish, exasperating girl from Mrs. Compson's stories. Mrs. Compson was more of a puzzle than Agnes Chevalier had ever been.

Twenty-Two

Mrs. Compson began Monday afternoon's quilt lesson by arranging Sarah's blocks on the table. She checked over the list of remaining blocks and worked out some problems on a calculator, then jotted down some notes on a pad. "Since you finished the Lancaster Rose block over the weekend, that makes eight. I'm surprised you were able to finish it so fast."

"I like appliqué. What are you doing?" Sarah gestured toward the calculator. "I'm good with math. Can I help?"

"Thank you, dear, but I'm finished. I'm calculating the necessary measurements for your Garden Maze setting." She frowned. "If I'm going to teach you how to machine piece today, I think we had better select the easiest of your remaining blocks. Let's go ahead and work on the Sister's Choice."

"Will it make any difference in the finished quilt that some of the blocks are machine pieced and some are hand sewn?"

"Not enough to matter." Mrs. Compson produced Sarah's template-making tools and spread them out on the table.

When Sarah had finished making her templates and cutting out the block pieces, Mrs. Compson showed her how to use the sewing machine. With the older woman hovering close by, Sarah practiced sewing on a few scraps of cloth before risking her quilt block pieces. It had been a long time since she had used a sewing machine in her junior high Home Ec class, but soon Sarah felt fairly comfortable with the tiny black machine. She pressed a seam open with her fingernail and inspected the neat, even stitches with a smile. This was definitely faster than hand piecing.

"Where can I get a sewing machine like this?" Sarah asked.

"Hmph. Depends. How much are you willing to spend?"

"That bad, huh?"

"I bought mine new many years ago, but if you can find one, and if the owner can bear to part with it, you might pay three hundred, five hundred dollars, depending upon its condition. Of course, I've heard of some people with incredible luck who have managed to snatch them up at garage sales for only a fraction of that." Mrs. Compson tilted her head to one side. "Of course, there's always—" She broke off suddenly and smiled, her eyes glinting in merriment.

"What? There's always what?"

"Nothing." But a faint smile played around the corners of her mouth. Sarah suspected she was up to something, but when she said so, Mrs. Compson merely smiled.

The next morning Sarah awoke with nervousness gnawing in her stomach. As she went to the bathroom to shower, she ordered herself to stop being so ridiculous. Mrs. Compson was the one who had to stand in front of Gwen's class and talk, not Sarah. All she had to worry about was running the slide projector.

She put on her interview suit and carefully arranged her long hair instead of merely pulling it back into a ponytail as she usually did for work. When Sarah and Matt arrived at Elm Creek Manor, Mrs. Compson was waiting in the back hallway with a box of slides and lecture notes. She wore an attractive lightweight pink suit and pearls.

Matt wished them good luck and strode off for the north gardens as Sarah helped Mrs. Compson into the truck. As they drove to Waterford College, Mrs. Compson gave Sarah some last-minute instructions. Sarah listened and nodded when appropriate, but her stomach was in knots.

The security guard at the west entrance to the campus gave them a short-term parking permit and a map. Gwen was waiting behind the classroom building when they pulled up.

"I'm glad you're here early," she said, taking the box of slides from Mrs. Compson. "When word got out about your talk, some of the other professors asked if their classes might join us. I said it was okay. Was it?"

Mrs. Compson shrugged. "Certainly. The more the merrier."

"I'm glad you feel that way. We had to move into the auditorium."

"The auditorium?" Sarah's voice quavered.

Mrs. Compson looked surprised. "Classroom, auditorium—what's the difference? Why are you so pale?"

Gwen peered at her. "Are you okay, Sarah?"

"Sure. Why wouldn't I be?" She hoped she sounded more confident than she felt.

She did feel better when she learned that she would be working at the top of the auditorium in the projection booth where no one would see her. Gwen showed her where the various light switches and controls were, then left to take Mrs. Compson backstage while Sarah set up the equipment. Almost all of the seats were full, and Sarah could hear the students buzzing noisily below. Before long a crackle of static came over an intercom to her left. "Sarah, are you there?"

She fumbled for the white button next to the speaker. "Yes, Gwen. I'm here and I'm all set."

"We're ready, too. House lights down, stage lights up."

Sarah glanced at the control panel and found the switches. "Okay, I've got them. Uh . . . over and out."

The students quieted as the lights went down and Gwen came out to introduce Mrs. Compson. Sarah clutched her hands in her lap, glad to see that Mrs. Compson was greeted with a smattering of applause as she came onstage and approached the podium. She tilted her head in Sarah's direction and smiled, though Sarah was sure Mrs. Compson couldn't see her. Mrs. Compson greeted the audience, and at that Sarah took a deep breath and turned on the slide projector.

At first Sarah sensed skepticism from the students, but to her relief, Mrs. Compson's wry humor quickly won them over. After discussing quilting's origins in ancient times through its use as padding for knights' armor in the Middle Ages, Mrs. Compson moved on to a discussion of quilting in colonial America and in the days of westward expansion. She concluded by describing contemporary quilting from the upsurge in interest sparked by the Bicentennial to present-day quilt artists who incorporate everything from traditional patterns to computer-aided design in their craft. Sarah found the discussion so fascinating that she almost missed a few cues, but she didn't think anyone noticed.

When it was over, the students gave Mrs. Compson an enthusiastic round of applause, and she inclined her head and smiled graciously. As class ended and Sarah switched on the house lights, a few listeners approached the stage with questions as the others left the auditorium. Sarah glanced at the stage and, finding Mrs. Compson surrounded by students, decided to use the time to pack up the slides. When she finished she left the projection booth and carried the box of slides to the stage, where Mrs. Compson and Gwen were saying good-bye to one lingering student.

"That was really interesting, Mrs. Compson," Sarah said. "You did a great job."

"Who would've thought that young people would find quilt jokes so amusing?" Mrs. Compson shook her head as if amazed, but she looked pleased.

Gwen looked pleased as well. "I can't thank you enough, Mrs. Compson. I think my students got a lot out of your lecture."

Mrs. Compson patted her on the arm. "Any time you want me to come back, I'd be delighted to. I thoroughly enjoyed myself."

Sarah noted the remark and tried to keep her features smooth and nonchalant. Inside she felt like shouting with triumph. She couldn't wait to tell Matt.

"I'm going to take you up on that," Gwen said. She walked them to the truck, and as they were about to drive away, she approached the passenger side window and peeked in. She gave Sarah a knowing glance and turned to Mrs. Compson. "Maybe Sarah can talk you into joining the Tangled Web Quilters at our meeting this week?"

"I've tried, believe me," Sarah said.

Mrs. Compson pursed her lips. "It's not the Waterford Quilting Guild?"

"No. We defected a long time ago."

"Very well, then. Perhaps I'll consider it."

Gwen grinned. "Hope to see you there." She backed away from the window and waved before returning inside.

Sarah drove them home to Elm Creek Manor.

"I think that went quite well, don't you?" Mrs. Compson asked.

"Oh, definitely. You had them in the palm of your hand."

"Well, I was an art teacher once, you know."

"No, I didn't, although I remember you mentioned studying to be one. But I thought you left college."

"I did, but I returned to school later and earned my degree. Not at Waterford College, though."

Sarah nodded. Mrs. Emberly had mentioned something like that at one of their quilting bees, but she didn't think she should tell Mrs. Compson that. Not yet.

Inspired by Mrs. Compson's successful presentation, they decided to ignore the work waiting upstairs and spent the rest of the afternoon quilting. As Sarah and Matt drove home that evening, she told him about the presentation and, most importantly, the promise Mrs. Compson had given Gwen. "She said any time Gwen wants her to deliver another lecture, she will. That must mean that she's thinking about staying, right? I mean, how could she give another presentation if she leaves Waterford?"

Matt nodded, considering. "It could be a good sign, I guess."

"You guess? If she feels needed, that's one more reason to stay, right?"

"Don't get your hopes up too high, honey. I don't want you to be hurt if things don't work out."

Sarah rolled her eyes. "Well, if that doesn't impress you maybe this will. She's also thinking about joining the Tangled Web Quilters."

"Does she know Mrs. Emberly is a member?"

Sarah paused. "I don't know. I don't think so."

"How are you going to work that?"

"I don't know." Sarah frowned and sank back into her seat, deflated.

They pulled into their parking lot. Matt draped an arm around Sarah's shoulders as she unlocked the door and went inside. "Sarah, something about this University Realty deal bothers me."

"Everything about it bothers me."

Matt took off his baseball cap and ran his hand through his hair. "I've been thinking about how much it would cost to remodel the interior of the manor so that it could be used for apartments, and frankly, I don't see how University Realty can hope to make any kind of profit. They'd have to charge incredible rents just to break even, and what college student has that kind of money to throw around? And most students want a place with all the modern amenities and aren't willing to sacrifice them just to say they lived in a historic mansion. Especially one that isn't within walking distance of campus."

"It never sounded very logical to me, either."

"The remodeling costs are only part of it. Tony's currently working on a similar project but on a much smaller scale, a three-story home near downtown that the owners want to convert into three apartments. You wouldn't believe all the laws and ordinances he has to follow and all the fees the owner has to pay just to get the place up to local code for rental units." He shook his head. "I don't know. It just seems to me that it would be more logical for University Realty to buy some land and start from scratch rather than try to make Elm Creek Manor into something it isn't."

Sarah's pulse quickened. "Maybe that's what they're doing."

"What do you mean?"

"Maybe they're only interested in the grounds, not in the manor itself."

Matt's eyes widened. "You mean tear down Elm Creek Manor—"

"And start from scratch, just like you said." Sarah's thoughts raced as she pictured how many modern efficiency apartments could be squeezed onto the grounds, each one pouring a generous rent into Gregory Krolich's pocket every month. "That has to be what they have planned."

"But that's crazy. Converting Elm Creek Manor is one thing, but tearing it down is another. Mrs. Compson would never sell knowing Elm Creek Manor would be demolished."

"I don't think she does know. We don't even know for sure. But think about how carefully Krolich chooses his words. Remember when Mrs. Compson said she was worried that students would trash the place, and he said it would never happen? I bet he meant it will never happen because there won't be any Elm Creek Manor left for them to trash."

"We have to tell her."

"Not until we know for sure. I don't want to upset her."

"I can talk to Tony. He's been in this town a long time and knows everybody in the business." Matt reached out and stroked Sarah's head. "Don't worry. We'll find out what's going on and tell Mrs. Compson before she signs anything. It's her home, and we have to respect her decision even if we don't like it, but she deserves to know the truth."

Sarah nodded. How could she not worry? Only a few moments before, she'd thought she would have Mrs. Compson and Elm Creek Manor all summer, at least. Now she felt as if they were already slipping away.

Twenty-Three

The next morning Sarah's mood did not reflect the bright and pleasant weather outdoors as she trudged from the truck to the back steps of the manor carrying her best blue interview suit on a hanger.

Mrs. Compson greeted her at the back door with a smile and a glint in her eye. "Let's go right upstairs and get started, shall we?"

Sarah had slept poorly, too worried about Elm Creek Manor to rest. To make matters worse, she felt ill prepared for her job interview later that day. She hooked the hanger over the doorknob and returned Mrs. Compson's cheery greeting halfheartedly. "I wanted to remind you that I have another job interview this afternoon," she added as she climbed the stairs behind the older woman.

Mrs. Compson gave a start. "Oh, of course. That's fine. I'm sure you'll do well." She continued down the hall, past the suite they had begun two days before but had not yet finished.

Sarah hesitated at the door. "Mrs. Compson?"

"Hmm?" Mrs. Compson turned. "Oh, yes, that. Don't bother with that room right now. I want you to work somewhere else today." She resumed her pace, motioning for Sarah to accompany her.

Sarah trailed after her, wondering what had gotten into Mrs. Compson that morning.

Mrs. Compson stopped in front of a door near the end of the hall. "This was my sister's room," she said, placing her hand on the doorknob. "I admit I've put off this suite as long as possible, but yesterday I thought of—well, never mind. You'll see for yourself." She pushed open the door and waved Sarah in ahead of her.

This room had been used more recently than the others. A pink-and-white quilt was spread across the queen-size bed, and a white lamp with a frilly pink shade sat on a bedside table. White eyelet lace curtains stirred in the breeze from the open west-facing window. A small, square quilt of pink, yellow, and white triangles arranged in the shape of a basket hung opposite the bed.

Mrs. Compson motioned for Sarah to follow her into the suite's adjoining room. Most likely it had been Claudia's sewing room, Sarah guessed, noting the sewing machine nearby. It resembled Mrs. Compson's other machine, except the interlocking pattern painted in gold on the shiny black metal was slightly different, and it was set into a wooden table with a single drawer.

Mrs. Compson pulled back the chair and gestured for Sarah to take a seat. "What do you think? Like it?"

Sarah ran a hand over the smooth, polished surface of the table. "It's gorgeous."

"It's yours."

"Mine?"

"Consider it an employee-of-the-month bonus. Now, it's not the same model as mine, but in my opinion it sews just as well. It just isn't portable because of the table. The light's on the back of the machine rather than above the needle, but a good lamp at your left will illuminate the area sufficiently."

"Mrs. Compson, I can't accept this. It's too—"

"What? Don't you like it?"

"Are you kidding? Of course I like it. I love it."

"Then take it and be grateful." Sarah started to speak, but Mrs. Compson silenced her with a raised palm. "Make an old lady happy by accepting her gift in the spirit in which it has been given. Surely you don't want to insult me?"

Sarah grinned. "Definitely not. Anything but that."

After Sarah dashed downstairs to fetch her Sister's Choice block pieces, Mrs. Compson showed her how to operate the machine. It had all kinds of attachments whose uses Sarah couldn't discern, and she soon realized that she could operate the machine better in her stocking feet than with her shoes on, since the foot pedal was actually no more than a single button she could depress with her right big toe.

Matt surprised them by arriving early for lunch.

"Look at my new toy, honey," Sarah greeted him, making Mrs. Compson laugh.

Matt gave them a tight-lipped smile. "That's great, Sarah. Mrs. Compson, I hope you don't mind if I take Sarah to her job interview early? I have a meeting with my boss in town and I can't be late."

"Oh, and we were having so much fun."

"I'll come back after the interview," Sarah promised. "After all, we should get some work done today, shouldn't we?"

With an anxious Mrs. Compson barking out directions and warnings as they went, Sarah and Matt carried the sewing machine downstairs and set it up in the west sitting room opposite the sofa. Sarah changed into her suit and joined Matt in the truck.

"I don't really have a meeting, Sarah," he said as soon as she shut the door. "I had something to tell you, and I don't think you're going to like it."

"What is it?"

Matt started the truck. "Tony checked with a friend in the city licensing department. University Realty has applied for a demolition permit."

"For Elm Creek Manor?"

Matt nodded, eyes fixed on the dirt trail as they drove past the barn into the forest.

"But they haven't even bought it yet," she exclaimed. "How can they apply for permits already?"

"Tony says the Waterford Zoning Commission can take as long as six months to grant approval to raze historic buildings. Apparently Krolich wants to be able to tear down the place as soon as his check clears."

"I can't believe he'd buy Elm Creek Manor without telling Mrs. Compson what he plans to do with it. We have to do something."

"I know."

Sarah thought for a moment. "Let's go see him right now."

Matt glanced at her, then quickly returned his gaze to the narrow road. "What about your interview?"

"We have time."

Soon Matt was parking the truck in front of the three-story Victorian building that housed University Realty's downtown office. Sarah raced up the front stairs as Matt fed coins into the meter. He joined her inside at the receptionist's desk, where Sarah was asking to see Mr. Krolich.

"Who may I say wishes to see him?" the receptionist asked as she reached for the phone.

"Just tell him it's important." Sarah craned her neck, trying to see the work space beyond the desk. Men and women in solemn business attire strode though the hallway, but Krolich was not among them.

"I'll need your names."

"Sarah and Matt McClure. He knows us."

The receptionist phoned Mr. Krolich's office, exchanged a few words, then replaced the receiver. "I'm sorry, but he's due in a meeting. If you'd like to schedule an appointment he'd be happy to see you sometime next month—"

Then Sarah spotted a familiar figure. She grabbed Matt's sleeve. "There he is." She marched down the hallway with Matt close behind, ignoring the receptionist's protests. Krolich's back disappeared around the corner into an office. By the time Sarah and Matt burst in, he had reached his desk.

He paused only slightly before settling down into the high-backed leather chair. "Hello again, Sarah, Matt." He gestured toward two chairs facing his desk. "Please, take a seat."

"We'll stand," Sarah said.

Krolich shrugged. "Suit yourself. So, to what do I owe the pleasure of this unexpected visit? Are you interested in that job after all, Sarah?"

"We want the truth about your plans for Elm Creek Manor."

Krolich frowned. "You must realize I can't discuss confidential business matters with anyone other than my clients and other involved parties. As much as I'd like to help you, well, you can understand the spot I'm in."

"Sarah is Mrs. Compson's personal assistant," Matt said. "And both of us are her friends. That makes us involved parties."

"So you might as well tell us your plans for tearing down Elm Creek Manor," Sarah said.

Krolich's eyes widened almost imperceptibly. "Oh, so you've heard about that." He picked up a gilded letter opener and fingered it. "Tell me, have you mentioned this to Mrs. Compson?"

"Not yet, but we plan to."

"I see." He returned the letter opener and folded his hands, resting his elbows on the desk. "I was planning to tell her myself, you know."

"Yeah, right," Matt said. "When? Before or after she signed the place away?"

"If Mrs. Compson wants to sell Elm Creek Manor, that's her business. Who are you to interfere?"

Sarah tried to keep her voice steady. "We're her friends, and we care about her, which is more than you can say."

"It's not that I don't care."

"Then why hide your plans from her?"

Krolich sighed. "Are you sure you won't sit down?" When Sarah and Matt didn't move, he nodded in acceptance. "Okay. I guess you're determined to see me as the villain here. But hear me out. I do care about Mrs. Compson. I'm trying to do right by her."

Matt snorted. "You have a funny idea of what's right."

Krolich's expression became earnest. "Hasn't it occurred to you that she already knows we plan to raze Elm Creek Manor?"

Sarah shook her head. "No way. She would've told me."

"Think about it, Sarah. My offer is the only one she's had, the only one she's likely to get. If she accepts it, she's agreeing to have her family home torn down. Do you think she'd admit to knowing that, even to herself?"

"So you're saying she's known all along, and she's lied to me?"

"Not exactly. I'm saying she doesn't want to know."

"That's ridiculous," Sarah shot back, but doubt trickled into her mind. She shoved it away. "You deliberately glossed over your plans for Elm Creek Manor because you knew she wouldn't sell it to you otherwise."

"I knew nothing of the sort."

"You had to suspect it, at least, or you would've told her."

"You're letting sentiment cloud your judgment. Not a good practice for an aspiring businesswoman." He shook his head as if regretful. "This discussion is getting us nowhere. I'm afraid I'm going to have to ask you both to leave."

Sarah opened her mouth to retort, but Matt caught her arm. "Let's go, Sarah. It's not worth it." He gave Krolich a hard look. "Anyway, we got the answers we came for."

Krolich frowned but said nothing.

Sarah and Matt hurried down the hallway, ignoring the stares of Krolich's employees. "We have to tell her right away," Sarah said as they climbed into the truck.

Matt shook his head and pulled into traffic. "Your interview, remember?"

"That's right." Her heart sank. "But what if he gets her to sign something before I'm done?"

"You go to your interview, and I'll go talk to Mrs. Compson."

"I think I should be the one to tell her," she argued. Then she sighed. "But we can't risk waiting. You're right. You tell her."

They pulled into the accounting firm's parking lot and exchanged a quick kiss before Matt drove away and Sarah hurried inside. She glanced at her watch, relieved to see she was still two minutes early.

A clerk took her name and guided her to a waiting room, where she took a few deep breaths to compose herself. An image of Matt breaking the bad news and Mrs. Compson's grief-stricken face flashed through her mind. She tried to shake it off.

Not five minutes later the clerk returned and led her to another office. "You'll be meeting with our new assistant director of operations, Thomas Wilson," he said.

Sarah started. She knew that name. The clerk opened the door for her and she entered the room.

From behind his desk Thomas Wilson looked up in surprise. "So you're Sarah McClure." He rose and shook her hand. "How funny. I've seen you twice before and I never got your name. Please, have a seat."

Sarah sank into the opposite chair, smiling uncertainly. Usually her interviews began with introductions between strangers, and the change was disconcerting. "Congratulations on your new job," she said, then wondered if she should have.

He smiled. "Thanks. Sure beats constant interviewing. Well, let's get started, shall we?"

He began with the few perfunctory questions she had heard so often before, and she provided her familiar responses. At first she felt hopeful, thinking that he was sure to be a sympathetic listener since until recently he had been on the other side of the interviewer's desk himself. Before long, however, her confidence began to erode. She noticed that he never once looked her in the eye or wrote down any remarks. The more Sarah tried to sound positive and confident, the more she began to wonder if this man really was the same person who had been so talkative only a few weeks ago.

When she was in the middle of responding to his question about why she left her former employer, he suddenly pushed her résumé aside. "Sarah, I'm a busy man. Let's save ourselves a lot of time and trouble and call it quits, okay?"

"What do you mean?"

"We both know you don't want this job."

"But I do. I wouldn't be here if—"

He raised his voice to drown out her protests. "Did you think I had forgotten our conversation—oh, what was it, two, three weeks ago? You made it clear that you really aren't interested in accounting work. I'm afraid I can't in good conscience hire you knowing you won't be satisfied with us."

"I will be satisfied. You know I can do the work and—"

"Being able to do the work isn't enough. If the desire isn't there, productivity won't be, either."

Sarah's cheeks grew warm. "I've always done the very best I could at every job I've ever held. I'd do the same here, I promise you."

"Thanks for stopping by. We'll let you know." He turned back to his papers as if Sarah had vanished.

Sarah knew she should leave, but his abrupt dismissal angered her. "Are you even going to consider me?"

He didn't look up. "We'll hire the most qualified candidate, and that's more than you need to know."

She stood and stared at him for a moment. Then she turned on her heel and left without another word, her eyes burning.

Matt was waiting in the truck, grim-faced. "I told her," he said as soon as she sat down. He sped out of the parking lot. "I don't think she's taking it very well."

"How did you expect her to take it?" Her voice was sharper than she had intended. Krolich, Wilson, that stupid guy with his stupid grocery store question—she should have realized that they were all alike. If business these days was some kind of game, then the players broke all the rules. No, that wasn't quite it. They followed rules, all right, but not any kind of rules Sarah could live with.

They drove the rest of the way in silence.

When they reached the manor Matt took her hand and squeezed it. "Everything will work out."

She tried to smile. "I know." She kissed him and hurried inside.

She found Mrs. Compson in the sewing room, sitting in a chair with her hands clasped in her lap, staring straight ahead at nothing. She looked up when Sarah entered. "Hello, dear. How did it go?"

"Fine. It went—" And then Sarah broke down, the words tumbling out and falling over each other, angry sobs choking her throat. Murmuring sympathetically, Mrs. Compson took her hand and pulled her over until Sarah's head rested in her lap. She stroked Sarah's long hair and listened while Sarah told her what had happened.

Sarah's tears subsided. She took a deep breath and closed her eyes, comforted by Mrs. Compson's motherly touch. It had been a long time since her own mother had so much as hugged her. "I'm just going to have to face it," Sarah said. "I'm never going to find a job."

Mrs. Compson's hand paused for a moment. "You already have a job, I thought."

"Sure, but how long is it going to last, what with you ready to pack up and leave as soon as you get the chance?"

"True enough." Mrs. Compson sighed and resumed stroking Sarah's hair. "I might as well tell you. I've decided not to sell to Mr. Krolich."

Sarah sat up and wiped her eyes. "Really?"

"Of course. What else could I do? I could hardly sell knowing his intentions. I'm grateful to you and Matthew for discovering the truth before it was too late. Elm Creek Manor will stand for a long time yet."

"So what happens now?"

Mrs. Compson shrugged. "I wait for a better offer." She eyed Sarah intently. "Can you make me a better offer?"

Sarah barked out a laugh. "Not unless you're planning to give me a huge raise. You know Matt and I could never buy this place."

"Must you be so literal? I don't mean for you to submit a bid, silly girl. I'm telling you to give me a reason to stay. You're a smart young woman. Use your imagination. This place—" Her voice faltered, and she looked around as if seeing through the walls and taking in the entire building. "This place was so full of life once. I'm just one old woman, but I don't want to sell my family home. There's time enough for Elm Creek Manor to be out of Bergstrom hands after I die."

"Don't talk like that."

"Don't interrupt your elders when they're making a point. And here's mine: I'm giving you the chance to convince me to keep Elm Creek Manor. Show me how to bring Elm Creek Manor back to life and I'll never sell it. I promise."

"I don't think—I'm not sure how."

"Well, don't panic, dear. I didn't expect you to have an answer already. Give it some time. But not too much time." She smiled and patted Sarah's shoulder. "Everything will come out all right in the end."

"Matt said something almost exactly like that when he dropped me off."

"A wise man indeed," Mrs. Compson said, her voice solemn. Then she smiled.

Sarah's mind raced. A better offer. How could they make Elm Creek Manor live again? She shook her head. She should approach this problem as a businesswoman would, collecting and analyzing the evidence before submitting a proposal to the client.

"Mrs. Compson, there's more I need to know."

"What's that, dear?"

"I need to know why you left, and why you didn't come back for so many years, and why you don't speak to your sister-in-law when as far as I can tell she might be your only living relative." Mrs. Compson's smile faded, but Sarah plowed on ahead. "Before I can help you figure out how to bring Elm Creek Manor back to life, I need to understand how it died in the first place."

Mrs. Compson took a deep breath. "I suppose. Perhaps if you know the whole story you'll understand. Or perhaps you'll just think I'm a foolish old woman who deserves to be unhappy."

Maybe that's what Mrs. Compson thought of herself, but Sarah didn't care what Mrs. Compson had or had not done. She would never agree that Mrs. Compson deserved such remorse.

She waited, and Mrs. Compson explained.

Twenty-Four

I suppose if James and Richard and Harold had never gone off to war I might have lived at Elm Creek Manor all my days and would have had a very different life. But they did go, and at the time my only consolation was that they would be together. I prayed that they would stay alive long enough to outlast the war.

As for the Elm Creek Manor homefront—well, I had the baby to think about, and Claudia and I both had our hands full trying to comfort Agnes. She seemed perpetually on the verge of tears, and usually did begin to sob uncontrollably if no one rushed to her side with a hug and some consoling words. I admit I became quite impatient with her. I too wanted someone to convince me that everything would be all right in the end, but when no one could, you didn't see me collapsing into hysteria.

I don't know. Perhaps I was also angry at myself for wishing that someone would comfort me as we all tried to comfort Agnes. A grown woman shouldn't need that. A grown woman in charge of an entire household should definitely not need that. When you're the strong one of the family you must be the strong one all the time, not just when it's convenient.

Spring turned into summer. Letters from the men were infrequent and often censored so thoroughly that we were hard-pressed to find a single comprehensible sentence. Still, we were relieved and thankful to learn that they were alive, together, and unharmed.

To help pass the time and distract our thoughts, Claudia and I would quilt and talk about more pleasant things. Sometimes my starry-eyed sister would launch into a fanciful description of her upcoming wedding. You would think we were royalty, her plans were so elaborate. As we worked, Agnes would linger around, sulking and pretending she wasn't interested. One day while I was working on a Tumbling Blocks baby quilt, Claudia whispered to me that Agnes deserved a second chance. To keep the peace, I relented and asked my sister-in-law if she wanted to learn how to quilt.

To my astonishment, she agreed. We set about planning a sampler just as you and I did, Sarah, but she refused to follow the simplest instructions. First she fought me over making a sampler, saying they were too simple. My instinct was to retort that a sampler would be all the more appropriate in her case, but a warning look from Claudia helped me bite my tongue. I lost that fight, so I tried to salvage the project by encouraging her to at least pick a simple block, like the Sawtooth Star or a Nine Patch. But she would have no part of any of my advice. Once she spotted that Double Wedding Ring pattern she made up her mind. She was going to make a Double Wedding Ring quilt and no one was going to stand in her way.

"Agnes," I said in my most reasonable tone, "look at this pattern more carefully. See all these curved seams, all these odd-shaped pieces with bias edges? Trust me, this isn't the best choice for your first quilt. You're just going to end up frustrated."

But she tossed her head and said that she hadn't had much of a wedding and no engagement whatsoever and she hadn't seen her husband in five months, and no one was going to tell her she couldn't have a quilt named Double Wedding Ring if she wanted it. I gave in very reluctantly, I assure you.

That quilt was doomed to failure from the first. We made our templates differently back then, but not as differently as the Puzzle did. She drew her shapes haphazardly, glaring at me when I warned her that even small errors could result in pieces that wouldn't match up. It had been enough trouble to convince her to use scraps, even when I reminded her there was a war on, but then she decided to make the entire quilt—yes, including the background pieces—out of red fabric. This quilt would have no contrast at all.

So many problems and she had not even begun sewing yet, which meant, of course, that the worst was yet to come. She handled the pieces so awkwardly that the bias edges stretched hopelessly out of shape, then she would mutter to herself as she jabbed pins into them to try to get them to behave. She jabbed herself more than once, too, and made sure everyone in the house heard it. Her stitches were large and crooked, but eventually I gave up telling her to take them out and do them over.

On one especially hot, muggy day a week later, Agnes, her forehead beaded with perspiration, triumphantly waved a ring in my face. "You didn't think I could do it, but here it is. So there."

I chose to ignore her childish behavior. "Very good, Agnes," I replied, taking it from her and placing it on a table for inspection. I tried to keep my face expressionless. An entire week's labor had gone into this? The ring buckled in the middle rather than lying flat, pieces didn't meet properly, stitches were so loosely sewn that the thread could be seen from the front of the block, and all that red blended together so that the pattern was unrecogniz-able. The forlorn assemblage of fabric begged for a mercifully swift delivery into the final resting place of the scrap bag.

"What do you think?" Agnes demanded when I had been silent for a while.

"Well," I said carefully, "it's fine for a beginner, but you need to remem-ber that small trouble spots multiply into big problems when you have a big quilt. Even if you're only off by an eighth of an inch, if you have eight of those mistakes, that's an inch worth of inaccuracy."

She scowled. "So how do I fix it?"

"You'll have to rip out some of these seams and do them over."

"Rip them out? It took me forever to put them in!"

"It's nothing to get angry about, Agnes. I've had to rip out plenty of seams. Every quilter does."

"Well, I guess I'm not a quilter, then." She snatched up her work and stormed out of the room.

Claudia had overhead everything. "You'd better go after her," she said, sighing.

I nodded and followed Agnes down the hall toward the front entry. I was relieved to see that Claudia had decided to accompany me.

"Where do you think she's going?" I asked as we crossed the marble floor. I didn't have to wonder long, as I spotted her yellow dress through the open door.

Agnes stood frozen in place on the veranda, her back to us. As we joined her, the unfinished quilt fell from her hand and dropped silently to the floor. Her face was no longer angry, but she stared straight ahead as if she had not heard us approach.

"Agnes, what—" Claudia's voice broke off as she followed Agnes's line of sight and spotted the car driving slowly up to the manor.

Icy fingers clutched at my heart.

Two men in formal military dress climbed out of the car and walked toward us. One was older, with brown curly hair graying at the temples and a grim expression. The younger man's face was pale behind a sprinkling of freckles. He swallowed repeatedly and avoided meeting our eyes as they climbed the right-hand set of curved stairs. Each man carried a yellow slip of paper.

I thought they'd never reach the top of those stairs. Claudia slowly reached out and clasped my hand.

Then they were standing at the top of the stairs and removing their hats. "Mrs. Compson?" the older man asked.

I nodded.

The man came up to me and glanced down at the paper in his hand. "Mrs. Compson, ma'am, I regret that it is my duty to inform you that . . ."

A distant roaring filled my ears, blocking out his words. I watched his lips working silently.

James was dead.

Through the fog I became aware that the younger man was fingering his paper uncertainly. He looked from Claudia to Agnes and back again. "Mrs. Bergstrom?"

Mrs. He said Mrs., not Miss. That means—

Agnes's eyes welled up with tears. The younger man's voice trembled as he repeated the older man's message.

Not Richard, too. This can't be happening.

Agnes began to wail. She sank to her knees, clutching the paper to her chest.

Claudia buried her face in her hands and murmured the same phrase over and over, her shoulders shaking. Then she looked up, tears glistening on her cheeks. "Thank God," she sobbed. "Thank God."

The roaring in my ears seemed to explode white hot. I slapped Claudia across the face, so hard my palm stung. She cried out. I grabbed the older man by his lapels. "How?" I screamed in his face. "How did this happen? He promised! He promised me!" The younger man leaped forward to pull me away. I felt fabric tear in my fists. "You're wrong! You're lying!" I kicked at them both.

Searing pain stabbed across my abdomen. *They shot me,* I thought, watching the dark red blood pool around my feet.

Agnes shrieked. Then I sank into cold, silent blackness.

I remember little about the next few weeks. I suppose that's a good thing. I do remember lying in a hospital bed holding my daughter's still little body and sobbing. She actually lived for almost three days, can you believe that? What a little fighter. If only—

But it doesn't matter now. She's with her daddy. That's enough.

Soon her grandpa joined them. Father collapsed from a stroke when he heard the news. They buried him before I was released from the hospital. I think I begged the doctors to let me go to the funeral, but they wouldn't let me. I think that's what happened. I don't remember it clearly. Can you imagine, missing my own father's funeral?

For weeks after returning home I felt as if I were shrouded in a thick woolen batting. Sounds were less distinct. Colors were duller. Everything seemed to move more slowly.

Gradually, though, the numbness began to recede, replaced by the most unbearable pain. My beloved James was gone, and I still didn't know exactly how. My daughter was gone. I would never hold her again. My darling little brother was gone. My father was gone. The litany repeated itself relentlessly in my mind until I thought I would go mad.

A few hesitant visitors from the quilting guild would come by, but I refused to see them. Eventually they stopped trying.

Then the Japanese surrendered, and Harold came home, thinner, more anxious, his hairline even farther back than when he had left. When he first returned to Elm Creek Manor I thought his receding hairline was the funniest thing I had ever seen. I laughed until my stomach hurt and the others stared at me. You'd think they would have been glad to see me laugh for a change.

Claudia lost little time planning her wedding. She asked me to help, and I agreed, but my mind wandered and I had trouble remembering to take care of all the little details. She exploded at me more than once, but it didn't bother me as much as it used to. Instead she turned to Agnes, who for some reason had decided to remain at Elm Creek Manor rather than return to her own family. Perhaps she felt Richard's presence here. I know I did.

Then one evening we had a visitor. Andrew stopped over for the night on his way from Philadelphia to a new job in Detroit. I was glad to see him. He walked with a limp now and sat stiffly in his chair as if still in the service. He was pleasant enough to everyone, but he had barely a cold word for Harold, who seemed to go out of his way to avoid our visitor. I found this strange, since I had always heard that veterans shared a bond almost like that of brothers. But I decided that perhaps seeing each other reminded them of the war, which everyone in Elm Creek Manor would rather forget.

After dinner Andrew found me alone where I was working in the library. He took my hand and pulled me over to the sofa, his face nervous and angry.

"If you want to know, Sylvia," he said, his voice strained, "I can tell you how it happened. I was there. I can tell you if you want to know, but I don't think it will comfort you."

"Nothing can comfort me." I knew that as certainly as I had ever known anything. "But I need to know how they died."

This is what he told me.

He, James, Richard, and Harold were in an armored division on an island in the South Pacific. Richard and another soldier in one tank and James and Harold in a second were completing a routine patrol of the beach. On a high bluff some distance away, Andrew and some others were preparing to relieve them.

Andrew heard the planes before spotting them in the night sky. He and his companions breathed sighs of relief upon realizing they were our boys.

"They're coming in awfully low," one of the other fellows said.

"You don't suppose they're going to try to land, do you?"

Andrew felt a cold prickling on the back of his neck. "If I didn't know better I'd think they were about to—" And then the beach exploded in flames.

Andrew flung himself onto the sandy ground. "Get down," someone screamed.

Another grabbed a radio. "Call it off. Call it off. It's us!"

Andrew scrambled to his feet, choking and wiping the grit from his eyes. One of the tanks was engulfed in flames.

He ran straight down the steep bluff to the beach, knowing he would never make it in time.

He saw the hatch to the second tank lift. James climbed out and jumped for the ground. He ran to the flaming tank, shouting over his shoulder. Harold's head poked through the opening just as James reached the other tank. He climbed to the top and tried to open the hatch. Andrew was closer now, and through the flames he could see the tendons in James's neck straining as he struggled to open the hatch.

James shouted something to Harold and stopped wrestling with the hatch long enough to gesture frantically for him to help. Harold stared at him, licking his lips nervously, seemingly frozen in place.

The breeze picked up, fanning the flames and carrying some of James's words to Andrew's ears. "Come on, Harold, help me!"

"Hang on," Andrew yelled as he raced by Harold's tank. "I'm coming! I'm—"

He heard the second plane droning overhead and saw Harold duck back into the tank. Then the explosion knocked the ground out from beneath his feet. Heat seared his eyes and wet soil rained down all around him.

Andrew was sobbing. "I'm so sorry, Sylvia," he wept, his voice breaking. "He saved me when we were just kids, but I couldn't save him. I'm so sorry."

I rocked him back and forth and tried to comfort him as best I could, but I had no words for him. All I knew was that James had died trying to protect my little brother as he had promised me, and Harold had let them both die rather than risk his own neck.

The next day Andrew left, and I never saw him again. I waved good-bye to him as his cab drove off, and turning back inside, I vowed not to tell Claudia and Agnes what I had learned. But still I felt uncertain. Should Claudia, at least, be told? Wouldn't she want to know this about her husband-to-be? Then I thought about her words on the veranda that terrible day. "Thank God!" she had said. "Thank God! Thank God!" Angry tears sprang into my eyes at the memory. No, Claudia would prefer her blissful ignorance. And Agnes was too fragile for the truth.

I found them in Claudia's sewing room, giggling like schoolgirls.

Agnes stood on a stool in the middle of the room as Claudia fitted her for a dress.

Their conversation broke off when I entered. "Do you—do you like it, Sylvia?" Agnes asked, holding out her skirts and smiling nervously. "It's my matron of honor dress for Claudia's wedding."

Claudia nudged her and flushed.

I started. "But I thought—but you already asked me to—"

Claudia tossed her head. "I changed my mind. After all, you've hardly been very helpful with my wedding plans. You're always too busy. You don't care about my wedding at all. Agnes does."

Agnes jumped down from the chair. "Stop it. Please. I won't listen to any fighting." She fled from the room.

Claudia threw down her tape measure and glared at me. "Now look what you've done. You just can't leave her alone, can you?"

"What on earth do you mean?" I gasped. "You're the one who asked me to be your matron of honor and then dropped me behind my back. Claudia, I'm your sister."

"She's our sister, too, now," Claudia snapped. "Can't you be unselfish for once in your life? My God, Sylvia, she lost her husband."

My anger swelled. "Have you forgotten? I lost my husband, too. And my brother, and my daughter, and Father. And you know who's to blame?" And then the truth I had vowed not to reveal burst from my lips. "That cowardly fiancé of yours! He let James and Richard die!"

"How can you blame him for that? It isn't Harold's fault he couldn't get the hatch open."

"What? He never even tried. Whatever he told you—Claudia, he never left his tank. Andrew was there. He told me everything."

"You're just jealous because my man came home and yours didn't. You've always been jealous of me, always—"

"He does not belong in this family!" I screamed. "You will not marry him. I am the head of the Bergstrom family now, and I forbid it!"

"You forbid." Claudia's voice was cold, her face pale with rage. "You can forbid nothing. Harold risked his life to protect Richard. How dare you—how dare you speak of him this way. He is as fit as any man to join the Bergstrom family."

"The Bergstrom family is dead," I choked out. "Dead!"

"If you can say that, then perhaps you're the one who doesn't belong here."

"Perhaps you're right." I turned my back on her then. I couldn't bear it anymore. I stormed to my room and threw my things into my suitcases. No one tried to stop me.

I left Elm Creek Manor that day and never returned until this spring. I never again spoke to my sister, or to Agnes, or to Harold.

⚜

The sitting room was silent for a long time. Sarah could hear birds chirping outside, and farther away, the sound of Matt's lawn mower.

"Where did you go?" she finally asked.

Mrs. Compson shrugged and wiped at her eyes with an embroidered handkerchief. "I stayed with James's family in Maryland for a while. They were happy to have me. Then I returned to college. I studied art education at Carnegie Mellon, where they taught things I had already learned from my mother and great-aunt, though my mother and great-aunt didn't use words like 'color theory' and 'composition.' After I received my degree, I taught art in the Pittsburgh area until my retirement. Since then I've had my quilting to keep me busy. I think I've done all right, but it wasn't the life I had hoped for."

"What happened to the others—to Claudia and Agnes?"

"Claudia and Harold married, but they had no children. Several years later Agnes married a professor from the college and moved out of Elm Creek Manor. Claudia and Harold took over Bergstrom Thoroughbreds, and you've seen the results of their keen business sense already. But I have no one to blame but myself for the business's failure. If I had remained here to manage things . . ." She sighed and placed her hand on Sarah's. "Well? Did my long-winded reminiscing solve any riddles?" Her voice was slightly mocking, but not unkind. "Will that help you think of a way to bring Elm Creek Manor back?"

"I'm not sure. I'm going to try."

"Well, you do that. I'm counting on your help." She patted Sarah's hand and sighed.

Twenty-Five

The next day Sarah interrupted her cleaning to ask Mrs. Compson if she would like to join the Tangled Web Quilters for their meeting that evening. Mrs. Compson thought about it for a moment, then shook her head. Although Sarah persisted, the older woman would neither change her mind nor explain her refusal.

So Sarah drove to Mrs. Emberly's home alone.

The red-brick colonial house was only a few streets away from Diane's, in an older part of the Waterford College faculty neighborhood. Sarah was the first to arrive, and Mrs. Emberly took her into the kitchen.

"Help yourself," Mrs. Emberly said, indicating the counter covered with snacks.

Sarah pushed a bowl of pretzels aside to make room for her plate of cupcakes. "Thanks. Maybe later, when the others get here."

Mrs. Emberly glanced back toward the front door. "So, you came alone?"

Sarah nodded.

"I thought Sylvia might come with you this time, since she was so friendly with everyone at the quilt festival."

"You heard about that?"

"Bonnie told Diane, and Diane told me." Mrs. Emberly sighed. "I suppose she would've come if not for me."

"It's not that. I don't think she knows you're a member."

"Really?" Mrs. Emberly brightened for a moment, then looked puzzled. "You didn't tell her?"

"No." Sarah gave her a wry smile. "Just like you never told me you're Mrs. Compson's sister-in-law."

Mrs. Emberly's cheeks went pink. "I assumed that you would've heard it from one of the others long ago, or from Sylvia herself. I suppose she never mentioned me, then?"

"She did, but she called you Agnes, and I didn't know you were Agnes. The Tangled Web Quilters always call you Mrs. Emberly."

"Diane started that. I used to baby-sit her when she was a little girl. She's always known me as Mrs. Emberly, and I suppose the habit was too strong. The others picked it up from her."

"I wish I would've known."

"I didn't mean to deceive you, but I was afraid you'd feel caught in the middle if you knew." Mrs. Emberly took a seat at the kitchen table. "Though I suppose there isn't anything for you to be in the middle of."

"What do you mean?"

"Sylvia and I have no relationship now. Oh, Claudia and I kept tabs on her as best we could through the years, but we had only secondhand information from mutual friends. That's not enough to hold a family together."

Sarah took the seat beside her. "I think Mrs. Compson would be glad to see you again."

"Really?"

"She's very lonely. She feels like she's the last Bergstrom."

"Perhaps she is." Mrs. Emberly twisted her hands together in her lap. "Claudia was a true sister to me, even after I remarried, but Sylvia—"

"Would you be willing to see her again?"

Mrs. Emberly hesitated. "Yes—that is, if you think she'd welcome me."

"I know she would."

"I'm not so certain. Sylvia holds on to a grudge with both hands."

Sarah couldn't argue with that. "What if we—"

Just then Summer burst into the room. "Hey, I'm the second one here. That must be like a new record for me or something."

Mrs. Emberly laughed and pushed her chair away from the table. "Then come on over here and celebrate with one of Sarah's cupcakes." She avoided Sarah's eyes.

The moment was over, and as the rest of the group arrived Sarah knew she wouldn't get another chance that evening to talk to Mrs. Emberly alone.

As the others quilted, Sarah made templates for her latest block, Hands All Around. Her conversation with Mrs. Emberly and Mrs. Compson's stories played over and over in her mind. Somewhere in their stories there had to be a solution.

Diane's voice broke in on her thoughts. "Isn't that a Hands All Around, Sarah? You're smart to hand stitch all those curved seams and set-in pieces."

Sarah hid a smile. "Actually, I've been machine piecing for several days now."

"Please tell me you're joking."

"Welcome to the twentieth century, Sarah," Gwen said.

The others laughed, but Diane glared at them. "You guys are a bad influence." That just made them laugh harder, and even Diane had to smile.

Sarah looked around the circle of friends. This was what Mrs. Compson needed. This was what Elm Creek Manor used to have and had lost.

Maybe Gwen was right, and Mrs. Compson and Mrs. Emberly should be forced into seeing each other again. They were both lonely, especially Mrs. Compson; they both needed to forgive each other. And if Mrs. Compson felt that she had family in Waterford, she might be willing to stay at Elm Creek Manor.

Or the first sight of each other might rekindle all of those smoldering resentments until any hope of reconciliation burned to ashes.

Sarah wished she could figure out what to do. If only she had more time.

By the middle of the next week, Sarah had finished the Hands All Around block and another block, the Ohio Star. Then she had only one block left to piece.

The next day, Mrs. Compson held the book open to the page so that Sarah could see the picture. "Here it is," the older woman said. "It's not the most difficult block, but it's a good one for using up scraps, so I saved it for last."

Sarah carried the book to the table and studied the diagram. The block resembled the Log Cabin pattern, but instead of only one center square, there were seven arranged in a diagonal row across the block. The strips of fabric on one side of the row were dark, and the strips on the other side were light. She looked to the title for the block's name. "Chimneys and Cornerstones," she read aloud, and smiled. "It's a Log Cabin variation, and its name also alludes to houses. That's appropriate, don't you think?"

Mrs. Compson was fingering her glasses and staring into space.

"Mrs. Compson?"

"Hmm? Oh, yes, the name is quite fitting."

"What's wrong?"

"Nothing's wrong. I just remembered something I hadn't thought about in a long time." Mrs. Compson sighed and eased herself onto the sofa. "My great-aunt made a Chimneys and Cornerstones quilt for my cousin when she left Elm Creek Manor as a young bride. She and her husband were moving to California, and we didn't know when—or if—we would see them again. It wasn't like today, when you can hop on a plane any time you like."

⚓

I was a very young child then. This happened before my mother passed away, before Richard was born, even before my first quilt lesson.

I admired my cousin Elizabeth very much. She was the eldest of the cousins, and I wanted to be just like her when I grew up. How confused and sad I was when she told me that she would be going away. I didn't understand why anyone would want to live anywhere but Elm Creek Manor.

"Why do you want to go away when home is right here?" I asked her.

"You'll understand someday, little Sylvia," she told me. She smiled and hugged me, but there were tears in her eyes. "Someday you'll fall in love, and you'll know that home is wherever he is."

That didn't make any sense to me. I pictured Elm Creek Manor sprouting wings and flying along after my cousin and her husband, settling back down to earth wherever they stopped. "Home is here," I insisted. "It will always be here."

She laughed then and hugged me harder. "Yes, Sylvia, you're right."

I was happy to see her laugh and thought that meant she wouldn't be leaving. But the wedding preparations continued, and I knew my dear cousin was going away.

Claudia helped the grown-ups as best she could, but I resented anyone who did anything to hasten my cousin's departure. I hid my aunt's scissors so that she couldn't work on the wedding gown; I took the keys to Elizabeth's trunk and flung them into Elm Creek so that she couldn't pack her things. I earned myself a spanking when I told her fiancé that I hated him and that he should go away.

"If you aren't going to help, then just keep out of the way and stay out of trouble," my father warned me.

I pouted and sulked, but no one paid me any attention. Eventually I pouted and sulked my way into the west parlor, where my great-aunt sat quilting. She was my grandfather's sister, the daughter of Hans and Anneke, and the oldest member of the family.

I stood in the doorway watching as she worked, my lower lip thrust out, my eyes full of angry tears.

My great-aunt looked up and hid a smile. "So, there's the little trouble-maker herself."

I looked at the floor and said nothing.

"Come here, Sylvia."

In those days, when a grown-up called you, you went. She pulled me up onto her lap and spread the quilt over us. We sat there, not speaking, as she sewed. I watched as she took a long strip of fabric and sewed it to the edge of the quilt. The softness of her lap and the way she hummed as she worked comforted me.

Finally my curiosity got the better of me. "What are you doing?" I asked.

"I'm sewing the binding onto your cousin's quilt. See here? This long strip of fabric will cover the raw edges so the batting doesn't fall out."

Raw edges? I thought. I didn't know quilts had to be cooked. Not wanting to reveal my ignorance, I asked a different question. "Is this her wedding quilt?"

"No. This is an extra quilt, one to remember her old great-aunt by. A young wife can never have too many quilts, even in California." She pushed her needle into her pincushion for safekeeping, then spread the quilt wide so that I could see the pattern.

"Pretty," I said, tracing the strips with my finger.

"It's called Chimneys and Cornerstones," she told me. "Whenever she looks at it, she'll remember our home and all the people in it. We Bergstroms have been blessed to have a home filled with love, filled with love from the chimneys to the cornerstone. This quilt will help her take a little of that love with her."

I nodded to show her I understood.

"Each of these red squares is a fire burning in the fireplace to warm her after a weary journey home."

I took in all the red squares on the quilt. "There's too many. We don't have so many fireplaces."

She laughed. "I know. It's just a fancy. Elizabeth will understand."

I nodded. Elizabeth was older than I and understood a great many things.

"There's more to the story. Do you see how one half of the block is dark fabric, and the other is light? The dark half represents the sorrows in a life, and the light colors represent the joys."

I thought about that. "Then why don't you give her a quilt with all light fabric?"

"Well, I could, but then she wouldn't be able to see the pattern. The design only appears if you have both dark and light fabric."

"But I don't want Elizabeth to have any sorrows."

"I don't either, love, but sorrows come to us all. But don't worry. Remember these?" She touched several red squares in a row and smiled. "As long as these home fires keep burning, Elizabeth will always have more joys than sorrows."

I studied the pattern. "The red squares are keeping the sorrow part away from the light part."

"That's exactly right," my great-aunt exclaimed. "What a bright little girl you are."

Pleased, I snuggled up to her. "I still don't like the sorrow part."

"None of us do. Let's hope that Elizabeth finds all the joy she deserves, and only enough sorrow to nurture an empathetic heart."

"What's emp—empa—"

"Empathetic. You'll understand when you're older."

"When I'm old like Claudia?"

She laughed and hugged me. "Yes. Perhaps as soon as that."

Mrs. Compson fell silent, and her gaze traveled around the room. "That's how I feel about Elm Creek Manor," she said. "I love every inch of it, from the chimneys to the cornerstone. I always have. How could I have stayed away so long? Why did I let my pride keep me away from everyone and everything I loved? When I think of how much time I've wasted, it breaks my heart."

Sarah took Mrs. Compson's hand. "Don't give up hope."

"Hope? Hmph. If I had any hope left, it died with Claudia."

"Don't say that. You know that isn't true. If you had no hope, you wouldn't have asked me to find a way to bring Elm Creek Manor back to life."

"I think I know when I'm feeling hopeful and when I'm not, young lady." But the pain in her eyes eased.

Sarah squeezed her hand. "I'm glad this block is in my quilt."

"I'm glad, too."

By the end of the week Sarah finished the Chimneys and Cornerstones block, and then all twelve blocks were finished.

On Monday Sarah prepared the blocks for assembly into the quilt top.

"Don't slide the iron around like that. Just press," Mrs. Compson cautioned as Sarah ironed the seams flat. "If you distort the blocks they won't fit together."

As Sarah handed her the neatly pressed blocks, Mrs. Compson measured them with a clear acrylic ruler exactly twelve and a half inches square. Each of Sarah's twelve blocks was within a sixteenth of an inch of the intended size.

"Fine accuracy, especially considering this is your first quilt," Mrs. Compson praised her. "You'll be a master quilter yet."

Sarah smiled. "I have a good teacher."

"You flatterer," Mrs. Compson scoffed. But she smiled, too.

To Sarah's surprise, Mrs. Compson announced that their next step was to clean the ballroom floor. "Or at least part of it," she added. She took a battered vacuum cleaner from the hall closet and gave it to Sarah, while she carried the twelve sampler blocks.

Mrs. Compson had mentioned once before that the ballroom took up almost the entire first floor of the south wing, but Sarah still took in a breath as she looked around the room. A carpeted border roughly twenty feet wide encircled the broad parquet dance floor, which still seemed smooth and glossy beneath a thin coating of dust. Above, a chandelier hung beneath a ceiling covered with a swirling vinelike pattern made from molded plaster. At the far end of the room was a raised dais where musicians or honored guests could be seated. In the far corner, a large object—a table, maybe, with chairs on all sides—rested beneath a dusty sheet. Rectangular windows topped by semicircular curves, narrow in proportion to their height, lined the south, east, and west walls.

Mrs. Compson moved from window to window pulling back curtains, but the drizzle outside permitted little light to enter. She went to a panel in the far corner, flicked a switch, and gave the chandeliers a challenging look. The lights came on, wavered, and then shone steadily, casting shadows and sparkling reflections to the floor below.

After Sarah vacuumed a small portion of the carpet, she and Mrs. Compson arranged the blocks on the floor in three rows of four, then stood back and studied them.

"I think I want the Schoolhouse block in the middle instead," Sarah said, bending over to switch two of the blocks. "And the Lancaster Rose next to it. Since it's more complicated I want to show it off."

Mrs. Compson chuckled. "Spoken like a true quilter. Then you can place the two blocks with curved piecing opposite each other, here and here. And since you have three star blocks, and another that resembles a star, you can put them in the corners like this . . ."

They spent half an hour arranging and rearranging the blocks until Sarah was satisfied with their appearance. In the upper-left-hand corner she placed the Ohio Star block, with the Bachelor's Puzzle, Double Nine Patch, and LeMoyne Star blocks completing the row. The middle row held the Posies Round the Square, Little Red Schoolhouse, Lancaster Rose, and Hands All Around blocks. The Sawtooth Star, Chimneys and Cornerstones, Contrary Wife, and Sister's Choice blocks made up the bottom row.

"I don't think this is going to be big enough for a queen-size bed," Sarah said.

"Don't worry. We're a long way from binding it yet."

"If I make any more blocks, I'll never finish the quilt in time."

"Oh, we'll contrive something."

"Like what? You mean the setting? That should make it bigger, but not by much."

"Not the setting. You just let me worry about that," Mrs. Compson said, and Sarah couldn't persuade her to say anything more.

They left the blocks in place and returned to the west sitting room, where Mrs. Compson showed Sarah how to make a Garden Maze setting. They began by making three templates: a small square, an even smaller triangle, and a narrow rectangle that tapered off to a point on both ends. To save time, Mrs. Compson traced the pieces—the tapered strips from the cream fabric and the other two shapes from the darkest blue—while Sarah cut them out. Sarah simply used her ruler rather than making a template for the narrow, dark blue pieces Mrs. Compson called block border strips.

Sarah sewed the hypotenuse of each small triangle to a tapered edge of the longer strips; when four triangles were attached, pieced sashing strips fourteen inches in length were formed. Meanwhile, Mrs. Compson sewed the dark block border strips around the edges of each block. They worked for the rest of the afternoon, and when it was time for Sarah to leave, Mrs. Compson told her to go ahead and leave everything where it was.

Sarah took in the fabric scraps, snipped threads, and quilting tools of all kinds scattered wildly around the room and had to laugh. "If you can live with this mess, I guess I can," she said as she left.

At home, Matt went to check the mailbox while Sarah went inside to study the cupboard shelves and try to figure out what to make for supper. When he returned he tossed her a thick beige envelope. "Something came for you." He leaned against the counter and watched her.

The return address announced "Hopkins and Steele" in bold blue lettering. Sarah tore open the envelope and scanned the letter.

"Well? What do they say?"

"They're offering me the job."

Matt let out a whoop and swung Sarah up in his arms. Then he noticed he was the only one celebrating. "Isn't this good news? Don't you want the job?" he asked as he set her down.

"I don't know. I guess so. I mean, I thought I did, but—I don't know."

"You want to stay with Mrs. Compson."

"Would that be so bad? You were the one who got me started working there in the first place, remember?"

Matt grinned and held up his palms in defense. "If you want to keep working at Elm Creek Manor, that's fine by me."

"It's fine by me, too, unless Mrs. Compson decides she doesn't need me anymore after we finish cleaning the place. I'm surprised I still have a job now, since the whole point of it was to help prepare the manor for sale."

"Maybe she likes having you around."

"She doesn't have to pay me for that." Sarah went into the adjoining room and slouched into a chair, spreading the letter flat on the table.

Matt took the opposite chair. He turned the letter around and read it. "They want you to respond within two weeks."

"That's two weeks from the date of the letter, not from today."

"Either way, you don't have to decide this minute. Take some time to think about it. Talk it over with Mrs. Compson, maybe."

"Maybe." Sarah sighed. Every day seemed to bring a new and more pressing deadline.

Twenty-Six

That week Mrs. Compson and Sarah spent their mornings finishing up the south wing's bedrooms and used their afternoons to finish piecing Sarah's quilt top. They sewed blocks and sashing strips together to make the three rows, then they fashioned four long sashing rows by alternating sashing strips with the two-inch squares. When the block rows were joined to the long sashing rows and then to each other, the sampler's garden maze setting was complete.

Thursday came and went, and once again Sarah went to the Tangled Web Quilters' meeting alone.

On Friday, Mrs. Compson instructed Sarah to cut long, wide strips from her background fabric and attach these borders to the outside edges of her quilt. Sarah's shoulders and neck ached from hanging curtains all morning, and sitting at the sewing machine didn't help. Their anniversary was quickly approaching and she hadn't even started the quilting yet.

Behind her she heard the cedar chest opening and the rustle of tissue paper. "Sarah?" Mrs. Compson asked.

"Just a sec. I'm almost finished with the last border." Sarah backstitched to secure the seam and clipped the threads. "There." She removed the quilt top from the machine and brushed off a few loose threads. "I still don't think it will be big enough. Almost, but not quite."

"Maybe this will help."

Sarah turned in her chair. Mrs. Compson was spreading four long strips of pieced fabric on the sofa.

"What are those?"

"Oh, just a little something I've been working on in the evenings after you leave. Did you think I just sat around all night waiting for you to return in the morning?"

Sarah rose for a closer look. "This looks like my fabric."

"That's because it is your fabric."

Sarah held up one of the pretty quilt tops, if that's what they were. Maybe they were table runners. There were two long and two shorter pieces, all with the same pattern of parallelograms and squares on background fabric.

Then Sarah remembered. "These look like the twisted ribbon borders we saw at the quilt show."

"You seemed to admire the pattern, and I thought it would suit your sampler." Mrs. Compson hesitated for a moment before hurrying on. "But only if you want them. I took the liberty of making them for you so that you could have the large quilt you wanted, but you don't have to use them."

"These are for my quilt? Really?" Sarah snatched up her quilt top and held it against the border, trying to see how the finished product would look. "Thank you so much."

"You don't have to use them, mind. Maybe you wanted the whole quilt top to be made by your own hands. I can understand that. Don't think you have to sew them on so you won't hurt my feelings."

"Are you kidding? I'm sewing them on right now and you just try to stop me."

Mrs. Compson smiled in response. Soon Sarah finished attaching the twisted ribbon outer borders, and she held up the finished quilt top for inspection. "What do you think?"

Mrs. Compson picked up the other edge of the quilt. "It's lovely. You've done well."

Sarah studied the quilt top. "I can't believe I made this—except for the border, I mean."

"Believe it. But it's a long way from finished."

"What's next?"

"Now we need to mark the quilting designs." Mrs. Compson rummaged around in her tackle box and produced a pencil.

Sarah clutched the quilt top to her chest. "You want to draw on my quilt? I don't think that's such a good idea."

Mrs. Compson rolled her eyes heavenward. "She makes one quilt top and now she's the expert." She reached out for the quilt top. "Will you relax, if you please? I've done this before."

Sarah handed it over. "Okay, but . . . be careful."

They spread the quilt top on the table and pulled up two chairs. Mrs. Compson handed Sarah the pencil and told her to give it a closer look. As she did, Mrs. Compson explained in a very patient voice that this was a fabric pencil, not a typical Number 2, and if the marks were made lightly they would wash out later. She then explained how to mark the quilting designs on the quilt, either by using a stencil or by slipping a printed pattern from a book or a magazine beneath the fabric and tracing it. They used dressmaker's chalk instead of pencil on the dark fabrics.

Sometimes the quilting designs were simple, like the straight lines a quarter inch away from the seams called outline quilting. Others were more complex, especially where they had open space to decorate, but to Sarah's relief none were as complicated as those she had seen on Mrs. Compson's quilts. She wasn't sure that she was ready for anything so difficult.

At the end of the day Sarah decided to take the quilt top home and finish tracing the designs over the weekend.

"That's fine," Mrs. Compson said. "But don't you think Matthew will notice?"

Sarah frowned. She wanted the quilt to be a surprise, but she was running out of time.

Mrs. Compson patted her on the shoulder. "I'll work on it. I don't know if I'll have it finished by Monday, but I'll do my best."

"I don't want you to go to so much trouble."

"Trouble?" Mrs. Compson laughed. "I haven't had so much fun in I don't know how long. It's nice to feel a part of things again." She ushered Sarah outside to wait for Matt so that he wouldn't walk in on them and see the quilt spread out on the table.

All weekend long Sarah's thoughts kept returning to Elm Creek Manor. She couldn't shake the feeling that her time for finding a way to bring Elm Creek Manor back to life was rapidly running out.

Unfortunately, Matt meant well but was little help when it came to finding a solution. He couldn't understand why anyone would never speak to her family again just because she didn't get to be matron of honor at some old wedding. And even if Mrs. Compson was still holding a grudge, her sister was gone, so why stay angry? "You don't see guys acting like that," he concluded, shaking his head in bafflement.

"You're missing the point," Sarah told him. "Think of everything she'd been through. She was angry at Claudia and Agnes for shutting her out, but she was even angrier at herself for needing them. She left instead of facing up to all the pain. I can understand why she left, but she sees it as abandoning her responsibilities." Then suddenly she understood. "That matron of honor business—that didn't mean anything. They fought about that because they couldn't fight about what was really hurting them—their loss, their rivalry. It was too painful to face."

Matt studied her. "Sort of the way you and your mother fight about her boyfriends."

Sarah stiffened. "It's not the same thing."

"Well, sure it is, if you look—"

"It's *not.*"

"Okay, okay." Matt backed down. "You know your mother better than I do."

"We're talking about Mrs. Compson, not about me."

"If that's the way you want it."

Sarah's thoughts churned. She didn't want to think about her mother, couldn't afford to spend a moment there when her time for saving Elm Creek Manor was dwindling so rapidly.

Then, suddenly, an image flashed into her mind, an image of herself as an old woman cleaning up her childhood home, sorting through her dead mother's things, still wrestling with anger and resentment and pain, forever denied reconciliation.

One day Sarah would be as angry and alone as Mrs. Compson.

Suddenly fearful, she flung the image from her mind.

By Monday morning she felt no closer to a solution. Worsening matters was the Hopkins and Steele letter, a persistent reminder that other deadlines were closing in. As Sarah and Matt drove to work, Sarah found herself looking forward to her quilting lesson later that day. Not just looking forward to it, she suddenly realized, but needing it. Tangled, anxious thoughts relaxed when she felt the fabric beneath her fingers and remembered that she was creating something beautiful enough to delight the eyes as well as the heart, something strong enough to defeat the cold of a Pennsylvania winter night. She could do these things. She, Sarah, had the power to do these things.

Sarah knew Mrs. Compson recognized the power of quilting, too. Quilting certainly seemed to bring Mrs. Compson's joy to life; maybe it could do the same for Elm Creek Manor. If Mrs. Emberly was one piece of the puzzle, maybe quilting was the second.

A vague shadow of an idea began to form in Sarah's mind as the truck pulled up behind Elm Creek Manor.

Mrs. Compson had finished marking all but a small portion of the quilt top, and she was completing that section when Sarah walked in.

"Did you remember to buy the batting and backing fabric like I told you?" Mrs. Compson asked, pausing long enough to peer at Sarah over the rims of her glasses.

Sarah nodded and showed her the Grandma's Attic bag. "And the fabric's washed and pressed, as ordered."

"Good girl." Mrs. Compson set down the pencil and removed her glasses. "Now it's time to prepare the quilt layers."

"I've done that part before, and I was thinking—"

"You've done this before?"

"Yes, with the Tangled Web Quilters. And that's who I wanted to talk to you about. I was thinking—"

"You never told me you've used a quilt frame before. This is indeed a surprise."

Sarah opened her mouth to speak, but then Mrs. Compson's words registered and she forgot what she was going to say. "Quilt frame?"

"Yes, of course." She folded the quilt top and draped it over her arm.

"Oh." Sarah frowned. "I thought you were talking about basting the quilt sandwich."

"With this quilt frame you don't need to baste, thank goodness. Life's too short to baste a quilt if you don't have to. Bring the bag." She turned and beckoned Sarah to follow.

Sarah hurried to catch up as Mrs. Compson walked to the ballroom. "Basting goes fast if you have lots of people to help. And that's what I wanted to talk to you about."

"What did you wish to say?"

"I was thinking that maybe this weekend we could invite the Tangled Web Quilters over for a quilting party. You know, like you used to have here? They could come over Friday after work and we could quilt and get a pizza or two, and they could spend the night, and then we could finish up on Saturday."

Mrs. Compson looked doubtful.

"Don't say no, Mrs. Compson. It would be a lot of fun. And I only have a little more than a week to finish the quilt in time for our anniversary."

Mrs. Compson stopped with her hand on the ballroom door and eyed Sarah suspiciously. Then her face relaxed. "A quilting party, you say?"

Sarah nodded.

"Sounds more like a slumber party to me. Aren't you a little old for slumber parties?"

Sarah shrugged and gave her a pleading look.

"What will Matthew say?"

"He can survive without me for one night, I think."

"Hmph. You may be surprised." Mrs. Compson paused. "As you say, it might be fun."

"You won't have to do any of the work. I'll take care of all the food and getting the rooms ready and everything."

"Hmph. No, you won't; I wouldn't let you do all that alone." She sighed. "How many people are we talking about?"

"Six. Seven including me."

"Eight including me. That's plenty of help for finishing the quilt."

"Most of them you've met already, at the quilt show, I mean, and you already know Bonnie and Gwen pretty well, and—"

Mrs. Compson held up a palm. "You can stop babbling now, Sarah. I agree. We may have your quilting party."

"Oh, thanks, Mrs. Compson." Impulsively, Sarah hugged her. "This will be great. You'll see."

"I believe I may regret this. You have something up your sleeve, my dear, and don't think I don't know it."

Sarah assumed her best wide-eyed-innocence expression. "Who, me? You're the one with all the surprises."

"Hmph. We'll see." Mrs. Compson passed the quilt top to Sarah, pushed open the door, and led Sarah to the large object in the corner of the ballroom. She grasped the edge of the sheet covering it. "This is the quilting frame I told you about, the one Claudia and I used before I left home. Let's see if it still works."

She pulled off the sheet, and a cloud of dust rose. Coughing and sneezing, Sarah peered through the cloud to find a rectangular wooden frame roughly four feet across and six feet long perched on four legs that raised it to table height. At the corners were strange assemblies of knobs and gears with slender rods running the length of the frame between them. On either side of the tablelike surface was a small wooden chair. And draped across the middle—

"Why, there's a quilt still on the frame," Mrs. Compson said when the dust had settled. "What on earth?" She bent over the faded cloth and studied the pieces.

Sarah could tell that it was a scrap quilt, and many if not most of the pieces were not typical cotton quilting fabrics. She guessed it was decades old, maybe as much as fifty years. Pieced blocks alternated with solid fabric squares of the same size. The block pattern resembled a star, but not quite. Eight narrow triangles with their smallest angles pointing toward the center formed an octagon in the middle of the block. There were eight squares, one joined to each edge of the octagon, and between the squares were eight diamonds, each with a tip touching a corner of the octagon. Four triangles and four parallelograms finished the design. The quilt sagged in the middle, as if the mechanism holding it taut and secure had weakened over time.

"Look over here," Sarah said. "The points of these diamonds are chopped off. Didn't you say that's a sign of Claudia's piecing?"

"Castle Wall," Mrs. Compson murmured. "Well, if that doesn't just fit. Castle Wall."

"Mrs. Compson?"

"Safety and security and comfort behind the Castle Wall. Except you have to come back home before home can be your safe castle, your refuge. Of all the choices."

"Mrs. Compson?" Sarah gripped her by the shoulders and gave her a small shake. Startled, Mrs. Compson gasped and tore her eyes away from the quilt. "Are you all right?" Sarah asked.

Mrs. Compson pulled away. "Yes. Yes, I'm fine. This was just . . . a bit unexpected."

"Is this Claudia's work?"

Mrs. Compson nodded and turned back to the quilt. "And the Puz—and Agnes's, too." With a trembling finger she traced one of the quilt pieces, a blue pinstriped diamond. Then she reached out and stroked a central octagon made from tiny red flannel triangles. "See this?" She indicated the blue diamond. "That was from the suit James wore on our wedding day. And this red flannel—why, I spent a good part of my married life threatening to burn this wretched work shirt." She touched a soft blue-and-yellow square. "This—" With an effort she steadied her voice, but Sarah saw tears spring to her eyes. "This was from my daughter's receiving blanket. My lucky colors, you know, blue and yellow—" She choked up and pressed a hand to her lips. "They were making this for me. They were making me a memorial quilt."

Sarah nodded. A memorial quilt, a quilt made from pieces of a deceased loved one's clothing, made as much to comfort the living as to pay tribute to the dead.

"They must have started it after I left, but—but why? After the way I left them? They must have thought I'd come back one day, but when I didn't— yes, that must be why they didn't finish it."

Sarah touched her on the shoulder. "Mrs. Compson?"

She jumped. "Yes? Oh, don't look so alarmed, poor girl. I'm perfectly all right." She took a lace-edged handkerchief from her pocket and wiped her eyes. "Don't worry. I was just caught off guard, like I said. I never thought— well, never mind. It can't be helped, not now." She forced her lips to curve into a smile. "There, see? All better."

"I'm not fooled."

"No? Well, I didn't think you would be."

Mrs. Compson stared at the quilt for a long while. Then, with Sarah's assistance, she removed it from the frame and folded the unfinished layers. She placed the bundle on the raised dais at the south end of the room and stood there stroking the fabric, her eyes full of pain.

Twenty-Seven

They worked no more on Sarah's quilt that day. Mrs. Compson isolated herself in the library, and Sarah worked alone in a west wing suite.

The next morning, though, Mrs. Compson met Sarah on the back steps. "I've been going over a list of things we'll need for the party," she said after greeting her. "Perhaps you and Matthew can pick them up sometime this week."

Sarah agreed and stuffed the list into the back pocket of her denim shorts. She'd been half afraid Mrs. Compson would cancel the quilting party after the unexpected surprise the previous day. Sarah was relieved that she wouldn't have to devise some other scheme. It had been difficult enough to come up with this one.

They went to the ballroom, where Sarah noticed that the quilt frame had been dusted and pulled away from the corner. Sunlight streamed in through the open windows, and a gentle cross breeze cooled the room. The memorial quilt was nowhere to be seen.

Mrs. Compson guided Sarah through the steps of placing the backing, the batting, and finally the quilt top around the rollers along the long sides of the quilt frame. By adjusting the gears, the three layers could be held firmly and smoothly without being stretched to the point of distortion. The middle of the quilt top was visible now, but when they finished that section they could bring the other parts into view by adjusting the rollers.

"James built me this frame," Mrs. Compson remarked as she directed Sarah to one of the chairs. "Before then, we would lay our quilts on the floor and crawl around on our hands and knees thread basting. Not too gentle on the knees or the back, I assure you." She dug through her tackle box. "I think we'll start you off with a nine between, if I have any. I usually use twelves—ah, here we are."

"A nine between what?"

"Hmm? Oh, that's what quilting needles are called. Betweens. They're thicker and sturdier than regular needles, which are called sharps. The number indicates the size. The higher the number, the smaller the size."

"Then I'll take the lowest number you have."

"A nine will be just right. Don't worry about making your stitches small at first; just concentrate on making them of equal length, both on the top and on the bottom. The more you quilt, the smaller your stitches will become. You'll see."

Mrs. Compson threaded two needles and handed one to Sarah. She showed Sarah how to tie a small knot at the end, to pull the needle from the back through to the front on one of the drawn quilting lines, then to give the thread a careful tug to pop the knot through the back and into the batting. It took Sarah a few tries before she could get the knot to stay in the middle of the quilt instead of popping right on through the top.

"Are you right-handed? Then put your thimble on your right hand and put your left hand underneath the quilt," Mrs. Compson ordered, and she proceed to demonstrate how to sew through all three layers. First, using the finger protected by the thimble, she pushed the needle through the top of the quilt. When the tip of the needle touched her left forefinger on the other side, she pushed the tip of the needle back through the layers to the top. By rocking her right hand back and forth in this manner, she gathered a few stitches on her needle. Then she pulled the needle and the length of thread all the way through to the top, leaving behind four small running stitches in a straight row along the penciled quilting design.

Sarah tried it, awkwardly gathering three stitches on her needle before bringing the needle and thread completely through the layers. She paused to inspect her work. "They're even and straight, but they're huge."

Mrs. Compson bent over for a look. "Those are toenail catchers for sure, but fine for your first try. Go ahead and see how it looks from the back."

Sarah ducked her head beneath the quilt frame. "They look the same to me. Huge, but equally huge."

"Good. That's what you want: nice even stitches the same length on the bottom as on the top."

They continued for a while, Sarah on one side of the quilt frame and Mrs. Compson on the other. At first Sarah tried to match the other woman's brisk pace, but soon gave up and proceeded more slowly, trying to make her stitches even and small. The quilt came alive beneath their needles as the quilting stitches added dimension to the pieced pattern. Before an hour had passed, Sarah's shoulders and neck ached and her left forefinger stung from so many needle pricks. She withdrew her hand from beneath the quilt and stuck her sore finger in her mouth, stroking the quilt with her other hand.

Mrs. Compson looked up. "You'll develop a callus there eventually, and it won't hurt as much. But perhaps that's enough quilting for now."

Sarah popped her finger out of her mouth. "No, let's go on just a little while longer, okay?"

Mrs. Compson laughed and shook her head. She tied a knot in her thread, popped it into the batting, and trimmed the trailing end. "No, it's important to rest every once in a while. Besides, you want to save something for your friends to do this weekend, don't you?"

"Even if we worked eight hours a day between now and then, there would still be plenty left," Sarah said, but she set her needle and thimble aside.

They spent the rest of the day working in the west wing. That evening Sarah phoned the Tangled Web Quilters and invited them to the party. She called Mrs. Emberly last and spoke with her for almost an hour.

On Wednesday, Sarah and Mrs. Compson bustled about arranging six bedrooms with fresh linens and pretty quilts for their guests. Twice they interrupted their work to spend some time quilting. They stitched and discussed the upcoming party with growing excitement. Mrs. Compson was cheerful and animated, and Sarah was about to burst with anticipation and nervousness. So many things could go wrong, but she tried not to think about that.

Finally she had to say something. "Matt's finished the north gardens," she said, trying to sound nonchalant. "How about if we take a look at them on Friday before our guests arrive?"

Mrs. Compson set down her rag and brushed the dust from her hands. "I'm ready for a rest. Why don't we go now?"

"No," Sarah exclaimed, and Mrs. Compson jumped. "I mean, I'd rather go Friday, Friday afternoon around four. I want to make sure we get this cleaning done. How about this—visiting the gardens can be our reward when we finish getting everything ready for the party, okay?"

Mrs. Compson studied her, bemused. "Very well, then. Friday it is." She walked off, shaking her head.

Idiot, Sarah berated herself. She had almost ruined everything.

Thursday passed quickly, with little time for quilting. At the Tangled Web Quilters' meeting that evening, Sarah explained her plan to everyone and made sure Mrs. Emberly understood her part. Mrs. Emberly's eyes were wide with worry, but she nodded. Sarah was sure she looked just as anxious herself.

At home that night, Sarah packed an overnight bag while Matt sat on the bed and watched her. "Mrs. Compson's important to me, too, and I'd like to help. Are you sure I can't come?" he asked.

"If you come you'll spoil my surprise for you." She kissed him on the cheek. "But you already have an important role. I couldn't pull this off without you."

"All I get to do is play chauffeur," he complained, but he cheered up a little.

Friday morning came. Matt dropped Sarah off with a kiss, an encouraging grin, and a promise to be at the appointed place on time. As he started to drive away, Sarah waved him to a stop and jogged over to his window. She took an envelope from her bag, held on to it for a moment, then passed it to him. "Do you think you'll have time to mail this for me today?"

"Honey, for you I'll make the time," he said, grinning. Then he noticed the address. "What's this? Your response to Hopkins and Steele?"

Sarah nodded.

"You're refusing their offer, right?"

"That's right." Sarah shifted her weight from one leg to the other.

"Have you thought this through? Shouldn't you wait and see if your plan works first?"

"If Mrs. Compson doesn't like this idea, I'll keep trying until I find one she does like. But if I take a new job, that will be the end of my days at Elm Creek Manor. If I'm not here, I think it will be much more difficult to come up with a new plan."

"I guess I can't argue with that." He leaned his head out of the window for another kiss. "I hope you know what you're doing."

"So do I," Sarah replied as he drove away.

She went inside and found Mrs. Compson in the kitchen humming and mixing something in a large bowl. "I thought I'd make us some sweet treats for tonight," she explained with a smile. "I know how much quilters like to nibble."

"You're going to fit in just fine with this crowd," Sarah said, laughing.

They hurried to finish all the last-minute preparations. Mrs. Compson had gathered wildflowers from around the barn and placed them in each quilter's room. Sarah made sure the kitchen was well stocked with snacks and beverages while Mrs. Compson checked for extra quilting supplies. As the day passed, Sarah's anxiety grew. Maybe her plan was a bad idea. Maybe she would make things worse.

But Mrs. Compson didn't have a phone, so Sarah had no way to call things off. She tried to force the negative thoughts from her mind. She had no choice but to go ahead with her plan, so there was no point to worrying about it.

At four o'clock she met Mrs. Compson in the front foyer. "Everything's ready, I believe," Mrs. Compson announced. She looked excited and happy.

Sarah hoped she wasn't about to change all that. "We still have an hour before everyone's due to arrive. Why don't we go see the gardens now?"

Mrs. Compson agreed and returned to the kitchen for her hat. They left by the cornerstone patio exit and strolled along the gray stone path toward the gardens.

"I hope Matt worked some miracles out here," Mrs. Compson said. "There was so much work—" Her voice broke off at the sight of the gardens.

Large bushes encircled the oval clearing where only weeds had grown before; although they would not bloom now, so late in the summer, in the spring the garden would be fragrant with the scent of lilacs. In the four planters, rosebushes and white bachelor's buttons were surrounded by lush ivy and other green foliage. The weeds and grass had been removed from between the gray stones beneath their feet, and the fountain of the mare and two foals had been cleaned and polished. The gazebo's fresh coat of white paint was dazzling in the sunlight. The terraces behind the gazebo had been rebuilt, and now displayed blossoms of every color and variety.

A breeze carried refreshing mist from the fountain and the scent of roses to them as they stood at the edge of the garden, taking in the beautiful sight.

"I can't believe it. I never would have thought it possible," Mrs. Compson gasped. "It's as lovely now as it ever was. Even lovelier."

Just then a small figure stepped out from behind the gazebo.

Mrs. Compson stared.

Sarah's heart thumped heavily in her chest. She clenched her hands together and swallowed. "Mrs. Compson, this is—"

"Agnes," Mrs. Compson breathed.

Hesitantly, Mrs. Emberly approached them. "Hello, Sylvia."

"Mrs. Emberly is one of the Tangled Web Quilters," Sarah said. "I thought—I thought maybe you two would like to see each other before the rest of the group shows up."

"It's been a long time, Sylvia." Mrs. Emberly stopped a few paces in front of them. She gave Mrs. Compson a slow, sad smile, and clutched her purse like a shield. "We have a lot of catching up to do."

Mrs. Compson stared at her, her lips pursing then separating slightly as if she struggled to speak.

Sarah willed Mrs. Compson to speak, to say hello, to say something, anything.

Agnes's lower lip trembled. "I've—I've missed you. We all did, when you went away."

"I found the quilt."

Mrs. Emberly blinked. "The—"

"The memorial quilt. The one you and Claudia were working on for me."

Mrs. Emberly's mouth formed an O. "Of course. The Castle Wall quilt."

"You did well. Both of you. Fine workmanship."

"Thank you." She looked grateful, and then her eyes filled with tears. "Oh, Sylvia, is there any chance we could ever be friends? I know I wasn't the sister-in-law you hoped for, but now that everyone else is gone—"

Mrs. Compson strode forward and gripped Mrs. Emberly's shoulders. "Now, you stop that. We'll have no crying here today. My behavior all that time ago had nothing to do with you. I was selfish and wanted Richard all to myself. I was wrong to treat you so badly, and I was a fool to leave home." She took Mrs. Emberly's hands in her own. "Richard loved you, and if I were any kind of decent sister I would have respected that."

"You were a decent sister," Mrs. Emberly insisted. "I was a spoiled, flighty little child concerned for no one but myself. You cared about your family and your home, and I should have been more understanding."

"You may have been foolish, but that's not as bad as being deliberately mean."

"Well, perhaps you were overbearing and bossy and always thought you knew better than everyone else, but at least you didn't blunder in unwanted only to divide a family and place enmity between sisters."

"Nonsense. Claudia and I always squabbled, as far back as I can remember. You had nothing to do with that."

Sarah looked from one tear-stained face to the other. "Mrs. Compson, Mrs. Emberly—"

Mrs. Compson didn't even turn around. "Remember, Sarah, never interrupt your elders when they're in the middle of making a point. Will you excuse us for a while? Agnes and I have some matters to discuss. It's time for me to stop being a self-righteous old bag of wind and make amends while the sun shines." She gave Mrs. Emberly a small, hesitant smile, which the other woman returned. Then Mrs. Compson gave Sarah a look over her shoulder that said as clearly as if she had spoken, *As for you, young lady, I'll deal with you later.*

Sarah nodded, then turned and hurried back to the house, leaving Mrs. Compson and Mrs. Emberly alone in the garden.

Twenty-Eight

Sarah waited outside on the back stairs for the other guests to arrive. A few minutes before five o'clock, Bonnie and Diane pulled up in Diane's car.

"How did it go?" Bonnie asked in a stage whisper as they walked toward the manor.

"I don't know yet. They're still out in the garden."

Diane sat down on the steps beside her. "Well, at least they didn't kill each other. That's something, anyway." She nudged Sarah and grinned.

"I think it's wonderful that you're trying to bring those two together, Sarah," Bonnie said. "It couldn't have been easy, considering how long they've been estranged."

"Bonnie's right. If you can pull it off, it'll be a nice thing you've done for them."

Sarah reddened. "It's no big deal. I'm just trying to save my job, that's all."

Diane rolled her eyes. "Do you expect us to believe—"

"Look, Judy's here," Sarah interrupted, relieved to be able to change the subject. She stood and waved to Judy as she pulled up in her minivan. Close behind came Gwen and Summer.

As always, everyone had brought a dessert; Sarah guided them to the kitchen, where they set their trays and boxes next to the pile of goodies already awaiting them. Then she led them through the manor and out the front entry to the veranda. The others' reactions made her smile. She had gawked even more her first days here, and that was a layer of dust or two ago. They still had more to do, Sarah reminded herself. Matt's work and her own had done much to restore Elm Creek Manor, but they weren't finished yet.

They waited on the veranda in Adirondack chairs she and Matt had arranged there. Their conversation broke off when Mrs. Compson and Mrs.

Emberly came around the north side of the building walking arm in arm. They hesitated at the foot of the stairs as the others watched them.

"Well?" Mrs. Compson finally barked, glaring up at them. "What are you all looking at?"

After the barest pause, Mrs. Emberly burst into laughter, and the others joined in.

Mrs. Compson smiled sheepishly. "Not much of a welcome, was it? Please accept my apologies. It's not every day hell freezes over." She clapped a hand over her mouth. "And now I'm cursing. Goodness, what has gotten into me?"

They went inside to the ballroom, where everyone oohed and ahhed appropriately as Sarah showed them her quilt. Then they decided they were hungry, so Judy used her car phone to order pizza. By the time the delivery car pulled up behind the manor, all the women—including Mrs. Compson—were chatting and laughing like old friends.

After a casual supper on the veranda, they got to work. Four people sat quilting on one side of the quilt frame and three on the other while the eighth person threaded needles, fetched quilting tools, or ran for snacks. Every so often the runner would trade places with one of the quilters so that everyone had a chance to rest their fingers. As they worked they talked about themselves, their quilts, their families, and their jobs, and often the ballroom would echo with laughter.

Occasionally everyone would take a break from quilting, and they would hurry to the kitchen for snacks and conversation, giggling like kids at recess, until their fingers felt ready to pick up their needles again. Sarah was delighted to see how quickly eight pairs of hands virtually flew over the fabric. Beside the more experienced hands, Sarah thought her own plodded along clumsily, but she had to admit her stitches were improving.

As the evening waned, one by one the quilters sighed and stretched and pushed their chairs away from the quilting frame—Mrs. Emberly first, then Diane, then Judy, and then the others until only Sarah and Mrs. Compson were left.

"It's nearly midnight," Mrs. Compson finally said, straightening and working out the kinks in her shoulders. "Perhaps it's best to stop for the night."

Although they were tired, no one wanted to go to bed just yet, so they went out to the veranda to watch the fireflies flickering in a silent dance on the lawn. They chatted more quietly now, and Sarah could feel the gentle sound of the rearing stallion fountain lulling her to sleep.

Her eyes were about to close for good when Mrs. Compson placed a hand on her shoulder. "Let's show our guests to their rooms, shall we?"

Sarah nodded and pulled herself up from her chair. Carrying Mrs. Emberly's overnight bag, she led the others inside and upstairs to their rooms. Sleepy though they were, the Tangled Web Quilters were pleased with their suites, with the lovely Amish furniture, the pretty quilts on the beds, and the cut flowers Mrs. Compson had so carefully arranged. Sarah showed them where the bathrooms were and wished them good night.

She carried Mrs. Emberly's bag into her room for her and placed it in the corner. "I'll see you in the morning," she said, closing the door behind her.

"Sarah?" Mrs. Emberly called before the door was completely shut.

Sarah pushed the door open again. "Yes?"

Mrs. Emberly stood in the center of the room, hands clasped at her waist. "Thank you for today."

Sarah smiled. "It was my pleasure."

Mrs. Emberly gave her a searching look. "Tell me something, Sarah. Did you select our rooms for us or did I end up with this room by chance?"

"Well, actually—" Sarah hesitated, glancing over her shoulder to see if Mrs. Compson was near. "Originally we picked these rooms because they're close together and already cleaned, and we were just going to have everyone pick whichever room they liked best. But when you were in the kitchen with Judy, Mrs. Compson told me to make sure you got this one. Why? Is something wrong?"

"Oh, no. Quite the contrary." She looked around the room, a thoughtful, sad smile on her lips. "This was my first husband's room when he was young." She pointed to a desk next to the door. "His initials are on that brass plate right there. We stayed here together before he went into the service."

"I see."

"And Sylvia wanted me to have this suite. What do you suppose she intended?"

"I don't know. Maybe you should ask her."

"No. That won't be necessary. I think I know."

Sarah smiled, then nodded and left.

Her own room was two doors down and across the hall. After changing into a short cotton nightgown, she padded down the hall in her slippers to the nearest bathroom. When she returned, she found Mrs. Compson sitting on the bed.

"Well, young lady, you certainly had a busy day full of surprises, didn't you?"

"You aren't angry, are you?"

"Of course not." She rose and gave Sarah a hug. "You forced me to do something I should have done on my own a long time ago. I suppose I just needed a push."

"How did it go? In the garden, I mean, talking with Mrs. Emberly."

"Better than I could have expected or hoped." Mrs. Compson sighed. "But we have a long way to go until we're as close as sisters ought to be. As you know from my stories, we were never friends, and we've both changed so much since we knew each other last. Who can say? Perhaps those changes will allow us to be friends in a way that simply wasn't possible then." She gave Sarah an affectionate smile. "As I said, we have a long way to go, but at least we've finally begun a journey we should have made fifty years ago." She turned and stepped through the open doorway. "Good night, Sarah."

"Good night."

Sarah shut the door behind her and switched off the light. She climbed into bed and inhaled the fragrance of the freshly washed, smooth cotton sheets. The room was cool and comfortable for a warm summer's night. Moonlight spilled in through the open window, and a soft wind stirred the curtains. Sarah rolled over onto her side and ran her hand along the empty space in the bed beside her. This was the first time she had slept without Matt since they were married, and it felt strange. She rolled onto her back and stared up at the ceiling wide-eyed, memories of the day crowding into her thoughts. She knew she would never fall asleep with so much to think about.

Then sunlight was dancing on the braided rug and someone was knocking on the door. Sarah leaped out of bed and fumbled on the bedside table for her watch.

"Get up, sleepyhead," Summer's voice rang out on the other side of the door.

"Come on in," Sarah called.

Summer entered, grinning. "Are you going to sleep all day while the rest of us work on your quilt?"

"Is everyone else up already?" Sarah ran a comb through her long hair and snatched up her shower bag.

Summer nodded. "Mom and I got up and went running early. She always does, rain or shine. The grounds are awesome. Mrs. Compson said to let you sleep until one of the showers was open. She said, and I quote, 'All of that mischief Sarah's been up to lately must have taken a lot out of her.' "

"That sounds like her." Sarah laughed. She hurried off to the shower while Summer joined the others downstairs.

As quickly as she could, Sarah showered, dressed, and went down to the kitchen, where the other quilters were talking and laughing over coffee, bagels, and fruit. After breakfast they returned to the ballroom to finish the quilt.

After they had been quilting and chatting for a while, Sarah looked around the quilt frame to Diane, Judy, Mrs. Emberly, and Gwen. "So," she said, changing the subject. "Did you guys have fun at quilt camp the other week?"

"Go on, tell us," Bonnie urged. "Mrs. Compson didn't get to hear you talk about it before."

Gwen launched into a vivid description of quilt camp, with the others occasionally speaking up to add a detail or share an anecdote. Sarah noted that Mrs. Compson seemed interested in the discussion, especially when Judy and Mrs. Emberly gushed about the new techniques they had learned in the different classes they had been able to take.

"Sounds like fun, doesn't it, Mrs. Compson?" Sarah asked when they had finished. To her satisfaction, Mrs. Compson agreed.

At noon they broke for a picnic lunch in the north gardens. Matt met them there, and after pulling Sarah aside for a kiss and murmuring "I missed you last night" in her ear, he proceeded to badger the quilters with questions about this mysterious surprise for which an overnight party was necessary. He pretended to be crushed when they refused to divulge the secret, but they knew he was only teasing them. After a lunch of chicken salad sandwiches, fruit, and iced tea, Matt led them on a tour of the gardens, explaining the restorations he and his coworkers had completed so successfully.

Before long Matt left for the orchards and the quilters returned to the ballroom. While the others put the last quilting stitches in Sarah's sampler, Gwen and Summer created a long strip of binding for the raw edges of the quilt by cutting a large square of the cream fabric into two triangles, then seaming them together so that they formed an offset tube from which they cut the narrow bias strip.

Then Sarah finished quilting the last section of the last design.

Mrs. Emberly, Mrs. Compson, and Bonnie removed the quilt from the frame and spread it flat on the dance floor. While Sarah carefully trimmed the backing and batting even with the edges of the quilt top, Diane folded the long binding strip in half, wrong sides facing inward, and pressed it with a hot iron so the crease would stay. She explained to Sarah that doubling over the strip increased its durability, which was important because the edges of a quilt experienced so much wear and tear. When that task was completed, the others relaxed on the veranda while Mrs. Compson showed Sarah how to sew the binding strip around the edges of the top of the quilt with the sewing machine. Sarah had to pull out stitches and try again when it came to mitering the binding at the corners, but in the end she was pleased with the results.

Sarah and Mrs. Compson carried the nearly finished quilt outside, where the others had arranged their chairs in a rectangle on the shady veranda. After a debate over whether blind stitches or whip stitches were best—the blind stitch advocates won—they showed Sarah how to fold the binding strip over the raw edges of the quilt and sew it to the quilt back. Each quilter worked on her one-eighth of the quilt circumference until the raw edges were covered by the smooth strip of fabric.

Sarah thought the quilt was finished, but to her surprise, the others flipped the quilt over to the back and turned to Summer. The youngest quilter reached into her sewing kit and pulled out a rectangular patch trimmed in blue, which she placed in Sarah's lap.

"What's this?" Sarah asked, lifting the piece and examining it. There were words printed on the right side, and she read them aloud:

SARAH'S SAMPLER
Pieced by Sarah Mallory McClure
and Sylvia Bergstrom Compson

Quilted by the Tangled Web Quilters

August 3, 1996
Elm Creek Manor, Waterford, Pennsylvania

"It's a tag to sew on the back," Summer explained. "I ironed some fabric to freezer paper and ran it through my laser printer. That printing won't wash out."

Sarah gave her a grateful smile. "Thanks, Summer. Thanks a lot." She looked around at her friends' smiling faces. "That goes for all of you. I can't thank you enough for all your help."

"Well, sew on the tag so we can declare this quilt officially finished," Diane urged.

Using an appliqué stitch, Sarah attached the tag to the back of the quilt in the lower-left-hand corner. She tied off the thread and rose, holding two corners of the quilt in outstretched arms. Mrs. Compson and Summer each took another corner, and the three women held the quilt open between them. The others stepped forward to look.

Sarah's first quilt was finished, and it was beautiful.

Judy began to applaud and cheer, and the rest joined in.

"You just finished your first quilt, Sarah," Bonnie said. "How do you feel?"

"Tired," Sarah quipped, and the others laughed. Sarah realized she felt a little sad, too. She almost wished she hadn't finished the quilt, because now she wouldn't be able to work on it anymore.

"What are you going to do for an encore?" Diane asked.

"I don't know," Sarah said, then Mrs. Compson caught her eye. She was standing with an arm around Mrs. Emberly, smiling proudly at her student. Then again, maybe the perfect project already awaited her. Somewhere inside Elm Creek Manor there was a memorial quilt that needed to be completed.

It was almost four o'clock when the Tangled Web Quilters finished gathering their things and loading their cars. They left thanking Mrs. Compson for the wonderful party and hoping they could do it again sometime. Mrs. Compson and Sarah stood on the back steps and waved to their departing guests as they drove away.

Then they returned inside and started cleaning up the mess.

As Sarah finished washing the dishes, Mrs. Compson entered the kitchen carrying the last bundle of linens. "I'll drop this off in the laundry room, but then let's go sit outside on the veranda for a while. I'll worry about the rest of this tomorrow."

Sarah drained the sink, dried her hands, and followed her outside. Mrs. Compson eased herself into one of the Adirondack chairs with a sigh. Sarah sat beside her on the floor and leaned back against the chair. Not speaking, they enjoyed the peaceful stillness of the sun-splashed front lawn and the distant forest, broken only by the soothing waterfall sound of the fountain and the music of songbirds.

Then Sarah decided that she wasn't likely to find a better time to speak. She turned and looked up at Mrs. Compson.

"About that better offer I'm supposed to think up," she said. "I can put on one of my interview suits and give you a formal proposal with visual aids and the works, or I can just tell you what I have in mind right now, as is. Which method would you prefer?"

Twenty-Nine

This will do," Mrs. Compson said, folding her hands in her lap.

Sarah rose and took the seat beside her. "You're an art teacher, correct?"

"If thirty years in the Allegheny County School District count for anything, yes."

"And you enjoyed giving that lecture for Gwen's class, the party this weekend, and teaching me how to quilt, right?"

Mrs. Compson nodded. "Especially your lessons."

"So I can conclude that you find fulfillment in many ways, three of the most significant being quilting, teaching, and being with people you care about, am I right?"

"You demonstrate wisdom beyond your humble years."

"Thank you. I try. I also noticed that you paid particular attention to the Tangled Web Quilters' conversation about the quilt camp they recently attended."

"Certainly. It sounded as if they had a marvelous time, and what an opportunity to interact with other quilters and perfect one's craft. Sensible critiques of one's work are a crucial part of any artist's development. Perhaps next year you and I could—" She inclined her head to one side, eyes narrowing. "Hmm. Are you about to propose what I think you're about to propose?"

Quickly, before Mrs. Compson could voice any doubts, Sarah launched into a description of her plan to turn Elm Creek Manor into a year-round quilters' retreat where artists and amateurs alike could share their knowledge and their love for quilting.

Nationally known quilters could be brought in to teach special programs and seminars, while Mrs. Compson and other members of the permanent staff would provide most of the instruction. Sarah would handle all of the accounting and marketing matters just as she had done at her previous job.

She presented the financial details and legal requirements she had investigated, showing, she hoped, that they had the resources and the abilities to make the project work. Getting the project under way would be neither easy nor quick, but before long Elm Creek Manor could become a haven for the quilter who longed for a place in which to create—if only for a week, a month, or a summer at a time. Mrs. Compson would be involved in the activities she loved most, and best of all, Elm Creek Manor would be alive again.

When she finished her proposal, Sarah studied Mrs. Compson's face for some sign of her inclinations, but Mrs. Compson merely gazed off at the distant trees.

Finally she spoke. "It sounds like a lovely dream, Sarah, but you've never even been to quilt camp. How do you even know you'd care for it?"

How could anyone not care for it? "Okay, that's true enough, but I've done a lot of research and I plan to do more. You and I could attend a few sessions together and talk to their directors and their participants. We should also talk to the quilters who don't attend and find out what's been missing. I'm willing to invest all the time and energy it takes. That's how much I believe in this."

Mrs. Compson still looked doubtful. "That's all well and good, but I fear you may be confusing running a quilters' retreat with attending one. I thought you hated accounting and all things business. I wouldn't want you to start a new business for my sake, only to find yourself unhappy in your work."

"I don't hate accounting, and I wouldn't be unhappy." That was the least of Sarah's worries. "What I disliked about my old job was the sense that I was just going through the motions, plugging in the numbers and spitting out sums, and none of it mattered. I wanted my work to have some—some relevance. I wanted it to mean something." She struggled to explain how she felt, how she had been feeling for so long. "This would matter. We would be creating something special. I would have a purpose here."

Mrs. Compson nodded, and to Sarah her expression seemed less skeptical, if only by the smallest degree. "What about teachers for these classes? I couldn't teach them all myself, and although you're a fine quilter, you're not quite ready for that yet."

"I've already spoken to the Tangled Web Quilters. Mrs. Emberly would be able to teach appliqué, Diane could teach introductory piecing classes, Bonnie could teach some of her Celtic knotwork and clothing classes here in addition to those at her shop, and you could handle the advanced piecing and quilting sections. If it turns out we need more help, we can always hire someone by advertising in quilt magazines, or better yet, we could find someone local through the Waterford Quilting Guild."

"Hmph." Mrs. Compson drummed her fingers on the arm of her chair. "I spot one fundamental flaw in your plan."

Sarah's heart sank. "What's that?" She had been sure she had covered everything. "If you don't want to risk your own capital, I'm sure we can find investors."

"That's not it. I'm certainly not about to use someone else's money for something I can well afford on my own." She sighed. "It's another matter altogether. I don't think you considered how difficult it would be for me to take care of so many overnight guests by myself. I can't be running up and down stairs at everyone's beck and call all the time."

"I guess I see your point."

"There's only one solution, of course. You'll have to move in, and you can be at everyone's beck and call instead."

"Move in here? To Elm Creek Manor?"

"I can see if the playhouse is still standing, if you'd prefer it. Naturally, I'd expect you to bring Matthew along. Yes, I see no other way around this problem except having you move in, and I'm afraid that's one condition I must insist upon, so if you don't want to live here—"

Sarah laughed and held up her hands. "You don't have to talk me into it. I'd be thrilled to live here."

"Very well, then. But you should check with Matthew before packing your things."

"I have a condition of my own."

Mrs. Compson raised her eyebrows. "So, this is to be a negotiation, is it?"

"You could call it that. My condition is that you have to have a phone line installed so our clients can contact us." Sarah rubbed her wrinkled, waterlogged hands together. "And a dishwasher."

"That's two conditions. But very well. Agreed. And now I have another requirement." She gave Sarah a searching look. "You may not like it."

"Go ahead."

"I don't know what kind of conflict stands between you and your mother, but you must promise me you'll talk to her and do your best to resolve it. Don't be a stubborn fool like me and let grudges smolder and relationships die."

"I don't think you know how difficult that will be."

"I don't pretend to know, but I can guess. I don't expect miracles. All I ask is that you learn from my mistakes and try."

Sarah took a deep breath and slowly let it out. "All right. If that's one of your conditions, I'll try. I can't promise you that anything will come of it, but I'll try, Mrs. Compson."

"That's good enough for me. And if we're going to be partners, I must insist that you call me Sylvia. We'll have no more of this Mrs. Compson this and Mrs. Compson that. You needn't be so formal."

For a moment Sarah thought Mrs. Compson was teasing her. "But you told me to call you Mrs. Compson. Remember?"

"I said no such thing."

"Yes, you did, the first day we met."

"Did I?" Mrs. Compson frowned, thinking. "Hmph. Well, perhaps I did, but that was a long time ago, and a great deal has happened since then."

"I couldn't agree more." Sarah smiled. "Okay. Sylvia it is."

"Good." Mrs. Compson sighed and shook her head. "An artists' colony. Sounds like something right out of my college days." She sat lost in thought for what seemed to Sarah to be the longest silence she had ever had to endure.

Say yes. Just say yes. Sarah clenched her hands together in her lap. *Please please please please—*

"I suppose all that's left is for us to select a name for our fledgling company."

Sarah felt as if she would burst. "Does that mean yes?"

Mrs. Compson turned to Sarah and held out her hand. Her eyes were shining. "That means yes."

Sarah let out a whoop of delight and shook Mrs. Compson's hand. Mrs. Compson burst into laughter and hugged her.

As they sat on the veranda brainstorming, Sarah's heart sang with excitement. Mrs. Compson seemed even more delighted, if that were possible. Sarah suspected that, like her, Mrs. Compson could already envision the beautiful quilts and the strengthened spirits of their creators bringing the manor to life once more.

The first question was easily settled—the name for their quilters' haven. Elm Creek Quilts.

ROUND ROBIN

AN ELM CREEK QUILTS NOVEL

Acknowledgments

My heartfelt thanks go out to

My agent, Maria Massie.

The people at Simon & Schuster who worked on this project, especially
my gifted editor, Denise Roy; her assistant, Brenda Copeland;
and publicists Elizabeth Hayes and Rebecca Davis.

My online quilting friends, especially the members
of R.C.T.Q., QuiltNet, and QuiltersBee.

Carol Coski and Terry Grant, who shared their experiences
of a quilt shop owner's life.

The members of the Internet Writing Workshop, especially
Christine Johnson, Candace Byers, Dave Swinford,
Jody Ewing, and everyone in the Lounge.

Geraldine, Nic, and Heather Neidenbach; Virginia and
Edward Riechman; Leonard and Marlene Chiaverini; and
my extended family in Cincinnati and elsewhere.

Most of all, I wish to thank my beloved husband, Marty,
whose love and faith sustain me.

For

Martin Chiaverini,

Geraldine Neidenbach,

Nic Neidenbach,

and

Heather Neidenbach,

with all my love

One

In a few months, spring would turn the land surrounding Elm Creek Manor into a green patchwork quilt of dark forested hills and lighter farmers' fields and grassy lawns. After last night's snowstorm, however, the view from the kitchen window resembled a white whole-cloth quilt, stitched with the winding gravel road to Waterford, the bare, brown tree limbs, and a thin trace of blue where the creek cut through the woods. The barn stood out in the distance, a cheerful splash of red against the snow.

So much about Elm Creek Manor had changed, but not the view from the window over the sink. If not for the stiffness in her hands and the way the winter chill had seeped into her bones, Sylvia could convince herself that the past fifty years had never happened. She could imagine herself a young woman again, as if any moment she would hear her younger brother whistling as he came downstairs for breakfast. She would look up and see her elder sister entering the kitchen, tying on an apron. Sylvia would gaze through the window and see a lone figure trudging through the snow from the barn, returning to his home and his bride after completing the morning chores. She would leave her work and hurry to the back door to meet him, her footsteps quick and light, her heart full. Her husband was there and alive again, as was her brother, as was her sister, and together they would laugh at the grief of their long separation.

Sylvia squeezed her eyes shut and listened.

She heard a clock ticking in the west sitting room off the kitchen and then, distantly, the sound of someone descending the grand staircase in the front foyer. For a moment her breath caught in her throat, and she almost believed she had accomplished the impossible. She had willed herself back in time, and now, armed with the wisdom of hindsight and regret, she could set everything to rights. All the years that had been stolen from them were restored, and they would live them out together. Not a single moment would be wasted.

"Sylvia?" someone called out from down the hall.

It was a woman's voice, one she had come to know well over the past two years. Sylvia opened her eyes, and the ghosts receded to the past, to memory. In another moment Sarah appeared in the kitchen doorway, smiling.

"The Elm Creek Quilters are here," Sarah said. "I saw their cars coming up the back drive."

Sylvia rinsed the last coffee cup and placed it in the dishwasher. "It's about time. They'd be very disappointed if they missed the show." She caught the smile Sarah tried to hide. Sarah often teased Sylvia for her insistence on punctuality, but Sylvia had no intention of changing her opinion. She knew, even if Sarah and the six other Elm Creek Quilters didn't, the value of a minute.

Sarah gave Sylvia a look of affectionate amusement. "The show won't start for twenty minutes, at least," she said as they went to the back door to greet their friends. They had called themselves the Tangled Web Quilters when Sylvia and Sarah had joined the bee nearly two years before, but together they adopted the new name to symbolize the creation of a new group and to celebrate the beginning of their business, Elm Creek Quilts.

Gwen and Summer entered first, laughing together like no mother and daughter Sylvia had ever known. Bonnie followed close behind, carrying a large cardboard box. "I cleared out a storage room at the shop last night," Bonnie told them. "I've got scraps, leftover ribbon, and some thread that's been discontinued. I thought we could use it when classes start up again in March."

Sarah thanked her, took the box, and placed it on the floor out of the way. Bonnie owned Grandma's Attic, Waterford's only quilt shop. Elm Creek Quilts ordered material and notions through her, and in return Bonnie gave them any leftovers or irregulars that couldn't be sold. Sylvia admired Bonnie's generosity, which had not lessened even after the new chain fabric store on the outskirts of town opened and began steadily siphoning away her income.

Diane entered just in time to overhear Bonnie's words. "You should let us root through that box first," she said, holding the door open for Agnes. "I can always use a bit of extra fabric, especially if it's free."

"Did you hear that?" Gwen asked Bonnie, as Judy entered, holding the hand of her three-year-old daughter, Emily. "Better turn on the security cameras next time you let Diane help in the shop."

Diane looked puzzled. "You have security cameras? I never noticed any." When the others began to chuckle, she grew indignant. "Not that I had any reason to look."

Gwen's eyebrows rose. "Sounds to me like you have a guilty conscience."

The hallway rang with laughter, and Sylvia's heart soared as she looked around the circle of women. She had welcomed them into her home, first as friends and later as business colleagues. In her heart, though, she would always consider them family. Not that they could replace the family she had lost more than fifty years before—no one could do that—but they were a great comfort, nonetheless.

The new arrivals were breathless with excitement and red-cheeked from the cold. They put their coats away in the hall closet and soon were settling into the formal parlor. Sarah took a seat on the sofa beside Sylvia's chair. "Didn't I promise you someday you'd be glad we got cable?" she said as she turned on the television.

"Indeed you did," Sylvia said. "But I'll reserve judgment until after the show."

"Sarah's going to drag you kicking and screaming into the twenty-first century if it's the last thing she does," Gwen said.

"She most certainly will not," Sylvia retorted. "I have more dignity than that. I'll move along calmly and quietly, thank you."

Emily squirmed on Judy's lap. "I want to sit by Sarah."

"Sarah wants to see this show," Judy told her. "Maybe later she can play."

"That's okay. Emily can sit here if she likes." Sarah slid over and patted the seat beside her. "I haven't seen her in two days. We have lots to talk about."

Emily jumped down from her mother's lap and ran across the room to Sarah, who laughed and helped her climb onto the sofa.

"When are you going to have one of your own?" Diane asked.

Sarah rolled her eyes. "You sound like my mother."

"You can't wait forever, you know."

"I realize that." Sarah shot Diane a quick frown before putting her arm around Emily. Emily giggled and smiled up at her. Sylvia caught the fragrance of baby shampoo and something else, something sweet and fresh beneath it, and she wondered why Sarah, who used to speak confidently about having children someday, had not said a word on the subject in months. Perhaps the couple had decided against having children, or perhaps they had no choice. Sylvia didn't want to pry, but her heart was troubled for Sarah and Matt, and she wished she knew how to help them.

"Where is Matthew, anyway?" Sylvia wondered aloud.

"He's inspecting the orchards for storm damage," Sarah said. "He said he'd try to make it back in time for the show, but . . ." She shrugged.

"He can't miss this," Judy protested.

"He won't. There's a new tape in the VCR." Sarah smiled, tight-lipped. "You know how he is about those trees. Besides, he was here for the filming last fall, and that was the exciting part, right?"

Nonsense, Sylvia wanted to say, but she kept quiet.

"The show's starting," Summer announced, taking the remote from Sarah. Sylvia saw their eyes meet, and something passed between them. Whatever it was, it made Sarah relax, and so Sylvia did as well. Summer was an exceptional young woman—optimistic and empathetic, and more thoughtful than most people her age. Sylvia would miss her when she went off to graduate school in the fall. The young couldn't help growing up and wanting to make their own ways through life, but Summer would be the first Elm Creek Quilter to leave their circle, and they would not feel whole without her.

Sylvia pushed the thoughts to the back of her mind, choosing instead to focus on the television. As the theme music played, a familiar man with graying hair and a red-and-black flannel coat appeared on the screen and walked across a gravel road toward the camera, a snowy cornfield in the background.

"Good morning, friends," the man said. "I'm Grant Richards."

"He looks better on TV than in person," Diane said.

Grant Richards smiled out at them. "Welcome to *America's Back Roads,* the show that takes you down the road less traveled to the heart of America, to the small towns where old-fashioned values still endure, where life goes on at a slower pace, where friends are friends for life, where the frantic clamor of the city ventures no closer than the evening news."

Gwen grinned. "Apparently he's never seen campus during Freshman Orientation."

"He's right about one thing, though," Judy said. "Around here, friends are friends for life."

"Hmph." Sylvia frowned at the screen. "I don't care for his folksy posturing. He makes it sound like we're a bunch of hayseeds out in the middle of nowhere."

"We are in the middle of nowhere," Agnes pointed out, and no one contradicted her.

Grant continued. "This Sunday morning we're traveling through the snow-covered hills of Pennsylvania, where you'll meet a man who makes musical instruments out of old auto parts, a Tony Award–winning actress who abandoned the bright lights of Broadway to become a high school drama teacher, and a group of quilters dedicated to passing on their craft, warming toes and hearts alike in a place called Elm Creek Manor."

The Elm Creek Quilters burst into cheers and applause.

Emily looked up at Sarah, puzzled. "We're last?"

"Probably," Sarah told her. "We won't have to wait too long, though." Emily's face fell anyway, and Sarah laughed and kissed her on the top of her head.

The excitement in the room built through the first two segments. The weeks between the arrival of the producer's first letter and the final wrap had passed swiftly compared to the months they had waited for this moment. Sylvia could hardly keep still. If she were almost three years old like Emily, she, too, would be bouncing up and down in her seat, but she settled for drumming her fingers on the arm of her chair.

Then, finally, it was time.

"There's Elm Creek Manor," Agnes said, just as the rest of them saw it. Grant Richards was walking up the front drive as he told the audience about Elm Creek Quilts, the business founded by Sylvia Compson and Sarah McClure, two women from Waterford.

"Sarah isn't really from Waterford," Diane said. "She moved here."

The others shushed her.

"After months of preparation, Elm Creek Quilts welcomed their first guests." Grant's voice-over kept pace with a montage of scenes: quilters arriving at the manor, moving into their rooms, attending quilt classes, laughing and chatting as they strolled through the grounds.

Then Sylvia appeared on-screen, Sarah by her side. "We wanted to create a place where quilters of all backgrounds and skill levels could come to quilt, to make new friends, to practice old skills and learn new ones," Sylvia explained. "Quilters can come for a weekly quilt camp or they can rent a room for as long as they like and work independently. Beginning and intermediate quilters usually prefer the former; advanced quilters, the latter."

Unconsciously, Sylvia sat up straight and touched her hair, pleased. She did look very smart there on the television in that nice blue skirt and blazer Sarah had insisted she purchase for the occasion. Her friends looked very nice, too, she thought, watching as the camera showed the Elm Creek Quilters sitting around a quilt frame, answering Grant's questions as they worked. Sylvia couldn't help smiling at the sight. They all looked so cheerful, so companionable.

On-screen, Grant admired Judy's red-and-white Feathered Star quilt in the frame. "I guess you finish a quilt much faster when you all work on it together, right?"

"That's exactly so," Agnes said.

"That's not what's most important about working around the quilting frame, however," Gwen said to the camera.

"Get ready, everyone," Diane said, watching. "The professor is about to expound." The real-life Gwen threw a pillow at her.

On-screen, Gwen's expression had grown serious. "The quilting frame speaks to something deep within the woman's soul. Too often, work in modern society isolates us in offices or cubicles. We speak to people on the phone or through the computer rather than face-to-face. The essential element of human contact has been lost. The quilting frame, on the other hand, draws us back together, back into a community."

Gwen wrinkled her nose at the television. "Do I really sound that pompous when I talk?"

"Yes," Diane said, throwing the pillow back at her.

Sylvia held up a hand. "That is a throw pillow, but let's not take the name quite so literally, shall we?"

Gwen's speech played on. "Women's work used to be much more communal, as when the entire village would gather food together, as when the women would all go down to the river together and do the laundry by pounding the clothes on rocks."

The camera caught Summer looking up from her quilting, her eyes wide and innocent. "That's how they did it when you were a girl, right, Mom?"

Both on-screen and off, the Elm Creek Quilters laughed.

Even Grant chuckled before resuming the interview. "But what about you? How did you learn to quilt? There were no Elm Creek Quilters around to teach you as you now teach others."

"My mother taught me," Sylvia responded.

"And Sylvia, in turn, taught me." Agnes gave her a sidelong glance. "Or at least she tried to."

"My mom taught me," Summer said.

Grant looked around the circle. "So most of you learned from your mothers, is that it?"

All but Sarah nodded. "Not me," she declared. "I mean, please. The idea of my mother quilting. . . ." She laughed and shook her head. "I don't even think she knows which end of the needle to thread."

On-screen, the Elm Creek Quilters smiled, but in the parlor, they didn't.

"Oh, dear," Agnes said.

"It seemed funnier at the time," Bonnie said, looking from the television to Sarah, who sat rigid and still on the edge of the sofa.

"I didn't know they filmed that part," she said.

Diane shot her a look of disbelief. "That little red light on the camera didn't clue you in?"

"I thought they had stopped filming by then. Really." Her eyes met Sylvia's. "Really," she insisted, as if something in Sylvia's expression conveyed doubt.

"I believe you," Sylvia said, although she wondered.

"What'll your mom say when she sees this?" Summer asked.

"Maybe she won't see it," Sarah said.

"Of course she'll see it," Agnes said. "No mother would miss her daughter on national television."

Sarah said nothing, but her expression was resolute, as if she had seized a thin thread of hope and had no intention of letting go.

Then the phone rang.

Agnes was closest, so she answered. "Good morning, Elm Creek Quilts." A pause. "No, I'm Sylvia's sister-in-law, Agnes. Would you like to speak to her?" A longer pause. "Sarah? Yes, Sarah's here." Her eyes went wide. "Oh, yes, hello. I've heard so much about you." She threw Sarah a helpless look. "Why, yes, I'll get her. Hold on, please." She held out the phone to Sarah. "It's your mother."

Sarah dragged herself out of her seat, took the phone and the receiver, and carried them as far toward the doorway as the cord would permit. Watching her, Summer fingered the remote as if unsure whether to lower the volume so that Sarah could hear her mother better or turn up the sound to give Sarah some semblance of privacy.

Sylvia turned back to the television and pretended to concentrate on the show. The other Elm Creek Quilters followed suit, but Sylvia doubted they were paying any more attention than she herself was.

"Hi, Mother. . . . Yes. I know. I know. I'm sorry, but—" Sarah winced and held the receiver away from her ear for a moment. "Look, I said I was sorry. . . . I didn't know the camera was on. . . . Of course that makes a difference." A pause. "Well, so what? I didn't mention you by name or anything. . . . It's not an excuse. It's the truth." Silence. "I said I was sorry. It was just a joke. Summer told a joke about her mom, and so I—" Sarah's mouth tightened. "I do not. That's unfair, Mother." Her face went scarlet. "He would not. Dad would never say such a thing. I'm sorry, okay? I'm sorry. What else do I have to do? . . . I can't apologize on national television and you know it." Silence. "Fine. If that's the way you feel, have it your way." She slammed down the phone and stormed across the room to return it to the table.

"How did it go?" Diane asked.

Sarah shot her a dark glare and flung herself onto the sofa. "How do you think?"

Emily didn't recognize the sarcasm. "Bad?" she guessed, looking up at Sarah with wide eyes.

Sarah softened and snuggled her close. "Not so bad," she assured her, but she gave the others a look that told them otherwise. "She'll never let this one go. Never. She's convinced I made her look like a fool."

"Well . . ." Summer hesitated. "You kind of did."

"Not intentionally," Sarah protested. "She thinks I did it on purpose, just to humiliate her. Honestly. She's so self-absorbed. She thinks everything's about her."

"Hmph," Sylvia said, thinking.

Sarah turned to her. "For goodness' sake, Sylvia, what's 'Hmph' supposed to mean?"

Sylvia refused to be baited. "Don't lash out at me, young lady. I'm not the one you're angry at, and neither is your mother." To her satisfaction, Sarah's anger wavered. "You know your words were thoughtless and silly, just as you know your mother's feelings are justified. You're embarrassed and ashamed, and rightfully so. If I were your mother, I would have given you an earful, too."

Sarah sank back into the sofa, defeated. "If you were my mother, none of this would have happened."

"Now, now," Sylvia said. "You'll put things right. Take an hour or so to cool down, then get back on that phone and apologize."

"I did apologize."

"I mean apologize sincerely."

Sarah shook her head. "I can't. You don't know her like I do. There's no use talking to her when she's this upset."

"Call her tomorrow, then."

"I can't." Sarah rose. "You don't understand."

"Explain it to us," Gwen said. "We'll listen. We want to understand."

But Sarah just shook her head and left the room.

"What should we do?" Judy asked.

"Nothing," Diane said. "We should stay out of it."

"There must be some way we can help." Summer looked around the circle of friends anxiously. "Isn't there?"

No one could answer her.

The show had ended, though no one had seen the last half of their segment. Sylvia considered rewinding the tape they had made for Matt and playing the last part, but decided against it. Already the Elm Creek Quilters were getting to their feet, preparing to leave. She would save the tape for another day.

Later, when she was alone, Sylvia mulled over the morning's events as she quilted in the west sitting room. She thought of a promise Sarah had made to her nearly two years before as they sat on the front veranda negotiating their agreement to launch a new business together.

"I don't know what kind of conflict stands between you and your mother," Sylvia had said, "but you must promise me you'll talk to her and do your best to resolve it. Don't be a stubborn fool like me and let grudges smolder and relationships die."

The unexpected request had clearly caught Sarah by surprise. "I don't think you know how difficult that will be."

"I don't pretend to know, but I can guess. I don't expect miracles. All I ask is that you learn from my mistakes and try."

Sarah had given her a long, steady look, and for a moment Sylvia had been certain that she would refuse and that their agreement to create Elm Creek Quilts would founder on this one point. Sylvia had been tempted to tell Sarah she would take back the condition, but she held fast, determined to see to it that Sarah would learn from her older friend's mistakes and not have to endure the hard lessons of a lifetime, if she could be spared them.

Her patience had been rewarded.

"All right," Sarah had said at last. "If that's one of your conditions, I'll try. I can't promise you that anything will come of it, but I'll try."

Nearly two years had come and gone since Sarah had spoken those words, and what had she to show for it? Sylvia let her hands fall to her lap, still holding her quilting. She sat there for a long while, lost in thought.

So many things could go wrong, she knew. But life carried no guarantees for anyone. That couldn't keep one paralyzed, fearing to act. That was no way to live.

Once Sylvia made up her mind, she saw no reason to wait. She put her quilting aside and went to the parlor, where she eased the door shut so she could make her call in privacy.

Two

Spring came to the hills of central Pennsylvania early that year. By mid-March, buds had formed on the stately elm trees lining the road to ElmCreek Manor, where Sarah, Sylvia, and the other Elm Creek Quilters waited for the first group of campers of the season to arrive. Sarah was pleased that Sylvia had agreed to direct their guests to the front entrance rather than the back.

"But parking is behind the manor," Sylvia had argued at first. "They'll only have to move their cars later."

"We'll do it for them, like valet parking. This way they won't have to carry their luggage all the way from the back door to the foyer for registration." Sarah didn't tell Sylvia she was more concerned about the first impression the quilters formed of Elm Creek Manor. She knew how they would feel as they approached in their cars, in groups and alone: first the gray stone manor itself would strike them, strong and serene in a sea of green grass. Then they would notice the wide veranda running the length of the building, lined with tall columns supporting a roof that bathed the veranda in cool shade. As they drew closer, they would see the two stone staircases that arced away from each other as they descended from the veranda. Their cars would come to a stop at the foot of those stairs in the driveway, which encircled a fountain in the shape of a rearing horse, the symbol of the Bergstrom family, the founders of Elm Creek Manor.

But Sarah didn't tell Sylvia this. Sylvia was pragmatic, not sentimental. Fortunately, Sarah's argument about carrying luggage through the house convinced her. Sarah could hardly keep from grinning as one quilter after another stepped out of her car, awestruck and thrilled that she would be able to spend a week in such a grand place.

"That makes eight," Judy said as the latest arrival took her room key and followed Matt upstairs. As caretaker of Elm Creek Manor, he spent most of his time maintaining the grounds and the building, but on check-in days, he carried bags and parked cars. The Elm Creek Quilters took turns sitting behind the registration desk and directing cars up the driveway. There wasn't really enough work to keep them all busy, but they thought it better, friendlier, to have everyone there on the first day to welcome their guests.

Sylvia checked her clipboard. "Four more to go, unless we have a cancellation." Her gaze returned to the wall opposite the front doors.

"What are you thinking about?" Sarah asked her. Sylvia had been uncharacteristically quiet that day, and she had been studying the wall above the entrance to the banquet hall off and on throughout registration.

Sylvia walked to the center of the foyer. "It occurred to me that this wall is the first thing our guests see when they enter the manor, as they look up to climb the stairs." She gestured, showing them the straight line from the twelve-foot double doors to the wall just beneath the balcony. "Our guests ought to see something a trifle more attractive than a bare wall when they arrive. We ought to have a quilt hanging there." She tapped her chin with a finger. "Perhaps one of my old quilts will do."

Summer joined Sylvia in the center of the room and contemplated the wall. "We could hang Sarah's sampler there, if she's willing to give it up. That's the quilt that brought us together."

"You'd have to fight Matt for it," Sarah said. She had given him her first quilt as an anniversary present nearly two years before, and he treasured it. She wondered if he knew how much that pleased her.

Sylvia shook her head. "We can't rob Matthew of his quilt. We'll have to think of something else."

"You know what else we need? A motto." Gwen held up her hands as if framing a sign. "Elm Creek Quilts: Where something something something."

Diane's eyebrows rose. "What kind of motto is 'Something something something'?"

"That's not the motto. That's just an example."

Judy spoke up. "How about 'Elm Creek Quilts: Where you can quilt till you wilt.' "

The others chuckled, but Agnes shook her head. "I don't think it quite fits. We want people to rejuvenate their spirits here, not work themselves into exhaustion."

"I've got one," Diane said. "Elm Creek Quilts: Where hand-quilting is celebrated and machine-quilting tolerated—sort of."

"That's your motto, not Elm Creek Quilts', " Bonnie said, laughing.

"Oh, yeah? Well, I have a motto for you. 'Bonnie Markham, whose phone is busy twenty-four hours a day, especially when friends are trying to call to see if she needs a ride to Elm Creek Manor.' "

"That's rather cumbersome for a motto," Sylvia remarked.

"My phone isn't busy twenty-four hours a day," Bonnie protested. "Just when Craig's on the internet."

"Exactly," Diane said. "Twenty-four hours a day."

Bonnie sighed and shook her head.

Gwen grinned. "My motto is 'When God made men, it was to prove She had a sense of humor.' "

Summer rolled her eyes. "Then mine will be 'Forgive our mothers, for they know not what they say.' "

Sarah figured that Summer's motto would be a good one for herself, except for that part about forgiveness.

"What about—" Bonnie said, just as the front door swung open and a new guest entered. Before they finished with her registration, two more arrived, and they forgot about bare walls and mottoes in the bustle of activity.

It wasn't until Sylvia was engrossed in conversation with one of the last guests that Agnes beckoned the other Elm Creek Quilters. "I think we should make Sylvia a round robin quilt for that wall," she said, keeping her voice low so that Sylvia wouldn't overhear.

"What's a round robin quilt?" Sarah asked, picturing a circular quilt with birds appliquéd in the center.

"It's a quilt made by a group of friends," Bonnie explained. "Each quilter makes a center block and passes the block along to a friend, who passes her own block along to the next person in line, all the way around the circle. Then each quilter pieces a border and attaches it to the block she received."

"Then the blocks are passed on to the next person," Judy said. "Everyone adds another border and passes on the blocks, and so on, until everyone in the group has added something to each person's center block and everyone has her own quilt top back."

Diane looked dubious. "If we work on only one center block, it won't be a true round robin."

"Who died and made you the quilt police?" Gwen retorted.

"True round robin or not, I think it's a great idea." Bonnie glanced at Sylvia, who was calling Matt over to help a guest with her bags. "Are we going to try to make it a surprise? That won't be easy."

"We'll keep it a secret until the top is finished," Agnes decided. "Sylvia would want to quilt it with us. I'll volunteer to make the center. Who else wants to help?"

"I do," Sarah said.

The others chimed in their agreement, all but Summer, who shook her head. "I'll have to sit this one out. With finals coming up, and graduation, I don't see how I'd have the time. I'll help you quilt and bind it, though."

"And baste," Diane added. "Don't even think about sneaking out of that."

The women laughed, but they quickly smothered their mirth when Sylvia broke into the circle. "What are you all giggling about over here?" she asked.

"Nothing," Summer said, her eyes wide and innocent.

"Supper," Sarah said at the same time.

"You know us," Gwen quickly added. "Always thinking about our next meal."

"Hmph. That's true enough." Sylvia checked her clipboard. "After our last guest arrives, we'll get supper started."

"Did someone mention food? Is supper ready?" Matt said, returning from his latest trip upstairs, where all but one of their guests were settling into their rooms. He usually wore a baseball cap over his curly blond hair, a habit against which Sylvia fought a tireless campaign. Today, apparently, she had won.

"No, supper isn't ready yet." A smile played at the corners of Sylvia's mouth. "If we aren't moving quickly enough for you, you're welcome to go to the kitchen and get started."

She said it so comically that everyone laughed, and as Sarah joined in, she felt her heart glowing with a warmth and happiness she once only dreamed of possessing. She and Matt had struggled so long to find their way, first as newlyweds in State College, and then even after the move to Waterford, where getting settled had been more difficult than they had anticipated. How fortunate it was that she had accepted that temporary job helping Sylvia prepare her estate for auction. She never could have imagined how that simple decision would open up her life to new friends and new challenges. It was as if she had finally found her way home after a long journey.

Over the sound of her friends' laughter, Sarah heard the door open. "That makes twelve," she said, turning to greet the last new camper.

A middle-aged woman stood just inside the doorway, a suitcase in her hand. "Hello, Sarah." As the door closed behind her, she shifted her weight from one foot to the other and broke into a hesitant smile.

Sarah stared at her, unable to speak.

"Do you know her?" Summer murmured.

"Yes." Though sometimes Sarah felt she didn't know her at all. "She's my mother."

As one, the Elm Creek Quilters gasped—all but Sylvia, who deliberately avoided looking in Sarah's direction.

"Mom." Matt bounded across the marble floor and down the stairs leading to the front door. "How nice to see you." He took her suitcase and leaned forward to kiss her cheek.

She laughed self-consciously and endured the kiss. "Please, call me Carol."

Matt beamed, unaware of the slight, or ignoring it. Sarah felt a smoldering in her chest—astonishment, dismay, and the tiniest flicker of anger. "What are you doing here, Mother?"

Carol's smile faltered. "I came for a visit, of course. And for quilt camp."

"Quilt camp? You don't quilt."

Sylvia gave Sarah a sharp look. "Then there's no better place for her to learn."

"That's what I thought when I saw Elm Creek Quilts on *America's Back Roads*." Carol followed Matt to the registration desk, where Bonnie helped her sign in and gave her a room key. "You remember *America's Back Roads*, don't you, Sarah?"

Sarah nodded, unsure how to interpret her mother's nonchalance. Her mother looked thinner than she remembered, and her reddish brown hair hung past her shoulders. All the other campers had worn casual, comfortable clothing, but Carol had shown up in her usual conservative skirt and blouse.

Then Sarah noticed that Summer was giving her an odd look. "Aren't you going to go say hi or something?" she whispered.

Sarah nodded and forced herself to cross the foyer. Naturally, Summer would think it odd that she hadn't wrapped her mother in a great big welcoming hug the instant she crossed the threshold. Summer and Gwen liked each other, shared interests, were friends as well as mother and daughter. Sarah could only imagine what that felt like.

"Welcome to Elm Creek Manor, Mother," she said, her words as stiff and formal as the hug they exchanged. Perhaps it was her imagination, but it seemed her mother clung to her a moment longer than she used to, and held her tighter. Over the top of her mother's head, Sarah glimpsed Matt grinning broadly as he watched the embrace.

As Sarah pulled away, her mother took her hands. "You look good," she said, holding her daughter at arm's length. After further appraisal, she added, "I suppose if you'd known I was coming, you would have gotten a haircut."

Sarah gave her a tight smile. "I got my hair cut last week. Why didn't you tell me you were coming?" She almost said "warn" instead of "tell," but her friends' presence urged restraint.

"I thought it would be a nice surprise." Carol's smile mirrored Sarah's own. "Besides, if you'd known I was coming, you might have found some reason to leave town for the week."

"That's ridiculous. How can you say that?"

"Here, Mom—Carol." Matt touched his mother-in-law on the shoulder. "Let me show you to your room. You'll love it."

Carol gave Sarah one last inscrutable look before following Matt upstairs. Sarah watched them go, Matt gesturing with his free hand as he described her room, her mother listening and nodding. Only when they disappeared down the second-floor hallway did Sarah relax.

"Well," Sylvia said. "I suppose I'll get supper started."

"Not so fast." Sarah caught her by the arm before she could escape down the hallway. "So this is why you so generously offered to take care of the registration sheets this time."

Sylvia brushed her hand away. "There's no need to get angry."

"There is so. Why didn't you tell me she was coming?"

"Why? So you could cut your hair?"

"Of course not. So I could prepare."

"We did prepare, when we made the manor ready for our quilt campers."

"I mean prepare mentally." Sarah looked around the circle of friends. "I can't believe you didn't tell me. Were you all in on this?"

Summer's eyes widened and she shook her head. "I sure wasn't."

"We're just as surprised as you are," Judy said.

"Sarah, you know very well I kept this to myself." Sylvia's voice was brisk. "If I had told one Elm Creek Quilter, I would have been obligated to tell the others, and we all know Diane can't keep a secret."

"Hey," Diane protested.

"Now, we'll have no more of this pouting." Sylvia held Sarah by the shoulders and looked her squarely in the eye. "Your mother's here, and I expect you to treat her with respect befitting the woman who raised you."

"You have no idea how difficult this is going to be. We don't get along."

"So you've said, and so I've just seen for myself. That's no excuse. You made a promise to me, don't forget, a promise that you'd reconcile with your mother."

"I've tried." Sarah wanted to squirm out of Sylvia's grasp. Her gaze was too knowing, too determined. "We talk on the phone, and Matt and I visited her last Christmas—"

"For a mere three days, as I recall, and you speak on the phone once a month at best. That's hardly enough time to rebuild your relationship." Her voice softened. "Nearly two years since you made that promise, dear, and so little to show for it. After that television fiasco, I had to invite her. Don't you see? If she had waited for you to ask, she would be waiting forever."

"I'm sure you mean well, but you should have told me."

"Next time, I shall." Sylvia gave Sarah's arms an affectionate squeeze. "I promise."

Sarah nodded, hoping there wouldn't be a next time. Her stomach wrenched when she thought of what the week would bring—a constant stream of criticism about her hair, her clothes, her speech, her attitude, and anything else that caught her mother's attention. No matter how well Sarah lived her life, Carol seemed to think she herself would have done much better in her daughter's place. Sarah sensed but had never understood the urgency behind the criticism, as if Carol was preparing her daughter for some impending disaster she alone could foresee. Carol was so unlike Sarah's easygoing, indulgent father that Sarah often marveled that they had ever considered themselves compatible enough to marry.

Sarah knew her father would have liked Matt as much as Carol disliked him. If only he were there to keep Carol's criticism in check as he used to when Sarah was younger. If Carol got started on Matt—"that gardener," as she used to call him, and perhaps still did—she could aggravate Matt's growing concerns about his job at Elm Creek Manor. He loved the grounds, the gardens, the orchards, but recently he had begun to wonder if he should have stayed at his old firm instead of coming to work for Sylvia.

"But Exterior Architects assigned you to Elm Creek," Sarah had reminded him when he first brought it up. "You're doing the same work at the same place. What's the difference?"

"The difference is the source of my paycheck. Exterior Architects used to pay me. Now Sylvia does."

Sarah had stared at him, perplexed. A year ago he had been all too eager to have Sylvia buy out his contract. "What's wrong with that?"

"I don't feel comfortable investing our entire future in one place, that's all."

"Why not? Lots of people who own their own businesses do."

"That's my point. We don't own our own business. Sylvia owns it."

"Of course she owns it. It's her estate. But so what? You know she'd never fire us."

"Yeah, I know." He walked away, saying that he had to check on the orchards, or the north gardens, or the new greenhouse. Sarah didn't remember which excuse he had used that time.

Now he was escorting Carol to her room, where her litany of complaints would surely begin. The room would be too small, or too shabby, or too far from the bathroom, or too near. Matt would nod to be agreeable, and her words would strengthen his own misgivings about living in Elm Creek Manor.

At that thought, the joy Sarah usually felt at the beginning of quilt camp went out of the day.

She could hear the new guests talking and laughing upstairs as they went from room to room getting acquainted. It was time for the other Elm Creek Quilters to leave for the evening, to return to their homes and their other responsibilities. Sarah and Sylvia walked them to the back door, then went to the kitchen to prepare the evening meal.

Sylvia wanted to discuss the week's schedule as they worked, but Sarah found her mind wandering. Her thoughts drifted back to the day she told Carol she was dating Matt McClure. "What about Dave?" Carol asked, referring to Sarah's previous boyfriend, whom she had dated for more than a year.

Sarah wrapped the phone cord around her finger and took a deep breath to steel herself. "Actually, we kind of broke up."

"What?"

"We're still friends," Sarah hastened to say, though she knew that wouldn't appease her mother. In truth, Sarah hadn't seen him in weeks. She had put off telling Carol about the breakup, knowing how much her mother adored him. Dave had charmed Carol just as he did everyone else.

"Maybe if you apologize, he'll take you back."

"I don't want him back. And why do you assume that he broke up with me?"

"Because I know you're a smart young woman and you wouldn't let a great catch like Dave swim away."

"He isn't a fish, Mother." And he didn't get away; it had been all Sarah could do to send him away. It had been a struggle to convince him that she didn't want to see him anymore. "You'll like Matt. Just give him a chance."

"We'll see." Carol's voice was flat, and Sarah realized Carol was determined to despise him and wouldn't give him any opportunity to change her mind.

Sarah hung up the phone with a sigh. She couldn't really blame Carol for not seeing through Dave; after all, it had taken Sarah fourteen months to figure him out. But now she could see that he was all style, no substance. As a freshman she had been dazzled by his popularity, his expensive car, the luxurious lifestyle his parents had provided him, but in the weeks preceding the breakup, she had grown restless. Dave was charming and witty, handsome and athletic, but something was missing. He wouldn't allow anyone to bring him down with bad news or serious conversation, not even Sarah. With him she had to feign perpetual cheerfulness or lose his interest. Once when she needed to talk about a frustrating argument with her mother, she watched as his face went blank and he began to look over her shoulder for someone more pleasant to talk to. That was when Sarah understood that Dave kept her around not because he loved her—although perhaps he thought he did—but because she worked so hard to amuse him. She had learned early in their relationship that there were plenty of other women on campus who would pretend anything, hide anything, if it meant having his warm smile directed at them. But Sarah was tired of acting, of being onstage every moment they were together. She wanted someone who could love the real Sarah, with all her bad moods and faults.

After knowing Matt only a short while, she realized she had found that someone in him. He was kind and sensible, and though he didn't have Dave's charisma, he was handsome in a strong, unpolished kind of way, and he made Sarah feel valued. The first time they kissed, she learned that what she thought was love with Dave had not been love at all, or even a close approximation. Infatuation, yes; admiration, definitely. But not until Matt came into her life did Sarah truly know what it meant to love someone and be loved in return.

It would have been pointless to explain this to her mother. She was convinced that Sarah had traded in a pre-med student from a good family for a man whose ambition in life was to mow lawns and prune bushes. Even after she met him, Carol never saw Matt's solid core of strength and kindness, and never sensed how much he truly cared for Sarah. Those qualities made Matt worth two of Dave, with his roving eye and his refusal to plan anything more than a week in advance. Sarah saw this, but Carol couldn't, or refused to.

Carol evidently never gave up hoping that Sarah would change her mind, not even when Sarah told her she and Matt were getting married. Then Carol grew frantic. She warned Sarah that she would never be happy if she settled for a man like Matt. She begged Sarah to wait, to date other men, if only to be certain that she wasn't making a hasty decision. She offered Sarah a check—enough for a more lavish wedding than Sarah could afford or even wanted—if only Sarah would cancel the ceremony.

Sarah managed to hold her fury in check long enough to point out that Carol herself had chosen a man much like Matt. "Did you settle for Dad?" Sarah demanded. "Would you have let your parents buy your affection?"

"I didn't have your choices," Carol said.

"I've made my choice," Sarah said, and as far as she was concerned the matter was settled. But Carol wasn't willing to give up, and her appeals continued throughout the engagement.

Sarah had torn up and discarded the letters long ago, but she could still see them in her mind, page after page of her mother's small, neat handwriting on the Susquehanna Presbyterian Hospital letterhead she'd probably stolen from the receptionist's desk. "Marriage will change your life, and not for the better," Carol had written. "Twenty-three is too young. You should have a life of your own first. You could go anywhere, do anything, and you ought to do it now, while you're young. If you marry that gardener, you'll be stuck in some little town forever, and everything you ever wanted for yourself will be swallowed up in what you do for him."

Marriage was expensive, she argued in letter after letter. Sarah could forget about the little luxuries that made life bearable. If she took a job in an exciting city, she would come into contact with all sorts of eligible men, lawyers and doctors rather than overgrown boys who liked to dig around in the dirt. After a few years, while she was still young enough to look pretty in a wedding gown and bear children, she should consider marriage. But not now, and not to that gardener.

"I understand why you find him attractive," her mother had written. "But young people today don't have to be married to have sex. You can do that, if you must, and get it out of your system without ruining your chances with someone better. Besides, if you marry him, the sexual attraction will fade once the novelty wears off, and then where will you be?"

Carol's signature followed, as if anyone else could have written such a hateful letter. There was a postscript, but Sarah's hands trembled, rattling the paper so that the words blurred and she could barely make them out: "Please know that my feelings are specifically about you and your friend. They are not a reflection of my relationship with your father. We had a happy, loving marriage that ended too soon."

At once, Sarah had snatched up the phone and dialed her mother's number. When she answered, Sarah didn't return her greeting. "Don't you ever, ever spew such filth about Matt again," she snapped. "Do you hear me? Do you understand?"

She had slammed down the phone without waiting for a reply.

The letters halted, and despite her earlier threats, a few months later Carol came to the small wedding in Eisenhower Chapel on the Penn State campus. She spoke politely with Matt's father, posed for pictures as the photographer instructed, and wept no more than was appropriate. Sarah could hardly look at her, could hardly bear to be in the presence of someone so spiteful to the man she loved. She knew Matt sensed the tension that sparkled and crackled between them, and hoped he attributed it to the inherent stress of the occasion.

The memory of those letters stung as sharply as if she had received them only yesterday.

"What do you think, Sarah?" Sylvia asked, startling her out of her reverie.

"Oh." Sarah carried a bunch of carrots to the sink to wash them. "Whatever you want to do is fine with me."

"You haven't heard a word I've said, have you?"

Sarah shook the water from the carrots. "No. I'm sorry." She avoided meeting Sylvia's eyes as she returned to the counter. "I've been thinking about our newest camper." She picked up a knife, lined up a carrot on the cutting board, and chopped off its top with a sharp whack.

Sylvia's eyebrows rose as she watched the cutting board. "I see." She wiped her hands on her apron. "Tell me. What brought about this estrangement? Did your mother abuse you? Neglect you?"

Sarah dispatched another carrot with a few strong chops of the knife. "No." As angry as she was at her mother, it wouldn't be fair to accuse her of that.

"What was it, then? It must have been something truly horrible, the way you two act around each other."

"It's hard to explain." Sarah divided the carrot slices among four large salad bowls and began cutting up the rest of the bunch. "Sometimes I wish she had done something bad enough to justify cutting her out of my life altogether. As a mother, I'm afraid she was all too typical. Lots of mothers constantly criticize their daughters, right?"

Sylvia shrugged.

"That's what my mother did. Does. Nothing I do is ever good enough for her. For most of my life I've been knocking myself out trying to please her, but it's useless. It's like she thinks I'm not living up to my potential just to spite her."

"I'm sure your mother is proud of you, even if she doesn't always show it."

"I wish I could be so sure."

Sylvia opened the oven door to check on the chickens. "You do love her, though, don't you?"

"Of course I love her." Sarah hesitated, then forced herself to say the rest. "I just don't like her very much. Believe me, the feeling is mutual."

"Sylvia, Sarah, would you two like some help?"

Quickly, Sarah looked up to find Carol standing in the kitchen doorway. Two other quilters stood behind her, smiling eagerly. Sarah's heart sank. How much had her mother overheard?

"We're fine, thank you," Sylvia said, as she always did. Quilters were generous people who knew that many hands could make even a dull, slow job pleasant and quick. Sylvia often had to remind her guests to enjoy their vacations and let others wait on them for a change, but there were always a few who brushed off her protests.

This time was no different. "Preparing a meal for twelve is too much work for only the two of you," Carol said, motioning for her companions to follow her into the kitchen. She had changed into a dark blue warm-up suit but somehow still managed to look dressed up.

"We can handle it," Sarah said. Her voice came out sharper than she intended. "And there's fifteen, including me and Sylvia and Matt."

Carol pursed her lips in a semblance of a smile. "Fifteen. I stand corrected." She went to the sink, tucked a dish towel into her waistband, and began washing a bundle of celery while Sylvia found tasks for the others.

Sarah forced herself to breathe deeply and evenly until the edge of her annoyance softened. "I see you've made some new friends," she said as her mother joined her at the cutting board.

"They're my nearest neighbors upstairs." Carol pulled open drawers until she found a knife. "Linda's a physician's assistant in Erie and Renée is a cardiac specialist at Hershey Medical Center. We have a lot in common."

"That's nice." Sarah watched as a puddle collected beneath the bundle of celery on her mother's side of the cutting board. Carol had neglected to shake the water off, as usual, and now the salad would be soaked. Sarah held back a complaint and concentrated on the carrots.

They worked without speaking. Sarah tried to concentrate on Sylvia's conversation with Renée and Linda, but she was conscious of how Carol kept glancing from her celery to Sarah's carrots. Finally her mother's scrutiny became too much. "All right. What is it?" Sarah asked, setting down the knife.

Her mother feigned innocence. "What?"

"What's the problem?"

"Nothing." Carol's brow furrowed in concentration as she chopped away at the celery. Water droplets flew.

"You might as well tell me."

Carol paused. "I was just wondering why you were cutting the carrots like that."

"Like what?" Sarah fought to keep her voice even. "You mean, with a knife?"

"No, I mean cutting straight down like that. Your slices are round and chunky. If you cut at an angle, the slices will be tapered and have a more attractive oval shape." Carol took a carrot and demonstrated. "See? Isn't that pretty?"

"Lovely." Sarah snatched the carrot and resumed cutting straight, round slices. First the hair, now this—artistic differences over carrot slices. It was going to be a long week.

When the meal was ready, Sarah, Sylvia, and their helpers carried plates, glasses, and silverware across the hallway through the servants' entrance to the banquet hall. The other guests soon joined them, entering through the main entrance off the front foyer. Sarah steeled herself and took a seat at Carol's table just as Matt hurried in from the kitchen, where he had scrubbed his hands and face. He smiled at Sarah as he pulled up a chair beside her, smelling of soap and fresh air.

"How's everything going with your mom?" he murmured.

Sarah shrugged, not sure how to answer. They hadn't fought, but that same old tension was still there. She swallowed a bite of chicken and forced herself to smile across the table at her mother. One week. Surely she could manage to be civil for one week.

After supper, everyone helped clear the tables and clean up the kitchen, so the work was finished in no time at all. The quilters went their separate ways for a time, outside to stroll through the gardens, to the library to read or write in journals, to new friends' rooms to chat. As evening fell, Sarah and Sylvia returned to the kitchen to prepare a snack of tea and cookies, which they carried outside to the place Sylvia's mother had named the cornerstone patio.

Sarah summoned their guests, encouraging them to don warm coats. It was time for her favorite part of quilt camp, when the week still lay before them, promising friendship and fun, and their eventual parting could be forgotten for a while.

The quilters who had remained indoors followed Sarah across the foyer toward the west wing of the manor. One room after another lay behind closed doors, and the quilters buzzed with excitement at the mystery of it all. Past the formal parlor, at the end of the hallway, Sarah held open one last door, allowing the guests to precede her outside to the gray stone patio surrounded by evergreens and lilacs just beginning to bud. After gathering the other guests there, Sylvia had arranged the wooden furniture into a circle and had placed the tea and cookies on a table to the right, where she waited, hands clasped and smiling.

Sarah caught Sylvia's eye and smiled as she closed the door behind her. Soon, she knew, one of the quilters was bound to ask why this place was called the cornerstone patio. Sylvia or Sarah, whoever was nearer, would hold back the tree branches where the patio touched the northeast corner of the manor. The quilter who had asked the question would read aloud the engraving on a large stone at the base of the structure: BERGSTROM 1858. Sylvia would tell them about her great-grandfather, Hans Bergstrom, who had placed that cornerstone with the help of his wife, Anneke, and sister Gerda, and built the west wing of the manor upon it.

When everyone had helped themselves to refreshments, Sylvia asked them to take seats in the circle. "If you'll indulge us, we'd like to end this first evening with a simple ceremony we call a Candlelight." The quilters' voices hushed as Sylvia lit a candle, placed it in a crystal votive holder, and went to the center of the circle. The dancing flame in her hands cast light and shadow on her features, making her seem at once young and old, wise and joyful.

"Elm Creek Manor is full of stories," she told them. "Everyone who has ever lived here has added to those stories. Now your stories will join them, and those of us who call this place home will be richer for it."

She explained the ceremony. She would hand the candle to the first woman in the circle, who would tell the others why she had come to Elm Creek Manor and what she hoped the week would bring her. When she finished, she would pass the candle to the woman on her left, who would tell her story.

There was a moment's silence broken only by nervous laughter when Sylvia asked for a volunteer to begin.

Finally, Renée, one of the women Carol had befriended, raised her hand. "I will."

Sylvia gave her the candle and sat down beside Sarah.

Renée studied the flame in her hands for a long moment without speaking. Around them, unseen, crickets chirped in the gradually deepening darkness. "My name is Renée Hoffman," she finally said, looking up. "I'm a cardiac specialist at Hershey Medical Center. I was married for a while, but not anymore. I have no children." She paused. "I've never quilted before. I came to Elm Creek Manor because I want to learn how. Two years ago—" She took a deep breath and let it out, slowly. "Two years ago my brother died of AIDS. Two years ago this month. I came to Elm Creek Manor so that I could learn how to make a panel for him for the AIDS quilt." She shook her head and lowered her gaze to the flickering candle. "But that's why I want to learn to quilt, not why I came here. I guess I could have taken lessons in Hershey, but I didn't want any distractions. I want to be able to focus on what my brother meant to me, and for some reason I couldn't do that at home."

The woman beside her put an arm around Renée's shoulders. Renée gave her the briefest flicker of a smile. "When I walked around the gardens earlier today, I thought I could feel him there with me. I started thinking about the time when we were kids, when he taught me how to ride a two-wheeled bike." Her expression grew distant. "I told him once, near the end, that I wished I had gone into AIDS research instead of cardiac surgery so that I could fight against this thing that was killing him. He took my hand and said, 'You save lives. Don't ever regret the choices that brought you to the place you are now.'" She stared straight ahead for a long, silent moment. "Anyway, that's why I'm here." She passed the candle to the woman on her left.

The candle went around the circle, to a woman who was going through a painful divorce and needed to get away from it all, to the young mother whose husband had given her the week at quilt camp as a birthday present, to the elderly sisters who spent every year vacationing together while their husbands went on a fishing trip—"Separate vacations, that's why we've been able to stay married so long," the eldest declared, evoking laughter from the others—to the woman who had come with two of her friends to celebrate her doctor's confirmation that her breast cancer was in remission.

Sarah had heard stories like these in other weeks, from other women, and yet each story was unique. One common thread joined all the women who came to Elm Creek Manor. Those who had given so much of themselves and their lives caring for others—children, husbands, aging parents—were now taking time to care for themselves, to nourish their own souls. As the night darkened around them, the cornerstone patio was silent but for the murmuring of quiet voices and the song of crickets, the only illumination the flickering candle and the light of stars burning above them, so brilliant but so far away.

Carol was one of the last to speak, and she kept her story brief. "I came to Elm Creek Manor because of my daughter." Her eyes met Sarah's. "I want to be a part of her life again. For too long we've let our differences divide us. I don't want us to be that way anymore. I don't want either of us to have regrets someday, when it's too late to reconcile." She ducked her head as if embarrassed, then quickly passed the candle as if it had burned her hands.

Sarah's heart softened as she watched her mother accept a quick hug from the woman at her side. They exchanged a few words Sarah couldn't make out, then listened as the next woman told her story.

I will try harder, Sarah resolved. They would have a week together to sort things out. She wouldn't let the time go to waste.

But as the days went by, she learned that promises were more easily made than kept.

The quilt camp schedule was designed to give the guests as much independence as possible to work on their own projects or do as they pleased. After an early breakfast, Sylvia led an introductory piecing class, lectured on the history of quilting, or displayed the many antique quilts in Elm Creek Manor's collection. After some free time, the quilters gathered at noon for lunch. On rainy days they met in the banquet hall, but when the sun shone they picnicked outdoors, in the north gardens, near the orchard, on blankets spread on the sweeping front lawn, or on the veranda. Requests to lunch on the cornerstone patio received polite refusals and the promise that they would gather there once more before camp ended. No other explanation was given, no matter how the guests wheedled and teased.

After lunch one of the other Elm Creek Quilters would teach a class— Gwen on Monday, Judy on Tuesday, Summer on Wednesday, Bonnie on Thursday, and Agnes on Friday. Diane didn't feel ready to lead a class of her own, so instead she assisted at each class. The arrangement pleased everyone. Sylvia was spared the task of teaching two classes a day, the other Elm Creek Quilters could keep their involvement at a level that didn't interfere with their jobs and other responsibilities, and the guests could enjoy a variety of teaching styles and techniques.

More free time followed the afternoon classes until the evening meal. Afterward, Sylvia and Sarah usually planned some sort of entertainment, a talent show or a game or an outing. All activities were voluntary, at Sylvia's insistence. "Our guests are here to enjoy themselves," she said. "This is their time. If they want to do cartwheels on the veranda all morning instead of taking a class, more power to them."

Despite all the free time available to the quilters, Sarah rarely found any for herself. She spent the days working behind the scenes—balancing accounts, designing marketing plans, ordering supplies, making schedules— to keep Elm Creek Quilts operating smoothly. Her hours were busy and productive, and she had never been happier in her work, perhaps because could see the result of her labors in the smiling faces of their guests, feel it in the quilts created there, hear it in the laughter that rang through the halls.

Elm Creek Manor was alive once more, just as Sarah had predicted, just as Sylvia had wished.

This week Sarah's work load kept her even busier than usual. Each day she promised herself she would spend time with her mother, but she always found more work to do, more tasks that simply couldn't wait. Sarah felt guilty for repeatedly turning down her mother's invitations to go for a walk or sit on the veranda and chat during free time, so she was relieved when her mother stopped asking. They did spend some time together, at meals and in the evenings, but always in the company of the other guests.

"I was hoping we'd have some nice quiet time together," Carol told her on Thursday evening as they went out the back door to the parking lot. That evening Gwen had arranged for everyone to attend a play on the Waterford College campus.

"We will," Sarah promised. "We still have another whole day left, and half of Saturday." As if to apologize for her absence, she made sure they rode in the same car and sat next to each other in the theater. She knew it wasn't what her mother had hoped for, but she couldn't ignore her responsibilities.

Later that night, as the quilters went off to their separate rooms to prepare for bed, Sylvia asked Sarah to join her in the library. "You haven't been spending as much time with your mother as I had hoped," she said, easing herself into a chair by the fireplace. No fire burned there now, and probably none would until autumn.

Sarah shrugged helplessly. "I know. I've been swamped with work."

Sylvia folded her arms and regarded her. "Is that so?"

"Well, yes." Sarah ran through the list of tasks she'd accomplished over the past three days.

Sylvia shook her head as she listened. "You know very well that most of that work could have been put off for at least another week. You had no pressing deadlines preventing you from enjoying your mother's visit."

"But—"

"But nothing. You went looking for all that extra work, and so naturally you found it. You piled it up all around yourself—big, solid stacks of paperwork to keep your mother from coming near. I know you, Sarah McClure, and I know what you're doing, even if you don't."

Sarah stared at her. "Is that really what I've been doing?" As Sylvia's words sank in, she recognized the truth in them. "I didn't mean to. At least I don't think so."

"Why are you distancing yourself from her, and after she said such nice things about you at the Candlelight?"

"But that's precisely why it's so difficult to talk to her." Sarah went to the window and drew back the curtain. Through the diamond-shaped panes of glass she could see the roof of the barn on the other side of Elm Creek. "Every time we're together, we bicker. That's been our way for years. Right now we've left things on a good note. I wouldn't want another silly argument to spoil that."

"Perhaps I should have told you about her visit after all, so that you could have planned what to say to her." Sylvia sighed. "It seems the element of surprise didn't work as well for you and your mother as it did for me and Agnes."

Sarah whirled around to face her. "Is that what you were trying to do?"

Sylvia nodded, no doubt thinking, as Sarah was, about that day almost two years before when Sarah had arranged for Sylvia to meet her long-estranged sister-in-law in the north gardens. Their reconciliation had encouraged Sylvia to remain at Elm Creek Manor instead of continuing her search for a buyer; if not for that, Elm Creek Quilts never would have existed.

"But that day in the garden was only the beginning," Sarah said. "You and Agnes didn't rebuild your relationship all in that one day. You grew closer over time, over all those months planning Elm Creek Quilts."

Sylvia nodded. "You're right, of course. I was foolish to believe your difficulties with your mother could be sorted out in a single week."

"Not foolish." Sarah tried to smile. "Overly optimistic, maybe, but not foolish."

"Hmph." Sylvia returned Sarah's smile, but her heart didn't seem to be in it.

Matt was already asleep when Sarah climbed into bed beside him. She closed her eyes, but sleep wouldn't come. Sylvia was so disappointed that she had not been able to return Sarah's gift in kind. She shouldn't be. Sylvia and

Agnes had been ready to reconcile. So many years of loss and regret had cleared their vision, had taught them how foolish the old squabbles were. In hindsight, it had been easy to bring them together, since they both ached for a reunion.

If Sarah felt anything of that longing, it was buried deep enough to ignore. How many decades of estrangement would pass before she cared enough about reconciliation to give her whole heart to it?

To those troubling thoughts, Sarah finally drifted off to sleep.

The next day she forced herself to avoid the office. She sat by her mother's side at breakfast, walked with her and Matt in the gardens during free time, and pushed two Adirondack chairs together on the veranda so that they could chat undisturbed during lunch. The time passed pleasantly enough, but Sarah felt restrained, as if at any moment she might say the words that would dredge up all those old animosities. Once, fleetingly, she wondered if that wasn't exactly what they ought to do—bring out all those old hurts and subject them to unflinching scrutiny. But just as quickly Sarah decided against it. She couldn't risk an enormous blowup that could take a long time to settle, not when Carol would be leaving the next day.

To make the most of their time together, Sarah joined her mother for Agnes's workshop that afternoon. At first Carol struggled to learn the appliqué techniques, but Sarah and Diane helped her. "I'm the expert on finding an easier way to do things," Diane said as she demonstrated a different way to hold the needle. "I've never met a shortcut I didn't like."

Carol laughed and assured Diane that she understood what to do now.

As they worked, Agnes strolled through the room checking on her students' progress and offering advice. When she reached Sarah's table, she took Diane and Sarah aside to talk to them about the round robin quilt. So much had happened since Sunday's registration that Sarah had nearly forgotten it.

"The center motif will take me a while to complete," Agnes said. "I think the rest of you should get started on the borders."

Diane looked dubious. "How can we add borders to something that isn't there?"

Agnes laughed and patted her arm. "Sarah can cut a piece of background fabric eighteen inches square and add her border to that. The rest of you can proceed as usual. When I'm finished, I'll appliqué my section onto the center square."

Sarah nodded, but she was still uncertain. "But what about colors? We won't want the borders to clash with the center. How can we pick coordinating colors if we can't see what fabric you're going to use?"

A quilter on the other side of the room signaled to Agnes for help. "Use the colors of Elm Creek Manor," Agnes called over her shoulder as she went to assist the student. "That's what I'm going to do."

Diane made a face. "She could have been a little more specific."

Sarah laughed in agreement, but she thought she understood what Agnes meant.

That evening the mood at Elm Creek Manor was nostalgic and subdued. It had been a special week for all, and though they had arrived mostly strangers, the quilters now felt they would be friends for life. In the midst of the many tearful hugs and promises to keep in touch, Sylvia whispered to Sarah that they ought to consider hiring a comedian to entertain them on future closing nights. "Anything to prevent such melancholy," she said, hugging her arms to her chest as if to ward off a draft.

The next morning their guests' spirits seemed to have brightened with the sunrise. As Sylvia and Sarah had promised, they gathered on the cornerstone patio for their last meal together. Sarah and Sylvia covered the table with a bright yellow cloth and loaded it with trays of pastries, breads, fruit, pots of coffee, and pitchers of juice. After breakfast, they took their places around the circle once again, this time for Show-and-Tell. Each quilter took a turn showing off something she had made that week and telling her new friends what favorite memory she would take with her when she left Elm Creek Manor.

Everyone proudly showed their new creations, from the AIDS quilt segment Renée had begun to the simplest pieced blocks the beginning quilters had stitched. The Candlelight on their first evening together was remembered fondly, as were the late-night chats in their cozy suites and the private moments spent strolling through the beautiful grounds.

Then it was Carol's turn.

She held up her first pieced block, a Sawtooth Star, and said that she'd like to start a baby quilt, if her daughter would cooperate by providing the baby.

Everyone chuckled, except for Sylvia, who let out a quiet sigh only Sarah heard, and Sarah herself, who clenched her jaw to hold back a blistering retort that the decision to have children was hers alone—hers and Matt's.

"As for my favorite memory, I'm not sure yet." Carol looked around the circle, everywhere but at Sarah. "My favorite memory might still be ahead of me. I've decided to stay on a while longer."

The other guests let out exclamations of surprise and delight, but Sarah hardly heard them over the roaring in her ears. "But—but—what about work?" she managed to say.

"I called the hospital. I told them it was a family emergency, and they agreed to let me have four months' leave."

Four months. Sarah nodded, numb. A family emergency. It wasn't exactly a lie.

The woman beside her patted Sarah on the back and congratulated her for the good news. She managed a weak smile in return. Four months. Time enough to patch things up, or to rend them beyond repair forever.

↕

Sarah cut an eighteen-inch square from a piece of cream fabric. She chose green for the stately elms lining the back road to Elm Creek Manor, her home, which felt less like home with her mother in it. She picked lighter greens for the sweeping front lawn and darker shades for the leaves on the rosebushes Matt nurtured with such care in the north gardens. She added clear blue for the skies over Waterford, though she felt they should be gray with gathering storms. Last of all she found a richer, darker blue for Elm Creek, which danced along as it always had, murmuring and rushing regardless of the joy or tragedy unfolding on its banks.

Using the same cream for her background fabric, Sarah created a border of blue and green squares set on point, touching tip to tip. Squares for the solidity and balance of the manor, for the dividing walls she and Carol had built over the years, for the blocks they had stumbled over on their journey toward each other, for the way Carol's news had left her feeling imprisoned and boxed in, forced to face the inevitable confrontation that somehow she had always known was coming.

Three

Diane received the quilt top from Sarah after class Monday afternoon. "You must have worked on this all weekend," she remarked, unfolding the quilt top and holding it up for inspection. "How'd you find the time? I thought your mother was still here."

"She is."

An odd note in Sarah's voice pulled Diane's attention away from the quilt. Sarah had shadows under her eyes and she kept glancing warily over her shoulder.

"Are you okay?" Diane asked. Usually, Sarah was calm and self-assured, but she had been snappish and edgy all day.

"I'm fine." Sarah snatched the quilt top and began folding it. "I just don't want Sylvia to see this. It's supposed to be a surprise, remember? Keep it out of sight."

"Okay, okay. Relax. She's in the kitchen. She can't see through walls." Diane took back the folded quilt top and tucked it into her bag. Honestly. More and more Sarah reminded Diane of her eldest son, Michael, but he was a teenager and such behavior was expected. What was Sarah's excuse?

Diane waved good-bye to Gwen, who had led that afternoon's workshop, and left the classroom. It had been a ballroom once. The dance floor remained, but quilters now practiced on the orchestra dais, where work tables had replaced risers and music stands. She had never seen an orchestra there, but Sylvia and Agnes had, and their stories were so vivid that Diane sometimes felt as if she had witnessed the manor's grand parties herself.

On her way to the back door, she stopped by the kitchen to bid Sylvia good-bye. Sarah's mother was helping Sylvia prepare supper, and they were laughing and chatting like old friends. Maybe that explained Sarah's moodiness. Maybe she wanted Sylvia all to herself and thought Carol was getting in the way.

Diane drove home to the neighborhood a few blocks south of the Waterford College campus where professors, administrators, and their families lived. Sarah had once told her that the gray stone houses with their carefully landscaped front yards reminded her of Elm Creek Manor, but Diane didn't see the similarity. The houses on that oak tree–lined street were large, but not nearly as grand as Elm Creek Manor, or as old—or as secluded, to her regret. Diane willingly would have parted with a neighbor or two—namely, Mary Beth from next door, who had perfect hair and perfect children and had been president of the Waterford Quilting Guild for eight years.

Diane parked in the driveway and walked up the red-brick herringbone path to the front porch, to the door with its brass knocker and beveled glass. The house was quiet, but she couldn't enjoy the peace and solitude, not when she was due to pick up Todd from band practice in fifteen minutes. Diane dropped her bag on the floor of the foyer, draped her coat over it, and yanked off her ankle boots. They used to call her a stay-at-home mom before she began working for Elm Creek Quilts, but a stay-in-car mom was more like it.

She padded to the kitchen in her stocking feet to check the answering machine. There was one message—Tim, she supposed, as she waited for the tape to rewind. He usually called her in the afternoons from his office in the chemistry building on campus to let her know what time he'd be home from work.

But the voice on the tape, though much like her husband's, was years younger.

"Mom?" Michael said. "Uh, don't be mad."

An ominous beginning. Diane closed her eyes and sighed.

"Um, I kinda need you to come pick me up." He hesitated. "They won't let me go until you pay the fine."

"Pick you up from where?" she asked the machine—an instant before his words sank in. Pay a fine?

"I'm at the police station. Don't tell Dad, okay?" Without a word of explanation, he hung up.

Diane shrieked. She ran to the foyer, threw on her coat, and stuffed her feet into her boots. She dashed outside to her car and raced downtown, her heart pounding. What had he done? What on earth had he gotten himself into this time? After the vandalism at the junior high last fall, she and Tim had put such a scare into him that he vowed never to get into trouble again. Their family counselor had warned them to expect ups and downs, but this— She felt faint just thinking about the possibilities. He must have done something horrible, just horrible, for the police to lock up a fifteen-year-old until his parents came to bail him out.

Sarah was wise to avoid having children, Diane thought grimly as she pulled into the parking lot behind the police headquarters.

Diane hurried inside, her heart pounding. Michael could be injured, ignored by the busy police officers as he slowly and quietly bled to death in a lonely cell. She gave the first officer she saw Michael's name. "Is he all right?" she asked, breathless. "Is he hurt?"

"He's just fine, ma'am." The officer looked sympathetic. Maybe he was a parent, too. "He's just in a little bit of trouble."

"Can I see him? What kind of trouble? How little? How long has he been here?" She took a deep breath to stem the flow of questions. She had gone to Elm Creek Manor at noon; Michael could have left the message any time after that. He could have been locked up for hours with violent offenders. The last thing Michael needed was that kind of influence.

The officer raised his hands to calm her. "He's been here less than an hour. He's waiting in an interrogation room."

"What exactly did he do?"

"He was skateboarding in a marked zone. We wouldn't have held him except he didn't have the money for the fine."

Diane gaped at him. "Skateboarding?" Her voice grew shrill. "You locked up my child for skateboarding?"

The officer squirmed. "In a marked zone, yes."

"Why didn't you call me at Elm Creek Manor? Why didn't you call my husband?"

"Your son insisted. He wanted you to get the news rather than his father, and he didn't want to interrupt your class."

Diane smothered a groan. Of all the times for Michael to get considerate. "I can't believe this." She rooted around in her purse for her wallet. "Well, it certainly does my heart good to know that the citizens of Waterford are being protected so heroically from skateboarders. Now, if only you could do something about all those thieves and murderers and terrorists running loose, well, then I'd really be impressed."

"We don't get many murderers and terrorists around here, ma'am."

"How much is the fine?" she snapped.

"Fifty dollars."

Diane counted out the bills, gritting her teeth to hold back the tirade she was aching to release. She'd save it for Michael. Oh, would he ever rue this day! "Here's your ransom," she said, sliding the bills across the desk. "May I have my son back, please?"

A few minutes later, the officer brought out her son. As usual, his skinny frame was enveloped in oversized clothes, so large and baggy that they could have been his father's, except Tim never wore black jeans and Aerosmith T-shirts. Along with his skateboard, Michael carried his jacket wadded up in a ball under his arm, and his baseball cap was turned backward.

"Is that my earring?" Diane gasped when she saw the flash of gold in his earlobe.

He nodded.

"Where's the other one?"

"In your jewelry box." He paused. "You never said I couldn't wear your earrings."

"I didn't know I had to." She hadn't wanted him to get his ear pierced in the first place, but Tim had pointed out that they ought to reward him for asking permission, to encourage him to do so more often. Besides, it was only one ear he wanted, thank God, not his nose or his eyebrow or his tongue. "I also never said you couldn't set the house on fire or run a counterfeiting ring out of the basement, but you knew you weren't allowed, right?"

"Yeah," he muttered. "I guess so."

"You guess so?" Then Diane remembered the officers watching them. "Let's go, Michael," she said briskly, placing a hand on his shoulder and steering him toward the door.

They drove in silence to Todd's middle school. Michael sat in the back seat staring out the window. Diane was so angry and embarrassed that for the first time in her life she didn't know how to begin the lecture.

"Does Dad know?" Michael finally asked as they sat at a long red light.

"Not yet."

"Are you gonna tell him?"

"Of course I'm going to tell him. A father has a right to know when his eldest son, his heir, his pride and joy, has earned himself a criminal record."

In the rearview mirror, she saw him roll his eyes. "You don't have to make such a big thing out of it."

The light changed, and Diane sped the car forward. "Mister, you have no idea how big this is already."

They drove on without speaking.

When she pulled into the school's circular driveway, Todd was waiting out front alone, banging his trumpet case against his knee and looking up at the sky. The sight of his woebegone face prompted a twinge of guilt.

"You're late," he said as he climbed into the back seat beside his brother, as mournful as if he had been waiting hours, days, long enough to be certain that she had abandoned him forever.

"I'm sorry," she said as she drove on. "I would have been on time, except I had to swing by the slammer to bail out Michael here."

"You were in jail?" Todd asked his brother, his tone at once shocked and admiring.

"Shut up."

"I don't have to."

From the back seat came a dull thump of a fist against cloth and flesh. "Hey," Diane snapped, glancing from the road to the rearview mirror and back, trying to figure out who had thrown the punch. "No hitting. You know better than that." She heard Todd mutter something about one of them knowing better than to wind up behind bars, too, and then another dull thump. "I said, knock it off!"

When they got home, she promptly sent them to their rooms. Michael went upstairs without a word, shoulders slumped, hands thrust into the pockets of his enormous jeans, but Todd's mouth fell open in astonishment. "Why do I have to?" he protested. "I didn't do anything."

Because your mother needs a few minutes to herself or she'll go completely berserk, Diane wanted to say, but instead she folded her arms and looked her youngest son squarely in the eye. "Your room is not a gulag. You've got homework, books, TV, and about half a million computer games. Just until supper, so I can have some peace and quiet, so I can figure out what I'm going to tell your father, okay?"

"I don't see why I get punished when he screws up," Todd muttered, his mouth tugging into a sullen frown.

An unexpected wave of sympathy came over her, sympathy for Michael. Todd had always been the good kid, and he couldn't understand why his older brother did the things he did. None of them understood, not really, but it saddened her that Todd seemed to feel so little empathy for Michael, so little solidarity. Sometimes she wished Todd would side with Michael, forming the typical united front of kids versus adults. More than anyone else Diane knew, Michael needed an ally.

She wrapped Todd in a hug. "Please?"

"All right," he said, resigned. As he dragged himself upstairs, Diane was tempted to remind him that he always went straight to his room after band practice, to put away his trumpet and get his homework done so that he could play basketball with the neighbor kids after supper. She was tempted, but she said nothing.

The phone rang as she was preparing supper.

"Hi, honey," Tim said. "How was your day?"

"Oh, you know, the usual." She wiped her hands on a dish towel and switched the phone to her other ear. "Your son gave me another dozen gray hairs, that's all."

She pictured him leaning back in his chair, removing his glasses, and rubbing his eyes. "What did he do now?" After she explained, Tim sighed, heavy and deep. "I suppose it could have been worse."

"Are you kidding?" It was his standard reply, but somehow Diane hadn't expected to hear it. "What's worse than being hauled in by the police?"

"Being hauled in by the police for something worth being hauled in for."

He was right, of course. "What are we going to do?"

"Try to take it easy until I get home. We'll have supper and talk. We'll figure out what to do." His voice was comforting. "It'll be all right. You'll see."

"Maybe." Diane wasn't so sure. In a few years she could be receiving Mother's Day cards from Death Row, not that Michael had given her a Mother's Day card since the sixth grade.

Supper was a strained affair, with Michael scowling at the table and waiting for the punishment to be levied. Diane concentrated on moving her food around on her plate with her fork because she knew that one look at Michael would have her snapping at him to sit up straight, take off his ball cap, get his elbows off the table, and for the love of all that was good in the world, stay out of prison. Only Todd treated the evening as any other, chattering on about new band uniforms and the swim team's upcoming candy bar sale. Diane wondered if he really was unaware of the tension blanketing the room or if he was trying to lighten the mood so that his parents would go easy on his brother. She hoped it was the latter, not that it would work.

After supper, Todd went outside to join his friends; Michael trudged back upstairs without waiting to be told. As Tim and Diane cleaned up the kitchen, they discussed their options. Michael had lost so many privileges already for past transgressions that there weren't many left to revoke. Grounding him wouldn't do any good because he spent most of his time in his room anyway. They could take away his skateboard, but to Diane that seemed like a slap on the wrist compared to the fright and embarrassment he had given her.

"Why does he do these things?" she asked.

"I don't know," Tim said, a thoughtful look crossing his face. "Why don't we ask him?"

They called him into the living room. He slumped into an armchair and studied the floor as they seated themselves on the sofa facing him.

"Michael," Tim said, "your mother and I have been trying to figure out why you got yourself into this situation today." Diane admired the way he kept his voice so calm, so reasonable, without a trace of the worry she knew he was feeling.

In reply, Michael shrugged.

"Come on, son. You must have some reason. Didn't you see the sign?"

"No, I didn't see it," Michael muttered. "But I knew I wasn't allowed to skate there."

"Then why did you?" Diane demanded. When Michael shrugged, she fought off the urge to shake him out of pure frustration.

Tim looked puzzled. "If you didn't see a sign, how did you know you weren't allowed to skate there?"

Finally, Michael looked up. "Because we aren't allowed to skate anywhere. Every single place is off-limits. The sidewalks, the parking lots, the campus—everywhere. It's not fair. I bought my skateboard with my own money and I can't even use it."

"Why not use it in the driveway?" Diane asked.

Michael rolled his eyes. " 'Cause I don't just want to go back and forth, back and forth all day like a five-year-old idiot."

"Don't talk to your mother that way," Tim said. Michael scowled and slumped farther into his chair. If he kept it up, Diane figured he would be horizontal before the conversation ended. He muttered something inaudible that could have been an apology.

Tim left the sofa and took a seat on the ottoman close to Michael's chair. "Look, we're trying to understand things from your point of view, but you have to help us, okay? If you knew you weren't allowed to skate there, why did you do it?"

"Because it's skate where I'm not allowed to or not skate at all."

Diane modeled her tone after Tim's. "Why not do something else?"

"Because I don't have anything else," he burst out. "Don't you get it? Todd has band and swimming and about a billion friends, Dad has his job and his workshop, you have all that quilting stuff—all I have is my skateboard. I suck at school, I can't play sports, the popular kids don't know I'm alive, but I can skate. I'm good at it. It's the only thing I'm good at."

"That's not true," Diane said, astonished by the bitterness in his tone. "You're good at lots of things."

He shook his head. "No, I'm not. You think I am because you're my mom, but it's not true. I'm not good at anything. Except for this. I'm one of the best skateboarders in Waterford, and the other skateboarders know that. I have friends when I skate. I'm important. I'm not just Todd's loser older brother for a change."

Diane didn't know what to say. She and Tim exchanged a long look— enough for her to see that he wouldn't be able to take away Michael's skateboard, either.

They sent him back to his room. He eyed them as if not quite believing that they meant for him to go without being yelled at first, but eventually he shuffled out of the room. They heard his footsteps as he went upstairs, slow, despairing, like a man on his way to the gallows.

Diane and Tim talked until it grew dark outside and Todd came in from shooting hoops in the driveway. He greeted them and continued on to the kitchen, but on the spur of the moment Diane called him back. She would ask him, she decided. She would ask him if what Michael said about himself was true.

"What's up?" Todd asked, tossing the basketball from hand to hand. He stood in the doorway, red-cheeked and glowing from exercise, grinning as if recalling a great shot he had made minutes before or a joke a friend had told. He had inherited Diane's beauty and his father's temperament, and as Diane admired him it occurred to her that he would always have an edge in life his brother lacked, his brother who had inherited his mother's temper and smart mouth along with his father's slight stature and narrow shoulders. Michael was two years older, but in the past few months Todd had almost caught up to him in height and weight, and threatened to leave him far behind soon.

"Mom?" Todd said after a long moment passed in silence. "You wanted to talk to me?"

"No." Diane shook her head and forced herself to smile. "That's all right."

He gave her a bemused grin and continued on to the kitchen.

"There must be someplace in this town where a kid can ride a skateboard in peace." Diane bit at her lower lip, thinking. "Todd has his basketball courts, the swimming pools, the band practice rooms—we have to find a place for Michael. What does a skateboarder need, anyway?"

Tim didn't know, either, but he promised to find out. Tomorrow he would let his graduate students fend for themselves while he helped Michael find a place to skate. He kissed Diane, squeezed her arm in a gesture both affectionate and comforting, and went upstairs to talk to their son.

The next afternoon, as she assisted Judy with her workshop at Elm Creek Manor, Diane's thoughts wandered from the quilt campers to her husband and son. The search could take them days or weeks, and as they looked, they would have time alone to talk. Maybe Michael would lower his shields for a while and allow Tim the chance to become closer to him, close the way Gwen and Summer were close.

That evening at supper, Tim and Michael took turns describing their search. They hadn't found anything yet, but Tim was learning a great deal about skateboarding. Right before coming home, they had checked out a parking lot behind a medical office.

"There was this paved ditch next to it that I liked," Michael began.

"And I liked the fact that there were so many doctors nearby, just in case," his father finished. They looked at each other and laughed.

Diane blinked at them, speechless. Since becoming a teenager Michael had scowled instead of smiled, but now here he was, laughing.

On Wednesday, Tim and Michael investigated the edges of town, and this time they took along Troy, Brandon, and Kelly, who, Diane learned at supper, were Michael's best friends.

"How nice," Diane said, thinking, *Michael has friends?*

"Aren't those the geeks from computer club?" Todd wanted to know.

Michael's scowl returned. "Shut up."

Diane ignored the outburst. "Were you thinking about joining computer club with your friends?"

"I dunno." Michael shrugged and took a drink of milk. "Maybe. They said they could help me make a skateboarding website. Sometimes they go on trips, like, to computer companies to see how they run. Next month some movie animator guy's coming in to talk. He got, like, an Oscar or something for special effects." He took a bite of casserole and chewed thoughtfully. "That would be a way cool job."

Diane pretended not to be thrilled. "Hmm. I don't know. I don't think you'd have enough time for something like that. When would you get your homework done?"

"After school. After meetings." His alarm was unmistakable. "It wouldn't take too much time. I could do both."

She bit her lower lip. "Well . . ."

Tim was shooting her frantic looks across the table, clearly convinced she'd lost her mind.

"Please?" Michael looked almost desperate. "I'll get my homework done, no problem. I'll even show it to you."

She feigned reluctance and said, "We'll see." Michael nodded, but his brow furrowed in determination, as if his mind was already working on how to change that "We'll see" to "Yes." For years she'd urged him to get involved in school activities, and he had countered every effort with resistance. Now he would do everything short of begging to be permitted to join, and since he'd had to work for the privilege, he would become the computer club's most enthusiastic member. Maybe he would even become their president, and wouldn't that be something to mention to Mary Beth from next door, who practically sent out daily press releases about her kids' achievements.

She gave Tim the tiniest flicker of a triumphant smile when she was certain Michael wouldn't notice. Tim hid his grin, but he couldn't mask the admiration in his eyes.

On Thursday evening the mood shifted. Tim and Michael had exhausted the local possibilities and weren't sure where to look next. "You'll think of something," Diane told them, disguising her concern behind a cheerful smile. Without skateboarding, there would be no friends, no computer club, no motivation to do homework, no inside jokes with his dad. Michael would revert back to his old, practiced ways, she was sure of it.

The next afternoon, the Elm Creek Quilters held a business meeting during the campers' free time after Agnes's workshop, so Diane headed home later than usual. Todd would be finishing his homework already, and Tim and Michael would be continuing their search. She hoped their luck would change, and soon.

To her surprise, Tim's car was in the garage when she got home. She pulled in beside it, wondering. Had they found a place for Michael, and was he even now spinning around and popping wheelies or whatever those tricks were called? Had they been forced to admit failure, and was Michael sulking up in his room while Tim paced around the house trying to figure out how to tell her? She got out of the car and leaned up against the door to close it, nervousness twisting in her stomach. She couldn't stay out there forever, she told herself, but she could delay the bad news a while.

Then she heard strange sounds coming from somewhere outside the garage. She walked down the driveway, listening, until she realized the noise was coming from behind her own house. It almost sounded as if the woods abutting their property had been turned into a construction site. She went around the side of the house and found Tim and Michael at the far edge of the backyard with all manner of building supplies and tools piled up on the grass around them.

She was almost afraid to know, but she approached them and asked what they were doing. They looked up from their work with nearly identical happy grins. "Dad's building me a ramp," Michael exclaimed. "Isn't this cool?"

"That's one way to describe it." She folded her arms and surveyed the damage to the lawn. They had enough material there for a small house. "Are you sure you don't need a building permit?"

Michael laughed and returned to his work.

She fixed her gaze on Tim, who was kneeling on the grass and sanding a board. "You know, for some reason I can't remember the conversation where you told me you were going to build a skateboard ramp in our backyard. I must have forgotten it, because I know you wouldn't begin a project like this without talking to me first."

He gave her a look that was both pleading and sheepish. "Honey, we looked everywhere. Every suitable place was off-limits. The only solution was to build our own place."

"Maybe I would have come to the same conclusion, if I had been asked, if we could have discussed this the way normal, rational, sane people usually discuss these things."

"It couldn't wait," he said simply, and Diane knew that he, too, had sensed something last night, some unspoken, unintended signal that this could be their last chance to reach their son, to convince him they were interested in his life, that despite their greatly advanced age and their abhorrence of all things fun, they didn't want his teen years to be entirely miserable.

She sighed and shook her head, and when Tim's face brightened she knew he understood that she was granting permission for the project to continue. What else could she do, really? They had installed a basketball hoop for Todd; was a skateboard ramp for Michael any different? Aside from its size, of course, and the expense, and the loss of a good portion of their backyard.

She turned and walked back to the house so that she wouldn't have to think about just how large the skateboard ramp would be if it required so much material. Their backyard was big enough; all of the backyards on this side of the street were, because they bordered the Waterford College Arboretum. The yards were separated by fences and mature trees, so they wouldn't disturb the neighbors. Really, she couldn't complain.

Tim and Michael worked until supper, then headed back outside as soon as the meal was over. After clearing away the dishes, Diane took her sewing basket and the round robin quilt out to the balcony off the master bedroom, so that she could keep an eye on the construction as she planned her border. But the quilt rested in her lap unnoticed. Tim and Michael worked until it grew too dark to see, and all the while Diane watched them, thinking.

The skateboard ramp took shape that weekend. By Saturday afternoon they had erected a structure of crossbeams that supported a U-shaped curve resembling the cross section of a pipe. It was higher than Diane had expected, and longer, but she clamped her mouth shut and vowed that instead of complaining, she'd insist Michael wear his helmet.

That evening some of Todd's friends came over to watch videos. From the family room where she was loading piles of folded laundry into her basket, she heard them raiding the refrigerator and arguing about which movie to watch first.

Then one of the boys interrupted the debate with a cry of astonishment. "What the hell is that?"

Todd's reply was barely audible, and she had to strain to catch it. "Something for my brother."

"But what is it?" another boy asked.

"It looks like a skateboard ramp." This voice was lower; it belonged to Mary Beth's son, Brent.

"Great theory, Einstein," Todd retorted. "It only took you one guess."

Brent laughed. "I didn't know you were a skateboard geek."

"I'm not."

"Your brother is."

"So? That doesn't mean I am. I mean, look at him. He's a total loser. I'm nothing like him."

Diane's grip tightened on the handles of the laundry basket.

"You better watch out," the first boy drawled. "You have the same genes, right? It might show up later."

The boys snickered.

Diane sailed into the room and slammed the laundry basket down on the kitchen table. Todd and his friends jumped at the sound. "Well, hello, boys," she declared, nailing a grin to her face. "Getting yourselves a snack?"

They muttered hellos and sneaked furtive glances at Todd, all but Brent, who had the nerve to look her straight in the eye and smile. "We were just checking out the skateboard ramp," he said. "It's really cool. Do you think Michael would let us try it when it's ready?"

Insolent little weasel. "You could ask him," she said, still grinning.

"Maybe later," Todd said, shoving his friends out of the kitchen. "Mom, I didn't mean that the way it sounded."

She would have been more impressed by his apology if he hadn't waited until his friends were out of earshot. "You have no idea how much it hurts me to know you score points with your friends by ridiculing your brother. You, of all people, should defend him." She snatched up the laundry basket and stormed from the room.

Tim and Michael worked until dusk, and the next morning Diane woke to the sounds of hammers and saws outside her window. They worked all day, taking breaks only for meals and church. Michael tried to convince her to let them skip mass just that once, and Tim looked like he might agree, but Diane would have none of it. "With this thing in the backyard we're going to need all the divine assistance we can get," she said, herding father and son inside with orders to clean up and change within twenty minutes or she'd cancel construction for the day.

Tim and Michael got back to work after church, and when Diane returned from welcoming a new group of quilt campers to Elm Creek Manor, they were still at it. By Sunday evening the skateboard ramp was finished. Diane and Todd joined Tim and Michael outside for the final inspection.

Michael was holding his skateboard and grinning. "What do you think?"

"Unbelievable," Todd said, eyeing the structure, and Diane agreed. The U-shaped half-pipe nearly spanned the width of the yard and looked at least twelve feet high.

"It's safe," Michael assured her. "Really."

Diane circled the ramp, looking it over. When the supporting beams hid her from view, she seized the nearest one and threw her weight against it. It didn't budge.

"Dad already tried that," Michael called. "It's sturdy."

Diane joined them in front. "It seems to be," she admitted.

Michael apparently took that as the signal to begin the test run, because he put on his helmet. He climbed up a ladder built into one side of the structure and moved onto a platform at the top of the U. He placed his skateboard at the edge, stepped on it, and scanned the length of the ramp.

"I can't watch," Diane murmured, but she couldn't look away, either.

Then Michael launched himself forward, over the edge and down the slope. His momentum carried him up the opposite side, where he turned at the edge and raced back down again. He shot up the first slope, but this time he soared above the U, crouching down to grab the skateboard with one hand as he turned.

"Big air," Tim whooped as Michael rode down the slope again. "That's what the kids say," he added in an undertone.

Diane nodded, her anxiety giving way to amazement as she watched Michael swoop down one side of the U and up the other. He was positively graceful.

Finally he slowed and came to a stop at the bottom of the U. "What did you think?" he called, smiling with triumph and breathing hard from exertion. Somehow he tossed the skateboard into the air with his feet and caught it.

Diane couldn't speak for a moment. He looked so proud and happy. "I'm impressed," she said. "I'm also terrified you're going to break your neck."

Michael laughed. "It's not as dangerous as it looks."

"Thank God for that."

Michael rode a while longer, until Diane told him he had to go inside and do his homework. To her amazement, he obeyed without protest.

"What happened to our kid?" she whispered to Tim.

"I don't know, but I'm not complaining." He put an arm around her shoulders and they crossed the lawn side by side.

The next day, Diane went to the manor earlier than usual to have lunch with the new campers and some of the Elm Creek Quilters. She had the whole group laughing with the story of how she and Tim had punished their wayward son by building him his own skateboard ramp.

"Why does Waterford have such a problem with skateboarding?" Summer asked. "There aren't any laws against in-line skates. How are skateboards any different?"

"I suppose it's because skateboarders tend to be teenage boys who dress a certain way and listen to a certain kind of music," Gwen mused. "They might be the nicest kids in the world, but they project an image which makes some people uncomfortable."

Diane was forced to agree. Michael was a basically good kid, but he looked like the stereotypical punk teenager. If he dressed differently, cut his hair, and lost the earring, adults would treat him with more respect. Unfortunately, despite her many attempts to explain, he didn't see the connection.

When she brought Todd home from band practice later that day, Michael was in the backyard with three other boys—no, two other boys and a girl. "Kelly, I suppose," Diane mused. She had assumed Kelly was a boy, since Tim had not indicated otherwise. She watched them through the kitchen window as they took turns zooming up and down the ramp. When it was Kelly's turn, Michael called out something that made her laugh. One of the boys nudged him and Michael grinned.

Well. That was certainly interesting.

Just then, Michael and his friends put down their skateboards and began walking toward the house. Diane let the curtain fall back across the window and busied herself emptying the dishwasher. They came into the kitchen laughing and talking and looking for food.

"We have apples and grapes in the fruit bin," Diane suggested, not surprised when they grimaced. She found them a package of cookies instead, and Michael took four glasses from the cupboard and filled them with milk. Kelly helped him carry them to the kitchen table and paused to thank Diane for the cookies. She was a pretty, dark-haired girl, and Diane decided she liked her.

When they finished their snack, Diane took the round robin quilt outside to the deck so that she could plan her border and watch the kids skate. She swung back and forth on the porch swing in the shade of her favorite oak tree and held up the quilt top. Sarah's border of squares on point used a cream background and varying shades of blue and green, so Diane decided to use similar colors. But what pattern should she choose? She had never participated in a round robin before, and she wished Agnes had given more specific instructions. Should she use squares, too, since Sarah had, or was the point to make each border completely different?

"Yoo hoo. Diane, yoo hoo."

Diane smothered a groan and tried to hide the quilt on her lap. "Hello, Mary Beth," she said to the woman peering over the fence. "How are you?" It was an automatic question. She couldn't care less how Mary Beth was that day or any other day. They had never been friends, and Mary Beth had never forgiven Diane for challenging her for the office of president of the Waterford Quilting Guild. Diane would have won, too, if Mary Beth hadn't made an impassioned speech to the guild the night before the election, asking them if they were willing to hand over the responsibilities of the Waterford Summer Quilt Festival to someone who had never won a ribbon. After Mary Beth's reelection, Diane and her friends were so fed up with the silly politics that they left the guild to form their own bee.

For years Diane had resented Mary Beth, but suddenly she realized she ought to thank her. If not for Mary Beth, she and her friends wouldn't have formed their own bee, so they couldn't have invited Sarah to join it, and then Elm Creek Quilts might not have existed.

But Mary Beth's phony smile pushed all gratitude out of Diane's mind. "What do you have there?" Mary Beth asked, craning her neck to see what was in Diane's lap.

Reluctantly, Diane held up the quilt top. "It's a round robin quilt I'm making with the Elm Creek Quilters. One person makes a center block and the others take turns adding borders to it."

"Oh, I know. I've made dozens of them." Mary Beth squinted as she studied the quilt. "You do realize you're supposed to put something in the middle? Not just leave it a big blank square?"

"Oh, really? My goodness. I had no idea. I thought it looked strange, and now I know why. Thank you for clearing that up."

Mary Beth eyed her, as if trying to gauge her sincerity. "You're welcome," she finally said. She nodded to the skateboard ramp as if seeing it for the first time. "What on earth is that?"

"It's a skateboard ramp."

"It looks like an accident waiting to happen." Mary Beth shook her head and made tsking noises with her tongue. "Do their parents know how high it is?"

Diane felt a pang of worry, but she refused to let Mary Beth see it. "Of course. In fact, some of them think it's not high enough."

Mary Beth's eyes widened. "No kidding? Well, I guess that's fine, then. I wish I were as brave as you. If that thing were in my backyard, I'd never have a moment's peace. I'd be too worried about liability."

Diane felt a twinge of nervousness. "We've taken care of all that."

"Of course. Tim is so practical."

Diane nodded and turned her attention to the quilt, hoping that Mary Beth would take the hint and go away.

"Aren't you worried that a skateboard ramp will attract—how can I put this—a certain undesirable element?"

Diane's head jerked up, and when she spoke, her voice was cold. "That undesirable element you're talking about is my son and his friends. They're under my supervision, and they aren't bothering you, so why don't you just leave them alone?"

For a moment Mary Beth just gaped at her—stunned, for once in her life, into silence. "You don't have to snap at me. I was just trying to help, in case you haven't thought it through."

"Thanks all the same, but we have thought it through, and if I wanted your advice, I'd ask for it."

"Fine." Mary Beth sniffed and set her jaw. "You're wrong, you know, about one thing. This monstrosity *is* bothering me, and it's probably bothering a lot of other people, too."

"No one else has complained."

"Not yet, maybe, but we do have rules in this neighborhood, you know, ordinances and things." Mary Beth gave her one last glare and marched back into her house.

Diane tried to return her attention to the quilt, but Mary Beth's remarks nagged at her. Eventually she put the quilt away and crossed the lawn to speak to Michael's friends. Their faces fell when she told them there would be no more skating until their parents came by and inspected the ramp for themselves. Brandon said his mom could be there in five minutes, but Kelly and Troy said their parents were working and couldn't come over until that evening, at the earliest.

"I'm sorry," Diane told Michael, and she meant it with all her heart.

Michael scowled, humiliated. "You said we could skate."

"It's okay," Kelly said, sparing a quick glance for Diane before turning back to Michael. "We can watch a video or something. We can skate tomorrow when everyone's allowed."

Michael muttered something, gave Diane a dark look, and motioned for his friends to follow him inside.

Diane went inside, too, after stopping by the deck to retrieve the quilt and glare at Mary Beth's house. If Mary Beth thought she could scare Diane into taking down that ramp, she was more foolish than Diane had given her credit for, and Diane had never been stingy when it came to estimating Mary Beth's faults.

By Tuesday evening, the parents of Michael's friends had inspected the ramp and had given their children permission to skate there. Diane enjoyed meeting them, especially Kelly's mother. "For weeks it's been Michael this and Michael that around our place," Kelly's mother said, shaking her head and smiling. "Kelly says Michael's the first boy she ever met who doesn't think it's odd for a girl to skate. He told her that boys who say girls can't skate are just worried about the competition."

"Really?" Diane was pleased. Somehow she'd raised a feminist. Gwen would be proud of her.

On the following night Diane joined the other Elm Creek Quilters for a staff meeting at the manor. Afterward, she updated her friends on the saga of the skating ramp. "I used to think like Mary Beth," she admitted. "But when I look at Michael now, it's hard for me to imagine why I ever disliked skateboarding. He hasn't seemed this well adjusted since the second grade."

"It isn't the skateboarding per se," Gwen said. "It's the attention you and Tim have been paying him lately."

"Thank you, Dr. Spock, but Michael's never lacked parental attention."

"But this is positive attention for an activity he enjoys. He's probably thrilled that you finally support one of his pastimes."

"You expect me to encourage his usual hobbies?" Diane shot back, thinking of the heavy metal music, the vandalism at the middle school, the fights with Todd. "Besides, it's not like you have any experience dealing with this sort of mess. Summer never gave you a moment's trouble."

Gwen held up her hands, apologetic. "You're right. I'm sorry."

"I used to get in trouble a lot when I was Michael's age," Judy said. "Talking back to the teachers, skipping classes, fistfights, you name it."

"Fistfights?" Bonnie said. "You? I can't believe it."

"It's true." Judy smiled wryly. "I got picked on a lot at school. The other kids would go like this"—she put her fingers to the outer corners of her eyes and stretched the lids into slits—"and tell me to go back to China."

"Their grasp of geography is depressing," Gwen said.

"You try explaining the difference between China and Vietnam to a bunch of obnoxious adolescents. They'd do Bruce Lee imitations and steal my lunch, saying I couldn't eat it anyway since I didn't have any chopsticks." Judy shook her head. "It sounds silly and stupid now, but at the time it was very painful. I guess I acted out because I didn't have any friends, anyone to support me. I didn't want to complain at home, because my mom had already been through so much."

"So what happened?" Diane asked. "You obviously straightened out somehow."

Judy shrugged, and her long, dark hair slipped over one shoulder. "My dad figured out what was going on and had me transferred to another school. No one teased me there, so I didn't need to cause trouble anymore."

"Do you think I should have Michael transferred to another school?"

"That's probably not necessary," Bonnie said. "Wait and see. It sounds like things may be turning around already."

"And making him leave his friends might make everything worse," Carol said. "The more advice you give your children, the more you try to help them do what's right, the more they insist on going their own way."

Sarah gave her a sharp look. "Sometimes parents try to help too much when no help is needed."

"Sometimes children don't know what's best for them. Sometimes they'd be wise to learn from their parents' mistakes instead of fumbling around on their own."

"Who's fumbling?" Sarah asked.

Carol said nothing, and an awkward silence descended on the foyer until a group of new campers arrived, sending the Elm Creek Quilters back to work.

The next day's classes kept Diane so busy that she had no chance to ask any of the Elm Creek Quilters about the strange exchange between mother and daughter, so she put it out of her mind. On the way home, she stopped at the grocery for a few things for supper and more cookies. The night before, Todd had complained that Michael and his friends had eaten all the snacks in the house, leaving nothing for Todd's friends.

"There's fruit," Diane had said, but Todd had scowled and muttered something about how things sure had changed around there. It was obvious he did not mean they had changed for the better. Diane hoped that an ample supply of snacks would appease him, if only temporarily.

As she pulled into the driveway, Diane saw the curtain in Mary Beth's living room window move aside. Her eyes met Mary Beth's before the curtain fell between them. Diane frowned and parked the car. Didn't Mary Beth have anything better to do all day than to spy on her neighbors? She carried the bag of groceries into the kitchen, then returned outside to check the mail. In her peripheral vision she saw Mary Beth's curtain draw back again, but she ignored it. That woman really needed a hobby.

Diane collected a handful of envelopes from the mailbox and leafed through them as she walked up the driveway. Credit card application, bill, bill, credit card application—and a thick envelope with a return address of the Waterford Municipal Building. She stopped in the middle of the driveway and opened the envelope, dreading the news. Rumor had it that the property taxes in their historic neighborhood were going to be reassessed, despite residents' complaints to the Zoning Commission.

The first line made it clear that the letter was not about taxes, but her relief soon turned to dismay. The Waterford Zoning Commission had received complaints that the Sonnenberg family had erected a skateboard ramp in their backyard. Since that structure met the definition of an Attractive Nuisance, and since they had not applied for the proper building permits, it must be razed within forty-eight hours.

"Is this some kind of a joke?" Diane exclaimed, gaping at the letter. The ramp was on private property. The Zoning Commission couldn't force them to tear it down, could they?

Diane looked up, her mind racing—and saw Mary Beth watching her through her living room window.

She crumpled the letter in her fist and marched across the lawn to Mary Beth's house. She could see the panic in her neighbor's face—before Mary Beth quickly hid behind the curtain. Diane stormed up the porch stairs and pounded on the front door. "Mary Beth," she shouted. "Get out here, you vicious little troll! I know you're responsible for this." She paused, but there was no response. She hammered on the door with her fist. "I know you're in there. Come on out!"

Mary Beth wisely remained inside. Eventually, Diane gave up and returned to her own house, seething. The nerve of Mary Beth, to turn Diane's family in to the Waterford Zoning Commission! "May her fabric bleed, her rotary cutter rust, and all of her borders be crooked," Diane muttered, slamming the door behind her and storming to the kitchen to call Bonnie. Diane was reluctant to interrupt her at Grandma's Attic, but this couldn't wait, and she wasn't going to risk getting a busy signal later that evening because of Craig's constant web surfing. Bonnie had served on the commission in the past as a representative from the Downtown Business Association. If the Sonnenbergs had any options, Bonnie would know what they were.

Quickly, Diane explained what had happened, then asked, "I know there are certain restrictions because this is a historic neighborhood, but is there anything I can do?" She steeled herself. "If I crawl over there on my hands and knees and beg Mary Beth to withdraw the complaint, and if by some miracle I manage to persuade her, would the Zoning Commission let us keep the ramp?"

"That's not how it works," Bonnie said. "Once the commission has made a ruling, the original complaint no longer matters. You have two options at this point. You can either comply with their request and tear down the ramp, or you can file for an exemption. That means you'll have to present your case to the commission at a public hearing."

Diane couldn't believe it. "You mean the kind of hearings they hold when someone wants to build a new mall or a new road?"

"I'm afraid so. According to their bureaucratic way of looking at things, your ramp is no different than a major construction site. You'll have to convince the commission that the skateboard ramp isn't a hazard to local residents, doesn't create unnecessary noise or traffic problems, and doesn't destroy the aesthetics of the neighborhood."

Diane groaned. "I know. I remember that part."

"I don't understand why Mary Beth went to the authorities instead of trying to work things out with you personally. Maybe you two aren't friends, but you are neighbors." Then Bonnie paused. "What do you mean, you remember?"

"Look, I have to go. Michael's going to be home from school any minute, and I have to figure out what I'm going to tell him."

"Oh, no, you don't. You're not hanging up until you tell me what you meant by 'I remember.' "

"Mary Beth has been a thorn in my side for too long." Diane sank into a chair, propped her elbows on the kitchen table, and let her head rest in her palm. "She never would have known about that ordinance if not for those stupid wind chimes."

"What?"

Diane's anger faded into chagrin. "Two years ago, Mary Beth hung some wind chimes outside her kitchen window. I swear to God, they were the wind chimes from hell, clanking and banging with the slightest breeze. They must have had amplifiers or something. They scared away every bird for miles—"

"Miles?"

"Well, yards, anyway. And they kept me and Tim awake all night. The only way we could escape the noise was to shut every window facing the backyard, and that wasn't fair. So I asked her very nicely to take them down—"

"Oh, I bet you did."

"I did, I swear. Whose side are you on? Naturally she refused, so I called the municipal building and asked them about noise ordinances."

"And when you found one, you called Mary Beth and threatened to turn her in, didn't you?"

"Of course not." Diane paused. "I went over and told her in person."

Bonnie burst out laughing.

"But I only threatened to turn her in," Diane protested. "I wouldn't have done it."

"Either way, you're the one who started it, and now it's come back to haunt you."

Bonnie's amusement was exasperating, mostly because Diane knew she was right. "I'm glad you find this so humorous, but you're not helping. My son's going to lose his skateboard ramp, remember?"

"I'm sorry. You're right." Bonnie made a strangling sound as if fighting to contain her laughter. She promised to help Diane file for the exemption and prepare for the hearing, if that's what she and Tim decided to do.

When Diane called him with the news, he came right home. They talked about it as they made supper, while outside Michael and his friends zoomed up and down the skateboard ramp, unaware that their fun could be short-lived. Diane and Tim considered the time and effort it would take to file for an exemption, the stress and publicity the hearing would generate—but most of all, they thought of Michael and how he would be affected by the loss of his skateboard ramp and by the knowledge that his parents had meekly submitted to the Zoning Commission's first and only letter.

"If we want to keep the skateboard ramp, we'll have to fight for it," Tim eventually said, and Diane agreed, but she had an additional motive. She wanted to fight because she refused to let Mary Beth win so easily. She'd give up quilting before she'd hand that woman an uncontested victory.

During supper, they told the boys about the letter and what they were prepared to do to keep the skateboard ramp. Michael's expression changed from alarm to relief when he realized they weren't going to give in, at least not until they had to. "Is there anything I can do?" he asked.

"I'll let you know what Bonnie suggests," Diane said. "It'll be a lot of work, but with all four of us helping out, we'll take care of it." Michael nodded, but Todd muttered something, nudged his plate away, and put his elbows on the table. He had hardly touched his supper, and suddenly Diane realized that he hadn't said a word since she brought up the letter. "Is something wrong, Todd?"

"Why do you just assume that everyone wants to help? Maybe I don't care about this stupid skateboard ramp. Did you ever think about that?"

Startled, Diane turned to Tim, who looked back at her with the same surprised helplessness she was feeling. "But—but Michael is your brother," she stammered.

"So?"

"So?" Diane stared at him, disbelieving. "So we help each other. That's part of what makes us a family."

"What about helping me? How come nobody thinks about me?"

Diane was at a loss, so Tim stepped in. "What do you mean, son?"

"Did you ever think about what it's gonna be like at school?" Todd's voice was high and thin. "Why does she have to fight with Brent's mom all the time? I'm not gonna have any friends left thanks to her."

Tim's mild voice grew stern. "Don't talk about your mother that way. Apologize this minute."

"But it's true. She's gonna ruin everything."

"I said, apologize."

Todd glared at the table and clamped his mouth shut as if afraid an apology might slip out by force of habit.

Tim's eyes sparked with anger. "Go to your room. Now."

Todd shoved his chair back from the table and stormed away.

"I'm sorry," Michael said when Todd was gone.

"Why?" Diane said briskly, picking up her fork. "You didn't do anything wrong." For once it was true. In a matter of weeks, her sons had traded personalities.

The next morning, Diane went downtown to Bonnie's quilt shop, where the red sign with the words GRANDMA'S ATTIC printed in gold seemed to welcome her. The quilt hanging beneath it in the shop window comforted her, too, since she had often seen Judy working on it at the Elm Creek Quilters' meetings. Everything about Bonnie's shop—from the folk music playing in the background to the shelves filled with fabric and notions—was familiar to her, a reminder of her friends and the good times they had shared throughout the years. Her friends would support her no matter what happened, she knew, and that knowledge strengthened her.

Bonnie was at the large cutting table in the middle of the room helping a customer when Diane entered. The bell attached to the door jingled, and Bonnie looked up and smiled. "Pull up a stool," she called out, motioning for Diane to join them at the cutting table. Diane did and waited for the customer to pay for her purchases and leave.

When they were alone, Bonnie showed Diane some papers she had picked up from the municipal building. She explained how to fill them out and described the exemption hearing process, and as she did, Diane began to feel better. She and Tim had a lot of work ahead of them, but not nearly as much as she had feared. With Bonnie there to reassure her, the task didn't seem as hopeless and overwhelming as it had the night before.

As Diane turned to go, she thanked Bonnie wholeheartedly. Bonnie waved off her thanks with an easy laugh and said, "You would have done the same for me. Now, try not to worry, okay? Work on the round robin quilt; that'll relax you."

"Oh." Diane had forgotten all about it. "That's a good idea."

Bonnie's eyebrows rose, and she gave Diane a look of amused exasperation. "You do know you're supposed to have it done by the end of this week, right?" Then her expression softened. "Look, why don't you just give it to me? You have enough on your mind already."

"No, I can do it," Diane said, heading for the door.

"Are you sure?" Bonnie called after her. "We can extend the deadline."

"That's not necessary. I'll get it done." Diane thanked her again for all her help and left the shop. There was no way Diane was going to let Mary Beth prevent her from participating in the round robin. Mary Beth had already interfered too much in Diane's life; she wasn't going to ruin this quilt, too.

That weekend, Diane and Tim collected documents on local privacy laws supporting their right to keep the skateboard ramp. The Elm Creek Quilters did their part, too. Summer researched possible precedents in the Waterford College library; Judy's husband, Steve, wrote a feature article on the conflict for the local newspaper; and everyone joined in to keep Diane's spirits up.

On the same morning Steve's article appeared in the *Waterford Register,* Agnes stopped by the Sonnenberg home with unsettling news. The boys were scrambling to get ready for school, but they hovered around the kitchen as Agnes told their parents about Mary Beth's weekend activities.

"She went to every house in the neighborhood with a petition supporting the commission's decision," Agnes said, her blue eyes solemn behind pink-tinted glasses.

The news made Diane uneasy, though she wasn't surprised. "How many signatures has she collected?"

"I didn't get a good look at the petition because naturally I didn't sign it, but I believe she had almost one page filled." Agnes pursed her lips and shook her head. "The nerve of her, bringing that petition to my door."

Diane hugged the older woman. Mary Beth knew very well that Diane and Agnes were friends. Agnes had baby-sat Diane when she was a child, and they were both Elm Creek Quilters. Mary Beth had to have known that Agnes would tell Diane about the petition. Was this a message, a boast that Mary Beth didn't care if Diane knew what she was up to because she knew Diane was powerless to stop her?

One page filled, Agnes had said, an entire page covered with signatures demanding the destruction of the skateboard ramp. The thought of it made Diane dizzy with apprehension. How could it be that so many of their neighbors had sided against them?

The phone rang as soon as Agnes left; it was Gwen, calling to gloat over Steve's article. "It's perfect," she crowed. "You'll have every parent and private property hawk in Waterford on your side."

"I haven't had a chance to read it yet," Diane said, pinning the receiver to her ear with her shoulder so her hands would be free to pack the boys' lunches. Tim sped through the kitchen and planted a kiss on her cheek on his way out. "Bye, honey," she called after him.

"Honey?" Gwen echoed. "Hanging up so soon?"

"That was for Tim, but yes, I do have to go." Had Gwen forgotten what school mornings were like in a family with teenagers? "First, though, does the article say anything about Mary Beth's petition?"

"No. What petition?"

"I'll tell you after your workshop. See you at Elm Creek Manor." Diane hung up and called out to her sons. "Lunches are ready. Hurry up or you'll be late."

Michael snatched his from the counter and ran out the door, but Todd hesitated, his brows drawn together in disbelief. "Brent's mom made a petition against us?"

The phone rang again.

Diane glanced from her son to the phone, to the clock over the kitchen table, and back to her son in the amount of time for the phone to pause between rings. "Not against us, honey, not against you. We're just having a difference of opinion. This is the way adults settle these things. We shouldn't take it personally. We can talk about this later, okay? You'd better hurry or you'll miss your bus."

He nodded, put his lunch bag in his backpack, and left, but he didn't look convinced. Why should he? Diane knew her explanation was a half-truth at best. Neither she nor Mary Beth was demonstrating textbook adult behavior, and Diane herself was taking this matter all too personally. She snatched up the phone a second before the answering machine would have clicked on. "Hello?"

It was a neighbor, calling to apologize for signing Mary Beth's petition. She never would have signed it, she said, if she had known the whole story, but now that she'd read the newspaper article, the Sonnenbergs had her support. Diane thanked her, but as soon as they hung up, the phone rang again.

"Hello?" she said, glancing at the clock.

"Tear that damn thing down or we'll tear it down for you," a voice growled in her ear, low, gruff, a man's voice. Then there was a click and the dial tone.

Stunned, Diane slowly replaced the receiver—and the phone rang again. Heart pounding, she unplugged the cord from the jack.

After Gwen's workshop, while the campers were enjoying their free time, Diane told Gwen, Sarah, Carol, and Sylvia about the call. All but Sylvia listened with wide eyes, stunned by the story. Sylvia looked concerned, but somehow she didn't seemed surprised.

"Did you use star sixty-nine to trace the call?" Gwen asked.

Diane shook her head. "I didn't think of it." Her heart sank as they all urged her to do so next time. Why were they so certain that there would be a next time?

"I must say I'm amazed by all this," Carol said. "This seemed like such a nice little town."

Sarah gave her a slight frown. "It almost always is. This is an anomaly."

"I hope you're right," Carol said, but she looked dubious. "It doesn't seem like a very nice place to raise children."

Sarah gave her a disapproving look but said nothing more.

Diane dreaded to go home, but eventually she could think of no more excuses to stay, and she wanted to be there when the boys arrived. Before she left, Sylvia took her aside and placed her hands on Diane's shoulders.

"Promise me you won't let those fools scare you," Sylvia said.

"I won't," Diane said. Though she was taller, she felt young and small beneath the older woman's knowing gaze. "I'm not scared, just angry."

"Good." Sylvia squeezed Diane's shoulders. "I want to believe in the good in people, I do, but I've seen how the people in this town can turn on a person. I know how it feels to have a whole town against you. Don't let them make you afraid. Don't let them make you feel ashamed when you've done nothing wrong." And with that, she strode away, back to her sewing room.

Diane watched her go, wondering.

When she got home, the house was quiet, but instead of the restful peace she usually sensed there at that time of day, the silence seemed strange and watchful. She chided herself for her nerves and told herself she was being silly, but still, she walked through the house checking every room to see what was amiss. She felt alert, wary. Something wasn't right.

When she returned to the kitchen and drew back the curtain to peer outside, she saw it.

Paint as red as blood stained the skateboard ramp; angry splashes and hateful words marred the smooth curves. Diane found herself running outside, strangling a scream of rage as she drew closer, close enough to see shattered eggs and mud and broken glass. She stopped at the base of the U, clenching and unclenching her fists, fighting to breathe. Her eyes darted around the yard, though she knew the culprits were long gone. The paint was dry; the dark patches of mud were cracked on the surface; the eggs had hardened into yellowish, foul-smelling streaks.

Michael. She couldn't let him see this.

She raced to the back of the garage for the garden hose, unwinding it like a thick green snake on the lawn. Most of the mud surrendered to the force of the spray, but the eggs were more stubborn and the paint glared scarlet through the droplets. She brought out buckets and soap and brushes and scrubbed at the stains with all her strength. She scrubbed harder, faster, until her muscles burned, sweat trickled down her forehead, and all she could do was scrub and scrub and scrub and spit out curses through clenched teeth.

"Mom?"

She gasped and turned so quickly that she upset the bucket, sending a stream of pink, soapy water running down the base of the ramp to the lawn. Michael and Todd were staring at her, too stunned to get out of the way.

Diane couldn't think of what to say. She sat back on her heels and drew the back of her hand across her brow, pushing the sweaty blond curls aside.

"What the hell happened?" Michael said. Openmouthed, he climbed onto the ramp and slowly spun around, taking it all in.

Diane watched him until she caught her breath, then she picked up her brush and got back to work. Her fury was spent; she worked slowly now, deliberately. A few moments later, she heard Michael set the bucket upright and fill it with water and soap. Soon he was on his knees beside her, plunging a second brush into the bucket and scrubbing furiously.

Five minutes passed, and then ten, and then Todd joined them. Unnoticed, he had gone back inside to change out of his nice school clothes. It was such a typical Todd thing to do that Diane almost burst out laughing, but she didn't let herself, because she knew if she did, tears would soon follow.

They worked until Tim came home. Diane had forgotten to make supper, so they ordered pizza. When they sat down to eat, Diane yanked the curtains shut so they couldn't see into the backyard.

"We need a guard dog," Todd said, chewing thoughtfully on a long string of mozzarella. "A huge, mean dog. A Doberman pinscher or a rottweiler."

"Or a pit bull," Michael said. "Or a couple of pit bulls."

"Or a velociraptor on crack," Tim suggested, reaching for a second piece.

It was so ridiculous that Diane had to laugh—deep, aching, whole-body laughs that soon had the entire family joining in. They laughed completely out of proportion to the humor in Tim's remark, and that awareness was what finally helped Diane stop laughing long enough to finish her supper. But for the rest of the evening, as the four of them tried to remove the signs of the vandalism, all anyone had to do was snarl and claw the air like a dinosaur after prey and they were all helpless with laughter again.

The next day, Diane left for Elm Creek Manor as late as possible and rushed home as soon as Judy's workshop ended. To her relief, no additional vandalism had occurred during her absence. Perhaps the culprits thought none was needed; traces of paint were still plainly visible on the smooth curve of the ramp, spelling out words she liked to fool herself into thinking her sons didn't know.

She was sitting on the swing on the deck, the round robin quilt untouched in her lap, when Todd came home. "I skipped band practice," he said by way of greeting, but she hardly heard him. His shirt was torn, the collar stained with blood that probably came from his split lip. His left eye was puffy and bruised.

"What on earth?" Diane jumped up, letting the quilt fall, and raced to him. She checked him all over for more serious injuries before marching him inside to patch him up.

"Brent," he said, though she had already guessed. "He got mad because I was passing around a petition after school."

"A what?"

He reached for his backpack, wincing in pain, and took out a crumpled sheet of paper. "I figured if they could have a petition, we could, too."

Diane skimmed the page, taking in about two dozen children's signatures below a paragraph asking the commission to let Michael Sonnenberg keep his skateboard ramp.

Her heart was too full for words. She wrapped Todd in a hug and held on tight.

"Mom," he said in a strained voice, "that kind of hurts."

Immediately, she released him. "Sorry." Then movement in the family room doorway caught her eye. It was a young man with hair neatly trimmed and nary an earring to be seen.

Diane stared. "Who are you and what have you done with my son?"

"Funny, Mom," Michael said, but he grinned, pleased.

Todd looked astounded. "Dude, what did you do to your hair?"

"I got it cut." Michael flopped into a chair. "I don't want to give those guys any ammunition."

A month ago, Diane never could have imagined she'd ever say the words she was about to speak. "I wish you wouldn't have. You don't need to change for them."

But Michael merely shrugged. "It's just my hair. It's not me." His eyes met hers, and for a moment Diane felt that they understood each other.

⚓

Her heart full of sorrowful pride, Diane took up the round robin quilt that had been so often studied and too long neglected. She chose fabric in a deeper shade of cream than what Sarah had used, for Sarah's fabric was too bright for this new feeling, for this not-yet-comprehensible sense that in fighting for her son's happiness she had done exactly what her family needed her to do, so that regardless of the hearing's outcome, she would know she had not failed them.

She cut four large triangles from the cloth, knowing that although they came from the same fabric, and looked alike, and might even seem identical to an outsider, there were subtle differences among them—a more crooked line here, a sharper point there, an edge not quite as long as it should be. Some quilters would call them mistakes, these variations that made each piece unique, but now Diane knew better.

She sewed the longest side of each triangle to an edge of the round robin quilt, setting the design on point, forcing a new perspective. One triangle for Tim, one for Michael, one for Todd, and the last for herself. The two smaller tips of each triangle met the analogous angles of the triangles on its left and its right, like four members of a family holding hands in a circle, united at last.

Four

He had thought about Sylvia often since that Sunday morning weeks ago when he had seen her on television. It was a shock, at first, to see the short gray hair where once there had been long, dark curls, but her spirit was the same, there was no doubt about that. The young woman who had spent so much of the program at Sylvia's elbow, though, the one who had made that joke about her mother—she was a mystery. She and Sylvia seemed close. Could she be a granddaughter? Had Sylvia married again after all? He didn't think so. He hoped not. If he'd had any idea that Sylvia would ever consider taking another husband, he would have stuck around.

A pang of guilt went through him. "I didn't mean that the way it sounded, Katy-girl," he said aloud. He could picture her wagging a finger at him in mock reproach, and he grinned. No, Katy knew he wouldn't trade anything for the more than fifty years they had spent together. Those years had given him two children, a home, and a peace he had never dreamed he could possess. Katy never minded his limp, or his background, or the way he needed to be by himself every once in a while. When he woke in the darkness shaking and sweating from the nightmares, she had held him and shushed him and stroked his head until he could sleep again. In the mornings she would say nothing of his terror, leaving him his dignity.

He missed her. Sometimes he wished he had been the one to pass on first. Katy would have managed fine without him, better than he had done without her. Then again, he wouldn't wish this loneliness on anyone, least of all his wife.

It sure would be nice to have her in the passenger seat, riding along beside him as they crisscrossed the country. Of course, if Katy were still alive, he wouldn't have sold the house and bought this motor home. She loved that little house. Over the years, as their nest egg had grown, he'd often suggested they find a bigger place, but she wouldn't hear of it. "Why move now, just when I have my garden the way I like it?" she had asked. Another time it was because the kids were in school, and then it was because all their friends lived in the neighborhood. But one by one their friends retired and moved to condos in Florida or rooms in their children's homes. His buddies at the VFW grew fewer and fewer. Some died, and all too soon Katy joined them.

The house was an empty shell without Katy, and he couldn't bear to remain. The kids agreed that selling the house was a good idea and they both assumed he would be moving in with one of them. Bob's wife, Cathy, tempted him with descriptions of the California sunshine, while his daughter, Amy, promised him his own apartment over the garage and plenty of New England fishing trips with her husband. He had waited until after the sale to tell them he had other plans. They thought he'd lost his mind when he bought the motor home, and they tried to talk him out of it. They didn't succeed. Oh, he knew if he lived long enough there would come a time when he would no longer be able to look after himself, and then he'd be grateful for the kids' help. But not yet. He had much to do before then.

"They're great kids, Katy, but they think anyone over seventy is ready for the old folks' home," he said. Still, although he wished he didn't seem so old and helpless in their eyes, he was glad that they wanted him. That proved he must have done something right all those years. He hadn't learned much from his own father about how to be a good parent, but he must have done all right in the end.

His philosophy about raising children had been simple: Do nothing that his own parents had done and everything they had not.

The day Katy told him she was carrying their first, he had broken out in a cold sweat. He had been thrilled at the prospect of being a father, of welcoming a new life when he had seen so much death, but there had been fear enough to match his happiness. He worried about Katy, of course; he knew women could die in childbirth. But Katy was strong and healthy, and deep down he knew she'd be fine. What made him tremble from fear was the image of himself beating his son, of touching his daughter until she cried, of bludgeoning his wife's soul until she became a pale shadow of the vibrant woman he had married. He had seen this happen. Except for the few brief glimpses of the Bergstroms, this was the only family life he knew.

"You are not your father," Katy had told him passionately. "You are the kindest and most loving man I've ever known. I wouldn't have married you if I didn't know this with my whole heart."

He had wanted so much to believe her, but still he had feared the monster that might lurk within himself, cruelty passed to him along with his father's build and sandy hair.

When he held his daughter for the first time, so much love coursed through him that he knew he could never hurt a child of his and Katy's. But he would take no chances. He could not discipline his children the way the other parents in the neighborhood did; even when they had earned themselves a spanking he couldn't bear to raise a hand against them, or even to scold them. He would send them to their rooms instead, and go for long walks until his anger eased. When the children needed a scolding, it was up to Katy to provide it. "I always have to be the villain," she would grumble, glaring at him as she marched upstairs to face a disobedient child. He and Katy had been able to resolve each and every disagreement that ever came between them, except for this one. He hoped that despite her exasperation she understood somehow, and if not, that she forgave him anyway.

When he came to a wayside, he pulled off the freeway and fixed himself a sandwich. He carried it and a can of soda outside to a picnic table near a patch of trees. There he sat, thinking, eating his lunch and watching the cars speed past.

He would be the first to admit that Katy and Sylvia were a lot alike. That's what had attracted him to Katy the first time he saw her at that dance. He had been struck by the dark hair, the confident way she had thrown back her head and laughed just from the pleasure of the evening. He was instantly transported back to the moment he had first seen Sylvia on horseback on the Bergstrom estate, riding around the ring, oblivious to her young brother's playmate, who had climbed the corral fence to watch.

"She's like a lady from a story," he had said to Richard, awestruck.

"Who, Sylvia?"

"She's like—" Only seven, he fumbled for the words. "She's like a princess."

This had sent Richard into hysterics, and he fell to the ground, where he rolled from side to side on his back, laughing.

His face went hot, and he quickly joined in the laughter so Richard wouldn't think him a sissy. Richard was his only friend. Everyone else at school shied away from him, frightened by his bruises or by something in his eyes, something his father had put there.

He knew Richard was wrong. Sylvia was a princess, and Elm Creek Manor was a paradise. He would do anything to live there with them, away from the shouts, away from his father's stick and his mother's weeping. He would bring his sister, and Mr. Bergstrom would adopt them and they would be safe. Even when he grew up he would never have to leave, never.

He had invited himself to live with them the day he turned eight. It had been the worst birthday ever. His parents had forgotten about it, and he had known better than to remind them. The teacher scolded him for forgetting to bring cookies for the class to share, and everyone but Richard had laughed at him. In truth, he hadn't forgotten the cookies. They didn't have a single cookie in the house or anything to make them with, but he wouldn't tell the teacher that, not with everyone watching and laughing.

That evening he stayed for supper at Richard's house, knowing those few pleasant hours would be well worth the licking they would surely cost him. The Bergstrom house seemed so full of light and laughter. Sylvia quarreled with her elder sister, Claudia, sometimes, but that was nothing, nothing compared to what he saw at home.

After the meal he offered to help Sylvia clean up.

She thanked him and raised her eyebrows at her brother. "It's nice to know someone around here is a gentleman. We can't get Richard to lift a finger."

For a moment he feared Sylvia's chiding would work and Richard would join them. But Richard must have been accustomed to Sylvia's teasing, for he stuck out his tongue at her and remained in his seat. And Sylvia merely laughed. She didn't strike him across the face or scream at him or anything. She *was* like a lady from a story, no matter what Richard said.

When they were alone in the kitchen, she washed the dishes and he dried them. As they worked, she talked to him as if he were a grown-up. It more than made up for the awful birthday.

He wiped the dishes slowly to make the moment last, and soon she finished washing and picked up another towel to help him. "I wish I were a boy," she muttered, as if she had forgotten he was there. "The girls have to do all the work but the boys get to play."

He nodded, thinking of what his sister suffered at their father's hands. He wouldn't want to be a girl, either. "I would always help you," he said instead.

"No, you wouldn't. You'd be like all the rest of them."

"I wouldn't," he insisted, his heart pounding as he screwed up his courage. "If I could live here, I'd help you with the work every day, I promise. I'd do all the work myself so you could go play. If I could live here, please, I promise—"

Sylvia was staring at him.

It was all wrong, and he knew it. "It's just a joke," he blurted out. "Richard dared me to say it. I didn't mean it. I'd hate to live here. Really."

She watched him, bemused. "I see."

"No, I don't really hate it here—I mean—" He didn't know what he meant. He felt a prickling in his eyes that warned him he might cry, and it sickened him. He couldn't cry like a baby in front of Sylvia, he couldn't.

But Sylvia didn't seem to notice. "What did you win?" she asked, turning back to the dishes.

"Wh-what?"

"The dare. What did you win for the dare?"

"Oh." He thought quickly. "Richard—he has to give me his lunch tomorrow at school."

"I see." She sounded impressed. "That's quite a prize. I'll have to make him an extra-big lunch tomorrow, won't I? Do you think maybe you could share it with him, so that he doesn't get too hungry to learn his lessons?"

"Oh, sure, sure." He nodded so vigorously that his head hurt.

"Thanks." She gave him a quick smile, then looked out the window. When she spoke again, her voice was casual. "It's too bad it was only a joke. We like having you around. You're always welcome here."

He felt so pleased and proud he couldn't speak. He kept wiping that one dish until Sylvia laughed and took it from him, saying that if he kept it up he'd rub a hole through the china.

After that, Richard's lunches contained twice as much food as even a hungry growing boy could eat. And Richard always shared everything with him, split right down the middle.

Richard would have been a good man, if he had lived.

Sighing, he wadded up his trash and carried it to a garbage can. In a few minutes he was back on the road, heading east to his daughter's place in Connecticut.

As he pulled onto the Indiana Toll Road, he wondered if Sylvia remembered him. Probably not. He wrote to invite her to the wedding, but she didn't come. She didn't even write back. Claudia had, though, to tell him that Sylvia had left Elm Creek Manor but that Claudia would send his invitation to Sylvia's in-laws in Maryland. They would know how to reach her.

Claudia added a postscript informing him that she was Claudia Midden now and had been ever since she married Harold.

He went cold at the news. Yes, he had known that Claudia and Harold were engaged, but he never thought she'd go through with it. Hadn't Sylvia told her how Harold had let Richard and Sylvia's husband, James, die?

The four men had enlisted within hours of each other—he and Richard first, thinking World War Two would bring them adventure and glory; James and Harold later, when they learned of the younger men's actions. James went to watch over Richard for Sylvia's sake, but if Harold shared James's intentions, his courage failed at the crucial moment.

He could never forget the view from that high bluff, the droning of planes overhead, the relief that turned to terror as their own boys fired upon them, the tank on the beach below exploding in flames. James, climbing out of the other tank and racing to help, as he himself had done, sprinting straight down the steep bluff to the beach, knowing he would never make it in time. In his nightmares he was forever running toward that tank, knowing Richard was inside, running with his feet sinking into the soft, wet sand, never gaining any ground. In the nightmares he could hear James's last words as he fought with the hatch, desperately trying to free his wife's beloved brother: "Come on, Harold, help me!"

But Harold ducked back inside his own tank. The planes made another pass, and the world exploded in flames.

Harold's cowardice had saved him, but the cost was great—Richard's life, and James's, and Mr. Bergstrom's, and that of the child Sylvia was carrying. Richard and James died in the second explosion; the shock of the news killed Mr. Bergstrom and caused Sylvia to miscarry James's child. Tragedy piled upon tragedy drove a wedge into the family, estranging the grieving sisters when they needed each other most. And now Harold had maneuvered his way into the family he had so devastated.

The outrage, the injustice of it all, nearly drove him mad. He frightened Katy with his fury, and only the shock in her eyes allowed him to regain control of himself. For an instant the part of him that was so like his father had escaped. He sealed it up again, eventually, but his anger never completely died. He couldn't bear it. He had longed to be a part of the Bergstrom family ever since he was a young boy playing with Richard on the banks of Elm Creek—but that honor had gone to Harold, the one who least deserved it.

That was why he had stayed away so long. Why return to Elm Creek Manor when Richard was dead, when James was dead, when Mr. Bergstrom was dead, when Sylvia had left for good? The place once so full of light and laughter must surely have become as cold and silent as a tomb. He could not go back. There was no point to it.

At least, there hadn't been for many years.

Shaken by memories, he pulled the motor home onto the shoulder of the road. He set the parking brake and turned on his hazard lights, then sat motionless, gripping the steering wheel, staring ahead through the windshield. The motor home trembled whenever a car sped past, but he barely noticed.

Later—it could have been ten minutes or several times that—he took out his wallet and held it for a moment before retrieving the old photo he knew was there. He had carried it all those years, ever since he and Richard were young men in Philadelphia.

He had seen the black-and-white snapshot in Richard's room, where his friend was boarding as he attended school. In the photo, Sylvia was standing beside a horse, one of the last Bergstrom Thoroughbreds, though of course no one knew that then. She wore close-fitting pants and carried a rider's helmet and crop in one hand; the other arm was draped around the horse's neck. She was smiling at the photographer with perfect joy, as if she had never known sorrow and never would.

"James took that picture," Richard had told him, seeing how he admired it.

He had nodded, his heart sinking a little. Of course, it had been nonsense to think that she would have waited for him. He was a child to her and always would be. He had not seen her in years, not since the social workers had taken him and his sister from their parents and sent them to live with an aunt in Philadelphia. He consoled himself with the knowledge that James was a good man—Richard had nothing but praise for him—and that Sylvia was happy.

"Can I have it?" he heard himself asking.

Richard grinned, removed the photo from the frame, and gave it to him. He'd carried it ever since, and it showed. He should have taken better care of it.

He studied the smiling face in the photo.

He could do it; there was no reason not to. He could take the Pennsylvania Turnpike to the road that led to Waterford. He would recall the way to Elm Creek Manor once he got closer. Sylvia might not remember him, but that wouldn't bother him too much. He just wanted to see her, to talk about old times and see for himself that she was all right. Now, when the past sometimes seemed more vivid to him than the present, it would be good to talk to someone who remembered the old days.

He put the photo away and turned the key in the ignition.

He'd do it. First, though, he had to get something better to wear. He had to be presentable when he saw Sylvia again, not worn and shabby in his old fishing clothes. For the first time he wished he'd given in to Cathy's urging to let her take him shopping.

"An hour at the mall won't kill you, Dad," she'd admonished him.

"You never know, it just might," he'd retorted, enjoying her teasing and delighted, as he always was, that his son's wife called him "Dad."

He smiled as he pulled back onto the road and headed east.

Five

Sarah knew Matt hated to hear her grumble about her mother, but one evening as they got ready for bed, she forgot herself. The more she told him about the annoying things her mother had done and said that day, the more irritable she became. She didn't realize that she had been rambling on for ten minutes, her voice increasing in volume and pitch with each sentence, until Matt cut her off.

"Sarah, I'm tired," he said, climbing into bed. "Can you just pull the plug, please?"

"Pull the plug? You mean, tell her to go home?"

"No, I mean stop playing this broken record." He lay down and drew the covers over himself. "Your mother says the wrong things, she embarrasses you, she doesn't understand you—I get the idea. We all get the idea."

Sarah stared at him. "Since when do we not talk to each other about our problems?"

"If you want to talk, we can talk. You're just ranting and raving." He rolled over on his side, ending the discussion.

Sarah watched him, speechless, before she finally finished undressing and got into bed. She lay down on her side with her back to him. She waited, but he didn't mold his body around hers as he usually did. She felt cold and alone, and it was an increasingly familiar feeling. She missed their old closeness and wondered what had become of it.

Sometimes she felt like she couldn't talk to Matt about anything anymore. She would have turned to Sylvia, but the older woman already had enough misgivings about bringing mother and daughter together; Sarah couldn't bear to add to them. She would have confided in the Elm Creek Quilters, but they had already accepted Carol as one of their own. Two years ago the Elm Creek Quilters had welcomed Sarah without judgment, without conditions, with no other wish than to offer her their friendship. In spite of everything, Sarah couldn't bring herself to insist that they deny that gift to another newcomer, even when that newcomer had her so crazy she often thought she'd rather fling herself into Elm Creek than spend another minute in her presence.

As the spring days grew longer and warmer, Sarah put her energy into counting the days until her mother's departure. If Diane could tolerate the skateboard ramp fiasco, Sarah could surely endure the rest of her mother's visit.

On a Thursday afternoon, Sarah left the office and went downstairs to the ballroom, where Diane was assisting Bonnie with her workshop. Sarah watched as Diane moved briskly and confidently from table to table, assisting the campers. If Diane was worried about the upcoming exemption hearing, she hid it well. There was a new determination in her eyes, an awareness and confidence Sarah hadn't seen there before.

When the class was over and the students had gone off to enjoy their free time, Diane took a folded bundle out of her bag. "I finished adding my border," she said. "Do you want it next, Bonnie?"

Bonnie agreed, took the quilt, and held it up. Sarah took one look at it and began to laugh.

"What?" Diane asked. "What's the problem now?"

"All you did was add four triangles and set it on point," Sarah exclaimed.

"So? No one said we couldn't set it on point."

"Setting it on point isn't the problem."

Bonnie shook her head. "No piecing, no appliqué—I consider that cheating."

"At least I got it done on time," Diane said, then she paused. "Almost on time. I'm only a little late."

They all laughed, but Sarah felt a wave of sympathy for Diane, who had been much too distracted lately to enjoy working on the quilt. Diane's piecing had improved so much over the past two years, and she had probably been eager to show off her new skills. Once again Mary Beth had forced Diane to modify her goals.

A similar thought must have crossed Bonnie's mind, for she folded up the quilt top and packed it carefully in her tote bag. "Your border's just fine," she said. "In fact, I think it was an excellent choice. An unbroken space for hand quilting will set off the center block perfectly."

Diane was so pleased by the compliment that she couldn't speak.

Suddenly, Sarah heard an odd rumbling coming from outside. "Do you hear that?" she asked her friends.

They all listened.

"Thunder?" Bonnie guessed.

"I don't think so," Sarah said. They went to a window on the west-facing wall, where they could hear the sound more plainly as they looked out on the back of the manor. Elm trees obscured most of the view, but in the distance Sarah could see a cloud of dust rising along the back road, near the barn and moving closer.

"What is it, a cattle drive?" Diane asked.

"I don't know, but I'm going to find out." Sarah left the ballroom and headed for the west wing, Bonnie and Diane close behind. Sylvia met them at the kitchen doorway as they passed.

"What on earth is that noise?" she asked them. Without waiting for an answer, she tossed her dish towel onto the kitchen table and followed her friends to the back door.

Sarah opened it and led the three women outside, where they shaded their eyes with their hands and looked down the back road. A motor home was crossing the narrow bridge over Elm Creek.

Sylvia sucked in a breath. "Watch the trees, watch the trees," she called out as the vehicle scraped through the stately elms lining the back road. Sarah was glad Matt hadn't seen it.

The motor home slowed as it entered the clearing behind the manor and circled the small parking lot, carefully making its way past the campers' cars. When it reached the far end of the lot, it maneuvered into a block of open spaces and halted.

A moment later, the door opened and a man got out. Sarah guessed from his gray hair and the slight stiffness to his movements that he was in his early seventies, a few years younger than Sylvia. He wore tan slacks and a striped golf shirt—the uniform of the leisure set—but the hard knots of muscle in his forearms suggested years of demanding physical labor.

"Someone's husband?" Bonnie murmured.

"Maybe." Sarah watched the man approach. They had a few campers around his age. Alarm pricked her. What emergency would require a man to come pick up his wife from quilt camp without phoning first?

Sylvia brushed past Sarah as she descended the steps to welcome their unexpected guest. "Hello," she greeted him from a few yards away. "Welcome to Elm Creek Manor. May I help you?"

A grin broke over the man's face, and Sarah found herself smiling, too. He looked almost bashful, and his brown eyes were warm and kind. "Hello, Sylvia," he said.

He knew her. Sarah, Bonnie, and Diane exchanged surprised glances, and Sarah could tell by their expressions that they didn't recognize the man, either. She wished she could see Sylvia's face, but the older woman's back was to her.

There was a long moment of silence.

Then Sylvia's hand flew to her throat. "Good gracious me, it couldn't be."

The man's grin deepened, and he nodded.

"Andrew Cooper, as I live and breathe," Sylvia exclaimed. It happened too suddenly for Sarah to detect who stepped forward first, but in an instant the distance between Sylvia and the man had been closed and they were embracing. Then Sylvia placed her hands on his shoulders and stepped back to see him better. "How are you? Better yet, what on earth are you doing here?"

"I saw your program on television," he explained. His voice had a rough edge to it, the sound of a man who spoke only when he had something important to say. "I was traveling east to visit my daughter, and I figured I'd pull off the turnpike and see the old hometown."

"I'm glad you did, but you could have told me you were coming," Sylvia scolded him. "You certainly know how to give a body a shock."

"Sorry." He smiled, and suddenly Sarah realized he'd been looking forward to that scolding for miles. As if sensing her thoughts, he looked up at her.

Sylvia followed his line of sight and started as if she had forgotten her friends were there. "Oh, dear. Andrew, you surprised the manners right out of me. These are my friends and colleagues—Bonnie Markham, Diane Sonnenberg, and Sarah McClure. Ladies, this is Andrew Cooper, a dear old friend of the family. He and my brother Richard were once as thick as thieves."

Andrew. With a jolt, Sarah realized who the man was, who he had been—the child who had hidden from his abusive father in Richard's little red playhouse so many years before; the young man who had shared Richard's excitement and naive bravery as they went off to war; the veteran of so much horror who had told Sylvia how her brother-in-law's cowardice had led to the deaths of Richard and her beloved husband, James. That figure from the past was greeting her and taking her hand in his callused, work-hardened one. She was as stunned as if Hans and Anneke Bergstrom themselves had suddenly appeared and waved at her as they strolled arm-in-arm across the lawn.

"We have so much catching up to do," Sylvia was saying to Andrew. "But surely you didn't travel all this way alone. I'll be terribly disappointed if you didn't bring your wife with you."

Andrew's smile wavered. "My wife passed on three years ago."

"I'm so sorry. I didn't know."

"How would you have?" He shrugged apologetically. "I've never been very good about writing letters. The last time I wrote was to invite you to the wedding."

"I wish I had come," Sylvia said. There was an ache in her voice Sarah hadn't heard in a long time. "I wish I had known her."

"You would have liked her."

"I'm certain I would have." Sylvia took Andrew by the arm. "Come inside and tell me all about her." She led him into the manor.

That evening, after the campers had turned in for the night, Sarah, Matt, and Carol joined Sylvia and Andrew in the parlor to hear more of Andrew's story. The day Andrew broke the tragic news to Sylvia had been his last in Waterford, and from there he had gone to Detroit for a job on the line in a factory that was being returned to auto production since tanks were no longer in such demand. Within a few years he had worked his way up to shift supervisor, and soon after he became foreman he married a young widow whose husband had died in Normandy, a beautiful young schoolteacher with dark hair, a ready laugh, and a quick temper that was appeased as quickly as it flared up. They had a daughter and a son, the most perfect grandchildren in the world, and almost fifty years together. She had died of an extended illness, but Andrew so couched this part of his story in euphemism that Sarah wasn't exactly sure what had taken her life. After his retirement, Andrew had bought the motor home and spent most of his time traveling between his son's home, on the West Coast, and his daughter's home, in the East. His many years of hard work had earned him the freedom to come and go as he pleased, and he'd made the most of it—and he planned to keep doing so as long as he and the motor home held up.

"I'm glad you finally decided to take the road home to Waterford," Sylvia said.

He smiled at her. "So am I."

They held each other's gaze for a moment. Sarah would have sworn Sylvia's cheeks colored before she looked away.

Then Andrew turned to Matt. "Is Elm Creek still good for trout?"

"One of the best streams in the state," Matt said. "They stock it every year."

"In the old days they didn't need to," Andrew said, shaking his head. "Domestic fish. Bet they train them to swim right up to your hook and take the bait. Where's the challenge in that?"

Matt grinned. "Think of it this way. They stock upstream, and that's where most people fish. The trout that make it down here have to be pretty smart to run that gauntlet. It might be harder to catch them than you think."

"Good. It's more fun that way."

"We can go out tomorrow morning if you like."

"I would," Andrew said, pleased. "We'll have trout for you and all your campers for lunch, Sylvia."

"Thank you, but I think I'll go ahead with my original menu, just in case."

Andrew smiled and turned to Sarah. "How about you? Do you fish?"

"Not much," Sarah admitted, making a face at the thought of putting a worm on a hook.

"I'll teach you so you'll like it," Andrew promised. "I taught a young woman to fish once. She caught her first fish with her bare hands. Well, actually, it was with her foot, and she didn't mean to catch it, but it wasn't bad for a first try."

"What on earth?" Sylvia asked.

He shrugged and waved the question off. "It's a long story. You don't want to hear it."

"Yes, we do," Sarah said. "You're just keeping us in suspense so we'll beg you to tell us."

The twinkle in his eye told Sarah she had guessed correctly. "My wife and I used to have a cabin up north near Charlevoix," he began. "We used to talk about retiring there, but when Katy fell ill, we went less and less, until I finally decided to sell it. No sense in owning a cabin you never use. But when my son was in college, we still had the place, and the whole family used to go up there all the time and go fishing.

"His third year in school over in Ann Arbor, my son met a real sweet girl and he wanted to bring her home to meet us. We had already planned a trip to the cabin, so we told them to come on up and join us. Cathy was a pretty little thing, but she was a city girl. Sweet and smart, but not much for the outdoors." He indicated Sylvia with a jerk of his head. "Not like this one, here. Never saw an animal she couldn't tame."

"Nonsense," Sylvia said, but she looked pleased.

"So one afternoon, me and Bob—that's my son—and Cathy were out in the rowboat. Cathy didn't want to fish, though. She said she just wanted to watch. Pretty soon she started to get bored, or hot, or something, because she took off her shoes and socks so she could dangle her feet over the side of the boat to cool off."

Matt grinned. "I think I can see where this is heading."

"Well, she couldn't, and we did try to warn her. 'Better not,' my son said. 'There's muskie in this lake.'"

"'What's a muskie?' she asked. I told her it was a big, mean, ugly fish with sharp teeth, a sour temper, and curiosity to spare. 'You put your foot over the side, and a muskie might think it's lunch,' I warned her, but she didn't listen. She thought we were just making it up to tease her." He looked abashed. "She had good reason. We'd been teasing her a lot already."

"So what happened?" Sarah asked.

"She put her feet over the side, and for the first half hour or so she was fine. 'See, I knew you were making it up,' she said, and then she let out a shriek that would curl your hair. She yanked her feet back into the boat—and she brought a fourteen-inch muskie with her."

Carol gasped. "You're kidding."

"I wish I was. That ugly thing had its teeth clamped around the heel of her foot, and it wouldn't let go no matter how hard she waved her leg around. Bob wrestled with it and managed to get it off, but it wasn't easy, what with Cathy clutching him and sobbing and carrying on."

"I would have been sobbing, too, if it had been me," Sylvia declared.

Andrew smiled at her. "No, not you, Sylvia. I've seen you break horses. You wouldn't be scared by a little fish."

"I never broke horses," Sylvia said, smiling back. "I gentled them. There's a difference."

"Fourteen inches doesn't sound so little to me," Sarah said. "Was Cathy all right?"

"She was fine. She needed a few stitches, and she hobbled around for a while with a bandage around her foot, but she was okay. She was a good sport about it afterward, too."

"What happened to the fish?" Matt asked.

The others laughed, but Andrew seemed to consider it a logical question. "I told Cathy and Bob that I threw it back. It was too small. Wouldn't have been legal to keep it. But I didn't really. I kept it, then went to the DNR, turned myself in, told them the story, paid a fee, and took the fella home." He grinned. "I had it mounted and gave it to Cathy and Bob two years later as a wedding present."

His listeners burst out laughing.

"Now, that's a fish story," Sylvia said. "You two aren't allowed to get into any trouble like that tomorrow, understand?"

"Yes, ma'am," Matt said meekly, but Andrew only grinned at her.

"I'll never look at filet of sole the same way," Carol said, laughing. "You just scared me away from fishing forever."

Andrew chuckled. "If you change your mind, you're welcome to join us."

"No, thanks." Carol shuddered.

Andrew turned to Sylvia. "You run a quilt camp. Why don't you run a trout camp, too?"

Sylvia's eyebrows arched. "A trout camp?"

"Sure. Maybe once in a while you could have a weekend for couples. The ladies could quilt during the day while the men go fishing. At night you could play records in the ballroom and have a dance."

Sarah and Sylvia looked at each other.

"That's a lovely idea," Sylvia said.

Sarah agreed, wondering why they hadn't thought of it first. They could have fishing for the men, or golf—there were so many possibilities they hadn't even considered.

"Andrew, between your story and your suggestion, you've earned your keep," Sylvia said. "Sarah, would you mind fixing up a room for our newest guest?"

Sarah nodded and rose, but Andrew shook his head. "I brought my bed with me."

"You can't mean it," Sylvia said. "Surely you don't want to stay in the parking lot when you can have a nice, comfortable room indoors?"

"The motor home's comfortable enough for me," he said, and in his mild way proceeded to deflect all of Sylvia's arguments to the contrary. To Sarah's amazement, Sylvia eventually gave up. She almost never backed down from a position once she had made up her mind.

The next morning, Sylvia phoned Agnes and told her to come to Elm Creek Manor earlier than usual, because Sylvia wanted to show her something before her appliqué workshop. Agnes arrived while Sarah, Sylvia, and Carol were preparing lunch and Andrew was entertaining them with stories of his travels. When Andrew identified himself, Agnes shrieked, burst into tears, and threw her arms around him, and for a moment Sarah could see the girl she had been, the impulsive, emotional young woman Sylvia had nicknamed "the Puzzle." If Sylvia had been surprised to see Andrew, Agnes looked positively astounded. Agnes, Andrew, and Richard had been great friends those few years in Philadelphia before the men went off to war. Sarah could only imagine how Agnes felt at seeing this figure from the past sitting so casually at the kitchen table.

Agnes insisted Andrew tell her everything that had happened to him since she had last seen him. He laughed and complied. She clasped one of his hands in both of hers and hardly took her eyes off him as he spoke.

"She's the one he really came to see," Sylvia told Sarah and Carol in an undertone. "It makes sense. They were friends in their youth, they're both alone again, and she was his best friend's widow."

Watching the pair, Sarah wasn't so sure. Andrew was looking at Agnes with genuine affection, but it seemed to be the love of friends or of family. There had been something different, something more, in his expression when he first spoke to Sylvia, she was sure of it.

On Saturday, after the campers had departed, Sylvia and Andrew took a picnic lunch out to the north gardens. They had asked Sarah and Matt to join them, but Sarah begged off, claiming too much work. What she really wanted was to give Sylvia and Andrew some time alone. They had so much to talk about, and they could do so more easily without the younger couple present.

After Sylvia and Andrew left, the manor was quiet for the first time all week. On Sunday morning they would need to prepare for the arrival of the next group of quilters, but Sylvia insisted they keep Saturday afternoons for themselves, to recover from the previous week and rest up for the one to come. Sarah considered spending some time with Carol, but the sight of Sylvia and Andrew strolling arm in arm with their picnic basket reminded her of picnics she and Matt used to go on when they were first married. They would pick up bagel sandwiches and bottles of iced tea from a deli on College Avenue and hold hands as they crossed the campus to President's House. Behind it was a secluded garden with a wooden gazebo where they would sit and eat and talk about everything—their hopes for the future, their worries, their plans. Sometimes Sarah would pretend that President's House was theirs and that they were sitting in their own backyard, though she kept this dream to herself. She never could have imagined that one day she and Matt would live in a house many times larger and grander than the one on the Penn State campus.

Sarah went upstairs to their suite, but Matt wasn't there. She searched the manor for him, planning their picnic menu as she looked. Before long she found him alone on the veranda, sitting in an Adirondack chair and reading the newspaper.

"Are you hungry for lunch?" she asked him. "I thought we could go on a picnic." It would be like old times. They would talk and laugh and kiss and Matt would be content again.

But Matt didn't even look up. "I'm kind of busy right now." He turned the page of the newspaper.

Sarah's happiness dimmed. "Can't the paper wait?" She playfully snatched at the pages until she realized what section he held. "The classifieds? Are you looking for another job?"

"No." Matt set the paper down. "If I want another job, Tony said I can come back to work for Exterior Architects any time I want."

"Why would you want to go back to your old job?" Then his words fully registered. "Tony said you could come back. So you've already talked to him about it? Without discussing it with me?"

Matt frowned. "I knew you'd react like this."

"Like what? How am I reacting?"

"Like a nag." He stood up. "Like a control freak."

"How can you say that?" Stung, Sarah felt tears spring into her eyes. "That's not fair. All I did was ask you a simple question and you snap at me like I'm your worst enemy instead of your best friend."

Her eyes met Matt's as she fought back the tears. He must have seen how she struggled, how he had wounded her, because he took her in his arms. "You're right." He kissed her on the top of the head. "I'm sorry. I didn't mean it."

But Sarah was not comforted. "I don't know what's been going on lately. You're just not nice to me anymore."

"I'm sorry," he said. "It's not you."

Sarah pulled away so she could see his face. "Then what is it? Can you tell me what's wrong? Is it my mom? Is it something I've done—or haven't done?"

"No. Of course not." He drew her close again, and held her so tightly that the buttons of his shirt pressed into her cheek. "I'm just being a jerk. I'll stop it. I promise."

His voice was gentle and loving in a way that it hadn't been for far too long, but Sarah's heart ached. She didn't know why he was so unhappy, but if he disguised his feelings rather than risk hurting her by sharing them, their troubles were sure to continue.

As Matt gave her one last kiss and released her, she recognized the same aching worry she had felt throughout those long months of his unemployment in State College. Matt's recent behavior, too, reminded her of that bleak time; his impatience with her, his restlessness, his hurtful words like lightning strikes on her soul. Back then, the smoldering emotions had too often erupted into arguments that left them hoarse from shouting and exhausted from the endless, circular quarreling over imagined slights and old resentments. Matt had blamed their fights on the strain of his unsuccessful job search, and usually Sarah had agreed with him, since it seemed the obvious culprit. After the worst fights, however, when the peace between them strained like new skin over burns, Sarah had wondered aloud if his unemployment was really the problem. Maybe it was their marriage. Maybe it was their life together that evoked his dark moods.

"Don't say that," Matt would respond. "You're the best thing that ever happened to me. It's being out of work, I swear. Once I get a job, everything will be different. Everything will be fine."

She had believed him then because she wanted it to be true, because the alternative was unthinkable. And when he finally found the job that brought them to Waterford, it seemed that she had been right to believe him. For a long time after the move, their marriage had been happier and stronger than ever. Matt seemed to think so; he couldn't have faked contentment for such a long time. Why had things changed in the past few months, when she thought all those old dark times had been left behind in the move, when Matt had a job doing what he loved for a kind and generous employer?

She couldn't bury her worries, not this time, even though she and Matt went on their picnic after all and had a pleasant, if subdued, afternoon together. She had to talk to someone, but definitely not her mother. Not Sylvia, either; the older woman had been so happy ever since Andrew had arrived, and Sarah didn't want to spoil it. Summer was kind and sympathetic, but she had no experience with marriage; Gwen had been divorced for so long that she had little more marital experience than her daughter. Diane would probably give her a few wisecracks before blabbing her story to anyone who would listen, and Judy was so happily married that Sarah's problems would no doubt baffle her.

Bonnie. She had been married a long time. Maybe she could help.

Sarah managed to take her aside on Sunday afternoon during new camper registration. She grew tearful as she told Bonnie about Matt's behavior and her own helplessness in the face of his growing dissatisfaction. When she finished, Bonnie was silent for a while, her expression a mixture of concern and compassion. Sarah watched her and waited for her to speak, hoping for a solution—or at least a course of action—and dreading that instead she'd receive a confirmation of her worst fears, that all signs pointed to a marriage in jeopardy.

"The first thing you need to do is stop agonizing over this," Bonnie finally told her. "Matt loves you—that much is obvious. Even if you have hit a rough patch, you'll work it out."

Sarah took a deep breath, relieved. That was what she had been telling herself, too, but it meant more coming from someone else, someone more objective.

Bonnie placed a hand on her shoulder and gave her an encouraging smile. "All marriages go through ups and downs. It's not like a movie, where everyone lives happily ever after. You're going to have times where you feel so close and loving that you'll think your marriage is invulnerable. Then you'll enter another cycle where everything you say is the wrong thing and the happy times seem over for good. But they won't be; they'll come back. You'll see."

"But I don't want ups and downs. I just want the ups."

"The only way to stay that consistently happy over a lifetime is for both of you to be heavily medicated," Bonnie said dryly. "And that approach brings problems of its own. As a relationship grows, it changes. Sometimes those changes can create tension, maybe even pain, but that doesn't mean you love each other any less. The only way to avoid those growing pains is to stagnate, and that's far worse."

Sarah nodded. Bonnie hadn't given her the panacea she'd hoped for, but she had given her hope. "Is there anything I can do to get us out of this bad cycle more quickly?"

"You could ask him to talk about how he feels. You might not have the answers he needs, but it sometimes helps to talk."

Sarah smiled. "That's true." She herself felt better after talking things out with Bonnie. Describing the problem helped her to better understand it, and putting it into words somehow gave it borders, made it finite. "Thanks, Bonnie."

"Anytime. I mean that. Whenever you need to talk—"

"Talk about what?" Carol said.

They looked up, startled. They had been so intent on their conversation that they hadn't seen her approach, but there she stood, looking from one to the other, eager to be included.

"Nothing," Sarah said automatically.

Carol's smile evaporated. "You must have been talking about something. You've been whispering in this huddle for at least twenty minutes."

"Oh, you know," Bonnie said easily. "The usual lover's quarrels. She just needed to sound off."

Carol fixed her gaze on Sarah. "Are you and Matt having problems? Why didn't you tell me?"

Because you'd say you told me so, Sarah thought. *You'd say you warned me about him and you'd gloat that you had been right all along.* "We're not having problems. Everything's fine."

"It doesn't sound fine." The familiar worry lines appeared around Carol's mouth. "I would think this was something a daughter would want to discuss with her mother." She glanced at Bonnie as if to say that Bonnie's intrusion pained her as much as Sarah's neglect.

If Bonnie noticed, she didn't show it. "You'd think that, wouldn't you?" she said, shaking her head and casting her gaze to heaven. "That's never how it works, though. Sarah's willing to talk to me, but my own kids would run screaming from the room rather than listen to my opinion."

Carol gave her a tight smile. "I see we have a lot in common." Her eyes met Sarah's briefly as she turned to rejoin the others, long enough for Sarah to see she had been deeply hurt.

"Mom, wait," Sarah called after her, but Carol kept walking.

Bonnie put her arm around Sarah's shoulders as they watched Carol return to the registration table. "Don't worry. She won't stay angry. You can talk to her later."

Sarah nodded, but she felt as if at any moment she'd collapse beneath the growing pile of worries. It was as if the stitches holding the scraps of her life together were unraveling faster than she could put them in, and if she didn't work quickly enough, a gust of wind would send the unsewn pieces scattering in all directions, whirling in the air around her, just beyond her grasp.

Six

Bonnie woke to find Craig's side of the bed empty. She listened for the sound of the shower, but instead she heard the faint clattering of fingers on the computer keyboard in the family room. He had risen early to check his email before work again. It was becoming a habit with him. She preferred his old habit—lying in bed with her as they held each other and planned their day—but as she had told Sarah the day before, relationships changed.

She kicked off the covers, drew on her robe, and padded into the family room in her slippers. Craig was sitting at the computer, his back to her, a cup of coffee and a doughnut within easy reach on the desk. He had already dressed for work.

"Morning," Bonnie greeted him.

He jerked upright as if she had sent an electric current through his chair. "You startled me."

"Sorry." She hid a smile and joined him at the computer just as he quit the application. "Any interesting mail?"

"Not really." He shut down the computer. "The usual memos, you know, reminders about meetings, things like that." He picked up his breakfast and carried it into the kitchen.

Bonnie followed. "Doesn't sound like anything worth getting up early for."

"Just wanted to get it out of the way." He poured the rest of his coffee into the sink and left the mug on the counter. "I'd better get going."

"So early?" It was only seven o'clock.

He nodded and wrapped his doughnut in a napkin. "Bob called an emergency meeting about graduation."

"Oh, dear. What is it this time?" Bonnie went to the sink, rinsed the coffee down the drain, and placed the mug in the dishwasher. "Not the floor again, I hope?"

Three years before, heavy rains had flooded the auditorium only days before commencement, warping the wood parquet floor into a series of small hills. The Office of the Physical Plant staff had to scramble to rearrange stages, seating, and enough microphones and speakers for a modest rock concert. It had made for several exhausting days and late nights, but they'd pulled it off in time for the ceremony.

"No, nothing like that, fortunately," Craig said. "Just the usual logistical snarls. You know how it is."

"Will you have to change your plans for the weekend?"

He shot her a quick look. "What?"

"Your trip to Penn State. Don't tell me you forgot."

"Oh." His features relaxed. "No, I didn't forget. And no, it won't be a problem. We'll have everything sorted out by then." He took his sack lunch out of the refrigerator and kissed her on the cheek on his way out of the kitchen. "I'll see you tonight."

She trailed after him. "Craig?"

He paused at the door. "What?" He had picked up his briefcase and was waiting for her to speak, his hand on the doorknob.

Suddenly she felt tired, as if it were the end of the day rather than the beginning. "Nothing. Never mind. Have a good day."

"Sure, honey. You, too." He hurried out the door. She heard him lock it behind him, then the faint sound of his footsteps going downstairs. She felt rather than heard the heavy door to the back parking lot slam shut, and then silence, broken only by the hum of the refrigerator and the odd clicking noises of their automatic drip coffeemaker as it cooled.

Bonnie sighed.

She threw out the used grounds and filled the coffeemaker with fresh grounds and water, then went to take a shower while she waited for the pot to fill. As she showered, she thought about the advice she had given Sarah the previous day. Was it sound advice, and was Bonnie the right person to give it? She had never considered herself an expert on relationships, but then again, she and Craig had been married for nearly twenty-eight years. That had to count for something.

Their marriage fit the usual pattern, she supposed. Newlywed joy, followed in turn by the challenges of raising kids, the relief when they went off to college, and the pride mixed with loneliness when they found jobs and spouses and lives of their own. Bonnie hoped that their younger son, still a junior at Lock Haven University, would find a job close to home after he graduated, unlike his brother, who now lived in Pittsburgh, and his sister, who had moved to Chicago.

Their home seemed so quiet now, even though it was over a store downtown and right across the street from the Waterford College campus. Bonnie used to fear that without the daily business of raising their children, she and Craig wouldn't be able to find anything to talk about for the rest of their lives. Fortunately, that hadn't been the case. Craig talked about his job and Penn State football, Bonnie talked about Grandma's Attic and Elm Creek Quilts, and they both wondered aloud when they would have their first grandchild. Maybe they weren't as romantic as they used to be, but they were both so busy, too busy to carry on like love-struck teenagers. Craig had never been the love poetry and red roses type of man, anyway, and Bonnie liked him too much to demand that he change. What was most important was that they were comfortable together. Over the years they had settled into an easy friendship illuminated by increasingly rare but intense flashes of passion, reminding them why they had come together in the first place and why they had remained together so long.

After breakfast, Bonnie dressed in a comfortable pair of slacks and a quilted vest she had finished over the weekend. The pattern had come from a new book she was stocking in the shop; if customers complimented her on her attire, she could direct them to the book so they could make vests of their own. Then she finished reading the newspaper, tidied up the kitchen, and began her two-minute commute to work.

She smiled to herself as she went downstairs to the shop, remembering a joke she and the kids used to share. "This is the only house in town where you go downstairs to get to the attic," Tammy would say.

On cue, Craig Jr. would chime in, "You should have called it Grandma's Basement." Then they would all laugh.

It was a silly joke, but it was theirs, and they enjoyed it. How noisy and cluttered and bustling the house used to be, and how quiet and tidy it was now. Craig didn't seem to mind, but Bonnie missed the mess.

At least the shop was the same—as cozy and friendly as ever. Grandma's Attic was the only quilt shop in Waterford, and over the years its steady and loyal customers had become her friends. The business had not made her rich—in fact, some years it was all she could do to break even—but it meant the world to her. She was her own boss, and her success depended entirely upon her own efforts. She also knew that in addition to selling fabric and notions and pattern books, she was providing Waterford's quilters with a gathering place, a sense of community. How many other people could say that about their jobs?

Her only disappointment was that none of her children had ever wanted to work at Grandma's Attic; not even the promise that they would own the shop someday had tempted them. Summer Sullivan enjoyed her part-time job there so much that Bonnie once thought she might want to go full-time after graduation and eventually take over the entire business, but when Summer was accepted into graduate school at Penn, Bonnie decided not to bother asking her. Summer was a bright young woman with a promising future, one she wasn't likely to abandon for a small-town business. Bonnie had put her heart and soul into Grandma's Attic, but when the time came for her to retire, she would have to close it down or sell it to a stranger. Neither option appealed to her, but fortunately she wouldn't have to think about that for a while. Sylvia's energy inspired her; if Sylvia could start up a new business in her golden years, Bonnie could certainly keep hers going for another few decades.

At least that's what she'd thought before the chain fabric store opened a branch on the outskirts of Waterford six months ago. They didn't carry the specialty quilting fabrics found in Grandma's Attic, but they sold calicoes and other cotton prints at nearly wholesale prices. They could afford to; their buyer ordered bolts of fabric for the entire national chain, winning enormous discounts because of the bulk orders. Bonnie couldn't match their prices without going into the red, but as the months passed, she slipped gradually nearer to that mark anyway.

At first she had told herself that once the novelty of the new store wore off, her sales would bounce back, but that didn't seem to be happening. "Maybe it's time to close the shop," Craig suggested when she mentioned the problem as she fixed his breakfast. "You could always find a job somewhere else."

The very idea of closing Grandma's Attic had horrified her. The quilt shop wasn't just a job; it was her passion, her calling, and her inspiration. She had broken down in tears that afternoon as she counted the week's receipts. Fortunately, Summer was there to console and encourage her. Better yet, the younger woman offered to help. Bonnie accepted, more grateful for the compassion than hopeful anything would come of the offer, but to her surprise and delight, Summer returned the next week with page after page of ideas. "Once I started brainstorming, I couldn't stop," Summer had said, so excited she could hardly stand still long enough to hand Bonnie the papers. "Grandma's Attic isn't beaten yet and won't ever be, if I can help it."

Summer's master plan included putting the shop online so that quilters from all over the world could purchase their fabric, notions, and books. They also created Grandma's Attic Friends, a club offering discounts to frequent shoppers. As the shop's losses gradually declined, Bonnie decided to implement more of Summer's ideas. Still, as much as she appreciated the help, Bonnie worried that Summer was sacrificing too much of her study time to what was really only a part-time job.

"Are you kidding?" Summer had replied when Bonnie tentatively approached the subject. "I'd much rather help Grandma's Attic than study. Besides, classes will be over in a few weeks."

"But doesn't that mean you have finals coming up? And won't you need to prepare for graduate school?"

Summer laughed and told her not to worry. Bonnie tried, but she still had misgivings. Gwen would never forgive her if her brilliant daughter got less than straight A's because Grandma's Attic was monopolizing her time.

Smiling, Bonnie let herself in through the back door and locked it behind her. She flicked on the lights and chose a CD to play in the background. Simple Gifts, a folk group from Lemont, suited her mood that morning, and soon the sounds of hammered dulcimer, guitar, violin, and flute were coming through the speakers over the main sales floor. Humming along with the music, she went through the aisles straightening bolts of fabric and tidying shelves. The bathroom was clean, but she gave it a quick going-over anyway before vacuuming the carpet in the main room, her office, and the small classroom in the back. She taught fewer classes there than in the days before Elm Creek Quilts, and now the room was more often used as a playroom for customers' children. Bonnie lingered over the toy box. The stuffed animals were store samples she had made to help promote pattern sales, but the other toys had belonged to her own children. It pleased her to have an excuse to hold on to them long after her own kids had put them aside.

After retrieving her money bag from its locked hiding place in her desk, filling her cash drawer, and dusting the items in the display window, Bonnie unlocked the front door and turned the sign in the glass so that passersby could see the shop was open. It was exactly half past eight o'clock, and another workday had begun like so many others before it—and, God willing, like many more to come.

Since the morning hours were traditionally slow, Bonnie went to her office to take care of bills and prepare deposits. The bell on the door would ring if any customers entered, and she could see the entire sales floor through the large window beside her desk.

Even pausing to help a customer or two, Bonnie was able to finish her paperwork within an hour. Then, with her inventory checklist in hand, she turned on her computer and logged onto the internet. Some of her suppliers accepted orders by email, which shaved at least a day or two off delivery time. Summer had shown her how even a business based on something as traditional as quilting could benefit from technology.

But not today, apparently. To her exasperation, her server was down for the second time in less than a week. "That does it," she said. Before the week was over, she would find a new service provider. It was bad enough that she couldn't place her fabric order, but how many sales had she lost because customers couldn't log on to her web page?

A second attempt and a third were equally unsuccessful. Bonnie realized it was useless and chewed on her lower lip, thinking. What now? She could fax the order, but that would delay the shipment. Regular mail would take even longer.

She could log on using Craig's account; his email used Waterford College's server, and she knew his password—JoePa, the nickname of Penn State's famous football coach. Craig had been so proud of his clever choice that he hadn't been able to keep it a secret.

"I'll be able to hack into your account now," Craig Jr. had warned.

"Do it and I'll disinherit you," his father had retorted, with a grin to show he was only teasing.

Bonnie wondered if Craig would mind if she used his account, and decided that if he had, he wouldn't have announced his password to the entire family. If their places were reversed, she would let him use her account without a second thought. Besides, as long as she sent just one message and didn't download anything, he would never know.

It took only a moment to change the settings on her email software, and soon she was connected to the internet. Breathing a sigh of relief, she typed in her fabric order and sent it off with a click of the mouse. Then, by force of habit, she checked for incoming messages.

"Oh, no, no, no," she exclaimed, frantically tapping the sequence of keys to cancel the request. But it was too late. A message was downloading. With growing chagrin, Bonnie watched the indicator bar showing the transmission's progress. Now she'd have to print out the message and give it to Craig when he got home or forward it back to his account so that he would receive it the next time he checked his email. Either way, he'd know she had been using his account. He might not mind, but what if he did?

She should have just used the fax machine regardless the delay.

The computer beeped cheerfully and flashed an announcement on the screen: "You have new mail!"

"No kidding," Bonnie muttered. The question was, what should she do with it? She could just delete it. Eventually the sender would ask Craig why he hadn't written back, and they would attribute the message's disappearance to the vagaries of cyberspace.

But what if the message was important?

Bonnie resigned herself to reading the note. If it was important, she'd fess up; if it was just another piece of spam, she'd delete it, breathe a huge sigh of relief, and never again use Craig's email account without permission.

She double-clicked the message—and with the first few words, her sheepish embarrassment was driven away by wave after dizzying wave of shock and disbelief.

"My dearest Craig," the letter began. What followed was a jumbled muddle of words and phrases that were incomprehensible and yet all too clear. A strange roaring filled her ears; she read the note over and over again, her body flashing hot and cold as the words sank in.

Her hands trembled as she clicked the mouse—first, to send the message back through cyberspace to her own account, and a second time, to print it. When the sheet of paper emerged from the laser printer, she deleted all traces of the message from Craig's account. Then she shut down the computer, shaking.

Craig was carrying on some kind of relationship—no, she ordered herself, say it—an affair. An affair over the internet. A passionate affair, if this message was any indication, with a woman named Terri.

Woodenly, Bonnie rose from her chair, and before she was entirely sure of her purpose, she locked the shop door and flipped the Open sign to Closed, then set the plastic hands of the display clock to indicate that she would return in ten minutes.

That's all she would need, she thought as she went upstairs to the home she and Craig had shared for most of their marriage. Ten minutes to see how far it had gone. Unless he had erased all the other messages, because surely there had been others. One didn't write "I can't wait to meet you in person" in a first message. She prayed that he had erased the evidence of his infidelity.

But he hadn't. When she called up the email software on Craig's computer, she found a file of messages from Terri dating back to the previous November. A second file contained messages Craig had sent to her; Bonnie choked out a sob when she saw that he had written to Terri on their wedding anniversary. And on New Year's Eve he had sent a special note: "It's nearly midnight, my darling, and I'm standing beside you ready to give you the first kiss of the New Year." On the stroke of twelve, Terri had responded, "Happy New Year, Sweetie! My arms are around you and I'm kissing you!"

Bonnie had been in bed by then. She had given Craig his kiss at ten o'clock and had gone off to bed, still weary from the previous weeks of holiday sales and entertaining, but glowing from the joy of the kids' visit home.

She read all the messages, every one, and pieced the story together. Craig and Terri had met on some kind of internet mailing list for fans of Penn State football. Eventually they began exchanging private notes, first about the Nittany Lions and then about themselves. Bonnie learned that Craig's wife was so wrapped up in her two jobs and her friends that she couldn't carry on a conversation without mentioning them. Terri was divorced, with two preteen girls.

Bonnie calculated the approximate difference in their ages, not that it mattered. Terri was significantly younger.

Craig's wife didn't share his interests; she didn't know former Lion KiJana Carter from President Jimmy Carter. Terri found that enormously funny, and confessed that her ex was an Ohio State grad. Messages had flown back and forth regarding rumors that Notre Dame might join the Big Ten; they eventually agreed to disagree whether this would be good for the Penn State team or disastrous.

And then the messages grew more serious, more longing. There was a brief discussion of Craig's guilty feelings regarding the wife; Terri wrote that what the wife didn't know wouldn't hurt her, and no more was said on that subject. They wrote of how much they looked forward to each new message, and how they ached when none arrived. From the sheer volume of messages, Bonnie figured they weren't aching very often.

Finally she shut down the computer. She sat very still for a long time, staring at the dark screen, numb and dazed.

Her life had been eroding for months, and she had been entirely unaware. All the while she was doing her best to be a loving wife and partner, Craig and this woman were joking about her. They called her "the wife" like she was a pet or a piece of furniture—"the dog" or "the chair."

A wave of nausea swept over her. She bolted to the bathroom and leaned over the sink, retching and gasping, but nothing came up. Eventually the heaves subsided, and she clutched the basin to steady herself until she caught her breath. Then she turned on the tap full blast, cupped her hands beneath the icy spray, and splashed her face, over and over again, until her hands were red from the cold and her stomach had settled.

As she turned off the water, she glimpsed her face in the mirror and was frozen in place by what she saw there. Eyes shadowed and haunted. Skin pale and dripping wet. She looked like she'd seen a ghost. No, she looked like the ghost itself—the ghost of a suicide by drowning.

She leaned closer to the mirror, close enough to see the fine lines around eyes and mouth and the deeper grooves crossing neck and brow. Gray had returned unnoticed to her hair, though she'd dyed it after seeing herself on *America's Back Roads*. She had never been slender, though she wasn't heavy, either, and the weight in her face made her look puffy and drawn. Or maybe it wasn't the weight. Maybe it was the shock, the betrayal.

She wondered what Terri looked like. She wondered if Craig knew.

"You must confront him," she told the ghost woman in the mirror. When he came home from work that evening, she would be waiting for him. She would tell him she knew that "Terry," the fraternity brother he planned to meet at Penn State that weekend, was actually "Terri," single mother and potential homewrecker. She would remain calm and grave as she spoke, giving him no sign that he had torn her heart out. And then Craig would—

Would what?

Would he break down and beg forgiveness? Would he become angry and claim ignorance so she would have to drag him over to the computer and point to the incriminating evidence? Would he grow silent and distant and disappear into the bedroom, emerging with suitcase in hand? In any event, a confrontation would ruin everything. There would be no salvaging their relationship if they openly acknowledged Craig's betrayal. Her pride and his shame would be too great to overcome. If she wanted them to stay together, she would have to think of something else.

But *did* she want them to stay together after what he had done?

Yes. Yes. He was her husband, and she loved him. She did not want her marriage to end.

He had betrayed her, but he had not yet committed adultery, something she would not have been able to forgive. Her only hope was to keep him from doing so and to have him decide on his own that he wanted no woman but herself. He had to chose her of his own free will, without any tears or threats or begging from her. It was the only way.

"It's the only way," she explained to the ghost woman, and left the bathroom in a daze. She returned to the shop downstairs, her movements stiff and requiring great effort, as if her joints had locked up after years of inactivity, or as if she had slipped inside someone else's body and had not yet learned all the connections between brain and nerve and muscle.

As soon as she entered through the back door of the shop, she heard rapping on the front door. It was Judy, knocking frantically and peering through the glass.

"Where were you?" she exclaimed after Bonnie unlocked the door and pushed it open. "You're always here this time of day, and the sign says you were going to be back fifteen minutes ago. When you didn't answer my knock, I got worried."

"I'm sorry. I was upstairs." Bonnie's voice sounded distant, artificial. She held open the door so Judy could enter. "Emily's not with you today?"

"I'm between classes. She stays home with Steve when I work. You know that." Judy looked concerned. "What's wrong? You look terrible."

That was not what Bonnie needed to hear at that moment. "That sounds like something Diane would say."

"I don't mean you look bad, but—" Judy hesitated. "No, I do mean it. You look awful. Are you ill?"

Bonnie clasped a hand to her forehead. "Now that you mention it, I think I am coming down with something." A small touch of adultery, to be exact. She felt hysterical laughter bubbling up inside her, but she choked it down.

"Is Summer working today? If it's not too busy, maybe she could handle things on her own and you could get some rest."

"She won't be in until this afternoon." Bonnie forced a smile onto her face. "Do you have time for a visit? I could brew a fresh pot of coffee, or we have tea . . ." And by the time their beverages were ready, Bonnie would be able to tell Judy what was really wrong.

But Judy had already been waiting a long time, and she had to leave right away or she'd be late for her class. After urging her once again to take it easy, Judy left. Except for the occasional customer, Bonnie spent the next few hours alone with her thoughts, which was the last thing she needed or wanted.

Somehow she managed to get through the rest of the morning. When Summer arrived in the middle of the afternoon, Bonnie asked her if she would mind working on her own for a few hours. "I'll be back in time for closing," she promised.

"Go ahead and play hooky for the rest of the day if you want," Summer said, laughing, and Bonnie gratefully agreed.

She drove to Elm Creek Manor, where Gwen and Diane were finishing the afternoon workshop. Bonnie helped them clean up the classroom, trying to figure out how to tell them what had happened and how to ask for their help without making Craig look bad. But it was no use. No matter how she explained it, Craig would look like a heel.

So finally she just took a deep breath and told them.

As she spoke, Gwen and Diane stared at her in disbelief. The Markham marriage was one of the constants in the Elm Creek Quilters' lives, and now Bonnie was telling them that it was in jeopardy. When she finished, they tried to comfort her by telling her that everything would be all right, but Bonnie didn't believe them. Nothing would be all right ever again unless she did something about it.

"Diane," she asked, "do you think you could give me a makeover? Hair, clothes, makeup—the works?"

"Of course." Diane looked Bonnie up and down and played with her hair. "I think you should go a bit shorter, you know, a bit more modern. I'll introduce you to Henri. He does wonders."

Bonnie turned to Gwen. "I want to start an exercise program, too. Do I need special shoes if I want to start running?"

Gwen looked dubious, but said, "If you're serious about this, we can go shopping as soon as we're finished here."

"And then we'll visit Henri," Diane broke in.

"And then Henri," Gwen agreed. "You should start out by walking briskly, and gradually build up to a run, if you like. Walking is just as good for your cardiovascular system, and it's easier on the joints." Gwen paused. "And don't expect to look like Christie Brinkley by Saturday. These things take time. I've been running for years and I'm bigger than you are."

"That's because you eat anything that isn't glued to the table," Diane said.

"But Gwen's in good shape," Bonnie said. "I'm flabby and jiggly."

Diane shrugged. "Some men like a little jiggle in a woman. Don't worry about it."

Bonnie gave her a wan look. "That's easy for you to say." Diane never exercised, as far as Bonnie knew, but she hadn't gained an ounce in all the years Bonnie had known her. It wasn't fair that a woman with two children should have such a flat stomach.

Gwen looked uncomfortable. "Bonnie, I hope you'll forgive me for saying this, but someone has to." She hesitated. "Are you sure he's worth it? After what he did, are you sure you still want him?"

"Is that what this is all about?" Diane exclaimed. "I thought the point was to get you ready to play the field."

"No," Bonnie said softly. "I want Craig back."

Gwen shook her head. "I know I'm the last person in the world you'd want for a marriage counselor, but have you given this enough thought? If you're doing this for the sake of the kids, well, they're old enough to handle divorce."

"And even if they weren't old enough, kids can adapt to anything," Diane added. "It's far better for kids to be in a loving, peaceful, single-parent household than to witness a messed-up marriage every day."

Bonnie winced. She had never thought of herself as someone with a messed-up marriage, but she supposed she was.

"Nice, Diane." Gwen glared at her.

"What?" Diane protested. "Would you stay with someone who did to you what Craig did to Bonnie? If Tim pulled this crap with me, I'd kick him out the door and throw his computer after him, and I'd do my best to bean him on the head with it. Let little Miss Homewrecker have him if she wants him. Anyone who would do something like this is no prize, as far as I'm concerned. If I were Bonnie—"

"But you're not me," Bonnie said.

They looked at her, silent and surprised, as if they had forgotten she was there.

They didn't know what they would do, not for certain, Bonnie wanted to tell them. No woman would ever know what she would do until she was faced with the situation herself. Gwen could advise her to put Craig out of her life because Gwen loved her independence and didn't know what it was like to build a life with a partner and to see that life threatened. Diane could say she'd kick Tim out if he did what Craig had done, because she knew Tim never would. Of course, six hours ago, Bonnie would have sworn the same thing about Craig.

"You're right," Gwen said. "We're not you. If this is what you want, we'll help you."

"Of course we will," Diane said. "You can count on us."

"Thank you."

"But—" Gwen hesitated. "Craig knows what you look like. A makeover won't keep him if he wants to go."

"Maybe," Diane said. She frowned in concentration and toyed with Bonnie's hair again. "But it can't hurt."

They went downtown to an athletic shoe store, where Gwen advised, "Find the most comfortable ones and worry about the price later."

Bonnie complied, but when she finally did look at the tag, the price nearly sent her reeling. "Is this for the shoes or the entire store?" she called out to a passing salesman, who ignored her.

Beside her, Diane was trying on pair after pair. "I'm getting some, too, so you don't have to go through this alone."

"The price will keep you motivated," Gwen said. "You'll walk every day because you'll want to get your money's worth."

"I'll walk with you," Diane promised. She stood up and took a few practice steps, then paused to examine her feet in the mirror. "Do you think these shoes make me look fat?"

Gwen burst out laughing, and Bonnie forced herself to join in. They were trying to cheer her up. The least she could do was let them think it was working.

After they made their purchases, Gwen had to return to campus, but she promised to phone later that evening. Diane took Bonnie by the arm and led her down the street to Henri's salon. Henri himself bounded over to welcome them. When Diane told him Bonnie needed "emergency resuscitation," Henri shook his head and made tsking noises. "It is a man, no?"

"No—I mean, yes," Bonnie said. "How did you know?"

He raised his eyebrows. "I know," he said significantly, and led her off to wash her hair.

Diane had been correct; Henri did work miracles. When Bonnie left the salon she looked a good five years younger—"Ten if you were not so very sad," Henri said. He had enhanced her best features with a wonderful haircut and clever makeup techniques. As she watched the transformation, Bonnie tried to rein in her delight with the sobering thought that this makeover was costing her a small fortune. *Craig is worth it*, she told herself firmly, and stopped calculating the bill for the long list of products Henri insisted were essential for re-creating her new look. But she needn't have worried. "Put it on my account, Henri," Diane sang out as they left the salon.

"But of course, *ma chérie,*" Henri called after them, waving cheerfully.

"I'm a very good customer," Diane confided as she took Bonnie next door to a fashionable boutique. Bonnie had often admired the expensive dresses displayed in the front window, but this was the first time she had actually gone inside. She felt out of place, but Diane breezed through the shop as if it were her own closet.

The dress Diane chose for her was light blue, and the flattering style seemed to take five pounds off her hips. With the new hair and makeup, the dress dangerously out of her price range, Bonnie looked amazing.

"You have to get it," Diane insisted.

"I can't." Bonnie fingered the price tag, gazed at herself in the dressing room mirror, and sighed. "It's out of the question."

"It would be a crime to let anyone else wear this dress," Diane grumbled, but she didn't pursue it. When Bonnie slipped back inside the stall to change, Diane offered to return the dress to the rack. Bonnie gave it to her reluctantly. She had wanted to admire herself in the mirror a few moments longer.

When Bonnie left the dressing room, Diane was waiting by the cash register, a shopping bag in her hand and a mischievous grin on her face. "You didn't," Bonnie said.

"I did." Diane handed Bonnie the bag.

"Thank you. I'm very grateful, but where on earth would I wear a dress like this?"

"L'Arc du Ciel, when you take Craig there for a romantic dinner and dancing Saturday night. Craig does like to dance, doesn't he?"

"Well, yes, but at L'Arc du Ciel?" Bonnie protested as Diane steered her from the shop. "I could feed the whole family for the price of one of their entrées. We've never eaten there before."

"Maybe you should start."

"But Craig will be at Penn State on Saturday," Bonnie said without thinking. She shook her head. "You're right. L'Arc du Ciel it is."

They parted at the corner. Bonnie hurried home to drop off her packages and returned to Grandma's Attic just in time for closing. Summer's delight at her new appearance made Bonnie blush. As she counted the day's receipts, locked the front door, and flipped the sign to Closed, she planned what she would say to Craig that evening. As she walked two blocks to the bank to drop off the deposit, she wondered if he would even notice her new appearance. She didn't expect him to match Summer's enthusiasm, but she hoped he'd show some appreciation, at least. Maybe she should put on a negligee and drape herself over his computer; he would have to notice her then.

She was preparing supper when he came home from work. He stopped by the kitchen to give her a quick kiss, then headed straight to the computer.

"Supper will be ready soon," she told him. "I don't think you have time—"

"It won't take long." He didn't bother to look at her as he spoke. "I have some important business to take care of."

"I bet you do," she muttered, too low for him to hear.

The table was set and Bonnie was in her usual chair waiting for him when he finally slunk into the dining room. "Sorry," he said. "I didn't mean for that to take so long."

"That's no problem," Bonnie said cheerfully. "I know how work can get away from you sometimes." So many evenings lately she had waited for him to drag himself away from the computer to come to supper or to bed, all the while feeling sympathy—sympathy!—for her poor, overworked husband. She'd been such a fool.

He gave her a quick smile as he took his seat, then did a double take. "You look different."

"Do I?" Bonnie rose and began serving him.

He nodded. "Did you get your hair cut?"

"Yes, I did." She could hardly get the words out, so pleased and relieved was she that he had noticed, and so angry at herself for feeling that way. She forced herself to smile. "What do you think?"

"You look very nice."

"Thank you, honey." She smiled at him, wondering if he detected the undercurrent of anger. She filled her own plate, taking smaller portions than usual.

Tim glanced at her plate. "Is that all you're having?"

"Oh, I decided to take off a few pounds." She said it breezily so he wouldn't think she was going to start obsessing about food, or worse yet, put him on a diet as well. Women who constantly criticized their figures annoyed him; he considered them self-absorbed and desperate for attention. Bonnie took an enthusiastic bite of chicken to show him she still had an appetite. "I'm going to start walking every day, too."

"Really." He eyed her with mild surprise.

She nodded. "That's right. There's going to be a whole new Bonnie around here soon." Not by Saturday, but soon. "Don't worry; I'm only changing my appearance, not the things that really matter. I know how fond you are of the old Bonnie." She heard herself speaking and wondered how she could sound so cheerful, so confident, so affectionate, when her heart was splintering into jagged pieces in her chest.

"I am fond of you," he said, holding her gaze for a moment before returning his attention to his food.

She jumped at the opening. "I know that, but it's nice to hear you say it," she said. "And while you're being so sweet . . . I was thinking, why don't we plan a special evening out soon? It's been a while since we've done something special, just the two of us."

"It's been just the two of us every day and every night since Barry started college."

"You know what I mean." She reached for his hand. "I mean going out, having fun."

He looked dubious. "What did you have in mind?"

"I thought we could go out for dinner and dancing at L'Arc du Ciel." She steeled herself. "I went ahead and made reservations for Saturday night."

"Saturday?" He set down his fork. "This Saturday?"

She nodded, her heart sinking as his frown deepened.

"But you know I have plans for this Saturday."

"I thought maybe you'd be willing to change them."

He shook his head and helped himself to more mashed potatoes. "We can go out to dinner any night. The Blue-White Game is only once a year."

"But it'll just be one half of the team playing the other half, right? Wouldn't it just be like watching a practice?"

"It's much more than a practice and you know it. It's the first time we get to see next year's starting lineup in action."

"Can't you tape it?"

"No, I can't tape it." His voice was rising, growing more agitated. "They might show it on local TV in State College, but we won't get it around here. It's not a Big Ten game."

Bonnie heard herself speak, and her voice sounded as if it were coming from someplace very far away. "Please don't go to Penn State this weekend. Please stay here and go dancing with me instead."

His face was hard. "I've already paid for my ticket, and I've been planning this a long time. We'll go out next weekend, all right?"

He was adamant, and she knew it. All the nervous energy drained from her. "All right."

She watched him eat, cutting into the tender chicken with his fork, chewing angrily on a slice of buttered bread. She was seized, suddenly, by the urge to dump the bowl of corn over his head. "I think I left the oven on," she said, and rushed back to the kitchen, where she waited for the urge to subside before returning to the table.

She slept poorly that night and woke, numb and confused, to the sound of the keyboard clattering in the other room.

Gwen was right.

A new hairstyle and makeup wouldn't keep him. The promise of a trim, healthier Bonnie wouldn't keep him. Neither would a romantic night on the town or a lovely new light blue dress that seemed to take five pounds off her hips.

If she wanted to win him back, it would have to be with her brain. She was over fifty, and although she had treated her body kindly throughout the years, it could do only so much for her. But although her beauty wasn't as great as it had been when she and Craig first met, her mind was better than ever. Years of managing a household, running her business, interacting with her wonderful, creative, intelligent friends had sharpened her mind and developed her soul. She had accomplished so much in her life; she was a partner worthy of any man. She would make Craig remember that.

Filled with new resolve, Bonnie kicked off the covers and started her day. By the time she had showered and had styled her newly cut hair, she knew what she had to do. She dressed in her favorite blue slacks and the quilted jacket she had made over the course of many months at meetings of the Elm Creek Quilters. Wearing it now, she felt as if her friends were with her, silent but encouraging, supportive, lending her their strength. She took a deep breath and strode into the family room to announce her intentions.

Craig was still at the computer, naturally, sipping coffee and munching buttered toast. On any other morning she would have scolded him gently and warned him about cholesterol, but today she was tempted to load the toast with as much butter as it would hold and force-feed it to him, along with a few slices of bacon and a cup of lard.

"I have a great idea," she declared.

Craig jumped in his chair. "Oh? What's that?" With a swift movement of the mouse, he turned on the screen saver. A school of fish appeared where an email message had been.

"Since you can't change your plans for Saturday, I'll change mine." Bonnie smiled brightly as he swiveled around to face her. "I'll come with you to Penn State."

Craig's face went from furious red to queasy pale more swiftly than she would have imagined possible. "What? What do you mean? You can't."

She deliberately misunderstood him. "Well, sure I can, honey. I'm not too busy."

"But—you have—" He gulped air. "What about the shop? Saturday's your busiest day. You can't afford to close on a Saturday, not when business has been so bad."

"Summer's working, and Diane offered to help her." Bonnie hadn't asked her yet, but she knew she would agree.

"What about quilt camp? I won't be back until Sunday afternoon. You'll miss registration."

"They can manage without me just this once."

Craig's mouth worked silently for a moment. "Ticket," he said, relief replacing his sickly cast. "You don't have a ticket to the game. You can't go."

"Oh, that." Bonnie dismissed that with a wave of her hand. "You and your friend can watch from Beaver Stadium, as you planned, and I'll find a nice sports bar downtown and watch the game on TV. You said it would be broadcast locally, right?" He nodded weakly. "Then it's all settled. I don't know why I didn't think of this earlier. It's been so long since I've seen campus."

"We could go together some other weekend—"

"And have you miss the Blue-White Game? I wouldn't dream of it." She crossed the room to where he sat limp and dazed before his computer, then squeezed his shoulders affectionately and kissed him. "Do you think we'll run into any of our friends? I'm sure we will. I bet if you had gone by yourself, you would have run into everyone from the old gang. They would have been asking where I was and promising to call me as soon as they got home." His eyes widened slightly; that had not occurred to him. She kissed him again, this time to say good-bye. "I'll see you tonight. I'm going to work."

"So early?" he asked in a hollow voice.

"Diane's coming by to plan for the exemption hearing," she lied. She shrugged helplessly and hurried out the door.

In the stairwell, her legs felt so weak that she had to clutch the handrail and lean against the wall. She had done it. She had never been more nervous in her life, but she had done it. She had not backed down, and he had not suspected a thing.

When she had composed herself, she continued down the stairs to Grandma's Attic.

All that week she planned and prepared, enlisting the help of her friends. Diane came over one afternoon and helped her choose an outfit for the day of the game. Bonnie had planned to wear jeans, thinking they would make her look younger, but Diane convinced her to wear a more flattering pair of casual slacks instead. She would also wear a white knit top under the blue Penn State cardigan Tim had given her for her birthday. She modeled the outfit, relieved to see Diane nod in satisfaction. "You look great," Diane said. "I just hope little Miss Terri asks you where you got the sweater."

Bonnie managed a smile as she pictured Terri's jealousy. She hoped Craig had never given Terri any gifts.

Judy had her husband, Steve, look up articles on Penn State football, and he also collected amusing anecdotes from his sportswriter friends, stories that had not made it into print. Every evening Bonnie doted on Craig as if they were newlyweds. He seemed perpetually bewildered, as if he didn't know what to make of her. On Friday evening he asked her if she still meant to accompany him; when she assured him she did, his shoulders slumped and he went off to his computer, dejected.

Bonnie's heart leapt in alarm. He was going to tell Terri not to come, and that would ruin everything. They would make arrangements for another time, another place, an occasion when it might be impossible for Bonnie to intervene.

As night fell, Bonnie lay in bed in the dark, unable to sleep. Finally, Craig climbed in beside her. When she was certain he had drifted off, she stole from the bed, tiptoed into the family room, and switched on the computer. It let out a chord when it started up, and the melodic chime shattered the silence. Bonnie held her breath, listening, but not a sound came from the bedroom. Slowly she let out the breath. She would have to hurry.

After turning the volume all the way down, she opened the email program. A quick check of Craig's most recent outgoing messages confirmed her fears. He had written to Terri to tell her not to come to Penn State the next day.

"I don't understand," Terri had written back. "Are you having second thoughts or what?"

"Just don't come," he had responded.

Barely a minute had passed between his message and Terri's reply. "I'm not your wife. You can't tell me what to do. I have my own ticket and a babysitter and I'm going to this game with you or without you."

It was the last message they had exchanged.

Bonnie chewed on her lower lip, staring at the screen and wondering what to do.

She typed in Craig's password and double-clicked the mouse. Her heart pounded as the computer announced the results of her query: two new messages were downloading into the computer. Terri had sent them both.

The first said, "Are you still there?"

The second had been sent ten minutes later. "I'm sorry I got mad," Terri had written. "I just don't understand why you're backing out like this. If you would just tell me why, I could accept it. What's wrong? Please write back."

Bonnie took a deep breath and slowly, slowly reached for the keyboard.

"I'm sorry," she wrote. "I guess I just got nervous. Forget I said anything. Let's meet at the Corner Room at ten as we had planned. I'll see you then."

She signed Craig's name and sent the message on its way. Then she erased the note from the outgoing messages file and disabled the internal modem. She shut down the computer and returned to bed.

The alarm woke her early Saturday morning. She shut it off quickly—Craig stirred but didn't open his eyes. She bounded out of bed and raced to the shower, but she didn't finish as quickly as she had hoped. By the time she had fixed her hair and dressed, Craig was out of bed and at the computer. He did not look pleased.

"Is something wrong with the computer?" she asked.

"Something is, but I'll be darned if I know what," he said. "I can't get online."

"Do you want to try the one downstairs?" She hoped with all her heart he'd say no.

He glanced at the clock on the screen. "No, I don't have time." Still scowling, he shut down the computer and stomped off to the shower. Bonnie hid her satisfaction. If there were any new messages from Terri telling him how pleased she was that he had changed his mind, Craig wouldn't see them.

She put on a pot of coffee and made him his favorite breakfast—cinnamon apple waffles. When he returned to the kitchen, his anger had faded and he seemed his usual self again. "Do I smell cinnamon?" he asked.

"You certainly do, so sit down and eat before it gets cold." She gave him a warm smile and carried their plates to the table.

After breakfast, they locked up the house and carried their overnight bags to the car. At first Craig responded to her attempts at conversation with brief phrases or shrugs, but as the two-hour drive progressed, he relaxed and began to chat comfortably with her. They talked about the NFL draft that had taken place earlier that month; Bonnie knew from the articles Steve had given her that the graduating Nittany Lions had had an excellent year. The conversation turned to their kids, and then to their favorite memories from their student years at Penn State. By the time they turned off Route 322 and were driving down Atherton Street toward campus, they were chatting and laughing and enjoying themselves.

At a quarter to ten, they checked into the Hotel State College on the corner of Allen Street, right across College Avenue from the main gates to the campus. They were given a pleasant room with a queen-size bed and a large window overlooking Allen Street. As Craig unpacked, Bonnie went to the bathroom to freshen up. She scrutinized herself in the mirror. Her eyes were bright with excitement, and the new hairstyle looked fresh and pretty. She was ready to face the enemy.

She summoned up her courage and put the next stage of her plan into motion.

In the other room, Craig was sitting on the edge of the bed flipping through the local newspaper. "So, when and where are we meeting your friend?" Bonnie asked him.

"Oh. There's been a change of plans. My friend isn't coming."

"Why not?" she asked, putting all the disappointment she could muster into her voice.

"Something came up." He set the paper aside and rose. "Do you feel like a cup of coffee before the game?"

"I'd love one." Bonnie smiled at him. "Why don't we go to the Corner Room?"

Craig agreed—and why not? It had been their favorite restaurant when they were students. As they went downstairs to the lobby, Bonnie slipped her hand into his, her thoughts racing. Since the restaurant was affiliated with the hotel, she and Craig could reach it without going outside—but what about Terri? Would she wait inside or outside? Terri expected to share Craig's room, so she had not needed to enter the hotel to register. Bonnie cursed herself for not being more specific. Even if Terri were waiting just outside, they wouldn't run into her, not that Bonnie would recognize her if they did. All Bonnie had was the description Terri had sent Craig months ago, and how accurate would that be?

She needn't have worried.

They restaurant foyer was filled with other Penn State fans. A smiling hostess with a clipboard was walking down the line taking customers' names and apologizing for the wait. When she reached Craig, he said, "Markham, two, nonsmoking, please."

The hostess smiled in recognition. "Craig Markham?"

"Why, yes."

"The other member of your party is already here." The hostess took them out of line, picked up two menus, and motioned for them to follow her. "I thought she said table for two, but I guess she meant she was waiting for two. That's okay, though; you have a booth, so there's plenty of room." And with that, she placed their menus in a booth already occupied by a wide-eyed woman with shoulder-length blond hair held back in a barrette.

"Craig?" the woman said. Her eyes flicked from Craig to Bonnie.

"Enjoy your meal," the hostess chirped, and left.

"Well, hello," Bonnie declared, sliding into the high-backed seat. "You must be Terri. Craig told me you had to cancel. I'm so delighted you came after all."

Terri's mouth opened and shut.

"I'm Bonnie, of course." She extended her hand, and Terri limply shook it. Craig stood rooted in place. "Well, come on, honey, sit down." She grabbed his arm and pulled him into the booth, then smiled again at Terri. "It's so nice to finally meet you."

"It's . . . it's nice to meet you, too." Terri held out her hand for Craig to shake and shot him a look of pained bewilderment, which Bonnie pretended not to see.

"I thought Craig told me he would be meeting a friend from his old fraternity, but obviously I misunderstood." Bonnie interlaced her fingers and rested them on the table. "So tell me—how do you two know each other?"

Terri swallowed. "Um, well—" She looked to Craig for help. "Why don't you tell her?"

"No, no, you go ahead." Craig sounded as if he were being strangled. "I'm not much of a storyteller."

Betrayal and annoyance flashed in Terri's eyes. Craig didn't see them since he had buried his face in the menu, but Bonnie did.

"We met on the internet," Terri said.

"Oh, well, that explains it," Bonnie said. "No wonder I got mixed up. It's so hard to keep track of all Craig's internet friends. He has so many."

Terri's mouth pinched into a hard line. "Is that so?"

"Oh, yes. He writes to people all over the world—men, women—"

"Not so many women," Craig interrupted. Terri just looked at him.

They ordered coffee, and while they waited, Bonnie summoned up all that was good and loving in herself so that she could stop hating the woman on the other side of the table, this woman who was trying to steal her husband and ruin her life. She imagined they were in Grandma's Attic and that Terri was a newcomer to Waterford, charmed inside by a bright quilt hanging in the shop window, unsure and uncomfortable, hovering nearby and listening wistfully to the laughter of the Elm Creek Quilters. There had to be something, something in this woman that Bonnie could love.

The shape of her face reminded her of Sarah. Her hair was the same shade of blond as Diane's. Her husband had left her for another woman and she was raising two children alone.

There. That did it. Her hatred faded.

This time when she smiled at Terri, she felt genuine kindness. "So tell me about yourself," she said.

Terri glanced at Craig, but he had not yet recovered his wits and was clearly of no use to anyone. So she began. When she mentioned her children, Bonnie asked if she had any photos. Hesitantly, Terri took a small album from her purse and passed it to her. Bonnie admired each picture and begged for the story behind them, and soon Terri was smiling shyly and talking almost as if they were friends. Craig looked on; by the time the server came by to refill their coffee cups, he had composed himself enough to join in the conversation, which shifted from family to work. Terri was working as an office manager in Harrisburg, but she dreamed of owning her own business someday.

Bonnie knew this; she had read the email. "I run my own business," she said.

Again Terri glanced at Craig. "I thought you worked in a fabric store."

Bonnie burst out laughing. "Oh, don't I often wish it were that simple. No, I own a quilt shop, a place for specialty fabrics and notions and books, and just about everything else a quilter needs. I also teach quilting classes there, though I've cut back since I started teaching for Elm Creek Quilts."

"That name sounds familiar," Terri said. "Weren't you on *America's Back Roads* a few months ago?"

"That's right."

"I remember it now." Terri's eyes grew misty and she sighed. "That manor is so beautiful. You really get to work there? That must be so great. And the people seemed so nice."

"They're the best people I've ever known," Bonnie said, and she meant it. "You should come to quilt camp sometime."

"Oh, no, not me." Terri flashed her a quick smile and shook her head. "I don't know how to quilt."

"What better reason to come to quilt camp? We'll teach you."

"It looks so hard—"

"If she doesn't want to come, she doesn't have to," Craig broke in. Bonnie and Terri looked at him. Terri frowned. Bonnie tried to hide her amusement. She sighed, looked at Terri, and rolled her eyes. Terri giggled.

"So tell me about your idea for your business," Bonnie said. "I'd be happy to share my experience with you."

Eagerly, Terri told her about her idea to open a computer software and supply store with products of interest to women and children. Bonnie had to admit it was an interesting idea, full of possibilities. She answered Terri's questions about start-up capital and location and marketing; together they brainstormed and debated. They talked through a few more refills of coffee until Craig finally cleared his throat and reminded them about the game.

"He's right," Bonnie said. "You two better get going or you won't make it to the stadium in time."

"What about you?" Terri asked, climbing out of the booth.

"I'm going to watch it from the club down the street." Bonnie explained that she didn't have a ticket because she had decided to come at the last minute. She saw Craig and Terri exchange a long look. Now Bonnie's presence had finally been explained, and now Terri finally understood why Craig had canceled the date. But Craig still didn't know why Terri had shown up after he had told her not to, and Terri had no idea why Craig had changed his mind and why on earth he had brought his wife along.

They would have plenty of time to talk at the game.

Craig and Terri walked with her to the bar, two blocks away. They arranged to meet outside the stadium after the game. Bonnie waited until Craig and Terri climbed onto the Campus Loop bus that would take them to the stadium, and then she went inside the bar.

She was exhausted. Everything was going well so far, but the effort had drained her.

The layout of the bar had not changed since her last visit years ago; the dining room was empty, but the bar was nearly full. One wall was lined with big-screen TVs, all tuned to the same station. Bonnie took the last available table and ordered a drink.

Her eyes were fixed on the screen, but her mind was with Craig and Terri. There was no reason for them to go to the game, not with "the wife" safely out of the way. They could be in the hotel room that very minute. After they wore themselves out with lovemaking, they would turn on the game and watch it as they cuddled, so later they could describe plays and statistics to her as if they had been in the stadium. At the last possible moment they would race hand in hand across campus to the meeting place outside the stadium, still glowing from their encounter and from the glee of deceiving her.

Bonnie shook her head to force the thoughts away. She couldn't think like that. Surely by now they were too worked up and anxious and guilty to even contemplate having sex. Besides, they knew she had a key to the hotel room. They wouldn't risk it.

She kept reassuring herself until she almost believed it.

She nursed her drink through the first quarter, then switched to soft drinks for the rest of the game. It seemed hours until the fourth quarter, but finally it was time for her to leave if she wanted to meet Craig and Terri promptly. But Bonnie didn't budge. Her heart began to pound as the game ended, but still she didn't leave. Instead, she struck up a conversation with some of the other customers and focused her attention on an interview with Joe Paterno.

Suddenly she spotted Craig and Terri making their way through the crowd toward her, unsmiling, carefully apart from each other. She pretended not to see them until they reached the table and Craig spoke her name.

Bonnie feigned astonishment. "Is it that time already?"

"We waited for you for twenty minutes," Craig said, almost woebegone.

"I lost all track of time." Bonnie rose and forced out a cheerful smile. "You two must have enjoyed the game even more than I did, since you were in the stadium."

"It was all right," Craig said, but neither he nor Terri looked as if they'd had much fun.

They were ready for supper, so they walked several blocks east to an Italian restaurant. Craig and Terri seemed ill at ease with each other and grateful for Bonnie's conversation, which was nearly a monologue, the others spoke so infrequently. Soon she had them grinning in spite of themselves with the anecdotes from Steve's sportswriter friends. Bonnie could almost forget what had brought them together in that place.

They left the restaurant at dusk.

"Where are you staying?" Bonnie asked Terri as they strolled down College Avenue toward the Hotel State College. The three walked side by side, with Bonnie in the middle.

"I'm going home."

"Oh, do you have to? I was looking forward to hearing more about your computer store over breakfast."

Terri fidgeted with the straps of her purse. "No, I'd better get home. It's only an hour away. No sense in paying for the sitter if I don't have to." She shook Bonnie's hand. "Thanks so much for all your advice."

"Don't mention it. Any time. You have my number."

Terri nodded. Then her mouth tightened and she extended her hand to Craig. "Good-bye," she told him, and her words carried a ring of finality.

Craig shook her hand and nodded, but said nothing. Terri flashed them a quick, tight smile and walked away.

Bonnie and Craig watched her until she rounded the corner, then they continued on to the hotel.

"Terri seems very nice," Bonnie said.

"She thinks you're nice, too." He paused. "Actually, she thinks you're wonderful. She said you were 'an inspiration.'"

"No kidding. I don't think anyone's ever called me that before." Bonnie kept her voice casual. "The next time you write to her, why don't you invite her to visit us in Waterford?"

"I don't think we'll be writing to each other anymore."

"Oh."

A moment passed in silence as they walked on.

"Bonnie—" Craig hesitated. "There's something I need to tell you about this trip."

"No, you don't."

"Yes, I—"

"Craig, I already know."

Silence.

"Oh." His voice was leaden. "I guess I knew that."

She glanced at him, and saw to her amazement that his face was contorted, as if he were fighting back tears. His pace slowed until he came to a stop in the middle of the sidewalk.

"Bonnie—" His voice broke. "I'm so sorry—"

Her first instinct was to comfort him, to tell him everything would be all right, that they could slip back into their comfortable, routine married life as if he had not set out to betray her. She had won, and in her victory she could afford to be generous. But the words stuck in her throat. She had won him back, but watching him fight off tears, she couldn't imagine ever trusting him again.

"I don't think I can go through this again," she heard herself say.

"You won't have to. I promise."

She tried, but she couldn't believe him. She would never know when the next Terri would come along, and she couldn't bear to spend every waking moment suspecting him, watching him, waiting for the ground beneath her feet to shift and crumble again. She deserved better than a lifetime of suspicion and mistrust. She deserved better.

"Bonnie?" Craig pleaded. "Please say you forgive me."

"Of course I do," she said, thinking, *I don't know if I can.*

They walked on.

⚓

When they arrived home on Sunday, Bonnie unpacked her suitcase with barely a word for her husband. Then she went to her sewing room, where she took out the round robin quilt.

She chose green and blue for the colors of Elm Creek Manor. She chose blue for truth and green for new beginnings. She followed Diane's lead and chose a darker shade of cream for her background; Diane had given her such good advice lately that it seemed reasonable to accept her guidance this time, too.

She pieced a border of pinwheel blocks—pinwheels for her windblown life, which with faith and perseverance she tried to stitch into order. The pattern was a four patch, a square divided into four smaller squares, which were in turn divided into two equal triangles, one light, one dark, like the darkness of the past week and the light hope of the future. She wanted to believe in hope.

One side of each triangle was for Craig, one for Terri, and one for herself, but as the border took shape, the triangles melted into the pinwheel pattern, and all she could see was the motion spinning ever forward, but to what destination, she did not know.

Seven

Sylvia traced around the template, careful to keep the points of the diamond clear and distinct as she drew on the wrong side of the dark blue paisley fabric. She would hand-piece this quilt, she decided, to ensure the accuracy of the piecing and the sharpness of the points. She had made other Broken Star quilts before, but this one was special. When it was complete, it would hang in the front foyer to welcome their guests to Elm Creek Manor.

A twinge of pain shot through her hand, so sharp that she dropped the scissors. She massaged her right hand with her left, waiting for the ache to subside. More and more frequently these days, aches and pains interrupted her work. Sarah told her she ought to see a doctor, but Sylvia put it off. She loathed doctors. They never kept their appointments promptly, and she had much better things to do than sit in an uncomfortable waiting room chair paging through outdated magazines. When the doctors finally condescended to see her, they would immediately trot her over to the scale and urge her to put on some weight. A few minutes later, they would draw some blood and order her to watch her cholesterol. How on earth was she supposed to watch her cholesterol and put on weight at the same time? Honestly. She was seventy-seven years old and didn't need some child a fraction of her age telling her how to feed herself.

After all, nothing was wrong with her. Even her little scare a few months ago had turned out to be nothing. Fortunately, Sylvia had kept it to herself or Sarah would have rushed her to the emergency room. The headache had come out of nowhere, and it was more severe than any Sylvia had ever felt. When she stood up to get an aspirin, she couldn't keep her balance. When she tried to call for help, the words came out in the wrong order, startling her into silence. She was on the verge of asking Sarah to call the doctor, but when the sensations faded after only a few minutes, she decided there was no sense in complaining. Later she heard Gwen describing a migraine, and she realized that was what she had experienced. It was a relief, but annoying, too, to learn she had suddenly developed migraines at her age.

When the pain in her hand had faded, Sylvia began to arrange the pieces she had already cut, dozens of diamonds in blue, green, and purple jewel tones. Claudia preferred—had preferred—pastels, but Sylvia liked the intensity of the darker hues. If Claudia were to walk in on her now, she would surely work herself into a good pout. "Can't you choose something more cheerful for once?" she would say.

"You're the cheerful one, little Miss Sunshine. You make the happy quilts if you want them so badly."

Claudia would scowl at the nickname, but it wouldn't prevent her from carrying on. "And what's this—another Lone Star?"

"No."

"It looks like a Lone Star to me."

"It's not." Sylvia would pause and hide a smile. "It's a Broken Star."

"Well, close enough," Claudia would retort, exasperated.

Claudia was right; Sylvia did make many Lone Stars and Lone Star variations. And why not? It was her favorite pattern, after all, and there were so many ways to arrange the colors and values to create the appearance of depth and movement. And perhaps just a tiny part of her found a smug satisfaction in choosing a pattern that Claudia struggled with. Even with the far simpler LeMoyne Star block, Claudia would chop off the tips of her diamonds, line up seams improperly, and distort the fabric so that the star bulged in the center. Meanwhile, Sylvia would hum pleasantly as she worked and would pretend not to notice Claudia's jealousy as one Lone Star diamond after another fell into place swiftly and precisely, as if it were no effort at all.

Only Sylvia knew the truth: although she made it look easy, it was difficult to piece those blocks so perfectly. If she were alone, she might have relaxed and allowed herself a slight misalignment, the tiniest bulge. But not with Claudia hovering around, watching and waiting for her to make a mistake.

She caught herself. Claudia wasn't watching anymore. She knew that.

Suddenly she felt overcome by shame. Of course her sister had been jealous of her all those years. Sylvia had done everything within her power to encourage that jealousy. She knew she was the better quilter and made certain everyone else knew it, too. She had been an arrogant show-off since the day she first picked up a needle. She could have helped Claudia become a better quilter; she could have been modest about her own successes; she could have admitted that Claudia's quilts were as warm and comfortable as her own. She could have ignored the minuscule errors that no one else saw until she pointed them out.

But at the time, Claudia had always seemed the one at fault. How could Sylvia have been so wrong and not have sensed it?

Sylvia closed her eyes for a moment and forced the thoughts away. Her right hand shook as she reached for the scissors again. The pain returned like an electric shock from her knuckles to the elbow. She gasped and tried to drop the scissors, but her hand had frozen up, tightening with the pain. She used her left hand to open the clenched fingers, and the scissors fell to the table.

"Are you all right?"

She looked up to find Andrew in the doorway of the sitting room. He looked concerned as he approached, and she wondered how long he had been standing there.

"I'm fine," she said. "Just some aches and pains."

"Are you sure?"

She followed his line of sight and saw that he was studying her hands. Without realizing it, she had resumed the massaging motions. She forced herself to stop and let her hands fall to her sides. "It's nothing."

Andrew nodded, but he reached for her right hand anyway. "Let me see if I can help."

"No, really, you don't—" But he had already taken her hand in both of his, gently working it with his thumbs. His hands felt sure around hers, gentle but toughened from work. She approved. Soft hands didn't belong on a man.

She watched him, but his eyes were intent on her hand. Suddenly he looked up and smiled. "How's that? Feel better?"

To her surprise, she did. "Why, yes, I do." There was no pain at all. "How did you do that?"

"I just showed those pains who's boss." He smiled and held her gaze, and as he did, she felt the strangest sensation, a stirring—and then she realized he had finished rubbing her hand but was still holding it clasped in his own.

She pulled her hand away. "Thank you."

"Any time."

He smiled at her again, so easy and comfortable, and the faint sensation—whatever it was—returned. What on earth was wrong with her? Perhaps Sarah was right and a trip to the doctor was in order.

She checked her watch, hoping the gesture wasn't too artificial. "I'd better find Sarah. It's about time to leave for Diane's Zoning Commission hearing. Carol agreed to look after our guests while we're gone." Her voice was brisk, and so was her stride as she turned away from Andrew and went into the kitchen.

He followed. "Anything I can do to help?"

"No, thank you. You've been such a big help already. You've earned your-self a rest."

"You sound like my kids," he said. "They're always trying to push me into a rocking chair. There'll be plenty of time to rest when I'm old."

Sylvia couldn't help smiling. Sarah and Matt used to give her that kind of talk, until she insisted they stop. "You're a man after my own heart, Andrew."

He caught her eye and grinned, but made no reply. She looked away, embarrassed. Somehow her words had come out differently than she had intended, almost flirtatious.

It was because she had grown so accustomed to Andrew's presence, that was all. In the few weeks since his arrival, he had found a niche for himself at Elm Creek Manor. He fit in so naturally—assisting Matthew with his care-taking duties and generally helping out around the manor—that it was hard to believe he had been away so long and that more than fifty years had passed since she had last seen him.

Carol, too, was making a place for herself, though not as smoothly as Andrew had done, nor as quickly. After that first week, Sylvia had invited Carol to stay as a personal guest, refusing her offers of payment as adamantly as Andrew declined a room in the manor in favor of his motor home. In return, Carol insisted on earning her keep. She took over lunch and supper preparations, and before long added straightening up the attic to her duties. The room stretched the entire length of the south wing of the manor and was filled with trunks, boxes, and furniture. Sylvia had long put off sorting through the attic, since even with Sarah's help it would have been a daunting task, but Carol enjoyed the challenge. Every few days she brought down a new treasure—a lamp, a vintage gown, a rocking chair—and after she or Andrew cleaned and repaired it, Carol found the perfect spot for it some-where in the manor.

When Sylvia pointed out to Sarah that her mother was sparing them a great deal of work, Sarah said, "As long as she stays out of the way, she can keep busy however she likes." Sylvia decided to interpret her reply optimistically, though it was far from a resounding shout of gratitude.

She found Sarah and Carol seated on the veranda with their backs to the doorway. Sylvia was so pleased to see them talking instead of arguing or ignoring each other that she hung back, unwilling to interrupt.

"Your uncles took most of Grandma's quilts," Carol was saying. "But they left a few for me. I have one on my bed now, one with stars in all differ-ent colors. I wish I'd thought to bring a picture. If I send you one, could you tell me what the pattern is?"

"Sure," Sarah said, her eyes on the quilt block in her hands. "If I don't know what it is, Sylvia will."

"Thank you."

They fell silent for so long that Sylvia was about to approach them, when Sarah suddenly spoke again. "Maybe it's the same pattern Grandma used for my quilt."

"Grandma made you a quilt?"

"Yes, don't you remember? A pink-and-white Sawtooth Star quilt. She gave it to me for my eighth birthday."

"Did she? I don't recall seeing it on your bed."

"Maybe that's because you took it away from me as soon as I unwrapped it." Sarah's voice was cool. "You kept it in a box in your closet."

"Are you sure? I don't remember." When Sarah merely shrugged, Carol added, "Why would I have done a thing like that?"

"You said it was too nice for everyday and that I would ruin it."

Carol shook her head, bewildered. "I wouldn't do that."

"You did. I remember it perfectly."

Sylvia froze as Carol suddenly turned toward Sarah. She tentatively reached out a hand to her daughter, only to withdraw it when Sarah kept her attention on her sewing.

"Well," Carol said quietly. "I don't remember this, but if you say it happened, I believe you. I'm sorry." She clasped her hands on the arm of her chair and studied them. "I wasn't a perfect mother, but I did the best I could. All I ever wanted was for you to be happy."

Sarah put down her quilt block. "No, Dad wanted me to be happy. You wanted me to be perfect."

Carol recoiled as if the words had scalded her. "I wanted you to be the best you could, to do better with your life than I had with mine. I still want that."

"I've done fine, Mom. And so have you. You have your career, a child, friends, you had a great marriage to a wonderful man—"

"Sarah," her mother broke in, "there's so much you don't know. You and I are so much alike, and I'm afraid—"

"We are nothing alike," Sarah interrupted. "You and I couldn't be more different. You think we're the same, but we aren't. We aren't."

Sylvia wished she had spoken up as soon as she had stepped onto the veranda, but as the conversation deteriorated, she had felt frozen in place, transfixed by the awful scene. Now she forced herself into action. "There you two are," she said brightly, startling them as she strode forward. "It's getting late. We have to get ready to meet the others downtown." She heard the tremor in her voice and wondered if the two women detected it, if they could sense how sick she felt, disappointed and remorseful through to her very core. She'd had such good intentions for their reunion, but each day her hopes seemed more futile.

Sarah stood up. "I won't be long." Without another word or glance for Carol, she went inside.

Sylvia watched her go, her heart sinking. When she turned back to Carol, she found her still staring in the direction her daughter had taken. "Thank you for looking after the campers while we're gone, Carol."

"She's always running away from me," Carol said, her voice distant. "I fear for her. She's more like me than she'll ever admit, and I'm afraid Matt will turn out to be just like her father."

"But isn't that a good thing? Sarah has nothing but praise for your late husband."

Carol looked embarrassed, as if Sylvia had caught her thinking aloud. "No. You don't understand. She never knew my husband, not really, not the man I knew."

Too astonished to speak, Sylvia could only stare at her, until Carol rose and went inside the manor. When Carol was gone, Sylvia sank into one of the chairs.

She felt very old as she sat there waiting for Sarah, each regret weighing heavily on her heart. Nothing about Carol's visit had turned out the way Sylvia had planned. Usually it was such a joy to welcome new friends to Elm Creek Manor, to hear the foyer ringing with laughter and feel the guests' delight as they looked forward to a week of quilting together. As she had many times before, Sylvia wondered what Claudia would think about the manor's transformation. Remembering the hollow, echoing halls she had found on returning to the manor after her long absence, Sylvia knew that the change was for the better.

Sarah had brought all this about, proving that she was capable of great things. Now, if only the young woman would work a few more changes in her own heart.

Before long Sarah came downstairs dressed in a light blue suit, but Sylvia couldn't bring herself to mention the disagreement with Carol. Sarah drove them downtown to the municipal building, where they met Diane and the other Elm Creek Quilters in the hallway outside the council hearing room. Sylvia almost didn't recognize Diane's two sons, freshly scrubbed and dressed in sport coats and neatly pressed slacks. As the boys talked with their father, the Elm Creek Quilters tried to ease Diane's nervousness by chatting about anything other than the hearing. Soon the conversation turned to the upcoming end of the school year, which all but Diane eagerly welcomed. "You try looking after two teenage boys for three solid months," she said when they teased her for complaining.

"I did, plus a daughter," Bonnie said.

"That's different. You didn't have my two." Diane shot Gwen a look.

"And don't you say a word. Everyone knows Summer is the world's most perfect child."

"Not really," Summer said hastily, looking embarrassed.

"Diane's right, for once." Gwen put an arm around her daughter's shoulders. "And believe me, I know how lucky I am." Her voice trembled.

"Oh, no, Mom, not again."

"I can't help it." Gwen dug in her pocket for a tissue. She wiped her eyes, laughing at herself. "My baby's growing up and going away. You can't expect me to take this calmly."

"Your baby's twenty-two," Summer pointed out. "I'm an adult, and I'm perfectly capable of looking out for myself."

"Don't tell her that," Bonnie said, too late, as Gwen began to sniffle in earnest.

"Now you've done it," Diane said to Summer. "You should never say, or even imply, that you no longer need your mother's help."

"No, no, it's okay. Summer's right." Gwen smiled through her tears and hugged her daughter, hard. "I'm proud of her independence. I want her to be able to look out for herself without me—that's always been what I wanted most for her. I'm going to be the happiest, most grateful mother on campus the day I drop her off at Penn."

Diane touched Summer on the arm. "If she's going to carry on like this, maybe you should drive."

Summer pulled away from her mother. "Mom, about that—"

"Don't worry, I was only kidding. I know you'll want to drive yourself." Gwen brushed a strand of Summer's long auburn hair out of her face and smiled. "I wouldn't embarrass you in front of all the other grad students in your department."

"It's not that. I—"

"Better quit while you're ahead, or she'll be walking you to your first class as if she were dropping you off for your first day of kindergarten," Diane advised. Gwen laughed, and after a moment's hesitation, Summer joined in.

Sylvia stole a glance at Sarah and found her watching Summer and Gwen wistfully.

Just then the court clerk opened the door and summoned them into the room. Diane, Tim, and the two boys entered first, the Elm Creek Quilters close behind. The zoning commissioners sat at a long, raised table at one end of the room, and as Sylvia took a seat with her friends in the row of chairs behind the Sonnenbergs, she caught a glimpse of Mary Beth, Diane's next-door neighbor, seating herself on the other side of the aisle. She was the rude woman responsible for stirring up all this trouble. Sylvia frowned at her, but Mary Beth didn't notice.

The exemption hearing lasted less than an hour. Diane and Tim presented their appeal, including facts such as the report Summer had found about a similar case in Sewickley, but in the end, Mary Beth's petition and the long-standing ordinances restricting recreational construction in their historic neighborhood swayed the commission's decision. They ruled against the Sonnenberg family, five votes to two, with one abstaining.

The boys were shocked by the loss, which Sylvia found heartbreaking. Diane accepted the Elm Creek Quilters' hugs and condolences, ignored Mary Beth's smug glare, and nodded when Tim murmured that it was time to go. She took each of her sons by the hand and left the municipal building with her chin up. Watching her, Sylvia felt a surge of pride for her friend. The Sonnenbergs had not won, but they had not been beaten, either.

On the drive back to the manor, Sylvia and Sarah talked about Diane's predicament and wondered if she had any other options. Sylvia was at a loss for suggestions. Besides, her meddling hadn't done anyone any good lately, so perhaps it would be best if she kept her ideas to herself.

Later that evening, Sylvia was too frustrated to sleep. Alone, she wandered outside through the back door of the manor and sat on the steps, watching the sun set through the trees. Their branches were covered with so many leaves that she could hardly make out the barn anymore, unlike that winter day several months ago when she had looked out on this same scene from the kitchen window. That was the day she had phoned Sarah's mother and put her misguided reconciliation plan into motion. How arrogant she had been to think that she could heal the rift between those two stubborn, deeply hurt women.

Gradually darkness fell over Elm Creek Manor, and a cool breeze began to stir. Sylvia wrapped her arms around herself to ward off the chill. Andrew's motor home was dark. She wondered if he was sleeping or if he was sitting awake as she was, thinking of his wife or his two children. His daughter had phoned earlier that day to ask Andrew when she should expect him. Sylvia didn't know what he had told her. Perhaps he would pack his suitcase in the morning and leave right after breakfast. Sylvia felt a pang at the thought, but she knew he had obligations to his family. Already he had stayed longer than he had intended, and surely he was running out of things to do. How many times could he go trout fishing with Matt before he tired of it? How many picnics in the north gardens could one man possibly bear? She was no charmer, she knew that. She had too many sharp corners and brittle edges, not like Claudia and Agnes, beautiful and charming in very different ways. Or at least they had been. The Agnes of fifty years ago had merged in Sylvia's mind with the woman she knew today, but Claudia would forever remain a young woman not yet thirty, beautiful and bossy and alive, just as she had been when Sylvia last saw her.

Suddenly a faint creak broke the still night air. Sylvia glanced in the direction of the sound to find Andrew leaving his motor home. Unconsciously, she sat up straighter as he approached. He carried something in his right hand, and as he came closer, she saw that it was a sweater.

"You looked chilly," he said, draping it over her shoulders.

"Thank you." She drew the sweater around herself as he sat down beside her. She tried to think of something to say. "Beautiful night, isn't it?"

He nodded, and they sat for a moment in silence, listening to the crickets and watching the fireflies dance, glowing and fading as they moved over the grass.

"You're not usually so quiet," Andrew said, breaking the silence.

"Yes, I am," Sylvia said. "I don't think one needs to chatter on and on unless one has something to say. You must be confusing me with Agnes."

"No, no." Andrew chuckled. "I could never do that."

Sylvia wasn't exactly sure what he meant, but his voice warmed her as much as the sweater did.

A companionable silence fell over them again.

Andrew shifted beside her, resting his elbows on his knees. "Something on your mind?"

"Why do you ask?"

"Something's keeping you up tonight. Is anything wrong?"

"Oh, no. I'm fine," Sylvia said briskly, forcing out a smile. "I'm just enjoying the night air."

"Is that so." He regarded her wryly. "I think I know you well enough to see when you're not happy. But you go right ahead and keep your secrets, Sylvia. I know better than to try to pry them from you."

Sylvia's smile faded. She did have her share of secrets—no one lived to her age without accumulating at least a few. But some secrets weighed too heavily on her heart, and the longer she kept them inside, the more they pulled her down.

She found herself telling Andrew about Sarah and Carol, how she had hoped to bring them together and how she had failed. She told him how much it pained her to see them estranged, and how she loved Sarah as if the young woman were her own child, how Sarah's joys brought her such delight, and how Sarah's sorrows pained Sylvia as if they were her own.

As she spoke, Andrew listened without interrupting. He didn't tell her that the problem wasn't as bad as she thought, in that infuriating, patronizing way so many men had. Nor did he try to solve the problem for her. All he did was listen, fold his hand around hers, and share her burden. And that, she realized, was exactly what she needed.

Eight

As she left her office in the computer sciences building late Tuesday afternoon, Judy thought about the round robin quilt. It was already beautiful, even without Agnes's center motif, which apparently was going to remain a heavily guarded secret. Whenever Sylvia wasn't around to hear, the other Elm Creek Quilters would beg Agnes to show them her progress—but each time she refused. She wouldn't even give them a hint. "You want to be surprised, don't you?" she would ask, smiling.

"No," Diane would retort.

But Agnes merely laughed and brushed aside their questions, no matter how persistent they became. All she would reveal was that she was using appliqué rather than piecing, which they had assumed anyway. Not even Bonnie could equal Agnes in appliqué.

Maybe she should use appliqué, too, Judy thought as she crossed the Waterford College campus, heading for home. It would be easier to decide if she knew what Agnes was doing, especially since Judy was now making the fourth border rather than the last. According to their original schedule, it was Gwen's turn to work on the quilt, but Gwen had begged Judy to switch places.

"My life is in chaos right now, what with final exams coming up and Summer's graduation," Gwen had explained. "I'll owe you one."

Judy had laughed. "In that case, I'll do it." She had finals of her own to write and grade, but she didn't mind trading places with Gwen, although it meant coming up with a new design. The border she had originally planned had a scalloped edge, which made it unsuitable for its new position. She had studied the quilt that evening and had thought about it throughout the day, but try as she might, she couldn't think of what to add.

As she walked up her driveway, Judy decided that if inspiration eluded her much longer, she'd use Diane's trick and just set the quilt on point again with solid fabric triangles.

When she entered the house, she saw Steve in the living room on his knees, stuffing foam peanuts and wadded-up balls of newspaper into a trash bag. He looked up at the sound of the door, and before she could greet him, he held a finger to his lips. She nodded to show she understood. Emily was sleeping.

He crossed the room and wrapped her in a hug. "Welcome home," he murmured, as if she'd been gone for months instead of hours, and gave her a kiss that made her knees weak. It was the same welcome he'd given her every day for years, but she had never grown tired of it, and couldn't imagine she ever would.

"How long has she been napping?" Judy asked.

"About fifteen minutes." Steve kissed her again before returning to his work.

Judy inspected the mess. "What's all this?"

"My mom sent Emily a present."

Something in his tone made her wary. "What was it?"

"Well—" Steve hesitated. "There's good news and bad news." He rose, took Judy by the hand, and led her down the hall toward their bedroom.

"This must be the good news," Judy teased, but he passed their room and stopped outside Emily's.

"No, the good news is my mother finally understands that you're not Chinese."

Judy laughed. "At last. What's the bad news?"

Steve quietly pushed open the door. Emily was sleeping, tucked under the Log Cabin quilt Judy had made for her. She looked so adorable that for a moment Judy forgot her mother-in-law, so swept up was she in the fierce love she felt for her only child. Once she had feared that she loved Steve so much she couldn't possibly have enough love left over for anyone else, but her first glimpse of newborn Emily proved to her once and forever that she had been wrong, so wrong.

Then she saw the doll in Emily's arms. It was new, and it was wearing a kimono.

Judy turned to Steve and sighed. Steve grinned and closed the door.

"That does it," Judy said. "Next year for her birthday, I'm getting your mother an atlas."

"Or you could get her tickets to *Miss Saigon.*"

"Oh, aren't you the funny one," she retorted, nudging him with her hip. He laughed and embraced her again, and kissed her, and after one more kiss they forgot about the mess in the living room for a little while.

As they lay in bed holding each other, Steve said, "I forgot to tell you. Your mom called."

"To give you more career advice, I presume?" Judy's mom considered writing a hobby, and she was anxious for Steve to find employment better suited for the husband of a computer science professor and the father of the most beautiful and gifted grandchild the world had ever seen. She'd been sending him advice columns and Help Wanted ads for years. Steve good-naturedly replied with thank-you notes and clips of his articles.

"Not this time." Steve stroked her shoulder. "She said you got a letter."

"At her house?"

"That's what she said."

"That's strange. I haven't lived there since college. Did she say who sent it?"

Steve shook his head and began to speak, but just then Emily called out from her bedroom. "Back to work," he said, kicking off the covers. They dressed quickly, and Judy went to see to Emily while Steve went to the kitchen to prepare supper. Steve jokingly called the routine they'd followed for nearly three years "tag-team parenting," but it worked well for them. Steve took care of Emily during the day while Judy worked; after supper, Judy minded Emily while Steve went off to the spare bedroom to write, or to the Waterford College library to do research. They spent the weekends as a family, away from their computers, away from their textbooks. The schedule didn't leave much time for Judy and Steve to spend alone as a couple, but that made the unexpected moments snatched from their busy days all the more precious.

It wasn't until after she'd given Emily her bath and put her to bed that Judy remembered to return her mother's phone call. Her mother lived alone in the house outside Philadelphia where Judy had grown up. When her mother's voice came on the line, Judy closed her eyes and imagined she was back there again, sitting at the kitchen table over a cup of tea, listening entranced to her mother's stories of the land of her birth and of Judy's, a country and time and place Judy no longer remembered. Every detail of that house was etched sharply into her heart. The sound of the winter wind in the trees, the smells of cooking, the sight of her father—young and alive in her memory, tall and strong as he mowed the lawn in summer or pushed her on the swing. One day, she knew, the big old house would become too much for her mother, and it would have to be sold. She hoped that day was a long time off, but she knew every year brought it closer.

"How is your husband, the writer?" her mother asked.

"He's fine. He has an essay coming out in the next issue of *Newsweek*."

"That's not bad," Tuyet said grudgingly. "I suppose that's good enough for now, until something better comes along." Judy suppressed a laugh. "And my granddaughter?"

"She's wonderful." Judy glanced down the hall to Emily's bedroom. "Except that today she told me she won't be eating any more green food."

"What? Green food—you mean, moldy food?"

"Of course not," Judy said, laughing. "I wouldn't feed her moldy food. I mean green as in peas, lettuce, broccoli."

"Oh." Tuyet was silent for a moment. "Tell her that I said she should eat whatever you serve."

Judy smiled. "Okay, I'll tell her." Not that it would make any difference. "Ma, Steve said you received a letter for me today."

Her mother went silent.

"Ma?"

"I'm still here." Her mother sighed, and Judy heard a chair scrape across the floor. "I don't know how to tell you this gently, so I'll just say it. The letter is from your father."

"What?"

"It's true. I'm holding it in my hand this moment."

Judy's heart seemed to skip a beat. The moment she had always dreaded had come. Her wonderful, vibrant mother, who had endured so much so bravely, was in decline, and more seriously and suddenly than Judy had feared. "Ma," she said carefully, "Daddy's dead."

"No, no," Tuyet said impatiently. "Not him, not your real father. Your other father."

Her other father. For a moment Judy's mind whirled as she tried to make sense of her mother's words.

Then she understood.

"Do you mean my biological father?" That had to be it, and yet it couldn't be. Judy had never heard from him, not once in all those years. His only contact with them had been through a lawyer more than thirty years ago, when he agreed to give up his parental rights so that her father could adopt her. Her father—that title belonged to the man who had raised her, who had married her mother. He had been her father in every way that mattered for as long as she could remember.

"Yes, your biological father. That is what I meant."

Judy took a deep breath and sank into a chair. "What does he want?"

"I don't know. I didn't open it. The letter is addressed to you, not me."

"Would you—" Judy swallowed. She felt ill, dizzy. "Would you open it and read it to me, please?"

"No."

"Why not?"

"If he wanted me to read this letter, he would have put my name on it, too. You can read it yourself when it arrives in Waterford. I will mail it to you in the morning."

Judy sighed, exasperated. She recognized that stubborn tone in her mother's voice. She would have to wait for the letter to arrive.

She told Steve about it as soon as she hung up the phone, but she said nothing to her friends. They knew little about her history; they knew she was the child of an American serviceman and that her mother had brought her from Vietnam to the United States when she was very young, but they knew nothing of the struggle to get here, nothing of the fear, that sense of being hunted. That was what Judy remembered most of their flight—the fear.

Since Tuyet had no money to pay for bribes and exit permits, she struck a bargain with an older woman and her family, who saw in the young Judy a ticket out of Vietnam. In exchange for gold, Tuyet claimed these people as her mother, her brother, and her niece, so they would be allowed to accompany them to America. Their money paid the way, but without Judy, they knew they had no chance of making it to the DP camps, let alone the States.

This family of convenience lasted until they were all safely in New York, when Tuyet and Judy were cast out. They took refuge in the small apartment of a distant relative, three rooms crowded with frightened, weary, bickering adults, waiting for a man Judy had never met to come rescue them. Months later, they instead received a letter denying his responsibility for Judy, his daughter, the child named after his own mother.

Judy remembered that, too, her mother crushing the letter in her fist and saying, "We do not need him. Remember that. We do not need him."

She said it with such determination that Judy believed her.

Since the man who had promised to marry her had changed his mind, Tuyet found work, first in a restaurant kitchen, where she met the woman who found her a better job in a hospital in Philadelphia. Some time later Tuyet moved them into an apartment of their own, a small place, with two rooms—a kitchen and a living room where they shared a sofa bed. Judy later realized that it must have seemed shabby and cramped compared to her grandparents' home in Saigon, the one her mother had fled in shame when the dashing army doctor's child in her womb became too obvious to ignore. But to Judy, the new place seemed bright and spacious. For the first time, she had felt safe and happy—except at night, when shadowed figures came out of the dark, spitting at her, striking her, shrieking in her native language *con lai, my lai,* names she did not understand.

Then Tuyet met John DiNardo. Like the man who had abandoned them, he, too was a tall American doctor, but this time the story ended differently. John DiNardo was kind and gentle, and Judy adored him, especially after he married her mother and adopted her as his very own child. After that, all the old fears had dissolved into the past.

What would the man who had denied her so long ago want with her now?

Tuesday night and Wednesday passed. She taught her classes at Waterford College and her workshop at Elm Creek Manor by rote. Her undergraduates were too preoccupied with their upcoming finals to notice, but the quilt campers sensed her distraction. She knew she must seem wooden and dull after Sylvia's crisp efficiency and Gwen's humor, but she couldn't snap out of it. Steve told her she had no reason to worry, but his words were no comfort. It wasn't worry she felt—in fact, she felt nothing. She was numb, as if her heart and mind had been encased in stone.

When she returned home from work on Thursday afternoon, she could tell from Steve's expression that the letter had arrived. She picked up the thick envelope from the table near the door and carried it into the kitchen. The return address was her mother's. She opened the envelope and found a second one inside.

She took a deep breath and sat down at the kitchen table. This envelope was addressed to Judy Linh Nguyen DiNardo—covering all bases, she supposed, with the first stirring of emotion she had felt since her mother's phone call. The name in the return address was Robert Scharpelsen of Madison, Wisconsin.

Wisconsin. She pictured rolling hills dotted with red barns and cows. So that's where he had been all these years. If he had married her mother, if he had come to New York for them as he had promised, she would have grown up in Wisconsin instead of Pennsylvania. She would have become a completely different person. She would not have met Steve; she would not have borne Emily.

Thank God Robert Scharpelsen had not come for them all those years ago. Thank God he had denied her. Her mother had been right. They did not need him. They had not needed him then and they did not need him now.

She sat there staring at the envelope for so long that eventually Steve spoke. "Are you going to open it?"

"Later." Judy stuffed the envelope into her purse and stood up. "Maybe." She went down the hall to Emily's room to read her a story, to play a game—anything to make herself forget.

Steve said no more about the letter that evening, and not once was Judy tempted to retrieve it from her purse and read it. Late that night, though, long after Steve had fallen asleep with his arms around her, she lay in the darkness, thinking. Robert Scharpelsen had blond hair, her mother had told her, blond hair and blue eyes. Judy saw nothing of him in her, and yet he was a part of her as much as her mother was. She pictured him, aged now, thin, the blond hair long gone to gray, sitting at a table, pen in hand, writing to the daughter he had abandoned a lifetime ago. What had he been thinking as he put the words down one by one? Why write now, when he had never needed to before? Was the letter an apology? An explanation? Was he dying, and wanted now to seek absolution? If so, he should have written to her mother. She was the one he had wronged.

She had a father. She did not need this man. She did not need his letter. She would destroy it unread—rip it up and burn the pieces. Let him wonder what had happened to her. Let him be the one abandoned. Let his words go unheard; however desperate he was to contact Judy now, her mother had been a thousand times more so as she waited for him to fulfill his promises. Let Judy's silence be his punishment, a small measure of justice seized on her mother's behalf, recompense for the many ways he had made her suffer for loving him.

She stole from bed, quietly, carefully, so Steve would not be disturbed, so he wouldn't ask her what she was doing, so he wouldn't stop her. In the kitchen, she took the letter from her purse and held it, feeling its weight, its thickness. He must have had a lot to say, and no wonder, after thirty years of silence.

Or perhaps he wanted to be sure that she would open the letter, so he had written page after page until he knew the letter would be too thick to tear. She could tear it up later, but she would have to open the envelope first. And once the envelope was open, it would take superhuman strength not to read at least one line of it.

She would read one line—just the first line—to see how he addressed her. That would tell her a great deal. There was a world of difference between "Dear Miss DiNardo" and "My dear daughter."

She took a deep breath and slipped her finger beneath the flap and opened the envelope. A single sheet of folded paper was tucked in front. Judy removed it, left the rest of the contents in place, and set the envelope on the kitchen counter.

Her hands trembled as she unfolded the paper and began to read the typed words. "Dear Judy," she read aloud, and the words seemed to stick in her throat. She forgot her resolve and read on:

> Dear Judy,
>
> I put my father's name on the outside of the envelope because I wanted you to have the choice to throw this letter away unread. My father's name alone would indicate the nature of this letter, and if you wanted no part of him, or of me, you

wouldn't have to read any further than the return address before tossing it in the trash. That is, as long as you know who my father is, and what he is to you.

You see, I wrote "my father," but I should have written "our father." I am your sister, your half sister. My father tells me you already know about him, though not about me. I hope his memory is accurate, and that this is not the first time you are hearing this news. If it is, please accept my heartfelt apologies. No one should have to receive news like that in a letter.

I've tried to write to you so many times. I've tried to imagine what it must be like to be you, and whether you would even want to hear from me. You have a life of your own and maybe you don't want a sister—a stranger—coming into it after all these years. I finally realized that I can never know what it's like to be you. I can't know whether you would want to hear from me. But I do know that if our places were reversed, I would want to hear from you. I would want to know I had a sister.

I would have written to you sooner, but I only learned of you two months ago, after my mother's death. Before then my father never spoke of you—out of respect for my mother, I guess. I'm trying to understand things from his point of view, but it's hard not to be angry at him. All my life I've had another sister and I never knew it.

My father has told me little of his relationship with your mother, but it is enough for me to infer that they did not part amicably. I would understand if you hate my father and do not want to see him. However, I hope you will be willing to see me. I really want to meet you.

Because of my father's declining health, he is unable to travel to Philadelphia and I am unable to leave him. It is my hope that you will use the enclosed voucher to purchase a plane ticket to Wisconsin. You might wonder why I sent it—I admit I wasn't sure if it was the right thing to do or if it would be offensive. I finally decided to send it to show you how much I want you to come, and so that you can do so without any cost to yourself.

If you can't come, I hope you will at least write back to me. I am more eager to hear from you than I can express in a letter.

> *Your sister,*
> *Kirsten Scharpelsen*

P.S. You have other family here, too. I have a brother and a sister.

Steve had come into the room while she was reading, and now he stood behind her, rubbing her shoulders and waiting for her to finish. Judy read the letter again, this time aloud. Her voice shook, but whether from nervousness or anger or something else entirely, she wasn't sure.

"I have a sister," she said at last, without emotion, spreading the letter flat on the counter.

"Two sisters and a brother," Steve said. He picked up the envelope and fingered through the remaining contents.

Anger surged through her. She snatched the envelope and flung it down on the counter. "She sends me a travel voucher, like I'm—like I'm some kind of refugee."

"You were, once."

"Not anymore. I don't need her charity."

"She doesn't know that."

"That's not the point."

"Don't be angry with her. I think she means well," Steve said. "All she knows is that her father abandoned you in Vietnam. She probably feels a lot of guilt for what he did, for what he didn't do. It sounds like she's trying to make up for his mistakes."

Anger still roiled in the pit of her stomach. " 'If our places were reversed,' she says. As if she could ever understand my place. 'I can infer they did not part amicably.' What a joke. He abandoned us. We could have died for all he cared. If we hadn't got out before the VC took Saigon, I can't even imagine what would have happened to us. They weren't exactly kind to the children of the enemy and the women who bore them."

She was shaking. Hot, angry tears blinded her until she couldn't read the letter anymore. Steve put his arms around her and murmured soothingly. She clung to him, and his strength bore her up until she could calm herself. She had never been so angry, so hurt, in all her life. It bewildered and alarmed her. In the back of her mind she knew the letter should not hurt so much. She should be joyful. After all these years, she had a sister, a sister who wanted to know her.

"He couldn't even write to me himself," she whispered, stunned by how much that pained her.

"Maybe he's not able," Steve said. "He doesn't sound like he's in the best of health. If—" He hesitated. "You might not have much longer to meet him."

"Do you think I should?"

He stroked her cheek. "I think you should consider it very carefully and then do what you feel is best."

His expression was so compassionate it made her heart ache. Steve loved her so much, and yet Robert Scharpelsen could not bring himself to love her even a little.

But she had two sisters and a brother.

"I wish she would have given me more information," Judy said. She picked up the letter and scanned it, hungry for details. "I don't know how old she is, the names of her brother and sister—there's so much she doesn't say."

"My guess is she's younger than you."

"Oh. Well, of course, she would have to be. He was with my mother for two years before he went back to the States and remarried. Married," she corrected herself. Her mother had considered Robert Scharpelsen her husband, but they had never officially wed.

"You're right, but that's not why I thought so. It's her style of writing. She's obviously educated. She has a solid grasp of grammar and access to a laser printer. I'd say middle-class, possibly upper-middle-class, or aspiring to be. She's young, though, maybe in her mid to late twenties. Notice the way she uses overly formal diction sometimes and other times she sounds like an anxious teenager?" He pointed to the fourth paragraph. " 'But it is enough for me to infer that they did not part amicably' is soon followed by 'I really want to meet you.' She's trying to be formal and dignified but her youth keeps sneaking through, probably because she's furious at her father for keeping you a secret."

Judy stared at him. "You got all that from two sentences?"

"What can I say?" He shrugged. "I'm a writer. After you and Emily, words are my life."

In spite of everything, Judy smiled. She hugged him to show him she was all right, then took his hand and led him back to their room. The sleep that had eluded her came quickly now that she knew what the letter said.

The following evening, Judy went to Elm Creek Manor. Ordinarily she would have brought Emily along, but she expected to be out past her daughter's bedtime. She felt guilty for taking up Steve's writing time when it was her turn to watch their daughter, but he assured her that he'd had a productive afternoon. "She'll be going to bed soon, anyway. I can write then. Besides," he added, smiling, "I'll be able to work better if I know you're having fun with your friends instead of worrying about the letter."

For his sake she tried to put the worries out of her mind as she drove through the woods to Elm Creek Manor. An evening with her friends was exactly what she needed. Tonight the Elm Creek Quilters had invited a group of theater arts students from Waterford College to put on three one-act plays for their guests. Judy joined the others in taking care of the last-minute tasks before the performance. Then she took a seat with a few guests she had befriended that week and settled back to enjoy the show. Before long she lost herself in the drama onstage, but all too soon the show ended. As the delighted campers showered the actors with applause, all the worries crowded in—the letter, her siblings, her father, the voucher—forcing out thoughts of the play, of her friends, of everything but the decision she had to make.

After the students left and the quilters went upstairs to their rooms, the

Elm Creek Quilters and their friends returned the ballroom to its normal state. From where she was working on the dais, Judy saw Sylvia and Andrew putting away the audience's chairs. They were talking and laughing quietly, somewhat apart from the others.

It touched Judy's heart to see Sylvia and Andrew together and happy. Maybe she was imagining things, but there seemed to be more than friendship between them. Judy had never told her so, but she admired Sylvia very much and hoped that she had indeed received the blessing of new love in her golden years. If anyone deserved that, Sylvia did. She had lost so much, and yet she had never succumbed to despair. In many ways, Sylvia reminded Judy of Tuyet.

Suddenly, an image flashed into her mind—her mother and Robert Scharpelsen, both alone again, rekindling their long-dead love. A wave of nausea swept over her.

"Judy?" Matt took her by the arm to steady her. "Are you all right?"

Judy nodded, unable to speak. No, that couldn't be what Kirsten intended. Mrs. Scharpelsen's passing was too recent, Robert's health too uncertain. Either way, Judy's mother would never consider it. She had not even wanted to read Robert's letter. To do even that would dishonor the memory of her husband.

"Judy?" Gwen said, alarmed. "Are you ill?"

The others, hearing Gwen's words, looked up. "I'm fine," Judy assured them, but to her dismay, they began to gather around.

Carol brought her a chair and maneuvered her into it. "Could someone please get her a glass of water?" she asked, pressing a hand to Judy's brow and peering intently into her eyes. Summer nodded and ran off.

"Really, everyone, I'm fine," Judy insisted. She almost laughed when Carol lifted her wrist and began taking her pulse, but it came out as a sob. "It's late. I'm tired, that's all. I'm not sick."

"Let Carol be the judge of that," Diane said.

"Have you been under stress lately?" Carol asked.

That was an understatement. "Maybe a little."

"What's wrong?" Bonnie asked.

"Yesterday I—" Then Judy fell silent. She looked around at her friends' faces. They looked so worried, so concerned for her well-being. This wasn't how she had wanted to tell them, but with everyone watching her, expectant and anxious, she had no other choice.

She took a deep breath and told them about the letter, and as she shared her worries, she felt them lessening. She had almost finished when Summer came racing back with a glass of water. Judy thanked her and drank it, as grateful for the pause in which to collect her thoughts as for the water itself. Then she told them that she wasn't sure what to do next. Her thoughts were in such turmoil that she feared she'd never sort them out.

"Take all the time you need," Gwen urged. "You don't have a deadline."

"But I do," Judy said. "Kirsten hints that he's in poor health. If I don't see him soon, I might never have the chance."

"That's his loss," Summer snapped. "He had all your life to see you. You don't owe him anything."

Everyone looked at her, astonished by the sharpness in her voice. Summer, who was usually as sunny and cheerful as her name, was sparking with anger. When Gwen sighed and put an arm around her, Judy remembered that Summer, too, had never known her father.

"Summer's right," Diane said. "He had his chance, years ago. Why is he so interested in seeing you all of a sudden? He probably needs a kidney or something. Well, I say don't give it to him."

"Diane," Sylvia admonished.

"War can do strange things to a man," Andrew said. "He made some bad choices in the past; there's no denying that. Even so, maybe it's time to forgive him."

"He doesn't deserve it," Diane said.

Andrew shrugged. "I don't know if that's for us to decide."

"Forgiving him and going to see him aren't the same thing," Sarah said. "Judy could just write him a letter. If she goes to see him, that might make everything worse."

Carol made a strangling noise in her throat and sat down on the edge of the dais, her back to them. Sarah didn't seem to notice.

Matt pulled up a chair beside Judy. "I think maybe I know a little of what you're feeling. I don't know why my mom took off when I was a kid, and I probably never will, but when I got older I finally realized it wasn't because she didn't love me. It wasn't because I wasn't good enough. Something in her just told her she wasn't ready to be a mom, to have a family." He rested his elbows on his knees, thinking. "If she wrote to me tomorrow . . . I think I'd go see her. I think I'd like to give her the chance to make peace with me and with herself."

Judy nodded. Some of what he said made sense to her, but other parts simply didn't fit. Unlike Matt's mother, Robert Scharpelsen must have been ready for a family or he wouldn't have raced off to Wisconsin to start one as soon as his tour of duty was over. And unlike herself, Matt had no reason to feel as if he would be rejected simply for who and what he was. Judy was *con lai*, a half-breed. Her American blood made her an outcast in the land of her birth, and her Asian heritage could earn her the same treatment from her white relatives. She didn't know much about Robert Scharpelsen, but what she did know suggested that he probably thought of her as diseased wood to be excised from the family tree.

She was proud of who she was, but her pride did not blind her to the fact that some people considered her beneath them because of her ethnicity. Robert Scharpelsen could be one of those people. Why should she go see him so he could fling the acid of his prejudice in her face?

"Give him a chance," Carol said, as if overhearing her thoughts. "He might surprise you. Maybe it wasn't neglect that kept him from contacting you sooner than this. Maybe it was shame. He's probably as nervous as you are, and he has just as much at stake."

"We're forgetting something," Agnes said. "This isn't about Judy's father, and how he feels, and what he deserves or doesn't deserve. He isn't the one who wrote to her." She turned to Judy. "This is about your sister. She wants to see you. Don't punish her for what your father did."

Her gaze was so imploring, so full of regret for her own missed opportunities, that Judy's anger and confusion dissipated. Her thoughts became clear for the first time all week. She knew what she had to do. It was the only possible choice and always had been.

But before she informed Kirsten that she would be accepting the invitation, she had to speak to her mother.

First she told Steve, who didn't seem surprised by her decision. "Do you want me and Emily to come with you?" he asked as they held each other in bed that night.

Judy thought of how proud she was of her family and how pleased she would be to show off her wonderful husband and her beautiful daughter. Surely, Robert would want to see his grandchild. But what if he rejected them both? Nowhere in Kirsten's letter had she written that her father looked forward to seeing Judy. Maybe he didn't want them to come.

Judy could bear his rejection; she was used to it. But she would not subject Emily to anyone's contempt.

"I think it's best if I go alone," she told Steve.

"Maybe next time." He shifted in bed and held her close to him. "Or maybe we can invite them out here."

"Sure," Judy said, though she didn't want to think about a next time. One visit, one weekend, was difficult enough. She had to survive this initial meeting before she could contemplate building a long-term relationship with her father's family. Besides, after her visit, perhaps neither side would want that.

On Saturday morning, while Emily was "helping" Steve work in the yard, Judy called her mother. Tuyet asked about Steve and Emily but said nothing of the letter. There was not even a hint of curiosity in her voice.

Either she hid it well or she had truly put Robert Scharpelsen so far out of her thoughts that she honestly didn't care what he had to say.

When Judy told her who the letter's real author was, however, her mother grew excited. "I do not care about that man," she declared, "but this, this is different. This is wonderful news. I always regretted that I did not give you a brother or sister, and now you have one."

"I have more than one," Judy told her, and read her the letter.

Tuyet remained silent for a long moment after Judy finished. Then she let out a heavy sigh. "What are you going to do?"

Judy had already made up her mind, but out of respect, she asked, "What do you think I should do?"

"You should cash in the voucher and use the money to come see me, instead."

Judy erupted into peals of laughter. "Oh, Ma." It seemed ages since she had laughed, and it felt as if iron bands compressing her chest had been released. "You know I can't do that. I'm going to return the voucher to Kirsten. We can still come visit you later this summer."

"So you aren't going to Wisconsin. Good. That is the right decision."

Judy hesitated. "Actually, I . . . I think I'm going to go."

"Why would you want to do that?"

"I want to see my sister. You yourself said it's wonderful that I have a sister. What good is having a sister if I refuse to see her?"

"Write her a letter or call her on the phone."

"I'll do that, too." She would have to, she suddenly realized, in order to make arrangements for the visit. Nervousness stirred in her stomach. She wasn't ready to talk to Kirsten yet.

"I see." Her mother's voice was crisp. "So this is how you respect the memory of your father. You try to replace him."

"How can you say that?" she asked, shocked by the cutting words. Even after five years, her grief over her father's death was as tender as a new bruise on her heart. "I'm not trying to replace Daddy. No one could replace him. That's the cruelest thing you've ever said to me."

"I'm sorry," Tuyet replied, uncharacteristically meek.

"I'm not going to see him; I'm going to see Kirsten. She's the one who invited me." Agnes's words came into her mind. "I don't think it's right to punish her for what Robert did."

There was a long pause.

"Bob."

"What?"

"He called himself Bob, not Robert."

Judy took a deep breath. "Fine. Bob it is."

"Is that what you are going to call him when you see him?"

"I—I don't know." She couldn't picture calling him Father, but Mr. Scharpelsen would be too stiff and formal. The thought of calling him Bob, the name her mother had used, didn't feel right, either. Maybe if she was careful and creative she could avoid using his name altogether.

"Maybe he will tell you what to call him."

"Maybe."

"If you are going, why not use their voucher? Make them pay for the privilege of seeing you."

"I want to pay for it myself." She had to, she knew, or the Scharpelsens could never see her as their equal.

Her mother seemed to understand that, perhaps even to approve. Before she hung up, she wished Judy a safe journey. "I hope the visit goes well," she said. "If it seems appropriate, give the family my best wishes. But only if it seems appropriate. Use your best judgment."

"I will," Judy promised, relieved that her mother had given the trip her blessing. Until that moment, Judy had not realized she sought it.

She hung up and went outside to join her husband and daughter. She shoved all thoughts of Kirsten and Robert out of her mind for the rest of that day and most of the next. When she returned from welcoming the new campers to Elm Creek Manor on Sunday afternoon, she went to Steve's office to search the internet for airline and hotel information. A far more difficult task followed: writing a response to Kirsten's letter. She struggled for hours to find the right words, the right tone. In the first draft she sounded chilly and reserved; in the second, too eager and grateful. After several revisions and a great deal of pacing, she settled on a simple, brief reply:

Dear Kirsten,

Thank you for your recent letter and your kind invitation. I was pleased to learn that I have two sisters and a brother, and I look forward to meeting you soon. If it would work well with your schedule, I thought I could come the evening of Friday, May 8th, and stay until the afternoon of Sunday, May 10th. I hope the short notice will not be an inconvenience. Because of obligations at the college where I teach, my next available weekend will not be until July. If the later date would be better, please let me know.

I appreciate the generous offer of the travel voucher, but I plan to make my own arrangements. Perhaps you could use it to visit me and my family here in Pennsylvania sometime. I know my daughter, Emily, would love to meet her new aunt.

Yours truly,
Judy DiNardo

She tried to sign the letter "Your sister," as Kirsten had, but she couldn't do it.

Kirsten responded by return mail. "I'm so glad you decided to come!" she wrote. "I can't wait to meet you in person." Her enthusiasm pleased Judy, who wished she felt the same. She was looking forward to the visit only in the sense that she was looking forward to getting it over with.

The Elm Creek Quilters supported her without fail, as they always did, but they showed varying degrees of approval for the trip. Diane and Sarah said nothing more about their misgivings, but their expressions revealed their reluctance. Gwen, Summer, and Bonnie told her they were certain the visit would go well. But it was Sylvia and Agnes who convinced her she had made the right decision. Privately, each told Judy that even if she never saw the Scharpelsens again, she would rest easier knowing she had made the effort. "You're right to do this now, before it's too late," Sylvia said, and Judy's heart went out to the older woman. She hoped Sylvia would find some comfort in knowing that Judy had learned from Sylvia's mistakes.

That week, Judy proctored the final exams for her two classes and turned in her course grades. She planned her wardrobe and bought film for her camera. On Thursday afternoon, she dug out her garment bag from the back of the hall closet—and that was when she realized what border she would add to the round robin quilt. When she closed her eyes she could picture it so clearly that she wondered how she ever could have considered any other pattern.

She left the garment bag in the hallway and hurried downstairs to her basement studio, where she searched through her fabric stash for the perfect shades of green and blue and gold. She traced pieces and cut cloth at a feverish pace, too busy to think, too busy to worry. Before she knew it, Steve was calling down from the top of the stairs to tell her supper was ready.

Guiltily, Judy swept the quilt pieces into her sewing kit. Steve had let her work undisturbed all afternoon, caring for Emily in Judy's place instead of writing. He had a deadline, too, but he had not complained.

She hurried to the kitchen in time to help him carry the dishes to the table. "Steve, I'm sorry," she said. "Next week, I swear—"

He stopped her with a kiss. "Don't be sorry. I understand." He grinned and gave her a tickle under her chin before turning to lift Emily into her chair.

Judy felt tears spring into her eyes as she took her seat. Steve was the kindest man she had ever known. She was more grateful for him that evening than she had ever been.

Later, Judy read Emily a story and tucked her into bed. She knelt on the floor beside her and brushed her soft, dark bangs off her forehead. "Honey, there's something I want to tell you."

"I know already."

Judy's eyebrows rose. "You do?"

Emily nodded, her dark eyes solemn. "Daddy told me."

That surprised her; they had agreed that Judy would tell her about the trip. "He did?"

Emily nodded again. "You're very busy. That's why you can't play."

Judy felt a pang. "Oh, sweetie." She stroked Emily's hair. "You're right. I've been very busy lately and I haven't paid enough attention to you, have I?"

Emily shrugged and said nothing, hugging the kimono-clad doll.

"You've been a very good girl not to complain."

"Daddy said not to," Emily confided.

Judy laughed. "Oh. Well, even so." She hesitated, wondering what to tell her. How much would she understand? She knew that Grandpa was Steve's daddy and that he lived in Ohio; she also knew that her other grandfather was Judy's daddy, who had gone to heaven before she was born. Would it confuse her to learn that she had a third grandfather? And what if the weekend visit went poorly and there was no more contact between the families?

Emily was still too young, Judy decided. Someday she would tell her everything, but not tonight.

"I'm going on a trip to see an old friend of Grandma Tuyet's," she finally said, picturing her mother tossing her head in scorn at the description. "When I get back, we'll have lots of time together, okay?"

Emily smiled. "Okay."

"You go to sleep now." Judy kissed her good night and rose, turning off the light as she left the room and leaving the door ajar, the way Emily liked it.

The next day Steve and Emily saw her off at the regional airport. As she went to board her plane, Judy waved good-bye to her family with a sinking heart, seized with a sudden urge to cancel the trip. It was a mistake. It was too soon.

But instead she crossed the tarmac and boarded the plane.

The eighteen-seat prop plane looked like a wind-up toy. It needed a bumpy ninety minutes to carry its passengers to Pittsburgh, where Judy breathed a sigh of relief and transferred to a jet. The second leg of her journey was smooth enough for her to retrieve her sewing bag from her carry-on and piece a few seams of her round robin border. As she worked her needle through the soft fabric, the familiar motions soothed her.

There was a long layover in Chicago, but eventually she boarded another plane, the last, the one that would take her to Dane County Regional Airport and the family she dreaded meeting. This time she was too nervous to piece. For the rest of the flight she looked out the window, thinking.

When the plane descended through the scattered clouds over Wisconsin, Judy caught a glimpse of sunlight sparkling on a large lake—no, two large lakes separated by an isthmus. As they drew closer, she saw that the narrow strip of land was crowded with buildings; the most prominent, a dome-topped structure with four wings, was in the center. Judy craned her neck to watch it as they passed. When she couldn't see the building any longer, she turned her attention to the lake, a rich blue etched with the white wakes of boats.

The plane lurched suddenly. Judy faced forward and clutched the armrests of her seat, but it was not the turbulence that wrenched her stomach. She wished they could stay up there in the clear sky above the blue water, circling, drifting, eventually turning around and heading back east toward home.

The plane touched down.

Judy gathered her things and left the plane, the strap of her tote slung over one shoulder, her garment bag in her other hand. In the terminal people were shaking hands, embracing, calling out welcomes. She felt invisible, alone.

"Judy?"

She looked in the direction of the voice. A tall, slender woman was weaving toward her through the crowd. Her straight blond hair brushed gently at her jawline as she walked, and she looked to be at least five years younger than Judy.

The woman came to a stop in front of her. "Judy?" she asked hesitantly.

Judy nodded.

The woman smiled, delighted. "I'm Kirsten," she said, embracing her. "Welcome to Madison."

Judy returned the hug awkwardly. "Thanks." She wondered how Kirsten had recognized her, but after a quick glance around, she realized she was the only Asian-looking person who had gotten off the plane. She felt as if she had disembarked in the Land of Tall Blondes.

Before she could react, Kirsten took the garment bag from her. "Do you have any more luggage?"

"No, just this."

"Great, then we can get going. I'm so glad you're here. How was your flight?"

"Fine," Judy managed to say. Her sister was smiling brightly and practically skipping with delight as they made their way through the airport, while Judy felt as if her legs had turned to lead.

"My car's right outside," Kirsten said. "I'll give you the nickel tour on the way to my apartment. I live downtown, near campus. I have the spare room all made up for you."

"Oh. Um, actually, I have a reservation—" Judy fumbled for the paper in her pocket. "At the Residence Inn on, um, D'Onofrio."

Kirsten stopped short. "You're going to stay in a hotel?"

"Well, yes, I mean—"

"But D'Onofrio's all the way on the west side of town. Don't you— wouldn't you prefer to stay with me?"

Judy forced herself to smile. "I thought it would be better this way, you know, so that you can still have your privacy and we won't fight over the bathroom."

She said it so comically that Kirsten smiled, and the tension eased. Kirsten resumed walking, keeping up a steady stream of questions about Judy's trip as they left the airport. Kirsten's car was parked just outside at the curb, its hazard lights flashing. They loaded Judy's luggage into the trunk and drove off. Kirsten described the various sights they passed—the large domed structure, which turned out to be the capitol building; the University of Wisconsin; and State Street, a row of shops and restaurants between the capitol and campus.

"We'll go there tomorrow, after the Farmers' Market on the capitol square." Kirsten gave Judy a quick glance. "Unless you're hungry. Would you like to go to the hotel and rest, or do you want to get something to eat?"

Judy hadn't eaten on the plane, and she was famished. They pulled into a parking garage—Kirsten called it a parking "ramp," which made Judy picture a large wedge jutting into the sky—and walked down the street to a small Turkish restaurant. The spicy aromas from the kitchen enticed them inside, and soon, over an appetizer of tabouli and hummus with wedges of pita bread, they were finally able to talk.

By the end of the meal, Judy felt more relaxed than she had since her mother told her about the letter. To her relief, Kirsten was friendly and talkative, accepting Judy's reserve for what it was—natural shyness, not a reluctance to be with her. For now that Judy was there, she found herself glad she had come and pleased by how well she and her sister got along. Kirsten was an intern at University Hospital, where her father had practiced before his retirement. She skimmed over their father lightly, but still Judy felt a fluttering in her chest at the mention of his name.

"What about your brother and sister?" Judy asked. "Are they still in school, too?"

"No." Kirsten took a hasty swallow of iced tea. "Daniel and Sharon both finished school a while ago."

Judy nodded. That made sense. Kirsten was twenty-eight, and Daniel and Sharon were probably only a few years behind her, beyond college age.

She had so many questions, but Kirsten was so eager to hear about Judy, her mother, and her life in Waterford with Steve and Emily that Judy barely learned anything about the other Scharpelsens. Kirsten answered questions about herself readily enough, but she evaded inquiries about Robert or her siblings. She did it so subtly and with such friendliness that it wasn't until the meal was over and they were walking back to the car that Judy realized she knew little more about her family than she had before the plane landed.

A shadow of doubt crept into her mind as they drove to her hotel, on the west side of the city. Judy gave Kirsten a hard look, but Kirsten was driving along, smiling and chatting happily, and suddenly Judy felt ashamed. She was paranoid to think Kirsten was hiding anything more than nervousness. This visit had to be as emotionally grueling for Kirsten as it was for Judy, perhaps even more so, since she had initiated the contact.

When Judy was finally alone in her hotel room, she kicked off her shoes, fell onto the bed, and closed her eyes, drained. Kirsten was as nice and as welcoming as Judy could have hoped, and yet their few hours together had wrung her dry. Tomorrow afternoon, when she would meet the rest of the family at Robert Scharpelsen's house, would be worse. She stretched out on the bed, soothed by the quiet darkness of the room, glad that she'd refused Kirsten's invitation to stay at her apartment.

Before getting ready for bed, she called Steve to tell him about her day. She spoke to Emily, too, or tried to—either her daughter had been struck by sudden shyness or she didn't quite grasp that the phone, unlike the television, allowed for two-way communication. Still, Emily's presence on the line cheered her, even if the only response was the sound of her daughter's breathing.

The next morning she woke feeling rested but jittery. Kirsten picked her up at eight-thirty, and they drove downtown for breakfast. The square around the capitol building had been closed to traffic, and the sidewalks were lined with booths and tables offering everything from fresh produce and baked goods to houseplants and cheese. Judy and Kirsten bought pastries and coffee at a stand on the corner and walked down the sloping street to a modern structure overlooking one of the lakes. They found seats on a stone bench and enjoyed the scenery as they ate and talked. Emily told her the building was the Monona Terrace, a convention center designed by Frank Lloyd Wright. Judy listened, nodding as Kirsten pointed out various sights along the lakeshore, glad for the cardigan she had worn over her long skirt and blouse. The sun shone brightly in a cloudless sky, but the breeze off the lake was cool.

When they had finished eating, they returned to the Farmers' Market and joined the orderly, steady flow of customers moving counterclockwise from stall to stall around the square. Every so often, Kirsten would stop at a stand and purchase something for the evening meal. On an impulse, Judy bought flowers to give to her father. When they had gone all the way around the square, they stowed their purchases in Kirsten's car and toured the capitol building. From the observation deck, Judy looked out over the lake and enjoyed the fresh smells of spring in the breeze, wishing that Steve and Emily had come with her. Everything was going so well that her earlier doubts seemed foolish.

Afterward, Judy and Kirsten walked down State Street window-shopping and people-watching. A little before noon they stopped at a restaurant for sandwiches, and as they ate, the conversation turned to Judy's journey from Vietnam to America. Judy told Kirsten the little she remembered; she had pieced together the rest from her mother's stories. Not wishing to offend, Judy glossed over the most difficult part of her history, in which she and her mother waited to hear from Robert Scharpelsen only to be disappointed by his cold response.

When Judy reached the part where her mother met John DiNardo, Kirsten shook her head in admiration. "Your mother sounds like an amazing person," she said. "How did she manage to land that hospital job?"

Judy shrugged. "Her experience on the army base helped, I suppose, and they were impressed by her fluency in so many languages. They really wanted someone who spoke English and Spanish, but she convinced them that someone who could speak Vietnamese, English, and French could easily pick up Spanish if she studied on her own. She did, too." Judy thought back to those nights when she and her mother would sit side by side at the kitchen table, Judy with a picture book, her mother with a Spanish text.

"I can understand why she would need English in the bar because of the GIs, but how did she happen to pick up French?"

"Vietnam was a French colony before—" Then Kirsten's words fully registered. "What do you mean, in the bar?"

"You know, the bar where your mother worked."

The skin on the back of Judy's neck prickled. "What?"

"In Saigon. Where they met. Where your mom met my dad."

"He told you they met in a bar?"

Kirsten nodded, confused.

"He said my mother was a bar girl?" Kirsten nodded again, color creeping into her cheeks. "My mother worked in the hospital on the army base with your father." Each word came out as sharp, as clear, and as cold as a splinter of ice. "She was a translator for the doctors and nurses and anyone else who needed her. My mother has never set foot in a bar except as a paying customer, and only rarely has she done that."

"But he said—" Kirsten fumbled for the words. "He told me—"

"And even if she had been a bar girl, what difference does that make? Bar girl or translator, he loved her enough to live with her."

"What are you saying? What do you mean, live with her?"

Judy stared at her, hard, the blood pounding in her head. Then she understood. "He told you she was just a one-night stand at a bar, didn't he?" This time Kirsten couldn't even nod, but Judy saw in her face that it was the truth. "He lied to you, just as he lied to my mother. They lived together for more than two years. He promised to marry her and bring her to the States. Then one day he didn't come home from work. She asked at the hospital, and you know what they told her? He had shipped out that morning. He had known about it for months, and yet he never saw fit to mention it. But she trusted him. She thought that if she could just get to America, he would take care of her—of us, because I was born a month after he left. She thought if he saw his child, if he saw me, he would marry her."

"But he couldn't," Kirsten choked out. "You don't understand. He couldn't marry her."

"Why? Because she was a bar girl?" Judy snapped. "No, you're the one who doesn't understand. He used my mother and abandoned us. Then he scurried off here and found himself a new wife, a white wife, someone he wouldn't be ashamed of at cocktail parties and neighborhood barbecues. That's the man your father is."

"No. No, you—you don't understand."

"I understand perfectly." Suddenly, Judy couldn't bear the sight of Kirsten, stricken and confused, struggling to speak, to make sense of the new information. She wanted to storm away from the table, to her hotel, to the next plane home. It would have been so easy, but something kept her in her seat, watching, listening, waiting to see what Kirsten would do next.

Suddenly, in a flash of insight, Judy realized that she was enjoying this. Seeing Robert cut down in Kirsten's eyes filled her with grim satisfaction. Let no one—least of all the daughter he had loved instead of herself—think of Robert as a good man, as a loving father. Let Kirsten know him for what he truly was.

Kirsten sat in silence, staring at the table, her face flushed, her eyes shining with tears.

Suddenly Judy was flooded by shame. "I'm sorry," she said. "I didn't mean it."

"No. You meant every word." Kirsten took a deep breath. "But you don't know the whole story."

"You're right. I don't." She thought of what Andrew had said, and reminded herself that Robert had been a young man when he knew her mother, a young man far from home in tumultuous times. Judy didn't know his side of the story, and though she doubted he could say anything to win her sympathies, she had no right to take out her anger on Kirsten. "I'm sorry."

"It's all right," Kirsten said, still not looking at her. She took another deep, shaky breath and fell silent.

They sat at the table without speaking until the server began clearing away their dishes. Then they paid the bill and left.

Judy wished she had not confronted Kirsten. She had ruined everything, just when they were getting along so well. Three times she tried to strike up a conversation as they walked back to the car, but Kirsten seemed unable to respond.

As they pulled out of the parking garage, Kirsten finally spoke. "Should I take you back to the hotel?"

Judy shot her a look. "I thought we were going to your apartment."

"I thought . . . I thought maybe you wouldn't want to anymore."

Kirsten looked very young as she stared straight ahead, her eyes fixed on the busy street crowded with cars and bikes and darting pedestrians. Judy reminded herself that she was the elder sister. She had started the argument; it was up to her to put Kirsten at ease.

"I don't want to go back to the hotel," she said. "I didn't come all this way to leave without meeting the rest of the family. We have to expect these kinds of bumps along the way. We can't just give up the first time we run into difficulties."

Kirsten said nothing for a long moment. "You're right." She glanced away from the road to give Judy a pleading look. "I want you to know that I never intended to hurt you. If I could do it over . . ." She shook her head and drove on.

They went to her apartment, a small, one-bedroom flat on the third floor of a seventy-year-old building across the street from one of the lakes. Long ago, the building had been a pump station; though it had been remodeled for housing, the large steel pumps remained in the lobby. Kirsten came out of her silence to tell Judy this history, and by the time they reached her place, much of her earlier animation had returned.

Kirsten offered Judy a seat in the living room, a cozy place with a comfortable sofa, brick walls, and a sloped ceiling. They spent the afternoon talking over cups of tea. Judy finally began to hear more about life in the Scharpelsen family—their house on Lake Mendota, the misadventures of the three kids, Kirsten's mother's slow and painful death from cancer. As the hours passed, Judy finally began to feel as if she was getting to know these strangers. Sometimes, Kirsten broke off in the middle of a story as if to collect her thoughts; other times, she seemed vague or unwilling to reveal too much. Judy couldn't blame her. No wonder Kirsten was careful now, even tentative; neither one of them wanted to say anything that would spark more anger.

As evening approached, they went to the kitchen and prepared a large tossed salad using the produce they had purchased at the Farmers' Market. Then it was time to go to their father's house.

Judy's throat felt as if it were constrained by a fist, clenching ever tighter as they drove west, then north through a thickly wooded neighborhood of large homes on small lots. Through the trees, Judy could see the sun glinting off water, and she realized they were driving along the lakeshore.

They pulled into the driveway of a large, modern house on the lake. "This is it," Kirsten said, turning off the engine.

Judy fumbled with the seat belt and got out of the car. She followed Kirsten through the garage to a door leading into the house. Kirsten opened it and led her into the kitchen.

Classical music was playing on the stereo, and cooking smells floated on the air—bread, barbecue sauce, roasted corn. Judy stood frozen in the doorway, the bouquet of flowers in her hands, until Kirsten motioned for her to come forward.

A woman on the other side of the kitchen counter had her back to them as she took glasses down from a cupboard. She had blond hair like Kirsten's, only it was curly with a touch of gray.

Kirsten set the salad bowl on the counter. "Sharon?" she said. "There's someone I'd like you to meet."

Sharon turned—and as her eyes locked on Judy's, her expression went from pleasant to shocked in the instant it took for Judy to realize that this woman was not only older than Kirsten, but also surely older than herself. That was impossible, unless—

"My God," Sharon said. "I can't believe you did this."

"I had every right," Kirsten said. "She's our sister."

"How could you, after everything I said? Don't you care about Dad at all?"

"I care about Dad with all my heart. Don't you get it? That's why I had to do it."

Judy looked from one sister to the other, stunned. "You didn't know I was coming," she said to Sharon.

Sharon pressed her lips into a hard line and shook her head.

Judy turned and headed for the door.

"No, wait." Kirsten grabbed her arm. "Don't leave."

"I can't stay, not under these circumstances." Now she understood Kirsten's evasiveness.

"Please, Judy. I know now it was wrong, but at the time it seemed like the only way. Please don't go."

"Yes, now that you're here, why not stay?" Sharon yanked open a drawer and scooped up handfuls of silverware. "Why not ruin everything? Why not upset our father?"

"Stop it," Kirsten said.

"How dare you tell me to do anything after this stunt?" Sharon slammed the knives and forks onto the counter, then fixed her gaze on Judy. "How dare you show up now? Don't you realize how hard this will be for him?"

"I came because I was invited."

Sharon barked out a laugh and resumed her work, yanking open cupboards and slamming them shut. Just then, two boys bounded into the kitchen. When they saw Judy, they stopped short and eyed her with interest.

"Hi," said the eldest, a boy of around twelve. "Who are you?"

"She's your Aunt Judy," Kirsten said before Judy could reply.

The children's eyes widened. "Really?" the younger one asked.

Kirsten nodded, but Sharon rushed forward and thrust the silverware into the children's hands. "No, not really," she said. "Go set the table."

The elder boy shot Judy a look. "But Mom—"

"Now." Sharon clasped each boy by the shoulder and steered them out of the room.

When she was gone, Judy turned to Kirsten. "I'm not staying. I can't."

"Meet Daniel and Dad first," Kirsten begged. "Please. You came all this way."

All this way, and for what? To learn that one sister had deceived her and that another hated her on sight. What was worse, she now understood why Robert had never married her mother. Kirsten was right; he couldn't have. Sharon was older than Judy, and perhaps Daniel was as well. In an instant, Judy had gone from being the daughter of the wronged first wife to being the daughter of the other woman, and somehow that changed everything.

"Please," Kirsten repeated, pleading.

Judy gulped air, dazed—but she nodded. Kirsten took her hand and led her down the hallway in the direction of the music. In a front room, a man who appeared near Judy's age sat talking with another man several years older, their voices a low murmur beneath the sound of the stereo. On the other side of the room sat another man, worn and gray-haired. He stared out the window as if he were alone.

The first two broke off their conversation as Kirsten brought Judy into the room. "Daniel," she said firmly to the younger man. "This is our sister, Judy."

The color drained from the man's face. "Uh—hi, hello," he stammered, rising. He shook Judy's hand, his mouth opening and closing as if he wanted to speak but had no idea what to say. Kirsten didn't give him a chance to compose himself, but as she propelled Judy to the other side of the room, he found his voice. "Kirsten, don't," he said. "Dad's not having a good day."

Kirsten spun around to look at him. "Good day?" she echoed. "How long has it been since his last good day? You know as well as I do that they won't be getting any better." She continued on, taking Judy with her. Her pace slowed as they approached the old man, who didn't look up.

"Dad?" Kirsten said softly, kneeling down and placing a hand on his knee.

A muscle tightened and relaxed in the man's cheek, but his gaze never left the window.

Kirsten leaned to the side, interrupting his line of sight. "Dad? There's someone here to see you."

He blinked at Kirsten, who smiled and motioned to Judy. By instinct, Judy knelt beside Kirsten and tried to hand him the bouquet of flowers. He would not take it, so she placed it on his lap instead. Slowly his gaze traveled from Kirsten to the flowers to Judy, his brow furrowing in confusion. The muscles in his face worked as if he were struggling to focus on her features, fighting to recognize her.

Then he spoke. "Tuyet?"

A wave of grief, of pain, washed over her as the old man groped for her hand.

"No, Dad," Kirsten said gently. "This is Judy, Tuyet's daughter. Your daughter."

Judy saw at once that the old man didn't understand, if he even heard the words. She gave him her hand and clasped her other around them both. She felt the man's bones through his skin, which felt as dry and thin as paper.

"Tuyet," the man repeated.

Judy wanted to weep. Unable to speak, she squeezed the man's hand and got to her feet. Blinded by sudden tears, she hurried out of the room, back to the kitchen. She heard Kirsten call after her, but she couldn't stop. She raced out of the house, down the driveway, along the winding, wooded street until she reached the main road. She kept walking until she managed to hail a cab, which she took back to the hotel.

There were two messages waiting for her, one from Steve and one from Kirsten. She called Steve, but reached the answering machine. "It was a nightmare," she said. "I never should have come." Then she told him she'd see him tomorrow and not to call back, because she was taking the phone off the hook, in case Kirsten tried to reach her.

It was too early for sleep, but she pulled the heavy drapes shut until the room was dark, put on her pajamas, and crawled into bed. There she lay, thinking of how her world had shifted. She felt that she ought to be weeping, but the tears wouldn't fall.

Sleep came hours later.

She did not remember her dreams the next morning, but she woke feeling heavy and sore and as weary as if she had not shut her eyes all night. She had planned to spend the day with the Scharpelsens; since that was out of the question, she called the airline and arranged to be transferred to an earlier flight. After gathering her belongings, she checked out of the hotel and called a cab from the lobby.

When she went outside to wait, she saw Kirsten's car parked right out front. Kirsten was leaning against the passenger-side door, but she straightened at the sight of Judy. "Hi," she said.

Judy composed herself. "Hi."

"I figured you might leave early."

"I didn't see any point in staying."

Kirsten nodded in acceptance and opened the car door. "I'll take you to the airport."

"I already called a cab."

As if she hadn't heard, Kirsten went to the back of the car and opened the trunk. She didn't look at Judy as she picked up the garment bag and put it inside. Judy sighed and got in the car.

They drove in silence past the wooded neighborhood of her father's house, through the downtown, and across the isthmus. Kirsten didn't speak until they pulled up beside the airport terminal.

"I'm so sorry," she said. "I never meant for things to turn out like this."

"I know." Judy unfastened her seat belt and got out of the car.

Kirsten did the same, and came around the back to unlock the trunk. "Will I ever hear from you again?"

"I don't know." Judy grabbed her garment bag and put it on the sidewalk.

"Can I write to you?"

Judy shrugged.

"If I do, will you write back?"

Her voice was so forlorn that Judy relented. "Of course I will." The relief on Kirsten's face was so intense that Judy decided in an instant that this would not be the last time they saw each other. They were sisters. Even if the other Scharpelsens wished she would disappear forever, she and Kirsten could still be friends.

They embraced and promised to talk soon. Judy picked up her bags and entered the airport alone.

Sharon was waiting at the gate.

Judy approached, set down her bags, and eyed her unflinchingly, waiting for her to speak.

Sharon gave her a shaky smile. "I thought you would be here," she said. "It was the earliest flight. I figured you couldn't get out of here soon enough."

Judy didn't quite know how to respond to that, so she said nothing.

"I'm sorry about yesterday," Sharon said. "It wasn't your fault. None of this was your fault."

"If I had known Kirsten hadn't told you, I wouldn't have come."

"I know." Sharon looked away. "It was just such a shock, you see? I've known about you for years. My mother knew about you, too. Dad wanted to bring you and your mother to America, but my mother forbade him to have any contact with you. To her it was a matter of her husband's having an affair and flaunting his mistress in her face. She—she didn't understand, she couldn't have known what—what—"

Judy placed a hand on her arm. "It's all right. I understand."

"Will you stay? I'd like the chance to talk to you."

"I can't." Judy gestured awkwardly toward the gate. "I already changed my flight, and—"

"Of course. I see."

"But—" Judy hesitated. "Maybe we'll try again someday."

Sharon held her gaze for a moment. "I hope so." She clasped Judy's hand, then turned and walked away.

Judy watched until she disappeared around the corner, then found a seat and waited for her flight to be called.

⚓

Judy chose green for the homeland she had left behind and did not remember. She chose blue for the skies over the new homes she had made for herself with her mother and stepfather, with her husband and child, and with her friends at Elm Creek Manor. She chose gold for sunlight and illumination.

She set the block on point again, knowing that unexpected shifts could be as enlightening as they were jarring. She could not add solid triangles as Diane had done, however, not when the most fundamental assumptions of her life had been thrown into disarray. One day the pieces would settle into a pattern and she would feel whole again, but not yet.

Instead her triangles were composed of partial Mariner's Compass blocks, the diameter of the compass running along the longest side of each triangle.

The compass was for all the journeys she had made in her life and all that she had yet to make. She knew that it was unfair to judge an entire journey by the first step. Often what seemed to be the right path turned out to lead in the wrong direction—but just as often, perseverance along a hard trail would lead to an important destination.

The potential rewards made the journey worthwhile.

Nine

Carol watched as the round robin quilt took shape, admiring the Elm Creek Quilters' handi-work and wishing she could add a border of her own. Each time they brought out the quilt, she told herself it didn't matter that no one had asked her to participate. Since she didn't sew well enough yet, she would have declined rather than ruin the quilt. Still, it would have been nice if they had given her that choice. As always, she was the odd woman out, lingering just outside the circle of friends, wishing someone would invite her in.

Not that anyone other than Sarah had made her feel unwelcome. Sylvia was generous and kind, and the Elm Creek Quilters were friendly. With Sarah so hostile and eager for her to go away, though, Carol knew she would never feel wholly a part of the place her daughter called home.

This visit was not going at all the way Sylvia had assured her it would over the phone that winter morning several months before. Carol didn't blame Sylvia; the older woman had done all she could, more than anyone could have asked. Maybe it was time to give up. Carol could go home, back to her job and her empty house, and Sarah could resume her usual life. Maybe they would both be happier that way. Carol had not gotten along with her own mother; why should she expect anything different between herself and Sarah?

Sarah did not need her—not for advice, not for a shoulder to cry on, certainly not for friendship. Carol could leave Waterford with a clear conscience, knowing her daughter was in good hands. If Sarah's marriage faltered and failed, as Carol dreaded it would, the Elm Creek Quilters would bear Sarah up. Carol's presence would be unnecessary and unwelcome. She had warned Sarah against marrying Matt, and when her predictions about him came true, Sarah would hate her for it. She would never believe that Carol had hoped with all her heart that she had been wrong about him. Carol wanted to like Matt, despite his modest aspirations, despite his resemblance to her own husband, which she alone seemed able to detect. When she looked at Matt, Carol saw another man who was diligent and reliable instead of fascinating, a man who knew right from wrong—and would hold everyone to it no matter what the cost. How long could a man like that keep the interest of someone like Sarah? And what penance would he force from her if she failed him? In the years to come, would Sarah learn to accept her widowhood with some measure of relief, as Carol herself had done?

Carol could have used a group of friends like Sarah's to see her through the hard times after Kevin died, and those that had come before. But except for one brief period before she married, Carol had never had a group of girl friends, or even one best friend. She had been too bookish, too introverted, too sensitive. The discrepancy between the way things were and the way things ought to be had been very clear to her, but she had felt helpless, powerless to do anything to make up the difference. It had been easier to live in the safe, scripted world of stories than to try to change her own world.

She was the child of her parents' middle age, the baby they had neither expected nor wanted. Her mother accepted Carol's arrival with her usual resignation, but her father made it clear he wanted nothing to do with this new mouth to feed who hadn't the decency to be born a boy. He had the two sons he wanted and could afford; another boy would have been accepted grudgingly, but not this girl child who would drain him dry and contribute nothing. Well, at least when she got older she'd be able to help her mother around the house.

Since her older brothers had entered college by the time she started kindergarten, Carol grew up as an only child, but without an only child's sense of uniqueness and privilege. Her best childhood friends were Laura Ingalls, Nancy Drew, and the other smart, headstrong girls in books, girls who faced enormous challenges and always overcame them in the end. Carol longed to be like them. She wished she could melt into a novel and live there, and spend her days helping Pa harvest the wheat or solving mysteries with her friends Bess and George. At night before she drifted off to sleep, she would tell herself stories of the places and people she had read about, writing herself into the scenes. She was Nancy's younger sister, held hostage by a con man, rescued just in time by her lawyer father, Carson Drew. She was Laura's cousin visiting from western Minnesota, twisting hay into sticks to fight off the cold of the blizzards that howled around the small house in DeSmet. In her imagination she could be anything. She learned to welcome twilight.

As she grew older, she realized she could never climb inside a book and stay there, but at least she could get out of her parents' cold home. She could escape; she *must* escape. Her brothers had found jobs after college and came home only to visit. If she studied hard and earned good grades, she could do the same.

Her teachers were pleased to have such a diligent pupil, though they wished she'd smile more and play with the other children instead of spending lunchtime and recess with her nose in a book. In high school, her honors English teacher took notice of her, the quiet, brown-haired girl with the pale face and wide eyes who wrote such thoughtful essays. He recommended books to her—the classics, new works by emerging authors—and her world expanded. She confided in him as she had in no one else, and he encouraged her. He even told her he thought she could win a partial scholarship to college if she kept up her hard work.

His words left her with mixed feelings. A partial scholarship would do her no good if her parents were unwilling to pay the rest. They had sent her brothers to college, but Carol's future was never discussed. She studied even harder, determined to earn a full scholarship. If she did, perhaps she wouldn't have to tell her parents about her plans until it was too late for them to stop her.

In the summer before her senior year, she saved her baby-sitting money and the little her mother gave her for clothes until she had enough for her college application fees. She sent them off with a fervent prayer and waited.

When the news arrived months later, it both delighted her and filled her with dread. She had been accepted to Michigan State, but the scholarship they offered was even less than her most pessimistic estimates. Her tiny savings and a job on campus would help her make up some of the difference, but it was clear she would need her parents' help.

It took her a week to summon up enough courage. Her English teacher helped her plan what to say. She waited until after supper, before her father left for the living room and his evening newspaper, before her mother beckoned her to help with the dishes. Then she brought out the letter and told them she had been accepted to college.

Her mother looked surprised and pleased, but her father frowned. "Why do you want to go to college?"

"To continue my education," Carol said, as she had rehearsed. "To better myself. If I have a degree, I'll be able to make a good living."

"You mean you want to work?"

Carol nodded.

"Your mother doesn't work. She didn't go to college. You think you're better than her?"

Carol thought of her mother's life, of the endless cooking and cleaning and washing and sewing and picking up after her husband. Her parents were the same age, but her mother looked ten years older. "No. Of course not. I just want something different."

He shook his head. "You don't know what it will be like. There are smart kids in college, smart kids like your brothers. You won't be able to keep up."

His words stung, but she didn't let him see it. "I'm going to be class salutatorian, so I think I'll be able to manage. I know it won't be easy, but my teachers have confidence in me."

"College costs money."

"Not as much as you might think." She told him about the partial scholarship, too nervous to look at him as she spoke.

Before she could finish, he interrupted. "I won't waste money sending a girl to college. I'll pay all that money for a fancy education and for what? Will it make you prettier? Will it teach you to stop moping around? It's going to be hard enough for you to get a husband as it is. No man will want to marry you if he thinks you're smarter than he is."

A sour taste filled Carol's mouth.

Carol's mother reached over and touched her husband's hand. "What if she doesn't marry?" she said gently. They both turned to look at her. Carol felt herself shrinking beneath their scrutiny. She knew what they were thinking. They could not count on a man to come and take their ugly little mouse off their hands. They could not provide for her forever, and she would need to earn her keep.

Carol was torn between shame and hope as she waited for her father to speak. She knew she was plain and that no man would ever love her, but that was not why she wanted to go to college. It didn't matter. What was most important was that she got her education. It made no difference why or how.

Finally her father let out a heavy sigh. "How much will it cost again?" Wordlessly, Carol handed him the letter. He scanned it, frowning.

"There are lots of nice young men at college," her mother said.

"For all the good that'll do her." He set down the letter. "Well, I guess it wouldn't hurt. You can go."

Carol nearly burst with relief and gratitude. "Thank you," she said, her voice thick with emotion.

"What will you study? Typing? Nursing?" He grinned at his wife. "What kind of classes do they have for girls, anyway?"

"I'm going to study literature," Carol said. She wanted to be a college professor someday, and live the life her English teacher had described: hours spent exploring old libraries, discussing the great books with attentive pupils, writing and reading to her heart's content in an office full of books in an ivy-covered hall.

But her father's thick brows had drawn together. "Not with my money you won't. You'll be a nurse or a secretary, something practical."

"Literature is practical." She looked from her father to her mother and back, anxious. "I'm going to keep studying until I have my doctorate. I'm going to be a college professor."

"How many years will that take?"

"I—I don't know."

"She doesn't know," he repeated to his wife. Then he turned back to his daughter, stern. "I'll pay for the same as your brothers got, and no more."

"You won't have to pay. I'll get a scholarship—"

"Like you did this time?" He shoved his chair away from the table with such force that he knocked over the salt shaker. He rose and pointed at her. "You'll be a nurse or a secretary, and that's final."

Anger boiled up inside her. "One doesn't attend the university to become a secretary."

He slapped her across the face, hard. Her mother gasped. Carol clamped her jaw shut to hold in the cry of pain. Slowly she turned her head and met her father's gaze. He struck her again, harder, so hard he almost knocked her out of her chair.

"Then you'll be a nurse," he said. "Or you'll be nothing."

Her head was reeling, so she didn't see him leave the room. As she tried to regain her senses, she heard her mother go to the sink and turn on the tap. In another moment she was at Carol's side, holding a cool washcloth to her cheek.

"You shouldn't provoke him," her mother murmured. "You know how hard he works. He said you could go. If you had just thanked him and left it at that—"

Carol took the washcloth and shrugged her mother off, furious with her for cataloging her mistakes, for not standing up to her father. She felt her dreams of a scholarly life slipping through her fingers like the grains of salt her father had spilled on the yellow-checked tablecloth. Very well, she thought bitterly. She would be a nurse, if she had to. Anything to get out of there.

If she had been able to follow her dreams, perhaps she would have turned out like Gwen Sullivan, associate professor of American studies at Waterford College, Elm Creek Quilter, mother of a loving daughter, and woman of many friends. It could have been Carol teaching a workshop full of eager students and waiting for her turn to add a border to the round robin quilt.

Carol admired Gwen more than she envied her. Gwen's confidence and wit reminded her of the heroines from her childhood books. She attended all of Gwen's workshops, even when the lesson plan was the same as a previous week's. On that day, when Diane asked if she would mind helping some of the new quilters, Carol was so pleased that she almost forgot to say yes. She watched how Diane went from table to table assisting the campers and did the same. Fortunately, Sarah wasn't around to roll her eyes and scoff at the sight of neophyte Carol offering advice to women who had quilted for years.

Judy arrived as the workshop was ending, and she helped them straighten up the room for the next morning's class.

"How was your trip?" Diane asked. Carol wished she had thought of it first.

"I expected more cows," Judy said, trying to grin. "I didn't see a single one."

Gwen put an arm around her shoulders. "How was it really?"

Judy told them. Carol's heart went out to her as she spoke of her elder half sister's anger and her father's confusion. Carol didn't know how Judy could bear such disappointment after the hopes raised by Kirsten's invitation.

"What are you going to do now?" Gwen asked after Judy finished.

"I don't know." Judy sat down on the edge of the dais and rested her chin in her hands. "Part of me thinks I should wait for Kirsten to make the next move. Another part of me wants to block out every memory of last weekend and never think of them again."

"I can understand that," Diane said.

Judy gave her a wry half smile. Carol wished she could think of something comforting to say, but she couldn't. She settled for giving Judy a hug. Judy held on to her so tightly that Carol knew it had been the right thing to do.

Then Judy sighed and reached into her sewing bag. "The trip wasn't a complete waste," she said, producing a folded bundle of cloth. "I finished my border."

"Let's see," Gwen said, helping her unfold the quilt top. Judy had set the quilt on point as Diane had done, but not with solid triangles. Instead, a design resembling a compass or a sun radiated from each side, the longest, central points nearly reaching the corners. All of the points were split down the middle lengthwise, with dark fabric on one side and light on the other, giving the design a three-dimensional, shaded appearance. The tips were perfectly sharp, and the border lay smooth and flat.

"Your piecing is amazing," Diane said, echoing Carol's own thoughts. "Maybe this will finally convince these machine people to switch to hand work."

Gwen looked ready to retort, but before she could speak, they heard the door open on the other side of the room. It was Sylvia, carrying a purse and wearing a light blue dress and a white hat.

"Quick," Diane whispered, but Judy was already bundling up the quilt top. There wasn't enough time to return it to the bag, so she held it behind her back. They nailed nonchalant expressions to their faces and greeted Sylvia as she approached.

"You four are obviously up to something," she said, her eyes narrowing as she inspected them. "Are you going to tell me what it is, or will I have to guess?"

"We're not up to anything," Diane said. "We're just cleaning up after Gwen's workshop."

"Hmph." Sylvia looked around at the clean tables and the carefully swept floor. "You're going to have to do better than that."

Carol fidgeted beneath the woman's scrutiny. "It's—well, it's a surprise—"

"For Summer's graduation party," Gwen interrupted.

"I see. Very well, then, what is it?"

Judy gave her an apologetic look. "If we told you—"

"It wouldn't be a surprise. Yes, yes, of course. I understand." Sylvia adjusted her hat. "As a matter of fact, I have business of my own for Summer's party. That's what I stopped by to tell you. Andrew and I are driving in to town to fetch some decorations. We'll be back before supper."

Diane's eyebrows shot up. "You and Andrew, huh? Is this your official first date?"

"It is most certainly not a date. It's an errand."

"It sounds like a date to me," Gwen said.

"Why do I even bother?" Sylvia wondered aloud. "It's not you four troublemakers I wanted to talk to, anyway. I'm looking for Sarah. If I'm going to be driving downtown, I'd prefer to borrow her truck rather than ride in that enormous contraption of Andrew's."

"You can take my car," Carol offered, returning to the back table, where she had left her purse.

"Are you sure it's no trouble?"

"It's my pleasure," Carol said as she handed Sylvia her keys. The Elm Creek Quilters were always helping each other, and lending her car to Sylvia made her feel more like one of them. So did the way Sylvia went out of her way to include her. She could have said, "You three troublemakers—and Carol." Carol didn't mind being considered a troublemaker the way Sylvia had said it, especially if that meant she was part of the group.

"Have a nice time," Judy said as Sylvia turned to go.

"Don't do anything I wouldn't do," Diane added.

Sylvia gave them a sharp look. "It's not a date." Before they could disagree, she left the room, more briskly than she had arrived.

Their mirth turned to relief as Judy brought out the quilt from behind her back.

"I swear that woman has quilt radar," Diane said. "She can sense a quilt within a hundred paces."

Gwen took the quilt from Judy. "We won't have to hide this much longer. I'll add my border, Agnes will finish the center, and we'll be ready to quilt."

Carol hoped that they would let her help.

The other women left, and as Carol went upstairs to her room near the library, she thought about Summer's party and tried to remember when she had last hosted one for Sarah. The wedding didn't count; Sarah and Matt had planned and paid for everything on their own. When Sarah graduated from Penn State, she might have had a party with her friends, but if she had, she hadn't invited Carol. Carol felt a twinge of guilt until she remembered Sarah's high school graduation. Carol had held an elaborate open house in Sarah's honor, even though Sarah had not been valedictorian or even salutatorian or even in the top tenth in her class. Carol had been disappointed. Sarah was such a bright girl; she could have been at the top of her class if she had spent as much time on her studies as she had her social life. She could have earned a full scholarship anywhere—Harvard, Yale, one of the Seven Sisters—if only she had been more industrious. But Sarah settled for the state school as indifferently as she had settled for B's when she could have earned A's, with no idea how much Carol envied her the opportunities she squandered.

No one had thrown Carol a graduation party, not her parents, who were still upset at her for wanting to go to college in the fall, and not her friends, since she had none. Her graduation from high school would have passed unnoticed if not for the ceremony itself, which her parents did attend, and her English teacher's kindness. On the last day of school he gave her three books: a dictionary, a thesaurus, and a leather-bound volume of the complete works of Shakespeare. Her heart leapt as she held the last and turned the gilt-edged pages to read the inscription. "These will take you anywhere," her teacher had written. "Congratulations, and may this be the first of many successes for you."

His kindness brought tears to her eyes. He alone knew how much it pained her to sacrifice one part of her dream so that she would not lose the whole. If only she were brave enough to defy her parents—but she was not. She would become a nurse rather than stay home until the unlikely arrival of a suitable young man bearing a marriage proposal. She would show her father that she was neither as stupid nor as useless as he thought. She would become the best nursing student in her class if it killed her.

And she did, but her father never knew it. He died of heart failure during her last semester, so he didn't see her graduate. Even if he had, he wouldn't have known how her joy was tempered as she accepted her degree; he would not have been able to detect a single regret, for life in his house had taught her how to hide her feelings. But beneath the placid surface, emotions churned. She never wished for him to die, not even when he beat her, but since it had happened, why then and not years earlier, so that she would have been free to choose her own path?

The thoughts shamed her, but she could not silence them.

She found a job in a hospital in Lansing, where almost by accident she made the first friends of her life. She and two other new nurses banded together for mutual support as they struggled with the nearly overwhelming demands of the hospital, and their need soon blossomed into friendship. At least once a week they went out in the evening together, to see a movie or to shop. Once, when they went bowling, a group of three men invited them out for a drink. After a quick whispered conference, they agreed. Boldly, Carol drank as much as the other girls and laughed nearly as loudly. It was the most fun she had ever had, and the next day, her friends insisted that one of the men had hardly been able to keep his eyes off her all night. She was pleased, but she didn't believe them. She didn't even remember Kevin's last name. She had preferred one of the others, a dark-haired lawyer who had put his arm around her as the men walked the nurses to their bus stop. He was well-read and charming, and she wished that it was he, not Kevin Mallory, who stopped by the hospital later that week and asked her out to lunch.

She accepted the invitation, and when he asked her out again, she agreed. With more surprised fascination than desire, she realized he was courting her. A year later, when he asked her to marry him, she would have laughed except he was so earnest.

"I'll be a good husband to you," he promised. "I'll take care of you. You won't have to work anymore. I love you and I want us to be together."

She stared at him, astounded. He loved her? He hardly knew her. She searched her heart and wondered if she had fallen in love with him without realizing it. She was almost certain she had not. He was a good, kind man, and she liked him, but passion didn't sweep over her when she looked at him. When he fumbled to kiss her good-night, she felt the pressure of his mouth but none of the electric warmth her friends described when confiding about their own trysts.

Still, she did like him, and she knew he would never hurt her. And a woman could not go through life alone.

"I'll need to think about it," she told him. He nodded reluctantly and told her to take all the time she needed; he would wait for her forever if he had to. Carol knew hyperbole when she heard it but decided to kiss him rather than scoff. He responded eagerly, relieved that she had not refused him outright.

Her girlfriends thought Kevin too dull for a boyfriend but perhaps just right for a husband, since he wasn't bad-looking and he earned a good living.

Her mother, who had never met him, was his strongest advocate. "Say yes," she urged over the telephone from the town in northern Michigan Carol had successfully escaped. "You might never get a better offer."

Carol couldn't ignore the truth in her words. The next time she saw Kevin, she told him she would marry him. And later, when his insurance company transferred him to Pennsylvania, she gave up her job and the only friends she'd ever had and made a home for him in a three-bedroom house in Pittsburgh.

Sarah was born a few months after the move. Carol's mother stayed with them during the difficult months before the birth, when the dangerous pregnancy forced Carol to remain in bed, and afterward, when a thick cloud of despair inexplicably came over her. The bright new baby in her arms brought her little joy, and she did not know why. Sometimes she woke in the middle of the night to find she had been weeping. Other times she could not sleep at all, but paced around the living room of the darkened house, smoking one cigarette after another. She did not know why she wasn't happy, and she hated herself for it. She had all she had ever wanted—an education, a pleasant house, an adoring husband, a beautiful child who would have everything, everything that she herself had been denied. What was preventing her from enjoying such blessings?

Her beloved books were forgotten. If not for her mother, meals, laundry, housekeeping, and even Sarah herself would have been neglected, too. Carol nursed Sarah when her mother brought her the child, but otherwise she lay in bed sleeping or sat outside in a chair, alone with her thoughts. After a few weeks of this, her mother taught her how to bathe the baby, change her, dress her, care for her. Gradually, her mother's quiet but firm insistence helped her develop an interest in the child, and a thin shaft of light began to pierce the heavy fog surrounding her. Carol could not find the words to voice her gratitude, but for the first time, she realized how deeply she loved her mother.

For his part, Kevin left for the office soon after breakfast, and Carol did not see him again until evening. He would ask her about her day, although there was never anything to tell him. He would nod and kiss her gently, then talk quietly with his mother-in-law before going off to play with Sarah until suppertime. Carol considered telling her husband and mother that she didn't like them talking about her behind her back, but she couldn't summon up the energy to complain.

Then one day, when Sarah was three months old, Carol had a dream. She was sitting at the kitchen table of her father's house, unable to touch the plate her mother had set before her. It was raining outside, and thunder crashed until the walls shook. Her father scowled and said, "You don't deserve that baby. You can't even take care of her."

Suddenly, Carol heard a faint wail coming from outside. Sarah was out there in the storm, alone and frightened. Carol ran outside to find her daughter, but the wind drove rain into her eyes until she couldn't see. She tried to follow the thin cry to its source, but every time she thought she was nearly there, the cry withdrew into the distance. Frantic, she ran faster and faster, but always the sobbing child remained just out of reach, lost and helpless, dependent and abandoned.

Carol woke shaking. Kevin slept on as she climbed from bed and stumbled down the hall to Sarah's room, where she listened to her daughter's breathing and touched the tiny bundle beneath the quilt to convince herself that Sarah was not lost in a storm. Reassured, she sank to the floor and hugged her knees to her chest, rocking back and forth, weeping softly.

The next morning Carol told her mother that she thought she could manage just fine now on her own. Her mother brightened, eager to return home to her garden and her friends. Carol saw her husband and mother exchange happy glances, pleased that she had returned to her old self. Carol knew she hadn't, not yet and perhaps never, but she would be better than she had been. She would be a good mother to Sarah, if only to prove that her father had been wrong about her. She was not a failure, though he had been convinced of it and had nearly convinced her, too.

After her mother left, she made a schedule for herself just as she had back in college. Every day that she managed to complete the tasks on her list was a subdued triumph. She fought off the old listlessness by throwing herself into her role of mother and wife. This was her new venue, she decided, and she could achieve there as well as any other place.

In fair weather she took long walks, pushing Sarah in her stroller. They had lived in that town for nearly a year, but in her distraction Carol had not yet learned their neighborhood. With her daughter's pleasant company, she explored the streets near their home, and one day she chanced upon a sight that sent a stab of longing though her: a used book shop, its front window stacked with books of every size and description.

She maneuvered the stroller through the store's narrow aisles, pausing whenever a book caught her eye, hungrily devouring a chapter or more before moving on to the next delight. The hours passed in the luxury of words and the smell of old paper. Eventually, Sarah grew bored and fretful, so Carol found picture books for her, which Sarah gnawed and flung to the floor. When other customers began to stare, Carol blushed and paid for the picture books, then hurried from the store. When she was almost home, she realized that she had forgotten to buy anything for herself.

Her embarrassment kept her away the next day, but she returned the day after. Soon she began to visit several times a week, sometimes to purchase a book for herself or for Sarah, other times merely to surround herself with so many stories, so many words. The polite hush of the shop was nearly religious in its serenity, and after more than a few days away, she found herself craving it.

The elderly woman who ran the shop came to know her by name, and Carol began to recognize other frequent customers. They would nod politely at each other, but this was not a place to strike up friendships. No one would dare intrude on another visitor's quiet contemplation of the walls of books.

Only one person broke this unspoken rule of the bookshop: the owner's nephew, Jack, who had dark hair and a quick flash of a grin. He was not there every day, but when he was, he would greet Carol with a slight bow as if she were someone of great importance. At first his slightly mocking demeanor embarrassed her, but she got used to it and began to return his bows with a mocking curtsy of her own.

Sometimes he searched the stacks for children's books and set them aside for Sarah. When he detected a pattern in Carol's purchases, he began to point out books he thought she would enjoy, classics in excellent condition. She appreciated his help and often thanked him with a small homemade gift—a slice of cake from yesterday's baking, a basket of fresh rolls. When she saw the pleasure her gifts brought him, her cheeks grew warm and she hurried deeper into the store, pushing Sarah's stroller before her.

One day he left the cash register and followed.

"Thank you for the cookies," he said when he caught up to her, keeping his voice low so that he wouldn't disturb the other customers.

"Don't mention it," she told him. His dark hair was so thick that it always looked tousled. Instinctively she lifted a hand to touch her own hair.

He misunderstood the gesture and extended his hand. "I'm Jack."

"I'm Carol." She shook his hand and quickly released it. "Carol Mallory. Mrs. Kevin Mallory."

He grinned at her, then bent down to look into the stroller. "And who's this big girl?"

Sarah squealed with delight, and Carol couldn't help smiling. "My daughter, Sarah."

"Pleased to meet you, Sarah," he said, extending a finger, which she seized. Laughing, he let her hang on for a moment before he freed himself and stood up. "It's nice to finally know your name." Grinning, he turned and walked back to the front of the store.

Carol watched him go. It *was* silly that she had not learned his name before then, but names had not seemed necessary in the bookshop.

Suddenly she was grateful that she had not told Kevin about him.

The meetings in the bookshop turned into long chats over coffee at a nearby diner. They would discuss politics and literature—and themselves. Jack, she learned, traveled the country acquiring books for the shop; that explained his frequent absences. He had never married, though he had come close once, years before. "I came to my senses just in time," he said, laughing. He had not yet decided if he wanted to take over his aunt's shop after her retirement.

"Why wouldn't you?" she asked.

He shrugged. "I don't know if I want to be held in one place."

Carol understood. He wanted the pleasure of discovering a first-edition Mark Twain at an estate sale, not the drudgery of placing books on shelves and making change. That was all right every once in a while, but not day in, day out. That was no kind of life for a man like Jack. That was for a man more like—well, like Kevin.

Sometimes they went for long walks after the coffee, and Carol would have to race home as fast as the stroller would go in order to have dinner ready by the time Kevin returned from the office. She found herself thinking about Jack when she wasn't with him. More than once, when Kevin made love to her, she closed her eyes and imagined Jack inside her, her hands tangled in his dark hair, his mouth on hers. Afterward, waves of guilt would wash over her, but she would tell herself she had done nothing wrong. She was unfaithful to Kevin only in her imagination, and no one could condemn her for that.

She knew that Jack had a girlfriend, a woman he had been seeing off and on for nearly three years. As the weeks passed, Jack mentioned her less and less frequently. Once, after a long walk through the park, as they sat on the grass under a tree watching Sarah play, Carol asked about her.

"I haven't seen her in weeks," he said.

Her heart pounded, but she kept her voice steady. "Why not?"

He met her gaze. "I think you know why."

She trembled inside and couldn't speak. She wanted to rip her eyes away from his, but she couldn't. She felt as if he could see into the very heart of her and knew what she was thinking—and what she imagined as she made love to her husband.

Jack took her hand. "Carol, I want to be with you."

"We can't." She felt her eyes filling with tears. "I'm married."

"He doesn't have to know." He began to stroke her arm with his other hand, and she shivered, dizzy with arousal. "Please, Carol."

She wanted to say yes. She wanted to taste him. She wanted to open herself to him and love him until she was sated, complete.

But— "I can't."

It came out as a sob. Sarah looked up from her play, startled. Hurriedly,

Carol snatched her up and placed her in the stroller. Jack had told her how he despised the manipulation of tears, and she would not let him see her cry.

"I won't ask again," he called to her as she walked away.

She hesitated. Was it a promise or a warning? She knew it made no difference. Without looking back, she continued on her way.

At home, she put Sarah down for her nap and flung herself onto the bed she and Kevin shared. Alone, she wept, mourning everything she had never had and would never feel. She wept until she was too exhausted to do anything but stare at the ceiling. She lay on the bed in silence, wondering how she would fill up her days with no more long talks over coffee to look forward to, no more meetings in the bookshop. She could never return to the store, that was certain.

The next morning, not long after Kevin left for work, the phone rang.

"I'm leaving," Jack said.

"Why?" she asked. "Where are you going?"

"I don't know. I just—I can't stay here." He paused. "I said I wouldn't ask you again—"

"Yes," she said quickly. "Yes. I'm coming. Don't go." She hung up the phone and rushed Sarah into her clothes. She left her with the next-door neighbor, a widow whose children were grown, with the excuse that she had an emergency doctor's appointment. When she reached the bookstore, Jack was waiting outside. Through the window she could see his aunt at the cash register, helping a customer.

"Are you sure?" he asked her when she reached him, breathless from running.

She nodded and gave him her hand.

He drove them to his apartment, where he began kissing her before he had even closed the door. She felt drenched and new and alive in his arms, and when they had finished making love, he held her close and stroked her hair. He held her for what seemed like a long time, and yet when he shifted to reach for his clothes, her heart broke that it was over so soon.

Her drove her home—or nearly there; he pulled over to the curb a few blocks from her house. They kissed swiftly, fervently, before she got out of the car and hurried down the street to the neighbor's, where Sarah waited.

That evening as she served Kevin his pot roast and potatoes, she wondered how he could be so blind to the change in her. A warmth had come over her, a sensation that she had never known, and she knew she could never return to what she used to be.

Jack didn't leave after all, now that she had given him a reason to stay. Over the next two months they met as often as Carol could get away, as often as she could get the woman next door to care for Sarah. "She's going to think you have a terminal illness if you keep having so many doctor's appointments," Jack teased. In response, Carol hit him lightly with a pillow. Their lovemaking was joyful, playful, so unlike her perfunctory moments with Kevin, when she waited for him to finish so she could go to sleep.

The comparison was not fair, and she felt ashamed for making it. From then on, she tried her best not to think of one man when she was with the other. It was if she were two women, one demure and dutiful, the other passionate and reckless.

Sarah provided the link between those two halves of herself. She was too young to know what was going on, too young to divulge their secret, but she was a constant reminder of Kevin, and Carol felt herself withdrawing from her daughter as she drew closer to Jack.

Once, when Carol could not get a sitter, Sarah accompanied them on a picnic in the city park. They found a secluded spot in a grove of trees and spread their blanket. Carol ached for Jack, but she could not kiss him, not with Sarah there.

An elderly man walking his dog paused to watch them as they murmured to each other and watched Sarah play. He apologized for his intrusion and said, "It's nice to see such a happy family enjoying this lovely day together."

Carol flushed, but Jack merely grinned and thanked him.

Later that day, Kevin came home from work early with good news: His hard work had paid off, and he had been promoted. He kissed Carol deeply, then swung Sarah up in his arms. "Did you hear Daddy's good news? Did you, my little sweet pea?" he said, nuzzling her until she crowed with delight.

Watching them, Carol felt a pang of guilt. Kevin worked so hard to take care of them, never realizing that his happy family was a sham. What would he do if he learned the truth?

Day by day, her worries accumulated, affecting her encounters with Jack. She thought about what they had done and wondered where it was going to lead. "What are we going to do about this?" she asked him once as he drove her nearly home.

"What are we going to do about what?" he asked, genuinely puzzled.

She shot him a look. "About us, of course."

"What do you mean?" He glanced at her as he pulled the car over to the curb. They had reached her usual disembarking place, but he left the motor running.

I love you, she almost said, but something in his eyes made her hold back the words. "Nothing," she said instead. She kissed him quickly and got out of the car.

Jack didn't phone her for the rest of that week, and when she stopped by the bookstore, he wasn't there. Another week went by with no word. Finally she fought back her embarrassment and returned to the bookstore, where she casually asked his aunt why they had not seen him around the shop recently.

"He's off on another buying spree," the older woman said. "He's traveling up and down the East Coast looking for bargains. Is there anything you'd like me to hold for you when he brings back the new stock?"

"No, thank you," Carol murmured. She left the store, dazed.

When Jack finally came for her a few days later, her first question to him was, "Why didn't you tell me you were going out of town?"

"Hey, slow down," he said, laughing, holding up his palms as if to ward her off. Then he paused. "You're serious, aren't you?"

She nodded, furious, too hurt to speak.

"I go on these business trips all the time, you know that." His voice was soothing, but there was an undercurrent of warning in it. "You aren't going to get all serious on me, now, are you? I thought we both understood that we don't make those kinds of demands on each other."

She went cold. They were in a dangerous place now, she could feel it. "But to go away for so long without telling me—"

"I don't ask what you and your husband do when I'm not around, do I?"

Stunned, she shook her head, and when she spoke, her voice sounded very far away. "No, of course not."

She understood then that he did not love her, not in the way she had thought. They would not be running away together to live penniless but happy in a room above a bookshop in another city where no one knew them. Jack would not become Sarah's doting stepfather, and Carol would not be his loving wife. He had no intentions of marrying her and never had.

Whose bed had he shared last week? How many other women had stood before him with lowered eyes, fighting to keep the grief and shock off their faces, pretending that they, too, had been in it just for laughs? He had never promised her anything more than what he had given, but still, somehow, she felt that she had been deceived.

When she told him she could not go home with him that day, he shrugged, unconcerned. The stroller supported her weight as she walked home, numb.

The dark clouds enveloped her again, worse than before, and this time her mother was not there to see her through. She stopped her daily trips to the bookstore. While Kevin was at work she let the phone ring unanswered, knowing it was Jack. Eventually he stopped calling. She often forgot to eat and had to remind herself to care for Sarah. Her life felt like it was happening in slow motion, and every part of her cried out silently for Jack.

Surely, she thought, this was her punishment for lying before God when she married a man she did not love.

As her condition worsened, Kevin grew worried, then alarmed. He called his mother-in-law for advice; he pleaded with Carol to see a doctor. She sat on the sofa, staring at the floor as he spoke. Then he was on his knees before her, grasping her hands. His eyes were full of tears as he begged her to get help. "I can't bear to see you like this," he said, his voice breaking. "Please, let me call the doctor."

He loved her, Carol realized, and thought the remorse would kill her.

"I don't need a doctor," she told him, and she began to cry. Hot, heavy tears fell soundlessly upon their clasped hands.

Kevin looked at her. "It's bad, isn't it?" he asked quietly.

She nodded, and then she told him.

He was furious, but he did not show his rage the way her father would have. The color drained from his face and he tore himself away from her. Her monotone confession still hung in the air between them. Now she was silent, waiting, unable to look at him.

When he finally spoke, it was with an effort. "You will not—" He broke off, glaring at her, breathing heavily. "You will not take my daughter with you when you go."

Distantly, she marveled at his restraint. Her father would have beaten her senseless by now. "I can't leave without Sarah," she heard herself say. It was a stranger's voice.

"I will not have my daughter raised by a whore," he said. "When you go, you go alone."

"I have nowhere to go." But he had stormed off to their bedroom. Their voices had woken Sarah, who started to wail. Carol sat frozen in place, unable to go to her. Moments later Kevin returned with her suitcase, only half closed, with clothing hanging out of it. He grabbed her by the arm and yanked her to her feet. She cried out and tried to free herself as he closed her hands around the handle of the suitcase and propelled her to the door.

"Get out," he roared, wrestling her outside. She pleaded with him to stop, but he shoved her along the front walk to her car.

"Kevin, please—"

"Get out!"

"Please, don't make me go, don't make me leave my baby!"

His face was contorted in grief and rage. He was sobbing now, too, she saw, and then suddenly he crumpled. He released her, dropped the suitcase, and slid to the ground with his back against the car. He buried his face in his hands and wept in loud, aching sobs, as if she had ripped his heart out.

She threw her arms around him and kissed him, shushing him, promising that everything would be all right. He pulled her to him and held her so tightly she thought she would smother in his embrace, but she clung to him, welcoming the pain, needing it.

He did not divorce her as she had expected.

At first she was grateful and thought him the most generous of husbands. Only as the years went by did she realize that he had let her stay so that he could punish her, so that he could show her what it was like to live without love. He let her remain his wife, but after that night he never loved her again. Kevin let Carol stay with Sarah, but he never let her forget how unworthy she was to live in that house with the husband and daughter she had wronged. All the love he had once showered on his wife he now gave to their daughter, who grew up adoring her father and believing her mother critical and unfeeling. What Sarah did not know was that Kevin punished Carol every day for the rest of his life. He punished her by not forgiving her.

She tried to regain his trust. She lived a sinless life from that day forward, but nothing would soften his heart. It was as if she were a child again, desperately striving for perfection so that her father would love her. Her efforts were as futile then as they had been so long ago.

In one last, desperate attempt, she sought perfection through Sarah, pushing her, teaching her, trying to raise her to be the most perfect child a father could want. Then he would see how Carol had atoned for her betrayal, and he would let her be a part of the family again. In this, too, she failed. Kevin already loved his daughter and had always thought her perfect, flaws and all. All Carol managed to do was to nurture resentment in Sarah, who grew up thinking she would be forever inadequate in her mother's eyes. That was not what Carol had intended. Nothing had worked out the way she had intended.

There was no harder person to live with than a man who did not forgive, except for a daughter who despised her.

Ten

Usually the end of spring semester brought Gwen a sense of deep satisfaction. Another school year completed; another batch of hungry young minds fed, although it might have been more accurate to say another batch of resistant young minds pummeled into submission. But not this year. Within a week, the day she had long dreaded and hoped for would arrive: Her daughter would be graduating, and after one last brief summer in Waterford, she would head off to graduate school at Penn. Judging by her own experience, Gwen knew that Summer wouldn't be coming home much after that. She would soon think of Waterford as her mother's home and Philadelphia as her own. Gwen would be lucky to see her more than a few times a year. How awful that would be, after seeing her virtually every day since she was born! Summer had had her own apartment in downtown Waterford ever since she began college, but she still came home several times a week to do her laundry, quilt, or borrow something. But there would be no more long heart-to-heart talks over cups of tea when a quick errand turned into a leisurely visit. Now the house would be an empty nest, a hollow shell, a lonely outpost on the frontier of motherhood.

"Now you're getting melodramatic," Gwen muttered as she tied her running shoes and began to stretch. She went jogging every morning, rain or shine. Actually, it was more of a brisk waddle than a jog, but at least she was moving. She had a favorite two-mile circuit through the Waterford College Arboretum that took her about forty minutes to complete. Other runners left her in their dust, but she didn't let it bother her. Everyone had to move at their own pace, whether along a running trail or through life.

A mist shrouded the woods that morning, and Gwen's breath came out in barely visible puffs as she ran. The only other sound was that of her footfalls on the wide dirt path. Spring was her favorite time of year in Pennsylvania. Other people preferred autumn, when the changing leaves covered the hills in brilliant color, but the renewal of spring soothed Gwen's spirit like nothing else. Winter had been vanquished at last, and the hot, humid days of summer were not yet upon them. The regular school year had ended, and the summer session had not yet begun. These few weeks provided her with a restful interim in which to take time for herself.

Perhaps she wouldn't go to campus at all today. She could work just as well at home as in her office. Or maybe she'd put her work aside entirely and quilt instead. She felt too nostalgic to work on her conference paper today, anyway. In the middle of the section on antebellum textiles, she was sure to go off on a weepy tangent about the clothing mothers sewed for their daughters before they parted forever. That would certainly make a fine impression on the review committee.

When she returned home, she showered and put on comfortable clothes—loose-fitting cotton pants and a long-sleeved flannel shirt, untucked. Far too many of her other clothes were getting snug around the waist. She would have to consider joining Bonnie and Diane for their evening walks. Better that than cutting back on treats such as the hazelnut biscotti she had with her tea for breakfast.

When she finished eating, she poured herself a second cup of tea and took it with her to the extra bedroom she and Summer used as a quilt studio. With a pang, Gwen realized that Summer would probably take her fabric and supplies with her when she went to school in the fall. Gwen had often wished for a more spacious workplace, but this was not how she had wanted to come by it.

She sighed and found the round robin quilt in her tote bag, where she had kept it since receiving it from Judy. She unfolded it and spread it out on the table, then stepped back to take it in. It was beautiful, no doubt about it. The blues, greens, golds, and various shades of cream harmonized well, and the assorted patterns complemented each other. Judy's Mariner's Compass border was dazzling. When Agnes finally contributed her center design, the quilt would be a masterpiece.

Gwen rested her chin in her hand and thought. What should she add? The last border had to be striking; it also had to somehow tie all the other borders together. That was no easy task, but Gwen felt up to it. The challenge would take her mind off Summer's departure.

She raided her fabric stash, selecting colors and prints that would work well with those her friends had selected. But that was the easy part. The question was, how would she stitch all those colors together? She knelt on the floor by the bookshelves, paging through pattern books, pondering her options.

Some time later, she heard the front door open and slam shut. "Mom?"

"In here," Gwen called out, rising awkwardly. She had been sitting with her legs tucked under her, and her right foot had fallen asleep. She was stomping her foot, trying to wake it up, when Summer entered.

Summer's eyebrows rose as she watched. "Summoning the muse?"

"Not this time." Gwen laughed and hobbled over to hug her. Summer seemed taller and more slender every day, but maybe on a subconscious level Gwen was comparing Summer to her ever-broadening self. "It's a hardwood floor, so I think the most I can hope for is a dryad or two." Summer smiled, but Gwen detected some tension in her expression. "What's wrong, kiddo?"

Summer threw herself into a chair. "How did you know?"

What a silly question. "I'm your mother, of course." No matter how far away Summer moved, that, at least, would never change. "I picked up a few blips on my mom sonar. What's going on?"

Summer picked up a Bear's Paw pillow from the floor and hugged it to her chest. "It's about graduation."

Finally, it was coming out. Ever since Judy received that letter from her half sister, Gwen wondered if this moment would come. She'd thought about bringing up the matter herself, but she had put it off, hoping that it would just go away. Or rather, stay away, since he hadn't been around for more than two decades. "I think I know what's bothering you."

Summer's eyes widened. "You do?"

"I think so." Gwen hesitated. "Kiddo, if you want to invite your father to your graduation, it's fine with me." They would have to find him first. The last Gwen had heard, he was running a coffeehouse and surf shop in Santa Cruz, but that had been ten years ago.

"Invite *him?*" Summer exclaimed. "Why would I want to do that? Why should he get to swoop in and snatch half the credit when you're the one who earned it?"

Pride surged through her, but Gwen decided to be modest. "In all honesty, you're the one who deserves the credit. You worked very hard. I'm very proud of you."

But Summer was not mollified. "Who needs him? He probably doesn't even know my name."

Gwen considered. "I'm almost certain he does."

"Almost certain. How wonderful," Summer retorted. "If he somehow shows up, promise me you'll pretend you don't know him. He might not recognize you, and he definitely won't recognize me."

Gwen nodded, surprised by her daughter's vehemence. "He won't show up. I'm not even sure if he knows where we live." She hoped Dennis wasn't a fan of *America's Back Roads*.

"Good." Abruptly, Summer rose and gave her mother a wry smile. "Get a load of Miss Whiner here. I'm sorry I've been such a grump lately."

"That's all right." Gwen hugged her. "You're entitled."

Summer laughed, and after admiring the round robin quilt and discussing options for Gwen's border, she was on her way, off to meet some friends for lunch.

Only after she left did Gwen realize that Summer had never explained what was bothering her.

Whatever it was, at least she wasn't gloomy over Dennis. She never had been before, not even when she was a little girl and her teachers assigned essay topics like "My Daddy's Job" or had the students make Father's Day art projects. Dennis had never been a part of Summer's life. She had truly never known him, since Gwen and Dennis had split up months before Summer was born.

Once, Summer had asked her why they divorced, and Gwen told her quite honestly that a more baffling question was why had they married in the first place. Admittedly, much of that flower-child time was a bit hazy to her now, but one would think she'd be able to remember something as significant as that. Maybe they had been caught up in a wave of universal peace and love that blocked out all reason. Gwen could just picture the expression on her daughter's face if she told Summer *that*.

Gwen liked to joke that she and Dennis had been married for about five minutes, but it was actually closer to a year. She was taking time off from college, intending to expand her mind by hitchhiking across the country and engaging in other experimental behavior she now prayed that Summer wouldn't dream of trying. She met Dennis at an antiwar rally, and somehow found him attractive as he stood in the middle of the Berkeley campus yelling epithets and burning Lyndon Johnson in effigy. Later she realized she had confused agreement with his politics with admiration for him, and his passion for justice with passion for herself. At the time, however, she thought she'd found true love.

After their barefoot ceremony—it was too cold to go barefoot in February, but Dennis insisted—they traveled the country with two other couples in a van plastered with peace signs and antiwar slogans. Gwen wasn't sure how they had managed to support themselves, since self-preservation had been the least of their concerns. They went where they chose, with nothing to hold them down, nothing to bear them up but each other.

The carefree times ended when Gwen realized she was pregnant. She had always possessed a strong pragmatic streak, and after a long dormancy it finally began to reassert itself. Suddenly she began to care about where their next meal would come from, where they would live and how, what kind of life she wanted for her child, what kind of mother she would be. Dennis's drug use, which had been only a minor irritant before, began to trouble her.

When she tried to get him to quit, he told her she was just jealous because the two times she'd tried grass, she'd gotten migraines. "Relax, baby," he said, blowing smoke in her face. Then he bent over to speak to her abdomen. "That goes for you, too, baby."

Something about the way he threw his head back in a fit of helpless giggling raised Gwen's ire. The next time they stopped for gas, she stuffed her few possessions into her backpack and left without saying good-bye to Dennis or her friends. How long had they waited for her, she wondered, before they realized she wasn't coming back?

She went home to her parents, who made her feel profoundly guilty by weeping when she arrived. She hadn't meant to abandon them, but it wasn't easy to write letters on the road. When Summer was a year old, Gwen returned to college; by Summer's eleventh birthday, Gwen had earned her Ph.D. and a position on the faculty of Waterford College.

Sometimes old friends passed through town, and they would talk long into the night about those days, about how they had tried to change the world and how they had indeed changed some small part of it. Some of their fellow travelers were still fighting the good fight; others had traded in their love beads for IRAs and BMWs. Occasionally these visiting friends had news of Dennis: He had remarried, he had divorced, he had opened a head shop, he was in Oregon chained to a giant sequoia to save it from loggers. He had never contacted Gwen to inquire about their child, and she had never asked anyone to pass along a message.

Should she have? Should she have insisted that he play a role in his daughter's life?

The questions plagued her, but one look at Summer assured her that she had done all right. Summer was the kind of daughter every mother wished for. She was thoughtful and smart and strong, and Gwen admired her. Yes, she must have done something right somehow, despite their rather precarious beginning as a family.

Summer insisted she didn't want Dennis at her graduation, and Gwen knew she was telling the truth. But if that wasn't what was bothering her, what was?

As the weekend approached and Summer said nothing more on the subject, Gwen decided that it must have been pregraduation jitters. By Saturday afternoon, Summer must have overcome them, because she was the picture of happiness at the graduation party the Elm Creek Quilters threw for her. Husbands were invited as well, and Judy and Diane had brought their children. While Craig and Matt supervised the grill, the others sat on the veranda and talked, or threw Frisbees on the front lawn. Michael and Todd took turns riding a skateboard around the circular driveway, and Gwen persuaded them to teach her how. She nearly broke her neck after a kick-turn went awry, so she decided to sit on the grass and watch the boys instead.

"What did you do with the skateboard ramp?' she asked them.

"We took it down and stored it in the garage," Michael said.

"Did you find a new place to ride?"

He shrugged. "You mean like other than our driveway and here? No."

"You must be disappointed."

"Wouldn't you be?" He came to a stop in front of her. He looked so dejected that Gwen was tempted to give him a comforting hug, but she wasn't sure he'd welcome it.

"Yes, I'm sure I would," she said. "So what are you going to do now?"

He shrugged again. "I dunno. I don't think there's anything I can do. I mean, they're like the city government and everything."

"They're not just 'like' the city government; they *are* the city government." She saw at once that the remark had gone over his head, but she was warming up to her subject and didn't want to pause to discuss his grammar. "They're elected officials, not gods. Law is a social construct, and in this country, at least, it's subject to the will of the people."

He sat down beside her, his brow furrowed. "You mean like voting and stuff?"

"That's right."

"But I can't vote yet."

"More's the pity," Gwen said. "We might have fewer stupid laws if you could. I bet you and your friends would shake things up around here, wouldn't you?"

He grinned. "Maybe."

"When I was a little older than you, my friends and I did more than just vote. We held demonstrations, sit-ins—anything to get our message out. We were trying to make our government get out of Vietnam."

"I know about that. We studied it in history class."

"Great," Gwen said, feeling ancient.

He regarded her seriously. "Were you a hippie?"

"Yes, I suppose I was." She was about to begin a long, nostalgic lecture about the passion for justice young people had felt in her day and how it compared to the callow selfishness of today's youth, but Matt chose that moment to announce that dinner was ready.

They ate on the veranda, seated in Adirondack chairs or on the stone staircase. Afterward, the Elm Creek Quilters gave Summer her gift, a signature wall hanging quilt they had worked on all winter. Summer gasped with delight as she opened the box and took out the beautiful quilt. Gwen had pieced a large Mariner's Compass block to symbolize Summer's life journey, and around it she had sewn solid, off-white borders on which everyone had written her congratulatory messages. Gwen became teary-eyed as Summer read the loving wishes aloud. Summer hugged each of them, even Andrew and Matt and the other Elm Creek husbands. Todd didn't want a hug, but Michael politely agreed to accept one.

The men must have sensed that their wives were about to talk quilts for a while, for they broke off into conversations of their own.

"I don't know how you managed to keep this a secret so long," Summer said as she carefully folded the quilt and returned it to its box.

Sylvia laughed. "We quilters are full of surprises."

"She has no idea," Judy murmured to Gwen.

"You have to promise to hang that in your apartment in Philadelphia," Bonnie said. "We want to make sure you never forget us."

"I could never forget any of you," Summer said with such feeling that Gwen had to reach for the tissues again.

"That's not good enough," Agnes teased. "You have to promise."

"Go on, Summer," Diane urged. "Raise your right hand and repeat after me: 'I, Summer Sullivan, being about to graduate from the esteemed institute of higher learning known as Waterford College, do hereby solemnly swear to hang this quilt on the wall in my new apartment far, far away in Philadelphia—'"

"Don't say 'far, far away,'" Gwen protested. "It's not that far."

"Now you made me lose track. Well, you get the idea, Summer. Go on, promise."

Summer looked around, flustered, as her friends began to chant, "Promise, promise, promise."

"All right," she finally called out above their voices, laughing. "I promise I'll hang this quilt in—in my apartment. And I promise I'll never forget the people who made it. Satisfied?"

"I thought my version was more eloquent," Diane said.

"You thought wrong," Gwen retorted.

The women broke into peals of laughter, but they could feel sadness creeping in. Summer would be the first of their group to leave since the founding of Elm Creek Quilts. They would have until autumn to enjoy moments like this, with all of them together and happy, but all too soon their circle would be broken.

As much as Gwen enjoyed the party, she was glad to have Summer all to herself the next day. While the other Elm Creek Quilters prepared for the arrival of a new batch of campers, Gwen and Summer got ready for the commencement ceremony. Gwen wanted Summer to wear her cap and gown as they walked through downtown Waterford to campus, but Summer begged off. "I'll be wearing them for hours," she said. "Can't I put them on in your office instead?"

Since it was Summer's day, Gwen reluctantly agreed. Gwen, too, would be wearing a cap and gown for the ceremony, since as a member of the faculty she would be marching in the procession. In her office, she helped Summer with her cap and gown first, then put on her own.

"You'll have one of these, too, someday," she said as she fastened the loop of her doctoral hood to the small button on the gown at the nape of her neck. She adjusted the hood's folds and smiled at her daughter. Summer flushed and gave her a quick smile before looking away.

The ceremony Gwen had participated in so many times took on a poignancy that she had not felt since receiving her doctorate. Afterward, they somehow found Judy in the crowd of other faculty. Gwen gave Judy her camera and had her snap a picture of Gwen and Summer, then Judy handed the camera to a physics professor and had him take a shot of the three of them together, arms intertwined. Judy and Summer smiled happily, but Gwen was sobbing and laughing at the same time.

That evening, Summer pleased Gwen by coming home instead of returning to the downtown apartment she shared with two friends. Gwen knew how to make only one baked dessert, a three-layer German chocolate cake, but she made it well, and she had prepared one that night in Summer's honor. As twilight fell, they sat on the back porch enjoying tea and cake, but most of all, each other's company.

"I'll miss you when you head off to Penn," Gwen said. "Before we know it, it will be time for fall quarter to begin."

"Actually, Mom, I've been wanting to talk to you about that."

Gwen reached out and stroked Summer's long, auburn hair. "What is it, kiddo? Are you nervous about graduate school?"

"Well, actually, no, that's one thing I'm definitely not." She hesitated. "First, though, promise me you won't get angry."

"Angry about what?"

"Just promise."

"No, I'm not going to promise, not without knowing what's going on." Suddenly she felt her stomach tighten into a knot. "Don't tell me you're pregnant."

"No, Mom," Summer exclaimed. "I don't even have a boyfriend."

"Oh." Gwen thought for a moment. "A girlfriend?"

Summer rolled her eyes. "Of course not—"

"What is it, then? Are you sick?" She sat up straight, clutching the armrests of her chair. "Did your father call?"

"No, it's not anything like that. I'm just not going to graduate school."

Silence.

Then, in a small voice, Gwen said, "You mean you've changed your mind about going to Penn?"

"I've changed my mind about graduate school altogether. I'm not going. I'm sorry."

Gwen felt dazed. "But . . . why?"

"It's just not what I want for my life." Summer reached out and took Gwen's hand. "I'm sorry about this. I know you must be very disappointed in me, but—"

"You have to go to graduate school," Gwen interrupted, confused. "It's what we've been planning for years. What—what—what else would you do?"

"That's just it, Mom. It's not what we've been planning; it's what you've planned for me." She took a deep breath. "I'm going to stay here in Waterford. I'm going to ask Sylvia for a larger role in Elm Creek Quilts and keep working for Bonnie. I want to own the business someday."

"Elm Creek Quilts? You could never afford it, you know that."

"Not Elm Creek Quilts. Grandma's Attic. Working there has been more rewarding than anything I've done in my major. I enjoy working with quilters and thinking up new ways to promote the shop. It's a challenge, and I'm never bored when I'm there. Unlike school," she added in an undertone.

Slowly the words sank in. Summer wanted to own a quilt shop. Instead of Summer Sullivan, Ph.D., she wanted to be Summer Sullivan, storekeeper. It couldn't be true. Gwen must have misunderstood.

With a sinking feeling, she realized that she hadn't.

"Mom, say something."

"What's left for me to say?" Gwen said. "It seems like you've made your decision, and since you obviously didn't want my opinion when you were making all of these secret plans, why would you want it now?"

"Don't talk like that, please," Summer begged. "I haven't made any secret plans. No one knows but me and you." She hesitated. "And the registrar at Penn."

"You mean you already declined your acceptance?"

Summer nodded.

Gwen sank back into her chair. "You turned down Penn without even checking with Bonnie and Sylvia first?" She knew from Summer's expression that it was true.

"I'm sorry," her daughter said again.

Her eyes were large and troubled. Gwen couldn't bear to look into them any longer, so she rose and began stacking up their dessert dishes. "Well, there's nothing more we can do about it now," she said briskly. "Tomorrow's Monday. You'll just have to phone Penn and tell them you made a mistake. I know people there. I can make a few calls myself if necessary. We'll get this straightened out somehow."

Summer placed a hand on her arm. "There's nothing to straighten out. I'm not going."

Gwen didn't trust herself to speak. She pulled away from Summer, snatched up the dishes, and hurried inside to the kitchen.

Summer followed. "You've always said that everyone has to choose their own path."

Gwen set the dishes in the sink with a crash. "Yes, but not *this* path."

"I can't believe you said that. That's so hypocritical."

"No, it's not. It is not hypocritical to want what's best for your daughter."

"Why do you assume that graduate school is what's best for me?"

"Because—" Because the world was an uncertain place. Because a woman had to be as prepared as possible to face its dangers. Because Gwen couldn't bear to think that her daughter would waste even a particle of her promise, her potential. Because Summer was meant for much greater things than what her mother had achieved.

"Think of it this way," Summer said. "You didn't want me to leave, and now I'm not going to."

That did it. Gwen burst into tears. Summer held her and patted her on the back, but Gwen was not comforted. Was that it? Had she made Summer feel guilty for leaving her? "I'll be all right," she said. "You don't have to stay in Waterford for me. I have my work, my friends—yes, I'll miss you, but I'll be all right. Don't stifle yourself for me. I never wanted that."

"That's not what this is about. Staying here wouldn't stifle me. I don't need a Ph.D. for what I want to do with my life." She stepped back to meet her mother's gaze. "Can you understand that, please? Can you try?"

"You don't have to rule out continuing your education entirely," Gwen said. "Maybe you want to take some time off first. I understand. I did the same thing myself. Maybe you won't go to Penn in the fall, but that doesn't mean you never will." She clutched at Summer's sleeve. "Promise me you won't rule it out completely."

"Mom—"

"Please."

Summer rolled her eyes. "Okay, I won't rule it out entirely. Maybe when I'm seventy years old and retired I'll decide I want to go back to school."

Gwen tried to smile. "I suppose that will have to do."

"Are you okay with this?"

"Sure," Gwen lied. "Never better."

Summer looked dubious, but she said nothing more. Together they rinsed the dishes and stacked them in the dishwasher. When Summer left, Gwen went to the quilt room they had shared for so many years, but not even the bright colors of her fabric stash or the pleasure of working on the round robin quilt comforted her.

The next day, Diane and Carol greeted her with alarm when she went to Elm Creek Manor to teach her workshop. She had dabbed her eyes with witch hazel, but still they were red and swollen.

"That must have been some ceremony," Diane remarked, inspecting her.

"The ceremony was fine," Gwen said, then told them about Summer's decision.

"Oh, how terrible," Carol said, stricken. "You must be heartbroken."

Gwen nodded. Carol looked like she understood completely, which Gwen had not expected.

"Just tell Summer she has to go to Penn, period," Diane said.

"I can't do that. She's a grown woman. I can't tell her what to do." Gwen tried to calm herself. She couldn't get all worked up now, not with class about to start. "What bothers me most is that she didn't feel she could talk to me about her decision. I wonder. How much do our children conceal from us about their lives, about themselves?"

"How much do we conceal from them?" Carol said softly.

Gwen and Diane looked at her, surprised, but she did not seem aware of their scrutiny.

When she got home, Gwen thought about what Diane had said. No, she couldn't order Summer to go to graduate school, but she could make it possible for Summer to enroll, should she change her mind. Gwen could undo that mistake, at least.

She phoned the registrar's office at Penn, but they could not reinstate Summer without permission from the director of Summer's department. Fortunately, Gwen and the chair of the philosophy department were old friends. She called him at home, explained that Summer had accidentally sent in the wrong forms, and asked if he wouldn't mind sorting out the problem with the registrar. He agreed and promised to take care of it that afternoon. Gwen hung up the phone, relieved. Now she would have the rest of the summer to change her daughter's mind.

Summer did not come to see Gwen that day but on Tuesday she phoned. They spoke briefly on trivial subjects; neither mentioned graduate school. Gwen sensed that Summer was tentative, testing the waters, making sure that her mother was all right. Gwen did her best to sound cheerful, but she wasn't sure if Summer was convinced.

On Wednesday, Gwen was fixing herself lunch when she heard the front door open and slam shut. "Hey, kiddo," she sang out as her daughter entered the kitchen. "You're just in time. Want a sandwich?" Then Summer's expression registered—face pale, jaw set—and Gwen fell silent.

"I just received a very interesting phone call," Summer said in a tight voice.

Gwen's stomach flip-flopped, but she tried to sound nonchalant. "Did you?"

"Penn wants to know if I'm interested in on-campus housing." Summer folded her arms and fixed Gwen with a furious glare. "Why do you suppose they'd do that, a month after I told them I wasn't coming?"

"A month?" Gwen exclaimed. Summer had kept this secret a full month? "I—I don't know, kiddo. I guess someone must have gotten their wires crossed."

"Yes, and that someone is you. I can't believe you did this. What were you thinking?"

"Me?" Gwen tried to sound wronged, innocent, but her voice came out shrill and false. "What did I do?"

"You tell me. Did you call the registrar or did one of your professor friends take care of it for you?"

"Take care of what?" Then Gwen realized there was no point in pretending anymore. "Summer, honey, what else was I supposed to do? You can't expect me to sit idly by while you ruin your life."

"Are you out of your mind?" Summer exclaimed, incredulous. "How am I ruining my life? I'm not dropping out of high school to join the circus."

"You might as well be. What kind of job can you get with a B.A. in philosophy?"

"I've already told you my plans—"

"Yes, and then you run off and burn your bridges before getting even the smallest confirmation from Sylvia or Bonnie."

"Don't you think I considered that? Do you think this is just a whim? I'm sure they'll want me, but either way, I'm not going to Penn." Summer's voice was brittle with anger. "Listen very carefully, okay? I don't want to be a philosophy professor. I don't want to be any kind of professor. That's you. That's not me."

"But it should be you. The best and the brightest always find their way into the academy. That's where you belong. You shouldn't squander your talents—"

"That's not what I'm doing," Summer shouted. "You're so—so impossible. You can't ever see anything from anyone else's point of view. Look, if that's how you want to see it, fine. I'm not going to try to convince you. But don't forget they're my talents to squander. It's my life to ruin. Not yours.

Not yours, mine. Understand? If I'm making the biggest mistake in my life, that's my prerogative. So just stay out of it."

She turned and stormed out of the house without waiting for a reply.

Gwen sank into a chair at the kitchen table. Summer had shouted at her, had ordered her to stay out of her life. Gwen couldn't remember when they had last argued like that, if they ever had. She wanted to chase after Summer, but found herself too sick at heart, too upset to move. What could she do? What could she do?

She should apologize—yes, and quickly, anything to win back Summer's approval. Before long Gwen would forget her disappointment, and everything would be fine between them again.

But just as she reached for the phone, she knew she couldn't cave in simply to win back Summer's favor. No. She had to do what was best for Summer, and that meant getting her into Penn. Summer might not understand now, but someday she would. When she had her advanced degree and a fine job at a prestigious university, she would, and she'd be grateful. Gwen had to put Summer's interests ahead of her own need for her daughter's approval. Gwen would endure anything, anything, rather than let her daughter throw away her future.

But what could she do? Reasoning with Summer wouldn't work, not after today. Summer would have to choose Penn on her own. Gwen had to make graduate school the only logical choice, the only possible option.

The next afternoon, Gwen drove out to Elm Creek Manor to speak to Bonnie. She couldn't talk to her freely at Grandma's Attic, since Summer might be working. Besides, she wanted to speak to Sylvia, too.

Gwen managed to take them aside before Bonnie's workshop. Diane had already spread the word about Summer's decision. When Gwen told them that it broke her heart to see Summer's brilliant academic career ended so soon, they comforted her and assured her everything would be all right in the end.

"I hope so," she said. "I think with your help, everything will be fine." She saw Sylvia and Bonnie exchange a quick glance. "What I mean is, I don't think it would be such a terrible thing if you were to realize that you couldn't give Summer the extra work she wants."

"You can't mean that," Bonnie said, appalled.

Gwen plowed ahead. "Bonnie, maybe you'll find that you don't have enough money to give Summer more hours at Grandma's Attic. And Sylvia, maybe you and Sarah don't need the extra help with Elm Creek Quilts."

"We most certainly do," Sylvia said.

"But maybe Summer doesn't need to know that."

Sylvia frowned. "Gwen Sullivan, I'm surprised at you."

Bonnie gave her a pleading look. "Please don't ask us to lie to Summer."

"It's for her own good," Gwen said. "You know sometimes we don't give our children the whole truth when it might hurt them. Summer doesn't know how irrevocable her decision is. I can't bear to sit back and watch her jeopardize her entire future. She's meant for so much more than—than—"

"Than life as a quilt shop owner?" Bonnie finished.

Gwen felt heat rising in her face. "I didn't mean it that way. You know I respect what you do."

"Apparently, you don't respect our work quite as much as you thought," Sylvia said.

Her voice was gentle, but Gwen felt it as strongly as a shout. She clasped her arms around herself, thoughts churning. She had insulted her friends by questioning their integrity and the value of their work; she had gone behind her daughter's back in an attempt to undermine her chosen career. Summer had been right to tell her to stay out of it. She had made a mess of everything.

What had happened to all her fine ideals, her sterling principles? Somewhere along the line she had become an elitist snob, believing that her daughter was above certain work, honest jobs that other mothers' children accepted gratefully. How had this happened to her? She had not raised Summer to believe that success was determined by the size of one's paycheck. She ought to be grateful that Summer had taken those lessons to heart, that she was seeking happiness and fulfillment rather than fighting her way up the ivory tower for its own sake.

She felt deeply, profoundly ashamed of herself.

Bonnie and Sylvia watched her, waiting for her to speak.

"I'm sorry," she said. "Please forgive me. Please forget that we ever had this conversation."

Immediately they embraced her. "Consider it forgotten," Sylvia said.

Gwen wished she could forget as easily, but she couldn't.

All she had ever wanted was for Summer to be happy, but now there she was, trying to drape her daughter in job titles and degrees, as if they would shield her from the hardships of life. It wasn't as if Summer had decided to become an arms smuggler or a drug dealer. Summer could do far worse than to assume a greater role with Elm Creek Quilts and prepare to take over Grandma's Attic someday.

Summer was right. Gwen was a hypocrite. Even worse, she was now estranged from her beloved daughter because of it. They weren't as widely divided as Carol and Sarah, or a dozen other mothers and daughters Gwen knew, but they had never let a disagreement linger on so long before, and it made Gwen sick with dismay. She couldn't bear to have Summer unhappy with her. Summer had said that she was sorry for disappointing her mother, but Gwen knew that she was the one who had disappointed—by not supporting Summer's decisions, by pressuring her, by keeping such a narrow focus on graduate school that Summer had never felt able to discuss other possibilities.

There was a rift between them now, and Gwen had put it there. Somehow she had to sew it up before it worsened. Words would not be enough. Gwen would have to show Summer that she accepted her daughter's choice wholeheartedly.

She would begin by visiting Grandma's Attic on Saturday while Summer was working. In front of everyone, Gwen would make a strong show of support for her daughter. That would be a start.

Though only a week had passed since Summer's graduation party, so much had changed that it felt much longer to Gwen. As she entered Grandma's Attic, she noticed the shop was nearly empty of customers. Gwen had forgotten that the interim between graduation and summer session was traditionally slow for shops in downtown Waterford. So much for her big scene in front of crowds of onlookers. Well, at least Bonnie and Diane were there, and Diane's tendency to gossip made her the equal of a crowd or two.

Summer seemed pleased to see her. After greeting Bonnie and Diane, Gwen brought out the round robin quilt and asked Summer to help her find a blue and green print, preferably with some gold in it. As they moved through the store, Gwen made a point of complimenting the sample quilt blocks displayed at the end of each aisle. Bonnie had told her Summer had made them, but even if she hadn't, Gwen would have recognized her daughter's style and bold color choices.

Gwen tried to act normally, but she was nervous, and she was sure Summer knew it. She almost regretted coming in, for if she hadn't she wouldn't have had to realize that for the first time she felt awkward and uncomfortable in her daughter's presence. She wished she had never spoken to Bonnie and Sylvia that day in Elm Creek Manor. How could she have even considered asking them to deny Summer her well-deserved promotion? She was the worst mother in Waterford—no, the worst mother ever.

As Summer cut Gwen's fabric, the phone rang. Bonnie answered the extension at the cutting table, where she and Diane had joined the mother and daughter. "Good afternoon, Grandma's Attic," Bonnie said, then smiled. "Oh, hi, Judy." The others looked up at the mention of their friend's name. "No, it's just me, Diane, Summer, and Gwen. Oh, and Craig, in the stockroom." A pause, then a smile. "Of course I can let her off work. I'm not running a sweatshop here. What is it?" Her brows drew together in concern. "Oh, my goodness. Do you think—" She glanced up at her friends. "Hold on, Judy. I'm going to put you on speakerphone." She pressed a button and replaced the receiver. "Okay, Judy, go ahead."

"Diane, are you there?" Judy's voice sounded tinny.

"Yes," Diane shouted at the phone.

Gwen winced at the noise. "She's not on Mars, for crying out loud."

"Steve just got a call from his editor at the *Waterford Register*," Judy said. "They asked him to go check out a protest at the square. I thought you might want to know."

Gwen leaned closer to the phone, intrigued. The square was a small downtown park near Waterford's busiest intersection, a good choice for a protest. Waterford College students frequently selected it when they wished to air their complaints about the local government's various housing and noise ordinances. Then she remembered that the students had deserted Waterford after commencement. Who could be left to hold a protest?

Diane was wondering something else. "Why did you think I would want to know?"

"Because whoever it is, they're protesting against the skateboard ordinance."

"Uh oh," Gwen said.

"What?" Diane shrieked at the phone. "Are my boys there?"

"I don't know. Steve's on his way there right now."

"So am I." Diane headed for the front door, leaving Bonnie to hang up the phone.

They called out to Diane to wait, but she didn't seem to hear them.

"I'll go with her," Summer and Gwen said in unison.

"Don't even think about leaving without me," Bonnie said, turning toward the stockroom in the back. "Craig! Come out here a second. Quick!"

Craig appeared, startled. "What is it?"

"There's a big protest on the square, and we think Diane's son is involved. Will you watch the store while we go check it out?"

"Are you kidding?" He hurried toward them—then continued on to the front door. "I'm not going to miss this."

They locked the shop and raced down the street and up the hill to the square. They saw a crowd gathered near the bandstand and heard music blaring and someone shouting. They saw Diane ahead of them, working her way through the people who had come to see what all the excitement was about.

When they reached the square, they forged ahead to the front of the crowd, where they found Diane gaping at a group of children skateboarding on the paved surface surrounding the bandstand. Gwen counted five boys and a girl—and two of the boys were Michael and Todd. The crowd stood on the grass as if held off the cement by a force field that only the skate-boarders could penetrate.

Even Diane did not leave the safety of the grass to seize her children. "Michael and Todd, get over here right this minute," she yelled over the sound of hip-hop blaring on a boom box.

"We can't, Mom," Michael said as his companions continued weaving back and forth on their skateboards. "We have to stand up for our civil rights." His gaze shifted to Gwen, and he brightened. "Hi, Dr. Sullivan! Isn't this cool? We're having a skate-in!" With that, he pushed off on his skateboard and zoomed around the bandstand.

Diane glared at Gwen. "I don't know how you did it, and I don't know why, but I do know you're responsible for this somehow."

"Who, me?" Gwen tried to look innocent.

Summer stuck two fingers in her mouth and let out a piercing whistle. "You go, Michael," she shouted. He waved happily.

The crowd was growing, but Steve spotted them and made his way toward them, grinning. "Hey, Diane, mind giving me a quote for tomorrow's paper?"

"I'll give you a quote," she shot back. "Those clowns in the municipal building brought this on themselves. If they would have permitted my family to keep our skateboard ramp on our private property, these kids would be skating at our house right now, instead of creating a scene in a public park."

"Good, good," Steve said, writing it down.

Just then Todd turned off the music. The crowd grew quieter as Michael climbed the stairs to the bandstand. "My name's Michael, and I'm a skateboarder." His friends burst into cheers and applause. "I'm not a criminal, I'm not a troublemaker, I'm not a druggie. I just want to ride my skateboard. But because of the fascists in the city government, I'm not allowed to, not even in my own backyard."

"Where did he learn a word like *fascists?*" Bonnie wondered aloud.

"You never know what they'll pick up in the public schools," a man beside them said scornfully. They glared at him.

"My parents tried to reason with them, but they wouldn't listen," Michael went on. "They forgot that in this country, at least, elected officials are not gods. They are subject to the will of the people."

"This sounds familiar," Summer murmured, giving her mother a side-long look.

"My friends and I can't vote yet, but we can show the city officials just what our will is. Skateboard laws affect kids more than anybody else, but kids can't vote for the people who make laws against skateboards. That's discrimination without representation."

Craig cupped his hands around his mouth. "That's un-American!"

"That's right," Michael shouted back. A smattering of applause went up from the crowd.

Diane shook her head. "I don't believe this."

Gwen couldn't, either.

"So, since we can't skate in my backyard, we're going to skate right here. It says right on that sign over there that this is a public park. We're the public, too, so we're going to skate."

Gwen let out a cheer, and Craig began to clap. More of the onlookers joined in this time.

But Michael wasn't done yet. "We have some extra skateboards here if any of you want to join us." Then he left the bandstand, turned on the music, and jumped on his skateboard. Soon he and his companions were zooming around, shouting and cheering.

"I had no idea Michael was such an orator," Bonnie told Diane.

"Neither did I." Diane stared at her sons.

"He's right, you know," Summer said. "If you believe in something, you have to be willing to stand up for it. It probably wasn't easy for him to do this, knowing how you'd feel, but he believed in it strongly enough to risk your anger. He's a brave kid."

"Brave or completely out of his mind. He's going to get in trouble, and not only from me."

"Even if he does, you have to let him make his own mistakes. You raised him well. You taught him right from wrong. Now you have to let him loose in the world to make his own way."

Diane looked dubious. "He's only fifteen."

"I didn't mean let him *that* loose," Summer said, laughing. She caught Gwen's eye. "You know what I mean?"

Diane shook her head, but Gwen nodded. Her heart lifted when Summer smiled at her.

Then, suddenly, Summer stepped onto the pavement. "What do we want? Skateboard freedom! When do we want it? Now!" she shouted, motioning for Michael to pause. The others joined in the chant as Michael gave her a skateboard, and soon, she too was circling the bandstand, her long auburn hair flying out behind her.

Suddenly Gwen knew what she had to do.

"Are you crazy?" Diane shrieked, grabbing her arm. Gwen shook her head and peeled Diane's fingers off her arm.

"What do we want? Skateboard freedom!" she shouted, climbing on the skateboard Michael offered her. She wobbled back and forth unsteadily until Summer took her by the hand and helped her steer. Hand in hand they skated around the bandstand, chanting until they were hoarse.

Craig kissed his wife on the cheek and grabbed a skateboard. Soon he was zooming past Gwen and her wonderful, strong-willed, bright star of a daughter. "Bonnie wanted to join us, but I told her I would instead," he said gallantly. "If one of us has to have a police record, we'll let it be me."

"I guess chivalry isn't dead after all," Gwen said. She and Summer looked at each other and laughed.

Every time they passed Diane, they encouraged her to join them. Every time they did, the crowd was a little larger, a lot noisier. Diane finally gave in and mounted a skateboard about five minutes before the police arrived and wound up arresting them all on charges of disturbing the peace.

"Did you really want me to go away and miss all this?" Summer shouted to her mother as they were being led away to separate police cars.

"I never wanted you to go away," Gwen shouted back. "Never." She could say nothing more because the police officer was guiding her into the back seat of the patrol car, careful not to bump her head on the door frame. Gwen was so elated, she wouldn't have felt it if he had. She and Summer were friends again, and that was all that mattered.

That was why Gwen didn't finish her border that evening as she had planned.

When she worked on it the next day, she cut a few pieces from the new fabric Summer had helped her select and added them to those she had already sewn in place. Just when she thought she had planned the pattern perfectly and that her work was nearly complete, Summer had given her something new to work with, something she had to learn to integrate with what she already had. Invariably this would alter the pattern, but perhaps that was not such a bad thing.

She chose blues and greens, golds and creams as her friends had done, for they had yet to lead her astray. If she did make a mistake, she could rely upon them to gently remind her what she was supposed to be about. All the quilt classes and quilt books in the world couldn't teach her as well as her friends did.

She pieced crazy quilt blocks to match her crazy quilt of a life, with patches going this way and that, apparently haphazard, with no discernible plan or pattern. That was what a careless glance would see—a random scattering of cloth. Only with more careful, thoughtful scrutiny could one discern the order within the chaos. For the patches of various sizes and shapes were stitched to muslin foundations, perfectly square, one block aligned with the next but not a part of it. The blocks were so very much alike but they were not the same, and she had learned to accept that.

The crazy quilt blocks encircled the round robin quilt in a wild and joyful dance, a mosaic of triangles and squares and other many-sided figures Gwen could not name. It was an embrace of blue and green and gold, unbroken.

Eleven

arah drove Sylvia to the police station to bail out their friends. Before they left, Carol admonished them for laughing about their friends' plight. "I don't see what's so funny," she said. "Now they'll have criminal records. This will stay with them for the rest of their lives."

They were laughing more from astonishment and dismay than from humor, but Sarah was too annoyed to bother trying to explain. "Relax, Mother," Sarah said as she helped Sylvia into the truck. "It's not like they knocked over a liquor store." Carol gave her a sour look and returned inside the manor. Sarah wished that just once her mother would relax her impossibly high standards. She cared too much about meekly submitting to propriety and looking good to the neighbors. So a third of the Elm Creek Quilters had been arrested—so what? They had done what they thought was right, and Sarah was proud of them. She wished she had been there.

"I can't wait to hear the whole story," she said as she and Sylvia drove through the forest toward the main road leading to downtown Waterford. "I'm surprised Craig was arrested with them. This seems like the kind of thing Gwen and Summer would get involved in, and you never know what Diane's going to do next, but Craig?" Sarah shook her head. Craig seemed too stuffy, too rigid, to get involved in something so wacky. It was almost as difficult to picture Craig on a skateboard as it was to imagine Carol complimenting her daughter.

"Perhaps he was trying to redeem himself for his foolishness earlier this spring," Sylvia mused. "I believe he's done it. Gwen, too."

"Gwen?" Sarah glanced at Sylvia before returning her gaze to the road. "Why would Gwen need to redeem herself? What's she done?"

"Oh, you know the way you daughters are," Sylvia said lightly. "You always think your mothers are guilty of something."

Maybe that was true, but it didn't answer Sarah's question. Was Sylvia referring to Gwen's less-than-enthusiastic response to Summer's decision to forgo grad school? That wasn't even in the same realm as Craig's betrayal of Bonnie. Sylvia must have meant something else, but whatever Gwen had done, Sarah knew Sylvia wasn't going to tell her about it. Sylvia disliked gossip and deplored the breaking of confidences. "I know too well how the idle ramblings of vicious minds can destroy lives," she had said once, and Sarah remembered that, more than fifty years before, a handful of members of the Waterford Quilting Guild had driven Sylvia and Claudia from the group with their malicious words, unfounded rumors that the Bergstroms sympathized with the Germans during World War II. Claudia had told their brother, Richard, about the rumors, never dreaming that he would enlist to prove his family's patriotism. When Sylvia said that gossip could kill, she meant it literally.

Sarah respected her friend's feelings, so she didn't persist. Then she allowed herself a small smile, thinking that if Sylvia wouldn't talk about Gwen, maybe she'd talk about herself. "What were you and Andrew doing in the garden when I came to find you?" Sarah asked.

Out of the corner of her eye, she saw Sylvia straighten. "What do you mean, what were we doing?"

Sarah shrugged. "It's just that when I was looking toward the gazebo from the other side of the garden, it seemed like you two were sitting very close together. I thought maybe Andrew was having trouble with his hearing or something, or maybe he was helping you get something out of your eye."

"We most certainly were not sitting very close together. We were no closer than you and I are now."

"Oh. I guess it must have been an optical illusion. Maybe the spray from the fountain refracted the light rays or something."

"All right, young lady, I know what you're insinuating, and I don't appreciate it."

"What? What am I insinuating?"

"You know very well."

"I don't," Sarah insisted, then began to laugh. "Tell the truth. Were you two being naughty?"

"Honestly, Sarah, I don't know where you get these ideas."

"Well, why not? He obviously likes you, and you're always together—"

"Are we, indeed?" Sylvia looked left and right, up and down. "I don't see him now."

"Almost always, then. And you've been fixing your hair differently and wearing your best outfits. You can't tell me Andrew isn't the reason."

"I most certainly can. I've been wearing my spring clothes, not my best. You've merely forgotten them over the long winter." Sylvia patted her hair.

"And I changed my hairstyle because Agnes recommended it. If I did it for anyone, I did it for her."

"Is the lipstick for Agnes, too?"

"Sarah, you try my patience. He's much younger than I am—almost seven years. He's Richard's age."

Sarah glanced at her, skeptical. "Do you really think seven years matters at this point?"

"Well—" Sylvia hesitated. "I don't suppose it does. Or rather, it wouldn't, if I cared for him the way you think I do, which I don't. Now, I must insist that you say no more about this."

"But—"

"I insist," Sylvia repeated, in a voice that would tolerate no disobedience.

So Sarah kept her curiosity to herself for the rest of the drive. Maybe Sylvia was telling the truth, or maybe she didn't yet recognize what her friends saw. Either way, Sarah hoped Andrew would postpone his trip east a little while longer. His company was good for Sylvia, so as far as Sarah was concerned, he was welcome to stay forever.

With Sarah's luck, it would be Carol who decided never to leave.

When they reached the police station, they went inside and followed signs that led to a waiting room. Bonnie was already there, talking to Judy's husband, Steve. Michael and Todd, who hadn't been arrested, stood close by, whispering to each other and looking around with wide eyes. Bonnie spoke excitedly, gesturing in frustration as Steve nodded and wrote in a small notebook. When Bonnie spotted Sarah and Sylvia, she looked so relieved that Sarah wished she had driven faster. "Thank God you're here," Bonnie said. "Diane is raising such a stink in there, I'm afraid they're going to lock her up for good."

"They can't do that, can they?" Michael asked.

"Of course not," Sarah assured him, hoping it was true.

"We came as quickly as we could," Sylvia told Bonnie. "Naturally we couldn't refuse a request to bail our friends out of the pokey."

Bonnie almost smiled. "It's not really bail, just a fine. They're going to be released on their own recognizance once they pay. I feel so awful. I wanted to pay for everyone, but—"

"But you didn't want Sarah and me to feel left out, since we already missed most of the fun. That was kind of you."

Bonnie nodded, grateful, and Sarah knew that Sylvia was the one who had been kind, interrupting Bonnie before she had to admit that she didn't have enough for all the fines. It was no secret that the Markhams had to watch every penny, but the Elm Creek Quilters pretended not to notice. In turn, Bonnie pretended that her friends really did need two yards of an

expensive fabric rather than one and that, as they insisted, as the most experienced teacher she deserved higher pay for the classes she taught for Elm
Creek Quilts.

Sylvia wrote a check, and as they waited for their friends, Bonnie gave
them more details about the protest. The police had shown up about a half
hour after Michael's speech and had asked them to turn down the music and
stop skating. When the protesters refused, the police listed several noise ordinances they were breaking, reminded them of the skateboard law, and
warned them that they needed a permit to hold a public gathering in the
square. Gwen began quoting from the Bill of Rights and told the police that
if the city of Waterford wanted them to stop skating, they were going to have
to arrest them. The police agreed and took her up on the suggestion. The
adults were taken into custody, but despite their insistence on being arrested
as well, the children were driven home to their parents. Bonnie had accepted
responsibility for Todd and Michael.

"Will they have to go to trial?" Sarah asked.

Bonnie shook her head. "Not a trial, a hearing, but only if they decide to
contest the fines."

"I suspect they will," Sylvia said.

Just then they heard their friends' voices floating down the hallway. "What
do we want? Skateboard freedom! When do we want it? Now!" they chanted,
their voices growing louder and louder. Steve burst into applause at the sight of
them. Sarah joined in, noticing that the ovation was unanimous, even though
most people in the room had no idea what was going on.

Michael and Todd ran over to hug their mother. "I knew they couldn't
keep you locked up for long," Michael told her.

"Were you in a cell?" Todd asked. "Did you get to see solitary confine-
ment? Do they call it 'the hole'?"

Diane embraced her sons. "No, we were all together in a conference
room. This isn't Attica, Todd. Michael, where's your skateboard?"

"In Bonnie's car."

"Good," Gwen said. "You're going to need it. Come on, everyone. Back
to the square."

Summer, Diane, and the boys cheered, but not Sarah. "You're not serious?"

"Of course. We can't give up now."

Sylvia placed a hand on her arm. "Perhaps discretion is the better part of
valor, at least for now."

"Are you kidding? We have not yet begun to fight!"

"There are other ways to fight," Bonnie said. "Can't you pick one of
them for the rest of the day?"

Gwen stared at her for a moment, then burst out laughing. "All right," she said good-naturedly. "No more public demonstrations today." The boys groaned in disappointment. "Relax. I didn't say we're giving up. We're going to start a letter-writing campaign."

Diane rolled her eyes. "Good luck with that one."

Michael looked dubious. "Writing letters?"

"That sounds like school," Todd said, uneasy.

"No, no, it'll be great," Gwen said. As they all left the building together, she placed an arm around each boy and began to explain.

Later that evening over supper, Sylvia and Sarah told Andrew, Matt, and Carol about the protest and the scene at the police station. They took turns narrating the story, laughing so hard that they had to wipe tears from their eyes. Andrew chuckled, but Matt just kept his eyes on his plate and said nothing, and Carol declared that she was ashamed of their friends. "I don't know what they hope to gain by making a spectacle of themselves," she said.

"They're hoping to draw attention to their concerns," Sarah said. She hated the thin-lipped, prissy, disapproving expression her mother had assumed. Sarah had seen too much of it over the years.

"Maybe that's true, but they're drawing attention to themselves, not to the issue. And they're bringing Elm Creek Quilts negative publicity. This will damage the reputation of everyone who works here."

Sylvia forced out a laugh. "I don't think it's as serious as all that."

"I wish I had your confidence." Carol shook her head, frowning as if she smelled something foul. "Maybe the rest of you can excuse their conduct, but I'm ashamed of them. Especially that Gwen. For a college professor, she doesn't have much sense. What kind of example is she setting for her students?"

"'That Gwen' has more sense than some people I could mention," Sarah snapped. She barely noticed as Matt abruptly rose, carried his dishes to the sink, and left the room without a word. "More courage, too. It's not easy to stand up for something you believe in, knowing that all eyes are upon you and that you'll have to accept the consequences of your words and actions. Some people are brave in that way. Others can only write nasty letters about people behind their backs."

Carol set down her fork. "What are you talking about?"

"You know very well I'm talking about those letters you wrote about Matt." She glanced up to be sure he was out of the room, then realized that she wished he had not left. It was about time he knew how his mother-in-law had tried to prevent their marriage.

"I was concerned, and I don't deny that." Carol's voice was deliberate and calm. "Instead of writing a private letter to my daughter, should I have announced my concerns on national TV? Would that have been better?"

"You should have kept your concerns to yourself."

"I'm your mother. I wanted to help."

"Maybe you should try helping a little less. You're always trying to improve me, trying to make me better. All my life you've shoved my faults and problems in my face, and for years I tried to fix myself so I could be good enough for you. But you know what I finally realized? It's hopeless. As soon as I correct one flaw, you find another." Sarah shoved her chair away from the table and stood up. "You win, okay? You win. I'm a worthless nothing. My marriage is failing and my friends are criminals. You've been right about me all along."

Sarah turned away from them and stormed out of the room.

She sought seclusion in the library, but her thoughts were churning, making it impossible to concentrate on her work. Eventually she slipped out the back door, carefully and quietly, so that no one would know she had left. She used to wander the north gardens when troubled, but when Sylvia and Andrew starting going there so frequently, she had found herself another place, a quiet spot in the woods where a bend in Elm Creek created a still pool of deep water. The branches of a nearby willow fell like a curtain, nearly concealing a part of the pool and a large, smooth stone that overlooked it. Sarah had found the stone one day when a sudden gust of wind eased the branches aside. Resting on the cool stone with the murmur of the creek in her ears, she could feel her troubled thoughts clearing, her agitated spirits growing calm.

She wished she had not needed to visit the pool so often lately.

For the past two years, whenever she had needed sympathy or support, she had always been able to turn to the Elm Creek Quilters. Carol changed all that. Her friends still felt comfortable sharing their secrets and concerns, but Sarah couldn't confide her worries in the presence of the person most responsible for them. Sarah couldn't talk about Matt, either, not with her mother there to give her those looks, the ones that said "I knew it" and "I told you so." Instead she found herself withdrawing from the circle of friends—and Carol was only too eager to push her way into the space her daughter had vacated.

Sarah could understand why her mother wanted so badly to belong, to be a part of the group. Sarah had always managed to assemble a group of girls wherever she lived, but her mother had never done the same. Other mothers had friends, women they met for lunch, women they played bridge with in the evenings, but Carol did not, and for the longest time Sarah had not known why.

Then one day when Sarah was in the sixth grade, she had come home from a slumber party to find her mother scrubbing out the kitchen sink.

Carol didn't ask about the party, but at that age Sarah still trusted her, so she began chattering away, buzzing from hours of talk and laughter and a near-overdose of sugar, replaying the party's events as much for herself as for her mother. All the while, Carol said nothing.

Suddenly, Sarah noticed her mother's odd silence, and it occurred to her that maybe her mother felt sad because she was too old for slumber parties. But even if she wasn't so old, whom would she invite over? Who would invite her?

"Mom," Sarah asked, "how come you never go out with your friends?"

"What friends?" Her mother turned on the faucet full blast to rinse the sink. "What makes you think I have friends?"

"Well . . ." Sarah hesitated. "Don't you?"

"I don't have time for friends," Carol said shortly. "Some people have friends. I have a husband, a job—and you."

Shocked into silence, Sarah mumbled an apology and slunk off to her room. Until that moment it had never occurred to her that she'd prevented her mother from having friends of her own. Maybe that was why her mother rarely smiled, why her voice was so sharp with criticism. Carol probably resented the way Sarah's needs had swallowed up every bit of her life until there was nothing left for her to call her own.

But if that was the reason, why hadn't things improved between them in recent years? Now that Carol was a widow, now that her daughter had married and moved away, she surely had plenty of time to herself. And if so much time on her own didn't suit her, she had her job and the Elm Creek Quilters' friendship to fill up the hours. But Carol might not have any friends back home, which was where she needed them. Was that why she had stuck around, even though it was surely obvious to both of them that their reconciliation wasn't going to happen?

Or, unlike Sarah, did Carol still hope that they would find a way?

Sarah lay down on her back upon the stone, her head resting on her hands. When she looked up she could see the willow branches gently moving with the wind. She watched until twilight fell, then, reluctantly, she left her hiding place and made her way carefully through the darkening woods, following Elm Creek until she reached the bridge between the barn and the manor. From there she could see the back of the manor clearly; some of the windows were aglow, including the kitchen and the west sitting room, Sylvia's favorite place to quilt. The suite Sarah and Matt shared was lit up, too.

Matt must be there. Sarah quickened her pace. She would try again to talk to him. She prayed that this time, when she needed him most, he would be willing to listen.

But when she went upstairs, she arrived just in time to see Carol turning off the light before leaving Sarah's suite. Sarah stopped short in the hallway. "Mother? What are you doing?"

Carol looked up, startled, but she said nothing as she closed the door and went down the hall to her own room.

Sarah hesitated. Should she go after her? She decided against it and went to her own room instead, glancing around to see if her mother had disturbed anything. Matt wasn't there, but there was an envelope on the bed with Sarah's name on it.

Sarah tore it open and found a letter.

> Dear Sarah,
>
> Tomorrow I will be going home. It's obvious you don't want me here, and I no longer have the heart to stay when I know we'll continue to fight. I want you to know that I'm truly sorry I could never be the mother you wanted. My intentions were good, but we all know where good intentions lead you.
>
> I'm sorry I wrote those letters. You're right, I should have kept my opinions to myself. If I wouldn't have objected to Matt so much, maybe you wouldn't have been so eager to marry him. You always did the opposite of what I told you to do. I should have known better.
>
> You have wonderful friends and a wonderful life. They have shown you such generosity, and yet you won't share even the smallest scrap with me. I wish things were different between us. I think I should leave before they get worse. At least we tried.
>
> Love,
> Mother

Sarah read the letter again to make sure she had understood it correctly. Yes, Carol would leave in the morning. Why wasn't Sarah relieved at the news? Instead she felt hurt—and angry. How like Carol to throw another barb at Matt in what was supposed to be an apology. How like her to heap on one last serving of criticism.

Sarah sank into a chair by the window. What should she do now? Run down the hall to her mother's room and beg her to stay? Help her pack? She felt a sting of guilt for her thoughts earlier that day, when she had sat by the creek and wished her mother would go away. She still wanted her life to go back to normal, but not if it meant having her mother leave in a huff. If Carol left now, Sarah knew that the chances for reconciliation would be more remote than ever.

Just then, she saw headlights outside the window moving past the barn, across the bridge, and toward the manor. She recognized their truck as it circled the two large elms in the center of the parking lot and stopped. Matt was home. Where had he been?

She raced downstairs and through the manor to the back door. Matt was just coming up the back steps, carrying a grocery bag. "Did you go into town?" she asked. "I didn't even know you had left."

"I would have asked if you needed me to pick up anything, but I couldn't find you."

Sarah wished he didn't sound so defensive. She tried to keep her voice light. "So, what did you buy me?" she asked, grinning and trying to peer into the bag.

"Ice cream. The real kind, as Sylvia calls it. She tried some of that fat-free stuff you bought and said it tastes like plastic. I offered to get her something better."

Ordinarily, Sarah would have reminded him that Sylvia was supposed to watch her blood pressure, but she couldn't afford to annoy him. "Matt, I need to talk to you."

"Let me put this away first before it melts."

"It will only take a minute." As soon as he got inside, he'd think of a dozen other things he had to do, anything but talk to her. "My mother's leaving in the morning."

He stared at her. "Why? Why now? Did you tell her to go?"

"No, of course not," she said, annoyed that he would think that of her. Quickly she read him the note, omitting only the part about Carol's letters.

Matt set down the bag. "Do you have any idea what brought this on? Yes, you two fight a lot, and sure, you're jealous of the time she spends with the Elm Creek Quilters, but that was true yesterday and the day before, too, and she knew it. They weren't reasons to leave then. Why are they now?"

His confirmation of Carol's complaints irked her. "If you had stuck around instead of taking off as soon as you finished eating supper, you'd know."

"I didn't want to listen to any more fights. Is that a crime?"

Sarah tried to calm herself. She had to get this conversation back on track. "I think the skateboard demonstration upset her. You know how she is. She kept going on and on about how their arrest will damage the reputation of Elm Creek Quilts."

"She has a good point."

"What?" Sarah stared at him. "Matt, these are our friends she's criticizing."

"Friends or not, they used poor judgment. You haven't thought this through. How do you think prospective campers will feel when they learn half your employees were thrown into jail for disturbing the peace?"

"My friends aren't criminals," Sarah said in a tight voice.

"Yes, they are. They broke the law. Even if they don't agree with it, it's still the law."

"I can't believe you're saying this. You sound just like my mother."

"Maybe she knows what she's talking about." Matt's voice rose until it was nearly a shout.

"Matt, calm down."

"Don't tell me to calm down. Don't you get it? We're dependent on this business for everything. Everything. What if all this crap with the police scares your customers away? What then? And what if something should happen to Sylvia? Who will get the business? Who will get the manor? Not us, that's for sure. We may live with her, but we aren't her family. She probably doesn't even have a will. She'll have heirs crawling out of the woodwork, and the first thing they'll do is close down the quilt camp and kick us out of the manor."

"That's insane," Sarah snapped. "I'm sure Sylvia's planned for that."

"You're sure?" Matt barked out an angry laugh. "You don't know that. That's not how you people run things. In any other company we'd have some security, some kind of safety net, but not here. It's too risky, and I'm sick of living this way."

"What are we supposed to do? What other way can we live?"

"I've been trying to figure that out for months. How am I supposed to know what to do? You're the one who got us into this mess. If not for your Elm Creek Quilts, we'd be a lot better off. I don't know why I ever let you talk me into leaving my old job. Now everything's in one basket and it's all about to spill over. And you won't let yourself see it!"

"No one forced you to quit your old job," Sarah shouted back. "That was your decision."

"Yeah, and it was the worst one of my life." He shot Sarah a furious glare. "Make that the second worst." He shoved past her and stormed into the house.

His words burned in her ears. She stood there, stunned, so hurt she could hardly breathe. Then, somewhere over her right shoulder, she heard a noise. She glanced up in time to see a figure move away from the kitchen window.

Oh, no. Was it Carol or Sylvia who had overheard their fight? Sarah went inside, heart sinking, praying that the figure at the window had been Andrew.

When she entered the kitchen, Sylvia stood in the center of the room, alone.

"Sylvia—" Then Sarah could go no further.

"Please forgive me for eavesdropping," Sylvia said, her voice quiet. "I should have left the window as soon as I heard you, but—"

"He didn't mean it."

"Oh, I'm quite certain he meant every word." Sylvia sighed. "The question is, what shall we do now?"

"I don't know. I don't know." Sarah felt tears gathering. She couldn't remember when she had last been so upset or so scared. She clenched her hands together to keep them from trembling.

"Don't waste a single moment." Sylvia placed her hands on Sarah's shoulders. "You'll have to go to them, to both of them, and apologize. Now, before it's too late."

Sarah froze, stunned. "Apologize?"

"Of course. It's the only thing you can do."

"I don't understand." Sarah shrugged off Sylvia's hands. Apologize? Carol was the one who had given up and was running away. Matt was the one who had become angry and insulted Sylvia and the other Elm Creek Quilters.

"What's to understand? March yourself upstairs and tell Matt you're sorry for losing your temper. Then sit down and discuss the matter rationally. When you're finished there, go speak to your mother."

Sylvia's tone was matter-of-fact, but her words sparked Sarah's anger. "Wait a minute. Hold on. Matt's the one who lost his temper. Why should I be the one to cave in? Why aren't you telling him to apologize to me?"

"Because he isn't the one who sought my advice. If he were the one standing here, I would have told him the same. Someone has to bend. What do you have to gain from being stubborn?"

"Stubborn?" Sarah gasped. "I'm stubborn? You ignore your family for fifty years after one little argument and *I'm* stubborn?"

A muscle twitched in Sylvia's cheek, but her voice was cool. "That's simplifying things a bit, wouldn't you say? And we're not talking about my mistakes now, but about yours."

Sarah felt the blood pounding in her ears as Sylvia continued, telling her how to approach Matt and Carol, what to say, how to say it. She used words like *responsibility,* and *maturity,* and *selflessness*—words that jumbled up and spun around in Sarah's mind until she thought she would explode.

Suddenly she couldn't bear one more word of criticism, one more sentence of blame. "Stop it," she burst out. "What do you know about any of this? Your mother died when you were five, so what do you know about dealing with someone like Carol? And how long were you married? I've been married three times as long as you were, so who are you to tell me what to do? You're not my mother. Sometimes you don't even act like my friend!"

All the color drained from Sylvia's face.

In an instant, Sarah was shocked and sickened by her horrible words. She started to apologize, but Sylvia cut her off. "No, no, you're quite right."

Sylvia wouldn't—or couldn't—look at her. "Who am I to be giving out advice? As you pointed out, I have little experience."

"Sylvia, please. I was just upset about Matt and my mother. I didn't mean—"

"You meant every word, just as Matthew did when he spoke his piece." Sylvia sighed, and the sound wrenched Sarah's heart. "Well. This won't do. Such unhappiness won't do." Her voice was bleak. "I'll say good night now. I've had enough of being a meddling old busybody for one day. Thank you for letting me know how you feel."

"But that's not how I feel, not really," Sarah said, but it was too late. Sylvia was already leaving the kitchen, her shoulders slumped, her footsteps slow.

Sarah called after her, but the words caught in her throat, and only sobs came out. She clung to the kitchen counter, sick with remorse and shame.

A moment later, a movement caught her eye. It was Andrew, standing in the doorway of the west sitting room. He gave her a long, steady look as he passed her on his way through the kitchen after Sylvia. He spoke not a word, but she could sense his profound disappointment in her.

Never before in her life had she found herself so deserving of anyone's censure. Never before had she been more aware of her own selfishness, her potential for cruelty. Never before had she been so alone.

Twelve

ylvia slept poorly. Andrew's words had been kind, but they had not comforted her. "She's just a young woman," Andrew had said. "She loves you dearly. Don't hold this one moment against her."

Sylvia promised him she wouldn't, but how could she ever forget how Sarah had lashed out at her? How could they go on as if nothing had happened? This could be the end of everything, everything, not just the hopes for a reconciliation between Sarah and Carol, but Elm Creek Quilts, the new life and joy they had restored to the manor, all of it.

Her dreams tormented her and shook her awake long before dawn.

As she lay in bed, waiting for the early morning grogginess to leave her, she felt uneasiness stirring, expanding until dread and worry filled her. Slowly she realized that there was something she had to do that morning, something urgent, something regarding Sarah and Carol. But what was it? What was it? She felt as if she had gone into a room to fetch something, only to realize she had forgotten what she had come for.

Sometimes retracing her steps helped her to remember. Yes. She would wake Sarah. As soon as Sylvia saw her, she would remember what it was that she must do. In the semidarkness, she sat up and groped for her glasses on the nightstand.

Just as her fingertips touched the fine silver chain, a searing pain shot through her skull.

She gasped.

Her left hand was numb, the left side of her face was numb, but her head was on fire.

This was wrong. The thoughts came slowly. Something was very wrong with her.

She should lie down and wait for it go away.

No. No. She couldn't.

Somehow she made herself sit upright. She tried to force her feet into her slippers, but she could not get her legs to move properly. She could see her slippers there on the floor beside her bed, and yet somehow she could not determine where they were. She tried to focus, but nothing would obey her, not her perception, not her limbs.

Afraid now, and barefoot, she forced herself to stand. She fell twice on her way to the door. She fumbled with the knob, slamming her shoulder on the frame as the door finally opened into the hallway. The blow registered, but not the pain.

Sarah, help me, she screamed, but no sound came out.

Leaning against the wall, she shuffled down the hallway toward Sarah's room. Right foot, left. Again, though she had no strength for it. Right foot. An eternity passed. Left foot.

She was nearly blind from pain.

"Sharuh," she called out.

Her mouth was frozen stiff. She took as deep a breath as she could. She would have one more chance. That, and no more.

"Sharuh!"

It was the haunted wail of a stranger. It could not have been her own voice.

It was useless, useless. She could go no farther.

Then, as if in slow motion, she saw two doors open, one on either side of the hall. Sarah and Carol stepped from their rooms. Slowly their heads turned her way. Their eyes went wide with horror.

The last thing Sylvia saw as she collapsed was the mother and daughter running toward her.

Then she fell into darkness.

Thirteen

Agnes was already awake when Sarah called from the hospital at six o'clock in the morning. The poor girl was so upset she could hardly get the words out, but the dreadful news was all too clear: Sylvia had suffered a stroke. The doctors did not yet know how serious.

"I'm coming," Agnes told her. "I need to be there."

Sarah must have anticipated this. "Matt's already on his way to pick you up."

Agnes hung up the phone, numb. They didn't need her there, getting in the doctors' way. If Sylvia was going to be fine, they would have asked Agnes to postpone her visit until the afternoon at least. This was their way of telling her she would be coming to the hospital to say good-bye.

Agnes collected her appliqué patches, carefully folded the round robin center, and placed everything into her sewing box. Hospitals meant long waits, so she would take her quilting with her to keep her thoughts focused away from her grief.

Life was just one extended series of partings. She could not bear many more. She supposed she would not have to bear many more.

She put on a sweater and went to the living room, where she could see the driveway from a chair near the window. Was Sarah calling the other Elm Creek Quilters? Someone else should do it for her—Matt, perhaps, or Carol. Diane had made the calls for Agnes when Joe died, and Agnes had not been nearly as distraught then as Sarah sounded now. It wasn't that Agnes hadn't loved Joe; she had. But he had suffered so terribly for so many months before finally succumbing to cancer that his death was, in a sense, a relief, though she wouldn't dream of telling her daughters that. And, too, no matter how much she had loved those who passed, every loss since Richard's had been diminished in comparison. No other loss could compare to that enormous, overwhelming pain, that severing—but Sylvia's passing would come close.

Suddenly she remembered Andrew, and her heart went out to him. How would he bear this? He had admired Sylvia since he was a child and had fallen in love with her as a young man. Agnes remembered a time so long ago when Richard had teased him after the two boys returned to Philadelphia following a long weekend at Elm Creek Manor.

"Andrew here is sweet on my sister," Richard told her, nudging Andrew.

"Is that so?" Agnes asked. She had not met Richard's family yet. Secretly she envied Andrew and wished Richard had invited her to come on the trip, too. "And how does she feel about you, Andrew?"

"It doesn't matter." He shrugged, disconsolate. "She's married."

"You mean you like Sylvia?" She thought Richard had meant Claudia, the pretty one, the eldest.

Richard grinned. "At least Sylvia's closer to his age."

"Yes, but she's married," Agnes said, scandalized.

"I didn't tell her," Andrew protested. "What kind of a fellow do you take me for?"

Laughing, Richard patted him on the back and said, "We'll have to find a pretty girl to keep his mind off my sister."

"I have a few friends who might be interested," Agnes teased, and Andrew's blush deepened.

They were such good friends in those days, young and carefree, with all their days yet before them, or so it seemed. No wonder she had fallen in love with Richard. He was so handsome and confident and kind. She had never met anyone like him, not at the silly cotillions her parents forced her to attend, not at dancing school, not at any of the other society functions. The boys she met there, the boys her mother firmly steered her toward, were virtually inter-changeable in their backgrounds, their educations, their interests—even their mannerisms seemed identically practiced and polished. But Richard had a wild energy about him she had never sensed in anyone else. And to her amazement, she realized that he saw something unique in her, as well. He saw a part of her she had almost forgotten, a spirited girl with a mind of her own and the confi-dence to follow it wherever it led. For as long as Agnes could remember, her mother had labored to shape that girl into a carefully decorated, overrehearsed debutante—like her sisters, like the women her brothers would eventually marry. But her mother's idea of what Agnes should be was imposed from with-out, not brought forth from within. Richard had seen through the façade, and she knew she would never be the same.

Naturally her parents hated him. They pitied Andrew, the poor scholar-ship student who would be educated beyond his station and relegated to a life as a tutor to rich men's sons, but they despised Richard. Not that he was anything but respectful to them during those few times they were together. In fact, his manners were impeccable—which incensed her parents all the more, and delighted Agnes. Oh, but she would have loved him even if he had not been forbidden. Something in her soul recognized his, and they both knew from the moment they met that, somehow, they completed each other.

A red pickup truck pulled into the driveway, drawing Agnes from her reverie. She didn't wait for Matt to come to the door but met him halfway up the path. Matt's expression was grim as he helped her into the truck.

"Is there any change?" she asked when he came around the other side and took his own seat.

"Nothing yet."

Her hopes wavered, but she forced confidence into her voice for his sake. "Sylvia's a fighter. If anyone can pull through this, she can. She will."

"I hope you're right."

A roughness in his voice made her look at him. For the first time she noticed that his eyes were red.

When they reached the hospital, they found Sarah and Carol in the waiting room. Sarah was staring straight ahead and crying without making a sound, so stricken that Agnes was frightened for her. Carol was by her side, speaking to her in a low voice. Once Sarah nodded slowly, but otherwise she seemed oblivious to her surroundings.

Agnes and Matt joined them, and not long afterward the other Elm Creek Quilters began to arrive in pairs and alone. Frequently, Carol would approach the reception desk and ask about Sylvia, then return to the group, shaking her head.

"When can we see her?" Agnes asked.

"Not until she's stable. Or—" Carol's voice broke off. She tilted her head toward her daughter, indicating that she did not want to say anything about Sylvia's worsening condition in front of Sarah. Sarah was still staring straight ahead, unaware. She had stretched out the hem of her T-shirt and was twisting it into a rope.

Agnes rose, glancing toward the emergency room doors, just beyond the reception desk. She had seen how the paramedics hit that large red button on the wall to make the doors swing open. If she summoned up her confidence, perhaps no one would challenge her if she walked through them. But what good would sneaking in to see Sylvia do? The last they had heard, Sylvia was unconscious. She would not know that Agnes was there. But if Agnes held her hand and whispered to her, perhaps something would reach her. Perhaps she would be comforted.

If Sylvia were awake and alert, she wouldn't want anyone to see her in such a state, confined to a bed, doctors and nurses fussing and scolding, tubes going every which way. She'd order her friends out of the room and not let them return until she was properly dressed and standing on her own two feet. Agnes almost smiled at the thought. As long as Agnes had known her, Sylvia had possessed a regal, almost imperious air, though it had softened over the years.

When Agnes first came to Elm Creek Manor, though, Sylvia had played the lady of the manor indeed.

Agnes was fifteen then; she had known Richard for only a few months, and she liked him more than any other boy she had ever met. Her parents' coldness toward him hurt her deeply, and she was determined to change their minds.

Every Christmas the Chevaliers threw an enormous ball, the most eagerly anticipated social event of the year in Philadelphia and beyond. Anyone who was anyone came—with the exception of a few "muckraking newspapermen" who published unflattering articles in the newspapers they owned, editorials about Mrs. Chevalier's father, the former senator, and her brothers, judges and senators all, any one of whom could become president one day. In hindsight Agnes realized she had grown up surrounded by wealth and power, but at the time, occasions such as the Yuletide Ball were merely parties, with pretty ladies and handsome gentlemen, beautiful music, delicious food—and the opportunity to wear a lovely gown as she danced with Richard.

She would ask her mother to permit Richard to attend as her guest. He would charm everyone there, she was certain of it. He had such an easy way with people, with none of her own stammering bashfulness. His secret was that he was genuinely interested in whatever his companion of the moment had to say. It was no act with him. He was fascinated with the world and everything in it. Any chance to meet someone he had never met or to try something he had never tried delighted him. Surely her parents would come to like him as much as everyone else did if they would just give themselves that chance.

"Absolutely not," her mother declared. "Agnes, how could you ask such a thing? It's simply unthinkable."

"But why? You've always allowed me to invite friends before."

"Don't be stupid. This is the Yuletide Ball. We can't have a stable boy running around smelling of horses' dirt."

"He's the heir to Bergstrom Thoroughbreds, and his family is as good as any in Philadelphia. But even if he were a stable boy, I would still want him to come. He is a very dear friend."

"Indeed," her mother said dryly. "You won't want for friends at the ball. The Johnson sisters are coming, and young Mr. Cameron will be there."

"Oh, how delightful. The young Mr. Cameron." Agnes plopped down on an overstuffed sofa in a most ungraceful fashion. "Will he spend the entire evening talking about his blasted greyhounds, like he did last year?"

"Agnes," her mother gasped, shocked.

It took Agnes a moment to realize her mistake.

Her mother's face was white with fury except for two scarlet blotches in the hollows of her cheeks. "Where did you learn such a filthy word?"

From Father, Agnes almost said, but she managed to hold it back.

"I know you didn't learn that at Miss Sebastian's Academy. Did your noble stable boy teach it to you?"

Agnes's anger got the better of her. "Yes, he did," she snapped. "That, and a great many other things."

Her mother nearly fainted. Too late, Agnes realized her second mistake. She had meant that Richard had taught her other curse words—which wasn't exactly true—but her mother had understood her meaning quite differently.

"You are such a trial to me," her mother said, seizing her by the arm and marching her from the drawing room. It did not occur to Agnes to resist. "You'll stay in your room until you remember how a young lady should behave."

Mrs. Chevalier had to let Agnes out to go to school, but she was watched so carefully that she couldn't run off to meet Richard and Andrew all that week. The following Monday as she left Miss Sebastian's, she spotted Richard just outside the tall wrought-iron gates. Her heart quickened with nervous pleasure as she went to meet him, hoping her father's driver was not paying attention.

"You haven't come to see us all week," Richard said, his brow furrowed in concern. "What's the matter, don't you like that café anymore? Or did Andrew say something to offend you?"

Agnes laughed at thought of Andrew's saying anything offensive, but she was thrilled. Richard had missed her. She had feared he had forgotten her.

"I wanted to come. There have been—" She hesitated, wanting to protect him. "Some complications."

Richard's eyebrows rose, but he didn't ask for more details, which was a relief. As angry as she was with her parents, she loved them and was loyal to them. She couldn't bear to disparage them before anyone, especially Richard.

"Any chance these complications will sort themselves out soon?"

Agnes tried to smile. "Anything is possible."

He nodded, then looked past her to the waiting car. Her father's driver had opened the door to the back seat and stood with his hand upon it, waiting.

"Andrew and I will be at the café as usual," Richard finally said. "Come see us when you can." He gave her one quick smile before turning and walking away.

Her heart sank to see him go.

Two weeks went by, and not once could she slip away. Richard met her once again outside Miss Sebastian's, but only once. After that, she had no word from him. Her hopes dwindled as the Christmas holidays approached. Both her school and the boys' school would be closed for a month, and Richard would be going home to Elm Creek Manor. She knew his travel schedule—which train he would take, what time he planned to leave—and as that hour approached, she realized what she had to do.

Swiftly she packed a suitcase and left a note for her parents with the butler. Then she hired a cab to take her to the train station. She bought a ticket and hurried as fast as she could to the platform, where she searched frantically for Richard.

Then she spotted him in the center of a knot of passengers waiting to board the train.

"Richard," she called to him. Her voice was swallowed up in the noise of the station. Frantic, she screamed his name. He jerked his head in her direction, his face lighting up with recognition and astonishment.

He left his place in line and made his way through the crowd to her side. "Agnes, what are you doing here?" He glanced at her suitcase but said nothing about it.

"May I come home with you for the holidays?"

"Your parents won't mind that you'll miss their party?"

"I'm sure they will, once they find out."

He studied her for a long moment. For a while she feared he would refuse. He was offended by her gall and never wanted to see her again.

But then he picked up her suitcase and offered her his arm. "I'd be delighted to have you come. If I'd known you could, I would have asked you weeks ago."

She took his arm, too overcome with relief to speak. That, Agnes later realized, was when she first knew she loved him.

The train ride west was one of the happiest occasions of her life. Finally she and Richard had the chance to talk alone for hours. Richard truly listened when Agnes spoke, unlike all the other men she had known, who would smile indulgently and exchange looks over her head, chuckling as if she were an amusing child. Richard didn't agree with all of her opinions—especially regarding the troubles in Europe—but he never once treated her as if she was nothing more than a harmless, silly decoration. To someone who had spent her life learning how to be an ornament, this was a revelation.

When they arrived at Elm Creek Manor, Agnes was nervous and excited. She didn't regret her decision to come home with Richard, but she wished his family had expected her. Maybe then Richard's sister Sylvia wouldn't have greeted her with such obvious shock. Maybe then Agnes wouldn't have earned Sylvia's immediate and intense dislike. It was obvious that Sylvia was the queen of this household, just as Agnes's mother ruled the Chevalier home. With Sylvia against her, Agnes feared Richard would not remain hers for long—if it was, in fact, right to call him hers.

"Your sister doesn't like me," she told him that evening before they retired to separate bedrooms a respectful distance apart. Richard laughed and told her she was imagining things, which made her heart drop even lower. From that moment she knew he would be forever blind to Sylvia's barely contained malevolence.

Gradually, Agnes won over the others. She got along well with Richard's elder sister, Claudia, and the young cousins even asked her to join in their games occasionally. Sylvia's husband, James, was a true gentleman, kind and thoughtful, much like Richard himself. Only Sylvia remained aloof and resistant.

Agnes understood the source of her resentment: Sylvia was selfish. She had a husband, a sister, a loving family, but that wasn't enough for her. She also wanted her younger brother all to herself, and no young woman from Philadelphia was going to steal him away.

How ironic it was that Sylvia was treating Agnes as Mrs. Chevalier treated Richard. If those two headstrong, jealous women ever encountered each other—Agnes giggled at the thought. She wished she could share her amusement with Richard, but she didn't want him to know how her parents felt about him. No doubt he suspected the truth, but she would spare him the insulting details.

Instead she doubled her efforts to befriend Sylvia. When she sensed how proud Sylvia was of her quilting, she made certain to praise Sylvia's needle-work—the fineness of her stitches, the intricacy of the designs.

"How charming," Agnes said, admiring Sylvia's current project, an elaborate quilt with appliquéd baskets, flowers, and other intricate shapes. "What pattern is this?"

"It's a Baltimore Album quilt." Sylvia went on to explain the history of the style. Agnes listened, nodding as if fascinated. Once she glanced up and caught Claudia's eye, and she saw that Richard's elder sister was trying to hide a smile. Claudia knew what Agnes was about, even if Sylvia didn't.

When Sylvia's long-winded explanation finally drew to a close, Claudia spoke up. "Do you quilt, Agnes?"

Agnes realized she had an ally. "No, I don't know how. I wish I could, but

I know I could never make anything as lovely as this." She gazed at Sylvia's quilt in admiration.

"All it takes is practice," Sylvia said briskly, but Agnes could tell that the compliment had pleased her.

"I wish that were true," Agnes said. "But I don't have your talent, Sylvia. I suppose I'll just have to keep buying my comforters in the shops in Philadelphia."

To her surprise, Sylvia pursed her lips, offended. "Naturally you'd want to do that. Out here on the frontier, however, we don't have that luxury."

"Sylvia," Claudia warned.

Agnes quickly added, "What I meant to say was that I would prefer a handmade quilt like those you have in Elm Creek Manor, but since I can't quilt, I—"

"You'll buy something made by someone with better sense." Sylvia glanced away from her work to frown at Agnes. "I hope you remembered to pack all you'll need, or you might need to go home early. Our humble shops out here in the country are no match for those in the heavenly land of Philadelphia."

The rebuke stung. Perhaps Agnes had gone on about Philadelphia during her visit, but it was only to show the Bergstroms how wonderful she found Elm Creek Manor in comparison. If only they knew how much she longed to take the happy clamor of their family back home with her. She left the room before she burst into tears. She would not humiliate herself further by allowing Sylvia to see her cry.

It was not an auspicious beginning, Agnes thought, turning away from the window. She and Sylvia had come a long way since then. In the past two years, since Sarah had reunited them, they had become friends. Agnes never would have dreamed it.

She never would have dreamed that she would one day be able to quilt like Sylvia, either, but she had learned. Sylvia had tried to teach her, but when those lessons failed miserably, Claudia finished the job. Now Claudia was gone, and Sylvia would soon join her. Once again, Agnes would be alone.

She took a deep breath to fight off the tears. It wouldn't do to break down when Sylvia needed her friends to be strong. Then she remembered the round robin center in her sewing box. Yes, that was what she needed, something to keep her busy so she would stop glancing at the clock and wondering why the nurse hadn't been back with news of Sylvia in such a long while.

The other Elm Creek Quilters, who had been so eager to see her center design, barely noticed as she took out the round robin quilt and began to work. She had strip-pieced a background for her appliqué, with varying shades of blue for the sky and green for the grass. After trimming this piece into a large circle, she had sewn pieces of gray and white onto it, creating a portrait of Elm Creek Manor in fabric. A scrap of black cotton became the rearing horse fountain in the front of the manor, and a narrow strip of blue was the creek in the distance. Now she was adding the final touch: a grove of trees at the northeast corner of the manor, where the cornerstone patio was, where the main entrance to the manor had been before the south wing was built in Richard's father's day.

Richard had told her so much of the manor's history—how Hans Bergstrom had placed the cornerstone with the help of his sister and wife, how the manor had served as a station on the Underground Railroad, how the estate had flourished over the years, and how it had sometimes faltered. Once he mentioned that the north garden was a perfect spot for a wedding, and once that the ballroom in the south wing could accommodate several hundred guests. His hints thrilled her, but she had other ideas. When she married, it would be in a proper church, and the reception afterward would take place in her parents' home. They would insist upon it. As far as Agnes was concerned, if she did somehow manage to convince her parents to accept Richard, she would let her mother do whatever she wanted for the wedding in gratitude.

As it turned out, neither Agnes nor Richard had the wedding they had imagined.

His proposal and the ensuing ceremony took place over a span of a few short days in March of the following year, 1944. Richard had returned to Elm Creek Manor for his school holidays, but this time she did not accompany him. Instead she waved good-bye from the platform as his train pulled out of the station, then she returned home with her brother, who had accompanied them at Mrs. Chevalier's insistence.

The next time she saw Richard was several days before he was actually due back. It was mid-morning, and he had come straight to the front door instead of throwing pebbles at her window and signaling her to meet him outside. Her mother's voice was frosty as she informed Agnes she had a caller waiting in the drawing room.

Agnes's heart pounded as she went downstairs. Her mother's tone told her it was Richard waiting—but why? What was he doing back so soon? Something was terribly, terribly wrong.

When she entered the room where Richard waited, he was pacing back and forth, hair tousled, face flushed, eyes bright with excitement. She was too startled to speak, but he looked her way at the sound of the door. He crossed the room swiftly and seized her hands. "Agnes, I have something to ask you." He dropped to one knee. "I love you with all my heart, and I know you love me, too. Would you do me the honor of becoming my wife?"

Agnes stared at him. Why was he asking her now? He knew she was just sixteen. He knew he ought to ask her father first, and not for years yet. Why—

Then she understood. He and Andrew—all their bold talk about enlisting—

Her legs were suddenly too weak to support her, but Richard helped her to a chair. "Please—" she choked out. "Please—"

He smiled, but there were tears in his eyes. "You don't have to beg, darling. I've already proposed."

She wanted to strike him for joking at such a time. She hated him. She loved him so fiercely she could never let him leave her. "Please tell me you didn't enlist. Please tell me you're not asking me this because you're going off to war in the morning."

"Not in the morning." His face was close to hers. He stroked her hair gently. "I have two weeks."

Her chest tightened up with sobs, so many that she thought they would tear her throat open. But she swallowed them back and wiped her eyes with the back of her hand. Unsteadily, she rose from her chair. "Will you excuse me, please?"

"But Agnes—"

"I'm going to seek my parents' blessing." Without waiting for a reply, she left the drawing room. Her mother was in her sitting room writing letters.

Agnes took a seat beside her and waited for her mother to look up. She refused to acknowledge her daughter's presence, to punish her for the undesirable caller. Agnes wondered what punishment her mother would contrive for what she was about to say and realized it didn't matter. Nothing could hurt her more than the thought of Richard's going off to war.

Finally her mother looked up. "Yes, dear, what is it?"

"Richard Bergstrom has asked me to marry him. I would like to have your blessing, and Father's."

Her mother's face went white in fury, but her voice was perfectly controlled. "Absolutely not." She resumed writing and nearly tore the paper with her pen. "If you're not pleased with the young Mr. Cameron we'll find someone else suitable for you, but you shall decline Mr. Bergstrom's proposal and instruct him never again to speak of it."

Agnes felt as if she were watching the scene play out from a great distance. "No," she heard herself say. "I shall not decline."

Her mother slammed down her pen. "You shall. You have no choice. You are too young. Do you really believe any judge within two hundred miles of here would allow a Chevalier daughter to marry under such suspicious circumstances?" Her voice was high and shrill. "They value their livelihoods too dearly for that, I assure you. Not one of them has any wish to be the man who allows a disobedient child to destroy the Chevalier family's good name."

Agnes grew very still. For the first time she saw her mother clearly, without fear. Agnes held the power now, and her mother was the frightened one. No matter what happened next, Agnes would never submit to her mother again. She was free.

"Richard has enlisted. He leaves in two weeks." Each word was as cold and distinct as if it had been chiseled in marble. "I will spend every moment between now and his departure by his side—every day and every night. I would prefer to do so as his wife, but I will do so as his mistress if necessary. Since you are so concerned with the Chevalier family's good name, perhaps you should consider carefully whether you truly wish to withhold your blessing."

Her mother stared at her for a long moment, breathing rapidly, clutching the desktop. "Your father will never agree," she managed to say.

"You will convince him."

Agnes was correct; her mother did make him see reason. But he gave Agnes one condition. "If you marry that man," he roared, "you leave this house forever. You will be dead to us."

His words shocked her into silence. She could only stare at him, the man she had always admired and loved so deeply. He thought she had betrayed him, and perhaps she had.

She thought of Richard, and how he might not return from the war. She might have two weeks with him, two weeks in exchange for a lifetime with her family.

She was her father's favorite daughter, and yet he could cut her out of his life with a word.

She wanted to ask her father if he meant it, but that would have been foolish. Her father never said anything he didn't mean. She wanted to beg him to reconsider, but her father never backed down from an ultimatum.

So she spoke from the heart. "I will miss you all very much," she said. Then she returned to the drawing room to tell Richard she would be his wife.

They had a simple civil ceremony. Andrew was one witness, one of Agnes's school friends was the other. Agnes had wanted her sisters, but she could not ask them to defy their parents.

Later that day, James and Harold arrived, too late to stop Richard and Andrew from enlisting. James decided to enlist so that he would be in the same unit as his brother-in-law. Harold reluctantly said he would as well.

Agnes thought it was madness. "Don't do it," she had begged them. She clung to James's arm. "Please. Think of Sylvia."

Gently, James freed himself. "I am thinking of Sylvia," he said, and then he and Harold left.

Agnes was not comforted by the knowledge that James and Harold would be looking after Richard on the battlefield. Their selflessness and courage would not stop a bullet. They should have tried to free Richard from his enlistment, not join him in it. It was madness. Utter madness. And she alone seemed to see it.

They returned to Elm Creek Manor together for a few bleak days of grievous good-byes. Harold proposed to Claudia, but they did not rush off and marry as Agnes and Richard had done, as so many other young couples had done. They wanted to wait until after the men returned so they could do it right. Agnes marveled at their certainty that they would have that chance.

And then, all too soon, the men departed.

Of the four, only Andrew and Harold returned.

Agnes's hands trembled, and she stuck herself with the needle. She dropped the quilt as soon as she felt the pain, but she was not fast enough. A small drop of blood now stained the back of the block, a smear of red leaking through the gray fabric of the manor.

She shivered.

"Let me help you," Bonnie said. She took the quilt and carried it over to the drinking fountain.

"Did you hurt yourself?" Andrew asked.

"Only a little needle prick," Agnes said, but Carol had already taken her hand and was examining her finger. There was a tiny drop of blood on the pad of her left index finger. Carol insisted on taking her to the bathroom to wash the pinprick with soap and water. Then Carol carefully applied antibiotic ointment and a bandage, all from the small first aid kit she kept in her purse.

"What do you do for a cough?" Diane asked when they returned to the waiting room. "A lung transplant?"

The Elm Creek Quilters smiled, but no one had the heart to laugh.

"It's better to be safe than sorry," Carol said.

"She's right," a voice broke in. "Hospitals are the worst places for picking up germs. I read that somewhere."

It was Sarah who had spoken. They all turned to look at her. As far as Agnes knew, those were the first words she had spoken since arriving at the hospital.

"Then I'm fortunate Carol was here," Agnes said gently, returning to her seat.

Bonnie handed her the quilt center. "The stain came out, but I'm afraid it's a little damp."

"That's all right. I'll finish when it's dry." All that was left was a tiny bit of the last tree, and then she could stitch the design in place in the center of the round robin quilt her friends had made. She tried not to, but in the back of her mind she wondered if Sylvia would ever see the completed quilt hanging in the front foyer to welcome the new quilt campers.

The quilt campers.

"Oh, dear," she said. "It's Sunday."

Her friends exchanged looks of weary dismay, and she could tell they had forgotten, too.

Gwen said, "We'll have to call everyone and tell them camp is canceled this week."

"We can't do that," Judy said. "It's already nine o'clock. If they're driving a long distance, they might have left already."

"And those who are flying already paid for their airline tickets," Bonnie added.

"Can't you refund their costs?" Andrew asked. "If you tell them what happened, they'll understand."

"No." Sarah sat up and looked around at her friends. "We can't do that. We have to hold camp as planned."

Silence.

"Maybe you're right," Diane said. "That's what Sylvia would have wanted."

Sarah whirled on her, furious. "That's what Sylvia would *want.*"

Chastened, Diane looked away.

Summer stood up. "Sarah's right. We can't let Sylvia think we'll fall apart if she doesn't watch us every minute. I'll go back to the manor and start setting up."

Gwen chimed in that she would join her daughter, and soon it was agreed: Agnes, Andrew, Sarah, Carol, and Matt would remain at the hospital; the others would return to Elm Creek Manor to await the arrival of their newest guests.

"Call us as soon as you hear anything," Judy urged, and Agnes promised they would.

A strange silence hung over the waiting room after their friends left. Matt went to the hospital cafeteria and returned with steaming cups of coffee and warm muffins. Agnes accepted a cup of coffee gratefully, but her stomach was in knots and she knew she wouldn't be able to choke down a bite of food. The heat from the cup soothed some of the chill out of her hands.

Sarah was right, Agnes knew. No matter what happened to Sylvia, they couldn't let Elm Creek Quilts fall to pieces. It would be an insult to Sylvia, a betrayal, if they let her dream die. She needed to know that the life and joy she had restored to the manor would endure.

Sylvia blamed herself for Elm Creek Manor's downfall—and the Bergstrom family's decline—as if her departure had been the one killing blow that had ended it all. But Agnes knew the end had not come with such merciful swiftness. The Bergstrom legacy had ground to a halt over time in a way that was unbearable to witness. But Agnes had witnessed it. When Sylvia was far away, living first in Maryland with James's parents and later in Pittsburgh alone, Agnes had remained behind, and she saw it all.

There had been so many arguments between the two sisters. It was only later that Agnes learned how that last argument had differed from all the others. At the time, Sylvia's departure had shaken Agnes, but neither she nor Claudia ever dreamed Sylvia would stay away so long.

It had happened shortly after Andrew's visit. He had decided not to finish school; he did not explain why. He was traveling to a new job in Detroit and had only stayed the night. That evening after supper, Agnes saw him go to the library where Sylvia was working. They spoke privately for a long time. Finally the door banged open and Sylvia stormed out, furious, tears streaking her face. Andrew had followed her as far as the library door. His face, too, was wet from tears.

"What happened?" Agnes asked him. As soon as the words left her lips, she felt a flash of panic. She did not want to know. She had too much pain already.

But Andrew had already taken her hand. "Agnes, there's something you don't know about the way Richard and James died." He hesitated. "You should know the truth."

"No." She tore her hand away. "I don't want to know."

"But Agnes—"

"I don't want to know!" she screamed.

Andrew took her in his arms and held her. "All right," he said, trying to comfort her. "Shh. It's okay."

He did not understand, but she did not try to explain. What did it matter how Richard had died? All that mattered was that he was never coming back to her. That was burden enough for one woman. She could not bear to add to it the picture of her husband's last moments—the explosion, Richard bleeding, limbs torn off or blasted away, screams of agony ripping from his throat—she imagined too much without hearing Andrew's story.

He did not ask her again.

He left the next day. As far as Agnes could tell, he had not taken Claudia aside as he had Sylvia, as he had tried to do with her. She did not remember that until later, until years after Claudia's wedding.

For the longest time, Agnes blamed herself for the last fight between Claudia and Sylvia. Sylvia had become withdrawn, locked deeply in grief.

She had tried to help Claudia with her wedding plans, but after Andrew's visit, she seemed to lose all interest. If anything, she became hostile to Harold. Often Agnes saw her staring at him, brooding. Agnes would have sworn she saw hatred in Sylvia's eyes, and she did not understand it.

Eventually, Claudia sensed something, too. "She's jealous," she told Agnes as they worked on her wedding gown. "She can't bear knowing that my man came back and hers didn't."

Agnes felt a stabbing pain in her heart. Her man had not come back, either. She could only nod as she fought to hold back her tears. Claudia hadn't meant to hurt her. She still thought of Richard as her younger brother, not Agnes's late husband.

Agnes didn't think Sylvia was jealous, but she herself was. Secretly she resented Claudia, who would be able to grow old with the man she loved, who would bear his children and be allowed to love him. Agnes would never have that life.

When Claudia asked Agnes to be her bridesmaid, Agnes accepted, wondering why Claudia had not asked Sylvia first. But, of course, she had. When Sylvia learned of the change, she was stunned. Agnes blamed herself and fled the room in tears as their argument escalated. She heard their shouts, but from a distance she could not make out their words. She did not want to.

But something had been said in that argument, something that compelled Sylvia to leave that very day and not return.

"She'll be back," Claudia had said that day and every day for several weeks. "Where would she go? This is her home."

Agnes, who knew how certain words could prevent one from ever returning home, wasn't so sure.

Claudia's wedding day came, but to Agnes the occasion seemed shrouded in grief. First there was Sylvia's absence, then the overwhelming sense that Elm Creek Manor was not ready for a celebration, not so soon after so much death. And there was what Claudia had said to her moments before she walked up the aisle.

She was deathly pale as she turned to Agnes and asked, "Is it wrong for me to marry him? Will I regret this?"

Agnes was too shocked to speak. She could hear organ music coming from inside the church. It was almost time.

Claudia's eyes were distant. "Sylvia told me something the day she left, something about Harold—" She hesitated. "But she was always jealous of me. She never wanted me to have what she couldn't have." She turned a pleading gaze on Agnes. "Do you know any reason why I shouldn't marry Harold?"

"Only one." Agnes met her gaze solemnly. "What you're telling me right now. If you have any doubts at all about marrying Harold, then you should not walk down that aisle. Once you say those vows, it will be too late to change your mind."

Claudia's voice was barely audible. "It's too late already."

In the months that followed, Agnes came to wish she had not let Claudia leave that room.

At first, the newlyweds seemed so happy that Agnes convinced herself that Claudia's fears had been nothing more than a nervous bride's last-minute jitters. Claudia and Harold seemed suited for each other. It wasn't their marriage that Agnes worried about, but their behavior. They threw parties nearly every week, spending money enough to make up for all the restrictions of the war. They lived as if to fight off death, as if by laughing and dancing they could undo all the pain they had suffered. Agnes looked on in dismay and prayed for Sylvia's return.

Harold became the head of Bergstrom Thoroughbreds, but he neglected the business. Hungry for cash, he sold off prized horses for a fraction of their true value. He and Claudia spent the money frivolously, as if it were a game, as if Elm Creek ran green with cash instead of water. Fearing disaster, Agnes searched her memory for every bit of financial knowledge she had gleaned over the years from her father and his friends, but the couple rarely heeded her advice. Secretly, Agnes began to channel some of the money into stocks and bonds; Harold and Claudia were such poor accountants that they never noticed the missing funds.

They seemed happy, but as the first year passed, Agnes began to detect an odd note in the couple's conversations, an undercurrent of hostility and accusation in Claudia's tone, a sullen defensiveness in Harold's. Once, inexplicably, Claudia asked Agnes if Andrew had told her how Richard and James had died.

Her heart leaped into her throat. "No, he didn't," she said. "I wouldn't let him."

"Of course." Claudia laughed strangely. "Well, if it were true, if it were important, he would have insisted on telling you, right?"

Agnes did not know how to answer.

The cash reserves drained swiftly the second year. A day came when there were only three horses in the stable, and then two, and then none. Claudia dismissed the last remaining stable hands, some of whom had been with the family for decades.

Agnes saw to it that they left with enough money to tide them over for a year. Since she had no money of her own, she sold off some antique furniture to raise the funds. She picked pieces at random from the empty bedrooms, forbidding herself to wonder about their sentimental value to the Bergstrom family. The Middens, not the Bergstroms, ran Elm Creek Manor now, and they were running it into the ground.

She visited the antiques shop frequently, hating herself for selling off the Bergstrom legacy, knowing she had no choice. That was where she met Joe, a history professor at Waterford College. He occasionally appraised items for the store owner, and he admired the pieces Agnes brought in. One day he asked her if he could take her to lunch in exchange for the story of how she had come to find so many lovely pieces. She agreed. When she had told him everything, he offered to put her in touch with some of his colleagues in New York, who would be able to offer her a much better price than what she could obtain in Waterford. She was so grateful she threw her arms around him. He laughed and patted her on the back awkwardly, but he didn't seem offended.

Then Claudia and Harold began selling off the land.

Agnes fought for every acre, but each time a tract came up for auction, Claudia and Harold reminded her that they had no other source of income.

"Sell one last parcel and invest the cash," she begged them. "Live off the dividends. Economize."

They ignored her.

She pleaded with Claudia to ask Sylvia to return. Claudia flew into a rage and shouted that they did not need anyone's help, least of all her hateful sister's.

Agnes knew she had to act or there would be nothing left. She did it for Richard, and she did it for Sylvia, in case she ever came home, so she would have a home to return to.

She found as many of the remaining deeds as she could; Joe helped her find the right lawyer. With his help, Agnes transferred the deeds into Sylvia's name so that as long as Sylvia lived, no one but she could sell those properties. Agnes replaced the old deeds with the new ones, berating herself for not thinking of this earlier. As the third year began, the Middens were finally thwarted. They could not touch the area that Agnes had saved, the acres bordered by forest and gardens to the north, Elm Creek to the south and east, and the orchard to the west. They blamed Mr. Bergstrom, never suspecting Agnes's role. No one but she, Joe, and the lawyer ever knew of it.

With no more land to sell, the period of frenzied gaiety came to an abrupt halt. The last remaining servants were fired. Claudia and Harold began to argue. Agnes threw herself into the cultivation of the orchard. It was their only source of income aside from Agnes's investments, which she claimed Mr. Bergstrom had made. They didn't check her story.

Agnes had nearly forgotten Andrew's untold story when Claudia mentioned it again. She told Agnes about Sylvia's accusations, that Harold had been responsible for Richard's and James's deaths.

"Do you think it could be true?" Claudia asked, her voice distant.

"I don't know." But Agnes knew Andrew would not have invented such a horrible tale, and she doubted Sylvia would have, either. Now she understood why Sylvia had gone away, and she longed to do so herself. But she could not. She had not completed her education, so she had no way to support herself. She could not return to her parents, and her pride was too great to allow her to seek help from her Philadelphia acquaintances. She was trapped in that dying house, and she saw no way out of it.

That night she was awakened by the sound of Claudia shrieking and Harold sobbing. At last Claudia had confronted him, and he had admitted the truth. Agnes pulled the covers over her head as if she were a little girl, but she could not block out the fighting.

The next day Claudia moved to another bedroom in the west wing, as far away from Harold's room as possible. After that, they no longer lived as husband and wife. They spoke only when necessary and spent little time in each other's company. Agnes thought she would drown in their silence. After a few months, she asked Claudia why they did not simply separate.

"It is my penance," she said, and never spoke of it again.

Once again Agnes felt surrounded by madness, madness she alone could see.

When Joe asked her to marry him, she hardly dared hope that he meant it. His proposal sent a shaft of light into the dark room that was her life. She told him, honestly, cruelly, that she would never love him as she had loved Richard. Joe said he had enough love for both of them. No one had ever spoken to her so kindly or offered her so much while expecting so little in return.

Claudia begged Agnes not to abandon her, for living with Harold without Agnes there would be worse than living alone. Her pleas pained Agnes, but she proceeded to show Claudia the household budget and accounts. When Claudia saw that Agnes would not be persuaded, she resorted to threats. "If you leave, you can forget about your inheritance," she shouted. "If you betray my brother's memory, you forfeit his share of the estate!"

Agnes looked at her with genuine pity. "Oh, Claudia," she said. "Do you really think that's why I stayed so long?"

She married Joe, and not a day went by that she didn't thank God for bringing him into her life. She grew to love him sooner than she would have dreamed possible, and if she never felt the passion for him that she once had for Richard, she never regretted her decision. Joe gave her love, a home, and two beautiful children. She learned that she could love again, and she knew, somehow, that Richard was happy for her.

But Claudia and Harold lived out their days in bitterness. Agnes mourned them long before they passed away.

Now she, Andrew, and Sylvia were the only ones left from those old days. Sylvia had stayed away for more than fifty years, returning only after Claudia died. Even before their reunion, Agnes was proud that Elm Creek Manor was still there to take Sylvia in. She knew she ought to be grateful that she and Sylvia had been given the past two years to reconcile.

But she was not grateful. She was angry. Two years was not enough. God owed her a reprieve. The God who had taken Richard, who had taken James, who had taken so much from the Bergstrom family, could not, must not, take Sylvia, not yet. Not yet. It was too soon. It would always be too soon.

It was the angriest prayer she had ever made, but she meant every whispered word of it. Then, her anger spent, she sat with her friends and waited.

They all looked up when the doctor entered. They rose as one and waited for him to approach. In the seconds it took him to cross the floor, Agnes tried to read his expression, but his face gave away nothing.

Not until the very last moment, when he smiled.

Fourteen

She pulled through," the doctor said, smiling. "Thank God," Sarah murmured. Her knees felt weak. If not for Matt's arm around her waist, she would have fallen.

"When can we see her?" Andrew asked.

"In a few minutes. She'll be a little groggy for a while. Don't be alarmed if she doesn't respond when you speak to her." The doctor hesitated. "Mrs. Compson suffered a cerebral thrombosis. That means that a blood clot formed in an artery carrying blood to her brain, blocking the flow."

"Did you use TPA?" Carol asked.

"Actually, yes, we did. It was a viable option in Mrs. Compson's case, especially since we were able to treat her so soon after the onset of the attack." He turned to the others. "TPA is tissue plasminogen activator, a drug that dissolves blood clots like the one Mrs. Compson had. TPA has its risks, but the benefits of treatment far outweigh the dangers. Ideally, TPA will clear the blockage and allow the blood flow to resume."

"Ideally?" Matt echoed. "Has it worked for Sylvia?"

"It looks promising at this point, but we'll have to wait and see."

It looks promising, Sarah repeated silently, relief washing over her. *Thank God.*

The doctor continued. "Later we'll have to discuss her long-term care and rehabilitation, but I'm sure you'd like to see her first."

Sarah started to follow him out of the waiting room, but then she stopped short. "Wait a minute. Long-term care? Rehabilitation?" She looked from the doctor to Carol and back, heart sinking. They looked at her with such compassion and regret that she knew at once she had felt relieved too soon. Something wasn't quite right, something they knew that she didn't.

Carol took her hands. "Honey, recovery from a stroke can be a long and difficult process."

Sarah stared at the doctor. "But—but you said she pulled through."

"She did pull through," the doctor said. His voice was kind. "She will live. However, it's too soon to tell how much damage her brain has sustained."

Carol stroked a lock of hair away from Sarah's face. "Sarah, honey, when the clot blocked the artery, it prevented blood from reaching parts of the brain. If those parts die, they don't regenerate."

"Rehabilitation can help," the doctor said, trying to reassure her. "Typically, spontaneous recovery in the first month accounts for most of a stroke patient's regained skills, but rehabilitation is still very important. It might even mean that Mrs. Compson can return home rather than be institutionalized."

"Oh, my God." Suddenly, Sarah's world went gray, and her legs buckled beneath her. She felt Matt helping her into a chair. Someone placed a paper cup of water in her hands. By instinct she clasped her fingers around it, but her hands shook so violently that she spilled the water all over herself. Her teeth chattered. Someone took the cup away and ordered her to take slow, deep breaths. She tried to cooperate, but when she closed her eyes she pictured Sylvia slumped over in a wheelchair, staring into the distance, lifeless.

"I thought—" She struggled with the words. "When you said she pulled through, I thought—" She thought that meant Sylvia would be fine. How stupid of her. Of course she knew the devastating effects of stroke. She should have prepared herself. God, she was so stupid. They were only through the most frightening part of this ordeal. The most difficult part was still before them.

What if Sylvia never fully recovered?

Carol put one arm across her daughter's shoulders and grasped Sarah's arm with her other hand. "Come on," she said. "Let's go see Sylvia."

Panic flashed through her. "I can't." She tore free from her mother's embrace. "I can't."

Andrew studied her, concerned. "Sylvia will want to see you most of all."

Sarah shook her head as hot tears began to streak her face. "I can't."

Andrew began to speak, but Carol shook her head at him. "Later, maybe," she said. "You three go ahead."

"I'll be right back, Sarah," Matt said as he followed Andrew and Agnes after the doctor. "I'll let you know how she is."

Sarah nodded and wrapped the twisted hem of her T-shirt around her right hand. This was her fault. It was all her fault.

✢

When Matt and Sarah dropped Agnes off at home later that day, she felt as if she had aged a hundred years. Sylvia had looked so still and small in that bed that Agnes had hardly recognized her. And the way Andrew held her hand and spoke to her so gently—it was enough to break Agnes's heart.

They would not know for some time how much of Sylvia would return to them. It was too soon to tell, the doctor had said.

Agnes hadn't eaten all day, and her stomach growled with hunger. It didn't seem right that the normal processes of life should continue as if nothing had happened. Somehow, Sylvia's stroke should have brought everything to a standstill as the world waited, holding its breath, to see what would become of her.

Sylvia would not deal well with incapacity. If she could not walk, if she could not speak, if she could not quilt again, she might hate the doctors for saving her life. She might hate her friends for letting them. As long as Agnes had known her, Sylvia had hidden her weaknesses, her vulnerabilities. She had always found her identity in being the strong one of the family. Now she would have to acknowledge her weakness and let others be strong for her. Would she be able to? Would she let her doctors and her friends help her? Or would she let this stroke win?

No. That didn't sound like the Sylvia Agnes knew. Sylvia hated to lose. So often Sylvia's stubborn streak had been her undoing. This time it could be her salvation.

Agnes heated a can of vegetable soup, made some toast, and ate her supper as she read the morning headlines. More bombings, more political nonsense, more children suffering all over the world. She sighed and pushed the paper away.

She cleared away the dishes, put the leftover soup in the refrigerator, and wondered what to do next. In her heart, she longed to be at Sylvia's side. She should have stayed there with Andrew, but Carol had insisted she go home and rest. Agnes was tired, but she could not rest. She wanted to do something; she wanted to help. She should have gone to Elm Creek Manor to welcome the new campers. There would be so much work to do now, what with covering Sylvia's classes, leading the Candlelight—who would lead the Candlelight that evening? Surely not Sarah. She was so distraught she ought to be in a hospital bed herself. Thank God Carol was there to look after her.

Agnes felt the knot between her shoulder blades release for the first time all day. Yes, Carol was there. So were Matt, and Summer, and Gwen, and Judy, and Diane. She needn't worry. The Elm Creek Quilters would take care of everything. They could manage without her that night. Tomorrow she would join them and contribute whatever she could, but tonight she could rest.

She carried her sewing box out to the front porch and sat on the swing Joe had hung there so many years before. For a long while she pushed herself gently back and forth and listened to the sounds of the neighborhood. She had rocked her babies to sleep on that swing more times than she could count. After the children had been put to bed, she and Joe would return to the swing and hold hands as they talked about the day, their children, the future. It had been a good life with him, and she was grateful for it.

She took the round robin center from her sewing kit and finished piecing the last tree. She had chosen the colors of Elm Creek Manor—blues and greens, gold for sunlight, brown for earth and the strong trunks of the elms that had given the creek its name. The gray stone walls of the manor had taken shape beneath her fingers; the cotton was so much softer than the stone it represented, and yet it could endure so much.

It was an act of courage to take the scraps life provided and stitch them together, wrestling the chaos into order, taking what had been cast off and creating something from it, something useful, beautiful, and strong, something whose true value was known only to the heart of the woman who made it.

⚓

As twilight fell, the women formed a circle on the cornerstone patio. A few who had visited the manor before knew what was coming, but most waited, unknowing, anticipating, whispering questions to the women beside them, enjoying the stillness and peace of the night.

She lit a candle, placed it in a small crystal votive holder, and held it in silence for a moment, remembering how Sylvia had held that same light at the beginning of the summer. So much had happened since then. So much had yet to happen.

She sent up a quick prayer for Sylvia, inhaled deeply to calm herself, and looked around at the faces of the newest guests of Elm Creek Manor. The dancing flame cast light and shadow over them as they watched her and waited for her to speak.

"Elm Creek Manor is full of stories," she told them. "Some of these stories are joyful; some are full of regret; all are important. I have been lucky enough to call this beautiful place home for a little while, and now, for the week at least, Elm Creek Manor is your home, too. Now your stories will join those that are already here, and all of us will be richer for it."

Carol explained the ceremony and handed the candle to the first woman in the circle.

⚓

The first week was the most difficult. Gwen had never realized how much Sylvia and Sarah did behind the scenes to keep the quilt camp running. The

Elm Creek Quilters divided up Sylvia's classes and other managerial duties, but they felt as if they were running day and night, just barely keeping on top of all the work. How had Sarah and Sylvia made it look so easy?

Gwen had asked Sarah that same question, but Sarah just shrugged and made no reply, as if she hadn't really been listening. Gwen wasn't surprised; all week long, Sarah had shown little reaction to the events around her, including her work. Summer had all but taken over her role in the company.

"I'm worried about her," Summer confided late one night when she and Gwen finally went home after a long, exhausting day. "I'm trying to get her involved in camp to take her mind off things, but it's like she's on another planet."

Gwen worried about Sarah, too. She had withdrawn from her friends ever since Sylvia's attack, and the few times she did join them, she had a stricken, haunted look in her eyes. Inexplicably, she had not yet visited Sylvia in the hospital, even though the rest of them had done so several times each, and Sylvia asked for her frequently.

"Sarah will be all right," Gwen said, because she knew Summer needed to hear it. "She just needs some time. This has been a shock for her."

"For all of us." Suddenly, Summer threw her arms around her mother. "I don't ever want anything like this to happen to you, okay? You have to get regular checkups, and if there's even the slightest warning sign of anything, you have to get help, understand?"

Gwen hugged her and patted her on the back. "I hear and obey, kiddo."

She stroked Summer's hair and told her everything was going to be all right, that Sylvia would be fine, and so would Sarah. As she said the words aloud, she began to believe them.

⚜

Late Thursday afternoon, Bonnie drove home from Elm Creek Manor exhausted and drained. All of the Elm Creek Quilters were worn to a frazzle, their nerves shot. There was so much to do and never enough time to get it all done. Bonnie felt as if she had been running a marathon barefoot, with the finish line still far off in the distance at the top of a steep hill. If they could just get through this week of camp, they would have Saturday afternoon to rest and recover. Surely next week would go more smoothly, once they worked out some of the bumps.

Bonnie was now teaching four classes a week, in addition to running Grandma's Attic. Even with Summer's help, it was too much. She felt as if she were being pulled in three different directions at once. All she wanted to do was rest, go to sleep and not wake up until Sylvia was better.

She stopped by the shop to help Summer close for the day. It took them longer than usual, for they could no longer put off organizing the fabric bolts and tidying the shelves. When Bonnie finally did drag herself upstairs, she decided that they'd have to get take-out for supper. She was too weary to make even something as simple as pasta. It would be the fourth time this week they'd ordered out. She hoped Craig wouldn't mind.

When she opened the door, the delicious smells of cooking floated on the air, momentarily confusing her. Had she started dinner already and forgotten? She went to the kitchen, only to find Craig peering into the oven. The kitchen counter was littered with pans and Styrofoam meat trays and spice jars.

"What on earth?" Bonnie exclaimed, taking in the scene.

Craig jumped, startled, and shut the oven. "Hi, honey," he said, coming forward to kiss her on the cheek. "Dinner will be another fifteen minutes or so. I think. The recipe on the back of the soup can called it 'Easy Twenty-Minute Chicken,' but I think that's a typo. It's taken me forty minutes already." He shrugged and smiled. "Of course, I haven't done this in a while, so maybe it's me. The table's already set, so why don't you go change out of your work clothes and lie down for a while? I'll call you when it's ready."

Bonnie promptly burst into tears.

Craig looked alarmed. "What is it?" Then he glanced over his shoulder at the mess. "Oh. Don't worry about it, honey. I'll clean it up after we eat."

"It's not that," she managed to say. She hugged him and cried, feeling foolish and unexpectedly relieved. She had held it together throughout that difficult week, and now here she was, weeping like a crazy woman in the middle of her filthy kitchen, and all because her husband had made supper.

⚜

Sylvia was getting better—that was the one bright spot of the week. She could sit up in bed now, and she was awake and alert. There was some lingering paralysis on the left side of her body, and it was difficult for her to speak clearly. Judy had visited her earlier in the day, but had left feeling frustrated and upset. She could not understand a word Sylvia spoke, and it rattled her. Andrew understood everything and had translated Sylvia's muffled, slurred speech for her, but that only made Judy feel worse, ashamed, as if she had failed Sylvia somehow. By failing to understand Sylvia's speech, Judy had made it impossible to pretend that Sylvia was just fine. She hated herself for it.

"You'll understand more when you get used to it," Andrew had told her privately. "Sylvia's getting better every day. She's not upset with you, so don't you be upset with yourself, okay?"

She nodded, but she couldn't change her feelings like switching off a light.

She was so tired. They all were, worn out from work and from worry. Once Sylvia came home, everything would be so much easier. Even if she couldn't resume her normal activities, her presence would bring the Elm Creek Quilters much-needed comfort and reassurance.

When Judy got home, she heard voices coming from the kitchen—Steve and someone else, a woman. As she walked down the hall, Judy thought the second voice sounded familiar, but she couldn't quite place it.

When she reached the kitchen, she immediately recognized the blond woman sitting across the table from Steve. "Kirsten?"

The conversation broke off as Kirsten and Steve looked up. "Hi, Judy," Kirsten said, rising. She came over and embraced her.

Judy returned the hug, her thoughts in a whirl. "Hi. What are—what are you doing here?" Her utter bewilderment kept her words from sounding rude.

"Steve called and told me about your friend. I have a couple of weeks off before summer session begins at UW, so I decided to come and see if I could help."

"But I thought you were in pediatrics," Judy said. "How can you help take care of Sylvia?"

Kirsten smiled, her face full of understanding and sympathy. "I didn't come to take care of Sylvia. I came to take care of you."

At that moment, Judy realized that she truly did have a sister.

※

On Wednesday of the third week, Sylvia came home. Andrew had worried about getting her up those stairs, so he was relieved when Carol suggested they make the west sitting room into a bedroom for her. "Temporarily, of course," Carol added. "She'll be up and around in no time."

"That's a good idea," Matt said. "This way Sylvia won't feel like she's shut away in a sickroom. She'll be able to be in the center of things."

Carol didn't reply, but Andrew caught something unexpected in her gaze when she looked at Matt—surprise, or maybe even respect. This was quite a change from what Andrew had observed between them since his arrival at Elm Creek Manor. Usually, Carol pretended Matt wasn't in the room.

Matt and Andrew removed one of the sofas and replaced it with a twin bed from one of the second-floor suites. Carol took care of arranging everything else, so when they finally brought Sylvia home, the pleasant, cheery room right off the kitchen was ready for her. She seemed pleased by the surprise, but said she was tired and wanted to rest.

Andrew left the room while Carol helped Sylvia into bed. When Carol went to the kitchen to help Diane prepare lunch, Andrew returned and sat down on the edge of the bed.

Sylvia seemed agitated, and Andrew thought he knew why. "Don't get too comfortable in here," he said. "You'll be back upstairs in your old room soon." He knew he had guessed correctly when her shoulders relaxed and the strain around her eyes eased.

She wanted to sit up in bed, so he helped her arrange her pillows. She asked for something, but he couldn't quite make out the words. She patted the bedcovers, exasperated. "Quilt. Quilt." After a few more exchanges, he understood. She wanted a different quilt, one that was in her bedroom.

He went upstairs to Sylvia's room, took the quilt off the bed, and brought it back down to her. "This one?"

She shook her head. "No. Scrap quilt."

"But this is a scrap quilt." He studied it. "Isn't it?"

"Wrong one."

Andrew made two more trips up and down the stairs before he found the quilt Sylvia wanted. It was an older quilt, and it had been wrapped in a clean white sheet and tucked away in the back of her closet. "Why do I suspect you hid this quilt ahead of time just so you could enjoy watching me hunt around for it?' he said as he spread the quilt over her. He had never seen the pattern before, not that he had seen many quilts before his return to Elm Creek Manor. The design almost resembled a star, but the sewing lacked the precision he usually saw in Sylvia's work. The pieces of fabric looked like they had come from old clothing. He even thought he saw a few velvets and corduroys in there.

Sylvia stroked the quilt and sighed, comfortable at last. She thanked him with a look, then gave him another command: "Quilt scraps."

For a moment he felt a sharp sting of worry. "You have the quilt already, Sylvia. This is the last scrap quilt in your room. You know that."

The exasperation in her expression told him he was the one who was confused. "Not scrap quilt. Quilt scraps." She jerked her head toward the corner of the room, where he spotted the tackle box she used to store her sewing tools. He brought it to her and helped her open the latch. She took out a plastic bag of quilt pieces, diamonds in different shades of blue, purple, and green.

"Need any help?" Andrew asked, watching her fumble to open the bag.

She shook her head and waved him off.

"Okay then." He went to the kitchen for the newspaper and brought it back into the sitting room, where he settled into a chair near the window. As he read, he kept an eye on Sylvia. Several slow minutes passed as she struggled to pin two diamonds together using only her right hand. He felt a pang, realizing that before the attack she would have completed the task in seconds without a thought.

Finally she finished. She sat back against her pillow before moving on to the next task. She didn't complain, but he could sense her frustration as she tried to thread the needle. She had stuck the point of the needle into her bedcovers and was trying to jab the end of thread into the eye. Her left arm hung by her side, forgotten. That didn't seem right. He had seen boys in the war whose paralyzed limbs grew thin and wasted from disuse. Sylvia needed to work that arm if she ever wanted to use it again.

He'd have to ask her physical therapist for advice so he didn't make things worse, but for now, he had to do something. He set the paper on the floor and stood up. Sylvia looked up at him as he returned to his seat on the edge of her bed.

"Take the end of the thread in your left hand," he instructed.

She held up the thread defiantly, firmly clasped between her right thumb and forefinger.

"What are you, a wise guy? Your other left." Andrew took the spool of thread from her and placed it on her lap, giving her a teasing smile. "Don't tell me you're chicken."

She let out a scoffing laugh and reached for the thread with her left hand. It took an effort, but before long she was holding it.

"Good." Andrew found a pair of scissors in the tackle box and snipped off the frayed end of the thread. "Now, pick up the needle in your right hand."

She did so, and by force of habit brought the end of the thread toward her lips to wet it.

"Not the thread," Andrew said. "Wet the eye of the needle." She eyed him, dubious. "Trust me." She did so. "Now, hold the thread upright and move the eye of the needle over it."

Concentrating, hands trembling, Sylvia followed his instructions. After several attempts, she slid the needle onto the thread. He was so pleased for her he thought he might shout for joy.

She looked up and caught his eye, grinning. "Men don't sew."

"That's true. And women don't run businesses."

Sylvia burst into laughter. The sound brought Carol and Diane running. "What happened? What is it?" Diane asked. The two women hovered in the doorway, concerned and anxious.

"Nothing," Sylvia said. "Go make lunch."

After a long pause, they reluctantly withdrew, whispering questions to each other as Sylvia and Andrew returned to their work.

❧

The physical therapist agreed that quilting could be an important part of Sylvia's therapy, so she added it to the routine. As the weeks passed, Sylvia slowly pieced her quilt top, and even more slowly regained the abilities the stroke had stolen from her. At least that's how it seemed to Diane, but she was impatient. She wanted to see Sylvia walking briskly around the manor again, helping the students, running the camp, bossing them all around. It couldn't happen soon enough to suit her, and she knew Sylvia felt the same.

Eventually, Sylvia progressed from a slow shuffle around the sitting room to a careful walk around the first floor of the manor. Once she confided to Diane that as soon as she was able, she was going to run up those stairs and corner Sarah in the library, where the young woman spent virtually every waking moment these days. "She's been avoiding me," Sylvia said, with only a trace of a slur in her voice.

"Some people don't deal well with this kind of thing," Diane said, but Sylvia made a scoffing sound and shook her head. Sylvia was right; Sarah had been behaving oddly. It was one thing not to visit Sylvia in the hospital; many people had an aversion to those places. But Sarah wouldn't even come to the west sitting room, and she made the most unbelievable excuses to dodge Sylvia at mealtimes and other occasions. Each of the Elm Creek Quilters had asked her to go talk to Sylvia, and Diane had come right out and ordered her to, but Sarah refused, and she wouldn't explain why. Diane didn't understand it.

She also didn't understand why no one else was alarmed by the news that Sylvia planned to hang her Broken Star quilt in the foyer. "But that's where we planned to hang the round robin quilt," she told Bonnie as they prepared for a workshop. "All our work will go to waste if she wants to hang some other quilt there instead."

"We'll sort it out later," Bonnie assured her, smiling. "What counts is that Sylvia is quilting again."

Diane thought about it and decided Bonnie was right. What mattered was that Sylvia was persevering despite the obstacles she faced.

That Broken Star quilt might just be the most important one ever made at Elm Creek Manor.

❧

Matt wished he knew how to comfort Sarah, but how could he when she wouldn't tell him what was wrong? "I'm fine," she insisted, despite all evidence to the contrary, as she shut herself away in the library or set off on another solitary walk along Elm Creek. Matt longed to run after her, to take her by the hand and plead with her until she told him what was troubling her. Once there had been no secrets between them, but now it seemed that with each passing day, Sylvia grew stronger and Sarah drifted farther away from him.

Finally he couldn't bear it anymore. One evening after supper, he was standing in the kitchen when Sarah passed on her way to the back door. He followed and called to her from the back steps. She froze, but didn't turn around.

"What is it?" she asked, her voice hollow and so soft he barely heard her.

"We need to talk." He joined her on the gravel road leading to the bridge, but she wouldn't look up at him. "Can you come back inside?"

"I don't feel like talking." She looked off toward the barn. "I need to be alone."

"You're alone too much." He reached out and stroked her back. "Please. It'll only take a minute. I—I miss you."

She inhaled shakily, but said nothing.

"Will you please tell me what's wrong?" Gently, carefully, he took her in his arms. The top of her head barely reached his chin. She seemed so small and fragile as he held her that he wished he could hold her like that forever and never let anything hurt her.

"Nothing's wrong."

"Sarah, I know you too well to believe that." He kissed her on the top of the head and stroked her hair. "If nothing's wrong, why won't you go see Sylvia? She asks for you every day."

Sarah pulled away from him. "I can't."

"Why not?"

Instead of answering, she turned away and began to walk toward the bridge.

"Come on, Sarah." He took a few steps after her. "Don't leave. Talk to me."

"I'm sorry," she said over her shoulder as she broke into a run.

He was tempted to pursue her, but helplessness and worry rooted him in place. He watched as she disappeared into the trees on the other side of Elm Creek, wishing he knew what to do. He had never seen her like this before, so despairing, so alone.

As he returned to the manor, a small brown shape at the foot of the steps caught his eye. A faint memory tickled in the back of his mind as he nudged it with his foot. It was a soggy mess of brown paper and cardboard—and suddenly he recognized it. It was the carton of ice cream he had bought for Sylvia weeks ago. He had forgotten it there after the fight with Sarah.

Guilt stung him as he remembered what he had said to her. No wonder she wouldn't confide in him now. Sarah deserved better than what he'd given her that night—and not just that night. All spring he had been sulky and irritable, snapping at her and stalking off whenever things didn't go his way. Why should she trust him now, when he had let her down so many times in the past few months? Why should she ever forgive him?

Sarah deserved better.

Self-loathing and anger flooded him as he cleaned up the mess.

⚜

On a rainy Saturday afternoon in mid-June, Carol sat in her room writing a letter to her supervisor at Allegheny Presbyterian to explain that she planned to use the entire four months of her leave after all. She was tempted to ask for even more time, but she didn't want to push her luck.

She looked up at the sound of a knock on the door. "Come in," she called, hoping it was Sarah. To her surprise, Matt opened the door.

"May I speak with you?" he asked.

"Of course." She set down her pen and gestured to a nearby chair.

"I'm worried about Sarah," Matt said as he sat down. "She hasn't been sleeping well, she's lost weight, she talks about Sylvia all the time but never goes to see her. Do you think something's wrong, something serious?"

He looked so distressed that Carol's heart went out to him. "She loves Sylvia very much," she said gently. "This ordeal has upset her."

"If that's all it is, shouldn't Sarah be getting better now that Sylvia's made so much progress? There's something else wrong, I just know it." He shook his head, his brow furrowed. "I want to help, but she won't tell me what's wrong. I thought since you're her mom, she might be willing to talk to you."

Carol felt a flicker of pride beneath her worry. Matt actually thought she and Sarah were close enough to have heart-to-heart talks, that Sarah would confide in her mother what she wouldn't tell her husband. "I'll talk to her," she promised, and watched as relief came over her son-in-law's face.

Matt thanked her and left. For a long while Carol sat in silence, her gaze fixed on the doorway. The past weeks had shown her a man she had not seen before. Without fail, Matt had treated Sarah with compassion and gentleness despite her inexplicable behavior. There were no orders for her to cheer up, no bitter reminders that he had been right to worry about their dependence upon an elderly woman, no complaints about the additional duties he had been forced to assume. He was so unlike Kevin that Carol wondered how she ever could have seen any similarity between the two men. Instead of manipulating the recent events to his own advantage, to score points in the battle of wills, Matt had set aside the old disagreements for the sake of his wife. His behavior was all Carol could have hoped for.

She had misjudged him.

She sighed and left the room. Someday soon she would make it up to him, to both of them, but for now, she had to see to Sarah.

The library was the most logical place to begin the search. Sarah spent nearly all her time there these days, staring at the computer or at the cold, dark fireplace. Sometimes she left the manor without telling anyone and disappeared for hours. Carol had watched from the window once and saw her daughter cross Elm Creek and vanish into the woods, but where she went from there, no one knew. Everyone needed private time, but Sarah had been spending far too much time alone. Matt was right. It was long past time someone spoke to her about it.

When Carol opened the library door, she saw that the lights were off and the draperies were pulled over the windows. The only illumination came from the computer. Sarah sat motionless before it, leaning toward the screen, her hands flat on the desktop, as if they alone held her upright.

Carol softly closed the door behind her. "Sarah?"

She didn't respond.

"Sarah, honey?" Carol said, raising her voice slightly.

Sarah looked up slowly, and the sight of her wrenched at Carol's heart. She looked as if she hadn't eaten or slept for days, and her face was drawn and haunted. "Oh, sweetie," Carol said, stricken. She swallowed and forced her voice into a nurse's brisk tone. "You're going straight to bed, and when you get up, I'm going to fix you something to eat. What would you like, soup and a sandwich, maybe?"

"I'm not hungry," Sarah said distantly, returning her gaze to the computer screen. "I can't rest. I have work to do."

"Surely it can wait. Nothing is so urgent that it can't wait an hour or two." Or five or six, if Carol had her way.

"This can't wait," Sarah whispered. "This is important. This is urgent."

Carol came closer, near enough to see that Sarah was running an internet search. "What are you looking for?"

"Information about stroke."

"Oh." Carol hesitated, watching as Sarah highlighted some text on the screen and clicked the mouse. "Are you trying to find something to help Sylvia?"

"Yes." Sarah's voice shook. "I'm also looking for the causes, to see if stress, or a fight—to see if being upset can do it, if it can make someone—"

"Oh, Sarah." Carol ached to see her daughter in such pain. "You didn't make Sylvia have that stroke."

Sarah took a shallow, quavering breath. "I think maybe I did."

"You didn't." Carol put herself between Sarah and the computer screen, shaking her head. "You didn't. That's not how it works. It wasn't your fault. It was never your fault."

Sarah looked up at her mother for a long, silent moment before she began to sob. Carol bent down and embraced her, and Sarah clung to her as she hadn't since she was a child. Carol brought her away from the computer over to the sofa, where she held her and rocked her back and forth, and told her that everything was going to be all right. Everything would be fine.

⚜

Sarah felt better after her mother described Sylvia's progress. Sarah had noted some of these improvements from a distance, but she had been too ashamed to visit Sylvia and talk to her about them. That needed to change.

When she felt strong enough, she dried her tears, washed her face, and went downstairs to find Sylvia. She was out on the veranda with Andrew. The rain, though just a gentle shower, had been enough to keep them under shelter. When Andrew saw Sarah hesitate some distance away, he offered to get Sylvia a cup of tea. As he passed Sarah on his way into the manor, he paused long enough to clasp her shoulder and smile encouragingly.

Sylvia's gaze followed Andrew as he went inside, and her eyebrows rose when she spotted Sarah. "Well," she said, straightening in her chair. "Look who it is."

Sarah took a hesitant step forward. "Hi."

"Hi yourself." Sylvia returned her attention to the Broken Star quilt pieces in her lap.

"How are you feeling?"

"Oh, just fine, thank you." She gave Sarah a sidelong glance. "You can come closer. It's not contagious."

Sarah took the chair Andrew had left. "How's the quilt coming along?"

"Slowly but surely. I'll be ready to layer it soon." She let her hands fall to her lap and regarded Sarah over the top of her glasses. "I suppose next you'll be asking me what I think about the weather."

Sarah gave her a wan smile. "How did you know?"

"I know all sorts of things about you, Sarah McClure."

"There are a few things I'd just as soon have you forget."

"Hmph." A smile flickered in the corners of Sylvia's mouth as she resumed her work.

Sarah watched as she pinned a green and a blue diamond together, her movements slow and deliberate, but confident. "Do you want me to thread the needle for you?"

"No, thank you. That would be cheating. My therapist wants me to practice my hand-eye coordination. Michael and Todd offered to let me borrow their video games, but I declined."

Sarah laughed, but then she could think of nothing else to say. How could she explain why she had neglected her friend for so long? How could she ever express how sorry she was for the awful things she had said? How could she even begin to describe the terror she had felt watching Sylvia collapse, and the grief and loneliness she felt every time she thought about losing her?

"Sylvia," she began, "I'm sorry. I wish I could—"

"All is forgiven, dear." Sylvia reached over and patted her hand. "Let's not waste any more time on our silly misunderstandings. I'm going to be fine. Let's be grateful for that and be friends again, shall we?"

Sarah's heart was full. "I'd like that very much."

"Good." Sylvia gave her hand one last brisk pat before she picked up her quilt pieces again. They sat in silence for a long moment, listening to the gentle fall of rain on the veranda roof.

Then Sylvia spoke. "Did I ever tell you that when Andrew first saw you on television, he thought you were my granddaughter?"

"No." Sarah inhaled deeply, then breathed out what felt like a lifetime's worth of grief and regret. "You never told me that."

"Well, it's true. That's what he said."

"I think that's just about the nicest compliment I've ever received."

"I'm sure it's not the nicest one," Sylvia scoffed, but a faint tremor in her voice betrayed her true feelings.

When Andrew returned with Sylvia's tea, Sarah left the two alone and returned inside. She walked through the manor to the back door, intending to go to her secret place beneath the willow on Elm Creek, but then she thought of another place she'd rather be. As soon as she thought of it, the urgency to be there spurred her on, so that she hurried out the back door without bothering to put on her raincoat. She ran across the bridge, along the gravel road past the barn, beyond it to the orchard, where she knew she would find Matt.

She searched the rows until she spotted him. She almost didn't see him, so well did his earth-tone rain poncho blend into the trees around him. He was checking the soil at the base of a newly planted sapling when Sarah called his name.

"Sarah?" he called out in disbelief, rising as she approached. "What are you doing out here without your jacket? You're soaked." Then he grew alarmed. "Is something wrong? Are you all right?"

It was only then that Sarah noticed how the cool rain had soaked her clothing and plastered her hair to her face, and she suddenly felt self-conscious and foolish. "I'm fine," she said. "I just—" She broke off and shrugged. "I missed you."

His expression grew serious. Sarah held very still as he walked through the mud toward her.

"I missed you, too."

Then he wrapped his arms around her and held her close.

❦

As the June days lengthened and the dark nights grew milder, Sylvia finished piecing her Broken Star quilt. She layered and basted it by hand, by ritual, each step performed methodically, patiently. This quilt was not meant for a quilt frame, where her friends would pitch in and help her finish it in a fraction of the time. No, this was one project she could not rush. She would quilt it alone, in a hoop held snugly on her lap. Her friends could support and encourage her in her work, as she knew they would, but this quilt was hers alone to see through to the end.

It was just as well that she decided this, for her friends were already using the quilt frame for a project of their own, one made by many hands and with an abundance of love.

Fifteen

ylvia studied her face in the mirror, then tried to force her features into a smile. One side of her face moved naturally into place; the other did not. Sylvia sighed and pushed back the disobedient flesh with her fingertips. There. Now, if she could just think of some excuse to walk around with her hand on her face all day, she'd be fine.

She turned away from the mirror and reminded herself to focus on the gains she had made in the weeks since the stroke rather than dwell upon the little that had been lost. She had been able to return to her room on the second floor; she could walk with barely a stumble; her speech, though not as crisp as it had once been, was clear. Her quilting abilities had survived the experience virtually intact. She had even managed to finish her Broken Star quilt in time for the brunch the Elm Creek Quilters were having that Sunday morning as a farewell party for Carol and Andrew.

It was a shame they had chosen the same day to leave. Sylvia was thankful that the purpose for Carol's visit had at last been accomplished: Carol and Sarah had finally begun to resolve their differences. They still had more work to do, but the gulf between them had been bridged, and both seemed committed to the healing. Carol promised to return for a visit over the Christmas holidays, so they would be seeing her again soon.

As for Andrew—she did not know when she would see him again. He had stayed so much longer than he had intended, and recently his daughter had been phoning every week to ask when she should expect him. Sylvia understood that he had obligations elsewhere, commitments to fulfill. She knew that he had to leave, but she would miss him.

She sighed again and sat down in a chair by the window. The summer had come to Elm Creek Manor at last. It was hard to remember, sometimes, that those dark green hills had ever been covered with snow, that in the mornings the sound of wind in the bare elms had woken her rather than birdsong. She thought she could still detect the fragrance of apple blossoms on the breeze, though she knew the orchards were past flowering for the year. The trees had grown thick and lush so that she could barely see the barn on the other side of Elm Creek through the leaves.

Except for the newly paved parking lot behind the manor, the scene from her bedroom window was unchanged from the time she was a young girl greeting the days with a heart full of happiness and expectation. An entire summer day would have awaited her, full of promise and fun. If Richard wanted, she would take him riding; together they would head out to the far edge of the estate that Hans Bergstrom had established so many years ago. If Sylvia was in an especially good mood, she might have invited Claudia to join them—if only because Claudia would pack them a picnic lunch. The sisters and brother would spend the whole day outdoors, returning hours later, hungry and happy, just in time for supper. Later that evening, Sylvia would steal off alone to her favorite place on the estate, a large, flat stone beneath a willow on the bank of Elm Creek, where she would listen to the murmur of the water flowing over rocks and watch the fireflies as the stars came out far overhead. And she would dream of her future, and plan, and wish, and promise herself that she would travel and have adventures and fall in love with a handsome man who liked horses, but she would always come back to this place, to Elm Creek Manor, to home.

Would she be able to find that stone again, that willow, if she searched for them? Should she even try? Perhaps it would be better to leave the past in the past and embrace the future that she had almost not been granted. She did not want to seem ungrateful to the fate that had given her so many second chances.

A tap on her door interrupted her reverie. "Are you watching for our friends?" Agnes asked.

Sylvia turned away from the window and smiled. "No, just enjoying the view."

"It's a beautiful day." Agnes crossed the room and peered outside. "A beautiful day for a drive, don't you agree?"

Sylvia said nothing.

Agnes sat down in the opposite chair. "It's a shame Andrew has to leave so soon."

"Hmph. I'm surprised he stayed as long as he did. His daughter in Connecticut has been asking for his visit for weeks now."

Agnes reached over and took her hand. "Sylvia, Andrew will stay if you ask him to."

"I couldn't possibly."

"He wants you to."

For a moment Sylvia was too startled to speak. "I couldn't. I couldn't impose on him like that. I can't have him staying on because he feels sorry for me."

"That isn't how he feels, and that's not why he'd stay."

Sylvia hesitated, then nodded. For several weeks now, she had been unable to ignore her growing affection for Andrew. Ever since he had sat on the edge of her bed and helped her remember how to quilt, she had known his heart as plainly as her own. It was nonsense, she had told herself, for a woman her age to be falling in love—but that was not what had held her back.

When she spoke, her voice was thick with emotion. "He isn't my James."

Agnes's eyes were warm with compassion. "He doesn't have to be."

Sylvia pressed her lips together and nodded. Yes. Of course, Agnes was right. James had loved her too much to begrudge her this. He would not have wanted her to live without love for so long.

Agnes squeezed her hand and smiled. "Let's go downstairs and wait for the others, shall we?"

Arm in arm, the two women went downstairs to the kitchen, where Sarah and Carol were preparing the meal. They offered to help, but the mother and daughter assured them everything was nearly ready. While Agnes sat down at the kitchen table to chat, Sylvia excused herself and went outside.

She spotted Andrew from the back steps. He had raised the hood on his motor home and was peering inside. Sylvia felt a surge of hope as she approached him, for surely engine trouble would require him to postpone his departure. But as she drew closer, her heart sank. He was only putting a quart of oil in the motor.

"All ready to leave, I see," she said briskly, forcing a smile onto her face.

Andrew glanced up from his work. "Not quite ready."

"It was very nice having you with us for so long." Sylvia wished she could retrieve her words. She could have been talking to the meter man for all the warmth in her voice.

"I'm glad I came." He emptied the last of the oil, checked the level with the dipstick, and shut the hood. He set the bottle on the ground and wiped his fingers on a rag, watching her all the while.

"Will it be a long drive?"

"Too long." He tossed the rag onto the empty bottle and smiled. "I've gotten comfortable, staying in one place so long. It won't be easy getting used to the road again."

"I suppose it wouldn't be." She hesitated. "Perhaps you shouldn't. What I mean is, it's a shame for you to make such a long, hard drive when you could, perhaps, just stay here instead."

His eyebrows rose. "Stay here? For good?"

"Well—" Sylvia hesitated. "Well, yes. For good, or for as long as you wish. I wasn't planning to lock you in."

"Does that mean I can have a room?"

"Of course you can have a room. You always could have had a room. You're the one who insisted on staying in—in—" She gestured toward the motor home. "In this thing. That wasn't my idea."

He folded his arms and leaned back against the grill, studying her. "Would you like me to stay?"

"Of course I would." He was making this very difficult. "Would I have invited you if I didn't want you to stay?"

He shrugged, thoughtful. "No, I suppose not." He rubbed at his chin. "My daughter will be disappointed if I cancel my visit."

Sylvia felt a sharp stab of regret. "Oh. Of course. I understand." She gave him a tight smile and turned so he wouldn't see her expression change. "Well, brunch won't be much longer. I'll see you inside."

"Wait." He caught her by the arm before she could leave. "What I meant was, I can't cancel my visit, but I'll come right back afterward."

"You will?"

"I'll just be gone a week or two." His hands were light and strong on her shoulders. "Why don't you come with me? I'd like for you to meet my daughter and my grandkids. Maybe later this summer we could even head out to the West Coast and I'll introduce you to my son."

Her breath caught in her throat. "Why, that sounds like a fine idea. I'd like to meet your family."

"And I'd like them to meet you."

They held each other's gaze for a moment before Andrew kissed her. She was so startled that for an instant she just stood there, frozen—but then she kissed him back.

Then he offered her his arm and escorted her inside.

When their friends arrived, they gathered in the dining room around the table Sarah and Carol had prepared. For Sylvia, the entire day had been transformed now that she would not have to say good-bye to Andrew. The day she'd thought would be filled with partings and loneliness now marked the beginning of what felt like her next grand adventure.

She looked around the table at the smiling faces of her dear, dear friends and knew with all her heart that no woman had ever been so richly blessed.

When the meal was over, everyone helped clear away the dishes; then, at Sylvia's suggestion, they gathered on the veranda. While her friends seated themselves, Sylvia remained standing. "If you'll excuse me, I have to fetch something."

"Wait," Diane said. "Don't rush off. We have to show you something."

"I have to show you something, too," Sylvia called over her shoulder as she returned inside. She retrieved the bag and the folder from the ballroom, where she had left them earlier that day. She couldn't wait to see her friends' faces when she gave them her news.

When she returned to the veranda, all her friends had arranged their chairs around the one Sylvia usually chose, and on that chair rested a large white box.

"What on earth?" Sylvia exclaimed. She nearly dropped her own burdens she was so surprised. Her friends were beaming at her. "What is going on here?"

Sarah moved the box out of the way so Sylvia could sit down. "It's a surprise."

Sylvia took her seat. "But I have a surprise for you, too." Sarah tried to hand her the box, but Sylvia's arms were full. "Goodness, where should we begin?"

"You go first," Judy urged, and the others agreed.

"Well—" Sylvia composed herself. "Very well. I'll go first." She set the folder aside and opened the bag. "I finished my Broken Star quilt last night." Sarah and Carol came forward to help her unfold the quilt, and then other hands reached out to take a corner or an edge, holding the quilt open so all could admire it.

It was lovely; even Sylvia was not too modest to admit it.

The small blue, purple, and green diamonds had been joined together to form a large, eight-pointed star in the center of the quilt. Framing the star were large diamonds, identical to the eight sections of the star, each pieced from sixteen small diamonds. The arrangement of colors created the illusion that the star glowed, adding depth to the Celtic knotwork patterns quilted into the cloth.

Sylvia had made other quilts like it, but although these points were not as sharp as usual, nor the quilting stitches so fine and straight, she was prouder of this quilt than of any other she had ever made. This quilt was a testament not to her skills but to her courage, to her refusal to give up. She had hoped that her friends would understand that, because she wanted them to know what it would mean to her when this quilt hung in the foyer and welcomed their guests to Elm Creek Manor. She hoped her friends did not need her to explain, because what she had put into that quilt she did not think she could put into words.

"It's the most wonderful quilt I've ever seen," Sarah said softly, and when she looked up and met Sylvia's gaze, Sylvia knew that Sarah, at least, understood.

"It's lovely, but I hope you're not planning to hang it in the foyer," Diane said. Judy nudged her.

"That's precisely what I planned to do with it," Sylvia said. "Why do you object? I assure you, no machine touched this quilt."

Diane hesitated. "It's not that I object, not exactly—"

"Just give her the box," Gwen said, laughing.

Sarah handed it to Sylvia. "Here's our surprise for you."

Sylvia let her friends take the Broken Star quilt from her and accepted the box. Her friends drew closer as she removed the lid and moved the tissue paper aside.

Her fingers touched cloth, and Sylvia gasped.

In the box was a quilt almost the same size as the one she had made. Her eyes filled with tears as she unfolded it—oh, it was beautiful, simply beautiful. It was a medallion quilt, with borders in several different patterns: Square in a Square, Pinwheel, Mariner's Compass, and Crazy Patch. In the center was a portrait of Elm Creek Manor in appliqué, so painstaking and perfect that it surely must have been Agnes's handiwork. And the outermost border's whimsy spoke of Gwen, as the Mariner's Compass's precision did of Judy: every inch of that quilt bore signs of her dearest friends.

"You made this for me?" she finally managed to say. "It truly is the loveliest gift I've ever received." She looked around the circle. "Thank you all from the bottom of my heart. I'll cherish this always. Diane's right. This must be the quilt we hang in the foyer."

"No, we'll find another place for it," Bonnie said. "Your quilt should be the first one our campers see when they arrive at Elm Creek Manor. It represents everything we try to teach them about quilting—perseverance, setting goals, overcoming obstacles—"

"But your quilt does the same, only in a different way. Your quilt reminds us of cooperation, and friendship, and—"

"Who says we can only have one quilt on that wall?" Summer broke in. "Why don't we hang them both? There's plenty of room."

Gwen hugged her. "Didn't I tell you guys my daughter's a genius?"

"At least once a week for the past two decades," Diane said.

Everyone laughed, and the sound of their voices warmed Sylvia nearly as much as the beautiful quilt in her arms.

"Why don't we hang them now?" Matt suggested. The others chimed in their agreement and moved toward the door.

"Not just yet, if you please," Sylvia called out above the clamor. "I have a few more surprises for you."

She saw them exchange curious glances as they settled back into their seats. She picked up the folder and opened it on her lap, enjoying every extra moment she kept her friends in suspense.

"My attack gave me much to think about," Sylvia said. And so did that argument she had overheard between Sarah and Matthew, but she wouldn't remind them of that awful time. "I decided that it was time for me to put my affairs in order. I met with my lawyer several times in the past few weeks, and I've made some arrangements which I'm sure you'll find quite interesting."

Diane looked dubious. "Interesting in a good way, I hope."

"Oh, most definitely." Sylvia turned to the first page in the folder and put on her glasses. "I've decided that it's time for me to change my role in Elm Creek Quilts. I won't be teaching any longer or organizing the activities. Instead I plan to supervise, pitch in here and there as I'm needed, work one-on-one with our campers now and again, and just generally enjoy myself. However, I don't expect Sarah to add all my duties to her already substantial workload." She peered over the top of her glasses at Summer. "In other words, dear, that full-time job you wanted is yours, if you're still interested."

"Absolutely," Summer exclaimed.

"Good. Then that's settled."

As the others congratulated Summer, Sylvia moved on to the next item on her list. "Then there's this little matter of demonstrations and skateboards and what have you."

They fell silent as all eyes turned to Diane.

"I'm concerned about the effect of continuous incarceration upon company morale," Sylvia said dryly. "I believe I have a solution. We'll arrange for the construction of a skateboard park—a legal skateboard park."

Diane's eyes were wide with astonishment. "You mean here? On the estate?"

"Heavens no. Far too many of our campers come here to escape teenagers; it wouldn't do to give them another whole crop to contend with. I own a small piece of property adjacent to the Waterford College campus. I plan to donate it to the city with the understanding that they will use it for this purpose. I imagine they could put up a swing set or two as well, something nice for the younger children. My lawyer has been speaking with the city planners, and they've nearly reached an agreement."

"This is wonderful, Sylvia," Diane cried. "My sons will be thrilled."

"Good, because the city of Waterford plans to put them to work. They're going to assemble a planning committee to research construction, costs, insurance, maintenance—countless other matters. Your sons will participate, as will several other children from local schools. I imagine it will be quite educational." She licked a fingertip and turned to the next page in the folder. "If nothing else, it will keep them busy and off the streets, so they won't be mowing down helpless old ladies like myself."

Andrew grinned and shook his head at her. "You're many things, but you're not helpless."

She smiled at him.

"You're too generous, Sylvia," Bonnie said.

"Oh, I'm just getting started." Sylvia checked her list. "Ah, yes. The company. I'm going to divide it all up into shares, which will be distributed among the Elm Creek Quilters." She had to raise her voice to be heard over their exclamations and gasps of astonishment. "Not in equal shares, I'm afraid. Each will receive a ten percent share, except for Sarah, who will receive twenty percent, and, of course, I'm keeping twenty percent for myself. My twenty percent will revert to Sarah after my demise, but don't hold your breath, Sarah, dear, for I plan to live forever. Now, where's Matthew?"

Matt raised his hand to catch her attention. He looked stunned. They all did, which delighted Sylvia beyond measure. "Ah, yes. Matthew. You get the orchard. Let's see, what's next? Oh, yes—"

"The orchard?"

Sylvia raised her eyebrows at him. "Why, yes, Matthew. The orchard. The one on the west side of the estate, where you were working just yesterday. Surely you remember it."

"Yes, but—"

"It's yours. The land, the trees, everything. The deed has been transferred to your name. If you don't want it, you can sell it, but I hope you won't." She paused. "I also hope you'll remain as our caretaker, but I'll understand if you don't. You're an essential part of our operation, Matthew. You're our—our secretary of the interior, as it were. I hope that the orchard will give you the independence you desire and the security any man would want for himself and his family, so that you keep your role in Elm Creek Quilts because you want to, not because you must."

"Thank you, Sylvia. I'm very grateful," he said, and Sylvia knew he spoke from the heart. "But the orchard—what am I supposed to do with it?"

"Do with it?" Sylvia looked around the circle in surprise. "For goodness sake, what does anyone do with an orchard? Grow apples and cherries if you like. Develop your own hybrids. Build a cider mill. Experiment. Learn. Tear everything up and plant a vineyard if you like, but have fun." She snapped the papers and hid a smile. "And here I thought you had a green thumb. What do I do with an orchard, he asks. What a question." She glanced at Andrew, and she could see that he knew how much she was enjoying herself.

Matthew had barely recovered his wits, the poor dear. "Thank you," he said again, sinking back into his chair, amazed. She could already see his mind at work, imagining the possibilities.

"The whole orchard. An actual piece of the Bergstrom estate," Sarah teased him. "You must be the boss's pet."

Sylvia fixed her gaze on her. "You only think that because I haven't given you your present yet."

Sarah looked at her, her smile fading. The others grew silent.

"But you're going to have to wait for it." Sylvia shook her head. "I almost fear telling you this. I know what an impatient young woman you are."

"I don't want anything," Sarah said quickly, clenching her hands together in her lap. "I don't even want you to have a will. I don't want you to *need* a will. I don't want anything if it means that you—that you—" Carol put an arm around her shoulders as Sarah's eyes filled with tears.

Sylvia sighed. And here they had been having such a pleasant time. "Sarah, dear, I survived this recent blow, but I won't survive forever. Recently I've learned that I'm stronger than I ever knew, but no one is that strong."

To her relief, Sarah nodded.

"I need to know that the estate will be cared for when I'm no longer here to see to it myself. I need someone who understands that the true value of Elm Creek Manor doesn't reside in its price per acre. You are that person." Sylvia reached out and stroked Sarah's hair. "Matt gets the orchard, the Elm Creek Quilters get the company, and you, my dear, you get everything else."

Sarah nodded, tears slipping down her face. Suddenly she was at Sylvia's side, embracing her. "I'll take good care of it for you. I promise."

Sylvia's heart was full as she hugged her dear young friend, who would perhaps never understand that no estate in the world could even begin to equal what Sarah had given Sylvia. "I know you will."

⚜

By the end of the day, two new quilts hung side by side in the foyer of Elm Creek Manor. The first was a testament to the courage of one remarkable woman who refused to be daunted when confronted with the many faces of tragedy. The other was a reminder of the power of friendship, the awareness that any task could be completed if friends thought creatively, trusted in themselves, and gained strength from each other.

In the years to come, whenever new visitors arrived at Elm Creek Manor, the Broken Star and round robin quilts would welcome them. The visitors would admire the colors, the patterns, the intricate quilting, and perhaps, just perhaps, they would sense the love that had been worked into the fabric with every stitch. They would wonder about the women who had sewn a small measure of their souls into the cloth as they labored with needles and thread, as they sat around the quilting frame or worked alone, driven on by hope and determination. Some visitors would discover the true stories behind the quilts; others would be content to imagine and wonder.

But Sarah McClure knew, and for as long as she lived, she would keep those stories close to her heart. She would never forget the lessons she had learned from the Elm Creek Quilters and from the wise woman who had become her most cherished friend. For Sylvia's greatest bequest was the reminder that true friends are the most precious gift, and that even in the darkest of times love illuminates the way home.

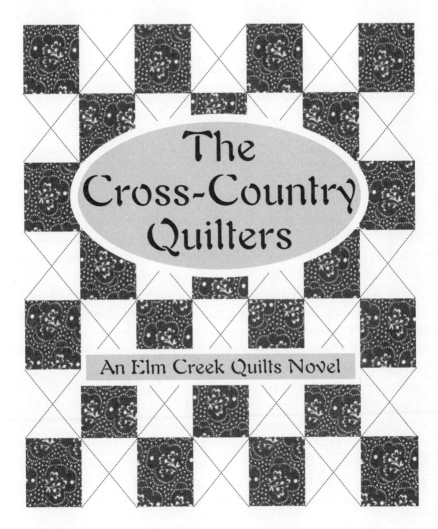

The Cross-Country Quilters

An Elm Creek Quilts Novel

Acknowledgments

This book would not have been possible without the help of many friends and colleagues, including:

My agent, Maria Massie; my editor, the incomparable Denise Roy; her assistant, Tara Parsons; and publicist Rebecca Davis. I am privileged to work with such talented people.

My fellow quilters, who never fail to inspire me, especially the members of the Mad City Quilters, R.C.T.Q., QuiltNet, and QuiltersBee.

The members of the Internet Writing Workshop, especially Christine Johnson, Candace Byers, Dave Swinford, Jody Ewing, Lani Kraus, Rhéal Nadeau, and everyone in the Lounge.

The whole Orbitec crew and associated friends, especially Rachel and Chip Sauer, my first and best Madison friends.

My wonderfully supportive family, especially Geraldine, Nic, and Heather Neidenbach; Virginia and Edward Riechman; Leonard and Marlene Chiaverini; and the entire Riechman clan.

My beloved husband, Marty, without whom I would not be able to live the writing life; and Nicholas, my heart's treasure and constant companion during the writing of this book.

My heartfelt gratitude goes out to you all.

For
Marty and Nicholas,
with all my love

One

Julia loathed retirement parties. Watching the guest of honor make the obligatory final curtain call evoked a predictable yet uncomfortable melancholy, but worse yet was the sense of the other guests' eyes upon her. She imagined their whispers: Isn't it about time we threw one of these parties for *her*, the dowager queen of the television drama? Doesn't she realize her time has passed?

As she raised her champagne flute to join the others in a toast to Maury, the man who had been her agent throughout her career, Julia forced herself to smile. Despite the critics' lukewarm appreciation of her talent, she knew she was a fine actress. No one would detect her dismay at realizing that she was one of the oldest people present, that she could no longer count on being the most beautiful woman in the room, that maybe it was best that she retire with some dignity instead of lingering on long past her prime.

No doubt the stars and would-be stars assembled there expected her own announcement soon, especially since *Family Tree* had just ended its lengthy run. She had hoped for at least another two years, but as the three endearing cherubs who played her grandchildren grew into sulky adolescents with various addictions and attitude problems, the program's once-spectacular ratings had begun a gradual but unmistakably downward slide. The final blow had come the previous winter, when the actor who played her son-in-law developed a particularly nasty infection in one of his pectoral implants. When his hospitalization forced them to shut down production for a month and show reruns during sweeps week, the studio heads decided not to renew any of their contracts. Most of the cast moved on to other projects, but for the first time in over two decades, Julia found herself facing a summer hiatus that threatened to extend indefinitely.

If she were planning to leave the business, this would seem to be the time to do it. Money wouldn't be a problem; she had invested her earnings so wisely that she wouldn't need to earn a paycheck to maintain her lifestyle—even with the ungodly amount of alimony she had to pay her third husband. But to retire now, before she had starred in a hit movie, something meaningful and important and true—that would be unbearable.

A handsome young waiter smiled as he offered her another glass of champagne. Drowning her sorrows didn't seem like such a bad idea, given that her series was over and Maury was abandoning her, so she placed her empty glass on the waiter's tray and took another. As she raised it to her lips, Maury caught her eye and inclined his head in the direction of his study. She took a hasty sip and nodded to indicate she would join him there. If he intended to scold her for drinking too much, she'd scold him right back. What was he thinking, retiring when she needed him so desperately?

"You look lovely," he greeted her, kissing her on the cheek as she entered the study. He closed the heavy door behind them, shutting out the noise of the party.

"Thank you, Maury. You look rather lovely yourself."

He grinned and tugged at the sleeves of his elegant tuxedo. "Evelyn insisted," he said. "I didn't want such an ostentatious send-off. I would have preferred eighteen holes and a quiet lunch at the club with a few friends."

"And disappoint everyone who wanted to bid you a proper good-bye?" Julia tried to keep her voice light, but she couldn't prevent some bitterness from slipping in. "It's not like you to put your golf game ahead of your friends."

"Now, Julia, don't be like that." He placed a hand at the small of her back and guided her to a soft tapestry-covered sofa in front of the fireplace. "You're going to be well looked after. Your new agent will be able to do more for you than I have these past few years."

The apology in his voice touched her. "I've had no complaints," Julia said, resting her hand on his arm. "There's no one in this world I trust more than you."

"Thank you, Julia." Maury cleared his throat and drew out his handkerchief. "That means a lot to me." Abruptly he strode over to his desk, and when his back was turned, Julia watched him fondly as he composed himself. Maury was a good man, one of Hollywood's last true gentlemen. He had been her first husband's oldest and dearest friend. He and his wife, Evelyn, had seen her through Charles's death and the two foolish marriages and bitter divorces that followed. He had insisted that the producers of *Family Tree* audition her for the role of Grandma Wilson despite their complaints that she wasn't the right type. He had unraveled hundreds of management snarls and eased countless disappointments throughout the years. Maury was a true friend in a city that knew little of friendship and everything about opportunism and greed.

He tucked his handkerchief away and picked up a thin stack of papers bound by three gold brads. "What's this?" she asked as he placed the papers in her hands.

"A little farewell present. You didn't think I'd leave you without one last great project, did you?"

That was precisely what she had thought, but she wouldn't tell him that. She glanced at the top sheet of the script for the writer's name. "Who's Ellen Henderson? What else has she done?"

"You won't have heard of her. This is her first major motion picture."

"Oh, Maury." Julia frowned and tossed the script onto the coffee table.

He took up the papers and sat down beside her. "Don't 'Oh, Maury' me before you read it. This is the project we've been searching for. It has heart, it has warmth, and it has a fantastic part for you." He placed the script in her lap and closed her hands around it. "Trust me."

"Who's directing?"

"Ellen is."

The alcohol helped flame her temper. "This is your big plan for getting me my breakthrough role? I've won four Emmys and a Golden Globe, and you give me a script written by a nobody. How dare you, after all I've sacrificed?" The last words came out almost as a sob, which she tried to disguise with another sip of champagne.

Gently Maury took the glass. "Don't hold her inexperience against her. Two years ago her student film won an honorable mention at Sundance. Plus, William Bernier is producing."

Julia raised her eyebrows at him, her anger forgotten. "I thought he had a three-picture deal with—"

"He does. This will be one of those projects. We'll have all the perks and publicity a major studio can provide."

"That's not bad," Julia admitted, picking up the script. Even if the production fell through, Bernier would remember that she had been willing to take a chance on a neophyte director for his sake. Not every actress of her caliber would take such a risk, and it certainly wouldn't hurt to have a man like Bernier in her debt.

"I'll leave you alone to read it." Maury patted her knee and rose. "If you don't love it, I promise I'll go out there in front of all those people and tell them I'm canceling my retirement until I can find you the project of your dreams."

"Don't tempt me," Julia teased as he left the room, though she knew such an announcement would embarrass her more than it would him.

Alone in the restful silence of the study, she settled back on the sofa and decided to skim through the first few scenes. If nothing else, Maury's script would provide an escape from an evening of phony smiles and niceties and too much rich food. She read the cover page aloud to test the sound of the title. *"A Patchwork Life,"* she said, and winced. She wanted *Masterpiece Theatre,* and Maury had given her something so hokey it could have been plucked minutes before from a Midwestern cornfield. If Bernier was half the savvy producer his reputation claimed, he would change that title before releasing a single dollar. Shaking her head and expecting the worst, she turned to the first page and began to read.

Within a few minutes she forgot the party, the humiliating dearth of offers, the patronizing responses of the few movie producers who owed Maury too much to avoid returning his phone calls. A woman named Sadie Henderson and her life in pioneer-era Kansas drew her in until they became more real than the tapestry sofa beneath her, more vivid than the music of the orchestra and the celebration just beyond the study door. She could almost taste the dust in her mouth as the script transported her to the small prairie homestead Sadie struggled to build with her husband, Augustus. Her heart broke when Augustus died, leaving Sadie with two young sons. Alone, Sadie persisted despite grasshopper plagues and drought when other neighbors gave up and returned to homes back east. She shared Sadie's grief when she sold off cherished family quilts to raise money to improve the farm. Sadie then took in sewing from her more successful neighbors, running the farm by day and stitching her neighbors' quilts late into the night. Her quilting kept the family alive until at last, years later, the farm flourished.

Long after she finished the last page, Julia held the script to her chest, lost in the details of Sadie's hardship and triumph. In Sadie's place, Julia would have crumbled in a week. She longed to meet Sadie, understand the source of her strength, and somehow harness that power for herself.

The door opened, startling her out of her reverie. "Well?" Maury asked, sitting beside her.

"It was quite good," she said cautiously, testing him. "But who would pay to see a movie like this, old ladies and nuns? It's a little—well, I don't know. A little too squeaky-clean." She thumbed through the script, shaking her head. "Maybe you should see if Sally Field is available."

"How can you say that?" Maury protested. "You said you wanted something meaningful, something worthy of your talent. This story has all the pathos and character development you wanted—or at least I thought you wanted."

"Relax, Maury. I didn't say I wouldn't consider it; I'm just not sure what this will do for me."

"It'll get you an Oscar nomination, that's what it'll do," he said, but his voice had lost some of its distress.

"It does have some great monologues," she admitted, but suddenly a horrible thought struck her. "Which part did you have in mind for me?"

"Sadie Henderson, of course. Not when she's in her twenties, but after that. Bernier will get his best makeup people. I'll insist on it."

She was too relieved to notice Maury's implicit admission that, without makeup miracles, she was far too old to play anyone younger than a matriarch. For a moment she had feared that Maury intended her to play the cruel elderly neighbor who tried to buy up the Henderson farm.

"So are you interested or not? Just say the word, and I'll send this along to Anne Bancroft, Judi Dench—"

"I'm interested," she interrupted. She refused to entertain even for a moment the thought of Dame Judi collecting a golden statuette for a role Julia had declined.

"Then I have someone I'd like you to meet." Maury crossed the room, opened the study door, and ushered a young woman inside. She was slender and dressed in what was likely her best suit, but her unfashionable haircut and lack of makeup marked her as a breed apart from all the other young women at the party. "This is Ellen Henderson."

"Miss Merchaud, it is such an honor to meet you." The young woman approached and shook her hand. "I've admired your work since I was a little girl."

Julia twisted a wince into a smile. "That long, hmm?" The young woman's grip was strong and confident, and suddenly Julia realized something. "Your name is Henderson. Are you a descendant of Sadie Henderson?"

"She was my great-grandmother. My script is based on her diaries."

"I'm so delighted to hear that," Julia exclaimed, forgetting her reserve. She so wanted to believe that Sadie had been a real woman who had lived and breathed and walked the same world she walked.

"Your writing makes Sadie live again," Maury said.

Ellen blushed at the compliment. "It's the actor who brings the script to life. Miss Merchaud, there's no one in the world I'd rather have portray my great-grandmother than you."

Years in the business had taught Julia to suspect flattery. "And why is that?"

"You have this core of strength, this resilience. I've seen it in every part you've played, ever since Mrs. Dormouse in *The Meadows of Middlebury*."

"You saw *Meadows*?" That couldn't be. Mrs. Dormouse was her first major role, but *Meadows* was a children's film that had quickly slipped into obscurity despite strong critical acclaim. Besides, Ellen hadn't even been born when it came out. For that matter, her parents had probably been too young to see it.

"My public library ran it during its summer film festival when I was in the fourth grade." Ellen gave her a shy smile. "I loved the book, but when I saw how actors brought all those characters to life, I was transfixed—and transformed. Especially when I saw how you made Mrs. Dormouse more real than she had been even in my imagination. That was the moment I knew I wanted to make movies when I grew up."

Ellen's genuine admiration hit home. "I'll take the part," Julia said, without thinking of contracts or box office or who might share top billing.

Ellen's face lit up. "Oh, Miss Merchaud, thank you." She seized Julia's hand and shook it again. "You won't regret this. I promise."

Julia laughed and eased her hand free. "I'm sure it will be a delightful experience." She raised her eyebrows at Maury, who recognized his cue.

"Miss Merchaud and I have some details to discuss," he said, showing Ellen to the door. "Why don't you go on out and enjoy the rest of the party?"

Ellen looked uncomfortable. "If you don't mind—if you won't be needing me, I think I'd rather go home. It's getting late."

As Maury promised her they'd be in touch, Julia wondered how long the awkward little wren had been forced to mingle among that crowd of peacocks as she waited for Julia to read her script.

When they were alone, Maury said, "You've just won her loyalty for life. Bernier took on the project on the condition that she would obtain a major star for the lead role."

"Really?" Julia felt a rush of pleasure at being considered a major star by a man like Bernier, but the sensation was quickly followed by anger that she had not taken the compliment in stride. Dame Judi no doubt heard such praise twenty times a day. "I wonder why she didn't mention it."

"She wanted to be sure you took the part because you truly loved her story, not because you felt sorry for her."

"If she keeps that up, this town will eat her alive." Still, the young woman's sincerity was oddly refreshing. Julia wished she had not been in such a hurry to dismiss her.

"She'll learn."

"The sooner the better, for her sake," Julia said. "So, when do we get started? Will we be shooting on location?"

"We'll have to for some of the exterior shots," Maury said apologetically.

"That's fine." Then she added, almost to herself, "Some time away would be good for me."

"I'm glad you think so, because I was planning to send you on a little trip."

"A week at Aurora Borealis?" Wouldn't that be just like Maury, to pamper her at her favorite retreat in Ojai.

"Not exactly. This will be more of a working vacation." He was smiling, but he still looked tentative. "You need to learn some new skills for this part."

"I already know how to ride a horse."

"But you don't know how to quilt, unless you've been keeping secrets from me."

"You know I don't keep secrets from you." Then she paused. "Do I really need to know how to quilt?"

He nodded.

"Can't we use a stand-in?"

"You need to know how to quilt for this role. It's important, Julia."

He said it so gravely that at once she understood what he would not admit aloud: He had won the role for her by telling William Bernier she already knew how to quilt. "I see," she said briskly. "I'll just have to learn, then. I might even enjoy it. Are you planning to bring a quilt tutor to the set? Is there such a thing?"

"I had a better idea," Maury said. "I'm sending you to quilt camp."

⚜

Megan hadn't felt so frustrated and helpless since the afternoon Robby had come home from Cub Scouts with a black eye and a missing tooth. At first he wouldn't tell her what had happened, and when she phoned the scoutmaster, his only explanation was, "Some boys aren't cut out for the Cub Scouts. Why don't you try again next year, when he's thicker skinned?"

"This is the Cub Scouts, not the Marines," Megan had snapped.

"Tell that to your son. He threw the first punch."

Megan had been so flabbergasted by this obvious untruth that she could think of nothing to say, so she hung up. Her gentle, owlish son was among the smaller boys in his grade, and she simply could not picture him as an aggressor. He had few friends at school, but never before had he been beaten up by his classmates. More than anything she wanted Robby to be safe, healthy, and happy, but at that moment, she realized she couldn't protect him from everything. A bullying gang of seven-year-olds had bluntly defined the limits of her motherly powers.

As she tended Robby's wounds, the story came out, but only in defense against the scoutmaster's charges. Robby argued that maybe he had thrown the first punch, but the other boy had started it by teasing him. Robby had told some of the other scouts that his father never came to any scouting events because he was an astronaut working on top-secret research on the space station. When another boy loftily pointed out that Robby's explanation couldn't possibly be true since the space station was still being built, Robby told him that was just a cover story so other countries wouldn't know how far ahead of them the Americans were. "It's an international space station, you stupid liar," the other boy said, and in response, Robby slugged him.

Like all of Robby's stories, this one had had a grain of truth in it, but only a grain. Although Keith was a corporate sales manager, Megan was an aerospace engineer, and one day the new technology she developed would be used aboard the space station. But although sometimes Megan wished her ex-husband had been shot into orbit, he and his new wife had made it only as far as Portland, Oregon.

That day Megan had told Robby that hitting was wrong, and that if he became frustrated or angry, he should just walk away. Several times since, she had also explained—after making certain her son did understand the difference between reality and fiction—how lies sometimes made people angry, because they didn't like to be deceived. "You don't need to exaggerate to get people's attention," she told him. "Just be yourself." Robby told her he had to tell stories because no one liked him just as himself. Megan patiently pointed to his bruises as evidence that they didn't seem to like him very much when he lied, either, and that in the future it might be better to err on the side of truth and caution. "If you like to make people laugh by telling a story, that's okay," she said, "as long as you tell them it *is* a story." Robby agreed, but it pained her to know that he thought no one would like him if he didn't put on an act. Maybe she was blinded by a mother's love, but couldn't everyone see what a sweet, sensitive, bright little boy he was? Couldn't the world appreciate him for that?

The Cub Scout incident had occurred two years ago, five years after Keith confessed to his affair and moved out. When she placed today's events in that context of misery, they seemed almost trivial. Why, then, was she so upset? This wasn't the first time she hadn't been invited to a party, although she never would have expected Zoe to exclude her. So few women engineers worked at their company that they all knew each other, and Megan had considered Zoe one of her closest friends at work. When she overheard Tina and Michelle discussing the Fourth-of-July barbecue at Zoe's house the previous Saturday, she first thought they were talking about a future event that she, too, would soon hear about from the hostess herself. But when Tina spotted her and both women abruptly stopped talking, Megan realized the truth.

Later, Zoe came to her office and tried, in her awkward way, to apologize. "There were only couples there," she explained. "I didn't think you'd have any fun, you know, being the only single person at a party full of couples."

Megan hid her disappointment behind a smile and assurances that she'd be delighted to join them next time, and if she needed an escort, she'd find one. Zoe looked relieved that she was taking it so well, never suspecting that after she left, Megan locked the door to her office and sat at her desk contemplating whether to burst into tears right there or climb out the window, flee for the sanctuary of home, and cry in private. She was a grown woman with a child, but she felt like she was back in high school. She regained her composure by reminding herself that she couldn't force people to include her, nor could she make them enjoy her company enough to excuse her involuntary single status. Nor could she resent Zoe when most of her other couple friends had also drifted away after Keith left. Maybe they feared divorce was contagious, or maybe they had always preferred Keith and tolerated her presence only because she was his wife. She would never know, because she wasn't the sort of person to confront others, even when they slighted her.

As she left work that afternoon, still unhappy, she decided that after Robby went to bed, she'd go online and vent her frustrations to her best friend, Donna. They had been email pals for years, ever since they had met in an internet quilting newsgroup. Whenever Megan needed to pour her heart out, Donna was there with patience and understanding, the same way Megan tried to be there for her. Often Megan wished that Donna lived nearby rather than in Minnesota, so that they could meet for lunch or go quilt-shop hopping like normal best friends. She wondered what that meant about her, that she was best friends with someone she had never actually met in person. Maybe Robby had inherited his social ineptitude from his mother.

As she pulled onto the long dirt driveway leading up to her parents' house, Megan checked the dashboard clock. She had arrived later than usual, but probably too early to say hello to her father, who at this hour would be closing up his hardware store in town. Her parents owned nearly ten acres sandwiched between two larger family farms, and although they still cultivated most of the property, the small farm had always been more of a hobby than a career. Megan treasured childhood memories of playing hide-and-seek with her father in the cornfield, the green stalks topped with golden silk towering above her head. Soon Robby would play there with his grandfather again.

She circled in front of the house and parked beside one of the outbuildings. Her father's two dogs bounded over to greet her as she climbed the stairs to the front porch. "Hey, Pete. Hey, Polly," she said, petting the golden retriever first and then the German shepherd. She heard laughter inside, and found Robby with his grandmother in the kitchen.

"Mom," Robby cried out. "Did you know when Grandma was little she had her own cow? It would come when she called it and everything, just like a dog." His grandmother caught Megan's eye and shook her head. Robby saw the exchange and quickly added, "It's just a story."

Megan's mother laughed affectionately and ruffled Robby's hair. "You're my little storyteller, all right." She hugged Megan in welcome, but then her smile faded. "What's wrong, honey?"

"Nothing. Just some stuff at work." It wasn't anything she wanted to discuss in front of Robby, and she wasn't even sure if she ought to confide in her mother. Her parents had raised her to be strong and independent, and she was ashamed to show them how meek and accepting she had become since Keith had left her. As hard as it had been for her staunchly Catholic parents to accept the breakup, it would be even more difficult for them to understand how deeply his betrayal still affected her.

But when they heard her father's truck pull up outside and Robby ran out to meet him, Megan found herself telling her mother what had happened. Her mother continued shelling peas, nodding thoughtfully as Megan perched on a stool and rested her elbows on the counter as she spoke. It was a scene that had played out many times in that kitchen since Megan was a child, first learning the painful truth that the whole world wouldn't cherish her the way her parents did.

"What did you do last Saturday?" her mother asked when she had finished.

"We took Robby to the county fair," Megan said. "You were there, Mom. Don't you remember?"

"Of course I remember, but I wasn't sure if you did. We had a great time, didn't we? Wasn't the weather perfect? Didn't Robby love the rides and the animals?"

Megan nodded, not sure where her mother's reminiscence was taking them.

"Well, then, seems to me this Zoe character did you a favor." Her mother finished the last of the peas and dusted off her hands as if brushing off both the chore and Megan's coworker. "If you had gone to the party, you would have missed the fair. And for what? A party with too many rules to be much fun, or at least that's how it sounds to me."

"It's not missing the party that bothers me," Megan said. "It's being excluded."

Her mother's face softened. "I know, dear." She cupped Megan's chin in her hand for a moment, then patted her cheek. "My quilt guild is meeting at Dorothy Pearson's house tonight. Why don't you join me? Your father can watch Robby."

Megan squirmed. Her mother's invitation sounded too much like her father's offer to escort her to the homecoming dance sophomore year of high school, when none of the boys had been willing to ask her and she had been too shy to ask any of them. Her mother's friends were sweet women, but they had known Megan since she was in diapers and had never stopped thinking of her as a little girl. "Thanks, Mom, but I have some papers to read before bed tonight. I have a grant proposal due next week."

"At least stay for dinner."

Megan tried to picture the contents of her pantry, wondering if she had enough energy for something as simple as pasta from a box and sauce from a jar. Then she thought of her mother's homemade bread and baked chicken, and vegetables fresh from her parents' garden. "We'd love to."

When Megan and Robby returned home early in the evening, Megan knew before she leafed through the mail that Keith's child support check would not be there. The day had gone too badly to end on such a high note.

That's why she assumed the envelope from *Contemporary Quilting* magazine was a subscription renewal notice and didn't bother opening it until two days later, when she paid her other bills. She would have opened it immediately if she had known that the renewal notice was in fact a letter informing her that her watercolor charm quilt had taken first prize in the magazine's annual contest, and that she had won a week's vacation at the famous quilting retreat, Elm Creek Manor.

⚜

"Way to go, Megan," Donna shouted as she finished reading the email note. It was about time her best quilting buddy had some good luck come her way. They'd been friends for years, ever since they met on an internet quilting newsgroup when Megan posted a frantic request for a certain piece of fabric. Everyone at her son's school had gone crazy over a Saturday morning cartoon called *Baby Dinosaurs,* and Megan's son was infatuated with a character named Little Trice, a pastel triceratops who somehow managed to look adorable clad in a bib and diaper. Megan had secretly begun working on a Little Trice quilt for Robby's birthday, but she had found only one yard of Baby Dinosaurs print fabric at her local quilt shop. She thought it would be enough, but she ran out when the quilt top was only half finished, and when she checked at the store, they told her the print had been discontinued. "All I need is a half yard more," Megan wrote to the other quilters in the newsgroup. "I'll swap anything for it, just name your price. Can anyone help me?"

Donna sympathized, for despite her compulsive fabric-shopping habit, she had often found herself in similar situations. She phoned all the quilt shops in her area code and finally found one that had two yards left on a remnant bolt. She drove an hour to St. Paul to buy it, then emailed Megan with the good news. A week after Donna mailed her the material, Megan sent her a box of beautiful Civil War–era reproduction fabric and a heartfelt thank-you note. Donna immediately sent her an email message to tell her how pleased she was with the surprise, and Megan wrote back to let her know how the Little Trice quilt was progressing. Their correspondence continued over the internet and through the mail, and before long, they had become confidantes. Donna knew everything about Megan's divorce and troubles at work, and Megan knew everything about Donna's eternal struggle with her weight and her two daughters' nerve-wracking journey through the teen years. Although they had never actually met in person, they were so close that Donna was as happy for Megan as if she had won the *Contemporary Quilting* contest herself.

After replying with a note of congratulations, Donna shut down the computer and returned to her sewing machine. The fourth bedroom had been the girls' playroom, but when they reached the age when they preferred to shut themselves away in their separate bedrooms, Donna had adopted it as her quilt studio. Even with the door open so she could monitor all the comings and goings in the house, she still had a sense of peaceful solitude, the perfect antidote to a hectic day.

"Mom?" Lindsay appeared in the doorway, slender and lovely in her denim shorts and pink top, her long blond hair pulled back into a ponytail. "Can I talk to you for a minute?"

Donna put down her quilt block and swiveled her chair around to face her elder daughter. "Sure, honey. What is it?"

Lindsay crossed the room and took her hands. "Not here. Downstairs." Lindsay led her out of the room. "Dad's already waiting, and Becca's about to go to work. I want to tell you all at the same time."

Laughing, Donna allowed herself to be guided downstairs to the family room. Paul was sitting on the sofa; Becca sat on the floor beside him, glancing at her watch and looking bored. Exchanging a quick glance of puzzlement with her husband, Donna seated herself on the opposite end of the sofa so that Becca was between them.

Only then did she notice that Lindsay was wringing her hands and compulsively shifting her weight from foot to foot. "Lindsay?" Donna said, suddenly anxious. "What is it, honey?"

"I have an announcement to make." Lindsay took a deep breath. "Brandon and I are getting married."

Donna couldn't breathe. She groped for Paul's hand and squeezed it.

Lindsay looked around at her silent family. "Well? Say something."

"You're out of your mind," Becca said flatly.

Lindsay frowned at her, then looked at her parents, hopeful. "Mom? Dad?"

Breathe, Donna ordered herself, then gasped, "I don't know what to say."

Lindsay smiled nervously. "'Congratulations' would be nice."

"Congratulations," Donna and Paul said in unison, in a monotone. Becca merely groaned and let her head fall back against the sofa.

"But you like Brandon," Lindsay protested.

Donna said, "Of course we like him—"

"I don't," Becca said.

"—but this is a little sudden," Paul finished. "Your mother and I weren't expecting to hear an announcement like this so soon."

"Brandon and I have been dating for two years."

"I've had library books longer than that," Becca said.

Donna patted Becca on the shoulder to quiet her. "Have you set a date?"

"Well, I've always wanted a June wedding, and Brandon will have some vacation time then—"

"June of next year?" Donna shrilled.

"I know that only gives us eleven months to plan, but we don't want anything elaborate."

"What about school?" Paul asked.

"Brandon says I don't really need to finish. After medical school, he'll earn enough to support both of us."

"I don't believe I'm hearing this," Becca said.

Donna couldn't believe it either. "You're going to quit school a year before graduation?"

Lindsay hesitated. "Well, Brandon thinks maybe I shouldn't go back this year, either. He thinks maybe—as long as it's okay with you—we could take my tuition money and use that for the wedding instead."

"'Brandon thinks,'" Becca mimicked, then her jaw dropped. "You're pregnant, aren't you?"

"No, I am definitely not pregnant," Lindsay snapped. She looked close to tears. "Isn't anyone happy for me?"

Paul released Donna's hand and leaned forward to rest his elbows on his knees. "Sweetheart, don't you think you ought to finish college before you get married? You're only twenty."

"That's legal in this state, Dad."

"Finish college first," Donna pleaded. "There's nothing wrong with a long engagement. If it's meant to be, two years won't make a difference."

Donna saw something in Lindsay's eyes change then, as if she were closing some part of herself away from them, and a pang of uneasiness went through her.

"It makes a difference to Brandon," Lindsay said. "He wants us to get married now, I mean, right now. Elope. I talked him into waiting until June. That's the best I can do."

Donna didn't like the sound of that, but before she could say anything, Paul spoke. "I still don't understand why you have to give up school. If you have your heart set on getting married, we won't stand in your way, but can't you continue school, too? Think of everything you'll miss. Your classes, all your friends, all the fun you girls have—"

"Yes, and the drama society," Donna broke in. "What about the plays you were going to direct this year? You were looking forward to them. And that internship next summer. Professor Collins said you had a good chance of winning it."

As Donna spoke, Lindsay's cheeks flushed. "I know," she said. "I know it's a sacrifice, but when you love someone the way Brandon and I love each other, you make sacrifices for him."

"What exactly is Brandon sacrificing for you?" Becca inquired.

Lindsay shot her a sharp look. "I'm leaving school because Brandon can't afford to pay for my last two years, and he doesn't feel right having my parents pay his wife's tuition." She took a deep, shaky breath and looked from Donna to Paul and back. "Please, I don't want to fight. Please tell me you're okay with this."

"Are you sure this is what you want?" Donna asked in a small voice.

"This is what I want."

"Then we'll make the best of it," Paul said.

"I don't want you to make the best of it," Lindsay said. "I want you to be happy for us."

She looked so miserable that Donna rose and embraced her. "We're happy if you're happy." As Lindsay clung to her, Donna caught Paul's eye and shook her head slightly. They could discuss this privately later and, she hoped, find some way to convince their daughter to reconsider.

"I still say you're nuts," Becca muttered.

Lindsay pulled away from her mother and turned to her sister. "I hope you'll be my maid of honor anyway."

"Maid of honor?" Becca considered. "Can I help pick out the dress?"

"Why? Are you afraid I'd stick you in something hideous?"

"That thought did cross my mind."

Lindsay laughed. "Yes, you can help pick out the style—but I get to pick the color."

"That's fair."

Lindsay turned back to her mother, tentative. "Will you help me choose a wedding gown?"

"You don't need to worry about that just yet," Donna said. "You have plenty of time."

"I know. It's just—well, now that it's official, I want to get it over with. The work, I mean. It'll be a lot of work, and I want to get started." Her smile trembled, and Donna knew what an effort it took for her to keep it in place.

Paul sighed and rubbed at his jaw distractedly.

"I know this is a shock, but you'll feel better once you get used to the idea," Lindsay said. "Brandon says his parents were surprised, too, but once they had some time to adjust, they were happy for us."

Donna wondered how long ago Brandon had told his parents. How long had Lindsay been engaged without telling her and Paul?

"You'll meet Brandon's parents soon," Lindsay promised. "They're coming to Minneapolis next month to visit him. I thought we could drive down and meet them for supper. That's on a Sunday, the fifteenth. The families should meet each other before the wedding."

"I can't," Donna heard herself say.

Lindsay's face fell. "What?"

"I can't." She could support her daughter here, at home, but she could not—she *would* not—rush out and meet the other family and plunge into a frenzy of wedding plans as if she wanted this marriage to happen, when she didn't, at least not now.

"Why not?"

"I can't." August fifteenth. Why did that date sound familiar? "I'm busy that day."

"Too busy to meet Brandon's parents?"

"That's the week I'm going out of town," Donna said. "I know you've heard me talk about it. My friend Megan and I are meeting at quilt camp. Don't you remember?"

Lindsay looked dubious. "I guess I forgot."

"Well, that's the week. I'm sorry, honey, but I'll have to meet Brandon's family another time." Brandon was a nice enough young man—what she knew of him—but they were both so young, and she couldn't bear to see Lindsay throw away all her dreams for the future. Lindsay had begged them to be happy for her, but how could Donna be happy when her every instinct screamed that Lindsay was not?

She climbed the stairs and retreated to the sanctuary of her quilt studio, where she switched on the computer and sank heavily into the chair. As she waited for the system to boot up, she realized she'd have to confirm that date with Megan and ask her where exactly this quilt camp was, anyway.

⚜

Adam fumbled for the phone. "Hello?"

"Adam?"

"Yeah?" he mumbled, trying to clear his throbbing head. Last night his two best friends had shown up with a case of beer and a stack of videos—war movies, the kind where the hard-edged, tough hero died at the end by throwing himself on a hand grenade or by carrying a bomb into an enemy bunker to save his equally hard-edged, tough buddies. Natalie despised the genre, and if she had been present, they would have watched something else entirely. And that, his friends' message seemed to be, was precisely the point; watching movies with an abundance of pyrotechnics and high body counts was celebration of the male independence he had narrowly escaped losing. As if that was what he wanted, as if it were his choice.

"Good morning, honey. It's Nana."

Of course. Who else would phone so early on a Sunday morning? "Hi, Nana."

"Did I wake you, dear?"

"Yeah, but that's okay."

"You should be getting ready for church by now anyway."

He squinted at the clock. "Church isn't for another four hours." He sat up on the edge of the bed and yawned. "What's going on?"

"I need you to drive me somewhere next month."

He smothered a laugh. "It's a good thing you called me so early," he said with mock solemnity. "If you'd waited until dawn, I might have been all booked up."

"Listen to how you talk to your grandmother," she scolded him. "I have no idea why you're still my favorite grandson."

"Each of us is the favorite, according to you."

"I can have more than one favorite. Now, about this ride. Are you free on August fifteenth or am I going to have to walk? That's a Sunday."

He felt a pang, picturing how that Sunday in August should have been spent—a leisurely breakfast on the patio with Natalie, an afternoon trip out to Amish country to look at the furniture she so adored, maybe a romantic candlelit dinner. But now . . . "I won't be busy."

"Are you sure?"

"Very sure. Where do you need to go?"

"It's time for my quilt camp again, remember? I always go during my birthday week. I need you to drive me there on August fifteenth and pick me up the twenty-first. That's a Saturday."

"Is this the camp in Pennsylvania?"

"Yes. Your sister took me last year, and she said to tell you it's your turn."

Now he remembered his sister complaining about the long drive to the middle of nowhere. "Why don't you fly this time?"

"You know I don't like airplanes," she said primly. "I would take the train, but the nearest station is a long drive from Elm Creek Manor. What do you suggest I do, take a taxi? I suppose I'll have to, if it's so much trouble—"

"It's no trouble," he assured her before she could get too excited. "I have a teachers' in-service at school the next day, but Sunday's no problem. I'll take you."

"And pick me up?"

"And pick you up." Why not? Anything was better than moping around the empty house. Maybe he should get a dog.

"Thank you. You're a good boy." She paused. "Do you want to come to supper tonight? I could make a nice pork roast."

"Thanks, Nana, but—"

"Dayton's only an hour north of you. Less than that, the way you drive."

"Maybe next week." He didn't feel up to seeing anyone that day. Or maybe for the rest of the summer.

Nana's voice softened. "Adam, I didn't forget what day yesterday was."

The reminder pained him. "You mean, what yesterday was supposed to have been."

"You're much better off without her."

"So I'm told."

"If she's that fickle, it's better you find out now rather than three or four years into it."

"Please don't criticize her."

"Why not, after what she did to you? I never liked her, you know."

"Yeah, I know." So did Natalie. So did the entire family and, if he knew his grandmother, all the ladies in her quilting circle and every other senior in her apartment complex. Nana had never been one to keep her opinions to herself, even when her words were sharp enough to cut. Yes, Natalie had her faults; he could admit that. She had a temper, and he never knew whether he would please her or set off a tantrum. But even now, when any sensible person would be too angry to remember any of her good qualities, just thinking about her made him ache with loss. He couldn't honestly say he still loved her the way he had before she broke off their engagement—his trust had been too badly damaged for that—but he still cared about her, and he missed her.

"My friends have granddaughters—"

"No, you're not setting me up," he interrupted. "I'm not ready. I mean it, Nana."

"I heard you," she said innocently. "But if I meet a lovely young woman and happen to mention my favorite grandson, and if she happens to be available . . ."

He was too tired to argue. After promising to come to dinner the next Sunday, Adam hung up the phone and slumped back into bed with a groan. This was supposed to have been his first full day as a married man. He should be sleeping peacefully in the bridal suite of the Radisson Hotel Cincinnati right now, his beautiful, dark-haired wife in his arms. He should be dreaming of their future, which had always seemed so full of promise. He should have risen just in time for a shower and breakfast before they left on their honeymoon. Instead Natalie and her sister were going to use their nonrefundable tickets to the Bahamas, and a call from his grandmother instead of a kiss from his bride had awakened him.

Adam closed his eyes and tried to go back to sleep. It wasn't even six o'clock in the morning, but already he knew he was in for a rough day. Maybe he *should* get a dog. Natalie hated dogs. Now that he was allowed to have one, he ought to get one, if only to convince his well-meaning but overanxious family and friends that he was getting on with his life.

⁕

Grace nodded as Sondra chatted about the two men she was dating, though she was only partially listening. For the most part her thoughts were on the television interview scheduled for later that morning, but in the back of her mind she fretted about the sewing machine and fabric stash left idle too long in her studio. She also worried about how tired she was, and how if the smell of relaxants and perming solution weren't so sharp in her nostrils, she might fall asleep. She tired so easily lately.

"Justine driving you to the station?" Sondra suddenly asked, speaking in a voice far too casual to be casual.

"Yes." Grace tried to catch her eye in the mirror. "Why do you ask?" Was it that obvious she rarely drove these days? She had walked to the salon, but her loft was only a few blocks away; surely that had not roused Sondra's suspicions.

"No reason." Sondra kept her attention on Grace's hair. "I was just wondering how she's doing."

"She's fine. Busy with school and Joshua, and volunteering at the women's shelter." Grace admired her daughter's commitment to social justice, but she hoped when Justine completed her degree and passed the bar, not all of her work would be pro bono.

Sondra trimmed a stray curl with the electric razor. "She seeing anyone?"

"Not that I know of."

"You sure?"

"Well . . ." Grace thought about it and shrugged. "Of course. She would have told me."

"Is that so."

Something in her expression made Grace suspicious. "What do you mean?"

"I wasn't going to say anything—"

Though Sondra had raised the seat until Grace could barely reach the ground with an outstretched foot, she managed to spin the chair around so she could face her friend. "Tell me."

"If you're going to force it out of me, two nights ago I saw her and Joshua out at a restaurant." Sondra raised her eyebrows. "They weren't alone."

"You mean, a man was with them?"

"What else would I mean?" Sondra shook her head. "For someone who's not seeing anyone, Justine sure looked interested."

Grace's hopes rose. Since Joshua had accompanied them, maybe this mysterious man was his father, and maybe that meant Justine had decided to patch things up with him. Grace had always liked Marc and had been heartbroken when Justine told her in no uncertain terms that they wouldn't be getting married. Two-year-old Joshua was an angel, but the older he grew, the more he would need a father figure in his life. Maybe Justine had finally realized that. "Did you get a good look at him?"

"Mmm-hmm." Sondra spun Grace's chair around to face the mirror and tended her close-cropped hair with a comb. "Tall, nice eyes, good-looking. If Justine gets tired of him, she can send him to me. He's more my type, anyway."

Grace hid a smile. Sondra thought every handsome man was her type. "How so, exactly?"

Sondra gave her a pointed look in the mirror. "He's old enough to be her father, that's how."

"Are you sure?" Grace's heart sank. So the man wasn't Joshua's father but someone else—someone *her* age. "Justine's never had a thing for older men."

"You didn't see this particular older man."

Grace didn't need to see him. She mistrusted him already. What was Justine thinking? She was supposed to find a father figure for Joshua, not for herself. "Maybe he was a professor. Maybe they were discussing a school project."

"At a restaurant on a Saturday night? And why would she bring Joshua along instead of leaving him with his grandma?"

"I don't know." Distressed, Grace searched her memory for any hint Justine might have let fall about this strange new man. "I can't remember what she told me she was doing that night. I know she didn't say she had a date." Grace definitely would have remembered that. "How was he with Joshua?"

Sondra's eyes widened in injured innocence. "Do you think I spent my evening spying on your daughter?"

"Yes, I do. And I would have done the same for you."

"Joshua seemed to love him." Sondra brushed a few bits of hair from the back of Grace's neck. "Think of it this way: He's old, but at least he likes kids."

"And that makes it fine that he has one foot in the grave."

Sondra laughed. "I said old enough to be her father, not great-grandpa."

"That's old enough."

"A good man is a good man," Sondra protested. "What does age matter?"

"You know it matters, or you wouldn't have mentioned it."

"Well, maybe it does matter, but it shouldn't." Sondra removed the plastic drape and gave Grace a hand mirror so she could examine the back of her head. "All that counts is that Justine is happy, right?"

Grace frowned, knowing Sondra was right but not feeling any better about it. Her daughter was an intelligent young woman, but even intelligent people didn't always make sensible decisions where matters of the heart were concerned. Grace knew that as well as anyone.

What was worse was that Justine hadn't told her about her new friend. If their relationship had advanced so far that Justine would bring Joshua along on their dates, why hadn't she mentioned him to her own mother?

"Good luck," Sondra told her as Grace left the salon, but Grace wasn't sure if she was referring to the interview or to Justine's mysterious dinner companion.

She met her daughter and grandson in the park across the street from the salon. Justine was pushing Joshua in a swing, her dozens of long, glossy braids gathered in a silk scarf at the nape of her neck. She had the strong cheekbones and rich brown skin her mother and grandmother had also been blessed with, but her stubborn, independent streak had come from her mother alone, and her passion from the father she barely remembered. Joshua resembled Justine physically, but his studious, thoughtful temperament reminded Grace of his own father. Marc and Justine had been good together. She wished with all her heart that he had been the man Sondra had seen with Justine.

When Justine spotted her, she smiled and lifted Joshua out of the swing. Grace laughed with delight as he ran to meet her, and, forgetting herself, she bent over to swoop him up in her arms. "Oooph," she grunted, shifting him so his weight rested on her hip. "You're getting bigger every day, aren't you, honey?"

"Bigger and smarter and more mischievous," Justine said with a smile as she joined them, but Grace saw the concern in her eyes.

"I'm fine," Grace told her.

"I know." Still, Justine took Joshua from her arms, and Grace was more than willing to let her.

As Justine drove them downtown to the television station, Grace decided not to mention the little she knew of Justine's secret. Her daughter would have a fit if she knew her mother's friends were keeping an eye on her. Grace contented herself with asking, "If you were seeing someone new, you would tell me, wouldn't you?"

"Sure." Justine paused, keeping her eyes on the road. "Probably. It depends."

"On what?"

"On whether I thought you'd hate him on sight, on how serious I was about him. I wouldn't want to get your hopes up by introducing you to someone who wouldn't be around long." She glanced in the rearview mirror and lowered her voice. "That's why I don't introduce anyone to Joshua right away, either. I wouldn't want to hurt him by letting him get too attached to just anyone."

"That seems wise."

"It also gives me time to make sure the boyfriend understands that Joshua will always come first in my life—before myself, before my work, and definitely before him." She sighed. "That's probably why I don't date much. Not that I mind. My life is full already, and I'm not one of these sisters who thinks she has to have a man to be complete. I learned that from you."

"I think I taught you too well," Grace said glumly, thinking of Marc, but Justine merely laughed.

When they reached the studio, Justine left Grace in front of the building and went to park the car. Grace went inside, up the elevator to the second floor. She waited there for the producer, a thin, dark-haired white woman with a harried expression, who bustled in ten minutes late, full of apologies.

"I wasn't waiting very long," Grace said, but the woman continued on as if she hadn't heard, leading her through a maze of corridors so rapidly that Grace stumbled and nearly fell.

"You'll be on in five, right after local news and right before the weather. Your assistant sent over the photos, so we're all set." The producer paused for breath as she stopped outside a large, solid door. "You'll need to keep quiet until your segment. Try not to knock anything over."

"I'll do my best," Grace said dryly as the producer opened the door and led her inside.

The studio was cool and dark except for the end of the room where the set was located. The two news anchors sat behind the desk taking turns reading from the TelePrompTer. Grace had hoped to see the same woman who had interviewed her last time, but her usual chair was occupied by the blond woman from the morning show. Soon after, when the news went to commercial and the producer led Grace to a chair on the set, she realized with some dismay that the blond woman was her interviewer.

"Good afternoon. I'm Andrea Jarthur," the blond woman said, smiling and extending a perfectly manicured hand.

Grace shook it. "Grace Daniels." From behind, someone clipped a microphone to her jacket. "Thanks for having me on."

"It's my pleasure. I love your work."

"Thank you," Grace said, nervousness stirring. "You do know I'm not here to talk about my work, right?"

"Of course," Andrea said, smiling. "But if we have time, I might get to that, okay?"

"I'd prefer it if you didn't."

Andrea's eyebrows rose. "I've never met an artist who didn't like to promote her work. Surely you don't mean it?"

Before Grace had a chance to reply, the stage manager called out, "In five, four . . ." He held up three fingers, then two, and then one.

Andrea turned to one of the cameras. "Welcome back. With us now is Grace Daniels, the celebrated quilt artist from right here in the Bay area. Welcome, Grace."

"Thank you."

"I understand that you're the curator of a new exhibit of antique quilts at the deYoung Museum in Golden Gate Park."

"That's right. The exhibit is titled 'Stitched into the Soul: A Celebration of African-American Quiltmakers in—'"

"Is any of your own work included?"

"No," Grace said, somewhat sharply. "These are *antique* quilts."

"Of course. Tell us, what makes these quilts so special?"

"They're important not only as works of art, but as historical artifacts. These quilts were pieced by slaves for their own use, and therefore they help document what life was like for them." Mindful of the limited time, Grace briefly explained what could be learned from the materials used, the patterns chosen, and the condition of the quilts.

"That's fascinating," Andrea interrupted just as Grace was warming to her subject. "Especially since the domestic arts are undergoing a renaissance of sorts these days, aren't they? Hobbies like quilting are becoming so popular lately, but you were really out there on the cutting edge—pardon the pun—years ago, weren't you?"

"Actually . . ." *Hobbies?* Grace thought. *Domestic arts?* "What this exhibit shows us is that—"

"I think what your fans really want to know is, when will you next treat us to an exhibit of your own work?" Andrea smiled innocently. "I understand it's been over three years since you've had a show."

"Two years."

"Can you give us a little hint as to your current projects? And maybe tell us how soon we can expect to see your latest work?"

Grace forced herself to smile through clenched teeth. "I don't like to discuss my projects before they're finished."

Andrea's bright smile never faltered. "The San Francisco art community will just have to wait in suspense, is that what you're saying?"

"I . . . I suppose so. But in the meantime, the deYoung Museum exhibit is a fascinating look at an important part of American art and cultural history." Quickly Grace ran through the particulars. Her voice sounded clear and serene in her ears, but inside she was fuming—at Andrea, of course, for her questions, but also at herself, for allowing herself to be so easily shaken.

After the interview ended, Grace abruptly rose and left the set without returning Andrea's farewell. Justine met her in the lobby, Joshua by her side. "How did it go?" she asked as Grace approached.

"I don't want to talk about it." Grace continued past her daughter and out the front door so quickly that Justine had to scoop up her son and hurry after her. Grace's heart was racing. Current projects—what current projects? How could she talk about her latest quilt when her latest quilt had been completed more than a year before? How could she admit that her well of creative inspiration—which she had once thought too deep to ever run dry—was as barren as her own future?

"I have to get away from here," she said, thinking aloud.

"The car's only a block away," Justine replied, baffled. But Grace hardly heard her. She had to get away from her loft, from her studio, from the museum where she faced questions like Andrea Jarthur's nearly every day, from everything familiar.

Suddenly a memory tickled the back of her mind, and she thought of her friend Sylvia Compson. Sylvia was running a quilt retreat somewhere in Pennsylvania. Perhaps Sylvia could provide the sanctuary Grace needed so that her art might return to her while she could still hold a needle.

Two

J ulia marveled that the agency's chartered jet managed to locate the tiny airport at all, much less come to a halt before speeding off the end of the runway. She studied the view from the window with misgivings. Except for the control tower and a small one-story building she assumed was the terminal, all she could see were trees. Had Maury taken leave of his senses, sending her out into the wilderness like this?

"The limo should be waiting," the man across the aisle said. "I've kept your arrival a secret, but don't be surprised if there's a crowd gathered around. They probably get a limo in this backwater only once every twenty years."

Julia felt a flash of annoyance, not the first since meeting her new agent a week after Maury's retirement party. "I'm Ares," he had introduced himself when she joined him at the restaurant. After she seated herself, he had reached across the table and offered her his hand and a flash of white teeth. Maury would have stood as she approached, and he would have pulled out her chair for her and not returned to his own until he was sure she was comfortable.

"Aries, the ram?" she had said, shaking the younger man's hand.

"No." His grin had suddenly become fierce. "Ares, the Greek god of war."

"How interesting," Julia had replied, gingerly releasing his hand and thinking, *Oh, dear.* She had allowed her contract to revert to him because of his reputation for being ruthless, for doing anything it took to get his clients the roles they sought. She couldn't have picked an agent less like Maury if she had tried, but Maury's approach, as a gentleman bargaining honorably with other gentlemen on the strength of his word, had become as ineffectual as it was archaic and naive. It also didn't hurt that Ares was the nephew of one of Hollywood's most powerful directors. She didn't have to like him, she reminded herself, to work with him.

Still, she worried that his focus on getting the deal might blind him to the importance of good PR. She gave him a disapproving look and said, "People in towns like these watch movies. They also kept *Family Tree* at the top of the Nielsens for many years."

"Near the top, anyway," Ares acquiesced. "The top of the middle, at least."

Stung, Julia pursed her lips and unfastened her seat belt.

No crowd had gathered by the limo parked on the tarmac, but the sight did attract a few curious glances from other travelers. A group of four women—some in cheerful patchwork clothing, all younger than she—talked and laughed as they greeted each other on the sidewalk. As the limo drove through the parking lot, Julia lowered her sunglasses to get a better look, but suddenly the tinted window began to rise.

She turned to Ares, who had his finger on the button in his armrest. "We can't have the locals gawking at you."

Julia thought the women seemed too preoccupied to spare the limo a second glance, but she removed her sunglasses and settled back into her seat, resigned.

For more than an hour they drove in silence past picturesque farms and rolling, forested hills. Julia lowered her window to take in the scenery, figuring they were surely isolated enough to satisfy Ares. Just when she thought she'd be stuck in that car with him until nightfall, the driver turned onto a gravel road that wound its way through a leafy wood.

"The least they could have done was pave the road," Ares grumbled. Julia hid a smile.

They crossed a narrow bridge over a creek so clear she could see stones at the bottom, and suddenly the trees gave way to a vast expanse of lawn. The road smoothed, and at the end of it Julia spotted a gray stone building with tall white columns and two semicircular staircases climbing gracefully to a broad veranda. She could see at least a dozen people—mostly women—unloading luggage or helping others carry their bags up the stairs, through the tall double doors, and into the house. With a pang, Julia suddenly remembered how much she had always hated the first day of school. Where would she sit in the classroom? Would she eat lunch alone every day? As lovely as this Elm Creek Manor appeared to be, Julia's stomach twisted at the thought of spending an entire week there, alone in a crowd. By instinct she slipped on her sunglasses again.

Sure enough, the clusters of women broke off their conversations and watched as the limousine came to a stop in front of the manor. When the driver opened the passenger door, Ares stepped out first and offered his hand to assist her. Julia took it ungratefully, suspecting it was a show for the crowd, who gaped as he escorted her up one of the semicircular staircases.

A woman older than she met them at the door. "Miss Merchaud?" she said pleasantly, without a trace of the awe or admiration Julia usually evoked from people outside the industry. "I'm Sylvia Compson. Welcome to Elm Creek Manor."

"Thank you." Julia followed her inside to a large foyer with gleaming marble floors and a ceiling three stories high. The furnishings spoke of wealth but of good taste and comfort rather than excess. Perhaps Maury hadn't been so misguided after all.

"You must be tired after such a long trip." Sylvia led her to the center of the room, where three women wearing name tags sat behind a long table. "Let's take care of your registration and show you to your room." She eyed Ares with some skepticism and nodded to the driver. "Matthew will help you with your bags."

She signaled to a young man with curly blond hair, who smiled as he approached and reached to take the bags from the driver.

Ares put out an arm to stop him. "It's under control, thanks." In an undertone, he added to Sylvia, "We don't need the entire staff knowing where Miss Merchaud will be staying. Security. You understand." He shrugged at Matthew. "No hard feelings, buddy."

"Sure," the other man replied, and Julia had the distinct impression he was trying hard not to laugh.

"Matthew is our caretaker. I assure you, he's quite harmless," Sylvia said.

Julia removed her sunglasses and pretended not to notice the hush that had fallen over the other guests, who were no doubt stunned to see "Grandma Wilson" playing the prima donna. "Give him the bags," she murmured to the driver. He looked from her to Ares, uncertain. "I said, give him the bags." At last the driver complied, and she smiled an apology to Matthew. To her relief, the registration process went quickly, and soon she, Ares, and Matthew with her bags were following Sylvia upstairs.

"Your suite is in the west wing," Sylvia told them as they reached the second floor landing. "You'll have your own bath. I trust you'll be quite comfortable."

"Thank you," Julia said, watching as other women went from room to room introducing themselves and welcoming each other, as excited and happy as children at summer camp. A few greeted Julia as she passed; she smiled guardedly in response, wondering if they recognized her without her limousine and stage makeup.

Sylvia ushered them into the room and pointed out the closet, the bath, and her private phone. It was a large suite with a four-poster bed covered with a blue-and-red quilt pieced of homespun plaids. "It's lovely," Julia said. "Thank you, Sylvia."

"You're quite welcome. Now, if there's nothing else you need, I'll return to our other guests."

Ares held up a hand. "Before you go, let's establish some ground rules."

The older woman's eyebrows rose.

"Miss Merchaud's status may cause some excitement," Ares went on. "Ordinarily Miss Merchaud goes out of her way to please her fans, but this week is different. We can't allow her to be disturbed. For that reason, she'll take her meals in her room rather than the common dining area, and she will not participate in any of the camp activities other than classroom instruction."

Sylvia folded her hands. "All of our activities are voluntary, Mr. Ares."

"Just Ares. Also, is there any way Miss Merchaud could have private instruction rather than attending classes?"

"I'm afraid that's not possible."

"Then at the very least, she'll need a table to herself at the front of the classroom."

"I'm sure that can be arranged."

"Ares," Julia interrupted, "I don't think—"

"You'll also inform your staff and other guests that they are not to address Miss Merchaud or trouble her in any way."

Sylvia's mouth twitched. "Do I understand you correctly? You wish me to announce that no one may speak with her?"

"Unless she speaks to them first, yes."

"That's absurd, and I won't do it," Sylvia declared. Behind her, the young blond man coughed as if he were strangling back a laugh. "Miss Merchaud is a camper like everyone else here." She turned her piercing gaze on Julia. "And I'm tired of talking about you as if you weren't in the room. If you wish to ignore people who speak to you, that's your decision, but I won't offend my other guests by clamping muzzles on them."

"I never wanted that," Julia said, distressed. "This wasn't my idea."

"I'm pleased to hear that, because otherwise you'll have a dreadful time this week. What an idea—to come to quilt camp and refuse to make any new friends." She shook her head in disapproval and frowned at Ares. "You see, I have a few ground rules of my own. If they don't suit you, I'd be happy to return your agency's check."

"That won't be necessary," Ares said stiffly. "I'm sure Miss Merchaud will be able to adapt to the circumstances."

"Good." Sylvia returned her attention to Julia, her voice noticeably warmer. "If there's anything we can do to make your stay more enjoyable"—her eyes flicked to Ares as if getting rid of him would be a step in the right direction—"please inform someone on the staff." With that, she and Matthew left the room, closing the door behind them.

"What a crazy old bat," Ares muttered.

"I found her quite pleasant," Julia said. "And I do wish you had consulted me before deciding I should isolate myself in my room all week. Maybe I would have enjoyed—"

"You're not here to enjoy yourself. You're here to work."

"Observing quilters would help me prepare for my role."

"You can observe them during your classes. The less you interact with these quilters, the less likely you'll reveal the truth. The press releases for the film will promote you as an expert quilter. Do you want these old biddies running to the media with the real story?"

Julia laughed. "I doubt even the tabloids would be interested. As secrets go, it's not very sexy."

"You can't afford the risk. Maury didn't want to tell you, but Bernier agreed to give you this part only because he thinks you already know how to quilt. If he discovers you lied, you're out of a job, and I don't think I need to tell you how difficult it will be to find you another role this good."

"I appreciate your honesty," she said crisply. How could he be so hurtful, so undiplomatic? "I suppose you're right. When I'm not practicing my quilting, I ought to be learning my lines."

"Don't bother. Bernier wants a major rewrite. Wait until you have a final script."

"Ellen will be involved in the revisions, of course?"

"Who?"

"Ellen Henderson, the writer and director."

Ares looked confused. "Stephen Deneford is directing. I heard it from Bernier himself two days ago."

"I see." Julia wondered how Ellen had been informed of the decision. "But she's still the writer."

"I guess she might be consulted. You know how Deneford and Bernier are."

Julia shrugged as if she did, although she had met Bernier only once and knew Deneford merely by reputation—and surely no more than half of those stories could be true.

None too soon, Ares left her to settle into her room. The room felt oddly still when she was alone, the silence broken only by the little noises she made unfastening her suitcases and opening and closing bureau drawers. From the hallway came the sounds of the other women talking and laughing, and the sound of quick footsteps going from room to room. Julia wondered why all the other guests seemed to know each other already, when quilt camp had only just begun.

She sat on the bed and listened.

✣

Donna had been at quilt camp for less than an hour but had already unpacked her suitcase and had met one of her next-door neighbors and the woman across the hall from her suite on the second floor of the south wing. She had just returned to her room for a patchwork jacket she had promised to show a quilter from West Virginia when she heard a voice through her open doorway. "I'm here," an elderly woman called. "The fun can begin!"

"Vinnie!" several other women cried out, and a clamor of voices echoed down the hallway.

Donna peered outside to see what all the commotion was about. A thin woman in her early eighties was trying to make her way down the hallway, but was stopped every few feet by one welcoming camper after another. She wore a bright red skirt, white tennis shoes and top, and had a red baseball cap perched on a fluffy cloud of white hair. Donna liked her on sight, and was pleased when the young man carrying her suitcase eventually led her into the unoccupied room next door. Several other campers followed them inside.

Donna's other next-door neighbor joined her in the hall. "Vinnie's here," she said, delighted. "That means we'll have a party."

"Do you two know each other?"

"I met her here last summer. She was one of the first twelve guests of Elm Creek Quilt Camp, and she's come back each year since, always during the week of her birthday. The staff throws a big surprise party for her—only it's not such a surprise anymore, though Vinnie always pretends it is. She's a riot. Come on, I'll introduce you."

She took Donna's arm and pulled her down the hallway. Donna was enjoying herself so much that she could almost forget that at that very moment her husband was in Minneapolis with Lindsay, Brandon, and Brandon's parents. And where on earth was Megan? It was almost time for supper, and she hadn't checked in yet.

✣

Megan pulled off the highway and followed the signs for food and lodging. She had been driving for hours, the past two with a growing suspicion that she had missed the correct exit. *Contemporary Quilting* magazine had awarded her a generous travel allowance, but instead of using it for an airline ticket and cab fare, she had put the money aside for Robby's back-to-school clothes. Now she regretted her frugality. She had anticipated having several more hours of daylight to drive by, but she hadn't considered the rolling Appalachian terrain. The sun had descended nearly to the tops of the mountains behind her; if she had missed the proper turnoff with the sun shining, how could she expect to find it in twilight? Twice she had stopped to ask directions—but while one person had heard of Waterford but didn't know how to get there, the other had insisted there was no such town in Pennsylvania.

Frustrated, her stomach growling, she pulled into the parking lot of a diner, ruefully remembering the camp brochure's photos of the elegant banquet hall at Elm Creek Manor. She would grab a bite to eat, study the map and get her bearings, and be back on the road in a half hour—and with any luck, she would choose the right direction.

She seated herself in a booth so she would have plenty of room to spread out her map. After the waitress took her order, she traced her route with a pencil, referring to the printed directions Elm Creek Quilts had provided. When the waitress delivered her turkey melt with fries, Megan moved the papers out of the way and thanked her. On impulse, she asked, "Do you know how to get to Waterford?"

The waitress shook her head. "Never heard of it."

Megan's heart sank. "Thanks anyway." Her gaze fell on a plate in the waitress's other hand. She inhaled the fragrance of baked apples and cinnamon and decided she'd order a slice of apple pie when she finished her supper. She deserved some dessert, as consolation for the loss of her first day of quilt camp. Besides, with her luck, she might be wandering Pennsylvania's back roads until dawn. She would need the energy.

As she watched the waitress walk away, her gaze fell on the man sitting in the booth across the aisle—or rather, on his shirt. It was the exact shade of blue she needed for her latest project, a charm quilt composed of hundreds of equilateral triangles. Instead of using pieced or appliquéd blocks, Megan preferred to make one-patch quilts, in which all the pieces were the same shape. Varying the color, pattern, and value of the pieces could create dramatic visual effects, but indifference to fabric placement could easily result in a drab, uninspired quilt. And since a charm quilt by definition required that no fabric be used more than once, she often spent weeks searching for the right material to finish a project. The gray-blue she now looked upon had eluded her for a month, even though her internet friends had sent her swatches of the various hues in their collections.

"Did I spill something on myself?"

Megan looked up, startled, into the puzzled but smiling face of the man wearing the shirt. "Oh, I'm sorry," she stammered. "I was just admiring your shirt."

"Thanks."

Megan wished she had stared more discreetly, but he had spoken to her first, and she just had to have that blue. "Where did you get it?"

"It was a gift from . . . a friend."

Something in his voice told Megan his friend was a woman. "It's very nice," she said lamely. She hoped he didn't think she was trying to pick him up. "I . . . see, I'm a quilter, and I'm always looking for the right fabric."

"Say no more," he said, with a knowing grin. "My grandmother is a quilter."

Great, Megan thought. As if she hadn't met enough people who considered quilting the exclusive domain of little old ladies and people with too much time on their hands. She was tired of explaining her passion to those who didn't know any better and decided not to bother trying to explain it to some stranger in a diner whom she'd never see again.

Megan returned her attention to the map as she ate, trying to figure out where she had gone wrong. According to her father's estimate, she should have reached the turnoff two hours ago. Should she backtrack or keep going east? She had seen a gas station across the street from the diner; maybe someone there would be able to direct her, although the responses she had received so far made that seem unlikely.

By the time she finished her sandwich, she had decided to give the gas station a chance—after dessert. She signaled the waitress, who approached with a slice of apple pie on a plate. "You read my mind," Megan said.

"What's that?" the waitress said, delivering the plate to the man in the booth across the aisle.

"Oh, I thought that was for me. I was just about to order a slice. Could I have it à la mode, please?"

"I'm afraid you're too late, honey. That was the last piece."

"Are you sure?"

The waitress looked tired. "You can check for yourself if you don't believe me." She jerked her head in the direction of the front counter, where an empty pie tin sat in the bakery case. "Would you like something else? Chocolate cake? Peach cobbler?"

"No, thanks. I was really looking forward to that apple pie."

"Here," the man said. "You can have it. I haven't touched it yet."

"Oh, no," Megan said. "Thanks anyway."

"No, really." The man got up and brought the plate to her table. "Take it."

"I'm not going to take your dessert."

"You're not taking it; I'm giving it to you." He set the plate on her table, smiling. "Go ahead. Enjoy."

"I don't want it." Annoyed, Megan pushed the plate toward him. "What planet are you from, that you offer perfect strangers in restaurants your dessert?"

"Cincinnati."

"No kidding," she said, without thinking. "Me, too."

"Really." He sat down across from her. "I live near Winton Woods. How about you?"

"Actually . . ." Involuntarily, she shrank back against the seat as his knees bumped hers. "I moved away when I was very young."

"To Pennsylvania?"

"Well . . ." She wasn't about to tell some strange man where she lived. She looked to the waitress for help, but the woman merely folded her arms and listened. "Look," she said to the man, in a voice she hoped was firm but not unkind, in case he was a nutcase or something. "I appreciate your generosity, but you ordered the pie first, so it's yours. I can't accept it."

He shrugged. "So we'll split it." He turned to the waitress. "Could you bring us another plate and fork, please, and a dish of ice cream on the side?" He looked questioningly at Megan. "Vanilla?" When Megan managed a nod, he turned back to the waitress. "Vanilla."

The waitress returned quickly with his order, and he deftly sliced the piece of pie and placed half on the new plate. "Here you go," he said with a friendly grin.

"Thanks," she said, resigned. "Do you want some of my ice cream?"

"No, thanks," he said. "When it comes to apple pie, I'm a purist. No ice cream, no cheese, no caramel—nothing to mar the pure simplicity of the apple and the pastry." With that, he took a large bite of pie, savoring the mouthful.

Megan watched him, her misgivings changing to amusement. "I had no idea it was possible to have such strong opinions about apple pie."

"You should hear my discourse on tiramisu."

Megan smiled and took a bite of the dessert—and found it just as delicious as its fragrance had promised. "It's wonderful. Thanks for sharing it. I'll pay half, of course—"

"Don't be silly. It's my treat."

"At least let me pay for the ice cream, since you're not having any." She gave him a practiced no-nonsense look that had proven most effective with Robby. "I insist."

"Fair enough." He glanced down at her map. "Are you planning a trip, or did you lose your way?"

"Lost my way. I don't suppose you know how to get to Waterford?"

"Sure. I just came from there."

She was so astonished she almost dropped her fork. "You have no idea how glad I am to hear that. I thought I missed the turnoff, and I'd have to turn around and go home."

"You didn't miss it. Head east for another hour and you'll see the sign. Here." He turned her map around and picked up her pencil. "The sign doesn't say Waterford, but it's the same exit as Two Rivers." He circled a spot on her map. "Go south for a few miles and you'll start to see signs for Waterford College. You should be there by seven."

"Thanks," she said, greatly relieved.

"Anytime." He signaled to the waitress, then shrugged apologetically. "Sorry to eat and run, but it's a long drive back to Cincinnati, and tomorrow's a school day."

"Oh. Of course." She felt oddly disappointed as he rose and took the check from the waitress. "Well, thanks again for the dessert and the directions."

"My pleasure." He left his check and a few bills on his table across the aisle. "Drive safely."

"You too."

Megan watched him leave the diner, then peered out the front window and watched him climb into a well-kept but older model compact car. Only as he drove off did she realize that she didn't even know his name. Not that it mattered. "Tomorrow's a school day," he had said, which meant he was probably a dad with children—a married dad with children. Then a thought struck her. It was the middle of August. Unless his children's school had a very strange schedule, they should still be on summer vacation, as Robby was—which meant that this nice-seeming guy was either lying to her or had a very bizarre sense of humor.

The evidence pointed to a friendly but rather odd man. *Too bad,* she thought and put him out of her mind.

✣

After the welcome banquet, Sylvia invited Grace to a cozy sitting room off the kitchen for a cup of tea and a chat. "I'm so delighted you accepted my invitation at last," Sylvia said after giving her a warm hug. "How many years has it been?"

"Five, I think," Grace said, easing herself down onto a sofa and taking the cup Sylvia offered her.

"That's right. Lancaster, wasn't it? The Quilter's Heritage Celebration?" Sylvia took a seat beside her, and her eyes had a faraway look. "And to think Elm Creek Quilts didn't even exist then."

"It's amazing what you've accomplished in such a short time."

Sylvia sipped her tea and nodded as if she agreed, as if, like Grace, she was amazed at the long journey that had taken her away from her beloved home and back again. When she and Grace first met, Sylvia had been estranged from her family for decades and had never expected to return to Elm Creek Manor.

Fifteen years before, Grace had been giving a lecture at the University of Pittsburgh on Civil War–era textiles and how they had inspired her own work. She created what she called story quilts, appliqué quilts that illustrated historical and sometimes autobiographical tales. Unlike the intricate, painstaking appliqué of the Baltimore Album style, her work more closely followed the folk-art appliqué tradition, with abstract figures representing people, places, moods, or ideas. That evening she displayed several antique quilts from her collection, including one pieced by a runaway slave who had settled in Canada. After describing the symbolism of the motifs the unknown quilter had used, Grace showed a quilt of her own, one she had sewn in tribute to the long-ago quiltmaker as Grace imagined her hazardous journey north to freedom.

At a reception following the lecture, Sylvia introduced herself and told her about the Civil War–era quilts she remembered from her childhood home, which had been a station on the Underground Railroad. Intrigued, Grace asked her if it would be possible for her to inspect the collection and possibly include photos of them in the book she was writing.

"That's unlikely," Sylvia said crisply. "For all I know, the quilts might not be there anymore."

Taken aback by her sudden change in temper, Grace apologized, wondering what she said to offend. Sylvia shook her head and said, "No, I should apologize to you. You had no way of knowing what a sensitive subject this is for me." She went on to explain that she and her sister had had a falling out years ago, and that Sylvia had not returned to her family estate since shortly after the war.

"Vietnam or the Gulf?" Grace asked, wondering how long this estrangement had gone on, and if the sisters might reconcile soon.

"The Second World War."

With that, Grace's hopes that she might be able to view those tantalizing quilts in the near future evaporated. In the years that followed, whenever she ran into Sylvia at a quilting function, she inquired about her relationship with her sister as delicately as she could, and eventually her concern for the quilts transformed into sympathy for her aging friend, who seemed to be growing more brittle-tempered with each year the old resentments simmered. Grace and her sisters were so close that hardly a week passed when they didn't communicate at least by phone, and she found it hard to imagine anything they could do that would compel Grace to sever all ties with them. No wonder Sylvia seemed so alone, despite her friends and accomplishments; she had cast off all her ties to her own history, and in doing so, she had lost herself. When Grace learned that Sylvia's sister had passed away, she feared that Sylvia would never recover from the loss and from the knowledge that now reconciliation would never come, but Sylvia had surprised her. From the debris of her grief, Sylvia had built a new future for herself and had come home at last to reclaim her family's history.

"I didn't build Elm Creek Quilts alone, of course," Sylvia was saying. "I have some very dedicated helpers. The truth is, I'm all but retired from the business now. Two young women, Sarah McClure and Summer Sullivan, direct our operations these days."

"You haven't retired from quilting, I hope."

"No, no, I could never do that. Even with the business, I still offer my opinion when asked—and often when I'm not asked—and I sign off on all our major financial and development decisions. Lately I've been seeing a bit of the country, traveling with a friend. I've spent more weeks away from Elm Creek Manor than here this summer."

"I'm glad you happened to be in town the week I came."

"Now, Grace," Sylvia admonished. "Do you really think I'd make myself scarce when you've come all this way? I couldn't leave without finding out what's troubling you."

Grace almost spilled her tea. "What do you mean?" Carefully she placed her cup and saucer on the coffee table. "I'm fine. I just thought I would enjoy a week of quilt camp."

"Grace, dear." Sylvia fixed her with that knowing gaze Grace remembered well. "We both know there's nothing our teachers could show you that you haven't seen already. You should be a teacher here, not a camper."

"I just needed a change of scene."

"Perhaps you do. I must say I've never seen you so tense. You haven't smiled once since you walked through those doors." Sylvia placed a hand on her friend's, and in a gentle voice, added, "But I know there's more. What's wrong, Grace?"

Grace took a deep breath and tried to smile. "My muse has fled."

Sylvia's eyebrows rose. "I see. And you thought you might find her here?"

"I thought in new surroundings, with other quilters around to motivate me, I might be able to reawaken my creativity." Grace shook her head, hopeless, and cradled her teacup in her hands. "I don't know. I'm probably grasping at straws, but I haven't started a new project in eighteen months. Eighteen months! You know how prolific I used to be."

A frown of worry creased Sylvia's forehead. "Can you think of any reason you might be blocked? Did something happen eighteen months ago? Have you been under an unusual amount of stress?"

Grace's heart pounded. Was she that transparent? "No, of course not. Just the usual stress." Sylvia looked dubious, so Grace blurted out the first plausible worry that came to mind. "Except for my daughter. She's seeing a much older man fairly seriously, and she didn't even tell me about him."

"But you've worried about Justine before, and your art hasn't suffered."

"I suppose that can't be it, then," Grace said, as if she didn't know precisely what the source of her anxiety was. But she couldn't tell Sylvia, not yet, not until she had no choice. "Maybe there isn't a cause. Maybe I've just run out of ideas and inspiration. But there must be some way to replenish myself even if I don't understand why I ran dry."

"If it's replenishment you need, I'll see that you get it," Sylvia said. "Perhaps I was wrong about our staff not having anything to teach you. Why don't you sit in on some of our advanced classes? We have some delightful workshops in color theory, photo transfer, computer pattern design—all sorts of exciting techniques to explore."

"Photo transfer?"

"Yes, techniques for transferring images from a photograph onto fabric. You've always been fascinated with quilts as historical artifacts and documenting quiltmakers' lives. Perhaps photo transfer could help you discover a new way to explore that area of your craft. And it's not just the information that might stir your creativity," Sylvia added. "The interaction with other quilters is what I find most invigorating about a class, whether I'm the student or the teacher. You never know what new ideas might come to mind when you brainstorm with other quilters."

"Yes, you're right." Grace felt a flicker of hope, and suddenly she realized that for the first time in months, she wasn't dreading the thought of approaching a stack of uncut fabric. "Sign me up."

Sylvia laughed. "Consider it done. But Grace, don't forget that the most important thing you can do this week is to relax and enjoy yourself. Think of your quilting as play, not work. Take the pressure off yourself and remember the joy quilting brings you. You have all the time in the world. Be patient and have fun."

Sylvia spoke encouragingly, but the words felt dull and empty to Grace. She didn't have all the time in the world. Despite the difference in their ages, she might have less time than Sylvia. Any project she began now might remain incomplete, like so many of the anonymous, abandoned relics from generations past she documented at the museum.

"Grace!"

Grace started and realized that she couldn't feel the teacup in her hand. Too late, she tried to hold the cup upright, but the warm liquid sloshed onto her lap. She gasped and instinctively tried to leap to her feet, but her ankle twisted under her clumsily, and she fell back onto the sofa.

"Goodness, dear," Sylvia exclaimed, handing her another napkin. She hurried into the kitchen and returned with a damp towel. "Did you burn yourself?"

"No . . . no, I'm fine." She wasn't fine. She was shaken badly, and her hand was still numb. She grasped the towel and tried to blot the tea stains from her slacks.

"Are you sure?" Sylvia's gaze was piercing.

"Quite sure." Grace laughed shakily. "Annoyed at myself for staining my favorite slacks, but otherwise unharmed."

"Hmph." Sylvia studied her a moment as if waiting for more, but when Grace said nothing, she sighed. "Well, you run upstairs and change, and I'll have one of my helpers wash those for you." She glanced at her watch and then out the window, where twilight was descending. "If you hurry, you won't miss our welcome ceremony."

"Welcome ceremony?"

"You'll see. You'll enjoy this. In fact, it might be just what you need to call that wayward muse back where she belongs." Sylvia rose, but she paused, looking down at Grace with a fond but troubled smile. "And if later you decide you want to talk, I'm always willing to listen."

Wordlessly Grace nodded and rose, wondering if anyone could keep a secret from Sylvia for long.

❦

The sun was just beginning to set when a staff member named Sarah McClure knocked on Donna's door and invited her to the welcome ceremony. Donna joined several other campers in the hallway and followed Sarah downstairs. "What's the welcome ceremony like?" Donna asked Vinnie. "There wasn't anything about it in the brochure."

But Vinnie refused to tell her. "I won't spoil the surprise," she said. "You first-timers will have to find out the hard way, like the rest of us."

A young woman beside Donna asked, "Is it an initiation? It won't hurt, will it?"

She looked so alarmed that the others laughed, but secretly Donna had been wondering the same thing.

Just as they were crossing the foyer, one of the front doors swung open and a slender woman entered, carrying a suitcase. She had light brown, shoulder-length hair and looked to be in her early to mid-thirties. Her gaze traveled from the empty registration table in the center of the room to the group of quilters obviously interrupted in the middle of an activity. With dismay, she asked, "Is it too late to register for camp?"

Although Donna had never seen her photo or heard her voice, she knew at once who the latecomer was. "Megan?"

"Donna?"

Megan barely had time to set down her suitcase before Donna had raced across the room and embraced her. "Megan! It's so wonderful to meet you in person! I was afraid you had changed your mind."

"No, I just misplaced it temporarily." She laughed, but she sounded exhausted.

Sarah joined them and welcomed Megan to Elm Creek Manor. She led Megan to the registration table, and within a few moments, Megan had signed in and received her room assignment. "I'm sorry you missed the welcome banquet," Sarah said, "but I could fix you something to eat in the kitchen."

"That's all right. I stopped at a diner on the way." Megan looked at Donna and added in an undertone, "Wait until I tell you about *that*."

To Donna's delight, Megan's dry tone sounded exactly the way Donna had always imagined it, and suddenly she was certain that joining Megan at camp had been a good idea.

Donna waited with the others as Sarah took Megan to her room to drop off her suitcase. When the pair rejoined them, Sarah led the group through the west wing and outside, onto a gray stone patio surrounded by evergreens and lilac bushes. The other guests had gathered inside a circle of forty chairs, where they sipped glasses of lemonade or iced tea and munched cookies. Donna spotted Sylvia Compson standing somewhat apart from the group, chatting with another woman who looked familiar, although Donna didn't remember meeting her earlier that day.

Megan clutched her arm. "Is that who I think it is?"

"Who?"

"The woman over there with Sylvia Compson. Is she Grace Daniels?"

Megan's prompting stirred Donna's memory. "She could be."

"I'm sure it's her." Megan glowed with excitement. "I didn't know there would be famous quilters here."

"That's not the least of it. Rumor has it Julia Merchaud is here, too."

"Julia Merchaud, from television?"

"The one and only. I didn't see her myself, but other people on our floor swear they saw her go into the room at the end of the west wing."

"That's right across from my room," Megan gasped, then hesitated and scanned the faces of the other guests. "But why isn't she here for the welcome ceremony?"

"I don't know. I hope it's not because she's so high and mighty she can't associate with us commoners."

Megan laughed. "Maybe she thinks we'll pester her for autographs instead of letting her enjoy camp." Then she frowned. "Okay, I'll admit it; that's exactly what I was going to do. Maybe she's right to stay away."

"If we see her, we'll treat her like any other quilter," Donna resolved. "Unless she wants us to treat her like a big star. Then we'll just leave her alone."

Megan agreed, and, eyeing the table near the door, suggested they get themselves some refreshments before it was too late. Just as they picked up their cups and plates of cookies, Sylvia clapped her hands to get everyone's attention.

"Let's have everyone take a seat so we can begin," Sylvia said. "It's getting late and I don't want any of you nodding off during the ceremony."

The campers laughed, some nervously because they didn't know what was coming next, others because they were far too excited to sleep. Their voices fell silent as Sylvia lit a candle and placed it in a spherical crystal holder. She moved to the center of the circle and looked around at the faces of her guests. "One of our traditions is to conclude the first evening of quilt camp with a ceremony we call Candlelight. Originally we intended this as a way for you to introduce yourselves to us and to each other; we're going to be living and working together closely this week, so the sooner we get to know each other, the better. But our ceremony helps you to know yourselves better, too. It helps you focus on your goals and wishes and helps prepare you for the challenges of the future."

Donna felt a thrill of expectation. Sylvia made it sound as if they were embarking on a journey together, when all Donna had planned for was a simple week of quilting with a friend.

Sylvia continued by explaining the ceremony. The campers would pass the candle around the circle, and as each woman took her turn to hold the candle, she would explain why she had come to Elm Creek Quilt Camp and what she hoped to gain that week. There was a pause after Sylvia asked for the first volunteer. Donna froze, heart thumping, and relaxed only when a woman two seats to her left raised her hand. Since the candle would be passed clockwise, Donna would have some time to prepare her remarks. She certainly couldn't tell the truth, that she was at camp because she was too cowardly to face her daughter's engagement.

The first woman held the candle for a long moment in silence. Around them, unseen, crickets chirped in the gradually deepening darkness. "I'm

Angela Clark, from Erie. I'm a new quilter. I've only made little things, pot holders and baby quilts. I came to camp to improve my skills because . . ." She took a deep breath. "My oldest son died in a car accident two years ago." A murmur of sorrow and dismay went up from the circle. "His best friend was driving. He was drinking—they were both drinking. He smashed the car into a tree. My son was killed instantly. His friend had a few broken bones, but otherwise he was fine." Someone murmured a scathing rebuke of the young driver. "No, you don't understand. I don't hate him. He made a terrible, terrible mistake, and my son paid for it. They both paid for it. My son died that night, but his best friend has been dying ever since, a little each day." She looked around the circle. "He's grieving, but he won't allow himself to heal. He can't forgive himself, and he can't believe that my husband and I and my other children have already forgiven him. He was Jeremy's best friend. Jeremy loved him as much as he loved his own brothers. I can't bear for him to be in such pain." She hesitated and lowered her eyes. "A lot of people want me to hate him, but I can't do it. I can never excuse what he did, but I want him to get on with his life. I've read about memorial quilts—the kind made from pieces of someone's clothing. I saved a lot of my son's T-shirts from school and other activities, and thought I would piece them into a quilt for my son's friend, to help him remember the good times he and Jeremy shared, and to help him find some closure. I don't know if it will work, but I'm going to try." With that, she passed the candle on to the next woman in the circle.

"I don't know how I'm supposed to follow *that,*" the woman said in mock displeasure as she took the candle. "I just came because I saw an ad in a magazine." A smattering of soft laughter went up from the circle, and Donna felt the tension and nervousness leaving her as she joined in.

She listened as one by one the others told their stories. One woman had come to learn how to quilt the pieced tops her late grandmother had left her; another, noticeably pregnant, had come to enjoy one last trip on her own before assuming the responsibilities of motherhood. "Also because my husband's nesting instinct kicked in," she said with a naughty grin. "He decided to paint every room of the house, and the fumes make me ill. At least, that's what I told him." Everyone laughed as she passed the candle to Vinnie.

"My name's Lavinia Burkholder, but everyone calls me Vinnie—except for my grandchildren, who call me Nana. I came to celebrate my birthday. I have the distinction of being one of Elm Creek Quilts' first campers." She rose and bowed as to a round of applause, then handed the candle to the woman on her left.

Before long the candle came to Grace Daniels. Like most of the others, she held the candle for a long while before speaking. "I'm Grace Daniels, from San Francisco," she eventually said, confirming what everyone else there had already guessed. "I'm an old friend of Sylvia's. She's been after me to visit her camp for years now, and I finally decided to indulge her." She smiled at Sylvia as the others chuckled. But then her smile faded. "What do I hope to gain this week? Some inspiration, I hope. I feel like I've run out of ideas, and . . . and I hope to discover some here." With that, she handed the candle to Megan.

"My name is Megan Donohue, and I'm from Monroe, Ohio. I came because my watercolor charm quilt won *Contemporary Quilting* magazine's quilt contest, and the first prize was this trip." She smiled at Donna. "I also came to meet my friend Donna, whom I met on the internet." And with that, she passed the candle to Donna.

Donna smothered a moan of dismay. Megan's story had been the shortest one yet, and Donna had planned on at least another minute or two to come up with something to say. "I'm Donna Jorgenson, and as Megan told you, I came to camp to meet my internet friend." Then she could think of nothing more.

She looked around the circle of faces. Some of them would become her friends that week, she realized, confidantes as dear to her as Megan. She thought of how they had opened their hearts, trusting in the sincerity and support of their listeners. How could she do any less?

"I also came because I'm a coward," she heard herself say. "My eldest daughter just got engaged to a young man my husband and I don't know very well. My daughter, though, I do know her, and something tells me her heart isn't in this marriage. It's just an instinct, but I don't think she's happy—and all I ever wanted was for my daughters to be happy, happy and safe." She confessed the rest. "I came to camp because it got me out of meeting her fiancé's parents. I know I'm just delaying the inevitable, but I want to buy my daughter time. It might be only a few weeks, but it might be enough for her to be certain that this is what she really wants."

"Don't underestimate your intuition," someone said. In the semidarkness, Donna was not sure who had spoken. "Our maternal instincts are there for a reason."

Others nodded and chimed in their agreement. Donna looked around the circle of concerned faces, and although nothing had changed, somehow she felt comforted. As she passed the candle to the next woman, Megan put an arm around her shoulders and whispered mournfully, "And here I thought you came just for me." She said it so comically that Donna had to laugh, although she was blinking back tears.

Before the next woman could begin her story, Grace leaned over behind

Megan and murmured, "You and I should talk." She gave Donna a knowing look. "I have a daughter, too."

Donna nodded, speechless. A world-famous quilter wanted to talk with her, Donna Jorgenson from Silver Pines, Minnesota. She had finally met her best friend and closest confidante in person. She had aired her fears to a circle of women who only an hour ago had been strangers, and they had taken her seriously, without judgment or ridicule.

She felt as safe as if she were at home surrounded by friends who had known her all her life.

The candle cast shadow and light around the circle as the next woman told her story.

⚜

After supper, with no one to talk to, Julia had gone through her yoga routine with extra care, then lay on the bed idly paging through the issue of *Variety* she had brought to read on the plane. Bored, she had tossed it aside and rummaged through her bag for the script and a notepad. Ares didn't want her to waste time memorizing lines that would probably change in the rewrite, but that didn't mean Julia would accomplish nothing that evening. She took a seat at the small desk in the corner and began reading through the script, noting each quilting technique that Sadie had used and Julia would need to learn. By the time darkness fell, she had finished the first act and had listed several unfamiliar terms on her notepad: basting, piecing, binding. Just then the voices had broken into her concentration and compelled her to go to the window to investigate.

For more than an hour, Julia had sat at her window, spellbound, listening as one by one the women shared the deepest secrets of their hearts with perfect strangers. How liberating that must feel, to unburden oneself without fear of rejection.

What would she have said when it was her turn to hold the candle, if she were spending the warm summer evening among them? She had come to Elm Creek Manor to learn how to quilt so that she could keep a movie role. She had to keep the movie role to breathe life into a stalled career. She had to revitalize her career or fade away into obscurity and become a has-been before she had ever truly made a difference, before she had ever participated in something worthwhile, something worth remembering. Something worth all she had sacrificed for her career—two marriages, her privacy, her pride when critics mocked her attempts to perfect her chosen art.

If only she could be as open and trusting as the women gathered in a circle beneath her window. Of course, none of them feared that one of the others would race to the tabloids with her deepest secrets. None of them worried that her failures would become fodder for late-night talk-show comedians. They could afford to trust each other.

Overcome by the sensation that she was intruding on an intimacy she did not deserve, she let the curtain fall back and withdrew from the window.

Three

Donna awoke bleary-eyed and disoriented in the unfamiliar room. For a moment, as she tried to sort out the furniture and shadows, she thought she was in the bedroom she had shared with her elder sister as a child. The blue-and-white Dresden Plate quilt on the bed focused her memory. It was the first full day of quilt camp, and the clock on the nightstand told her it was not quite five. Usually she needed an alarm to yank her out of sleep by seven. *I must still be on Minnesota time,* she thought, until the sleepy confusion left her and she realized that she had her time zones mixed up. At home it was not yet four.

Strangely enough, despite the travel and the excitement of the previous day, she felt as wide awake as if she had slept a full eight hours. Anticipation for the day ahead kept her from drifting off to sleep again, so she got up and dressed in her workout clothes. Silently she left her room and tiptoed down the grand staircase and across the foyer to the front door.

Outside the air was cool and misty, with the promise of warmth as soon as the sun rose above the trees. Donna stretched her calf muscles, enjoying the solitude and the chirping of birds in the distance. Then, with a sigh, she descended the circular stone staircase and began walking briskly across the lawn and along the edge of a thick grove of trees, inhaling deeply and pumping her arms.

Sometimes she wondered why she bothered. Years of watching her diet and exercising regularly had not burned any of the excess baggage from her hips and thighs, and yet she stuck with it, stubborn and hopeful to a fault, as she was in everything. Lindsay encouraged her mother by urging her to think of the internal benefits to her heart and lungs, and not to evaluate her fitness by the number on a scale alone. Donna tried, but it wasn't easy to be proud of her low cholesterol and excellent blood pressure when her size four-teens no longer fit as well as they once had. "Maybe they shrank in the laundry," Paul would say when she fretted, and she had to bite her tongue to keep from retorting that his clothes had been in the same load, and they still fit him fine.

She hadn't planned to stick to her morning workout routine at camp, but seeing Megan motivated her. Megan, nearly as slender as Lindsay, wouldn't blame pregnancy for her weight gain, unlike herself, who clung to that excuse although her babies were now sixteen and twenty. For some reason Donna had assumed that Megan would be closer to her own size. Maybe Megan had thought the same thing about Donna, and was dismayed to learn that her internet friend was so pudgy and out of shape.

Knock it off, she ordered herself. She was at camp; she was supposed to be relaxing. If she kept up with those miserable thoughts, at breakfast she'd be tempted to wolf down a foot-high stack of pancakes for comfort. If she wanted to make herself miserable, instead of contemplating her ever-widening thighs, she ought to think about Lindsay.

Lindsay. Donna's heart plummeted with such force that she quickly shifted her thoughts to her schedule for the day. After breakfast, she and Megan would meet for the first of a weeklong series of color theory classes. Lunch followed, and then she would attend an appliqué class while Megan took one on miniature quilts. Donna was disappointed that they hadn't chosen all the same classes but consoled herself with the thought that they had most of their seminars in common. She was especially looking forward to the watercolor workshop. Megan had already mastered the art of using small pieces cut from large-scale prints and arranging them so they blended together in the style of an Impressionist painting, and Donna hoped to pick up some tips from her. It wasn't by accident that Megan had won the *Contemporary Quilting* contest.

Her muscles now warmed from the exercise, Donna paused to stretch by a wood rail fence that, she assumed, indicated the northern border of the property. Last night, Sylvia's verbal tour of the estate had located the gardens to the north, but somehow Donna had missed them. Maybe the gardens were within the grove of trees she had just circled. She walked along the fence until she came upon a break in the trees. There she found a path of the same smooth, gray stones she had seen by the manor. At this end, the path was untended—probably unused, judging by the weeds and grass growing between the stones. Hoping she wasn't breaking any camp rules by straying off the more well traveled parts of the property, Donna pushed a branch aside and followed the path into the trees.

Fortunately for her arms and legs, which were acquiring a few scratches from the undergrowth, the path grew wider and clearer as she continued. Before long, she glimpsed a white wooden structure that, as she drew nearer, she realized was a gazebo. Then the trees opened into a clearing, and Donna stopped short—a pace away from tumbling into tiered flower beds carved into the hillside. From the top terrace she was eye-level with the gazebo's gingerbread molding, and she heard the splash of water somewhere beyond it. As the fragrance of flowers wafted to her, she looked around for the source of the sound—and found instead a series of stones artfully arranged along the edge of the hill as if nature had built a staircase there.

As she followed the stone path, more of the garden came into view: a black marble fountain in the shape of a mare prancing with two foals, and beyond that, four large, round planters filled with roses and ivy. The planters were larger at the base than the top, the lower halves forming smoothed, polished seats. Donna spotted someone sitting on one of those seats.

Grace Daniels.

She sat staring straight ahead at a bed of decorative grasses, not quite facing the gazebo. Donna almost called out to her, but the other woman's stillness held her back.

The trail to the manor resumed just past the spot where Grace was sitting, but Donna deliberately kept her distance. When she reached the edge of the garden she glanced back, tempted to remind Grace of her invitation to talk about their daughters. She bit her lip and considered, then decided to continue in silence. If Grace had wanted company, she would have called Donna over. Even if somehow Grace hadn't seen her as she passed in front of the gazebo, the sound of her sneakers clomping on the stone would have been hard to miss.

⚓

Grace's heart sank at the sound of footfalls, and in her peripheral vision she spotted someone on the other side of the gazebo. *Please turn around and go away,* she thought, but the figure emerged and began descending steps Grace hadn't seen in the hillside. She stared fixedly ahead, pretending she hadn't noticed the newcomer. It was one of the other campers, the plump woman with the Upper Midwest accent. *Leave me alone, leave me alone,* she thought, clutching her hands together in her lap.

She stiffened as the sound of footsteps grew louder, then relaxed as they continued past and fell silent. Grace took a deep breath and leaned back against the cool stone seat. Finally, someone who respected her privacy, who didn't insist that she talk all the time. That Candlelight business had been bad enough. If she had wanted a support group, she would have signed up for the one at the hospital.

Her fingertips were numb again. The pins-and-needles sensation had intensified since that disastrous meeting in Sylvia's sitting room. She felt her heart begin to pound, and rising panic stole over her. Quickly she closed her eyes and pictured herself in her favorite place: a restful spot in Santa Cruz, hiking through a redwood forest, emerging from the shade of the trees on the edge of a bluff overlooking the sparkling waters of the Pacific Ocean. She inhaled deeply and imagined the wind, the feel of the sunlight on her skin, the faintly sweet odor of moldering leaves, the smell of decay and new life.

She exhaled, trying to blow out all her anxiety with the breath, just as she had been taught. This time, the exercise worked, and she felt her pulse returning to normal.

She was not having a relapse. She was fine.

It was the fatigue and stress of travel, that was all. She had gone to bed too late and risen too early. She was not getting worse. She had plenty of time.

⚘

Julia overslept.

She had forgotten to set the alarm clock and, still jet-lagged, did not wake until someone knocked on her door. "Miss Merchaud?" a woman called. "Breakfast."

Julia scrambled out of bed and snatched up her robe. "Just a minute." Hastily she finger-combed her hair as she went to the door. She hoped the woman in the hallway didn't have a camera. The *National Inquirer* would pay big for a shot of her with mussed hair and no makeup. Holding her robe closed at the neck, she opened the door a crack, only wide enough to see a brown-haired young woman holding a covered tray, looking back at her inquisitively.

Julia had the younger woman place the tray on the desk and ushered her out again as quickly as possible. She wasn't hungry, but she nibbled on an English muffin and ate most of the fruit, leaving the omelet untouched. The coffee was suitably strong, though she missed her cinnamon cappuccino. Oh, well. As Ares had said, she was there to work. She could endure a week of roughing it.

She showered quickly but dressed and applied her makeup with care. In the hallway, the muffled sounds of other campers making their way downstairs had faded, and a glance at the clock told her she would have to hurry. She grabbed a pen and the notes she had compiled the previous night but, with an effort, forced herself to leave her sunglasses on the dresser.

Her registration papers included a map of the manor, and she followed the directions downstairs to the ballroom, which had been partitioned into classrooms with folding screens decorated in patchwork. The last of eleven women to arrive, she found Quick Piecing with barely a moment to spare. The instructor—the same young woman who had brought Julia her breakfast—had already begun her introduction as Julia slipped into a seat at the back of the room, grateful that she had a table to herself. She would have been mortified if the teacher had made another camper change places to accommodate Ares's demands.

The teacher, Sarah, passed out the first lesson, instructions on quick-piecing quarter-square triangles. "First, you'll need to pick a light fabric and a medium or dark," Sarah said. "Cut a six inch by twelve inch rectangle from each fabric using your rotary cutter, and then lay the two fabrics with right sides facing, the light piece on top."

As Sarah spoke, Julia watched with alarm as the other ten students reached into their bags and brought out folded bundles of fabric, plastic rulers, and odd-shaped tools that resembled pizza cutters. Was she supposed to have brought her own fabric? She glanced around her tabletop—a sewing machine, a gridded plastic mat, no fabric—and her face grew hot. Obviously she should have brought fabric from home; everyone else was prepared. She looked to the front of the classroom in dismay, but Sarah was already walking around the room observing her students as they layered fabric on their mats and happily sliced away at it with the pizza cutters.

"Is everyone ready to go on?" Sarah called out. Julia's meek "No" was lost in the chorus of affirmatives. "Okay, then, next I want you to take your pencil and, using your ruler, draw a grid of two-inch squares on the back of your light fabric."

A ruler. Julia snatched up her notebook and quickly tore out a sheet of paper. The pages were eight and one half inches by eleven; she could fold it into sections and estimate an inch. Then she remembered the gridded plastic mat and scooted her chair closer to it. To her relief, she saw that the grid was marked in one-eighth-inch increments along two edges. Folding her paper to strengthen it, she lined it up against the edge of the mat and began marking off inches. By the time her makeshift ruler was completed, the rest of the class had already proceeded to the next step. Racing to catch up, Julia tore two more sheets of paper from her notebook and wrote "Dark" on one and "Light" on the other. She drew a wobbly-edged grid as the other students moved on to their sewing machines. She was too far behind to ever catch up, but she persevered grimly. Ares had sent her to this godforsaken place with none of the proper materials, but she needed that role and she was going to learn *something* while she was there.

Suddenly a shadow fell over her table. "Is everything okay back here?"

Julia looked up to find Sarah standing on the other side of her table. "I . . . Yes, everything's fine," Julia said. "Please continue."

Sarah looked dubious. "Did you leave your things in your room? You have time to run upstairs and get them."

"No, thank you." The other students had paused in their work to watch. "Please, I don't want to hold up the rest of the class."

"Wasn't there a supply list in the course confirmation packet mailed to your home?"

A supply list. Of course, there must have been a supply list, and it must have been sent to the agency. "There probably was," Julia said, picturing her hands closing around Ares's throat, "but I didn't get it."

"I see," Sarah said, with a puzzled frown that said she didn't see at all.

"I have some extra fabric," said an older woman with a cloud of shockingly bright white hair. "What do you like? Red or blue?"

"Oh, no, that's quite all right," Julia demurred.

The woman was already making her way from the front of the room, a bundle of fabric in her arms. "Nonsense; I always bring plenty." She placed the bundle on Julia's table and held up a piece of kelly green fabric with wide red lines zigzagging across it. "Here's a nice one. Or do you prefer calico?"

"Calico," Julia said quickly, recognizing one of the unfamiliar terms from Ellen's script. The older woman smiled indulgently and handed her a piece of dark blue fabric sprinkled with tiny white flowers.

"Here's something you can use for the light fabric," another woman called out, waving a cream-colored piece over her head like a banner. Sarah supplied her with one of the pizza-cutter tools, and soon everyone had joined in, showering Julia with extra rulers and pins and needles and so much extra fabric she wasn't sure how she'd carry it back upstairs to her room. She felt her face flaming with embarrassment as she accepted their gifts and stammered out her thanks.

"I'm sorry you didn't get the list. There must have been some oversight," Sarah said. "After class, why don't you show me your course list and I'll send into town for the rest of the supplies you'll need."

"Thank you. I'd appreciate that." Julia wished everyone would stop looking at her. Suddenly she couldn't bear for the instructor to think that an experienced quilter would be so ignorant. She lowered her voice. "I'm sorry for the disruption, but I never quilted before."

The white-haired woman overheard, and her eyebrows shot up. "This is your first quilting class? Ever? My goodness, you're ambitious, skipping the basics and going straight to this high-tech stuff."

"Skipping . . ." Julia's voice trailed off, and she looked from the white-haired woman to Sarah. "This isn't a beginner's course?"

"Most new quilters start out in Beginning Piecing," Sarah said. "You've really never quilted before?"

Julia shook her head, thinking *Isn't it obvious?*

"Then . . ." Sarah hesitated. "I don't mean to question your judgment, but why did you sign up for Quick Piecing?"

Julia had never even seen a course description. Ares had signed her up for this course, and suddenly Julia understood why. "Because I need to learn quickly."

The white-haired woman laughed as if Julia had made a joke, but Sarah only smiled kindly. "I think tomorrow morning we should switch you to Diane's Beginning Piecing class, okay?"

"That would be lovely, thank you." Julia wished she could disappear.

⁜

On their way to their first activity, Megan confided that she had some misgivings about signing up for the color theory course, but she felt reassured when Donna confessed her own doubts. Their reasons differed, though; Megan feared the class would be dull, while Donna worried that it would be too technical to understand. To their delight, their apprehensions vanished within a few minutes, mostly because their eccentric teacher made the material lively and interesting. Gwen was a stout, red-haired woman who wore a bright blue beaded necklace and a long flowing skirt in a wild print, and her enthusiasm for the subject matter was infectious. "How dare she say such a thing," she had cried when a student timidly mentioned that her elementary school art teacher had insisted that red and purple didn't go together. "Who is she, the color police? Let her make quilts in matchy-matchy colors if she wants, but don't let her prevent you from being more adventurous!"

Her good-humored indignation sent the class into peals of laughter, which turned into murmurs of surprise and delight as Gwen passed out boxes of crayons and sheets of paper. She instructed them in a coloring exercise meant to free their inhibitions and expand their "color sense." Megan colored happily, feeling like a carefree first-grader as she and Donna talked and compared their work.

"As long as we're expanding our color sense, maybe you'll finally give purple a try," Donna said, waving a violet crayon before Megan's eyes.

Megan feigned a horrified shudder. "Get that thing away from me."

"You like blue and you like red. How can you not like purple?"

"It's simply a matter of personal preference. What do you care what colors I use or don't use?"

"I hate to see you limiting yourself."

Megan laughed. "This, from the woman who refuses to use white as a background fabric."

"That's just a habit, not a phobia. And I have good reason. Off-white and cream don't show the dirt as well." Donna gave her a determined look. "I'm going to get you to use purple in a quilt if it's the last thing I do."

Later, after Megan had completed her exercise and was looking around to see what the other quilters had done, she spotted Grace Daniels at a table on the other side of the room. She nudged Donna. "Look. There she is."

Donna's head jerked up, but then she frowned, disappointed. "I thought you meant Julia Merchaud."

"Grace Daniels isn't a big enough celebrity for you?" Megan teased. "Anyway, I don't think Julia Merchaud is really here. Her room is supposedly across the hall from mine, but I haven't seen her."

"Some people say they have."

"Yes, but some people say they've seen extraterrestrials and the Loch Ness Monster. Maybe these Julia Merchaud sightings are like that."

"Sure, Julia Merchaud is the Loch Ness Quilter."

Megan laughed, but her mirth faded as she watched Grace carefully select another crayon, her brow furrowed in concentration. "She seems sad."

"What makes you think so?"

"Everyone else is having fun, but she looks like she's taking the SATs."

"I saw her this morning, in the garden," Donna said. "I thought she wanted to be left alone. Maybe she's worried about her creativity, like she said at the Candlelight."

"She's not talking to anyone."

"Maybe she's shy."

Megan doubted that a famous quilt artist could feel shy among a crowd of admiring quilters, but before she could say so, Gwen announced that class was over. "Let's ask Grace to join us for lunch," Megan suggested as they gathered their things. Donna agreed, but when they looked over at the other side of the room, Grace had already left.

They looked for her outside, where the staff had arranged a picnic buffet on the veranda, but Grace wasn't at any of the tables or standing in line for food. "Tomorrow we'll sit near her in class," Donna said as they joined the queue. "The worst she can do is ignore us, right?"

"She won't. Who would be crazy enough to deny themselves the pleasure of our illustrious company?"

"Julia Merchaud, for one."

They laughed.

"What are you two girls giggling about?" someone behind them in line asked. Megan turned to find a white-haired woman eyeing them with mock suspicion. She wore red tennis shoes and a T-shirt that read "Quiltoholics Anonymous."

Donna laughed and introduced Megan to the woman, Vinnie from Dayton, Ohio. Megan had remembered her from the Candlelight, and was pleased that Vinnie remembered her.

"Oh, yes, you're the one who won the contest." Vinnie nodded toward the buffet and sighed happily. "Isn't this marvelous? I love a buffet. You can take whatever you want and leave the crap behind."

"Vinnie!" Donna protested.

"Relax, honey, I'm just teasing." Vinnie added a generous helping of baked beans to her plate. "But I'd better not let the staff hear me or I might get expelled." She raised her voice and looked around as if she feared unseen staff members were eavesdropping. "My, this food is so tasty."

"It's too tasty," Megan said. "I'll probably gain fifty pounds this week."

"I don't think you could gain fifty pounds if you tried." Donna's voice had a hint of envy in it. Megan watched as Donna returned the macaroni salad spoon to the bowl without taking any and reached for the tongs in a bowl of tossed salad instead. Donna noticed her scrutiny. "Before you ask, yes, I am trying to slim down."

"For the wedding?" Vinnie asked.

Megan winced. "Don't remind her." Then she shot Donna a sharp look. "Is that really why?"

"I'd happily gain two hundred pounds if I thought it would stop the wedding." Donna's voice was grim. She had reached the end of the line, and she quickly walked off with her plate to an Adirondack chair at the far end of the veranda.

Megan and Vinnie exchanged a look and hurried after her. "Don't you like the young man?" Vinnie asked as they took the empty chairs on either side of Donna.

"I hardly know him. I've seen him and Lindsay together for—I don't know, maybe a total of seven hours over the past two years."

"Maybe once you get to know him better, you'll grow more fond of him," Megan said.

"Maybe." Donna didn't look as if she believed it.

"There's always hope," Vinnie said. "Maybe she'll leave him at the altar."

"That only happens in movies."

"It happened to my grandson."

Megan and Donna stared. "You're kidding," Megan said.

"Well, maybe a little." Vinnie shrugged and nibbled on a piece of fried chicken. "It wasn't exactly at the altar. At least he was spared that indignity. But she did break off their engagement three months before the wedding."

"How awful for him," Donna said.

"Not really. She wasn't good enough for him—as I've told him plenty of times, not that he listens. He deserves better. And he definitely deserved better than to be strung along, only to be jilted after the invitations had been sent out."

Megan murmured her sympathies and refrained from pointing out that they were only getting her grandson's side of the story. In her experience, a woman who left a man usually had a very good reason for doing so. Then, with a pang, she thought of Keith, and his reason for leaving her—a blond Comparative Literature graduate student with no stretch marks and an uncanny ability to ignore Keith's irritating quirks.

Megan said, "If she was going to change her mind anyway, at least she did it before the wedding rather than after."

"He'll find someone else," Donna said.

"Of course he will, with a little help from Nana." Vinnie wiped her lips delicately with her napkin and set her plate aside. "How old is your daughter?" she asked Donna, reaching for the tote bag beside her chair.

"Twenty."

Vinnie took a red plastic photo album from her bag and flipped through the pages, shaking her head with regret. "I was afraid of that. She's too young for my Adam."

"She's too young to get married, period."

"I married at seventeen." Vinnie passed the open album to Donna. "But that was a different era. This is my grandson. Isn't he a good-looking young man?"

"Very." Donna gave Megan a sidelong look. "He looks close to your age."

Vinnie brightened. "You're single?"

"I am now." Donna held out the album to her, so Megan took it.

"Oh, dear. Divorced?"

"I'm afraid so," Megan said. "Actually, I'm annulled and divorced."

Donna looked bewildered. "How does that work?"

Megan hesitated, surprised by how much admitting his betrayal still hurt her. "When Keith first left me for another woman, a divorce was good enough for them. It was the quickest, easiest way to put me in the past. Later, though, she decided she wanted to get married in the Catholic Church, so he put in for an annulment. According to the Church, our marriage never existed."

"But you have a child," Donna said, aghast.

Vinnie shook her head and clicked her tongue. "It's far too easy to get an annulment these days, if you want my opinion. Not like when I was young. Then, you had to stick around and work on it whether you wanted to or not."

"And too many people spent their lives miserable in unhappy marriages," Megan said. "No, I'm better off single again than married to someone who cheated." *Someone who didn't love me as much as I thought he did,* she added silently. *Who didn't love me as much as I loved him.*

"If only Adam had that attitude," Vinnie said with a sigh.

Then Megan remembered the album, and she glanced down at the photo. What she saw made her gasp.

Vinnie's eyebrows rose. "Goodness, dear, he's handsome, but not *that* handsome."

"I don't believe this. This is the guy from the diner."

Donna's eyes widened. "The apple pie guy?"

As Megan nodded, Vinnie looked from her to Donna and back, perplexed. Quickly Megan told her the story of their meeting on the road to Elm Creek Manor.

"Did you like him?" Vinnie asked anxiously.

"Well, yes. I mean, I didn't talk to him very long, but he seemed nice."

Vinnie clasped her hands together, delighted. "Your meeting must have been fate! No, something stronger than fate—divine intervention. You live in Ohio, isn't that right? So does Adam."

Megan shot Donna a look of alarm, a look that meant *Save me.* "It might not have been fate."

Donna quickly added, "There are only so many routes to Waterford from Ohio, and not many places to stop to eat along the way. It was just a coincidence."

"I don't believe that," Vinnie said, a stubborn set to her chin. "There are no coincidences. I believe that in life, you meet the people you need to meet, the people who will help you become the person you ought to be."

"Maybe so, but maybe Megan needed to meet your grandson so he could help her find Elm Creek Manor, so she could meet us," Donna said. "Maybe we're the ones she needs to meet."

"I think that's true," Megan said quickly.

"Maybe you need to meet all of us," Vinnie declared, but then she smiled and reached over to pat Megan on the knee. "I think we're going to become quite good friends this week, my dear."

⚓

Donna was enjoying her conversation with Megan and Vinnie so much that she was almost late for her appliqué workshop. She rushed in, breathless, and took the first open seat she found, at a table in the back. Donna hated to be late, not because it suggested that she was scatterbrained—which she sometimes feared she was—but because she hated to be rude.

She greeted the few campers she recognized, then took out her supply list and checked her bag to make sure she had remembered everything. She was glad Megan wasn't there to see her; Donna had checked the bag twice before leaving her room and once at lunch, which Megan found hilarious. "Do you think something jumped out of your bag and wandered off while your back was turned?" she had teased.

"It could happen," Donna had retorted. Something had to account for those dozens of rotary cutters and thimbles she had lost over the years.

She put the list away and listened attentively as the teacher introduced herself as Agnes Emberly. A woman slipped into the seat beside her, but Donna pretended not to notice. She had been the recipient of too many annoyed frowns for her own tardiness to feel anything but sympathy for this latecomer.

It wasn't until Agnes passed out pattern sheets and Donna turned to hand them to her table partner that she realized she was sitting next to Julia Merchaud.

She was so surprised that she forgot to let go of the pages when Julia took them. Julia tugged at the pages in vain, and then her famous hazel eyes met Donna's. "I have them, thanks," she said.

Donna released the pages as if they were on fire. "Sorry."

Julia Merchaud nodded in response and turned to the front of the classroom as if she had already forgotten Donna was there. Donna felt like a fool, but she couldn't help staring. It was Julia Merchaud, wasn't it? It had to be. Her long blond hair was pulled back into a French twist, just the way she had worn it the day the oldest Wilson child got married. Donna had seen every episode of *Family Tree* since the premiere. Becca thought it was one of the corniest shows ever created, but Becca had a low opinion of television in general, and Donna had never let her youngest daughter's teasing discourage her from watching.

After a moment, Julia Merchaud gave her a nervous sidelong glance, and Donna quickly snatched her gaze away and pretended she had been studying the pattern sheets. Julia Merchaud was not only at Donna's quilt camp but at her very table. How could Donna hope to concentrate on Agnes's instructions with a celebrity of Julia Merchaud's stature sitting not three feet away?

Using all her willpower, she forced herself to focus on the front of the classroom, where Agnes was listing the items they would need for the first activity. As Donna withdrew her supplies from her bag, she stole a peek at the other woman, eager to see what fabric a television star used. Expecting to see Hoffman prints with gold-stamped ink or exotic Indonesian batiks packed in a Gucci tote, she was astonished when Julia Merchaud removed a mismatched stack of ordinary calicoes from a paper grocery bag. She placed them on the table, then carefully arranged a pack of needles, a pencil, a small pair of blue-handled scissors, and a spool of thread beside them. Then, in a gesture that seemed both protective and formal, she folded her hands in her lap and turned her attention to the teacher.

Donna couldn't help studying Julia's hands. A ring on her left hand, a large diamond set with pearls, caught the light. A ruby-and-gold tennis bracelet encircled her thin right wrist. The hands themselves seemed strangely out of place, with protruding veins and knobby knuckles. They seemed much older than the rest of her, especially compared to the smooth, faintly lined skin of her face.

At the front of the room, Agnes announced that someone from each table needed to come to the front of the room for a roll of freezer paper. Since she was on the aisle, Donna jumped up. "I'll get it," she said, smiling. Julia gave the barest of nods without looking her way.

The brief errand gave Donna enough time to collect her scattered thoughts. She remembered what she and Megan had promised the previous evening: If they saw Julia Merchaud, they would treat her like any other quilter. *She's just a quilter like any other,* Donna told herself as she returned to her seat, but she couldn't quite believe it. "Here we go," she said brightly, placing the box on the table between them. Julia murmured something that might have been thanks.

Donna had used the freezer paper method for appliqué before; she had tried almost every quilting technique at least once, although she rarely stuck with any one style long enough to truly master it. She had signed up for this course hoping it would help her improve her weakest skill. Following Agnes's instructions, she tore off a sheet of freezer paper, placed it on top of the pattern, and began tracing the first design. Out of the corner of her eye, she watched as Julia imitated her, step by step. Deliberately, Donna slowed her movements and made sure not to block Julia's view of her work. Sure enough, Julia's scrutiny continued as the class went on.

When it came time to sew the appliqué to the background fabric, Donna sensed her neighbor's growing frustration. Summoning up her courage, she whispered, "Do you need some help?" When Julia nodded, Donna went over the steps again, demonstrating each one. When Julia tried again, she managed to complete a shaky but perfectly respectable appliqué stitch. For the first time, Donna saw her smile.

Donna picked up her own needle again, surreptitiously watching Julia's progress. Assured that Julia was doing fine, Donna soon became engrossed in her own work. She had never made an appliqué block as elaborate as a Whig Rose before, but Agnes's instructions were so clear that the pieces seemed to fall into place almost effortlessly.

Class was nearing the end when Julia spoke again. "Excuse me," she murmured. "I don't mean to interrupt you, but you seem to know more about this than I."

"Just a little, maybe," Donna said diplomatically.

"I wondered . . ." Julia hesitated. "Is this the same method as needle-turned appliqué, just using different name?"

"No, they're two different styles. Agnes probably picked freezer paper because many people think it's easier."

"I see." She seemed troubled. "But this technique has been around just as long, I suppose?"

"I don't think so. As far as I know, freezer paper appliqué is fairly modern."

"Oh, dear." Julia set down her needle and sank back into her chair.

"What's wrong?"

"I have to learn needle-turned appliqué."

"Your Whig Rose block will look exactly the same," Donna assured her. "It doesn't matter what technique you use."

"It does matter. I can't believe this. I'm wasting my time. I never should have come."

"Don't say that." Instinctively Donna placed a hand on Julia's shoulder. "I know it can be frustrating sometimes, but you can learn. You just need practice."

"You don't understand." Julia removed a notebook from her paper bag and opened it to the first page. "I have to learn certain quilting techniques for a movie role. But this morning I found out I was in the wrong piecing class, and now I'm in the wrong appliqué class. . . ."

"Don't worry. It'll be all right." Donna patted Julia's shoulder and picked up the notebook. "Let's take a look at this list. Okay. All of these terms have to do with piecing. Are you taking Beginning Piecing?"

"I'm transferring to it tomorrow."

"Then you'll definitely cover the first half of the list. These steps here"—she pointed to the page—"have to do with the actual quilting process itself. Did you sign up for a class on quilting?"

Julia nodded.

"Hand or machine?"

"Hand."

"Then you're all set there, too. The only problem seems to be needle-turned appliqué." As Donna returned the notebook, inspiration struck her. "If you like, I could teach you during free time."

The famous hazel eyes looked guarded. "You would do that for me?"

"Sure. I've never won any blue ribbons for my appliqué, but I can at least give you a crash course in the basics."

"I'd be grateful," Julia said. "Are you sure it's no trouble?"

"Not at all. We can start today after class if you'd like." Then she remembered her plans with Megan. "I'll need to leave a message for one of my friends first, but after that, we can work until supper."

Julia agreed with such gratitude that Donna felt taken aback. Of course she wanted to help a beginning quilter; wouldn't anyone? Julia must not realize how quilters treated each other. Where would Donna have been if no one had been willing to teach her more than twenty years before, when she was pregnant with Lindsay and nearly driven insane by a hormone-induced compulsion to sew a baby quilt?

Then Julia looked hesitant. "I wonder if you would be willing to do something else for me. This might sound foolish, but I don't want anyone to know I'm not already an experienced quilter."

It did sound foolish. Every quilter had to start somewhere. "Why not?"

"It's rather difficult to explain. Would you promise not to tell anyone?"

Donna shrugged. "Sure, okay."

"Would you be willing to sign a confidentiality agreement?"

Donna stared at her. "A what?"

"A confidentiality agreement." Julia smiled and looked apologetic, but also wary. "It's for the lawyers. You know how they are. Everything has to be formal. You'll sign a document promising you won't reveal my, shall we say, inexperience, to anyone."

Donna wondered if most celebrities made a habit of carrying around a folder of confidentiality agreements in their purses. "Don't you think anyone who sees you in class will realize you're a beginner?"

"That would be mere speculation. You have firsthand knowledge." Julia's smile was disarming. "I'd be very grateful."

Resigned but still baffled, Donna nodded. "I'll have to tell my friends something. They'll want to know what we're doing together."

"Tell them you're helping me brush up on my skills. Skills I already have," she added.

Donna didn't know what else to do without rudely revoking her offer, so she agreed.

After class, Julia remained behind while Donna raced upstairs to her room. She hastily scrawled a note: "I'm sorry I'm going to miss Vinnie's show-and-tell session. Please tell her I'm sorry. Something came up. I'll explain when I see you at supper." Then she added, "The presence of the Loch Ness Quilter has been officially confirmed."

She slipped the note under Megan's door and hurried back downstairs to help the famous Julia Merchaud prepare for her movie role.

After supper, Grace returned to her room, intending to go to bed early. Instead, she lay on top of the covers, fully clothed, her fingers interlaced over her abdomen, her eyes closed. She felt a strange sensation of peace settling over her as she listened to the sounds of the old house: the creak of a floorboard, a door closing in the distance. Other noises, soft but distinct, she could not name. An old house like this one probably sheltered its share of ghosts, but if any spirits haunted Elm Creek Manor, Grace was certain they were benevolent.

Her hopes had risen tremendously since that bleak morning in the garden. The forced intimacy she had feared had not surfaced, and she had been allowed to spend the day with a minimum of intrusion upon her solitude. *Solitude* seemed an inappropriate word for it, since she had attended classes and meals surrounded by dozens of other quilters, and yet that was how it had felt, as if she were a stone fixed in a creek bottom, with the water dancing over her and around her and yet leaving her in peace, to move downstream at her own pace. That, she suddenly realized, was what she had been so desperately seeking: a respite from the sense that time was rushing her along too fast, forcing her to break into a stumbling run to keep up.

The creative breakthrough she longed for had not arrived with the suddenness of a thunderclap; she had predicted as much. Even so, she could feel the first stirrings of inspiration within her imagination, like the movement of water beneath the frozen surface of a lake. If she were patient and allowed the stirrings to build, eventually something would surely shatter the ice and allow her to create again. In the meantime, it felt good to be working with fabric, even if she was examining the colors and textures with an unfamiliar detachment, as if regarding them from a great distance or through a blurred lens.

Her mind wandered as she rested. She was picturing herself back in her studio arranging crayons in a three-tiered box when a knock sounded on the door. "Come in," she called, sitting up on the edge of the bed.

Sylvia peered inside. "Did I wake you?"

"No, I was just daydreaming." Grace stood, and as she did, she realized that sometime during the day, the pins and needles sensation in her hand had faded. She had not even noticed.

"The evening activities are about to begin. Would you care to join me?"

"Thanks, but not tonight."

"Are you sure? We're going to play games. It'll be fun."

"I think I'll turn in early instead."

"Then I'll see you in the morning." Sylvia withdrew, but before the door closed completely, she uttered something, not quite under her breath.

"What did you say?" Grace asked.

Sylvia swung the door open again, her expression innocent. "Who, me?"

"Yes, you. What did you call me?"

"I called you a party-pooper. Good night. See you at breakfast."

Grace crossed the room and grabbed the knob before Sylvia could close the door again. "I am not a party-pooper."

"You look like one from here. It must be a trick of the light."

"Is that so?" Grace picked up a light sweater and threw it over her shoulders. "I've forgotten more about having fun than you'll ever know." She marched past Sylvia into the hallway and pulled the door shut behind them.

As they went downstairs, Grace heard laughter and conversation coming from the banquet hall. Inside, the campers had gathered near a long table by the windows and were helping themselves to dessert and coffee. Grace felt a hand squeeze her shoulder, and when she looked over, Sylvia gave her an encouraging wink and left her there on her own.

Seeing that the other quilters were seating themselves, Grace quickly pulled up a chair at a table near the back and watched as Sylvia climbed onto a small riser at the end of the room. She clapped her hands for attention. "If you'll take your seats, we'll get started," she called out. "Four campers to a table, please." She signaled to two staff members, who began distributing sheets of paper and pencils to each table.

"Are you saving these for anyone?" a slender woman in her early thirties asked, placing a hand on the chair at Grace's left. Behind her, the plump woman Grace had seen in the garden that morning smiled tentatively.

"No," Grace said, startled. "Please, go ahead."

"Thanks."

They introduced themselves—Megan from Ohio and Donna from Minnesota. Grace was just about to give them her own name, when a voice sang out, "Save a place for me." A thin, white-haired woman wearing a red straw hat with a plastic daisy in the band hurried to their table. She seated herself and looked over at the dessert table longingly. "Why do they have to start on time? I didn't even get to check out the snacks, and now it's too late."

"Here, Vinnie," Donna said, sliding a plate of brownies and frosted sugar cookies toward her. "I shouldn't be eating this stuff anyway."

Vinnie brightened and raised her eyebrows at Grace. "Do you want anything, honey?" When Grace declined, Vinnie took a bite of a brownie and rolled her eyes to heaven with pleasure.

Party-pooper, Grace could almost hear Sylvia say. "Maybe just one," she said, reaching for the plate.

Donna passed out the pencils the staff member had left on their table. "Please tell me this isn't a quiz."

Grace scanned the list of numbered items. "'How many UFOs do you have?'" she read aloud. "I think it's just a questionnaire."

"'How many paper bags would your stash fill?'" Vinnie read. "That depends. How big are the bags?"

"Do we have to know exactly?" Donna said, her brow creased in worry. "Can we estimate?"

Megan grinned. "I think they expect us to."

"Besides, what are they going to do, go to our houses and check?" Vinnie added.

"What's a UFO?" Grace wondered aloud. Sylvia couldn't possibly mean a flying saucer.

"An Un-Finished Object," Megan said. "Or an Unfinished Fabric Object, whichever you prefer. It's a quilt you've begun but haven't completed yet."

"I thought that was a WIP," Donna said.

"A whip?" Grace asked.

"A Work In Progress."

"When does something shift from being a WIP to a UFO?"

"When you've given up all hope of ever finishing it," Vinnie said.

"By that definition, I don't have any UFOs," Donna said. "I intend to finish every project I've ever started."

"Oh, come on," Megan said. "You don't have any projects you've abandoned? Not even one?"

Donna looked hesitant. "Well . . ."

From the front of the room, Sylvia interrupted by announcing the rules of their first game, which was to fill out the questionnaire "as honestly and completely as you can." There would be prizes for the correct answer to each question. "But I'm not telling you what the correct answers are, so you can't cheat."

The quilters laughed, and Donna raised her hand. "What about WIPs?" she asked. "Should we include those in our UFO count?"

Sylvia considered. "Yes, go ahead and include any project begun but not yet completed."

"Oh, no," Donna murmured gloomily. "This is going to be embarrassing."

Then Vinnie raised her hand. "For question number two, how big a paper bag are we talking about? Do you mean a grocery or a department store shopping bag?"

Sylvia cast her eyes to heaven. "I see I'm going to have to revise my questionnaire for table number six. A paper grocery sack will do, Vinnie."

Satisfied, Vinnie began filling in her questionnaire with dramatic strokes of her pencil. More cautiously, Grace started hers. How many UFOs? None. Grace preferred to finish one project before beginning another, and she hadn't started anything new in ages. How vast was her fabric stash? That question was more difficult. She pictured the shelves lining her studio wall and the bundles of folded cloth, sorted by color and fiber content, stacked neatly upon them. At least fifty, she decided, and wrote that down. She proceeded through the rest of the questions, from "How many quilts have you finished?" to "How long have you been quilting?" She was filling in the last blank when Sylvia announced that time was up.

"I didn't know there was a time limit," Donna said, dismayed, as a staff member came to their table to collect the papers. "I didn't finish the last three questions."

"Then the best you can hope for is a C-plus," Vinnie said. "So much for the Quilters' Honor Roll."

Donna's eyes widened in alarm before she realized Vinnie was only teasing her.

Next, the staff members placed a sheet of paper facedown on the table in front of each camper. Vinnie gingerly picked up the corner of hers. "No peeking until I say so," Sylvia commanded, and Vinnie quickly snatched her hand back to her lap.

Sylvia went on to describe the rules of the next game. The front side of the papers provided a list of quilt block anagrams, and the quilters at each table would work together to unscramble the design names. The first team to get all the correct answers would win a prize.

"I'm going to be good at this," Vinnie declared. "I do the jumble in the *Dayton Daily News* every day."

Grace was relieved to hear that, because she knew she would be a liability for her team. She hadn't pieced a traditional quilt block since she first learned to quilt. Unless Sylvia had chosen blocks from the eighteen hundreds, in which case Grace's historical textile studies would aid her, she wouldn't be able to contribute much.

"On your marks," Sylvia called from the front of the room. "Get set, go!"

There was an excited scramble as papers were flipped and pencils seized. Grace skimmed the list of twenty anagrams, but nothing came to mind.

"I think I have number three," Donna cried. "'Plane Pipe.' That's Pineapple."

"That's right," Megan said. "Nice work."

As Grace wrote the correct answer on her sheet, she overheard a woman at the adjacent table say, "You guys, the third one is Pineapple." Grace looked up in time to catch the woman's guilty glance before she looked away.

"Well, I never heard of such a thing," Vinnie declared, glaring at the woman.

"Never mind her. Don't let it distract us," Megan urged. "Just keep your voices down from now on."

Murmuring answers across the table, Grace's team worked their way down the list, unscrambling Trip Around the World, Broken Dishes, Hole in the Barn Door, and Feathered Star. Sunbonnet Sue and Grandmother's Fan gave them considerable trouble, but soon they, too, were untangled. Megan and Vinnie quickly proved themselves the strongest members of the team. Although Donna solved several puzzles, Grace was unable to unscramble a single one. Instead she began giving only half her attention to the paper while scanning the other tables to judge how much progress the other teams were making.

"The team closest to the dessert table seems confident, but intense," she reported. "They might be close to finishing."

"That figures," Vinnie grumbled. "They can reach out and get more fuel anytime they need it."

"Here." Megan passed her the last cookie. "Refuel with this. We're doing fine." It was true; they had completed all but two anagrams.

"I have one," Donna said. "'A pathless totter' is Steps to the Altar. How appropriate."

When Megan nodded in wry agreement, Vinnie gave them a sharp look. "Not necessarily. It depends who's taking those steps."

Only one anagram remained. "'Our nouns be drudgery,'" Grace murmured to herself. Our nouns be drudgery. Something about it tickled a memory in the back of her mind, and suddenly she could picture the answer as clearly as if the letters had rearranged themselves on the page. "Burgoyne Surrounded."

Megan shot her a look. "What did you say?"

"Burgoyne Surrounded."

Donna looked dubious. "Is that a real block?"

"Of course. It's a pattern of squares and rectangles, usually done in two colors. According to tradition, it was named to commemorate British general John Burgoyne's defeat in the Revolutionary War—"

"Skip the history lesson and write," Vinnie cried. Quickly they filled in the last empty line on their papers and waved them in the air. "We're done! Sylvia!"

A groan went up from the other tables, the loudest of all from the group nearest the desserts. Sylvia held up her hands. "Now, now. Don't give up yet. We still have to check their answers." She crossed the room, took Megan's paper, and read the answers aloud. Then she smiled. "We have our winners."

Grace's team cheered and exchanged high-fives. One of the staff members came to their table to award them their prizes: ribbon-tied bundles of fat eighths, hand-dyed in a gradation of rainbow colors. As Grace ran her hand over the soft cloth, she wondered if maybe this fabric would spark the inspiration she so desperately needed. Maybe those fat eighths would become her next quilt.

Sylvia returned to the riser at the front of the room. "While you were working, Sarah and Summer read your questionnaires. The results are in, and we're ready to announce the winners." A young woman with long red hair handed her a sheet of paper. "Which camper has the greatest number of Unfinished Objects? With a grand total of . . ." She read from the sheet silently, then turned to the young woman. "This can't possibly be right, is it?" When the red-haired woman nodded, Sylvia shrugged and turned back to her audience. "With a grand total of one hundred seventeen . . ." A gasp of awe went up from the quilters. "Yes, you heard right, ladies. With a grand total of one hundred seventeen UFOs, Donna Jorgenson!"

Red-faced, Donna rose and went to the front of the room to claim her prize as the campers applauded and laughed. "I'm so embarrassed," she said as she returned to her seat. "As soon as I get home, I'm going to finish some of those quilts."

"At least you won a prize," Vinnie consoled her, leaning over to peer into her closed hand. "What is it?"

Donna handed her a small metal object. Vinnie studied it and nodded in approval before passing it around the table. When Grace received it, she saw that it was a pin with the words "Elm Creek Quilts" encircling a picture of a house and a grove of trees. It seemed familiar somehow, and suddenly she remembered seeing a similar design on a medallion quilt hanging in the manor's foyer.

Sylvia continued. "And now, for the quilter with the least number of UFOs, with a grand total of zero"—this the quilters interrupted with an exclamation of astonishment—"Grace Daniels!"

Her heart heavy, Grace pushed back her chair and went to the front of the room for her prize. Sylvia gave her a sympathetic, almost apologetic smile as she placed a pin identical to Donna's in her palm and closed her fingers around it.

When Grace returned to her table, Megan said, "I was sure I was going to win that one. I only have two UFOs." She shook her head in admiration. "How do you stay so organized?"

Grace's first impulse was to respond with a joke, but she decided to be honest. "It's not organization. It's lack of ideas. I'd do anything to have as many projects in the works as you do, Donna."

"No, you don't want that," Donna said. "All my prize shows is that I have a short attention span."

"At least you both got pins," Vinnie said grumpily. She rapped her fingernails on the table and frowned expectantly at the front of the room.

Sylvia went on to announce the rest of the winners, who claimed their prizes amid praise and teasing. Grace half expected to win a second pin for owning the most fabric, but a woman from New Mexico whose stash filled two entire rooms had them all beat.

Vinnie's fidgeting increased with each new camper who earned a pin. "Don't let it bother you," Megan said. "I'm not going to win anything, either. Besides, we won the group prize."

"I don't mind," Vinnie insisted, her voice falsely innocent. "I can be a good loser."

The other three members of her team exchanged knowing glances as Vinnie hungrily watched three campers, who had taken their first lessons just that morning, approach the riser to receive pins for being the newest quilters.

"And last but not least," Sylvia announced. "For the camper who has quilted the longest, a woman who began quilting at age six and has stuck with it more than seven decades—Vinnie Burkholder!"

"Hooray for Vinnie!" someone cried out.

"Vin-nie, Vin-nie," Megan chanted, and soon the whole room had joined in, calling out Vinnie's name in time with their clapping hands. Vinnie sat frozen in her chair, her mouth forming an O. Donna nudged her and motioned for her to stand up. Vinnie started and rose, then brightened and walked to the front of the room waving and bowing graciously to her admirers.

"Vin-nie, Vin-nie," Grace chanted, laughing and clapping her hands as Vinnie accepted her pin from Sylvia and stepped onto the riser beside her, beaming.

⚘

As Vinnie returned to her seat, Sylvia Compson looked out over the crowd of quilters. Some chatted with their teammates; others mingled, going from table to table, greeting old friends or making new ones. She watched as her dear friend Grace admired Vinnie's pin; she looked on as women who had been so shy and tentative at Candlelight now threw back their heads and laughed and joked along with the most outgoing of the group. Yes, she thought with satisfaction, the week of camp was off to a fine start, indeed.

Four

Vinnie began each morning with a conversation with God. *You didn't take away my aches and pains in the night like I asked You to,* she would pray, *but at least You let me see another day, and at my age I ought to be grateful for that.* Then she would thank Him for His many blessings, especially her children and grandchildren, and ask Him to watch over her family and protect them throughout the day.

That morning she added a special request: *Donna and Megan can shout coincidence all they want, but I think I see Your hand at work. If I'm mistaken, please let me know—and make it obvious so I won't miss it. Unless I hear otherwise from You, I'll fit a little matchmaking into my vacation.*

Satisfied, Vinnie threw off the covers and got up. As she showered and dressed, she thought about Megan and the confidences she had shared with Vinnie and Donna over supper the night before. Megan's ex-husband, Keith, sounded like a scoundrel. Back in Vinnie's day, men hadn't been able to lift a dustcloth to save their lives, and they might have spent one night too many with friends down at the local bar, but at least they had known what a man's obligations were. Nowadays, men seemed to think they could cast off one family and start another, bearing no responsibility for the first wife and the first children. Sometimes the women were just as bad. Vinnie often didn't recognize the world, it had changed so drastically.

But on holidays or other special occasions, when all her children and grandchildren and now even great-grandchildren gathered around her, she would shake off the melancholy of aging and be content. With each graduation or new addition to the family, Vinnie would feel the love of her descendants and admit to herself that she would not trade her presence among them for anything, not even to be reunited with Sam. She'd see him again in God's own good time, and Sam would understand if she lingered. As he had always told her, when you got right down to it, family was all they had and all that truly mattered.

These days families dispersed to the four winds, mothers and children separated by half a continent or more. She was lucky that her children had stayed relatively close, scattered around the state rather than the entire country. Some of her friends in Meadowbrook Village had children in California or New York or Florida, whom they rarely saw. One woman had never seen her own grandchildren. "Why doesn't that son of yours bring them out for a visit?" Vinnie had demanded.

Airfares were too expensive, she was told, and hotel fees for a family of four were out of the question. Her son would pay for her to visit them, but Vinnie's friend refused. "I'm too old to fly so far," she had said, her face crumpling in grief.

Vinnie had not known what to say, and rarely was she at a loss for words. She was two years older than her friend, but as much as she disliked flying, if a four-hour flight was the only way to get to her family, she would suffer through it. She promised herself right then and there that she would never say she was too old for anything.

Several times since, she had been tempted to chide her friend into getting out of her chair and making that trip, but she held her tongue. Not everyone felt as strongly about family as Vinnie did. Maybe a person needed to grow up without a family to truly appreciate one.

She corrected herself; she *had* had a family—two, in fact, although the second had been more unconventional than the first.

For six years she had been part of a family she supposed other people would consider ordinary: her parents, her elder brother, Frankie, and herself. They lived in a small house in the Hartwell neighborhood of Cincinnati, and Vinnie remembered being happy and content there, until her mother's death changed everything.

Later, Vinnie learned that her mother had succumbed after a long battle with cancer, but at the time, her mother's death seemed as sudden as it was incomprehensible. The funeral passed in a blur of grown-ups with dark clothes and hushed voices. Relatives hugged her and told her that her mother had loved her very much; neighbors dropped off casseroles and told her to be a good girl. Only when the bustle of activity ceased did a chill of realization settle in Vinnie's heart: Her mother wasn't ever coming back, and nothing Vinnie did could make their family whole again.

Her father seemed to wish he had gone away with Mother. He rarely left his chair by the radio, and he seemed not to notice when his children spoke to him. Frankie looked after Vinnie, fixing her cereal and toast three times a day and making sure she brushed her teeth at night. They played quietly in their rooms or in the backyard, avoiding their strangely silent father. Vinnie knew this wasn't normal, but she pretended not to notice.

Then one day, a neighbor spotted them outside, and when she questioned them, something in their hushed voices and guarded manner sent her hurrying inside to her telephone. A few days later, their father's elder sister arrived with a suitcase and a look of determination that reminded Vinnie of how Daddy used to be.

Vinnie was glad to see Aunt Lynn, since in her presence, Daddy remembered to shave and change his clothes. He returned to work. At suppertime they had hot meals; at night they slept in clean sheets scented with lavender. When Vinnie cried at night for her mother, Aunt Lynn came to her in the dark and rocked her until she fell back asleep.

Vinnie didn't know why Aunt Lynn didn't have any children of her own, except that ladies had to have a husband first, and Aunt Lynn didn't. That was one of the things that the other aunts didn't like about her. They also didn't like that she wore lipstick and worked in an office and had turned down two marriage proposals. Vinnie didn't understand why the aunts whispered such things when Aunt Lynn wasn't there; she thought Aunt Lynn was very pretty and nice, and her life sounded terribly exciting.

When she left several weeks later, Vinnie was sorry to see her go. She asked Aunt Lynn to stay, but Aunt Lynn said her boss needed her. "Your Daddy will look after you," she promised, then kissed Vinnie and carried her suitcase outside, where a taxi waited to take her to the railroad station.

As the days passed, it seemed that Aunt Lynn had taken Daddy's restored energy with her. He still went to work and sent the children off to school each morning, but in the evenings he sat alone in his chair by the radio, smoking and listening to music. Vinnie eventually grew accustomed to the gloom, but her memories of happiness grew ever fainter.

She ached for her mother. She ached with the large, constant pain of knowing her mother was gone, and in dozens of small ways when each day brought another sign of how much Vinnie still needed her. The sight of an incomplete Nine Patch block reminded Vinnie that her mother would never finish the quilting lessons that had begun only months before. Each morning Mother had plaited her brown locks into two smooth braids, but the braids her father attempted hung loose, with tufts of hair sticking out here and there, and her bangs grew nearly to her chin. When the popular girl who sat across the aisle at school told her she looked like a sheepdog, Vinnie pretended not to hear her and tried to poke the unruly bangs into the braids. When that failed, she tucked the strands behind her ears. She thought she looked better, but the popular girl snickered. Vinnie's face grew hot with shame, and she whispered, "At least I'm not worst in the class in spelling."

The popular girl's face grew sour, and at once Vinnie knew she should have ignored her. At recess the girl waited until the teacher was out of earshot before calling her a sheepdog again, and before long her friends had joined in, laughing and jeering. Vinnie stood very still, watching the popular girl's sour little mouth blabbering insults, the smug disdain in her eyes, the sunlight gleaming on her two perfect, blond braids—and then something inside Vinnie exploded. She charged into the girl, knocking her to the ground. By the time the teacher ran over and pulled her aside, the popular girl was sobbing, her face red where Vinnie had repeatedly slapped her.

Vinnie was sent home. When her father read the principal's note, he sighed so heavily that Vinnie grew even more ashamed. She stammered out an explanation, but her father seemed not to hear her. Then he said, "Bring me the scissors."

Her heart sank as she found her mother's sewing basket, untouched for so many months, and brought her father the scissors. He sat her down in his chair by the radio, combed out her sloppy braids, and began to trim her bangs. He frowned in concentration as he worked, cutting straight across above her eyes, trimming the uneven edges, then pausing to study his work before cutting again.

"Daddy, that's short enough," Vinnie said, alarmed by the sight of the snipped ends collecting on her lap.

"Be still. I'm trying to make this even."

Vinnie hoped for the best, but when her father finally sat back, satisfied, and sent her to look in the mirror, she discovered a short brown stubble where her bangs had once been.

She felt tears gathering, and tried to hide her face before her father noticed, but his eyes met hers in the mirror. "I can fix it," he said hastily. "If I cut the sides a little shorter, they'll blend in."

"Do you think so?"

"Sure," he said, and steered her back to the chair. Vinnie clutched her hands together in her lap and closed her eyes, cringing inside with each snip of the scissors. As her head grew lighter, her stomach grew more queasy. She was afraid to open her eyes, but when her father told her to, she obeyed.

She looked into the mirror, and a familiar face stared back at her in horror. Frankie's face. Daddy had cut her hair so that it looked exactly like Frankie's.

She burst into tears. "I can't go to school like this."

Her father stared at her, an odd, distant expression on his face. "Your mother is dead, and you're crying over your hair."

Vinnie's tears choked off abruptly. She climbed out of the chair and went to her room.

The next day she went to school and got into another fight when the popular girl's cronies teased her for looking like a boy. The following morning she walked to school with Frankie as usual, but as soon as he ran off to join his friends, she doubled back and hid in her bedroom. The school contacted her father when she had been absent a week. He was instructed to bring her in for a conference, where the principal lectured them on truancy while Vinnie stared at the floor and her father repeated assurances that Vinnie's absences were over.

"I don't know what to do with you," her father said as they walked home. His voice was flat and hopeless. "Frankie doesn't give me this kind of trouble. I wish . . ."

He never finished the thought, and Vinnie found herself wondering what exactly he wished.

She was only a little surprised when Aunt Lynn returned the next week. Her father gave Vinnie a quick hug, so hard it almost hurt, then took Frankie to the park to play catch.

When they were alone, Aunt Lynn smiled at Vinnie, but her voice was tentative when she said, "Your father and I thought maybe you could come to live with me."

Vinnie's heart sank. She liked Aunt Lynn, but this was her home. "For how long?"

Aunt Lynn shrugged. "We'll see."

"What if I don't want to?" she asked in a small voice.

Aunt Lynn watched her without speaking for a moment, and Vinnie could see the sympathy in her eyes. "Come on. Let's pack your things."

They packed all her clothes and books, and her favorite toys. Vinnie was too numb to cry. She worked slowly, hoping her father would return before she left, but all too soon the last box was filled, and she realized her father would stay out even past Frankie's bedtime to avoid her.

A black car waited at the curb, its back door and trunk open. Aunt Lynn loaded the boxes into the car, motioned for Vinnie to climb into the back seat, then sat beside her and shut the door.

A blond woman in the driver's seat turned around and grinned. "Hiya, Vinnie," she said. "Welcome aboard the Lynn and Lena Express. Hang on to your hat."

Vinnie was too heartsick to reply. She shut her eyes and let Aunt Lynn pull her close as they drove away from the only home she had ever known. She never once looked back.

In the decades that had passed since then, she never forgot how easily a girl could be sent away and ignored as if she had never existed. As she grew older, she realized that age was no protection: Wives could become inconvenient and be put aside as easily as daughters.

Now, with her eighty-second birthday only a day away, she had met a kindhearted woman who deserved better, just as Vinnie herself had deserved better so long ago. Vinnie recognized the grief she saw in Megan's eyes, and the spark of resolve that had not yet been quenched. She remembered what that felt like, and how only the love of two compassionate women had helped her grow from a lonely little girl into a strong, resilient woman. It was long past time she helped another as she had been helped.

If Vinnie had her way—and she usually did—she would see her new friend happy again before another birthday passed.

⚓

Megan saved seats for Donna and Grace in Color Theory, and was pleased when Grace came to sit beside them without waiting to be invited. At the beginning of class, Gwen assigned an exercise, working with paints to explore tints and hues. Each student selected a tube of her favorite color, squeezed a sample onto an artist's palette, and colored the first section of a chart. Next Gwen told them to mix in white paint, one drop at a time, and to fill the chart with the resulting color variations.

Donna tried to convince Megan to use purple, but Megan snatched the blue tube before Donna could hide it. Grace chose red, so Donna took yellow. "Someone at this table has to be daring," she said.

"What's so daring about yellow?" Megan teased.

"For a quilter, yellow is daring," Grace said. "Some quilters refuse to use it at all, and some use so much that it completely overpowers the other colors in the quilt. It's challenging to strike the right balance."

"Besides, it's next to impossible to find the perfect shade of yellow in a fabric store," Donna said. "You want a butter yellow and you have to settle for canary or daffodil."

"Recently I've resorted to dyeing my own to get the colors I need." Grace frowned at the tip of her paintbrush. "Although to be honest, 'recently' is a relative term. I haven't dyed anything in more than a year or started anything else, for that matter."

"I have the opposite problem," Donna said. "I have so many projects in the works that I won't possibly live long enough to finish them all."

"You should do what my mother does," Megan said. "She keeps each of her works in progress in a separate box labeled with the name of one of her friends. If, God forbid, she should pass away unexpectedly, each friend will receive the box with her name on it and think my mother was working on a quilt especially for her. She uses the names of women she doesn't get along with, too. She says it's a great way to make sure she has plenty of guilt-ridden, sobbing mourners at her funeral."

Grace laughed, but Donna shuddered. "That's morbid."

Megan smiled to herself. Donna only thought so because she didn't understand her mother's sense of humor. Megan wished she had inherited more of it and less of her father's somber pragmatism. Maybe then she'd be able to laugh off her failures instead of brooding over them. Maybe then she wouldn't worry about Robby's tendency to embellish the truth beyond recognition and how she could never hope to fully compensate for his father's absence.

"Is your quilter's block because of your daughter?" Donna asked Grace.

Grace hesitated. "Yes . . . well, that's part of it." She added a drop of white paint to her palette and fell silent as she blended the new shade. "I don't know what bothers me most: that she's seeing an older man or that she hasn't told me about him."

Megan thought of her own futile attempts at dating after the divorce. "Maybe she doesn't want to mention him until she knows whether she's serious about him."

"That's exactly the problem. She must be serious about him, because she already introduced him to her son. She's adamant about not letting him meet casual boyfriends." Grace sighed. "I think I've answered my own question. What bothers me most is that she didn't tell me. For all I know, he might be a perfectly wonderful man."

"He probably is," Megan said to reassure her, but Donna shook her head.

"I keep telling myself the same thing about Brandon—my daughter's fiancé," Donna said. "I feel like I'm trying to convince myself that everything is going to be okay, because deep down, I don't really believe it. Does that make any sense?"

Grace nodded emphatically. Megan watched the two women, linked by their similar worries, and thought with some trepidation about her own child. What, if anything, could Megan do to help Robby avoid repeating his parents' dismal mistakes?

Her pragmatism asserted itself. There was no point in worrying about Robby's future relationships now. She'd have time enough to worry when she allowed Robby to begin dating—which she'd be ready to do in about twenty years.

Just then, she heard footsteps behind her and felt a light touch on her shoulder. She looked up to find Sylvia Compson.

"Megan Donohue?"

"Yes?"

"Your mother's on the phone. You may take the call in the parlor, if you'd like some privacy."

"My mom?" Megan pushed back her chair and rose. "Is something wrong?"

"She didn't say so, dear. I'm sure she would have if it were an emergency."

Megan quickly gathered her things and followed Sylvia out of the classroom, finding no comfort in the older woman's sympathetic assurances. Robby. She pictured broken limbs, car accidents, malevolent strangers. By the time they reached the formal parlor in the west wing, Megan's heart was pounding, and she snatched up the phone without remembering to thank her hostess, who quickly departed. "Hello?" she said breathlessly into the phone.

"Honey?"

"Mom? What's wrong? Is Robby okay?"

"He's fine," her mother assured her, then lowered her voice. "I'm so sorry to call you like this, but Robby's upset. He's been crying all morning, and I don't think he'll calm down unless he talks to you."

"Why? What happened?"

"Nothing happened, honey, it's just that . . ." She hesitated. "He's afraid you aren't coming back. I hate to tell you this, but he thinks you've left him like his father did."

"Could you put him on the phone, please?" Megan said, fighting to keep her voice steady.

"Of course."

In another moment, her son's wavering voice said, "Hello?"

"Hi, Robby, it's Mom."

"Mom?" he said. "Where are you? Are you coming home?"

Yes, she almost cried out, *Right this minute. I'm on my way.* Instead she took a deep breath and said, "I'll be home on Saturday, like I told you before I left, remember?"

"Y-yes." He sniffled, and she could picture him wiping his nose on the back of his hand. "Are you sure you're coming back?"

"Of course I'm sure." She forced humor into her voice. "Did you think I'd get lost or something?"

"Well, you do get kind of lost sometimes, Mom."

She'd walked right into that one. "Not this time. I have a map and everything. Besides, I have to come home. I left all my stuff there."

He mulled that over. "That's true," he admitted.

She kept him on the phone until he was cheerful again, telling her all the fun plans he and his grandpa were making for the week. She listened and responded with just the right amount of enthusiasm, but inside she was aching and seething, wishing that Keith was there so she could shake him, so she could rage at him, so she could somehow make him see what his silence was doing to their precious child.

✤

Julia sat on her bed looking over her notes from the Beginning Piecing class. The class had covered several of the terms on her list that morning, and the teacher had assured her they would get to the others later that week. For the first time since her plane had touched down in central Pennsylvania, Julia began to feel some hope that this trip wouldn't be a wasted effort, after all.

To her surprise, she had actually enjoyed the lesson. The teacher, a strikingly pretty blond woman in her early forties named Diane, had a dry sense of humor that took some getting used to, but her explanations were clear and simple. The other five students had made templates for a Friendship Star block the previous day, but Diane had helped Julia while the other students cut out their fabric pieces, and before long, Julia had caught up to them. With Diane's class and Donna's private tutorials, Julia might just be able to convince Deneford she had been quilting for decades.

Suddenly a knock sounded on her door. "Megan! Are you decent?" a voice sang out as the door swung open. The white-haired woman stuck her head in the room, and when she spotted Julia, her eyebrows arched in surprise. "My goodness," she said. "You're decent, but you're not Megan."

"No." Startled, Julia rose and smoothed her skirt self-consciously. "I'm afraid you have the wrong room."

"Are you sure?" The woman, whom Julia now recognized as the same quilter from yesterday's disastrous Quick Piecing class, peered around in puzzlement as if she might spy the woman she was looking for hiding in a corner. "I was sure she said first room on the left in the west wing."

"I'm sorry." Julia's surprise was turning to impatience, but, remembering her image, she put on a pleasant expression. "There's no one named Megan staying in this room."

"Oh." The woman frowned, thinking. "Well, I already knocked across the hall, so maybe she went down to lunch already. Are you coming?"

"Well, actually—"

"You're not planning to skip lunch, are you? Someone as thin as you?"

"I'm expecting someone to bring me a tray."

"Are you ill?"

"No, but—"

"Then you can't stay up in your room all alone," the woman protested, and before Julia knew it, she had entered the room and taken Julia's arm. "You'll miss all the fun." Julia was too startled to do anything as the woman began to steer her toward the door and into the hallway. "I'm Vinnie, by the way."

"I don't mean to be rude, but—"

"Tuesday is pasta buffet," Vinnie said. "You pick what shape of pasta you like, what ingredients, and what sauce, and the cook mixes each order in a separate omelet pan. Everyone can have her lunch exactly the way she likes it."

They had reached the stairs, and Julia saw no way to escape without knocking the older woman on her backside. "That sounds delicious," she said instead, her stomach knotting at the thought of a crowd of quilters just waiting for her to slop marinara sauce down the front of her blouse. They passed Sarah on her way upstairs with a covered tray. "I'll be lunching with the other campers today, thank you," Julia said with all the dignity she could muster. In the banquet hall, she resigned herself to being the lunchtime entertainment for the day. Tomorrow, she promised herself, she would remember to lock her door.

The meal itself wasn't as tacky as she expected it to be; the cook prepared her penne with sun-dried tomatoes, fresh basil, and an excellent olive oil she was astonished to see this far from the West Coast. Vinnie ordered a plate of spaghetti and meatballs in a red sauce, then motioned for Julia to follow her a nearby table where two other women were already seated. One of the women was Donna, who started at their approach.

"These are two of my newest quilting friends, Donna and Grace," Vinnie said, and the two women greeted Julia with silent nods. "Donna and Grace, this is . . ." She looked up at Julia. "My goodness, dear, I didn't even get your name."

"Julia." Was it possible the old biddy didn't recognize her?

"Julia." Vinnie nodded in satisfaction and sat down. "Well, pull up a chair, Julia, before your noodles get cold."

"We can't have that, can we?" Julia said as pleasantly as she could manage, seating herself between Vinnie and Donna.

Just then, another woman joined them. A slender brunette, she was the youngest of the four, but unlike the others, she looked unhappy. "Sorry I'm late," she said, taking a seat between Grace and Vinnie. Then she bounded to her feet again. "Oh. I forgot my food."

"What's wrong with Megan?" Vinnie asked as the harried young woman headed for the pasta bar.

"She received a phone call in the middle of Color Theory class," Grace said. "I hope it wasn't bad news."

When Megan returned, her eyes met Julia's, and she nearly dropped her plate. "Oh my goodness, I didn't even see you there."

Vinnie reached for Megan's hand in a grandmotherly gesture that completely escaped the younger woman's notice. "Megan, this is Julia."

"Yes, I know. Julia Merchaud." She fumbled for her chair and sat down, still staring at Julia.

"You've met?"

"Well, no, but everyone knows Julia Merchaud."

Vinnie turned to her. "Is that so?"

Before Julia could reply, Donna said, "You're kidding, right? You've never heard of Julia Merchaud?"

"No." Vinnie looked from Donna to Julia and back. "Well, why should I have heard of her? She's probably never heard of me. Are you another famous quilter, like Grace?"

"She's famous, but she's not a quilter," Megan said.

"She most certainly is too a quilter," Donna said hastily, stealing a quick glance at Julia. "You're sure you've never heard of her? Julia Merchaud, Grandma Wilson from *Family Tree*? On television?"

Vinnie gave Julia a guilty smile. "I'm sorry, dear. I suppose I'm not watching the right channels. What day is your show on? I'll be sure to watch for you."

"It's been canceled," Julia managed. Eight years in the same role, one that earned her four Emmys and a Golden Globe, and someone from her core demographic didn't even recognize her.

"It was a great show, though," Megan ventured.

"It was my favorite," Donna said. "I wrote a letter to the network and complained when it was canceled, but no one ever wrote back."

Julia's annoyance ebbed, no match for Donna's admiration. "That's typical of the networks," she said, stabbing a piece of pasta with her fork. "They pay more attention to advertisers than viewers."

"That's a shame," Vinnie said. "Well, dear, if Donna and Megan here are any indication, you have loyal fans who won't rest until they see you on another show soon."

"Do you have any other projects pending?" Grace inquired.

"I do have one that's rather important. That's why I came to quilt camp—to brush up on my skills. My agent insisted, unfortunately. I'd planned on a week at my favorite spa." Julia sighed. She could be receiving a massage at that very moment. Instead her fingertips were sore with needle pricks, and she kept finding stray bits of thread all over her clothes. "I'll be playing a quilter in a feature film that begins shooting in a few months."

"How wonderful," Vinnie exclaimed. "A movie about quilters. It'll be a hit; I'm sure of it."

Warming to her subject, Julia divulged some details about the plot, and about how Ellen, whom she generously described as a "promising new voice in filmmaking," had based the story on her great-grandmother's diaries. As the four women hung on her every word, Julia forgot that she had not desired their company in the first place.

"That sounds so exciting," Donna said wistfully. "All I've ever done with my life is keep house and raise kids."

"That's all?" Grace said. "That's everything. There's no more important job in the world than raising your children. No job is more difficult, either."

"Or more rewarding," Vinnie said. "I raised four children and don't regret for a moment any of the sacrifices I made for them. I don't know how mothers these days can bear to leave their children in day care while they go off to work."

Megan gave her a wan look. "It isn't easy."

"Your situation is different," Vinnie said. "It's not your fault that husband of yours left. I'm sure you'd stay home if you could."

Grace laughed. "My husband left me, too, but even if he hadn't, I still would have kept up with my career. Yes, motherhood is my most important calling, but I would have gone crazy if I hadn't had some other outlet."

"I would have gone crazy if I hadn't stayed home," Donna said. "I wouldn't have been any use to an employer, anyway, on the phone all day checking in on the girls, staring out the windows fretting about what milestones I was missing."

"Every family is different," Megan said. "My son is loved and well cared for, and that's what matters most."

"Hear, hear," Vinnie said, raising her coffee cup and clinking it against Megan's.

"I like to think I set a good example for my daughter by being a mother and also pursuing my artistic career," Grace said. "She grew up assuming that there are many possibilities for women."

Megan nodded, looking hopeful for the first time since she had sat down. Then suddenly, her face fell. "Leaving my son for work is one thing—that's a necessity—but I'm never going to leave him for a vacation again."

"Let me guess. This is your first time away from your son overnight?" Grace asked, and Megan nodded. "He'll be all right. When you come home, that will reassure him, and your next trip away will be much easier."

"I don't think I could leave him another time," Megan said.

"You have to," Vinnie cried. "Next year, during my birthday week. You are coming back to camp next summer, aren't you?"

Megan looked dubious, as if she hadn't planned on it but liked the idea.

Donna said, "You should, Meg. It will be good for Robby—and for you."

"You have to come back, too," Grace told Donna. "I have to hear how that wedding works out."

"I guess that means you've already decided you'll be here," Megan said to Grace.

Grace let out a small, self-conscious laugh. "I suppose it does."

"By that time you'll have a new work in progress to show us," Vinnie declared. When Grace winced, Vinnie added, "Have a little faith in yourself. A whole year to begin one quilt. A lot can happen in a year."

Julia looked around the table, an observer rather than a participant. Only moments ago she had been the center of attention, but now the others seemed to have forgotten she was there—and not one had thought to ask her if she would return the next year. Why should they? They knew her trip was all business, no pleasure. No doubt they assumed she had better things to do—which she did, but it would have been nice if at least one of them had included her, if only to be polite.

Julia wondered what she was doing there, a childless woman among mothers whose shared experiences forged bonds among them she would never understand. They looked toward the future, each of them, because their love for their sons and daughters gave them a fierce and passionate stake in it. Julia's parents were dead; her link to the past was broken and her link to the future never forged.

She had always believed her work made her immortal, but watching these women, who had neither fame nor fortune to compare to hers, she realized that they, and not she, would live on forever. Her work would one day be forgotten, and all memory of her would one day disintegrate with the videotape that had captured her image, but part of these women would always live in their descendants' memories, in their very flesh and blood and bone.

Her work was nothing. What had she ever done to truly affect the life of another human being for the better? Throughout her career she had clawed and scratched and scrambled over competitors and colleagues alike to get where she was today, and for what?

Julia felt herself adrift in time, barren and alone.

⚜

In appliqué class after lunch, Julia still held the needle guardedly, but Donna was pleased to see that her pupil was making progress. Even so, Julia spoke so little during class that Donna worried that Vinnie had truly offended her. "Don't mind Vinnie," Donna apologized later, after they had begun their private needle-turn class in Sylvia Compson's formal parlor. "She's probably asleep by prime time."

"Hmm? Oh, that. I had forgotten."

Donna wasn't quite sure if she believed her. "About that confidentiality agreement . . . since you told the others about the movie at lunch, does that mean I can talk about it now?"

Julia sighed. "I suppose so."

"Does it really matter how recently you've learned to quilt?" Donna ventured. "What's important is how well you quilt when they're filming, right?"

Julia set down the leaf appliqué she was stitching to her Whig Rose block. "Yes, I suppose you're right. Except for my pride, of course. My agent—my former agent—told the producer I already knew how to quilt. He won't be pleased to learn we deceived him."

"What do you mean, 'we'?" Your agent lied, but you didn't. If the producer does learn the truth, you can just tell him your agent made a mistake."

"He's not a very gullible person."

"Maybe not, but you're a very good actress."

"That's true." Julia smiled briefly and picked up her block again. "If he hears the truth from me first, I won't have to worry about one of these other campers running to the tabloids and telling them what a terrible quilter I am."

"You're not a terrible quilter," Donna chided her, then hesitated. "Do you really think one of the other campers would do such a thing?"

"I'm no longer surprised by what anyone will do, for the right price."

Julia spoke airily, as if accustomed to betrayals. Donna felt a sudden surge of sympathy for her. It must be difficult going through life suspecting everyone, guarding your words and your actions. Quilters aren't like that, she wanted to say, but uncertainty held her back. For all she knew, campers were taking notes and snapping photos of Julia with hidden cameras. Julia's paranoia was rubbing off on her. "I don't think you have anything to worry about," she said, her loyalty to her fellow quilters outweighing her desire to appear agreeable.

"I have much to worry about. You have no idea how important this role is to my career. Now that the series is over, if something doesn't go right for me soon, I'll be lucky if I can get a spot in an antacid commercial." She shrugged and flashed Donna what was probably meant as a nonchalant grin, but the pain beneath it was obvious.

"You can't mean that," Donna said. "You've won five Emmys. You must have directors begging you to star in their shows."

"Four Emmys," Julia said. "And a Golden Globe. But that doesn't matter much when you're my age. How often do feature films star a woman, and I mean really star, as the main character and not just someone's girlfriend or wife? And how many women over forty do you see in any roles at all?" She shook her head and began stabbing her quilt block with her needle in quick, emphatic motions. "In Hollywood's version of America, women over forty have all but vanished."

Donna barked out a laugh. "It's not just Hollywood. We haven't disappeared, but we might as well be invisible for all the respect your average wife and mother receives in our society. At least you have your career. People have to respect you."

"For being an entertainer?" Julia said. "For reciting lines someone else wrote? What's the merit in that? What exactly have I contributed to the world?"

Their eyes met briefly, and for a moment Donna was struck with the unsettling sensation that Julia Merchaud envied her. "Your work is important," she said. "You present stories and situations that teach, that make people think."

Julia brushed that off with a wave of her hand. "Please. 'Next, on a very special *Family Tree,* Grandma Wilson cures cancer and feeds the hungry.'"

"I'm serious," Donna insisted. "Your work can be positive or negative, but if people watch it, it will influence them. My daughter studies drama, and she would tell you the same thing." Donna suddenly lost her enthusiasm. "Or at least she used to study drama."

They worked on in silence, but Donna's thoughts churned. Who was she to be making impassioned speeches, as if she had cornered the market on confidence and self-worth? She had spent far too much of her time apologizing for being a stay-at-home mom, all the while secretly consoling herself with the assurance that she was doing what was best for her children. But now, despite all her love and encouragement, one child was dropping out of college to get married, just as Donna herself had done. Maybe Grace was right: If a mother worked outside the home, she proved to her daughters that there were other possibilities for women.

She felt overcome with heartsickness. She couldn't bear the thought that she had set her own sights too low and had thereby influenced her daughters to do the same.

Lindsay used to study drama. Soon, Donna would say that her daughter used to be a promising student at the University of Minnesota, that she used to be active in college organizations, that she used to have a future bright with promise and possibilities. Too much of her daughter's life was shifting into the past tense with this impending marriage, and Donna couldn't accept that.

And why should she accept it, without first trying to persuade her daughter to take another path? In hindsight, she should have stepped in earlier, when Lindsay moved into Brandon's apartment at the beginning of the summer. She had not protested then because she didn't want to appear out of touch or old-fashioned. Well, she was old-fashioned, and although Lindsay might prefer that Donna accept every one of her daughter's choices without question, Donna would do so no longer.

She couldn't simply order Lindsay not to marry Brandon or postpone the wedding; young women who thought they were in love rarely listened to logic or common sense. Instead, Donna would focus on Lindsay's education. Surely she could find a way to convince Lindsay that furthering her education would be best for her—and by extension, for her marriage—in the long run.

Lindsay had to finish school. Donna couldn't let Brandon become Lindsay's whole life.

Five

Vinnie woke Wednesday morning with a sense of triumph. She had made it to her eighty-second birthday. She said her morning prayers quickly, eager to start the day. Before she left her room, she studied her face in the mirror and practiced looking surprised. If Sylvia and her staff discovered she anticipated their annual surprise parties, they might stop having them.

At breakfast, Vinnie graciously collected birthday greetings and a few ribbon-tied fat quarters from well-wishers she had met during previous years' camp sessions. "When's the party?" several whispered when no one on the staff could overhear, forcing Vinnie to feign innocence. Keeping up the pretense of surprise was part of the fun.

Vinnie loved celebrating her birthday and was impatient with people who refused to acknowledge their own. What was so shameful in living another year? It was considerably better than the alternative. Vinnie never missed an opportunity to have fun, especially when other people wanted to show their affection for her. She had learned that from Aunt Lynn and her aunt's friend, Lena.

Lena was the blond woman who had driven Vinnie from her home to Aunt Lynn's small house in Dayton so many years ago. She had tried to engage Vinnie in conversation as they drove, but Vinnie was too numb to respond. Her father had sent her away—and although he had not explained why, she knew. If she had only been good, he would have kept her, as he had kept Frankie.

As the weeks passed, Vinnie's shock and grief lessened but never quite left her. A chasm of grief and loneliness seemed to separate her from the other girls at her new school, and she still felt like a stranger in Aunt Lynn's home. Her new teacher was kind and encouraged the other children to include her in their play, but Vinnie usually wandered off to be alone and think.

She had to find a way to persuade her father to let her come home. She wrote to him often, telling him how good she had been and how she never got into trouble at school anymore. She told him that Aunt Lynn had taught her to clean and sew, and how she would do all the chores, hers and Frankie's both, if he would just let her come home.

He responded to her first letter, writing that he was pleased she was being a good girl and he was sure she wouldn't give Aunt Lynn any trouble. Frankie wrote frequently, reporting on the neighbor's new puppy and a trip to the zoo with Daddy, but Daddy rarely sent letters, and never once did he respond to Vinnie's questions about when she might return home.

One day, after many months, Aunt Lynn asked Vinnie how she would like to celebrate her upcoming eighth birthday.

"I want to go to the zoo with my daddy," Vinnie said, remembering Frankie's letter.

Aunt Lynn and Lena exchanged a look. "How about if we take you instead?" Aunt Lynn asked. "Your dad might not be able to go."

Vinnie felt her eyes welling up with tears. She didn't care about the zoo; all she wanted was to see her father. "If he can't take me, I don't want to go."

"Would you like to do something else?" Lena asked.

"I don't want to have a birthday at all."

"We have to celebrate your birthday," Aunt Lynn said.

"We didn't last year." Last year, so soon after her mother had died, no one in the family could have imagined celebrating. Talk of her birthday called back all that grief and loneliness, which were never far away.

Without another word, she left the room rather than cry in front of Aunt Lynn and Lena. She doubted they would ask her father about the zoo; even if they did, he would refuse, if he bothered to reply at all.

Aunt Lynn and Lena said no more about her birthday, so she assumed they had forgotten about it, as she wished she could. Then one Saturday morning, Aunt Lynn and Lena bounded into her room and threw back the curtains. "Get up, sleepyhead," Aunt Lynn sang out.

Lena sat on Vinnie's bed and bounced up and down on the mattress, grinning. "Come on. You don't want to sleep in on your birthday!"

"I thought I wasn't having a birthday this year," Vinnie said, sitting up and blinking in the light.

"We decided to celebrate anyway," Aunt Lynn said. "In fact, we're celebrating twice as much. You missed two birthdays, so we have to make up for lost time. Otherwise we'll have to celebrate three times as much on your next birthday, and that might be too much for us old spinsters." Aunt Lynn and Lena looked at each other and laughed.

"Well, get up," Lena admonished. "The Pot-Luck Pals will be here soon."

Vinnie needed no further enticement. She flung back the covers and scrambled to get ready.

Vinnie hadn't made any friends of her own in the neighborhood yet, but the Pot-Luck Pals were the kind she hoped to have someday. Aunt Lynn and Lena's friends came over twice a month for a pot-luck supper and wild games of gin rummy that lasted long after Vinnie had been sent to bed. Some of the ladies were married, but most were single women in their late twenties and early thirties, like Aunt Lynn and Lena. They were shopgirls and secretaries and schoolteachers, and they were unlike any grown-up women Vinnie had ever known.

Not long after breakfast, the Pot-Luck Pals began to arrive, each bearing a covered dish and two colorfully wrapped gifts. "Happy seventh birthday," Margaret said, kissing Vinnie on one cheek. "And happy eighth," she said, kissing the other. Carla, the oldest, put a funny paper hat on Vinnie's head and placed an identical one on her own dark curls; her sister, Ethel Mae, picked up Vinnie and spun her around for good luck, seven times for her seventh year, and eight more times for the eighth. Afterward, she collapsed on the sofa and said, "If I keep this up, I won't need any of Lynn's punch!"

Never had the Pals filled the little house with so much warmth and laughter. They laughed and joked and played party games; they turned on the radio and danced themselves breathless. At noon they had a pot-luck lunch, one of the best the Pals had ever prepared, and then Vinnie opened her presents. She blew out candles on two birthday cakes and drank lemonade until she thought she would burst. The party grew louder and happier as the Pals indulged in more of Aunt Lynn's famous punch, the kind Aunt Lynn told her she'd be allowed to have on her eighteenth birthday and not an hour before. When Aunt Lynn wasn't watching, Ethel Mae let Vinnie have a taste from her cup; it burned going down, and Vinnie couldn't imagine why the Pals liked it.

The party lasted all day, until one by one the Pals went home, leaving the house a whirlwind of dirty dishes and party favors. Vinnie was exhausted, but happier than she had been in years. She helped Aunt Lynn and Lena begin to clean up the mess, but before long the three of them collapsed on the sofa, Aunt Lynn and Lena leaning against each other, Vinnie's head resting in Aunt Lynn's lap.

"Look at that grin," Lena said, nudging Aunt Lynn and nodding down at Vinnie. "I didn't think the kid knew how to smile like that."

Vinnie's smile broadened even as her eyelids drooped with sleep.

"I wonder what she wished for when she blew out her candles," Aunt Lynn said, her voice sounding far away.

"Don't make her tell, or the wish won't come true."

As Vinnie drifted off to sleep, she held her secrets close to her heart. As the last candle on the first cake had flickered out, Vinnie had wished that she would never forget that day as long as she lived. Over the candles on the second cake, she had made not a wish, but a promise: One day, she would be as carefree and confident as Aunt Lynn, Lena, and the other Pot-Luck Pals. No one would ever again believe she didn't know how to smile.

She kept her promise so well that people who knew her later probably never imagined that Vinnie had ever been anything but happy. Her birthday wish came true, as well, although some years—the birthdays when Sam was overseas, the time all four kids came down with the chicken pox, the first lonely birthdays as a widow—Vinnie found it more difficult to celebrate. If not for that brochure about the first Elm Creek Quilt Camp, she might have let her promise slip away, and a fine show of appreciation for Aunt Lynn and Lena that would have been. She filled out the form and sent it in over the protests of her children, who had planned to throw her a party. "You don't want to spend your birthday alone," her daughter said.

"I won't be alone," Vinnie replied firmly. "I'll be with other quilters."

The moment Vinnie stepped on the grounds of Elm Creek Manor, she knew she had made the right decision. That evening, at the Candlelight welcoming ceremony, she told the other campers why she had come and was warmed by their sympathy. On the morning of her birthday, Sylvia Compson, a widow herself, hosted a delightful birthday breakfast. As she blew out the candle on her blueberry muffin, Vinnie made another wish and a promise: a promise that she would come back to Elm Creek Manor each year to celebrate her birthday as long as she was able, and a wish that she would always find herself among friends. She kept that promise, and every year Sylvia and her staff rewarded her with a suprise birthday party.

This year they made her wait in suspense all day, so long that Vinnie began to worry that perhaps they had forgotten. But when she entered the banquet hall for supper, the lights were out and the curtains drawn. And when the lights suddenly came on—

"Surprise!" the campers shouted, showering her in confetti. They blew noisemakers and broke into a chorus of "Happy Birthday" while she stood in the doorway reveling in the attention. Almost too late, she remembered to open her eyes wide and let her jaw drop.

"My goodness," she exclaimed. "You should know better than to scare an old lady so." Everyone laughed, because no one could imagine considering Vinnie an old lady, a fact that pleased Vinnie beyond measure.

Dinner was wonderful—stuffed pork chops, her favorite, though she couldn't imagine how Sylvia had known that. The quilt campers were delightful company, just as they were every year, and this time there were two celebrities present. Julia Merchaud hugged her and gave her a lovely pin as a gift, which told Vinnie, to her relief, that the television star had forgiven her.

As the guest of honor, Vinnie sat at a special table with Sylvia and two other co-founders of Elm Creek Quilts, but she insisted that her newest quilt buddies join them. Everyone applauded when Sarah wheeled out a birthday cake large enough for all the campers to share.

As she blew out the candles, Vinnie glanced at Megan, smiled secretly to herself, and made a wish.

After breakfast Thursday morning, Grace retreated to the formal parlor with a box full of photographs Sylvia had provided. All that week in photo transfer class, Grace had managed to avoid any actual hands-on work by observing the other quilters as they practiced the various techniques. Sylvia must have told the instructor, an auburn-haired young woman named Summer, to permit Grace to proceed at her own pace, for although Summer urged the other students forward, she left Grace alone, merely checking now and then to see if she was enjoying herself or if she had any questions. Grace, who would have balked if she were pushed, appreciated Summer's patience. Best of all, it had paid off. Grace now felt ready to do something she hadn't done in over eighteen months: begin a new project.

First, however, she would need a photo. Class members who had registered in advance had brought pictures from home, but aside from a few wallet-sized snapshots of Joshua and Justine, Grace had none. When she explained her dilemma to Sylvia, she suggested Grace choose a photo from a previous session of quilt camp. Alone in the parlor, Grace curled up on an overstuffed sofa and began sorting through the box. Many of the photos were candid shots taken during classes; in others, campers posed in various locations around the estate, their arms around each other, smiling happily for the camera.

Grace held one photo thoughtfully, studying the smiling women. She, too, had made friends that week at camp, something she had never expected. She had Sylvia to thank for that. Just that morning at breakfast, she and Donna had had a long heart-to-heart about their daughters. How refreshing it had been to commiserate about the trials of motherhood as if those were the only problems on her mind. She had even managed to forget about the other problems for a little while.

Grace set the photo aside. Although today's project would be merely an exercise in which any photo would do, she wanted a more meaningful image than a group of strangers. What a shame she couldn't use one of Megan's photos. During the evening festivities she was rarely without her camera, but of course, her film wasn't developed yet. Megan had offered to get multiple prints and send them each a set after they returned home, but Grace needed something now.

She took out another handful of photos and thumbed through them. A frontal view of Elm Creek Manor would be perfect, if she could find one. It was hard to believe that someone as organized as Sylvia would store her photos so haphazardly. Grace would have expected them to be neatly mounted in scrapbooks in chronological order according to subject.

She paused at a picture of Sylvia and the rest of the Elm Creek Quilts staff sitting on the front veranda. She thought it must have been taken in autumn, judging by the fallen leaves scattered in the foreground.

"Are you having any luck with those?"

Grace looked up to find Sylvia standing in the doorway. "I just found one of you and your staff," she said, showing Sylvia the photo. "I'm surprised at you. What do you call your filing system? Random or chaos?"

"Don't blame me. Those are Sarah's photos, not mine." Sylvia sat beside her to get a better look at the photo. "Hmm. Oh yes, I remember that one. Camp had ended for the season weeks earlier, and we were just about to leave on a road trip to the International Quilt Festival in Houston. That was the year I had my stroke." She settled back against the sofa cushions. "It's funny how I mark time these days—before Elm Creek Quilts and after, before my stroke and after."

Grace nodded, uneasy, wondering if Sylvia had guessed more than she let on. She knew exactly what Sylvia meant. She had her own demarcation, the time when she thought she was merely overtired or stressed out, and the bleak, sterile months that followed the doctor's diagnosis.

But Sylvia continued. "I was thinking, after your classes today, perhaps you'd like to join me in searching for those old Civil War quilts I told you about? If my sister didn't sell them, they could be up in the attic. I know the exact trunk they would be in, but we might have to move some boxes around before we unearth it."

Grace wanted to see those quilts so badly she almost agreed—but then she thought of all those flights of stairs, of the strain from moving boxes, and knew she wouldn't make it. She'd been pushing her luck all week, and although she longed to spend a leisurely afternoon exploring the manor's hidden treasures, she couldn't risk another exacerbation. "I can't."

"Why not?" Sylvia asked. "Don't you have free time this afternoon?"

"Yes, but I'm afraid attics aren't good places for me."

"We don't have any bats that I know of," Sylvia said. "Are you allergic to dust?"

Grace nodded, but her conscience stung from the lie.

Sylvia sighed and rose. "I thought you'd jump at the chance to find those old quilts."

"I would like to see them." Grace hated to see Sylvia so disappointed, so puzzled by her ostensible lack of interest. "If I had brought my medication, I'd be up there in a second, believe me."

"I understand. I can hardly take a breath around cats, myself. Perhaps I can drag Matthew up to the attic today to shift some clutter. If I find the quilts, I'll bring them down to you."

Grace thanked her, and with a promise to see her later, Sylvia left. Grace set the photo of the Elm Creek Quilters aside and returned to the box. She hated keeping secrets from a trusted friend and she hated lies, but she hated pity even more. Justine had said she was too proud, and maybe Justine was right, but it was her life, and she was determined to live it on her terms as long as she was able.

Just then, her fingertips brushed another photo, jostling it loose from the box. As the picture fell to the floor, she glimpsed a patch of cheerful red, in the midst of which, to her surprise, was Vinnie. She sat in the gazebo in the north gardens, a red straw hat perched jauntily on her white curls. Draped over her lap was a cheerful Ohio Star quilt in bright rainbow colors. Vinnie's mouth was slightly open, and she had a mischievous look in her eye as if she had been interrupted while telling a joke.

Grace couldn't help smiling. It was hard to believe that spirited woman had just turned eighty-two. If Grace had half her energy, she'd probably whip out a dozen quilts a year.

Suddenly Grace had an idea. She would use this picture for Summer's photo transfer workshop. After the photo's image was reproduced on fabric, Grace would frame the portrait in Ohio Star blocks pieced from the hand-dyed fat eighths she had won Monday night. She could machine quilt the finished design and make a small wallhanging, which she would present to Vinnie as a belated birthday gift.

With a newfound thrill of anticipation, Grace returned the other photos to the box and hurried off to class. Granted, this quilt wouldn't be museum quality or win praise from art critics, but at least she would be creating again.

⚘

The more Julia learned about quilting, the more she realized a week's worth of classes wouldn't be enough to enable her to pass herself off as a master quilter. She had never known how much work was involved in making a quilt, from piecing the top to stitching the three layers together. What once seemed a simple, even mundane bed covering now took on a new meaning as a true work of art. She felt a new respect for those who managed to finish even one full-size quilt in one lifetime, though only weeks before she would have dismissed them as pitiable women with nothing better to do than waste their time on tedious hobbies.

She had finished her Friendship Star block and was well on her way to completing the Whig Rose when Megan suggested she try other patterns, enough to sew a small sampler. Julia knew she would need to practice her skills after camp ended, but when she thought of all the work involved in sewing an entire quilt, even a wallhanging, she grew discouraged. "Don't think about the entire quilt," Megan said. "Just take it one block at a time."

"Sounds like a twelve-step program," Julia said, but she agreed to try. Megan suggested other patterns that would teach her various quilting techniques: the Drunkard's Path for learning to piece curves, the Stamp Basket for setting in pieces, and a few others. Donna, Grace, and Vinnie contributed ideas of their own, and by Thursday afternoon they had helped her design a sampler of nine blocks arranged in a three-by-three grid, separated by strips of fabric Vinnie called sashing.

"The studio should hire you four as consultants," Julia teased them.

Grace laughed, but Donna asked in earnest, "Do you think they would?"

"Don't be silly," Vinnie admonished. "How will Julia keep her secret if we're hovering around telling her what to do?"

They all knew Julia's predicament by now, and while they didn't quite believe that her career could be in jeopardy, they were eager to teach her all she needed to know for the role. Instead of one tutor, Julia found herself with four. Sometimes she wondered exactly what they hoped to gain from helping her, but eventually she decided to accept their assistance for what it appeared to be, kindness and generosity. Since she desperately needed them, she didn't have much choice.

She would have practiced late into the night if left to herself, but the others insisted she join them for the evening program. Her fingertips were so sore from hand-quilting that her pace had slowed considerably, so with more relief than reluctance, she agreed to meet them in the ballroom.

When she arrived, she saw that some of the classroom partitions had been removed to make room for several rows of chairs in front of a raised dais at the far end of the room. "What's all this?" she asked her new acquaintances as the rows began to fill with excited, chattering quilters. The news that the Campers' Talent Show was about to begin made her wish she had stayed in her room. The last thing she wanted was to endure a hapless amateur hour when she had so much work to do.

Vinnie must have sensed her reluctance, for she pushed Julia into a folding chair. "You're not leaving," she said. "Not until you give me your professional opinion of my acting. Your honest opinion, mind you."

Julia smiled at her weakly and hoped that Vinnie would be remarkably good, but if it came down to telling the truth or hurting the feelings of someone whose help she needed, she would lie.

The show was rather informal. Instead of waiting backstage, the performers sat in the audience. When one act ended, Sylvia Compson announced the next by calling the soloist or group to the front of the room. Several of the acts were skits, which, based upon the laughter from the audience, she assumed were supposed to be humorous. Since even the solemn Grace smiled, Julia decided that quilters must have inside jokes she simply didn't understand.

Some of the performers were surprisingly good. One woman gave a dramatic monologue from Shakespeare; afterward Julia overheard that she was a professor of English literature at Brown. Vinnie and Donna nearly brought down the house with their rendition of "Who's on First." Even Julia had to laugh when Vinnie brandished a yellow plastic whiffle ball bat and shrieked, "I'll break your arm if you say 'Who's on first!'" The audience roared with laughter so long that Donna grew flustered and forgot her next line. When Vinnie prompted her loudly enough to be heard in the back row, the laughter erupted again.

When the performers returned to their seats amid a shower of applause, Vinnie whispered to Julia, "Well?"

"I can honestly say that was the most original Abbott and Costello impersonation I've ever witnessed," Julia said.

Vinnie looked pleased, but Donna said, "She's just being nice. I stunk up the place."

They laughed as Sylvia called the next performer to the stage. "Megan, dear, it's your turn. Megan Donohue, everyone."

As Megan went to the front of the room, two staff members wheeled a baby grand piano to the front of the stage. Megan flashed the audience a quick smile before she sat down at the bench and tested the keys.

"I should have done that instead," Vinnie whispered. "I can play 'Heart and Soul' with my eyes closed."

Donna stifled a giggle, then jumped in her seat as Megan's hands suddenly crashed onto the keyboard in a resounding chord. To Julia's astonishment, the aerospace engineer from Ohio was playing Chopin's *Fantasy Impromptu* in C-sharp minor—and playing it well. Remarkably well, in fact. Soon Julia forgot herself and listened as breathlessly as the rest of the audience as the music flowed from the piano and washed over them. When the final notes died away, there was a moment of stunned silence before the listeners applauded wildly.

Megan returned to her seat, her cheeks flushed, pausing to accept congratulations as she went. "I bet you're glad you stuck to comedy," Donna teased Vinnie. Julia could tell from her proud expression that she had long known of Megan's gift.

When Megan finally was able to sit down, Julia leaned over and said, "You play wonderfully." Megan flashed her a quick, embarrassed smile and said nothing, but she looked pleased.

"Does anyone else wish to entertain us?" Sylvia called out from the front of the room. "Grace?"

Grace looked alarmed. "Not me."

"Julia? How about you?"

To Julia it seemed as if everyone in the room suddenly turned in their seats to look at her. "Well . . ." Their eyes were so eager and expectant that she was at a loss for words.

"Oh, come on, dear. Surely you can't have stage fright."

Julia wavered. "I didn't prepare anything."

"Give me a break, honey," Vinnie said, nudging her. Before Julia could protest, Donna and Megan had pulled her to her feet. The campers burst into cheers. Julia couldn't help basking in the admiration as she went to the dais and seated herself at the piano. She warmed up with a few chords, then said, "Here's a song I'm sure you all know. It suits this week very well, I think." *Corny, but true,* she thought, especially for herself.

Julia had chosen "Climb Every Mountain" from *The Sound of Music.* She chose it not only because she thought it would appeal to this particular audience, but also because it was her standard musical audition song. She had rehearsed and performed it more times than she could count, and knew the phrasing and emphasis by heart. As a pianist she fell far short of Megan, but the tune was simple enough that she could play it flawlessly. Her voice sounded rich and full, and as she held the final note, she saw with satisfaction that her listeners were entranced.

As she rose and bowed to thunderous applause, Julia felt a contentment in her heart she hadn't sensed in years. It had been far too long since she had performed for the sheer joy of it.

"You sure gave them a thrill," Vinnie said over the cheers of the other campers when Julia returned to her seat. Julia glowed, delighting in their response. She lived for the stage, for the admiration and appreciation that only an audience could provide. *Family Tree* was over and she might never have another series, but her fans had not forgotten her. They still loved her.

Sylvia stood on the dais trying to quiet the audience. "Thank you to all our performers," she said. "And now, if you'll mark your ballots, we'll select our winner."

Julia felt a jolt. "Winner?"

"That's right," Vinnie said, handing her a stack of blue slips of paper and a handful of golf pencils. "The winner gets a prize. Donna, if we win, do you think we'll each get a prize or will we have to split one?"

"We don't have to worry," Donna said.

Vinnie laughed, then raised her eyebrows at Julia. "Well, go on, honey. Take one and pass the rest down. Unless you're planning to stuff the ballot box?"

Julia took one ballot and passed the rest on to Grace. She stole a glance at Megan, who was writing on her slip of paper, apparently unconcerned. Except for Julia herself, no one else had received such enthusiastic applause, and Julia never would have participated if she had known a winner would be selected. She was a professional; it was inappropriate for her to snatch a prize away from an amateur in an amateur competition. What if Julia won instead of Megan? Then she had a horrible thought: What if she *didn't* win?

Quickly Julia scribbled her own name and handed the slip of paper to the staff member passing through the center aisle. Her heart pounded as Sylvia and her staff tallied the votes at the front of the room.

"Your attention, please," Sylvia finally said, and the quilters fell silent. "I'm pleased to announce that by an overwhelming margin, the winner of the Campers' Talent Show is—Julia Merchaud!"

Numb with relief, Julia went to the dais to receive her prize, acknowledging the audience's applause as graciously as she could manage.

"Congratulations," Grace said when Julia returned to her seat. She nodded in response.

"What did you win?" Vinnie asked.

Only then did Julia inspect her prize. Sylvia had given her an Elm Creek Quilts pin identical to those her friends had won on games night.

"Now we all have one," Vinnie exclaimed, then caught herself. "Oh. Except for you, Megan."

Megan shrugged. "We still have one more day of classes. Maybe I'll have better luck tomorrow." She smiled at Julia. "Congratulations."

Suddenly Julia was stung by shame. "You deserve this more than I do."

"What are you talking about? You won, fair and square."

"But I only won because . . ." Because she was more popular, because she was famous, because the campers had been so thrilled to see a star perform live that they failed to see the merit of Megan's performance. "I never should have entered."

She tried to give Megan the pin, but Megan merely laughed off the gesture, as if she weren't the least disturbed by the unfairness of the competition. Her refusal to become resentful only made Julia feel worse, and that unsettled her. After all, she had trampled over her competitors as long as she had been in Hollywood. More than once, she had stolen other actresses' roles through conniving and manipulation. She had destroyed rivals' careers by anonymously revealing their addictions to the media and had alienated more than one costar with her insistence on top billing. Many times Julia had deserved to lose, then reveled when she managed through luck or subterfuge to come out on top. But now, as the quilters bid each other good night and went off to their rooms, she felt oddly empty. Where was that familiar sense of triumph after a victory?

Clutching the pin in her fist, she went upstairs to sleep so she wouldn't have to think about it anymore.

⚓

On Friday morning, Vinnie waited, watching the clock, until she couldn't wait any longer. She dialed Adam's number and hoped she wouldn't wake him.

"Hello?" he said groggily after the fifth ring.

"Good morning, honey," she said brightly. "Did I wake you?"

"Nana?" In the background she heard bedsprings creak. "Is something wrong?"

"No, dear, I just wanted to be sure you're planning to pick me up from quilt camp tomorrow."

"Of course," he said through a yawn. "I'll be there around eleven."

"Could you make it any earlier?" Vinnie glanced at the door as if someone might overhear. "Around ten, maybe?"

"I thought camp wasn't over that early."

"It's not."

"Don't you have that special farewell breakfast? Why do you want to leave early?"

"I don't want to leave early," she said impatiently. "Goodness, Adam, can't you just do as you're told? Be here by ten or I'll—just be here by ten."

She hung up the phone before he could ask any more questions. That young man had a way of sneaking the truth out of her.

⚓

Friday passed so swiftly that before Megan knew it, her last full day of quilt camp was over. That evening, a comedy improv group comprised of students from nearby Waterford College put on an entertaining show, but the campers' laughter was not as joyous as it would have been earlier in the week or even a day before. Already Megan felt nostalgic for camp, which was too soon coming to an end. She missed Robby, but part of her wished that she could stay at the elegant manor for another week of quilting and fun with her new friends.

After the show, Sylvia announced that the final breakfast would be served on the cornerstone patio, where they had held the Candlelight ceremony. "We'll have one last good chat before you leave," she said. "Bring something for show-and-tell."

Julia looked dubious. "Show-and-tell?" she said in an undertone as the campers left the room and headed up the stairs. "As in grammar school?"

"Don't be such a wet blanket," Vinnie teased. "You're never too old for show-and-tell."

Megan suppressed a smile. She wondered how long it had been since someone had dared to tease the great Julia Merchaud.

Megan bid the others good night and went to her room to pack, but within a few minutes, she began to feel lonely. She set her suitcase aside and went down the hallway to Donna's room, but before she could knock on the door, it opened. "I was just about to come to your room," Donna exclaimed. "Come on in."

"I can't believe camp is over already," Megan said, dropping dejectedly into a chair. "I feel like we just got here."

Donna agreed, then settled in on the bed across from Megan. They talked for a while about how much the week had meant to them, then began to gossip about some of the other members of their internet quilting newsgroup. They were in near hysterics recalling a flame war about off-topic posts when a knock sounded on the door. Grace poked her head in and demanded to know what was so funny. By the time Megan finished recounting the tale, their threefold laughter elicited yet another knock.

"Come in," they shouted together.

Vinnie peeked in. When she saw them, her face brightened. "Ooh, a party," she exclaimed, and quickly ducked back outside again. In a moment she returned with a grocery bag. "We can't have a party without refreshments."

"You brought all this from home?" Megan said, eyeing the tins of home-made cookies, the bags of popcorn, and the jars of nuts.

"I thought I might get hungry on the drive."

"Where were you driving from, Alaska?" Donna asked, helping herself to a few chocolate chip cookies.

"Ohio, wise guy," Vinnie said, taking a jar of cashews for herself. "You know, all we're missing are a few Chippendales dancers and this could be a real party."

Just then someone knocked on the door.

"Vinnie, you didn't," Grace exclaimed.

Vinnie's face went nearly as white as her hair. "Oh, my goodness. I didn't mean it." Her look of genuine shock set the others laughing even harder than before. When Donna finally managed to greet the unknown visitor, Julia opened the door warily. She stood for a moment taking in the scene of half-hysterical quilters, a quilt block and needle in her hand.

"I was hoping you could help me with this," she said to Donna. "Maybe I'll see you in the morning." She started to shut the door, but Donna jumped to her feet and pulled her inside. When Julia stammered something about making an early night of it, the others drowned out her protests. Reluctantly, she perched on the bed and showed them the Whig Rose block that was giving her so much trouble. Calming themselves for her sake, each inspected the block and offered suggestions for improving her appliqué stitch. When Julia was ready to begin, Grace sat beside her on the bed and watched as Julia put their ideas into practice.

They chatted as Julia worked, alternating between comical and serious topics. They talked about the families and problems they had left behind at home and would be returning to the next day. Somehow, knowing she would probably never see these women again pained Megan, yet it freed her to be more open than she ordinarily would have been. As she told them about Keith, for the first time Megan didn't feel that she had to apologize for not being stronger, for not already filling up—with work and friends and new love—the hole he had left in her life. She was so grateful for her friends' acceptance that she wished they had had this talk earlier, so that she would have had more time to savor their friendship before they parted. But she also sensed, as the night turned into early morning, that a special closeness bound them, something almost magical. Perhaps they couldn't have talked this way on any other night.

⚓

Donna's alarm clock announced that morning had arrived all too soon. She was not a night owl by any stretch of the imagination and knew she would suffer all day for her late night. She simply couldn't have closed down the impromptu party, though, and since no one had volunteered to be the first to leave, the festivities had stretched on into the early morning hours. Even after she was alone, Donna couldn't drop off to sleep right away. Her thoughts and her heart were too full.

She met the others on the cornerstone patio for breakfast. The day promised to be warm and sunny, but Donna's mood was dark. She missed her family, but camp had been so much more special than she had expected, and she couldn't bear to see it end. She wondered if she would ever again have a week full of such perfect moments.

After breakfast, the campers gathered in a circle as they had the first night of camp, this time for show-and-tell. Each quilter showed something she had made that week and shared her favorite memory of Elm Creek Manor. Even the beginning quilters proudly displayed their handiwork. Julia held up her Friendship Star block, and seemed genuinely pleased when the other campers praised her piecing skills. When Sylvia prompted her to name her favorite memory, she hesitated before looking right at Donna and saying, "The kindness of other quilters who were so willing to share their knowledge. I can honestly say it's been a long time since I've experienced such generosity."

Donna was surprised and pleased to know that Julia had appreciated her simple lessons so much, but she couldn't help feeling sorry for Julia and wondering why someone so successful apparently had so little kindness in her life.

Vinnie showed off a half-finished Double Pinwheel quilt top she had worked on in her Quick Piecing classes, and declared that her favorite memory was her surprise birthday party. "That's what you said last year," Sylvia said, her eyes glinting with merriment, "and the year before. It's time for you to come up with something new."

Vinnie pursed her lips and thought, then said that if Sylvia wouldn't let her use her real favorite memory, she would have to go with the food. "It was especially good this year," she protested when everyone laughed.

For her turn, Megan held up an exquisite Feathered Star miniature quilt, only fourteen inches square. When the other quilters marveled at the precision of her piecing, Megan passed the quilt around the circle. "When you see it up close you'll spot the mistakes," she said, but everyone declared that they couldn't find a single one. When she held the quilt, Donna couldn't find even the smallest tip of a triangle out of place or truncated, and she shook her head and announced that Megan was being too critical of herself.

"She should win a prize for being the toughest judge of her own work," Vinnie hinted to Sylvia. "Maybe one of those Elm Creek Quilts pins." But Sylvia merely laughed.

Donna had brought two items to show: the Whig Rose block she had completed in the appliqué workshop and the color gradations chart she had made in Color Theory. She was especially proud of the latter, since her color choices tended to be conservative, and the chart had inspired her to be more daring. "My favorite memory is easy," she said. "Meeting all my wonderful new friends."

Grace went last, and, remembering her confession during the Candle-light ceremony, everyone waited with anxious expectation to see what she would show them. To Donna's surprise, she held up not a small block or an exercise from Color Theory, but a small quilt bordered with Ohio Star blocks. In the center was a photo-transfer block of Vinnie sitting in the garden with a quilt on her lap. "Thanks to Summer and Sylvia—in fact, thanks to all of you, for your encouragement—I finally broke through my quilter's block. Happy birthday, Vinnie."

"For me?" Vinnie's eyes shone as she took the quilt. "Why, it's lovely. Ohio Star blocks, and I'm from Ohio!"

"That's why I chose them."

"Oh, my." Vinnie was speechless for a moment as she held the quilt up to admire it, then hugged it to her chest. "I'll treasure it always."

"What about your favorite memory?" another quilter prompted.

Grace smiled at Vinnie admiring her gift. "I think this is it."

Everyone laughed, but a little sadly, because now every quilter had taken her turn. The week of camp was over.

Donna was reluctant to leave, so she lingered on the cornerstone patio with her friends as the other campers exchanged hugs and tearful good-byes. She and Megan would keep in touch, of course, but what of the others? She would never know if Grace would continue to triumph over her quilter's block or if Julia would convince her producer that she was an expert quilter. She would never know if Vinnie would find her grandson a new girlfriend. In turn, they would never know if she had convinced Lindsay to stay in school, and when the wedding came and she needed their support, they would be miles away, scattered around the country when she needed them most.

"I'm going to miss you," Donna said, embracing each of them in turn. "Without you, I don't think I ever would have found the courage to face Lindsay. I wish . . . I wish we could all be there to help each other with all the problems waiting back home."

She looked around the circle of friends and knew at once that each felt the same way.

"A few days ago we all said we were coming back next year," Donna said. "Let's promise each other right now that we will, that we won't let anything stand in the way."

The others nodded, Julia a bit hesitantly, as if she wasn't sure Donna meant her, too. "A year is a long time," she said. "We don't know where we'll be in a year."

"I know where I'll be," Vinnie declared. "I'll be right here celebrating my eighty-third birthday and congratulating myself on finding my grandson a new sweetheart."

She succeeded in making them laugh, and Grace added, "Well, then, I'll be here showing you all my latest projects."

Julia gave them a small smile. "And I suppose I'll be here telling you how filming went."

"Oh, you must," Vinnie exclaimed. "I have to know how everything turns out. That goes for all of you—I can't bear thinking that I might not know how everything turns out. Donna's daughter's wedding, Megan and little Robby—"

Megan looked resolute. "By this time next year, I promise I'll have done everything humanly possible to bring Keith back into his life."

"We won't have to face our problems alone," Grace said. "We'll be with each other in spirit."

"We'll keep in touch," Megan said. "Whenever we need encouragement, we can write, or call, or email. Are the rest of you on the internet?"

Grace nodded, but Julia shook her head and Vinnie said, "Heavens, no."

"You have to get online," Megan insisted. "It's the best way to stay in touch."

Donna, usually the most optimistic of the group, felt her spirits drop. "People always say they'll keep in touch, but they usually don't."

"We'll be different," Vinnie said stoutly.

Donna wished she could believe her. They might leave Elm Creek Manor with the best of intentions, but as the weeks passed and they fell into the patterns of ordinary life, they might forget how special—how magical—the week they had spent together had been. If they failed to nurture it, their friendship might become nothing more than a fond memory, something to reflect upon and cherish when leafing through an old scrapbook rather than something vibrant and alive.

"We need a symbol, something to remind us of our promise," she heard herself say.

"I have a wonderful idea," Vinnie said. "Let's make a challenge quilt."

"A what?" Julia asked.

"A challenge quilt. We'll take a piece of fabric and divide it into equal shares. We'll each piece a block from it, and next year, we'll meet at camp and sew them into a quilt."

"The challenge comes from being required to use a particular fabric rather than being free to choose whatever you like," Grace told Julia. "But sometimes there are other restrictions. Should we have any?"

"How about this," Megan said. "We can't start working on our block until we take steps to solve our problems. That will keep us from procrastinating."

On our quilt blocks or on solving our problems? Donna wondered. She knew which project she'd rather face.

"All right, then," Julia said. "As soon as the first day of filming is over, if I haven't been fired, I'll start piecing my block."

Vinnie clasped her hands, delighted. "Then I'll start mine the first time I ask Adam if he's heard from Natalie and he says, 'Natalie who?'"

They all laughed, and Donna felt her spirits rising. For the first time, she felt that even though they would be scattered cross-country, they would remain close friends.

"Cross-country," she murmured, then added in a louder voice, "That's what we are, the Cross-Country Quilters."

"A name makes it official," Vinnie declared. "How can we fail?"

After they had finished packing, the Cross-Country Quilters gathered in the parking lot for a final good-bye. When Megan's car was loaded up and they were waiting outside the manor for Vinnie's grandson and Julia's limousine—in which she had invited Donna to join her for the drive to the airport—Vinnie brought out her bag of quilting supplies. "We still need to choose a fabric," she said. "Who will do the honors?"

"I'll pick," Donna said eagerly. She dug around in the bag and laughed. "How about this?" She pulled out a print of black-and-white cows grazing in a meadow.

Julia looked alarmed, and Megan said, "No way."

Donna pouted, but she returned the fabric to the bag and tried again. "How about this?"

This time she held up a blue-and-red paisley print. Megan liked it, but there was only a fat quarter. "Do you think there's enough for all five of us?"

"You can't reject everything I pick," Donna complained. "We'll be here all day."

Vinnie glanced at her watch, then frowned at the empty road. "I might be here all day regardless if my grandson doesn't get a move on. I told him to be here at ten."

"Why so early?" Megan said.

Vinnie's eyes widened in innocence. "No reason."

Megan knew Vinnie well enough to be suspicious of her attempts at innocence, but she shrugged and turned to Donna. "Okay, I'll cooperate. Whatever fabric you show us next, I'll agree to it."

"You might regret that," Grace warned, but it was too late. Donna's eyes lit up, and she plunged both hands into the bag. A few moments later, she pulled out a yard of fabric and held it over her head.

"I have it," she shouted in triumph. "This is the one!"

Megan stifled a groan of dismay. It was a beautiful print of autumn leaves on a cloth of excellent quality, expertly designed, and highlighted with silver embossing. The leaves were burgundy, loden green, a rich beige—and purple.

Even Julia laughed out loud.

Megan knew when she was beaten. "All right," she said. "We can go with the cows."

"Absolutely not." Donna put the rest of the fabric away. "I'm not going to miss this chance to force you to use purple."

"There might not be enough," Megan tried to argue, but Vinnie would have none of that.

"There's an entire yard," she said, taking the fabric from Donna. "I have more at home, so we'll divide this into fat quarters for the four of you."

When each had her fat quarter of fabric, it was time to go. They exchanged addresses and phone numbers, and Megan made one last entreaty to Julia and Vinnie to get email addresses. Grace already had one through the museum where she worked as a curator, although she rarely used it. "You'll use it more now," Donna promised.

Just then a long black limousine crossed the bridge over Elm Creek and circled the parking lot. "There's my ride," Julia said with regret.

Megan, too, was reluctant to leave, but now that the time had come, she was eager to get on the road. She had a long drive ahead, and she hoped to be back to her parents' house in time for a homecoming supper. Just as she was about to bid the others good-bye, Vinnie grabbed her arm.

"There's my grandson," she exclaimed. "Don't you girls leave until I have a chance to introduce you."

Suddenly Megan felt an urge to sprint to her car, but Vinnie held fast. She threw Donna a helpless look as an older model compact car pulled into the parking lot. Megan glimpsed a familiar face through the windshield, and sure enough, when the car parked in front of them, the man she had met at the diner stepped out. "I'm sorry I'm late, Nana," he said, bending to kiss her. He picked up her suitcase, smiling. "Did you have a good time?" Just then he glanced at Megan, and utter astonishment came over his face. "Hey. It's you. The woman—"

"From the diner." Suddenly nervous, Megan forced herself to smile and extend her hand. "Megan Donohue."

Quickly he set down Vinnie's suitcase and shook Megan's hand. "I see you made it to Waterford okay."

"Yes, thanks to your directions."

Vinnie patted his arm proudly. "Adam's a teacher. He's very good at explaining things."

Adam looked embarrassed. "But not very good at being on time. Sorry I'm late, Nana. There was construction on the turnpike."

"That's all right," Vinnie said graciously. She introduced the other Cross-Country Quilters. Adam's startled expression returned when she named Julia.

"You must have had quite a week," he said to Vinnie. His gaze rested on Megan again, and he smiled warmly.

"I'll tell you all about it on the drive home," Vinnie promised, then beamed at her friends. "Drive safely, ladies. I'll see you next year."

"Drive safely," Megan echoed, and the others joined in.

Vinnie took her grandson's arm and let him help her into the car. As they drove away, Vinnie gave them a jaunty wave and a cheerful, satisfied smile. Her eyes met Megan's, and suddenly Megan knew as clearly as if she had spoken that Vinnie intended to be the first of the Cross-Country Quilters to complete her block.

Six

aul and Becca had kept the house fairly tidy during Donna's absence, but for two intelligent and capable people, they otherwise seemed to have no idea how to manage a household. On Tuesday the kitchen sink had sprung a leak, and Paul had to phone Lindsay for the name of their usual plumber. When it came time to pay him, Paul had forgotten where Donna kept the checkbook and had to race to the nearest ATM for cash. The next day Becca had attempted a load of laundry, but had turned all the socks and underwear a delicate shade of pink. When Donna's car pulled into the driveway, her husband and daughter ran outside to meet her. Donna soon discovered the reason for their joy and relief, and she wondered if her family had missed her or just the cook and maid services she usually performed. That evening, though, after Paul took her out to eat and Becca asked her to demonstrate how to run the washing machine properly, Donna relented. After all, it was nice to have all her hard work noticed and appreciated. She decided to leave them on their own more often, to provide them with more opportunities to fend for themselves—and to remind them not to take her too much for granted.

By the next day, Donna had restored the household to its usual order. She had invited Lindsay and Brandon for Sunday dinner, and as she roasted a chicken and tossed the salad, she resolved to look for the best in him and not to become a stereotypical mother-in-law if she could possibly avoid it.

When she heard Lindsay's car, Donna wiped off her hands on a towel and went to the window, where Paul had already pulled back the curtain and was peering outside. "She's alone," he said, relief in his voice.

Donna felt the same way, but she said, "We have to start getting to know him sometime."

"I already started, and I know as much as I need to."

"Paul," Donna gently admonished him. At the restaurant the previous night, he had told her unhappily of the unfavorable impression Brandon had made on him when the two families met during Donna's absence. Brandon bossed Lindsay around, telling her what entrée to order and advising her to go without dessert so she would look better in the wedding pictures. Brandon's mother was a meek and silent woman, but his father more than made up the difference. Obnoxious, Paul called him—Paul, who never insulted anyone unless he truly deserved it.

"There must be some good in him or Lindsay wouldn't love him," Donna told her husband. "We might have to look hard to find it, but it must be there."

Paul nodded to show he agreed with her logic, but he looked doubtful.

Lindsay entered then and greeted her mother with a warm hug. "Couldn't Brandon make it?" Donna asked.

"He had some studying to do."

"Before classes even start?" Paul asked, a little sharply. College had been a sensitive topic with him ever since Lindsay's announcement.

Lindsay shrugged. "He's busy," she said, which didn't really answer the question. She left her purse on the counter and began to set the table. What a pair she and Paul were, Donna thought as she assisted Lindsay. They were glad Brandon hadn't come and yet were slighted that he hadn't bothered to show up. If Brandon suspected any of this, he'd wonder just what kind of family he was marrying into.

During supper, Donna told her family amusing stories about her week at quilt camp. Even Becca was thrilled to hear that she had befriended the famous Julia Merchaud. Still, although Lindsay smiled and joined the conversation, she seemed distant and reserved, as if her thoughts were elsewhere.

After the meal, Lindsay helped Donna clean up, although that was traditionally Becca's chore. They chatted about trivial subjects, Donna wondering all the while what her daughter really wanted to discuss. Only after the last plate was placed in the dishwasher did Lindsay tentatively ask if Donna had a moment to talk about the wedding.

Donna's heart flip-flopped, but she dried her hands on a dishtowel and tried to appear calm. "Sure, honey. What did you want to talk about?"

"I've been looking through bridal magazines to get ideas for my gown." Lindsay hesitated. "I tried on some at a bridal shop near school, but they're much more expensive than I thought they would be."

Donna's heart went out to her, and she felt a stab of regret picturing Lindsay shopping for a gown alone. She had always imagined they would choose together, but it was her own fault. No wonder Lindsay hadn't invited her along, after the way she had reacted to the announcement of the engagement. "Don't worry about the expense," she said. "Your dad and I will pay for your gown."

"I know. But . . . well, until I get a full-time job, I don't feel right about spending so much money on something I'm going to wear only once. Do you think you could make me a dress? I'm not asking just to save money."

"Oh, honey." Donna reached out and tucked a loose strand of blond hair behind her daughter's ear. "I'd love to make a wedding gown for you." Then inspiration struck. "Or would you like to wear mine? I could take it in to fit you—"

"Oh, Mom, that would be perfect," Lindsay gasped. "Your gown is so beautiful. That's what I wanted all along, but I was afraid . . ."

Her voice broke off so abruptly that Donna knew she had finally touched on what had been troubling her all evening. "You were afraid of what?"

Lindsay's cheeks flushed. "I was afraid that you would say no, because— because you don't like Brandon."

"Lindsay, sweetie . . ." Too overcome to speak, Donna took Lindsay in her arms and hugged her tightly. Whenever she had thought of her daughters' wedding days, she had imagined planning every detail with joy, sharing a special closeness as the day approached, watching them dance with their father at the reception. She had never intended to ruin what should be one of the happiest times in Lindsay's life.

Blinking back tears, she held Lindsay at arm's length so she could look her daughter in the eye. "If I told you I didn't wish you'd wait a few years, I'd be lying," she said. "But it's not that I don't like Brandon. I don't know him well enough to dislike him."

Lindsay gave her a wan smile. "Great."

"I'm not saying this right. What I mean is, I wish I knew him better, and I wish you'd consider waiting until you finish college. Lindsay, even before you were born your father and I promised ourselves you would receive a good education. I think it means even more to me than to your dad, since I didn't finish college myself. You seemed so happy with the university, I'm just surprised you'd give that up."

"I told you what Brandon said."

"I remember, but I don't think he's thought this through. Maybe he'd like you to be out of school now, but what about later? What if he loses his job or becomes ill, and you need to support the family?"

Lindsay shook her head. "He would hate that. I don't think he would let me."

Donna winced. "'Let you?' He's going to be your husband, not your keeper."

"I didn't mean it that way. It's just . . . I think it would hurt his pride if I had to support us."

"Well, God willing he'll never be sick or lose his job, but it's best to be prepared, and you'd be able to get a much better job with a college degree. And what about when you want to buy a home, or when your own children are ready to start college? You might want to work for the extra income."

Donna could sense her daughter's conflicted emotions and see from her expression that she was torn between logic and loyalty. "I hadn't thought of that," Lindsay admitted.

Donna doubted that Brandon had, either. "Besides, what else are you going to do all year? You can't plan a wedding all day long, and you don't have a full-time job. What if you can't find one right away?"

"I don't know." Lindsay hesitated. "I couldn't just sit around the apartment all day."

Donna knew she had to take a chance before Lindsay could talk herself out of it. "I'll make a deal with you. Go back to school and finish your degree, and you won't hear a word of complaint from me about the wedding from this moment forward. Unless, of course, you pick an awful dress for the bridesmaids just to infuriate your sister."

Lindsay allowed a small smile. "Really?"

Donna hugged her. "I promise." It wouldn't be easy, but she would have her jaws wired shut if it would keep Lindsay in school. "Now, you have to promise me you'll keep your part of the bargain."

After a pause, Lindsay took a deep breath and said, "I promise." Silently Donna rejoiced in her victory and kissed her daughter on the cheek. Lindsay clung to her for a moment before pulling away. "I'm not sure how I'm going to tell Brandon."

"Just tell him."

"It won't be that easy. He's very sensitive."

Donna thought that Brandon struck her as one of the least sensitive young men she'd every met. And when had Lindsay ever been too anxious to speak her mind? Instead of saying so, she reasoned, "What's good for you is good for your marriage. Explain it to him logically, just as we've discussed. I'm sure he'll agree that you've made the right decision."

Lindsay looked dubious, but then she relaxed. "You're right," she said, and for a moment she sounded like the old Lindsay. "I'll tell him tonight. Registration doesn't end for a few more days, so I shouldn't lose any of the classes I signed up for last spring."

Donna was so pleased she didn't trust herself to speak. She stroked Lindsay's hair. "Come on," she said. "Let's have you try on that gown."

As they went upstairs, Donna remembered the promise she had made to herself and the other Cross-Country Quilters only a day before. Would she be the first to begin her Challenge Quilt block?

An anxious thought came to her then: Surely it couldn't be this easy. But as Lindsay modeled the wedding gown and chattered happily about the upcoming semester, Donna forced the lingering worries from her mind. Lindsay would be returning to college, and that was all Donna could fairly ask, for now.

⚜

Megan's work had piled up during her absence, but instead of griping about how the other engineers on her team hadn't picked up the slack, she was guiltily relieved to be too busy to spare Keith much thought. By Saturday, though, she knew she had to stop procrastinating. She warmed up by sending Donna an email and writing letters to Vinnie, Grace, and Julia, then steeled herself and began a letter to Keith.

Her first two drafts went straight into the trash. They were too accusing and shrill, and she knew she wouldn't get anywhere with him if she put him on the defensive. After two more failed attempts, she considered phoning him instead, but her stomach twisted at the thought of hearing his voice again. It had to be a letter, or nothing.

She took a break to do the laundry and fix Robby his lunch, then forced herself to swallow her pride and try again. She imagined she was writing to a colleague, and this time she managed to strike a cordial, professional tone free of whining and neediness. She couldn't bear it if he thought she was begging for his attention, although in a way she was—not for herself, but for their son.

It was difficult to invite him to visit Robby, because she knew it would hurt her to the core to see him again. She prayed he'd have the decency to leave his new wife, Gina, at home. She reminded him that school would be starting soon, and Labor Day weekend would be perfect for Robby's schedule as well as his own.

She mailed the letter and tried to put it out of her mind for a while. The annual bustle of activity that heralded the new school year provided a much-needed distraction, but when a week passed with no reply, she began to grow anxious. Then, two days later, an envelope arrived. Inside Megan found a check for two hundred dollars filled out in loopy, girlish handwriting. The memo read "Back-to-school clothes." There was no letter.

Fuming, Megan was tempted to tear up the check. She had asked for Keith's time, not his money. But then practicality set in; she could hardly complain about his sporadic-at-best child support payments and then refuse to accept the money he did manage to send. But why hadn't Keith sent so much as a sentence in response to her request? Maybe his new wife had intercepted Megan's letter, and Keith knew nothing of either Megan's request or the check. It was difficult to imagine Keith willingly sending Megan money, after the way he had fought for the house and the car in the divorce proceedings. He had won the car but lost the house, and ever since, his reluctance to send his child support payments clearly indicated he still held a grudge.

After a day of indecision, Megan sent another letter. Labor Day was fast approaching, she told Keith, and she would need a definite answer one way or the other. If traveling to Ohio would be too inconvenient, Robby could come to Oregon. Megan swallowed hard as she wrote the lines; she was reluctant to send Robby on a plane by himself, but she would, if there were no other way.

Labor Day came and went, and Robby started the third grade without a visit or even so much as a phone call from his father. Megan was furious and heartbroken for his sake, and her only consolation was that she had kept the proposed visit secret, just in case it didn't work out.

Two weeks into September, another envelope came, bringing Megan a letter from Gina. "Dear Megan," she had written, "I hope Robby's school year is off to a good start. I'm sorry the Labor Day visit didn't work out. Keith would have come, but I'm expecting a baby and he is saving up all his vacation days for after we deliver. Maybe next summer, Robby can stay with us for a week or so and meet his new brother or sister. All the best, Gina."

They were expecting a baby. Gina was carrying the second child Megan longed for and would never have. And Keith, who had gone back to work the day after Robby was born and had not changed a single dirty diaper in his life, was now planning, with this new child, to make up for all the attention he had withheld from his firstborn.

Or was he? A thought struck her then: Keith had national holidays off, so Labor Day weekend wouldn't have cost him any vacation days. And something about Gina's letter was strangely familiar, too. Megan recognized in Gina's strained apologies the same excuses she herself had made for Keith for so many years.

Gina was expecting, and it was while Megan was carrying Robby that Keith had first turned away from her. Surely Gina would remember that.

As Megan threw the letter away, she wished her former rival luck. Unless Keith had truly changed, she would need it.

⚜

If not for the lifeline her upcoming role in *A Patchwork Life* provided, Julia thought the new fall television schedule might have driven her to drink or to her plastic surgeon's office for another face-lift. She couldn't believe the cheap vulgarity that passed itself off as comedy these days, and as for the dramas, she had never witnessed such self-indulgent whining in all her life. She could click from channel to channel all day long and see nothing but beautiful twenty-somethings bemoaning the trivia of their empty lives. It sickened her almost to the point of throwing her flat-screen, high-definition television into the swimming pool, but it had been one of the few possessions she had argued out of her third husband's clutches during the divorce proceedings, and, knowing how much he had treasured it, she intended to hold on to her trophy until its wires fused together.

Occasionally an especially inane scene would have Julia seething. Her assistant had long ago adopted the policy of leaving the room whenever Julia turned on the television, so Julia had no one to complain to except the actors on the screen. Not only was that unsatisfying, it made Julia feel uncomfortably like some elderly eccentric who had lost touch with reality. She had enough insecurities about her age without adding that one to the list.

Eventually she abandoned her critique of the fall television season and resumed practicing her quilting. After her return from quilt camp, she had sent her assistant out in search of the supplies she would need to perfect her skills. Since most of her quilting scenes involved hand-quilting, Julia set her pieced and appliqué blocks aside. At camp, one of the Elm Creek instructors had traced a pineapple motif on a piece of unbleached muslin for her; now Julia placed it on top of cotton batting and another piece of muslin and held the layers snugly together in a lap hoop. With a short needle called a "between" and a piece of cotton quilting thread, Julia worked the needle through the layers along the traced line until the picture began to emerge from the smooth muslin. As the weeks passed, the rocking motions of hand-quilting became more familiar until her work acquired a soothing rhythm. Often she would sit outside on the patio of her hilltop estate in Malibu, quilting and enjoying the fragrances of orange trees and flamevine as a gentle breeze tinkled wind chimes overhead. As her stitches became smaller and more even with practice, she wished she could show the Cross-Country Quilters how much progress she had made.

Already quilt camp and the Cross-Country Quilters had taken on an air of unreality, like something out of a vivid dream only dimly remembered. It was hard to imagine herself confiding in a group of women who were, after all, little more than strangers, especially considering how fiercely she usually guarded her privacy. Still, Julia found herself missing Elm Creek Manor and wishing for a dose of Vinnie's sharp humor, Donna's optimistic kindness, and the encouragement and companionship of the whole group—especially after Ares would phone with updates on the movie, reawakening Julia's fears that she wouldn't be able to quilt convincingly enough and the director would denounce her as a fraud.

Julia had expected the Cross-Country Quilters to write, especially Donna and Megan, who were avid email correspondents, but the weeks passed without a word. She even took to sorting her own mail, but after a few days she returned the task to her assistant. Perhaps they were waiting to hear from her first, but somehow Julia couldn't bring herself to initiate the correspondence. Or perhaps they weren't as close as Julia had thought. Maybe they had only exchanged addresses to be polite. It had been so long since she'd had a friend that she was unfamiliar with the etiquette of such things.

At the end of September, Julia and Ares went to the first of several script meetings. On the way to the studio, Ares filled her in on the rest of the cast. The good news was that the role of Young Sadie had been given to Samantha Key, a virtually unknown actress with only a few bit parts to her credit. She couldn't afford to play the diva, not with Deneford, so Julia needn't fear she'd try to expand her role at Julia's expense. Julia had never heard of Cameron Miller, who would play her younger son, but Noah McCleod, the elder Henderson boy, had a reputation for being talented, professional, and down-to-earth. She had worked frequently with child actors on *Family Tree,* and Julia was confident she'd get along fine with the two young men.

She was less pleased to hear that Rick Rowen had won the role of Augustus. She had worked with him only once, when they had cohosted a holiday special three years before, but he had been an arrogant man then, and rumor had it he had become even worse after *People* magazine named him one of its Fifty Most Beautiful People. Only a month ago, his latest movie, an action film set in South America, had premiered at number one and held steady, which meant that he was no doubt being buried in offers for which he could name his salary. Given his elevated circumstances, Julia wondered why he had accepted a small role in a serious drama and decided that he must have signed the contract before his fortunes rose. Working with him was sure to be excruciating. Fortunately, Augustus would be dead by the second reel.

When she and Ares arrived at Deneford's conference room, Julia realized at once that they would not be reading from the script, as indicated by the agenda faxed to her the previous day. The sheer number of agents in the room told her they were in for some negotiations first, and as much as she disliked Ares, she was suddenly glad that he had accompanied her. Rick looked bored and cocky, Samantha gazed listlessly at the table, but their agents radiated caffeinated energy. They eyed Julia with carnivorous eagerness as she entered, and only then did she note that the children and their ubiquitous mothers were not present, which suggested they were in for a brawl.

Deneford sat at the head of the table. In her younger years Julia would have seated herself at his right hand, the better to make suggestive eye contact and accidentally brush her leg against his beneath the table throughout the meeting, but in this light she knew distance would be more flattering. She chose the chair directly across from Deneford at the foot of the table, where she would be sure to catch his eye now and then. Ares took a seat at her left hand; to her right sat Ellen Henderson.

When Julia greeted her, Ellen whispered bleakly, "Did you hear? I'm out as director."

"I know, dear," Julia said sympathetically, and it struck her that she sounded exactly like Vinnie.

"This was supposed to be my breakthrough project."

"It still can be. You're still the writer. You'll receive plenty of recognition for that."

Just then, Deneford spoke. "Since we're all here, let's get started." He turned to Rick's agent, a young man with dark, slicked-back hair who looked vaguely familiar. "Jim, since you have the most to say, I'll let you begin."

"Rick isn't happy with the script," Jim said. "His talents aren't being fully utilized."

Talents? Julia thought scathingly.

Deneford shrugged. "He liked the script just fine when he first read it."

"That was before *Jungle Vengeance*." Jim looked around the table as if to enlist the others' support, which surely he knew was a wasted effort. "Let's be honest here. Does it really make sense to kill off your male lead so early in the picture?"

"But that's how it really happened," Ellen interjected.

Jim gave her a withering look, then ignored her. "A lot of people are going to consider this a Rick Rowen film. They're going to see it because they want to see Rick Rowen. Do we really want to disappoint them?"

Ares said, "You're kidding, right? This is a Julia Merchaud film."

You'd better believe it, Julia thought.

"That's funny, I thought it was a Stephen Deneford film," Deneford said dryly. "Okay, Jim, you've made your point. And I agree with you to a certain extent. The last two thirds of the story—"

"Turn it into a chick movie," Rick interrupted. Samantha stirred long enough to give him a sidelong look, but then her gaze reverted to the tabletop. "I don't do chick movies."

"Chick movie?" Ellen bristled. "This is a movie about women—strong, intelligent women going about the difficult business of living in nearly impossible circumstances."

Rick shrugged, puzzled. "Right. A chick movie."

Jim leaned toward Deneford as if they were alone in the room. "We both know Rick Rowen's presence in this picture guarantees a huge opening weekend—if word of mouth is good. It won't be if his fans don't get to see enough of him."

"Now I'm barely making a cameo appearance," Rick complained. He flipped through the script, shaking his head. "It should be Augustus, not Sadie, who keeps the farm from going up in flames. He should be the one to scare off the claim jumpers. I mean, come on, who's going to believe a woman did all that?"

In a cold and steady voice, Ellen said, "That's how it really happened."

"How it really happened doesn't matter," Deneford said. "What matters is that it's believable."

"You mean as believable as one man saving a legion of Green Berets from the entire Colombian army?"

"That could happen," Rick shot back.

Ellen snorted disgustedly and sat back in her chair, folding her arms.

"I fail to see what's so unbelievable about a woman performing heroic acts," Julia said. "Especially to protect her children. Women were widowed all the time on the frontier. They could hardly afford to wait around for a man to rescue them."

Ellen shot her a grateful look. Julia gave her a small nod in return, her conscience pricking her. She had spoken up to protect her role, not the integrity of Ellen's script. The scene where Sadie faced down the unscrupulous cattle ranchers with nothing more than an unloaded rifle and a pitchfork contained one of the film's best monologues. Julia wasn't about to let Rick Rowen get it instead.

Jim's attention was still on Deneford. "Given Rick's draw, would it really be such a bad idea to steer the picture in a more action-adventure-type direction?"

Deneford stroked his chin, thinking.

Encouraged, Jim pressed ahead. "It would be like *Little House on the Prairie* meets *Die Hard*."

Suddenly Samantha spoke up. "I like *Little House on the Prairie*."

Everyone stared at her for a moment before her agent jumped in. "If Samantha likes it, I have no argument with expanding Rick's part."

"Hold on just a second," Ares said, without needing any prompting from Julia. "I'm not about to let Julia's best scenes go to Rowen. We're ready to walk away right now."

Julia felt a flash of panic as he shoved his chair away from the table, but to her relief, Deneford held up his hands. "Julia won't have to sacrifice any of her screen time. We'll just cut out some of the domestic scenes and add new material for Rick."

"Domestic scenes?" Ellen echoed sharply.

"Not all of them. In fact, since Augustus will be sticking around, we'll probably need a few love scenes between him and Sadie." He looked at Jim. "Any problems with that?"

Jim glanced at Rick, who grinned. "No problems," Jim said, than glanced at Julia. "Um, which Sadie are we talking about?"

"Julia."

Jim made a barely perceptible wince and glanced at Julia once again. "I'll have to speak to my client." As he bent his mouth close to Rick's ear, Julia pictured herself leaping across the table to claw his eyes out. She knew what he was whispering into the young actor's ear—would he be willing to do love scenes with, to put it politely, an actress of Julia's maturity? How dare he, and right in front of her. It took all her strength of will to keep her expression serene.

When Jim straightened, Rick grinned. "I'm cool with that," he said, leering at Julia. "When I was a kid I used to dream about doing it with the mom from *Home Sweet Home.*"

"How charming," Julia muttered, as disgusted as she was surprised that someone his age remembered her first series.

"Fine. Augustus lives, Augustus and Sadie have a roll or two in the hay, maybe literally, everyone's happy." Deneford raised his eyebrows at Ellen. "Can you make those changes without delaying our production schedule?"

Ellen looked faintly ill.

"If you can't do it, say the word and I'll get a team of studio writers—"

"I'll do it," Ellen said quickly. She slumped back in her chair in disbelief.

After a brief discussion of the production schedule, the meeting broke up. Julia and Ares went out to the parking lot, where Ellen caught up to them and asked to speak with Julia privately.

"I can't believe they want so many changes," Ellen said. "I've never written by committee before. Is this typical?"

"That's part of the business." Julia patted her on the arm and smiled. She was in a good mood, since the meeting had worked out largely in her favor. She hadn't lost a moment of screen time, and although Rick disgusted her, a few love scenes with a popular young actor couldn't hurt her image. "I'm afraid you'll just have to get used to it."

Ellen looked dubious. "I'm afraid they're going to ruin my movie."

It's Deneford's movie now, Julia almost said, but she decided to be kind. "Nonsense. You're a gifted writer. I'm sure the revisions will be just as wonderful as the original."

"If you say so, I'll believe you. I feel like you're the only person who shares my vision about this project. You're the only one who cares about my great-grandmother's history as much as I do."

Julia forced herself to keep her smile in place. "Of course I do." She patted Ellen on the arm again and hurried off to her car before the conversation could make her even more uncomfortable.

✿

Grace returned home from the doctor's office in a gray fog of depression. Her condition was unchanged—no better, no worse. She was lucky, according to the doctor, especially after she told him about the minor exacerbations she had experienced at quilt camp. "No exacerbation can be considered minor," he reminded her for what must have been the thousandth time. "You need to take it easy. Stress can aggravate MS."

MS. He tossed off the initials so casually, as if her life weren't at stake. Grace knew he was not trying to be unkind; he was so used to treating multiple sclerosis patients that he had learned to be matter-of-fact with the disease, while she still treated it warily, like an enemy who had moved into her home, someone she could not ignore but must address with cautious respect.

For nearly eight years Grace had experienced strange symptoms—tingling in her hands and feet, pain in her eyes and problems with her vision, and slight uncoordination. The symptoms would flare up unexpectedly, then completely disappear. So much time elapsed between occurrences that she attributed the odd sensations to stress, fatigue, poor circulation, and overwork, and in fact, the first few doctors she consulted had made the same diagnosis. Not until a frightening incident four years before had Grace, at Justine's insistence, pursued a more aggressive search for answers.

She had been driving to the deYoung Museum to study some new acquisitions when suddenly her hands felt as if they were being pricked by hundreds of needles. Her hands gripped the steering wheel clumsily, and suddenly alarmed, she set a turn signal and pulled over to the shoulder of the freeway. When she tried to ease off the gas and apply the brake, her right foot was numb and unresponsive. Grace used all her force of will to command her sluggish foot to move—and it did, but too late to prevent the car from slamming into the guard rail.

Although the car sustained substantial damage in the accident, she was physically uninjured but emotionally traumatized. Her little difficulties, as she had called them, had never affected her so strongly before. What if she had been on a road with no guard rail? What if she had struck another car and injured its occupants? She could not trust herself to drive again until she knew for certain what was wrong with her.

She consulted one doctor after another. Some found nothing wrong with her; others suggested she try antidepressants. Grace, who knew her emotional state was a symptom and not the cause of her physical problems, persisted. She underwent blood tests and CT scans, none of which yielded any conclusive answers. Finally a practitioner of alternative medicine provided some help. She suggested that Grace was suffering from some autoimmune response to toxins in her environment. Purging her home and her diet of harmful chemicals, combined with daily meditation, might help her manage her symptoms.

At first Grace was skeptical, but to her grateful surprise, the prescription seemed to work. At least she certainly felt healthier, more relaxed and at peace. She even began driving confidently again. But three months into her treatment, Grace's symptoms returned with such force that she went to the emergency room, certain she was having a stroke. That was where she was referred to Dr. Steiner, who took a clinical history, ordered an MRI and a spinal tap, and determined she had MS.

She had been seeing him ever since, as well as participating in clinical trials and learning all she could about the disease. At first she retained some confidence, because it seemed that her disease followed a relapsing-remitting course, which meant that she could expect some or even complete recovery between attacks. But as the months dragged by with no new advances in treatment, no miraculous remissions or sudden leaps forward in the medical understanding of MS, her faith began to ebb. Dr. Steiner had never tried to conceal her prognosis, and she knew she was looking at a future of possible incapacitation, the abandonment of all the activities she cherished, and total dependence—the one thing she simply could not bear.

Grace had told Justine and her immediate family but had sworn them to secrecy. Not even her closest friends suspected what she was going through, and that was exactly how Grace wanted it. She would not have anyone treating her any differently than they always had.

"Eventually they'll know something's wrong," Justine had told her. She meant that eventually the disease would progress so far that Grace would no longer be able to conceal it. A wheelchair was a difficult contrivance to ignore.

"So that's when I'll tell them," Grace had said, and refused to discuss the subject further. Justine insisted that the support of her friends was what she needed most, but what Grace wanted most was her old life back. She wanted a sense of normalcy and ordinariness; she wanted the same blissful ignorance of the future most people enjoyed.

She prayed for guidance, for serenity, for a miracle, but her sewing machine gathered dust and her fabric stash permanent creases from being left folded in the same positions for so long.

Since returning from Sylvia's nearly eight weeks before, Grace had tried to maintain her resolve to work through her creative block. She thought of how Sylvia had worked through the impairment brought on by a stroke and knew she had to keep trying. She went to her studio and sat on a stool, propping her elbows up on a work table and studying the shelves full of fabric. No matter how low she felt, the colors never failed to lift her spirits.

After a while, she took out the fat quarter of the autumn leaf print Vinnie had given her. According to the loose rules the Cross-Country Quilters had established, she couldn't begin sewing her block yet, but she could choose some suitable complementary fabrics. She spent a quiet hour searching through her inventory, comparing the colors in the fat quarter to the many shades in her collection. She had chosen a rich burgundy cotton with a visual suede texture and a purple floral print with striking blue highlights when someone buzzed her loft from the front door. When, a moment later, the elevator sounded, she knew her visitor was Justine, who had a key.

Grace left the material on a work table and went to meet her daughter at the loft door. To her delight, Joshua was with her.

"How did it go?" Justine asked after Grace had greeted her visitors with hugs and kisses.

Grace shrugged. "Same as before."

Justine's tense expression eased. "That's good news, at least."

"I'd hardly call it that."

"It's better than hearing that you've gotten worse."

Grace felt a flash of annoyance. "Little pitchers," she said, tilting her head toward Joshua, who was playing with blocks on the floor.

Justine gave her a look that said she was being ridiculous. "You don't like to talk about it, but you should."

"I'll talk about what I please, when I please."

"You'd feel better if you were more open and honest about this. Not just with me, but with yourself."

"The way you've been open and honest with me?" Grace shot back.

Justine stared at her. "What are you talking about?"

"Nothing. Never mind." She leaned over to pick up a block that had tumbled away from Joshua's pile and returned it to him.

"No, you brought it up. Something's obviously bothering you. Let's air it out."

Grace took a deep breath. "I know you're seeing someone."

Justine's eyebrows rose. "What?"

"I know you're seeing someone, and I know . . ." She glanced at Joshua and lowered her voice. "I know it's serious."

"Mom, you couldn't be more wrong."

"Don't give me that. Sondra saw you together at a restaurant back in July. Joshua was with you."

Justine set her jaw. "Your friends are spying on me?"

"That's hardly fair. Sondra happened to see you, and she asked me who the man was, and of course I had to tell her I didn't know, since you didn't have the decency to tell me on your own."

"Mom—"

"And what's worse than being the last to know about these important developments in your life—and Joshua's life, I might add—is that your new boyfriend is my age."

"Mom, you have it all wrong."

"I most certainly do not. Sondra told me he's old enough to be your father."

"That's because he *is* my father."

"What?"

"The man Sondra saw us with is my father."

Grace stared at her as the words slowly sank in. "Oh my God."

"I didn't tell you because I thought you'd be upset." Justine sighed. "Which, judging by the way you're staring at me, you obviously are."

"What does he want?"

"What does he want? He wants to see his daughter. He wants to get to know his grandson. He'd even like to see you, if you're willing. I told him you probably wouldn't be, but he said—"

"You're right. I don't want to see him." Grace squeezed her hands together to keep them from trembling. Gabriel, back in their lives after so many years. "I don't understand. How did he find you? Or did you go looking for him?"

"He came to the legal aid clinic one day while I was working."

"Is he in some kind of trouble?"

"He wasn't coming for himself. One of his students was being abused by her live-in boyfriend, and he was investigating resources to recommend to her."

So Gabriel was teaching again. "He couldn't have recognized you." The last time he had seen Justine was when she was four.

"No, but I recognized him from your pictures, and when he gave me his name, I knew."

Grace felt her face grow hot. Those pictures, that one album she had saved and had assumed was safely hidden in her closet. When had Justine seen it? "You should have told me you had met with him."

"I didn't want to upset you."

Grace closed her eyes, nodded, and tried to still her churning thoughts.

His abrupt departure twenty years before had torn out her heart, and it had taken her a long time to recover. For all intents and purposes, he had been dead to them. And now he had returned.

Grace steeled herself and spoke the question she dreaded to ask. "Are you going to see him again?"

She knew what the answer would be even before Justine nodded.

❧

Autumn was Vinnie's favorite time of year. By mid-October, the days were still pleasantly warm but the evenings took on a slight chill—"good quilting weather," Vinnie called it.

In her last letter, Donna had written that nearly all the leaves were off the trees in her backyard and that she wouldn't be surprised if it snowed by Halloween. Vinnie figured that was normal for northern Minnesota, although it seemed to her a bit early to be thinking about snow. No doubt Julia was still basking in the southern California sunshine; Vinnie couldn't say for certain, since Julia had not responded to a single one of her letters. Since Vinnie had heard from the other Cross-Country Quilters several times already, she was beginning to suspect that maybe her letters were getting lost amid the piles of fan mail Julia probably received each day. Undaunted, Vinnie wrote another letter, but this time she decorated the outside of the envelope with little quilt blocks drawn in colored pen. As an extra measure, in the return address, she wrote her name as "Lavinia Burkholder, AKA Vinnie from Quilt Camp." There. If that didn't get through to Julia, Vinnie didn't know what would.

Writing letters was a habit she had picked up while living with Aunt Lynn—where, Vinnie reflected, she had also acquired the habit of writing letters without expecting a response. She had written three or four letters to her father for every one he sent her. Frankie had written more frequently; she had learned more about her father from her brother's letters than from his own. She grew accustomed to her father's indifference, which was made easier to accept by the love Aunt Lynn and Lena showered upon her.

But although Vinnie felt secure and content in her new life with Aunt Lynn, she had learned to expect change.

She was too absorbed in school and her friends to pay much attention to the news of the stock market crash, but the trouble forecast by adults' worried expressions and hushed conversations was soon confirmed. Aunt Lynn explained that they might face difficult times ahead, but Vinnie shouldn't worry because Aunt Lynn had a secure job in a government office. Vinnie believed her aunt, but she soon realized that other families on their block were not as fortunate as they. Even the Pot-Luck Pals seemed to have to work harder to be cheerful, and they brought smaller covered dishes to their twice-monthly gatherings.

For months Vinnie had overheard Aunt Lynn and Lena discussing the possibility of Lena's losing her job at the factory where she worked as a secretary. She sounded confident that the boss couldn't manage without her, but one night, long after Vinnie was supposed to be asleep, sounds came through the wall that separated her bedroom from Aunt Lynn's. She could have sworn she heard Lena weeping.

The next morning, Lena and Aunt Lynn met her at the breakfast table with somber expressions and bad news. As it turned out, Lena hadn't been fired after all. The company had gone bankrupt and the entire factory shut down, which meant that all the employees—including Lena and her boss—were out of work. Until she found another job, Lena could no longer afford her room in the boarding house across town. Aunt Lynn hesitated before asking Vinnie if she would mind if Lena came to live with them.

"It's fine with me," Vinnie said, surprised that they would need to ask her. Lena spent the night so often that it was almost as if she lived there already. "Do you want my room?"

Aunt Lynn and Lena exchanged a quick look. "No, honey. Lena will stay with me," Aunt Lynn said. "That's very nice of you to offer, but you need a quiet place to do your homework."

That seemed reasonable to Vinnie, so the following weekend, Lena moved in. For the first few days her presence made the house seem festive, but before long Vinnie began to wish she could do more to help. Aunt Lynn went to work every day and took all the extra hours her employer would spare, while Lena took care of the home. Although they never complained, at least not in front of her, Vinnie knew both women were tired from overwork and worried about money. Once Vinnie asked Aunt Lynn if she should quit school and find a job.

"Your job is to go to school," Aunt Lynn said. "You help us by doing well with your studies."

"And keeping your room picked up," Lena added, tweaking her nose.

Vinnie wasn't satisfied. She wanted to contribute something to the household, enough so that Aunt Lynn would relax and be cheerful the way she used to, enough so that Lena would crack jokes and smile again.

Since she knew of no other way to contribute, Vinnie devoted herself to her schoolwork. She often stayed after class for extra help, which her teachers were willing to provide, pleased to have such a diligent pupil. One afternoon, as she worked through some long division problems on the blackboard, Miss Kelley leaned over her desk to check her work and caught her dress on a rough edge.

Vinnie heard fabric tear. "Oh, no," Miss Kelley groaned, bending over to free her hem. As her teacher examined it, Vinnie glimpsed a three-inch-long tear in the fabric. "Of all the days to rip my dress."

"You can sew it when you go home," Vinnie said.

"That's the problem. I'm not going home. I'm going straight to my fiancé's parents' house for supper. I can see his mother's smirk already. Wouldn't she just love to catch me walking around with a hole in my dress!"

"Why would she love that?"

Miss Kelley caught herself. "Never you mind," she said sternly, then added, "When you have a mother-in-law, you'll understand."

"If you have a needle and thread, I could sew it for you," Vinnie offered. At first Miss Kelley demurred, but when Vinnie insisted, she retrieved a needle and thread from her purse. Vinnie studied the tear. It was a simple rip right along the grain of the fabric, and soon Miss Kelley's dress was mended, the seam almost invisible.

Miss Kelley, much relieved, offered to pay her, but Vinnie grew embarrassed and refused. "I hate to sew," Miss Kelley said. "Won't you take something for saving me the trouble?"

"You don't take anything for helping me with my math."

Vinnie had never spoken so boldly to a teacher before, and she felt her face growing red-hot. She expected Miss Kelley to scold her, but instead she looked thoughtful. "If this had been your job, would you have allowed me to pay you?"

Uncertain, Vinnie could only nod.

"Then do you suppose if I brought you some other mending, I could hire you to complete it? As long as your aunt agrees, of course."

Vinnie promised to ask, and she ran home, her spirits soaring.

Aunt Lynn seemed dubious at first. "Will you have enough time for your schoolwork?"

"How much mending could one teacher have?" Lena said, giving Vinnie a wink. "The kid looks like she'll pop if you say no, Lynn."

At that Aunt Lynn laughed and agreed that Vinnie could try it for a while, but if her grades suffered, she would have to stop. The next day Vinnie raced to school with the news and returned home with a bag full of stockings that needed darning. When she finished, Miss Kelley paid her five cents for each pair. Vinnie triumphantly presented the money to her aunt.

Soon other teachers learned of the arrangement, and within a month Vinnie had added two other teachers to her list. Then Mr. Borchard from English class became a client; a bachelor, he soon had recommended her to several of his unmarried friends. Before long Vinnie had sewing projects every night and was making more money than she had ever dreamed possible.

But her success kept her up late and away from her books. When her term report card showed a slight dip in her grades, Aunt Lynn worried that she was spending too much time working. "I can do both," Vinnie insisted. She knew her earnings made a difference to the family and couldn't bear to quit, not until Lena found work. Eventually Aunt Lynn agreed to let her continue, but no more than one hour on school days and four on the weekends.

Dismayed, Vinnie nodded and carried her sewing basket into the other room so Aunt Lynn wouldn't see how upset she was. On Aunt Lynn's schedule, she wouldn't have enough time for more than two or three clients. Blinking back tears, she set herself to work, determined to finish as much as she could.

After a while, Lena sat on the sofa beside her and watched her hemming a skirt. "That looks difficult."

Vinnie didn't feel like talking. "It's not."

"I haven't sewed since high school home ec. Would you show me?"

Her heart still heavy, Vinnie demonstrated the stitches. Lena caught on quickly and asked for a scrap of fabric so she could practice.

All that week and the next Vinnie taught Lena what she knew. Lena practiced, sometimes on scraps, sometimes on the clients' garments under Vinnie's close scrutiny. Then one afternoon Vinnie returned from school to discover that Lena had finished reattaching three loose collars and hemming two suits.

Lena was obviously proud of herself, but her voice was hesitant when she said, "What do you say you and I become partners, kid?"

Delighted, Vinnie agreed. The next day Lena dusted off Aunt Lynn's sewing machine and set about teaching herself how to use it. She visited the library and checked out books on sewing and dressmaking and tailoring. Together she and Vinnie were able to take on more work for more money. Before long, Lena's skills surpassed Vinnie's own, and she made plans to expand their business into making custom-made garments. One of the Pot-Luck Pals printed up advertisements, which Lena distributed around the city. She modeled her creations at Dayton's fine boutiques, whose clientele had thrived despite the Depression. With her striking blond good looks and professional manner, she impressed the boutique owners as well as their customers, and soon Lena began receiving regular orders for everything from casual attire to gowns. Within a year Lena's enterprise had become so successful that her earnings equaled her previous salary.

Looking back, Vinnie marveled how Aunt Lynn and Lena had managed to see their little family through the Depression unscathed. Even now she admired Lena for transforming loss into opportunity, and she was proud of herself for her role in it.

Sometimes all people needed was a little nudge in the right direction, and they would go far. Vinnie picked up the phone and dialed Adam's number. Her grandson could use a little nudge right about now.

⚜

A few days later, Megan received a letter from Vinnie:

> *Dear Megan,*
>
> *I was tickled to get your last letter. I'm sorry to hear your ex is being such a louse. But don't worry. I know you'll figure out something and you'll get to make your quilt block yet.*
>
> *Do you and Robby have any plans for Halloween? I hope not, because I'd like to invite you for a visit. Meadowbrook Village has a Halloween party and trick-or-treating every year, and I would be honored to have you two as my guests. My grandson, Adam, is coming too, but since he's a little old for trick-or-treating, I thought it would be much more fun if you brought Robby.*
>
> *If you don't wear a costume, you'll be the only person there who doesn't. I'm going as Raggedy Ann.*
>
> *Hope to see you soon!*
>
>

Love from your quilt buddy,
Vinnie
>

Megan considered the letter thoughtfully. Vinnie's invitation was an answer to a prayer. The boy next door, who had been Robby's playmate until a year ago, was having a Halloween party, too, and Jason had invited all the boys in the class—except Robby. Jason's mother spotted Megan raking leaves in the backyard, came outside, and made an awkward apology over the fence. "You know how kids are," she said, shrugging and trying to smile.

Yes, I know, Megan thought. She knew how kids were. She knew they needed to be taught that kindness mattered more than popularity, and that they ought to include the outcast even if they preferred not to, simply because it was right, because inviting every boy but one was cruel. Megan couldn't bear the thought of Robby watching out the windows as the other boys' parents dropped them off next door for a night of wild Halloween fun.

She wouldn't have hesitated to accept Vinnie's invitation—except for Adam. Vinnie had to be the least subtle matchmaker in the history of romance, and Megan cringed when she pictured Adam's embarrassment when Vinnie nudged them together, beaming and dropping hints. Then again, he would have to be a total idiot not to see what his grandmother was doing, and since he was still willing to attend, he must not mind all that much.

He had been rather nice at the diner.

"Robby," she called out, returning the letter to its envelope. "Do you want to go to a Halloween party?"

Seven

Grace hoped to channel her anger into the creation of a new quilt so that at least some good would come of her argument with Justine. In the past she had been able to work out her frustrations by slicing through fabric and pounding the pedal on her sewing machine, but like so much of her pre-MS life, that ability, too, had apparently been lost. Thwarted, she flung her rotary cutter aside, switched on her computer, and vented her frustrations in an email to Donna and Megan instead.

TO: Megan.Donohue@rocketec.com, quiltmom@USAonline.com
FROM: Grace Daniels ‹danielsg@deyoung.org›
DATE: 9:27 AM 18 Oct
SUBJECT: May I start my quilt block now?

I wish I were asking because I've broken through my quilter's block, but unfortunately, that's not so. However, I have made progress on the other aspect of my challenge ... if you can call it progress. It turns out my daughter isn't dating an older man after all. The man my friend saw with Justine and Joshua was her father.

Should I be happy that Justine wasn't keeping a boyfriend secret from me, or outraged that she's been in contact with my ex-husband of twenty years and didn't see fit to tell me? It's not much of a consolation that I'm halfway to fulfilling my promise to the Cross-Country Quilters. What do you think: Although I haven't started a new quilt yet, am I allowed to begin working on my Challenge Quilt block?

Donna must have been online, because she wrote back almost immediately:

TO: Grace Daniels ‹danielsg@deyoung.org›
FROM: Donna Jorgenson ‹quiltmom@USAonline.com›
DATE: 18 Oct 11:35 AM CDT
SUBJECT: Re: May I start my quilt block now?
CC: Megan.Donohue@rocketec.com

Good grief. I don't know whether to congratulate you or not. At least Justine wasn't hiding a secret romance from you, but it sounds like you have a bigger problem on your hands. Have you talked to the Ex yet?

As for the Challenge Quilt, I don't think you should be allowed to start until you have at least a plan for a new project. Sorry, but the motivation will be good for you. Good luck.

Megan didn't respond until later that afternoon, and when she did, Grace could almost feel the computer screen steaming from her indignation:

TO: Grace Daniels ‹danielsg@deyoung.org›
FROM: Megan.Donohue@rocketec.com
DATE: 2:00 PM 10/18
SUBJECT: Re: May I start my quilt block now?
CC: quiltmom@USAonline.com

So where's he been all this time? Did he only just remember he had a daughter?

Grace wondered about that herself, but in order to get an answer, she would have to talk to Gabriel, and she was not ready to do that. She doubted she'd ever be. Twice Justine had invited Grace to join them for outings with Joshua, but Grace had refused. She had nothing to say to Gabriel that silence wouldn't communicate just as well.

"Don't you even want him to apologize?" Justine persisted.

Grace wanted that very much, but she wasn't willing to admit it. "How do you know he will?"

"I just know."

Grace let out a scoffing laugh and shook her head. "I think I know him better than you do. He was never good at regret."

"He's changed. Give him a chance."

"I've given him more than twenty years' worth of chances," Grace said. "In all that time, did he ever come to see you? Did he ever send so much as a letter to let us know he was still alive?"

Justine watched her in silence for a long moment. "If you talk to him, he'll explain."

"I don't need his explanations now. Anything he could say would be too little, too late."

After that, Justine did not mention him for weeks. Grace tried to put him out of her mind, as she had done so well for so long, but her anger smoldered. She knew Justine was seeing him every week and that Joshua called him Grandpa, as if Gabriel had been there all along, as if he hadn't abandoned his family as easily as sloughing off soiled clothing.

As the weeks passed, it became clear Gabriel intended to remain a part of Justine's life. Just that morning, Justine had asked her if they could invite him to Thanksgiving dinner. The request left Grace speechless. "Thanksgiving is for family," she finally managed to say.

"He's family. He doesn't have anyone else."

"That's his own fault."

"Mom—"

"You know I'm supposed to minimize the stress in my life. Believe me, inviting him to your aunt's for Thanksgiving will not help."

"Don't use your MS as an excuse."

Anger and humiliation surged so intensely that tears came to her eyes. "I told you, do not mention that in front of Joshua," she gritted out, her voice shaking.

"He's my father, Mom," Justine pleaded. "He's Joshua's grandfather. Don't shut him out."

Grace couldn't believe what she was hearing. Since when was Gabriel's estrangement her fault? "You are a disloyal and ungrateful child."

"You're jealous and holding a grudge."

Her words stung. "He left us, Justine. Did you forget that?"

"He says you kicked him out."

"Only to force him to get help," Grace snapped. "Did he tell you that part? His drinking was destroying our family."

"He's sober now, Mom. He's been sober for ten years."

"Then he should have contacted us ten years ago."

"Why bother, for this kind of welcome?" Justine scooped up Joshua and stormed out.

Grace and Justine had often disagreed and sometimes even argued, but never before had they fought with such fury. Alone in her loft, Grace tried meditating to calm herself, but her thoughts were churning too strongly. The truth was, she *was* jealous. Grace had been there for Justine and Joshua all their lives, and now Gabriel could waltz in, the prodigal father, and Justine was willing for him to step right back into the family as if he had never left, as if she cared nothing for her mother's pain. Gabriel had done nothing to earn such a welcome, and Grace couldn't bear it.

If Justine knew the whole story, she would never attribute Grace's feelings to something as simple as holding a grudge.

She and Gabriel had met as students at Berkeley, in a time of turmoil and hope, when their unjust society seemed more malleable than at any time in history. An art history major, Grace had noticed the tall, strikingly handsome man in several of her classes but had never spoken to him, although campus was not yet so integrated that most African-American students did not have at least a nodding acquaintance. It wasn't until her junior year—while both were part of a group picketing against a local chain restaurant that had repeatedly demonstrated racism against black students and faculty—that he approached her and introduced himself. They struck up a friendship based on mutual interests and attraction, which soon blossomed into romance.

After graduation, Gabriel entered graduate school with the goal of becoming a professor of history. Grace turned down other, more lucrative opportunities and accepted a position at an art museum on campus in order to remain near him. They married a year later.

Gabriel had always drunk at parties and other social gatherings, no more than anyone else and less than most, and since he didn't care for marijuana, it never occurred to Grace that he might have a problem. Only after they began living together did she realize how much, and how often, he drank. At first it was merely a few beers after classes had ended for the day, and possibly another as he unwound before bed. Then he began drinking at lunchtime, joking that he needed the fortification to deal with the class of brainless freshmen whose papers he was obligated to grade as a part of his teaching assistantship. When Grace expressed her concern that his graduate advisor would probably disapprove, Gabriel retorted, "He disapproves of everything I do anyway. The only way I could please him would be if I turned white overnight."

When his professors evaluated him at the end of the semester, his advisor called him in to talk. Gabriel came home in a rage. Somehow—Gabriel insisted he had no idea how—he had developed a reputation as argumentative, undisciplined, and unreliable. No one in the department questioned his intellect and passion, his advisor explained, but they needed him to make a more obvious commitment to the profession if he wished to continue in the program. Gabriel blamed his advisor for blackballing him. Grace blamed the alcohol.

When she realized she was pregnant, she doubled her efforts to get him to stop drinking, but he turned his anger on her instead. Somehow he managed to scrape his way through school, earning his master's in history when Justine was a year old. To Grace's relieved astonishment, he was accepted into the Ph.D. program. Now, she told herself, he would have no choice but to give up the drinking and concentrate on his work and family. Instead, the increased pressures of the more rigorous academic program augmented his need for drink, and he left school after three months.

He found a job teaching history at a local high school, and for a while, the bitter disappointment of losing his long-held dream shocked him into sobriety. For two years he limited his drinking to the home and would drink only in the evenings, when he would play with Justine for a little while after supper and then settle in front of the television set, sipping one drink after another until he passed out. In the mornings he would get up, shave, and head to work on time, so Grace decided to count her blessings. She loved him deeply and learned to accept that he was not the husband she had once thought he would be.

Then one day, the principal of his school phoned her at work and told her in a stiff voice that Gabriel had fallen ill and needed to be picked up immediately. Grace arrived to find him in an empty classroom, nearly unconscious and reeking of alcohol. The principal said nothing as he helped her walk her husband to the car, but his anger was unmistakable. Grace was so ashamed she could barely look at him.

The principal expedited the paperwork, and when Gabriel was fired a few days later, he blamed a racist school board for his dismissal.

"It's always someone else's fault, isn't it?" Grace shot back. "It's never you. It's never your drinking."

He glared at her balefully and rolled over onto his side on the sofa. In another moment, he was snoring.

Gabriel didn't even attempt to look for a new job. Sometimes he left in the mornings before Grace took Justine to the sitter's and went to her own work, but he was always home by the time she returned, passed out on the sofa. They hardly spoke anymore, and Grace was afraid to leave Justine alone with him. Gabriel stopped coming to their bedroom at night, which was more of a relief than she ever would have thought possible. His loving touch had long since given way to awkward gropings in the dark, resulting in failure most of the time, and leaving her angry and confused even when they didn't. She felt desperately alone but was too loyal to talk about the situation with anyone, even her sisters, whose disapproving expressions suggested they knew something was wrong but respected Grace's pride too much to confront her.

Then something happened to shake Grace from her complacency.

One night she woke to the acrid stench of burning. Her heart pounding, she scrambled from bed to find the living room in flames.

"Gabriel," she screamed at the motionless lump on the sofa. Choking on smoke, she stumbled to his side and shook him, screaming his name over and over until she managed to rouse him. She helped him stagger outside and let him fall uncomprehending on the front lawn. Her heart racing with fear, she turned back inside, only to find that the fire had spread. The hallway to the room where Justine lay sleeping was impassable.

Frantic, Grace ran outside and raced around the backyard to Justine's window. Her eyes burned and streamed tears; her ears were full of the menacing roar of the fire as it consumed her home. She struggled to open the window, but it wouldn't budge. She searched around blindly until she stumbled upon a lawn chair. Without a thought, she lifted it over her head and smashed it through the glass.

She didn't remember climbing past the broken shards and hauling Justine to safety, only sitting on the front lawn with her daughter in her arms and a neighbor's blanket over her shoulders. She stared at the house unblinking as the firefighters struggled to extinguish the blaze. Justine sobbed and buried her face in Grace's shoulder.

When the house was nothing more than a smoldering ruin, a paramedic came to inspect Grace's injuries. Still dazed, at first Grace refused to let go of Justine, but eventually was persuaded to allow a neighbor to take her. She stared at the embers of her life as the paramedic examined her. "We'll have to take her to the hospital to remove the glass," she overheard him say. Only then did she feel the sharp stinging in her hands and legs and feel the wet slickness of her own blood on her skin.

Helen, one of her elder sisters, took them in. A few days later, Grace learned that the blaze had started when Gabriel fell asleep holding a lit cigarette. He dropped it and set fire to the drapes. In a way, they had been fortunate. If the cigarette had fallen on the sofa, the investigators said, the foam cushions would have burned much more rapidly than the drapes, almost certainly killing Gabriel and possibly the rest of the family. They were lucky.

"Lucky," Gabriel mumbled, and left Helen's house for a drink.

Under Helen's watchful eye, Grace could no longer maintain the facade of a happy family. She crumbled and tearfully confessed the pain of the past few years. Helen listened without judgment until Grace was spent. Then she said, "If he had killed your baby last night, that would have been his fault. If he kills her tomorrow, it will be yours."

When Gabriel returned, drunk and stumbling, the house was closed to him. Helen went outside only long enough to tell him to find another place to spend the night. She handed him a letter Grace had written, a painful message of love and resolve in which she told him he could come home to his wife and daughter when he was sober, and not a day before.

Gabriel tried to change her mind, but with Helen to support her, Grace held fast. She had forgotten what it was like to wake up in the morning not dreading the day, how peaceful it was to be able to walk from the hallway to the kitchen without averting her gaze to avoid seeing her husband passed out in the living room. When Justine asked for her daddy, Grace told her he was away but he would be coming home to them soon. She thought she was telling the truth.

⸙

The Thursday before Halloween, Robby picked two of the best pumpkins from his grandmother's garden, one for him to carve and one for Megan. When they reached home, Robby's description of his carving strategy abruptly broke off. "What's that?" he asked, pointing to the front porch.

Megan glimpsed a brown box by the door as she as she pulled into the garage. "Looks like someone sent us a package."

Robby was out of the car and racing around to the front door almost before she turned off the engine. Carrying the pumpkins, she entered the house through the garage, unlocking the front door for Robby on her way. He met her in the kitchen with the parcel in his hands. "It's for me," he exclaimed, showing her his name printed in block letters with a black marker above their address. "Look. It's from Oregon. It's from Dad."

"That's great," Megan said, hiding her astonishment. Robby set the box on the table and tore into it, tossing packing materials aside. Then, suddenly, he froze, and his smile faded.

"What's wrong?" Megan asked. She peered into the box to find ginger-bread and sugar cookies cut into the shapes of ghosts, pumpkins, and black cats, beautifully decorated with frosting. They were carefully packaged and unbroken, and seemed to be arranged several layers deep.

"Dad didn't make these," Robby said flatly. "*She* sent them."

"You don't know that. Maybe Dad bought them in a bakery." Megan indicated an orange envelope. "There's a card. See what it says."

Reluctantly, Robby opened the envelope and read the card, which he promptly threw back into the box. "They're from her," he said again, sliding down from his chair.

"Robby . . ." she began, but he left the kitchen with his mouth set in a sullen line. In another moment she heard the door to his room slam shut. Her heart sinking, Megan picked up the card. It had a picture of a haunted house on the front and a simple rhyming poem inside. The signature, in Gina's handwriting, said, "With love from Dad and Gina."

Megan sank into the chair Robby had vacated, the card in her hand, wondering what to do. If only Keith had taken the thirty seconds required to sign the card himself. It would have been far better for Gina to send nothing than to go to such trouble to send a present Keith obviously had nothing to do with. Sighing, she returned the card to its envelope, placed it on top of the cookies, and discarded the scattered wrapping. Then she took a gingerbread ghost down the hall and knocked on the door to Robby's room.

When he didn't respond, she said, "May I come in?"

"I'm busy." His voice was muffled through the door, but she could hear the tears in it.

"Oh. Okay." Megan thought for a moment. "Well, I'm going to start supper. It might be a while. Do you want a cookie to tide you over?"

"I'm not allowed to eat sweets before meals."

"Just this once we can make an exception."

"I don't want any stupid cookies."

"Do you mind if I have one?"

A pause. "I don't care."

"Okay, then." Megan took a bite of the ghost's head. "Mmm. This is delicious."

"You can have them."

"I can't eat them all myself. I'll get sick." She took another bite. "Maybe you'll want some after supper."

"I don't want anything *she* makes."

Megan waited for him to say something more, but when he didn't, she decided to leave him alone. "I'll be in the kitchen," she said, hoping he would join her there to talk. She waited, but he didn't leave his room until she called him for supper, and then he took his seat and ate without a word. His eyes were red-rimmed, and as soon as he had finished eating, he returned to his room without clearing his dishes, a chore that had become such a habit that he sometimes automatically rose to clear his place at restaurants.

After straightening the kitchen, Megan tried again. She knocked on his door and asked if he wanted to carve pumpkins. "No," he said through the door.

"But you planned your design and everything."

"I don't feel like it."

Megan covered the kitchen table with newspapers in case he changed his mind, but he only left his room once, to go to the bathroom and brush his teeth, and then it was his bedtime.

The next morning, Megan taped the box of cookies shut and placed it by his backpack and the bag holding his Batman costume. When he saw the box, he gave her an odd look. "Why is this here?"

"I thought you could share the cookies with your class."

"They won't want them."

"Not want cookies? You're kidding, right?" Megan made sure his jacket was zipped, then put on her own coat and opened the door to the garage. "Come on, let's go. We'll be late." Sullen, Robby picked up the bag and backpack, leaving the cookie box for her to carry.

As they drove to school, Megan reminded Robby that she was leaving work early so she could pick him up right after the class parties ended. "If there are any cookies left, bring them," she said. "We can take them to Vinnie's."

Robby perked up at the reminder of the party, enough so that he submitted willingly to a hug and kiss. "I'll see you later," she called as he shut the door. He waved good-bye with the tips of his fingers, his left arm wrapped around the box of cookies.

Throughout the day, Megan found herself thinking about Robby and wondering how his day was going. She doubted she would be able to persuade him to send Gina and Keith a thank-you note for the cookies. Most likely she would end up sending an acknowledgment herself. She wondered if this would be the way of things for the rest of their lives, Keith and Robby communicating by proxy through her and Gina.

Robby's school ended classes for the day after lunch, when the students gathered in the gymnasium for a Halloween parade. When Robby was in kindergarten, Megan had joined the other adoring parents with camcorders in the bleachers, searching the long line of costumed children for her son, and grinning with delight when she spotted him marching proudly with his friends. Afterward, the students held parties in their separate classrooms. Megan pictured Robby distributing the cookies Gina had so lovingly made, and hoped the other students wouldn't reject them as they had most of Robby's other offers of friendship.

The school parking lot was reserved for faculty and staff, so Megan parked on a side street a few blocks away and walked to school, self-conscious in her costume. Because of the trouble with the cookies, she had postponed the decision until that morning, when she put together an empire-waist dress, elbow-length gloves, and other period accessories and decided she was Elizabeth Bennett. Throughout the day, however, she began to have an uncomfortable suspicion that not even fans of *Pride and Prejudice* would be able to identify her, even with her hair up. Only then, when it had been far too late to change her mind, did it occur to her that whatever she wore would make a lasting impression on Adam.

She still wasn't sure what impression she wanted to make. As nice as Adam had seemed, Megan had mixed feelings about Vinnie's matchmaking.

She had grown accustomed to being alone, and in many ways, although she wasn't as happy as the happily married people she knew, she was much more content than those tangled in fractious relationships. The thought of enduring all the heartache of falling in love and breaking up and starting over with someone else in a unrelenting cycle of searching and hoping made her weary. She didn't think she should put herself—or Robby—through that again.

Robby was waiting for her on the playground, as they had arranged. Other children played nearby, but he sat alone on a swing in his Batman costume, scuffling his feet in the gravel. Megan spotted his backpack and the bag with his school clothes on the ground not far away.

He looked up when Megan called his name, smiled, and got off the swing. "Where's the box?" Megan asked him. "Are all the cookies gone?" At that, Robby's face fell, and he turned his back on her to pick up his backpack. "What is it? What happened?" She pictured him shyly offering the other children the cookies, and some bully shoving them back in his face. "Didn't the other kids want the cookies?"

"No."

"Why not?"

"They got broken."

"Got broken?" Megan echoed. "How?"

Robby shrugged.

"You must know how."

Robby said nothing, his eyes downcast. "They broke on my way to school."

"But I let you off right in front of the building."

"I dropped the box."

Megan watched him, waiting for more. Gina had padded those cookies with so much plastic wrap and paper that Robby could have dropped the box off the roof of the school and the cookies might have survived unscathed. "What did you do with the box?"

"Threw it away."

"Show me."

"But they're only crumbs now."

"Show me."

Reluctantly, Robby led her toward a garbage can on the edge of the playground. He stopped a few feet away and pointed. With her thumb and first finger, Megan gingerly moved aside wadded-up brown paper lunch bags, school assignments on lined paper, and crumbled candy wrappers until she uncovered the box. She stooped down, placed it on the ground, and lifted the lid. Inside it was just as Robby had said: Each cookie had been pulverized into crumbs until their original shapes were completely obliterated. Some of the crumbs had been compressed into piles, and in these she found the impression of the sole of a shoe.

She took a deep breath and rose, returning the box to the garbage can. "Who did this?"

Robby shrugged.

"One of the other kids?" She recalled the name of the sixth-grade terror who had stolen his lunchbox the previous month. "Was it Kenny?"

He shook his head.

Megan was quiet for a moment. "Did you do it?"

Robby held perfectly still, which told her all she needed to know.

"Let's go." She took his clothing bag in one hand and placed the other arm around his shoulders, and led him back to the car.

The drive to Dayton took more than twenty minutes, and Megan used the time to tell Robby, as she did every day, some of the interesting things that had happened at work. Eventually, perhaps because of the familiarity of the routine, he relaxed and told her about the school parade and his class party. He didn't mention the cookies, and neither did she. She didn't have the heart to scold him for destroying Gina's present; in fact, she thought she might have done the same in his place.

They arrived at Meadowbrook Village Retirement Community to find a high-rise apartment building surrounded by several one-story condos, four units to a building. They were set back into a woods, giving them an air of privacy despite their closeness. Vinnie's condo was the farthest from the parking lot, as Megan and Robby discovered as they walked from building to building searching for the right number.

Vinnie answered the door dressed in a blue-and-white-checked dress and a red yarn wig. Two bright red circles were painted on her thin cheeks. "Come in, come in," she said, ushering them inside. She hugged Megan. "Hello, dear. I've missed you."

"I missed you, too," Megan said, surprised by how much. Suddenly she felt a wave of nostalgia for camp—for the freedom and friendship and peace it had brought her. She wished all the other Elm Creek Quilters lived close enough so that they, too, could have come to the party.

Vinnie turned to Robby. "You must be Robby. I'm Vinnie, but you can call me Nana. I don't know anyone your age who doesn't call me Nana."

"Nice to meet you," Robby said, shaking her hand. If he was startled to be conversing with an eighty-two-year-old dressed as a Raggedy Ann doll, he hid it well.

"Let's see. What are you supposed to be? Now, don't tell me. Let me guess." Vinnie put her hands on his shoulders and spun him around slowly, inspecting his costume. "Are you one of those rangers, one of those Power Rangers?"

"You're a few years behind the times," Megan said. "They're not in anymore."

"I'm Batman."

"Oh, of course!" Vinnie shook her head helplessly. "I'm afraid I don't keep up with my superheroes as well as I should. If your mother had dressed as Robin I would have known right away." Her eyes went to Megan. "What exactly are you?"

"I'm almost afraid to let you guess."

"Are you Betsy Ross? No, you'd be carrying a flag. Are you a suffragette?"

"No, I'd be carrying a picket sign."

"Or a ballot box." Vinnie studied her for a moment longer, then sighed. "I'm afraid you'll have to tell me."

"Elizabeth Bennett, from *Pride and Prejudice*?" Megan had a feeling she'd be repeating that line many times that night.

"Of course," Vinnie said, but she still looked puzzled. At that moment, a buzzer sounded somewhere out of sight, just as the doorbell rang. "Oops, my brownies are done. Will you get the door?" Vinnie asked as she hurried off down the hallway. "It's probably Adam."

"Sure." To her annoyance, Megan felt a flutter of nervousness at the prospect of seeing him again. She hung back and let Robby open the door. On the doorstep stood the same brown-haired man from camp and the diner, almost unrecognizable in a fifteenth- or sixteenth-century-style cape, leggings, and plumed hat. In one hand he carried a telescope; with the other, he doffed his plumed hat, and smiled.

He looked endearingly ridiculous, and Megan suppressed a smile. "Adam? Is that you?"

"At your service." He replaced the hat and came inside. "Hello there," he greeted Robby. "Hey, don't I know you? You look familiar." He frowned. "You resemble—but no, that couldn't be it."

Robby was interested. "Who?"

"Well, I was going to say you look like the famous millionaire Bruce Wayne, but anyone can see you're Batman." Adam shook his hand. "It's an honor to meet you. I admire your work."

Robby grinned and took off his mask.

Aghast, Adam flung up an arm to shield his eyes. "Don't do that! You'll give away your secret identity."

"I'm not really Batman," Robby explained. "This is just my Halloween costume. I'm Robby Donohue."

"Of course." Adam smacked his forehead with his palm. "Halloween. I forgot."

Robby grinned, recognizing that Adam was pretending but going along with the joke. "Who are you?" he asked.

"Guess."

Megan saw Robby's gaze travel from the plumed hat to the leggings to the telescope. "Christopher Columbus?"

"Not a bad guess, but that's not it." He raised his eyebrows at Megan. "Care to try?"

She had been about to guess Christopher Columbus, too, but she noticed the deliberate way he held his telescope and said, "This is a long shot, but how about Copernicus?"

"Very good," he said, impressed. "Wrong, but close. I'm Galileo. Most of my students thought I was supposed to be one of the Three Musketeers."

Robby's face screwed up in puzzlement. "Wouldn't you need a sword or something?"

"Exactly. That's what I told them. Can you imagine a musketeer whacking people with a telescope? He wouldn't get very far that way."

Robby laughed, then tugged at Megan's hand. "Mom's turn. Guess who she is. No one else knew." He looked up at his mother. "Can I give him a hint?"

"No hints," Adam said. He studied Megan's costume, looking her up and down until she felt her cheeks growing warm. "Are you Jane Austen?"

Megan's jaw nearly dropped. "I can't believe it."

"Am I right?"

"No, but that's the closest anyone's come all day. I'm supposed to be Elizabeth Bennett." With a self-conscious laugh, she twirled around in her long dress. "I guess I should have chosen something less obscure."

"No, you look beautiful."

Robby grinned up at her, nodding so that Megan grew flustered and quickly changed the subject. "Do all the teachers dress up at your school?"

"Not all," Adam said with a shrug, and Megan guessed that only those with a sense of humor did. She wondered what he was like as a teacher. She suspected he was one of those whom the students liked, even when he graded tough and pushed them to work harder than they ever had before.

Vinnie joined them then, purse in hand. She hugged her grandson and raised her cheek for him to kiss. Then she declared that they had better get over to the clubhouse for the party before all the food was gone, and she shooed them outside.

The clubhouse was in the lobby of the high-rise, and it had been decorated with black and orange streamers, jack-o'-lanterns, and cardboard cutouts of black cats and ghosts. The other residents and their children had already gathered there and had seated themselves at tables covered with orange-and-white-checked tablecloths. Costumed grandchildren darted among the tables, and Robby looked after them longingly as Vinnie led her guests through the refreshment line and to an unoccupied table. Robby hastily ate one cookie, claimed to be full, and ran off to join several young vampires, princesses, and Jedi Masters in a game of tag.

Megan kept one eye on Robby while chatting with Vinnie and Adam. Vinnie found frequent excuses to leave them alone while she hurried off to greet one friend or another. Megan smiled, watching her travel among clusters of friends, just as she had every day at quilt camp.

"Why are you smiling?" Adam asked.

"I enjoy watching Vinnie have a good time."

"So do I." They both watched as Vinnie and two other women burst into laughter at some joke. "After my grandfather died a few years ago, I wondered if I'd ever see her like this again."

"I'm sorry," Megan said, turning to face him. "I knew Vinnie had lost her husband, but I had no idea how recently."

"That's why she moved here. She couldn't stand being alone in the house they had shared for so long." Adam's eyes were on his grandmother. "They married young, right before my grandfather was sent overseas in World War Two. Each was the other's first love."

"It's hard to lose your first love," Megan said, thinking of Keith. Then she remembered what Vinnie had told her about Adam and said, "Oh, I'm sorry."

"About what?"

"Vinnie told me about your . . . situation. About your fiancée."

"Oh." Adam let out a wry laugh. "I guess I should have expected that. I imagine everyone at camp knows?"

Megan nodded apologetically. "I didn't mean to dredge up unhappy memories."

"It's okay, really. Besides, Natalie wasn't my first love."

"She wasn't?"

"No. Before her I was in love with a beautiful brown-eyed girl named Michelle. She was the love of my life. Of course, we were only in the fifth grade at the time, so our relationship consisted mostly of holding hands at school roller-skating parties and claiming to hate each other."

Megan couldn't help smiling. "How did it end?"

"She left me for a sixth-grader with a moped."

Megan laughed. Just then Robby ran over to grab another cookie and to ask Adam to be his partner in the three-legged race. Adam good-naturedly agreed, and Robby led him off.

Vinnie returned then and took her seat with a happy sigh. "Sorry I left you alone for so long. I trust my grandson is behaving himself?" Without waiting for an answer, she patted Megan on the hand and said, "Now, catch me up on all the latest news. Have you heard from that ex-husband of yours?"

Except for the Halloween present Gina had sent on his behalf, she hadn't, so Megan had little progress to report on her quest to involve him in Robby's life. "I think the Challenge Quilt will be one block short," she said.

"Nonsense. You're trying, and that's all we expect you to do. The rest is up to Keith," Vinnie said. "Have you heard from any of the others recently?"

Vinnie knew about Donna's success in getting Lindsay to return to college, but Grace owed her a letter and so she had not yet heard about the true identity of Justine's older man. Vinnie listened, wide-eyed, as Megan filled her in. Afterward, she lamented, "Such interesting news, and I'm the last to know. Why didn't Grace tell me?"

"If you were online, she would have," Megan said, although Vinnie had often declared that she and computers didn't get along and that she had no intention of setting fingers to keyboard in this lifetime. Now, however, she looked undecided and said she'd think about it.

"Did Julia ever get an email address?" Vinnie asked.

"If she did, I don't know it. I don't think she's much of a letter writer."

"I've written to her five times, and all I get back are these silly form letters and autographed pictures. The same letter, the same photo, each time."

Megan laughed. "I bet that's the same letter and photo I received. I only tried once, though."

"Did you notice the return address? It was some agency in Burbank. I don't remember the name offhand, but I know it wasn't the mailing address she gave us."

Megan hadn't noticed. "Do you think she isn't getting our mail? Maybe she just doesn't want to write back."

"Nonsense. She enjoyed herself at camp with us, I'm sure of it. And I don't think she has so many friends that she can afford to ignore the four of us."

"What makes you think she doesn't have friends?"

Vinnie shrugged. "Instinct, I suppose. The way she hung around the outside of our circle and never seemed quite comfortable with us, as if she expected us to send her away at any moment. I think our Julia is a bit lost, the poor girl."

Megan pondered this in silence. Via email, she and Donna had decided that Julia's silence was intentional, that the Hollywood superstar had forgotten them as soon as her plane left Pennsylvania. Now she felt ashamed of their assumptions. "What should we do?"

"I suppose we'll have to wait to hear from her," Vinnie said. "But if she thinks we're ignoring her, we might be waiting a long time."

Just then, a young woman wearing a Meadowbrook Village name tag stepped to the front of the room and announced that it was time to award prizes for the best costumes. Robby and Adam returned to the table, discussing strategies for the rest of the games. They had come in third from last in the three-legged race, but were determined to stage a comeback. As prizes were announced in two divisions, one for the residents and one for the children, Megan watched Robby and smiled to herself. His eyes lit up as he and Adam whispered their plans, and he had looked so delighted as he played with the other kids. She wished he could have that joy every day of his life, the pleasure and security of knowing he was liked and wanted. He deserved that much, after what his father had put him through.

Vinnie and Robby won prizes for their costumes—Vinnie for Prettiest, and Robby for Most Heroic. In fact, Megan realized, every resident and child was awarded something, which meant that near the end of the list, some of the categories became rather far-fetched, such as Most Scientific and Biggest Mask. Vinnie's prize was a gift certificate to the residents' holiday craft sale, which would be held in December, and Robby, like all the children, won a small plastic jack-o'-lantern filled with candy.

It was near Robby's bedtime by the time the party began to wind down, but since it was a Friday and Robby didn't have school the next day, Megan agreed to Robby's request to stay until the end. Afterward, Vinnie invited them back to her condo for coffee—or hot chocolate, in Robby's case—and some of the brownies she had baked. At first Megan begged off, citing the drive back to Monroe and the piles of treats Robby had eaten already. "I only had two cookies and a popcorn ball," Robby protested. "That's hardly anything. I'm starving."

"You wouldn't send a starving child home without one more treat, would you?" Vinnie asked. She and Robby looked up at Megan with expressions of mournful hope, so similar that she had to laugh.

"All right," she said. "One small brownie, and you'll drink milk instead of hot chocolate."

Robby let out a cheer and slipped his hand into hers. As they left the clubhouse, though, his jubilance seemed to fade. Megan hoped it was only because he was growing tired, and not that he had suddenly remembered Jason's party, which was likely just finishing.

Back at the apartment, Vinnie and Adam went to the kitchen to fix coffee while Megan helped Robby hang up his coat. He was unusually quiet considering his recent excitement, so Megan took her time, waiting for him to speak.

"Mom?" he finally said. "Why did the kids here at the party like me and the kids at school don't?"

Megan felt a pang of sadness. "I don't know why the kids at school act the way they do, honey." She knelt beside him and brushed his hair out of his eyes. "But it's not your fault. The kids here liked you, right? So do the kids from soccer. That proves that you're a likable, fun kid, someone any sensible person would want for a friend."

He looked at her, unbelieving. "*Am* I fun?"

"Of course you are," she exclaimed. "You're the most fun of any kid I know. You were fun even before you were born."

Robby frowned, dubious. "How could I be fun before I was born?"

Megan rocked back on her heels. "When I was pregnant with you, we used to play games."

"Uh-*uh*."

"It's true. I called one of them the Kicking Game. You would kick and I would push back, gently, just like this." She touched him softly on the stomach. "And you would kick back, and I'd push back, and we go back and forth just like that. And sometimes your dad would rest his head on my stomach and talk to you, and once you kicked him right in the nose!" Robby grinned. "It didn't hurt, of course. You were so little."

"What else did I do?"

"Well, sometimes I would lie on my back and place my hand flat on my stomach, like this, and you would press up against it." She remembered thinking at the time that it felt like her baby was curling up in her palm for comfort. "You had a sense of humor, too. Sometimes I would try to let other people feel you moving around. As soon as you starting kicking, I would call for everyone to come running, but as soon as someone else put their hand on my belly, you would hold still. As soon as they lifted their hand, you would kick. So I'd say, 'The baby's moving! Come back!' but when they did—"

"I held still?"

"Oh, so you remember now?" She tickled him under the chin until he laughed. "Everyone thought I was making it up, you little goof. You made your mom look pretty silly."

"Sorry," Robby said, but he didn't look sorry. He looked delighted.

"You were fun then, and you're fun now." Megan hugged him tightly and made a silent promise that she would figure out something, some way to get the kids at school to give him a chance.

"Let's go see Vinnie before she thinks we got lost," she said. She released him and rose, only to find Adam standing at the end of the hall, watching them. Her heart thumped, and she wondered how much he had overheard.

"Nana wants to know if you'd like regular or decaf." Adam's voice was quiet, and he reached out to ruffle Robby's hair as the boy passed him in search of Vinnie.

"Either one is fine with me."

"Robby's having trouble in school?"

Megan shrugged and felt tears pricking her eyes again. "You know how kids are. They have a pack mentality, and unfortunately, Robby's the one they decided to pick on."

"But he's such a great kid."

"I know that. Of course, I'm biased." She tried to laugh. "Don't worry about it. It's no big deal."

Adam came closer, studying her. "It seems like a big deal to you. And to Robby."

Suddenly weary, Megan dropped the pretense. "It is. It's breaking my heart. And it doesn't help that his father . . ." She broke off. She didn't want to talk about Keith, not to Adam. "If only I could figure out some way to help him."

"Have you spoken with his teachers?"

"No." Megan remembered then that he was a teacher, and felt a stirring of hope. Maybe Adam had known other children like Robby and would know how to help him.

"His teacher might be able to give you more information. Tell you things Robby won't."

Megan was taken aback. "Robby tells me everything."

"No third-grade boy tells his mother everything." Adam smiled sympathetically. "Trust me. I used to be one. He knows you hurt when he hurts, and he might be trying to protect you."

It had never occurred to Megan that Robby might worry about her feelings. "I'll talk to his teacher," she said.

"Good." He placed a hand on her shoulder. "Come on. Nana's dying to show you some of her quilts."

They joined Vinnie and Robby in the living room, where they enjoyed their dessert and talked about the party. Though at first he seemed too wound up to rest, Robby soon fell asleep on the sofa, his head in his mother's lap. Megan stroked his hair as she, Vinnie, and Adam spoke softly so as not to wake him. Later Vinnie brought out several of her quilt projects for Megan and Adam to admire, then mentioned casually, "Adam is a quilter, too, you know."

Megan looked at him in surprise. "No kidding?" She had never met a man who quilted.

"I've made two quilts," Adam admitted, embarrassed. "They weren't very good."

"Of course they were," Vinnie protested. "If you stuck with it, you could be very good. Not as good as I am, but still, not too bad."

"They were for school," Adam explained. "We were working on tessellations in geometry class, and I had my students piece quilt blocks that used tessellating shapes."

"He likes to use examples from real life," Vinnie added. "Otherwise his students pester him with 'When are we ever going to need to know this?' every time he teaches them something new."

"Some still say that," Adam said. "But now they also ask, 'When am I ever going to make a quilt?'"

Vinnie laughed so loudly that Robby stirred. Megan glanced at her watch and couldn't believe how much time had passed. With regret, she told Vinnie she had to get Robby home. She helped Adam carry the dishes to the kitchen, then collected Robby's treats and woke him. "It's time to go home, sweetheart," she murmured in his ear. He nodded sleepily and said good-bye to Vinnie. When he called her Nana, Vinnie broke into a broad grin and hugged him. She hugged Megan, too, and whispered that she hoped they'd see each other again soon.

Adam walked her to the car, a half-asleep Robby between them. They helped him into the front passenger seat, then Megan went around to her side. "Well," she said. "It was nice seeing you." She extended her hand.

"It was nice seeing you, too." He held her hand for a moment before releasing it. "If I can think of some way to help Robby, I'll let you know."

"Thanks."

"I could call you. . . ." He hesitated. "Or maybe you'd rather have me tell my grandmother, and have her call you?"

"You can call. Vinnie has my number."

Adam smiled. "Great. I'll get it from her."

Megan nodded, trying to keep her teeth from chattering in the late October chill that had settled in after nightfall. Adam noticed and said, "I guess you'd better go." Megan nodded again and got into the car. Adam shut the door for her, then stood on the sidewalk and watched as they drove away.

Robby woke in time to wave good-bye. "I like Adam and Nana," he told her.

"So do I."

"I think Adam likes you."

Megan felt a jolt. How would Robby feel if Adam did? How would she feel? Keeping her voice casual, she asked, "Why do you say that?"

"He said you were beautiful."

"I think he was talking about my costume."

"No, I remember. He said, 'You look beautiful.'"

Megan didn't know what to say. "He was probably just being nice."

"Whatever you say, Mom," Robby said in such a world-weary tone that she had to laugh. She reached over and tousled his hair as he grinned and tried to duck away.

As Robby dropped off to sleep again, Megan thought about Adam. It had been a long time since anyone but her parents had told her she looked beautiful. She wondered if he meant it. He seemed sincere enough, and if he had been trying to flatter her, he could have done better than that. Keith knew how to lay on the charm and lay it on thick. Within ten minutes of conversation, he could have any woman feeling as if she were the most re-markable person in the universe. Unfortunately, Keith would make every woman in the room feel that way, even when his wife was watching.

How had Keith changed from the loving husband who played the Kick-ing Game with his unborn son to the sort of man who chafed under the yoke of marital fidelity? Or had he always had a wandering eye? Was her sense of judgment so impaired that she had overlooked such a significant flaw, or had she deliberately ignored it, hoping he would change?

She supposed she would never know for certain—but she would never make that mistake again.

🌿

Nana was waiting for Adam just inside the door. "Well?"

"Well what?"

"What did you think?"

Adam feigned ignorance. "About what?"

"Don't torment me. About Megan. What did you think of her?"

"She seems like a very lovely woman."

"And pretty."

He had noticed. "That, too." He bent forward to kiss his grandmother on the cheek, careful to avoid the red Raggedy Ann circle she had painted there. "I have to get going. Thanks for the party. I had a good time."

She scowled at him. "That's all you're going to tell me?"

"That's all," he said, cheerful but firm. Anything he told Nana would be reported back to Megan and probably half the residents of Meadowbrook Village.

"Well, take her phone number, at least," she said grumpily, handing him an index card with Megan's name and phone number, as well as her postal and email addresses.

"Thanks, Nana."

"Will you at least tell me if you like her?" Nana pleaded as he left.

"I like her," he said. "Good night." He kissed her again and shut the door.

As he drove home to Cincinnati, Adam admitted to himself that he'd had a much better time than he had expected. He had come to the party mostly to appease his grandmother, and only partly because the green-eyed woman from the diner intrigued him. He liked the way she had agreed to share the apple pie with him, as if she were a decent, down-to-earth person and expected him to be one, too. In Megan's place, Natalie would have given him a cold, withering glare and written him off as a lunatic. Natalie had certain ideas of what was proper and what was not, and splitting desserts with strangers would definitely fall into the latter category. After years of trying to please Natalie and soothe her unpredictable temper, Megan's willingness to take a chance had been refreshing.

Should he call her? He wasn't sure Megan wanted that. She had been friendly enough, but there had been a reluctance about her, as if she were afraid of bruising herself. Considering what Nana had told him about her ex-husband, Adam wasn't surprised. He was resuming dating rather gingerly himself, and he and Natalie had been together only five years. How much more difficult it must be for Megan, who had married this man and had a child with him, only to be betrayed. At least Natalie hadn't been dishonest with him; she had always been perfectly clear about what she wanted, and equally clear about her displeasure when he failed to deliver.

The breakup had been coming for months. In hindsight, he supposed he knew Natalie was going to leave him long before she did.

They had met at a wedding. One of Adam's cousins was the bride; Natalie was a friend of the groom. He was first attracted to her dark-haired beauty, and later, her unpredictability and passion for life drew him in deeper. When they were together she made him feel that like her, he, too, was exciting and passionate. Even years later, when infatuation grew into love and he thought they understood each other as well as any two separate people could, he still wasn't sure why Natalie had been interested in him at the start. She said his personality, especially his kindness and honesty, had drawn her to him, but he wondered about that, since those had been the very things that had later driven her away.

He had been teaching in the parochial school system for several years by then and had always been open about his plans to remain in the profession. Natalie had recently been hired as an assistant to the associate buyer for an upscale department store chain whose flagship store was in downtown Cincinnati, but her ambitions aimed higher. She had a six-year plan to become the principal buyer for the entire chain, and a ten-year plan to be named a vice president.

Before he met Natalie, Adam had spent weekday evenings quietly at home, grading papers and planning the next day's lessons. An eventful night might involve attending one of the school sporting events or chaperoning a dance. Natalie, meanwhile, took business associates out for drinks, hosted dinner parties, or attended social events where she would be likely to brush shoulders with the "right people," as she called them. To please her, and because he loved her and wanted to be with her, Adam became her willing escort. He was proud of her beauty and the ease with which she could charm even the most reserved or withdrawn. If the conversations at these gatherings tended toward the trivial, the irrelevant, the shallow, he could ignore that for her sake. As Natalie said, such socializing was important for her career, and if rising in her company would make her happy, Adam wanted to help in any way he could.

He knew his friends thought them an unlikely pair. In the past Adam had always dated women who had chosen the helping professions, women with a strong sense of social justice and commitment to social change—women more like himself. Natalie's beauty they understood well enough, but not her craving for material signs of status and wealth. Still, they were his friends and accepted his choices and always treated Natalie courteously enough. They did not know how Natalie picked them apart behind their backs, criticizing their clothing, their cars, what she called their appalling lack of ambition. Only Adam's former college roommate, a gentle man who had become a Benedictine monk, cautioned him against rushing into a lifetime commitment. "Don't lose sight of who you really are," John advised, and said nothing more on the subject.

But John's words stayed with Adam, and he began to reflect on what he became when he was with Natalie. He felt as if he were playing a role to please her, setting aside everything that truly mattered to him. He didn't like what that said about him, especially since compartmentalizing his life like that contradicted every value he tried to instill in his students.

They had been engaged nearly eight months by then, and had already completed pre-Cana premarital counseling. Natalie and her mother had whirled about in a frenzy of wedding preparations, leaving Adam feeling more like a spectator than one of the principal participants. But it was not embarrassment or anxiety that kept him from suggesting they reconsider or at least postpone the ceremony. He still loved Natalie, although he knew they weren't right for each other, and he couldn't bear to lose her. Besides, he had asked her to marry him, and he was a man of his word.

He supposed he ought to be grateful that Natalie had acted more decisively than he had. She had spared them both a world of pain and recriminations.

He hoped Natalie would be happy. He figured she would; she knew how to get what she wanted. He was less certain of himself.

He missed Natalie the most at times like these, when he was pulling into the driveway of his darkened house. He had left the porch light off to signal his absence to trick-or-treaters, but the house looked so lonely and forlorn he wished he had left it on. Once he had thought that Natalie would live there with him, an assumption that in hindsight seemed ridiculous, since his was a small, older home and never had been much to her liking. It occurred to him then that at that moment, Megan might also be arriving home with no warm welcome waiting from someone she loved. But she had Robby. He was glad for her that she was not alone.

When he went to the kitchen to check his messages, he noticed that his answering machine was flashing a steady pattern of two blinks. His first, foolish thought was that Megan had called, but as he pressed the play button he remembered that he had not given her his number.

He listened to two hang-up calls, then shook his head and rewound the tape. Nana, he guessed. She loathed answering machines almost as much as computers and refused to leave messages for him. She had probably called as he was en route to her home to make sure he wouldn't be late, as he had been when he had picked her up at Elm Creek Manor.

Suddenly cheerful, Adam carried the newspaper into the living room and settled down to read. Nana was something else. Even from miles away, she had welcomed him home.

⚜

Julia was enjoying her day off, so when the phone rang, she groaned, turned the page of her magazine, and allowed her assistant to pick up in the other room. She did a few deep-breathing exercises to ward off a tension headache, which in the past few weeks had become a nearly daily occurrence. Perhaps it was an overstatement to say she was enjoying her day off when in truth, relief was her strongest emotion. Filming had not been going well, and Julia needed this day away from the set to relax. Today she wanted to do no work at all, unless reading a copy of *Quilter's Newsletter Magazine* counted as research for the role of Sadie.

Since the first script meeting, there had been a decidedly negative atmosphere on the set. Julia now realized she had taken the collegial feeling of the *Family Tree* cast and crew for granted. Deneford was a stubborn tyrant of a director; Samantha, as Young Sadie, seemed to have misplaced her brain most days; and Rick was a preening peacock. Aside from Julia herself, the only members of the cast who were behaving themselves were the extras and the two young boys playing her sons. Worse than the actors, if less notice-able, was Ellen, who moped around the studio in a state of perpetual gloom, muttering about the script changes Deneford continued to demand of her. To Julia's consternation, and for reasons she couldn't fathom, Ellen had selected her as her special confidante, which meant that Julia was privy to every minute detail of her despair, delivered in tearful monologues as Ellen paced around in Julia's trailer. Yesterday she had spent the better part of an hour bemoaning the title change.

"*Prairie Vengeance?*" she had cried in disbelief. "There's no vengeance in this movie. What is Deneford thinking?"

Patiently, Julia reminded her what the director had said at the morning meeting. "He's trying to capitalize on the success of *Jungle Vengeance*. Rick Rowen's agent is thinking about having him do an entire *Vengeance* series."

"This film doesn't belong in that series," Ellen said. "Can't you see what they're doing? They're turning this picture into a vehicle for Rick, and that takes away the focus from Sadie. This story is supposed to be about Sadie."

Julia did feel a twinge of apprehension at that. She had heard rumors that Rick's name would be appearing above the title, which she wouldn't mind, as long as hers preceded his. Lately, though, she had heard other rumors that Rick's name would appear there alone. She wondered if her name would be placed below the title, or worse yet, buried somewhere after Samantha's.

But she shook off her doubts and said, "You have to expect these things. A film is a collaborative effort, but the director's vision has priority. We all have to adapt for the greater good of the final project."

"But we're getting so far from my great-grandmother's diaries."

"You're young, Ellen. You have to pay your dues. Just cooperate and don't make any enemies, and when *Prairie Vengeance* is a success, you'll have much more control over your later projects."

Ellen accepted this, as she did all of Julia's advice, with resignation about the way things were and gratitude that Julia took the time to explain them. Julia had to admit Ellen's behavior was rather flattering. Although Ellen was only a writer and not an actress, Julia almost felt as if Ellen were her protégé. In fact, it was better that Ellen was only a writer, as Julia had always been sus-picious of the young starlets nipping at her heels, begging for advice, no doubt longing for the day when they could steal her roles and send her tum-bling into the netherworld of rare guest appearances on sitcoms. Ellen, on the other hand, was obviously no threat, so Julia could afford to be generous.

But not today. She snuggled back into the sofa cushions and tried to lose herself in an article about the Smithsonian Institution's collection of antique quilts. Today she simply did not feel like discussing the capricious nature of the movie industry with Ellen, or with anyone else, for that matter.

Her assistant entered the room, the cordless phone in her hand. "Miss Merchaud, there's an urgent call for you."

"From whom?" *Please,* she thought, *don't say Ellen.*

"It's Miss Henderson again, ma'am."

Julia let her head fall back against the pillow. "Did you tell her I'm home?"

Reluctantly, her assistant nodded.

Sighing impatiently, Julia sat up. "Lucy, you and I need to have a serious talk." Lucy gulped, handed her the phone, and hurried from the room.

Julia took a moment to compose herself before putting the phone to her ear. "Ellen, dear. What a lovely surprise."

"Miss Merchaud?" Ellen's voice was so quiet the bustle in the background nearly drowned her out. Where was she calling from, the runway at LAX?

"Yes, it's me."

"There's a problem."

Naturally. "Would you mind speaking up?" she said, a little sharply.

"I can't. I'm on the set, and . . ." Ellen fell silent, and when she spoke again, her voice was an anxious whisper. "I can't talk now, but you need to get down here right away."

"They aren't filming any of my scenes today," Julia reminded her.

"Not yet they aren't," Ellen said darkly. "Just get down here. Please." With that, she hung up.

Uneasy, Julia turned off the phone and set it aside. Not yet they aren't? What was that cryptic remark supposed to mean? Whatever it was, it couldn't be good, Julia decided as she hurried to her bedroom to change.

She had given her driver the day off, so after telling Lucy she was going out for a while, she drove her Porsche as fast as she could down PCH to the studio. Fortunately, traffic was relatively light, so not quite forty minutes later, she was driving through the front gates and parking behind the sound stage reserved for *Prairie Vengeance*'s indoor shots. According to the production schedule, Deneford planned to shoot several of Samantha's and Rick's scenes that day, including a love scene Deneford had added to the original script. As she slipped inside the darkened building, Julia wondered if that was what Ellen was so worked up about. If so, Julia would finally give her the dressing down she deserved. Neophyte or not, she ought to know better than to drag Julia all the way down there merely to vent.

But when Julia reached the set for the interior of the farmhouse to find Samantha dressed as Sadie and sitting at the quilting frame as she recited her lines, Julia's breath caught in her throat. Those were Julia's lines; that was the quilt Sadie made to raise money to purchase seed wheat after their last crop was lost to a grasshopper plague.

"What is going on here?" she shrilled.

"Cut," Deneford called out sharply. He looked around to glare at who-ever had been foolish enough to ruin his shot, but when his eyes fell on Julia, his anger was immediately replaced by a mask of bland nonchalance. "Julia," he said, rising to greet her. "What brings you in today?"

"Why is she doing my scene?"

Deneford placed his hands on her shoulders in an attempt to calm her. "Julia, let's go to my office and talk."

Julia wouldn't budge. "I asked you a question," she said, raising her voice and not caring who heard her. In the corner of her eye, she saw Ellen emerge from the shadows, her expression a mix of indignation and triumph. If not for her, Julia would have shown up on Monday completely unaware of Deneford's duplicity, and as for that conniving little Samantha . . .

"We're just rehearsing," Deneford said soothingly. "Just to see how it plays."

"What good does it do to rehearse my scenes without me? Unless they aren't my scenes anymore."

"Okay. Look. I'm sorry you had to find out this way, but we're shifting some of your scenes to Young Sadie. Just a few of the quilting scenes, noth-ing major."

"Nothing major?" Julia gaped at him. The quilting scenes were among the most important in the entire film. "Do you mind telling me why?"

"To be honest—"

"I certainly wish you would be."

"To be honest, the quilting close-ups look more realistic when Samantha does them. Frankly, Julia, I know you say you're an experienced quilter, but Samantha's better. It's that simple."

"I like quilting," Samantha said dreamily. Sure enough, as Julia watched, Samantha deftly worked the needle through the three layers held fast in the quilt frame, as swiftly as any of the teachers at Elm Creek Quilt Camp. Julia was too far away to see, but with a sinking heart, she suspected Samantha's stitches were similarly tiny and perfect. "My grandma taught me when I was just a little girl."

You're still a little girl, Julia almost retorted, but realized just in time that emphasizing the difference in their ages probably wouldn't help her much.

Deneford took Julia by the arm and steered her toward the exit. "It's only three scenes," he said as they walked through the darkened hallway. "The material we've added with you and Rick together will more than make up the difference, and the new material is better. Trust me."

That was the last thing Julia intended to do. "Which three scenes?" she asked, thinking. *Please, not the quilting bee.*

"This one, and the scene after the neighbor's barn burns down, and the quilting bee."

Silently, Julia swore. "I want the quilting bee," she said, her voice shaking. She hated to beg, but that scene was *hers*. She needed it. "You know as well as I that Samantha has the emotional depth of a potted cactus. She can't handle the dramatic shifts of that scene."

"She did fine when we shot it this morning."

Julia went cold. "This morning?" The quilting bee scene called for more than thirty minor characters and extras. To coordinate such a shoot required advance planning, hardly the spur-of-the-moment decision Deneford had implied only moments before. "That was no rehearsal back there, was it?"

"It was a rehearsal; Samantha needed one. But to answer your next question, yes, we will be filming that scene with her in the role of Sadie."

Julia forced air through her constricted throat. "I see." Another breath. "Then let me shoot the scene, too. You choose the superior performance. That's fair, don't you think?"

"No."

Julia stared at him. "What do you mean, no? Just no? You're not even—"

"Julia, why are you doing this to yourself?" He seemed genuinely puzzled. "Why make this more difficult than it has to be?"

Her thoughts in a whirl, Julia couldn't respond. When Deneford opened the door, she blinked in the bright sunlight and stepped outside. "We'll talk on Monday," he called after her, but she didn't acknowledge him. The door fell heavily shut behind her, and she walked to her car, numb.

She heard the door open and shut again, and then footsteps on the pavement. "Miss Merchaud," Ellen called out. Julia stopped and turned around, her movements mechanical. "What did he say? Did he change his mind?"

"He's going to use Samantha."

"That ignorant hack!"

"He's no hack." Julia's voice sounded wooden to her ears. "He has an Oscar and four Emmys. Or is it five? I don't remember—"

Ellen seized her shoulders. "Miss Merchaud, we can't let him ruin our movie."

"It isn't our movie," Julia said, Ellen's touch drawing her back to awareness. "You sold him your script. He owns it now. Whatever he wants to do, he can do."

Ellen looked close to tears. "I wish I'd never sent him a single page."

"At least you'll still receive credit for the screenplay."

"I don't know if I want it."

Suddenly Julia's own voice echoed in her thoughts: *A film is a collaborative effort,* she had told Ellen, *but the director's vision has priority. We all have to adapt for the greater good of the final project.* The memory taunted her, and she thought she might be ill.

She closed her eyes to still her churning stomach. *Breathe,* she ordered herself. When she opened her eyes again, Ellen was staring at her, worried. "Are you all right?"

Instead of answering, Julia said, "He'll know someone tipped me off. You better get back in there or he'll figure out it was you."

Ellen laughed bitterly. "He barely even notices when I'm there. I don't think he'll notice that I'm gone."

"I'm serious, Ellen. He could have you barred from the set."

Ellen looked taken aback. "He can't. It's my movie."

"It isn't your movie," Julia said, each word clear and emphatic. "It's his movie. Accept that, and make the best of it."

Ellen stared at her for a moment, then swallowed and nodded. She turned and hurried back into the building. Only after she was gone did Julia realize she had forgotten to thank Ellen for the warning.

As she drove home, her thoughts gradually became more clear. She would fight. It was a slim chance, but there might be something in her contract prohibiting this. The first thing she would do was call Ares and get him searching for a loophole.

But when she called, his assistant said he would be in meetings all day and wouldn't be available until tomorrow. "He has to check in sometime," she snapped, thinking of how Maury would interrupt a meeting, any meeting, to take her emergency calls. "Have him call me then." She slammed down the phone without waiting for a reply, and then, since Deneford and Ares were out of range, she kicked over a copper vase full of dried decorative grasses and sent it clattering across the gleaming hardwood floor. Now what was she supposed to do?

Suddenly inspiration struck. "Lucy, there's a mess in the parlor," she called out as she raced to her study. Samantha had replaced Julia because she was a better quilter. Well, that was a situation Julia could remedy. She yanked open her desk drawer and took out her folder of quilt camp notes. Near the bottom was the sheet of paper with Donna Jorgenson's address and phone number.

Julia sat down and rested her hands on her desk to compose herself. Very well. None of the Cross-Country Quilters had seen fit to contact her, and her injured pride had prevented her from reaching out to them. But now she needed Donna's help and could wait no longer.

The phone rang twice before a girl's voice answered, "Hello?"

"Yes. May I speak with Mrs. Donna Jorgenson?"

"Hold on, please." There was a hollow sound, as if the mouthpiece had been covered, and then a muffled, "Mom, it's for you."

A moment later, a familiar voice said pleasantly, "Hello?"

"Donna?"

"Yes?"

"It's me. Julia." For a panicky moment she wondered if Donna would remember her. "From quilt camp."

"Julia?" Donna cried, delighted. "I can't believe it. It's so nice to hear from you. Where have you been? We all thought you fell off the face of the earth."

Was that so? "You could have written," Julia said, petulant.

"Are you kidding? We did! I wrote twice, Grace and Megan each wrote once, and Vinnie—well, gosh, she must be on her eighth or ninth letter by now. All we get back are these form letters and autographed pictures. Don't get me wrong; we're glad to get them, but honestly, how many identical photos do we need?" She laughed.

For the second time that day, Julia felt as if she had tumbled into a separate reality from the one she usually inhabited. "You wrote to me? At my home?"

"Well, I'm not sure. It's the address you gave us at camp. I assumed it was your home." Donna read off the address for Julia's home, not a digit out of place.

"I don't understand this."

"Neither did we, especially since that's not the address on the envelopes you sent us."

Donna recited a second address, but Julia only needed to hear the first word to realize what had happened. "That bastard."

"What? Who?"

"My agent." Somehow he'd arranged to have her mail routed to his office, and suddenly she understood who his accomplice must have been. "And my assistant. She gave him my personal mail."

"Why?"

"I don't know, but I'm going to find out, and then I'm going to fire her."

"Fire her?" Donna sounded horrified. "I'm sure there must be a logical explanation—"

"For stealing my mail?" Didn't Donna understand? All those weeks of feeling neglected and forgotten, and Lucy—with specific instructions to notify her the minute a letter from the Cross-Country Quilters arrived— "I have to fire her."

"Can't you just tell her not to do it again?" Donna begged. "Give her another chance. You're too nice a person to fire someone this close to the holidays."

Donna was wrong. Julia was not a nice person, and she was feeling especially not nice at the moment. But something in Donna's voice nagged at her, until, against her better judgment, she reluctantly said, "I'll get her side of the story first. I'm not promising anything, but I'll give her a chance to explain." And if Julia didn't like what Lucy had to say, *then* she'd fire her.

"I'm sure you'll be glad you did."

Julia doubted it, but she had bigger problems on her mind. "Donna, the reason I'm calling—"

"Yes?"

Donna's voice sounded so warm, so full of concern, that Julia's pride evaporated. "I need your help."

Eight

Megan had been too busy to check her email all day, so it wasn't until she was about to go home that she finally had a chance to download her messages. Several were waiting, including an exchange between Grace and Donna that had begun the day before, when Donna had written to announce that Julia was alive but facing problems with her agent and her director, not the least of which was having her personal mail misdirected. Today Grace responded:

TO: Megan.Donohue@rocketec.com, quiltmom@USAonline.com
FROM: Grace Daniels ‹danielsg@deyoung.org›
DATE: 8:14 AM PT 9 Nov
SUBJECT: Re: News from Julia

I'm glad she didn't forget us. Someone should tell Vinnie before she buries southern California beneath an avalanche of mail. We really have to get those two online.
Any thoughts on how we can help Julia with the movie problems?

Donna had written back:

We could fly down there and give her director a few good pokes with our needles.

Within minutes, Grace had answered:

I wish we could. I'd love to get out of town. You aren't going to believe this, but I agreed to let Gabriel come to Thanksgiving dinner. My sisters think I'm crazy, but Joshua dotes on his grandfather, and I didn't want to ruin the holiday for him.

Donna answered that she didn't envy Grace, but she didn't expect her own holiday to be much better. Lindsay and Brandon were coming for Thanksgiving dinner, which meant that Donna intended to put on a production worthy of Martha Stewart. "I have to make up for all these months of pretending the engagement would just go away if I ignored it," she wrote. "Lindsay sounds so stressed out lately, and I'm sure it's my fault. I have to stop acting like an evil mother-in-law before Brandon runs screaming for the hills."

Megan smiled and wrote:

Donna, honey, you are not an evil anything. But tell the truth, would you really mind if Brandon ran away?

She waited a few minutes just in case Donna was online and would respond quickly. When she checked her email, a message downloaded:

TO: Megan.Donohue@rocketec.com
FROM: wagnera@rogerbacon.k12.oh.edu
DATE: 5:43 PM 9 Nov
SUBJECT: Checking in

So, how did the meeting go?

Megan felt a stirring of pleasure at the sight of the familiar address. Since Halloween, she and Adam had begun corresponding by email, and she usually heard from him several times a week. They exchanged small talk, mostly, details about their work and their plans for the weekends. Megan had discovered that Adam's quirky sense of humor was just as amusing via email, although she found herself thinking she would have preferred to hear his voice. Especially now, since the meeting he referred to had felt more like an ambush than a parent-teacher conference.

When Megan had entered the classroom, she was surprised to see the teacher was not alone. The man with her introduced himself as the school counselor. "I'm glad we're finally able to meet," he said, shaking her hand.

"Finally?" Megan said. The teacher and counselor exchanged a look, and then it came out: In the past few months, they had sent Robby home with three requests for a teacher-parent conference.

"Why didn't you mail them?" Megan managed to ask. "Why didn't you phone me at work or at home?"

They explained that they would have, eventually, but unfortunately three postponements weren't unusual in these situations.

"And what kind of situation is that, exactly?" Megan asked.

Minor disciplinary problems, of course. If it had been something egregious, they hastened to assure her, she would have been contacted immediately.

Megan sat numbly as they explained. Robby was a bright and imaginative boy, but quieter than the others and somewhat withdrawn. Usually. Other times, he would tell wild, outlandish tales, and when the other students teased him, he lashed out. He had trouble controlling his anger, and sometimes he would have outbursts with no apparent provocation. That was why they suspected some trouble at home.

They paused then, waiting for her to speak, and their scrutiny made Megan feel powerless and fearful. The look in their eyes suggested they had already decided she must be an unfit mother and were only looking for the evidence to support their conclusion. "Robby doesn't do anything like this at home," she stammered, just as she remembered Gina's cookies. "I mean, the usual childhood disobedience, testing authority and such, but nothing like what you've described."

"That's not unusual," the counselor said. "What about Robby's father? He couldn't come today?"

"He lives in Oregon. We're divorced."

"I see." The counselor nodded and made some notes on a pad. "Does Robby have much contact with his father?"

"Very little since he moved away at the beginning of the summer. Before then, they saw each other maybe once a month." Megan inhaled deeply to still the pounding of her heart. "My former husband wasn't very good about keeping to the scheduled visitation agreement."

"Robby often tells stories about his father," the teacher said. "One week he's a secret service agent, the next he's a fighter pilot—"

"It seems likely his behavior problems are related to his father's absence," the counselor broke in. "Don't you agree, Mrs. Donohue?"

"I . . . yes, that seems likely." Megan could have told them that years ago. She counted to three silently before asking if they had any suggestions for how to help Robby. They recommended professional counseling to help him deal with his emotions, especially his anger at his father.

The teacher and counselor had seemed satisfied as she left, as if they had discharged their duties appropriately and now were free to turn their thoughts to other matters. They probably had no idea they had tapped into the deep spring of anxiety that welled up in the heart of every mother, that despite all her love and her best efforts she had failed her child. If she wanted to absolve herself of responsibility, she could shift the blame to Keith, but that would neither ease her conscience nor help her son. She was the custodial parent; she should have done more, somehow, to compensate for Keith's neglect.

Even now, after the initial shock of Robby's deceptions had dulled, just thinking of it threatened to bring on tears of frustration, so she kept her reply to Adam vague:

It was not especially helpful. I'll write more tomorrow.

Almost immediately, Adam responded:

Would you like to talk about it in person instead?

Megan's hands froze on the keyboard. She pictured him jumping into his car and racing to comfort her. It was an unexpectedly reassuring image, and for some reason that bothered her. She took a deep breath and wrote:

What did you have in mind?

Adam replied:

Dinner? There's a great Italian restaurant halfway between your place and mine. We could meet there Friday night at seven.

Megan's pulse quickened. He must mean just the two of them, because they could hardly discuss Robby with him present. She felt a strange mixture of pleasure and discomfort at the thought. A Halloween party at Vinnie's was one thing, dinner alone quite another. She wasn't sure she was ready for that.

She glanced at the calendar to see if she was free, already knowing she was, and suddenly she thought of Gina and the baby she was expecting. Keith had moved on with his life long ago, but Megan had been stuck in the same place for years, wavering, uncertain. After all this time, if she were not yet ready to resume dating, it was because she had decided she preferred to be alone for the rest of her life. Besides, this might not even be considered a date. Adam knew she was Vinnie's friend, and since he worked with children, his intentions were probably only professional.

She clenched and unclenched her hands to warm them and typed:

Send me the directions. If my parents can watch Robby, I'd like to come.

She clicked the mouse on Send before she could change her mind.

⚓

November 11

Dear Vinnie,

A thousand apologies for not writing to you sooner. You are such a darling to send me ten letters although I never wrote back! I can't imagine what you thought of me. I do have an excuse: My agent told my assistant to forward him all my fan mail because he didn't want it to "distract" me. Can you imagine? I was more distracted by wondering why I hadn't heard from any of my camp friends. Now the misunderstanding is all sorted out, or so I'm told, so if you write to me again, I should receive your letter just fine.

The movie is not going well, unfortunately. The male star is a spoiled brat, and the girl who plays Young Sadie is as dizzy as the day is long. She also happens to be a talented quilter, which means that my director has shifted some of my scenes to her. I've been practicing until my fingertips bleed, but I don't know if I'll improve enough to hold on to my role. Keep your fingers crossed for me.

I haven't made much progress on the sampler quilt you and the others designed for me at camp because I've been practicing my hand-quilting instead. I did begin another Friendship Star block with your autumn leaf fabric, my small contribution to the Challenge Quilt. Now I feel as if I shouldn't be allowed to finish it until shooting ends, because I might be completely squeezed out of this picture if things don't turn around for me soon.

I hope all is well in Ohio.

Sincerely,
Julia

⚓

November 14

Dear Julia,

Testing, testing . . . This letter is for Julia Merchaud. If you are Julia's assistant or agent, stop reading and give this letter to Julia right away! I mean it, Nosy!

There. If you're still reading, you must be Julia. My goodness, it was nice to hear from you. I'm sorry the movie isn't going as well as you hoped. Chin up, honey. I've been watching old episodes of **Family Tree** on Lifetime, and you're a wonderful actress. I didn't know you were the mother from **Home Sweet**

Home, *too! I used to watch that show all the time, and now I'm enjoying it again on Nick at Night. If I had put two and two together, I would have recognized you right away when we first met at lunch at camp. (I hope you've forgiven me for that.) Anyway, I can't imagine that any director with a brain in his head would let you get away, so keep practicing quilting, and I'm sure everything will work out fine. I can't wait to see the movie. I know it will be a big hit, because every quilter in America will go to see it. I'll be first in line in Dayton.*

I started my block for the Challenge Quilt, too, but I don't know if I should have. You know my challenge was to find a new girlfriend for my grandson. Well, after much thought, I decided that Adam and Megan would make a charming couple. I invited them and Megan's son, Robby, here for a Halloween party, and they seemed to hit it off, but now neither one will talk about the other, and it's driving me crazy. If Megan mentions him, would you please tell me? Even if she makes you promise not to? A grandmother has a right to know.

Well, that's enough for now. Keep me posted on the movie. I want to have time to pick out my outfit for Oscar night.

> Your quilting buddy,
> Vinnie

PS: This is some of my famous peanut-butter fudge. Share some with that sourpuss director of yours. It might sweeten him up.

PPS: Why did you pine away at the mailbox all these months instead of writing to us first?

⚓

Megan drove through a chilly drizzle to the restaurant, wondering if she'd made a mistake. As soon as she stepped inside, though, and the warm fragrances of fresh bread, olive oil, basil, and garlic enveloped her, she felt some of her nervousness disappear. It vanished completely when she saw Adam waiting. He wore a sport coat, which made her glad she had worn her favorite casual dress instead of slacks.

"What, no plumed hat this time?" she teased.

"Not today," he said, smiling. "You look very nice."

Megan thanked him. The hostess approached then and showed them to a small, candlelit table in a secluded section of the restaurant. They chatted as they studied the menus, but while Adam seemed perfectly comfortable, Megan felt her earlier nervousness resurfacing. Silently she scolded herself to stop acting as if she were on a job interview and relax. What was the worst that could happen? They could have a miserable evening and might decide never to see each other again. She'd survived far worse.

It wasn't exactly the power of positive thinking, but somehow that realization put her at ease. By the time their salads were served, she felt as if she were enjoying a pleasant evening with a good friend. She liked the way Adam's eyes lit up when he talked about teaching, and the stories he told about his students soon had her laughing. She wished her son had a teacher like him.

Eventually the conversation turned to Robby, and Megan told Adam about the miserable conference. When she finished, Adam winced. "I hope you don't judge the entire teaching profession by those two."

"Of course I don't. But tell me, am I wrong to think they should have made more of an effort to contact me earlier?"

"In their place, I would have tried." He hesitated. "Did you ask Robby about the notes they sent home?"

"As soon as I got home. At first he said he lost them, but after I reminded him that he should have at least told me about them, I couldn't get another word out of him." She still couldn't believe her sweet son had lied to her. "I told him how important it was for us to be honest, and that no matter what, I would always love him. I don't know if he believed me or not."

Adam reached across the table and took her hand. "I'm sure he knows that. Anyone who sees the two of you together knows that."

"Then why did he lie to me?"

"To keep from getting in trouble. Because he didn't want you to talk to his teacher. There could be many reasons."

Adam's hand was warm and comforting around hers. "I did take their advice. Robby will begin seeing a counselor next week. If nothing else, I think that will help him deal with his anger about his father."

Adam nodded, thoughtful, and then said carefully, "Is there any chance you might be able to get Keith more involved?"

"I don't know." Megan pulled her hand away and toyed with her fork, remembering their phone conversation. When she finally reached Keith, after three evenings of leaving unanswered messages, he had listened in silence as she described the situation and asked for his help.

"If you had let me have custody," Keith had said in a flat voice when she finished, "he wouldn't be in so much trouble now."

"You never asked for full custody." Megan said, taken aback. "I offered you joint custody. You said visiting on the weekends was enough."

"Well, what do you expect me to do now?"

"Can you come for a visit? Can he visit you, for Thanksgiving break, maybe?"

"Do you know what a pain it would be to try to get an airline ticket now?" Keith complained, "Look. I can't do this right now. Gina's baby is giving her terrible morning sickness. I can only concentrate on one crisis at time."

"Keith—"

"I'll call him. Okay? I'll call him soon." With that, Keith had hung up.

Gina's baby, Megan had thought as she replaced the receiver. Not *their* baby, or even *the* baby. Gina's. Keith would never learn.

Now, Megan looked across the table at Adam and tried to smile. "I don't think he's going to be much help. At least Robby has his grandfather. He's very busy, but they still spend quite a bit of time together."

"Have you thought about Big Brothers?"

"I looked into it, but there isn't a chapter in our town."

"I used to be a Big Brother," Adam said. "Just until last January, in fact, when my little brother moved out of state. I was going to sign up for a new one, but—"

When Adam didn't continue, Megan said, "But what?"

Adam looked sheepish. "But Natalie didn't want me to. She thought, with the wedding coming up and everything . . ."

Megan nodded. "I see." She was beginning to piece together a rather unflattering portrait of Natalie, and she wondered why anyone as nice as Adam would have chosen someone so unlike himself. "I suppose she thought you would be too busy."

Adam's face hardened. "Only too busy for the things that matter." Just as swiftly, the shadow passed, and he smiled again. "What do you think about me being Robby's Big Brother? I mean, not officially, through the organization, just informally."

The suggestion was so totally unexpected that Megan didn't know what to say. "Well—"

Adam held up his palms. "I have no ulterior motives, I swear," he said. "You can check me out if you want. All teachers at my school are investigated before they're hired, and I'm sure Big Brothers would be willing to provide an evaluation."

"It's not that," Megan said. "I . . . I just . . ." She studied him quizzically. "Would you really want to?"

"Sure. Robby's a great kid. We had a ball at the Halloween party." He took her hand again. "How about this: The three of us can go out together, and if we're getting along well and you agree, I'll ask Robby if he wants to do something the next weekend. If he says no, we'll forget the whole thing."

Megan considered the idea. As difficult as it was to admit it, she couldn't be everything to Robby, and a good friend, someone outside of the family, could become the confidant he needed. She had watched Robby and Adam together at the Halloween party and had reflected on how well they got along. They could try it, she decided. If it didn't work out, she would call it off.

"If you're sure," Megan said. "Yes. Let's see what we can do."

Adam squeezed her hand, smiling. "It'll work out. You'll see."

Something in her heart told Megan she could believe him.

☙

The Saturday before Thanksgiving, Donna was in the basement excavating her cartons of holiday decorations. This year, since Brandon would be coming for dinner, Donna intended to outdo herself. She knew she had a cornucopia basket down there somewhere, and with a bit of cleaning and some embellishment, it would make a lovely centerpiece. The night before, she had completed one of her longtime UFOs, a table runner for the sideboard, in the Pine Burr pattern. The new decorations and her best table linens would show Brandon the Jorgensons were eager to welcome him into the family.

She had spent the morning poring over her favorite cookbook and leafing through the recipes she had collected from her online quilting buddies over the past several months. When she suggested to Becca and Paul that they try a completely different menu this Thanksgiving, they exchanged unhappy glances.

Surprised, Donna said, "After all these years of teasing me for serving the same thing every Thanksgiving, when I finally suggest a change, you're turning me down?"

Becca fidgeted and said, "The regular stuff is nice." Paul only nodded, but Donna understood their unspoken plea: When so much about their family was changing, the comfort of familiar traditions was more important than ever. So Donna agreed to keep the menu the same—that would be easier, anyway—and settled for the new table runner and centerpiece to accompany their traditional table decoration, a pair of brass candlesticks that had once belonged to Paul's mother.

She found the cornucopia basket and dug it out of its box. She was eager to see Lindsay, who for weeks had been too busy to come home. As for Brandon, he was so abrupt on the phone whenever he called for Lindsay that Donna feared he had detected—and resented—her misgivings about the wedding. She intended to make it up to him over the holiday, for Lindsay's sake.

The phone sounded faintly from upstairs. Donna blew dust off the basket and listened, but when Becca didn't shout for her, she decided the call was for someone else. She had thought it might be Julia, who in the past few weeks had taken to calling almost every other day for quilting advice. It wasn't easy to continue their lessons over the phone, but from what Julia said, if she didn't improve soon, she could lose her movie role altogether. Donna didn't understand why any director in his right mind would cut an actress as talented and popular as Julia, but as Lindsay had told her, acting was a difficult, uncertain profession. Donna was glad Lindsay had chosen to pursue directing rather than acting—although it remained to be seen whether she would continue to pursue any career after graduation.

At least Lindsay was involved in the university's fall production; she had almost bowed out, but after persistent pleading from her friends in drama club and at least two professors, she had agreed to direct again. She was enjoying herself so much that Donna was certain she'd participate in the spring semester play, too. Donna would volunteer to handle the details of the wedding preparations if Lindsay thought she would be too busy to do both.

Just then, Donna heard footsteps coming down the basement stairs. "Mom?" Becca said. "That was Lindsay on the phone."

"Oh, good." Donna carefully maneuvered through the stacks of cartons, the cornucopia in her hands. "Did you two have a nice chat?"

"Not really." As Donna continued toward the stairs, Becca added, "Don't bother. She already hung up."

Donna halted. "Already?" She hesitated, surprised and a little hurt. "She didn't want to talk to me?"

"She said she was too busy, and not to call her back, because she's going out." Becca winced as if she'd rather not say anything more. "Mom, I have some bad news."

"What?"

"They're not coming for Thanksgiving."

"You mean only Lindsay is coming?"

"No, I mean they're both not coming."

Donna felt a weariness come over her. "Oh." She sat down heavily on a stack of dusty boxes. "Are they going to Brandon's parents' home instead?"

"I think they're staying at the apartment."

"Why?"

Becca shrugged, and only then did Donna see the anger in her face. "Lindsay says Brandon has a major project due before the end of the semester, and she has to work on the play."

"Can't they come just for the day?"

"Brandon says it's too far to drive."

"But it's only an hour there and an hour back."

"That's what I said. Lindsay never thought it was too long before." Becca's gaze was beseeching. "Mom, do you think you can talk her out of it?"

"I can try," Donna said, but somehow she knew she wouldn't succeed.

Sure enough, when she went upstairs and dialed Lindsay's number, the phone rang and rang. Becca leaned on the kitchen counter, watching her mother expectantly. The answering machine eventually picked up, and Donna forced herself to leave a cheerful message.

"She won't come," Becca said. "I hate Brandon."

"Becca—"

"I mean it, Mom. I know this is his fault. Lindsay never missed Thanksgiving before, not because of a play, not for anything." Scowling, she stormed out of the kitchen, adding, "I'd never let some guy control me like that."

"He's not some guy. He's her fiancé, and . . ." Abruptly Donna fell silent, stopped short by Becca's last words, unable to defend him. Brandon did seem somewhat domineering, and even Paul had called him bossy. But Lindsay was a strong person, too, and surely she would never do anything she didn't want to do simply because Brandon said so.

Perhaps Donna, Paul, and Becca had to accept the possibility that Lindsay preferred to be alone with Brandon. As much as it hurt Donna to think that her daughter didn't want to spend the holiday with the family, she couldn't ignore that this was, in a sense, the couple's first Thanksgiving together. Surely they wouldn't need to be alone every holiday, but maybe this first one was special. Besides, Christmas wasn't too far away, and it would come after the play and the semester had ended. Surely Lindsay would come home for Christmas, with or without Brandon.

Just then Donna realized she still held the dusty cornucopia. She studied it for a few moments, turning it over and over in her hands, then carried it back downstairs and packed it away.

⚜

On Thanksgiving Grace drove for the first time in four months, as a favor to her sister. Helen usually took Mother to holiday church services, but on Tuesday she had phoned and begged Grace to take her instead. Helen's son needed to be picked up from college on Wednesday, and although Helen's husband had intended to make the trip, at the last minute he could not get the day off from work. Driving all day would put Helen so far behind schedule that she'd need all of Wednesday night and Thursday morning to get ready for the more than forty relatives who would gather at her home to celebrate Thanksgiving.

"You wouldn't be in this mess if you'd let us each bring something," Grace teased. Helen was notoriously finicky about the holidays and insisted on preparing the entire meal herself.

"Thanks for volunteering. You can make the rolls," Helen countered, then hung up before Grace could protest.

So on Wednesday, Grace baked two kinds of rolls, sourdough and rye, then made a pumpkin pie for good measure, until the whole loft was filled with the spicy fragrances of baking. On Thursday she packed the rolls and the pie carefully in two baskets, summoned up her courage, and went to her building's underground garage. She expected to find cobwebs clinging to the rearview mirror and an engine choked with dust, but the car looked no different than the last time she had driven it, and it started up immediately as if that had been only days ago. At first Grace felt uncomfortable and nervous behind the wheel, but soon she relaxed. Traffic was light, the day was bright and sunny, and she had been feeling well for weeks, so well that she had even begun sketching a new quilt. If not for the occasional pins-and-needles sensations in her hands, she could almost believe the doctor had misdiagnosed her.

"Don't get overconfident," Dr. Steiner cautioned her at her last visit, when she told him how remarkably healthy she felt. "You still need to take it easy. If you overdo, you could have a relapse."

Grace knew he was right, but his warning only slightly diminished her optimism. Spontaneous remissions occurred in other, even more serious diseases; there was no reason why she couldn't hope for one in her case. "Hope never hurt anyone," she told the doctor, and he agreed but said that while she was hoping, she should err on the side of caution and be sure to take care of herself.

Dr. Steiner's warnings were never far from her thoughts, but it was a sign of just how good she felt that she was driving that day. The doctor had never forbidden her to drive; that prohibition had been her own, born of the fear that had haunted her since her accident. Even if she had felt only half as well, however, she still might have agreed. Mother had to get to church, and Grace couldn't picture convincing Helen that her fears about driving were realistic. And Grace couldn't ask Justine to drive them, because for all Grace knew, Gabriel might be with her.

Mother still lived in the home where Grace and her sisters had grown up. She was waiting in the front room, neatly attired in a wine-red suit and a pillbox hat with a short veil that did not quite reach her eyes.

"There's my baby girl," she said when Grace entered, and hugged her. Then she held Grace at arm's length for inspection. "You look well."

"I feel great. Never better."

Mother nodded, satisfied, and picked up her purse from the credenza near the door. She also retrieved a covered casserole dish and gestured to two plastic pie carriers beside it. "Will you take those for me?"

"I hope one of these is your sweet potato pie," Grace said as they left the house.

"Of course. It wouldn't be Thanksgiving without it. The other one is apple, and this is my green bean casserole. Helen said to bring just the pies, but you know your sister. She won't ever admit when she needs help." She gave Grace a sidelong glance as Grace helped her into the car. "Must run in the family."

"It skipped Mary, then," Grace replied, ignoring the obvious reference to her own stubborn independence, and shut her mother's door.

"Mary's more like your grandmother," Mother conceded when Grace entered the car on the driver's side. "She'd rather ask for help than try something on her own."

"I'm going to tell her you said that."

"Go right ahead. She knows it's true."

Grace laughed and started the car. As they drove to church, Mother updated Grace on all the news from the neighborhood—who had died, who had moved away, who had gotten married, and who had welcomed new babies into their families. Several of Mother's friends had asked about Grace, and Grace grew tense until her mother assured her that no one knew of her MS. "They're just being friendly," her mother said. Grace had never known her mother to lie, but she couldn't help wondering if Mother had inadvertently let clues fall, not only by what she told her friends, but by what she didn't say.

The church was full, as it usually was on Thanksgiving, mostly with older couples Mother's age, some accompanied by grandchildren. Grace listened to the preacher's words of forgiveness and gratitude and reflected ruefully on how well they applied to her that day, as if the preacher knew about her impending reunion with Gabriel and had written the sermon especially for her. In the spirit of the day, she promised herself that she would be civil to him.

Afterward, as Grace and her mother drove to Helen's home, Grace said, "Did Helen tell you Gabriel will be joining us?"

"Yes, she did, although I think she wishes he wasn't," Mother said. "She wouldn't have allowed it, except that I told her if you didn't object, neither should we. That's very Christian of you, Grace, to allow him to come. Forgiveness is never easy, and he's done much to be forgiven for."

Grace was silent. "I don't know if I've forgiven him," she finally admitted. "Justine grew up without a father, and nothing he does now can change that. I don't know if I can ever forgive him for that."

Mother patted her on the arm. "You're willing to try. That's a step in the right direction."

Her voice was reassuring and kind, so Grace didn't have the heart to tell her she had only reluctantly allowed Justine to invite Gabriel, and then only because she didn't want to ruin Joshua's holiday. That, and because she couldn't bear to let Justine think she was keeping him away out of jealousy.

When they reached Helen's home, the driveway was already full of cars and others were parked along the street in front of the house. When they opened the front door, they were greeted by hugs from aunts and uncles and cousins, as well as the delicious aromas of roasting turkey, dressing, and other tempting dishes. Grace and her mother brought their contributions to the meal into the kitchen. Before she could slip away to search for Justine, Helen tossed her an apron and put her to work. Sometime later Justine entered, carrying Joshua on her hip. "Tell Grandma 'Happy Thanksgiving,'" she coached as she held him out for Grace to take. Joshua obediently obliged as best he could, and Grace laughed and hugged him.

"You're my good boy," she said, kissing him on the top of the head. She set him down, and as he toddled off to the living room in search of his cousins, her eyes met Justine's. "Is he here?"

"He's in the other room. Last I saw him, he was talking to Uncle Steve. I think I'll join them."

Justine left, and Grace was about to resume mashing the potatoes when Helen took the masher from her and said, "You might as well get it over with." She gave Grace a knowing look and tilted her head in the direction Justine had taken.

Grace nodded and untied her apron. Helen was right; it would be better to face Gabriel for the first time now rather than across the supper table. She went into the crowded family room, stopping to chat or exchange hugs as she worked her way across the room. She spotted her mother and Justine in the crowd, but Gabriel was not with either of them.

In the living room, Gabriel was seated on the sofa beside Grace's sister Mary, with Joshua on his lap. His back was to her, so only Mary saw Grace enter. "Um, I just remembered," she said, rising. "I told Helen I'd help set the table."

Gabriel must have seen Mary's gaze wander, for he turned and spotted her. "Grace. Hi." He set Joshua down in Mary's place and stood. He smiled, hesitantly, and extended his hand.

She had to force herself to shake it. "Hello, Gabriel." Her voice sounded calm and even, which astonished her. Somehow, after so much time, she had expected not to recognize him. He was thinner, and the mustache was gone, and there was a slump to his shoulders that she had not seen before, but except for the gray in his hair, little else about him had changed.

He flashed a nervous smile. "You're looking well."

"Thank you." Only then did she realize that one by one, the other family members had slipped out of the room, except for Joshua, who sat quietly playing with an Oscar the Grouch doll. Grace picked up her grandson and sat down on the sofa, placing him in her lap. "I see you've met Joshua."

Gabriel took that as his cue to sit beside her. "Yes, we're getting to be good friends. Aren't we, Josh?" In reply, Joshua grinned up at his grandfather.

What a shame you missed his first two years, Grace thought. What a shame he had missed most of Justine's life. Justine had been just as beautiful a child. "So, are you back in town for good, or just passing through?"

"My passing through days are over, Grace," he said quietly, as if she had rebuked him. "I'm working as an adjunct professor at the city college."

"That's right. Justine said you were teaching again."

"Just nights. During the days I work as a drug and alcohol abuse counselor."

Her eyebrows shot up. "Really."

"You're thinking, 'Physician, heal thyself.' I've been sober for ten years."

It angered her that he assumed he still knew her well enough to guess her thoughts. It flustered her that he had guessed correctly. "I'm happy for you."

"It wasn't easy, but I made it." He reached out and stroked Joshua's head. "Not soon enough, I'm afraid. I missed out on so much."

More than you'll ever know, Grace wanted to snap at him, but she was too angry to speak.

"I wish that I could make it up to you." He rested his elbows on his knees, unable to meet her eyes. "I can't say I know what you went through, but I can imagine. I'm sorry I wasn't there for you, Grace. For Justine. I wish things had been different. I can't change them now, but I would if I could. I'm sorry."

She watched him, speechless. Ever since he had come back into Justine's life, Grace had hungered for his apology, but now that she had it, she felt empty.

Gabriel looked up, his eyes pleading. "I don't expect you to forgive me, and I don't expect to pick up where we left off—"

Grace laughed, once, loud and sharp. She hadn't meant to, but it escaped before she could restrain it. Pain flickered in his eyes, and he turned away again. "I'm sorry," Grace said. "But what you said was . . . unexpected."

"All I meant was, I'd like to be a part of your life again. We have a history. We have a child and a grandchild. If you're willing, I'd like us to be friends."

"I don't see how that's possible," Grace said, just as Helen called everyone in for supper. She picked up Joshua and carried him into the dining room without sparing Gabriel another glance.

Helen's dining room wasn't large, but somehow all forty-two members of the family, four generations from Mother, the eldest, to Joshua, the youngest child, crowded into the room. Justine came to Grace and took Joshua, giving her a questioning look that Grace pretended not to see. "Mother's going to say the blessing," Helen called out over the din of voices, which immediately quieted. The family members joined hands and bowed their heads as Mother began to speak.

Even in her anger, Grace enjoyed the meal. Helen was easily the best cook among them, and the others' contributions were nearly as delicious. Gabriel spoke to Grace only once, to compliment her on the rolls. Grace thanked him but did nothing to prolong the conversation.

When the meal was nearly over, Mother suggested, as she did every year, that everyone at the table tell the others what they were especially thankful for that year. "I'll begin," she said. "I'm thankful that once again we've all gathered together to celebrate this special day. It does my heart good to have my whole family around me." Then, with a quick glance at Grace, she added, "I'm also especially thankful that we all continue to enjoy good health, especially Grace."

There were murmurs of assent, and Grace felt her face growing hot. Mother knew she wished to keep her illness secret from all but family. Had she forgotten Gabriel was there?

The others expressed similar sentiments, and she herself said something about the blessings of Justine and Joshua, but she was distracted, waiting with faint dread for what Gabriel would say. He didn't disappoint. "I'm grateful to be alive," he said, and received affirming nods in response. "I'm also deeply thankful that Grace and Justine have given me the opportunity to earn their forgiveness."

Grace couldn't bring herself to look at him.

After dessert, Gabriel caught her alone in the family room. "I meant what I said," he said without preamble, in a quiet voice so no one would overhear. "Please give me a chance to earn your forgiveness. Don't put this off. We don't have a lot of time."

She felt as if an electric shock had shot through her, freezing her to the marrow. She stared at him. "What did you say?"

He looked back at her, and this time she knew what he was thinking.

"You know, don't you?"

He hesitated, then nodded.

Grace felt all the blood rush to her head. "I have to . . ." She struggled to stand, and brushed off Gabriel's hands when he tried to assist. He knew. Justine had told him, Justine or someone else. "I have to go."

"Grace . . ."

Blinded by tears, she stumbled into the hallway and fumbled in the closet for her coat and purse. She threw the coat over her shoulders and raced to her car, blocking out the alarmed voices calling after her, calling out her name. He knew. He knew, and she could not bear for him to know.

✦

Adam was enjoying his Thanksgiving break so much that not even the stack of geometry tests that needed grading could dampen his spirits. On Thursday his family had gathered at his mom's house for their annual feast, and he had spent the day eating, playing football in the backyard with his cousins and brothers, and watching games on television. Whenever she had been able to catch him alone, Nana had pestered him about Megan, and he teased her by refusing to answer her questions. He didn't tell her about their email exchanges, which he had come to expect and anticipate every day, or the night they had dined out together, or their upcoming meeting on Saturday, when he, Megan, and Robby planned to have lunch and see a movie. Nana was so annoyed at him that she forbade him to have any of her apple pie, which she knew was his favorite, but at the end of the day she relented and sent him home with the two pieces that somehow had been left over.

The next day, Adam graded half of the tests and began writing his final exams, went to the gym, and worked around the house a bit, relaxing, but watching the clock in anticipation of the next day. He was tempted to call Megan, but not wanting to interrupt her holiday, he settled for sending her an email message telling her he was looking forward to seeing her and Robby. When he checked his email that evening, she had not yet responded. He was disappointed but told himself she was probably at her parents', where she didn't have access to a computer.

On Saturday, they met at noon in a restaurant in Monroe. Megan had offered to meet him halfway, as they had before, but Adam wanted to spare her the drive. Robby seemed delighted to see Adam again, but when Adam asked him about school, Robby withdrew. Quickly Adam dropped the subject and asked him about video games instead. His familiarity with some of the games, though only slight, pleased Robby greatly. "Mom doesn't like video games," Robby told him sorrowfully, and Megan laughed.

After the movie, Megan suggested they go to an orchard on the outskirts of town for apple cider and cinnamon doughnuts. As they finished eating, Megan asked Robby to pick them a few apples to take home. When Robby ran off, Megan turned to Adam and said, "He seems to like you."

"I like him."

"Are you still interested in the arrangement we discussed earlier?"

Adam smiled at her sudden formality. "Of course."

"It wouldn't be a burden?"

"Not at all. In fact, it would give me an excuse to have some fun every once in a while."

Megan smiled then, and Adam realized he had been waiting all day for her to smile at him alone. "Okay, then. We'll see if Robby's willing."

When Robby returned with a basket full of apples, Adam asked him if he liked football. Robby winced and said, "Watching, not playing."

"How come?"

Robby glanced at Megan before answering. "The other kids in my class are bigger than me, and I get crunched a lot. I like kicking, though. I'm good at that. And I don't get tackled so much."

"Really? How good are you?"

Proudly Robby recited his statistics, which were remarkably good for a kid his age. "I'd like to see that," Adam said. "Would you show me? Maybe we could get together next weekend and practice."

Robby looked pleased. "That would be fun." He looked up at Megan. "Can we, Mom?"

"I have some things to do, but why don't the two of you go?" She glanced at Adam. "If that's all right with you?"

They arranged that next Saturday afternoon Adam would pick up Robby at Megan's place and they would kick the football around at the local middle school for a few hours. Then, to Adam's disappointment, Megan said it was time to go.

She paid for the apples, and as they walked to the parking lot, Megan allowed Robby to run ahead to the car. "Thank you," she said, offering Adam her hand to shake. "I appreciate this."

"It's my pleasure," Adam said, and meant it.

Megan rewarded him with another smile, and as she got into her car, she called out, "I'll see you online."

Adam waved good-bye and watched them drive off before getting into his own car. The memory of her smile lingered as he drove home. He liked Megan. He liked her quiet gentleness that would unexpectedly break into humor; he liked the way she was with Robby, the way she patiently listened to him and thoughtfully considered what he said. He liked the way her face lit up with love when she hugged her son close, and he found himself wishing she would look at him with such fondness.

When he returned home, there was a message on the answering machine, and for a moment Adam hoped it was Megan calling to talk and feared it was Megan canceling their plans for next Saturday. He never would have expected the voice that played back on the tape, a voice he knew so well but had not heard in so many months.

"Adam, it's me," Natalie said. "Are you there? Please pick up." A lengthy pause. "Come on, I know you're mad at me, but don't play games, okay? Not today." Another pause, and then a sigh. "Okay, I guess you're not home. I was just calling . . . well, I was just calling to see how you're doing. And to wish you a happy Thanksgiving." Another pause, and then she quickly added, "You don't have to call me back. I'm not home anyway. I'm in Aspen. It's great here. You'd love it. Well, anyway, I hope you had a good holiday." She hung up.

Stunned, Adam stood staring at the answering machine before playing the message again. It was not his imagination; Natalie sounded lonely. Sad, too. He sat down heavily on a kitchen stool and wondered what had prompted her to call, from her skiing vacation, no less. Could she have changed her mind? The thought, which once he would have greeted with relief and joy, now made him uncomfortable. As much as their breakup had wounded him, he knew now that they were not well suited for each other, just as Natalie herself had said when she returned the engagement ring. He hoped she wasn't thinking about . . .

He shook off the thoughts. Of course she wasn't thinking about getting back together. She was just calling to wish him a happy Thanksgiving. Maybe she had started to feel some remorse over the way she had treated him, but he was positive she felt nothing more than that. Not Natalie.

He rewound the tape and went into the second bedroom he used as an office to finish checking the geometry tests. By the time he went to bed, he had almost forgotten Natalie had called.

The next morning, he fixed himself some breakfast and read the paper before getting ready for church. He usually skipped the Sunday business section, but a prominent headline caught his eye: "Lindsor's Stock Down and Rumors of Buyout."

Lindsor's—the department store Natalie worked for. Adam read the article, dismayed to learn how declining sales had hurt the store but had made it a more attractive purchase for a large chain. Spokespeople acknowledged that representatives of the two stores were in contact but would neither confirm nor deny that an offer had been made. Regarding the rumors that some stores would be closed and others consolidated—resulting in hundreds of layoffs—they had no comment.

Adam shook his head in regret, thinking of Natalie. The weeks between Thanksgiving and Christmas were usually her favorites, frantically busy with sales and social gatherings. The frenzy burned out some of her colleagues, but the stress and excitement suited her, and she was in her element. This stress was different, though, and it pained him to think of her wondering if the job she had fought so hard for was in jeopardy.

No doubt that explained the odd tone in her voice; surely she would have known of the situation before it made headlines. Should he call her to offer some sympathy, to give her a chance to vent? He considered it before remembering that she was out of town. He couldn't reach her if he wanted to, and somehow that filled him with relief. They had promised each other they would be friends, but she couldn't expect more from him than that.

Nine

With a sigh, Vinnie set aside the letter Donna had enclosed in her Christmas card. She wished she could drop everything and fly off to Minnesota to comfort her friend. Not only had Lindsay canceled her plans to visit her family for Thanksgiving, but she hardly talked to her mother anymore, even on the phone. "I feel like she's pulling away from us," Donna had written. "I suppose this is natural, considering she's going to be married in a few months, but it makes me heartsick."

Vinnie wanted to write back with words of encouragement but could find nothing encouraging in the little she knew of this young man Brandon. Vinnie didn't consider Lindsay's withdrawal at all natural; in her experience, weddings brought families together rather than wedging them apart. Even Natalie had warmed to her new in-laws and Adam's extended family in the months leading up to the expected ceremony, and that engagement had been a disaster from the beginning. Vinnie had never met Lindsay, but the young woman's behavior seemed odd, even troubling, and her fiancé's was worse.

Vinnie didn't want to stir up trouble by alarming Donna with warnings that might be unfounded, but she suspected Donna's worries had merit. Donna was a kind, generous, and loving woman, not the sort to cling jealously to her daughter rather than allow her to make a new life with the man she loved. Even now, she continued to give Brandon the benefit of the doubt, long after others—Vinnie included—would have become suspicious enough to confront him, or at least to speak to her daughter.

Donna would have to approach Lindsay with much more tact than Vinnie herself could have mustered, but keeping silent any longer wouldn't do Donna's nerves any good, and if it turned out there was some reason why Lindsay and Brandon shouldn't marry, the sooner they found out, the better. She had learned that from Adam and Natalie.

Vinnie knew her Cross-Country Quilter friends wondered why she was so eager to see Adam married, or even dating, so soon after the breakup of his engagement. They thought she innocently believed that once married, everyone lived happily ever after. But they misunderstood her. She had learned from her own parents that happy marriages could end too soon in grief; her own marriage had taught her that even happy unions had ups and downs, and that each day required a renewed commitment to make it work. But from Aunt Lynn and Lena she had learned that love and companionship were essential for any other kind of happiness.

Vinnie had married young, at seventeen. She had known Sam for less than a year, but had known almost from the start that she loved him and that he was the only man she would ever love.

They met at a dance on a Friday evening in early June. Vinnie was dating another young man at the time, but the passing years had faded her memories of a time she felt affection for any man other than Sam, so that sometimes, even when she concentrated, she could hardly picture his face. Sam, too, had a girlfriend, and they were very close to getting pinned. They might have married one day if Sam's girlfriend had not caught a bad cold on the same weekend Vinnie's boyfriend was out of town visiting relatives, and if their respective groups of friends had not cajoled them into going to the dance anyway.

Vinnie had seen Sam before, since his girlfriend attended her school and Sam had occasionally escorted her to school functions. What Vinnie didn't know until later was that Sam had seen her before, too, and thought she had a wonderful laugh and the most beautiful face he'd ever seen—an observation he kept to himself rather than share with his girlfriend.

When Sam saw Vinnie at the dance, he had to wait through several songs until she was free. Then he quickly stepped in and invited her to dance. His girlfriend didn't like to swing dance, so he wasn't as polished as some of the other young men, but Vinnie was an excellent dancer and made up for any of his shortcomings. He liked the way her eyes lit up with fun as they danced, and so he stayed by her side for the next dance, and the next, and before either of them realized it, they had spent the entire evening together.

Vinnie had enjoyed dancing with the tall, handsome man with the slow smile and the easy manner, but since he was three years older than she and was dating a senior from her own school, she didn't expect to dance with him again after that night. She certainly didn't expect to run into him the next day at the library, where she studied every Saturday afternoon with her friends. When he asked her to go out with him, at first she was too startled to reply. For one quick, guilty moment she thought of her boyfriend, but she accepted.

When one date led to another and they began to go steady, the senior girls at her school rallied around their scorned, heartbroken friend and made life difficult for Vinnie. Their eyes narrowed as Vinnie passed them in the hallways, and the whispers followed her wherever she went. Tramp, they called her, assuming that she must agree to all sorts of sinful things in the dark with Sam. Only that could have turned his head, when he had been so faithful for three years. Three years Sam and his girlfriend had been together, and yet he had broken off the relationship within a week of meeting Vinnie. A week!

Vinnie let her own boyfriend down more gently, and he took it bravely, which made Vinnie feel worse. But only for a little while: she was young, after all, and she was in love, and all that mattered was Sam and herself and the future they had begun to talk about, first tentatively, and as time passed, with greater assurance and hope.

Then the whole world erupted in war, and the United States was drawn into it. Sam, at twenty, was eligible for the draft, and for the first time since meeting him, Vinnie feared all their hopes and plans had been in vain. She cried when he asked her to marry him, because she knew his haste came from an all too plausible concern that if they did not marry soon, they might never have the chance. Aunt Lynn gave her blessing but cried a little over Vinnie's leaving school. She also urged Vinnie to ask her father to give her away, because although she rarely saw him, he was, after all, the only father she had. Vinnie's instinct was to retort that he had given her away a long time ago, but because Aunt Lynn wanted it, she agreed.

Within weeks Lena had whipped up a wedding dress and Aunt Lynn had planned a modest celebration. Her father escorted Vinnie down the aisle and gave her hand to Sam, then exacted a tearful promise that Sam look after his little girl. Vinnie wasn't sure what astonished her more, her father's emotion or his belief that he was relinquishing the role of her protector to Sam. If anyone ought to do that, it was Aunt Lynn, and her aunt would assume Vinnie planned to take care of herself.

But Vinnie was too joyful to dwell on the unhappiness of the past or the way her father had failed her. She danced with her father at the reception, but saved most of her dances for Sam, who had improved so much since that first swing dance they had shared that Friday night in spring, and who had since become her partner in so many greater things.

As the hour grew late, her father kissed her good-bye and tried, in his own stumbling way, to apologize. "I never wanted to send you away when your mother died," he said. "Boys I understood, but I didn't know how to look after a little girl."

Suddenly she saw him not as her father but as a man regretting his mistakes, a man who had made unfortunate choices at a time when his reason was clouded by grief. He had not meant to hurt her, and ultimately, he hadn't, because everything had worked out for the best. She embraced him, and in her heart, she forgave him.

Several weeks passed before Sam was called up. She feigned bravery for his sake and pretended to believe him when he promised her he would return. He survived the Normandy campaign when many of his friends did not, but Vinnie ached for him, wondering how long his luck would last. She prayed, alone in their apartment, and her days grew darker and more bleak as the war dragged on.

It was Lena who urged her to return to high school. At first Vinnie demurred, believing that as a married woman her place was at home, but then she began to long for her books and her friends, anything to ease the loneliness and fear of waiting. The school board rejected her application for readmittance, saying that married women were not permitted to attend classes with the unmarried girls.

But Lena, who knew something of how it felt to have one's last hope snuffed out, refused to allow Vinnie to give up. She stormed into a school board meeting and demanded that Vinnie be permitted to return. She cited Vinnie's excellent academic record and argued that their obstinance was not only unreasonable and unfair, but also unpatriotic, considering that Vinnie's husband was risking his life for his country. "You make a mockery of all the women fighting on the home front," she accused them, and said she'd see that the whole city learned of it.

They relented, and Vinnie resumed classes the next quarter. By the time Sam returned safely home from the war, she had her diploma and a job at the local library, a job she willingly gave up when their first son came along a year later. Two more sons followed, and then, at last, a daughter.

She loved all her children deeply, and knew that a mother shouldn't have favorites, but she couldn't help herself. This precious girl child, the last of her babies, was the child of her own heart. Vinnie was fierce in her determination that her daughter would never know the grief and loneliness she had known. She would protect her daughter as best she could, as long as she could, and would lavish upon her all the love and attention she herself had longed for as a motherless—and fatherless—girl. She would love her daughter and all her children as her aunt had taught her to love.

She named her daughter Lynn, and when her daughter married and bore a son and named him Adam after Vinnie's own father, Vinnie extended her vow of protection to him. She wanted Adam to be happy, to know the blessing of love as his parents and grandparents had, and to be spared the loneliness that had been the burden of the great-grandfather whose name he bore.

For she knew Adam was much like herself, unable to completely enjoy his life unless someone shared it with him. She had learned well in her eighty-two years that she could not guarantee her own happiness, much less that of someone else, but she would do what she could to care for the people she loved.

Even when that meant meddling, she told herself with a laugh. Especially when that meant encouraging them down paths their hearts had already chosen to follow.

✢

The exacerbation struck when Grace was Christmas shopping. First she couldn't feel her hand on the escalator rail, and then her legs went out from under her. If not for the man three steps below, who caught her before she could tumble to the first floor, she might have broken her neck in the fall.

Hours later, after Dr. Steiner had examined her, the pins-and-needles sensations in her hands had not yet faded, and this time they were also in her feet. She tried to walk, but could only manage a sort of slow shuffle. Her mind, too, felt numb, as it had ever since the doctor had told her she might not have a complete recovery this time and that she might have to resort to a wheelchair sooner than they had hoped.

When Justine arrived, her mouth tight with worry, Grace couldn't bring herself to repeat the doctor's bleak report, so Dr. Steiner took Justine into the hallway and explained. When she returned, Grace saw resolution in her eyes, but she also saw that her daughter was pushing a wheelchair.

"You're allowed to go," Justine said, and patted the back of the chair. "Come on. I'll help you."

Grace turned her face to the wall. "I'm not leaving in that."

"Then you're not leaving at all. Hospital regulations. You have to be wheeled out of here. I can do it, or I can get an orderly. Your choice."

At any other time Grace would have smiled to hear her own stubbornness echoed in her daughter's voice. Today she blinked back tears and allowed Justine to assist her into the wheelchair. She felt trapped and exposed as Justine wheeled her to the front desk to take care of her discharge forms and arrange to rent a wheelchair. She tried to stand, but Justine put a firm hand on her shoulder and gently held her back.

"Where's Joshua?" Grace remembered to ask as Justine drove her home.

"He's being watched," Justine said shortly, and Grace knew this meant he was with his grandfather. Grace had forbidden Justine to mention Gabriel ever since the day after Thanksgiving, when Justine admitted that she had told him about the MS.

"You promised to tell no one outside the family," Grace had shrilled into the phone. After her abrupt departure from Helen's house, Justine had been phoning Grace's loft all evening, leaving one message after another as Grace listened in on the answering machine. Grace eventually picked up only because Justine declared that if she didn't, Justine would assume she was injured and couldn't reach the phone, and would summon the police. "How could you have told him?"

"I needed to talk to someone. Can't you see that you're not the only one hurting?"

"You could have talked to your cousins. You could have talked to me."

"I can't talk to you, Mom. You won't talk about it."

Grace hung up before Justine would know she was crying. She turned off the ringer to the phone, turned down the volume on the answering machine, and went to bed, where she lay awake for hours, her thoughts in turmoil. Gabriel knew. Was that why he had been so eager to see her again, to apologize before it was too late to obtain absolution?

He was twenty years too late, Grace had told herself. Her MS had nothing to do with that.

Even with the rented wheelchair, Justine struggled to maneuver Grace from the underground parking lot to her third-floor loft. In the elevator, Justine slid the metal gate shut and reached for the lever, but then she pulled her hand away and said, "You do it." Grace didn't like the new bossiness in her daughter's voice, but she obeyed—or tried to. From her seat in the wheelchair, she couldn't reach the controls to operate the elevator.

"You'll have to do it," Grace said, her face burning.

"Who manages this building?" Justine asked. "Don't they know we have wheelchair accessibility laws in this state?"

"This building was grandfathered out." Grace wondered how she remembered that. It had never mattered to her before.

When they reached the third floor, Justine urged Grace to open the gate herself. With some difficulty Grace managed, but when Justine told her to wheel herself off the elevator, she found that the elevator had stopped just below the floor of her loft, the gap just wide enough to block forward motion. Justine had to tip the chair onto its rear wheels and give it a good shove to lift her over the barrier. Justine then pushed her into the kitchen and asked her to reach the sink, which she couldn't; then it was on to the bathroom, to the quilt studio, to the bed, with Justine growing more determined, and Grace ever more humiliated.

"All right, you've made your point," she said when she couldn't bear any more. "I'm helpless in this chair. Do you think I don't know that?"

Justine's face softened. "That's not what I've been trying to say at all." She gestured around the roomy loft. "It's this place, not you. You live in a converted warehouse. It won't meet your needs anymore."

At last Grace understood. "I'm not moving."

"Mom—"

"I mean it. I'm not leaving my home." Abruptly she pushed herself away from her daughter. Didn't Justine know her at all? Wasn't it enough that she had to sacrifice her pride, her art, her livelihood, without Justine wanting her to give up her home as well?

Justine followed and for more than an hour argued the merits of moving to a newer, more convenient apartment, but Grace refused to listen. Over the next few days, Justine persisted, bringing her brochures for attractive condos and even scheduling an appointment with a real estate agent, but Grace rebuffed every attempt to persuade her. She had lost too much of the old Grace to abandon the quirky loft and its eclectic neighborhood for some shiny new condo with smooth floors and no personality. The loft held too many memories, and she would not part with them.

By that time Grace had recovered enough to forgo the wheelchair, and on her follow-up visit to the hospital, she returned it and canceled the rest of the rental contract. She waited for Justine to tell her she had made a mistake, but Justine didn't, nor did she say anything more about leaving her home.

The next day, Grace was in her studio sketching the central motif for a new pictorial quilt when the buzzer sounded. Usually interruptions of her work frustrated her, but today she was glad for the excuse to take a break. This new quilt, a thematic interpretation of the Twenty-third Psalm, had been begun in a burst of inspiration that had since dissipated, like the seven other quilts she had tried to design since returning from Elm Creek Quilt Camp. She was almost tempted to make something using a pattern from a magazine just so she could finally begin her block for the Challenge Quilt— and have something positive to tell the Cross-Country Quilters when they asked about her progress.

Since she wasn't getting anywhere with her quilt, she gladly buzzed back, and soon heard the elevator rising to the third floor. She expected Justine or Sondra or another friend, and so she could only stand there in shocked amazement when Gabriel pushed back the gate.

"Morning, Grace," he said, hesitating in the elevator. On the floor beside him Grace saw a large toolbox, and behind him was a stack of assorted pieces of wood and metal. "May I come in?"

"What do you want?"

"I want to talk to you about this place."

"I'm not leaving."

"I know. Justine told me." Gabriel stepped out of the elevator and slowly turned around, scanning the loft. Then his eyes met hers. "Want to show me the kitchen?"

"Why?"

"Because that's where I'll start. Then the bathroom, the bedroom, and your studio. I might not get it all done today."

Grace stared at him, exasperated. "What are you talking about?"

In response, Gabriel began unloading the elevator. When she didn't move, he walked past her and found the kitchen on his own. Grace followed, only to find him measuring the height of the countertops and the width of the aisles. "What are you doing?" Grace asked, although she was beginning to suspect.

"I'm retrofitting your loft."

"The whole building was retrofitted for earthquake safety years ago."

"Not for an earthquake; in case you need that chair again."

Grace felt hot anger rise in her chest. "So Justine told you about that, too?"

Without a word, Gabriel stepped past her and returned to the elevator for some tools and two-by-fours, and before she knew it, he had set himself to work.

"I didn't ask for your help," Grace snapped.

Gabriel snorted but never paused. "If I waited for you to ask . . ." He shook his head.

"Did Justine put you up to this?"

At that Gabriel looked up. "No, this was my idea, and frankly, I don't think Justine will approve. She wants you to move, and if I adapt the loft, you won't need to. So do you want me to keep working or not?"

His directness startled the anger right out of her. "What do you know about retrofitting a loft?" she said, disguising her confusion with scorn.

"I'm a licensed carpenter. I've been working as a contractor for more than eight years."

Grace didn't know what to think. "Well, aren't you full of surprises," she managed to say. Gabriel made no reply but continued working as she stood there trying to make sense of him, wondering what to do. She didn't want to talk to him, and she felt foolish standing there watching him, so eventually she returned to her studio to complete her sketch. But she could not focus her thoughts knowing he was in the other room, so instead she toyed with her colored pencil and listened to the sounds of hammer, drill, and saw.

After two hours of this, she shoved herself away from the drafting table and went to the kitchen. Gabriel had begun widening the aisle by removing part of the countertop and was now partially hidden, his head and shoulders inside a lower cupboard. "What are you doing?" Grace asked.

"Adjusting the shelves so you can reach them from a seated position with a grabber. I thought you could move your plates and cups down here, and put some of the lighter things in the top cupboards."

Grace admitted to herself that wasn't a bad idea, but she wouldn't say so. "You don't have to do this, you know."

"I know."

Grace held back an exasperated sigh and glanced at the clock. "I was going to fix myself some lunch. Do you want something?"

Gabriel came out from the cupboard, an electric screwdriver in his hand. "I would. Thanks."

As Gabriel washed up, Grace heated some leftover bean soup and made ham sandwiches. A distant memory came to her, of standing at the kitchen counter of the home that had burned, fixing him sandwiches to eat during his breaks between classes. She pushed the thought aside and set the kitchen table, clearing away some of Gabriel's scattered tools. She started eating without him, but he joined her a few moments later, his hands and face clean, his hair combed.

"Delicious," he said, tasting the soup. "You always were a great cook."

She refused to allow his flattery to move her. "I do appreciate what you're doing."

"You're welcome." Gabriel savored a bite of his sandwich. "I know what it's like to lose a home. I've lost several. I wouldn't want that to happen to you."

To happen to me again, Grace almost corrected him, thinking of the fire, but she managed to hold it back. "What made you take up carpentry?"

"When I started to get sober, a man from my AA group was looking for someone to help in his contracting business. He offered me a chance to learn and to make some money at the same time. I was living in a shelter at the time and wanted to get a room somewhere, so I took him up on it. He said if I showed up drunk, that would be my last day of work. He was a good motivator."

"You lived in a shelter?"

"I've lived in several." Gabriel gave her an indecipherable look. "What did you think I did after I left you?"

"I . . . I assumed you stayed with friends or family."

"I did, for a while, but eventually I used up my last favor. I traveled around, stayed in LA for a while, but when my money ran out, I ended up on the streets."

He said it matter-of-factly, but Grace was transfixed with horror. In all of her frantic and lonely wondering about him, about where he was and what he was doing, she had never imagined him homeless—a homeless alcoholic on some filthy city street. "How did you ever . . ." But then she could say no more.

"How did I get back?" Gabriel prompted. Grace nodded. He sighed and sat back in his chair. "I hit rock bottom, as they say, after some long, ugly years I've been blessed with a selective memory about. The short version is that I went to a mission one day hoping for a hot meal and stumbled into an AA meeting. I thought it was a joke, at first, but eventually it started to sink in that I wasn't a lost cause. As soon as I believed that, I wanted to get better. I had a lot of setbacks, but I made it. I've been sober for ten years, and each day, I have to remind myself where I'll end up if I take another drink." He shrugged and resumed eating with a nonchalance she knew to be false, from the way he couldn't look her in the eye.

Softly she said, "I'm sorry that happened to you."

Gabriel looked up, and his eyes were full of pain. "I'm sorry this happened to you." He closed his hand over hers, where it rested on the table, and said, "No one deserves a disease like this, Grace, least of all you. When I think of all I must have put you through, it kills me. I want you to know, I let you down then, but I won't now. I'm here, and I'm going to help you in every way I can. If you let me."

His hand was warm and strong around hers, but it was not the soft scholar's hand she remembered. She thought then of how easy it would be to allow herself to accept his help, not only in retrofitting the loft so that she could keep her home, but in all the other ways she would need assistance in the future. She knew her prognosis; she knew the ultimate course of her disease; she knew that the independence she had fought so hard to win would, in the years to come, grow ever more difficult to keep. Every time she held off relying on her daughter or his sisters or her friends was a triumph; every bit of dependence she acquiesced was like losing a piece of her soul. But with Gabriel it would be different. With Gabriel it wouldn't be a matter of accepting charity because she was an invalid. Gabriel owed her.

How tempting it would be to let him take care of her, and to lie to herself when she said it was merely his penance for leaving her and Justine. It frightened her how easily she could imagine it.

She pulled her hand away. "Thanks, but my family is here for me. Adapting the loft is help enough."

He nodded, but she sensed his disappointment and prayed that he would never know how hard it had been to refuse his offer, and how essential it had been that she do so.

⚘

A week after their dinner together, Adam came to Megan's house to pick up Robby. He came inside and chatted with her, but only for as long as it took Robby to tie his shoes, throw on the coat Megan insisted he wear, snatch up his football, and race out the door. "We'll be back in a few hours," Adam said, grinning as Robby shouted for him to hurry.

When Megan shut the door, the house fell silent, and it occurred to her that she had a few hours to herself for the first time in ages. It had been so long since she had last had free time that for a moment she was at a loss for what to do. She considered reading some technical papers she had brought home from work but decided to brave the malls and go Christmas shopping instead.

Ordinarily Megan disliked shopping because she invariably had to cram two hours' worth into twenty minutes between leaving work and rushing off to pick up Robby from his grandparents'. On this outing, she browsed through the stores at a leisurely pace, listening to Christmas carols, and soon found she was enjoying herself. After selecting gifts for her parents and picking up a few things from Robby's list, she stopped by her local quilt shop, where she purchased a few fat quarters in Christmas prints to send to Donna. Afterward she stopped by her favorite bookstore and treated herself to a novel, which she began to read in the coffee shop over hot chocolate and shortbread, and continued later at home, as she soaked in a hot bath. She hadn't felt so relaxed since quilt camp.

As the afternoon waned, an unexpected loneliness crept into the quiet house, so she started the beef barley vegetable soup that she planned to have for supper with the whole wheat bread she'd purchased at the bakery next door to the quilt shop. As the soup simmered, she sat at the kitchen table and read, glancing out the window at nearly every car that passed. When Adam's car finally pulled into the driveway, she marked her place in the book and went to meet them at the door.

"Did you have fun?" she asked Robby as they came inside, red-cheeked and grinning. She hugged her son and took his football so he could unzip his jacket.

"I made a field goal from the ten-yard line," Robby said.

"Did you?" Megan said, impressed. "That's a record, isn't it?"

"For me it is." Robby grinned up at Adam. "Adam showed me a better way to kick to make it go farther."

"He didn't need much coaching from me," Adam said. "He's a natural."

"Adam says he thinks I could make the middle school team when I'm older, if I practice."

"Oh, he did, did he?" Megan gave Adam a sidelong look, picturing enormous linebackers lumbering forward to crush her child. "Well, we'll see."

"That's what she says when she means something's too dangerous," Robby said to Adam. "She thinks I'm still a baby."

"That's not true," Megan protested as they laughed. "'We'll see' means I'll think about it."

"Can Adam stay for supper? Please, Mom?"

Megan smiled, glad to be able to repay Adam for giving her the luxury of an entire afternoon to herself. "If he'd like to, he's more than welcome. We're having beef barley vegetable soup."

"Not from a can," Robby added. "Mom says that has too much sodium and preservatives."

"Homemade soup?" Adam began to remove his coat. "You don't have to ask me twice."

The soup was flavorful, the crusty bread warmed in the oven and light, perfect for a crisp early December day. Robby and Adam soon had her laughing with stories of their afternoon outdoors. She enjoyed herself so much that she was glad Robby had invited Adam to stay, and she wished she had thought of it herself. After supper, Robby helped Megan clear the table, and to her amusement, Adam began rinsing off bowls and stacking them in the dishwasher. He looked up from his work to see her stifling a laugh, and he grinned sheepishly. "It's a habit," he said, shaking water off his hands and stepping back from the sink. "Sorry."

"No, no, that's quite all right," she said, and began to help. They chatted as they worked, and when Robby was out of earshot, Megan thanked Adam for spending the day with him.

"No need to thank me. I had a great time," Adam said, but Megan wished she could do something more to show him how much she appreciated the way he had befriended her son. She wondered if he had any idea how her heart swelled with gladness to see Robby so happy.

The next Saturday, Adam and Robby went to the Books & Company bookstore in Dayton to meet J. K. Rowling, who was signing copies of the latest Harry Potter book. Megan enjoyed another relaxing afternoon on her own, finishing her Christmas shopping and working on her quilt block for the Challenge Quilt. Although she hadn't completely accomplished her goal, Vinnie had reminded her that she was only required to try, and she had certainly done that. Keith had phoned Robby on Thanksgiving; Robby's counselor said he was making progress, and he hadn't had an outburst at school since the Halloween cookie fiasco; and he was getting along wonderfully with Adam. Until recently, Megan had feared she'd never be able to complete her block without breaking the rules of the challenge, but recently, with Adam's help, she had begun to feel hope.

She began by selecting fabrics for her block and soon found a clear, rich blue floral print that complemented Vinnie's autumn leaf fabric so well that she had to admit that maybe purple wasn't so bad after all. Choosing a pattern proved to be much more difficult. The one-patch styles Megan preferred didn't suit a sampler quilt, so she didn't have a store of favorite blocks to call upon. She paged through several of her quilting books for ideas, but none of the designs or block names fit as a symbol of her accomplishment. As she finished looking through the third book, she realized that it had grown dark outside. She had lost track of time, but apparently so had Adam and Robby, for they had not yet returned.

She put her books away and hurried downstairs to start supper, but despite her late start, by the time Adam's car pulled into the driveway, she had been keeping the meal warm in the oven for a good half hour. Relieved, she went to the door to greet them.

Adam began apologizing before she could even say hello. "The event went on longer than I expected," he said. "I should have called. I didn't think of it until we were on our way home."

Robby was glowing with excitement. "We had to wait in line for hours," he exclaimed, delighted rather than annoyed, as Megan herself might have been. "There were thousands of kids there." Megan and Adam looked at him skeptically, and he quickly amended that to, "Maybe one thousand."

"I'd say at least eight hundred," Adam added, and with a single look to Megan over Robby's head, he conveyed what it had been like to wait in line among so many excited kids and their beleaguered parents all afternoon.

Megan suppressed a laugh and said, "Supper's ready if you're hungry. Adam, will you stay?"

Adam agreed, and in a few moments they were sitting around the table, eating and listening as Robby told them what questions the audience had asked and how the author had responded. Robby reverently showed Megan the autograph on the title page. He raced off to read his book as soon as he finished eating, but Megan and Adam lingered, talking about work and the upcoming holiday.

Together they cleaned up the kitchen and then continued their conversation over coffee. Before she knew it, hours had passed, and it was Robby's bedtime. Adam, who seemed as surprised by the late hour as she, hugged Robby and wished him good night. Megan walked Adam to the door and watched out the window as he drove away. Then she went upstairs to make sure Robby brushed his teeth.

When Megan arrived at work Monday morning, she sent Adam an email note telling him that she had hardly seen Robby all weekend, so engrossed was he in his book. Adam wrote back before noon, and they sent messages back and forth throughout that day and the next. By Wednesday she expected to find a note from him whenever she checked her email, which she found herself doing more frequently than usual. On Thursday, Adam suggested that the three of them go out for pizza after he and Robby went to the movies that weekend. Pleased, Megan agreed, and the rest of the week dragged as she waited for Saturday afternoon.

But on Saturday morning, Adam phoned. "Megan, it's Adam," he said, his voice so weak and hoarse that Megan didn't recognize it. "I hate to do this, but I'm going to have to cancel. I think I have the flu."

"You sound terrible."

"I feel terrible. Will you tell Robby I'm sorry?"

"Of course. He'll understand." She understood, too, and sympathized, but she couldn't help feeling disappointed. "I hope you feel better soon. Get plenty of rest and drink lots of fluids, okay?"

He coughed and groaned. "Not if it means getting off the sofa."

"I mean it. You have to take care of yourself."

"Okay, doctor," he said wearily. "I'll try."

She wouldn't hang up until he promised he'd take her advice, but his promise came so halfheartedly that she doubted he'd keep it. Her hand still on the receiver, she considered calling him back, but then an idea came to her, and she phoned her mother instead.

Robby was in his room reading the last few chapters of his Harry Potter book. "I have some bad news," she said, and waited for him to set down his book. "Adam has the flu. He can't come today." Before he could get too disappointed, she quickly added, "But I called your grandma and grandpa, and they're going to take you to the movie instead."

Robby brightened, but then he looked puzzled. "Aren't you coming?"

"No," Megan said, embarrassed. "I'm going to make sure Adam's all right."

Robby agreed that this was a good idea. Vinnie had given her Adam's address months earlier, and Megan obtained directions to his house from an internet mapping site. Before long she had dropped off Robby at her parents' house and was on her way to Cincinnati.

Adam's house was a red-brick colonial with black shutters on a quiet street in the northern part of the city. Megan parked in the driveway and hesitated before knocking on the front door, wondering if she had made a mistake by coming there. She considered jumping back in the car and driving home, but Adam might have seen her from the window, and she didn't know what she would tell Robby when he asked how his friend was doing, so she shoved her worries aside and knocked.

She waited, but there was no answer. She knocked again, louder, and then rang the doorbell. Finally she heard someone fumbling with a lock, and the door swung open to reveal Adam, unshaven and pale in gray sweatpants and a long-sleeved T-shirt. He looked even worse than he had sounded on the phone.

"Oh, no," Megan said, appalled. "I should have let you sleep."

Somehow Adam managed a bleary-eyed smile. "Megan," he said, and he sounded glad to see her. "Didn't you see the quarantine sign?"

"I'm sorry I got you up."

"No, no, that's okay." He opened the door wider. "Come in, if you aren't afraid of the plague."

Megan entered the foyer, her face growing warm. "I thought I'd check in on you to make sure you don't need anything." She looked past him into the living room, where she saw a pillow and a quilt on the sofa, but nothing, not even an empty water glass on the end table, to indicate he had followed her directions. She folded her arms and regarded him with stern amusement. "Have you been taking fluids?"

"I was just going to get myself a glass of orange juice."

"A likely story." She spun him around and gave him a gentle push in the direction of the sofa. "Go lie down. I'll bring you some."

Adam nodded meekly and shuffled off, and as Megan found the kitchen, she heard him groan as he returned to the sofa. She opened the refrigerator door and sighed at what she found there—or rather, what she didn't find. There was a half-empty gallon bottle of milk, some condiments, two Chinese takeout containers—no orange juice, and nothing she could use to make him something nutritious to eat. "Don't you buy groceries?" she called to him, and received a weak apology in return.

Megan found a tea bag in a cupboard, but no kettle, so she boiled water in a saucepan and poured it into a mug. As the tea steeped, she took inventory of the kitchen and made a shopping list. When the tea was ready, she carried it to him and said, "I'm going to run to the grocery store. Is there anything you need?"

"A new set of lungs and some sinuses would be nice." He took a drink of the tea. "Thank you. This is great."

"I'll be back soon."

"Wait," he called after her. "The front door locks automatically. There's a spare key in the drawer of that table in the entry."

"I found it," Megan called back after a brief search. "Drink your tea and try to rest. I'll be back soon."

She tucked the key into her purse and drove to a grocery store she had passed on her way to the house, where she bought more milk, some tea and honey, a quart of orange juice, crackers, and the ingredients for chicken noodle soup. When she returned to Adam's home, she let herself in with the key as quietly as possible, left the grocery bags in the kitchen, and tiptoed into the living room to check on him. He was asleep, the empty mug on the floor beside the sofa.

Megan decided sleep was probably better for him than a glass of orange juice, so she carried the mug into the kitchen and left Adam alone while she prepared the soup. She checked in on him from time to time while the soup simmered, but with the exception of a few fits of coughing, he slept peacefully. She remembered seeing a newspaper on the front porch and went outside for it, then pulled up a stool and read it at the kitchen counter, pausing every so often to check the pot on the stove. Just as she decided the soup was finished, the phone rang, startling her with its abrupt shattering of the silence.

She snatched up the receiver, hoping the noise hadn't woken Adam. "Hello, Wagner residence." There was a pause, and then a dial tone.

As Megan hung up, she heard Adam call to her from the other room. When she joined him, he was sitting up weakly. "Who was it?"

"A wrong number, I guess. They hung up. Was it all right that I answered? I was hoping you'd sleep through it, but maybe I confused them."

"That's fine, thanks. I've been getting a lot of hang-up calls lately, mostly on my answering machine. I think something's wrong with my line." He paused. "What is that wonderful smell?"

"Chicken noodle soup. Are you hungry?"

"I didn't think I would be, but I am." He started to get up, but Megan ordered him to stay where he was, and she brought him a bowl of soup, some crackers, and a cup of tea. When she returned with soup and tea for herself, Adam had settled back against the sofa cushions, eyes closed. At first she thought he had fallen asleep again, but then he opened his eyes and said, "This is without a doubt the best soup I've ever tasted."

Pleased, Megan settled herself on the floor beside him. "Thanks. It's my mother's recipe."

"I don't think I'll ever be able to eat soup from a can again."

"That's my mission in life, to remind people of how food tastes when it's not made in a factory."

He laughed, but the laugh turned into a cough, and he fumbled for the box of tissues on the end table. "How's Robby doing?" he asked when he was able to talk again.

"He's almost finished with the book you bought him last weekend. Which reminds me, I need to pay you back for that."

"You're kidding, right?" He nodded at his bowl, now nearly empty. "After all this?"

"How about if I leave you the leftovers, and we'll call it even?"

Adam agreed, then finished his soup and set the bowl on the end table. Still weak, he lay down on the sofa again, then watched her as she finished her meal and placed her empty bowl beside his. "Do you want any more?" she asked.

"Not now." His eyes were still red-rimmed, but he looked more comfortable and rested. "How do you do it?"

"How do I do what?"

"How do you do everything you do so well? You're a rocket scientist, a real one, you're a wonderful mother, you're beautiful, and you make homemade soup. It's hard to believe you're real."

"I think we should take your temperature. You're delirious."

"I mean it." He watched her so steadily that she wanted to look away, but found herself unable to. "I would really like to kiss you right now, but I don't want to give you the plague."

Megan's heart jumped, but she said lightly, "I don't think you have the plague."

"Whatever it is, it's killing me, because otherwise I could be kissing you." He considered. "Of course, without this fever, I probably wouldn't have started this conversation."

"Probably not," Megan said gently.

"I still wish I could kiss you, though."

Her eyes locked on his, Megan slowly kissed her fingertips and pressed them to his cheek. He raised his hand and held it over hers, then clasped it and brought it to his lips and then to his heart. Then, slowly, his eyes closed, and he fell asleep again.

Megan eased her hand free, then returned to the kitchen, where she stored the leftovers and washed their dishes. When she finished, she poured Adam a glass of orange juice, placed it on the end table, and sat down on the sofa beside him. She woke him by touching him lightly on the shoulder and telling him she had to go.

"I wish you could stay," he murmured.

"So do I," she said. "But Robby's waiting."

"Would you tell him I'll see him next week?"

"Are you sure? So close to Christmas?"

"Of course."

"I'll tell him." She squeezed his shoulder and stood up.

"Megan—"

"Yes?"

"Thanks for everything. The soup, the company—everything."

Megan smiled at him. "It was my pleasure."

Outside, night had fallen, and light flakes of snow were drifting down and dancing in the winter wind. She closed her eyes and raised her face to the darkened sky, feeling snow crystals fall like kisses, cool and gentle upon her skin. She almost laughed out loud. "Snow crystals," she whispered, knowing at once what block she would create to represent the changes she wanted to make, and was making, in her life. Snow like a soft quilt blanketing the earth, clean, fresh, and new, as hopeful as a mother's dreams for her child.

Donna's first thought when she woke Christmas morning was that Lindsay was coming home. Her heart light, she threw off the covers and hurried to shower and dress. Lindsay was coming home, and they'd have an old-fashioned family Christmas as they always did, Brandon or no Brandon.

She sang carols as she made blueberry pancakes for breakfast, anticipating the day with great joy. She had spent Christmas Eve baking, and the whole house still smelled of gingerbread and apple pie. The tree in the living room was beautifully decorated and surrounded by colorfully wrapped gifts, snow was falling outside, and the day promised to be festive and fun, full of love and laughter with the people she loved most.

Paul and Becca came downstairs for breakfast, smiling and teasing each other. Paul liked to pretend that Becca still believed in Santa Claus, and Becca went along with it to amuse him. "I think I heard reindeer on the roof last night," he said, and Becca bounced up and down in her chair as if she were six rather than sixteen. Donna laughed, enjoying their closeness, and told herself that Lindsay's presence was all she needed to make the day complete. She brushed aside any worry that Lindsay would cancel as she had at Thanksgiving. Lindsay would be there; Donna refused to believe otherwise.

But when the phone rang and Becca answered, her heart began to pound. She prayed it was her brother calling from California to wish them a happy holiday, but when Becca told her flatly that Lindsay was on the line, she steeled herself for the worst. "Merry Christmas, honey," she said with forced cheerfulness. "I thought you'd be on the road by now."

"Merry Christmas, Mom." Lindsay's voice sounded strained. "I thought we would have left by now, too, but we're running late."

"You're still coming, aren't you?"

"Of course. I wouldn't miss Christmas. What time were you planning to have dinner?"

"Around two."

"Okay. We'll be there by one thirty."

"But we were going to open presents first."

"Can we do that after?" Donna heard a low voice speaking in the background, and a hollowness while Lindsay covered the mouthpiece and murmured a response. "It won't take long, will it?"

Donna's throat tightened. "Tell Brandon it will take as long as it takes. It's Christmas, and I'm not rushing through it to please anyone."

Lindsay was silent for a moment. "Okay. We'll be there at one thirty. Bye, Mom. See you soon." She hung up.

"Is she canceling again?" Paul asked.

"No. She'll be here."

Becca looked relieved, but Paul merely nodded grimly.

Donna pretended that nothing was wrong and went about fixing Christmas dinner. *They're only delayed,* she chided herself. Anyone could be delayed driving in Minnesota in December. She was overreacting. But Paul and Becca also seemed ill at ease, for instead of returning to the family room to watch Christmas parades on television, Paul put carols on the CD player, and they stayed in the kitchen, assisting her when she asked, and talking about some of their favorite Christmases of the past.

At a quarter before two, Brandon's car pulled into the driveway. "They're here," Becca called out, running to the front door to meet her sister. Lindsay entered, shaking snow from her blond hair, carrying gifts in one arm and hugging Becca with the other. Paul went to greet her, too, but Donna hung back in the kitchen, listening to the reunion in the foyer with uncertain relief. Because of Lindsay's phone call, she had expected Brandon to be in one of his bad moods, the kind he always seemed to be in whenever Donna phoned her daughter. She dreaded that he would be unpleasant and ruin the holiday.

But when Lindsay led Brandon into the kitchen, he was smiling, and after Lindsay hugged her, Brandon did as well. "Merry Christmas," he said cheerfully. "Thanks for having us. Everything smells great." His enthusiasm was so unexpected that Donna could just barely manage to stammer a Christmas greeting in reply. She caught Paul's eye, and he shrugged, clearly as surprised as she was.

Brandon asked Becca to show him to the Christmas tree so he could leave some gifts beneath it. Lindsay watched them go, then turned to give her mother another hug. "I'm sorry we're late."

"It's all right," Donna said, and now that Lindsay was there, it was. She held her daughter at arm's length and looked her up and down. "Goodness, honey, you're getting so thin."

Lindsay rolled her eyes, smiling. "No, I'm not. You say that every time I visit."

Donna let it go, but Lindsay did look thinner, and she had always been slim. Her face looked tired, too, as if she'd been ill or had slept poorly. "You need a good home-cooked meal," she said, wishing that Lindsay would be spending the night in her old bedroom so Donna could see to it she had a hearty breakfast, too.

The turkey was ready, so Donna and her daughters quickly set the dining room table with the good china and served the meal. Her family praised her cooking, as they always did, declaring this Christmas feast the best yet. For his part, Brandon said her turkey was perfect and her stuffing the best he had ever tasted. Pleased in spite of herself, Donna thanked him, and gradually, as he joined in the dinner conversation as pleasantly as she could have wished, her apprehensions ebbed away. She had to admit that Brandon was handsome and charming, and she understood why her daughter was attracted to him. The worst she could say was that he tended to interrupt when others were speaking, but she could hardly condemn Brandon for something Paul had done to her at least twice daily throughout their nearly twenty-five years of marriage.

After supper, Donna, Lindsay, and Becca cleaned up the mess while Paul and Brandon went into the family room to watch the last quarter of a football game. From the kitchen Donna heard them talking and, every so often, laughing out loud. "They seem to get along well," Donna remarked to Lindsay, who glanced toward the family room and nodded in a distracted way as she wiped off the countertop.

When they finished tidying the kitchen, Donna and her daughters joined Paul and Brandon in the family room to exchange presents. Lindsay explained their tradition to Brandon: The youngest person would give a present to the second youngest, who would unwrap the gift and then give a gift to the next oldest. When the oldest person had received and opened a gift, he would give a gift to the youngest. The pattern would repeat, each person giving a gift to the youngest person they had not yet given a gift to, until all the gifts were distributed.

Brandon shook his head and grinned. "Sounds more complicated than necessary."

"It's a tradition from my side of the family," Paul said.

"Which explains why it's so confusing," Becca added. "And why I always have to be last."

Everyone laughed, but Donna defended her husband, saying, "It's better than what we did in my family. Everyone just tore into the packages at the same time. Wrapping paper flew everywhere, and you could never see what everyone else had received. This way it lasts longer."

With the same grin, Brandon said, "That could be either good or bad, though, couldn't it?"

"Here, Becca," Lindsay said quickly. "I'm younger than Brandon. I'll start."

Becca handed her a box wrapped in red-and-white-striped paper, and for the next half hour, they opened presents one by one, with Paul's system creating occasional but easily remedied confusions, since Lindsay and Brandon had already exchanged gifts. Donna had not expected a present from Brandon, and thought that, at the most, Lindsay would include his name on her gifts, but Brandon had brought presents for everyone. To Paul he gave a computerized day planner; for Becca, he had brought a cashmere sweater set that made her squeal with delight; Donna received an elegant gold watch, set with a diamond chip.

"Brandon, this is too much," Donna exclaimed, admiring the watch. She and Paul had given him a nice sweater and a medical text on CD-ROM that Lindsay had said he wanted, and until that moment, she had considered them suitable gifts. Now she realized Brandon's family must celebrate Christmas on a much more lavish scale than the Jorgensons did, and she wondered if he would think them cheap. He seemed pleased by their appreciation of his gifts, however, so she decided not to fuss about it, and to make it up to him on his birthday.

After the last present had been unwrapped and admired, they were sitting around the Christmas tree chatting when suddenly Brandon slapped his thighs, smiled at Lindsay, and said, "Well, honey? Should we hit the road?"

"Already?" Donna protested. Brandon smiled amiably, but Lindsay looked uncomfortable. "You haven't even had dessert yet."

"Thanks, but we don't want dessert." Brandon stacked up his gifts and rose, then turned to Lindsay. "Are you ready?"

Lindsay hastened to gather her boxes. "Thanks for everything," she said, her voice apologetic. "Dinner was great, Mom."

"Dessert will be great, too," Becca said. "Mom made apple pie especially for you. Don't go yet. It's not even dark outside."

Lindsay hesitated, and glanced at Brandon, who smiled regretfully and shook his head. "I'm afraid we can't," he said. "My parents are expecting us, and it's a long drive. We're going to have dessert there." He headed for the front door. "Come on, honey. Let's go."

"At least let me pack you some gingerbread cookies," Donna said, her face growing hot. She realized with alarm that she was on the verge of bursting into tears. *It's been a nice afternoon,* she scolded herself. *Don't ruin it with a tantrum.* She hurried into the kitchen and filled a cookie tin with gingerbread men, then filled a second for Brandon's parents. By the time she joined the family in the foyer, Brandon had already left to carry their presents out to the car.

Donna hugged her daughter tightly. "I wish you didn't have to go so soon."

Lindsay clung to her, burying her face in her mother's shoulder as she used to when she was a little girl. "I'm sorry. I want to stay."

Suddenly Donna felt awful for making her daughter feel guilty. "It's all right," she said briskly, releasing Lindsay and forcing herself to smile. "I have to share you with your future in-laws. I'm sure they want to see their son as much as we want to see you."

Wordlessly Lindsay nodded and took the cookies, then gave her father and sister quick hugs before hurrying outside to the car, her coat still unfastened.

As they drove away, Donna shut the door against the winter cold.

They returned to the family room, their spirits greatly subdued. Before long Becca excused herself to go to her room to try on her new Christmas clothes, and Paul turned on the television to watch the rest of the football game. Or perhaps it was another game. Donna didn't know and she didn't much care.

She retreated to her quilt room to page through the pattern books Lindsay had given her, but before long she pushed them aside and switched on the computer. She sent Christmas greetings to Megan and Grace, and hoped they were having a happier holiday than she was. After shutting down the computer, she went to her sewing machine to work on the block she had begun for the Challenge Quilt. She had chosen the Hen and Chicks pattern as a teasing reminder of how she played the mother hen to her two girls, and how she had henpecked Lindsay into returning to the university. It had been easier to poke fun at herself then, when she thought everything would be fine as long as Lindsay continued her education. Lindsay was back in school now and doing well, but Donna felt worse than ever. Brandon was charming, but there was something else beneath the charm, something that troubled her.

"Mom?"

Donna started and turned around in her chair. Becca stood in the doorway, her expression unhappy. "Yes, honey?"

"Something's bothering me," Becca said. "First Brandon said they didn't want dessert, but then he said they were going to have dessert at his parents' house."

Donna hadn't noticed, but even now, this seemed insignificant compared to some of his other behaviors. "I suppose when he said they didn't want dessert, he meant that they didn't want it here, because they were going to eat at his parents' later."

"I thought of that, but I wanted to know for sure." Becca hesitated. "So I checked."

"You checked?"

"I called their apartment."

"Becca, you didn't."

"I couldn't help it. I was worried." She crossed the room and sat down on the floor to put her head in her mother's lap. "They were home. Lindsay answered, but when she found out it was me, she said she couldn't talk and hung up. Mom, there wasn't enough time for them to do anything but go straight home."

Donna stroked her daughter's hair. "Maybe they stopped home to pick up something on their way."

Becca pushed herself away from her mother. "Why are you always making excuses for him? Can't you see what a jerk he is? He lied to us, and Lindsay turns into a little mouse around him! Am I the only one in this family with a clue?"

"Okay, honey," Donna soothed, holding out her arms. Becca scowled at her stubbornly for a moment before allowing herself to be pulled into a hug. "I'm not as clueless as you think. I agree that Brandon . . ." She struggled to find the right words, but her feelings were so jumbled that she failed. "He does seem a bit domineering."

"A bit?"

"Well, the holidays are stressful, and you know what Lindsay says about medical school. He's under a lot of pressure. Maybe he was just having a bad day."

"All his days are bad."

"We don't know that. We don't see him every day, not the way Lindsay does. She knows him better than we do, and she wouldn't settle for anything less than a good, kind man who treated her well, would she?"

"Maybe she's confused," Becca persisted. "People do stupid things when they're in love. Remember that time in seventh grade when I called John Richardson's house fifteen times in one day and hung up as soon as someone answered the phone?"

"I thought you said it was only those two times your father caught you on the phone."

"That's what I told him, but it was really more like fifteen."

Donna laughed and hugged her. "Okay, you're right. People do foolish things when they're in love, but Lindsay is sensible, and agreeing to marry someone isn't in the same league as prank phone calls."

"They weren't prank calls. I just got too nervous to stay on the line."

"Either way." Donna sighed. "Honey, maybe Brandon isn't the man we would have picked for Lindsay, but it's not up to us. What's important is that Lindsay is happy. If they love each other, we'll only ruin things if we don't welcome him into our family."

Becca looked her straight in the eye. "Do *you* think Lindsay is happy?"

"I hope she is," Donna said carefully. "I can't believe she would marry him if she didn't believe she and Brandon would be happy together. That's not what I taught you girls."

"Maybe Lindsay didn't learn as well as you think she did."

The doubts that had nagged Donna for months now erupted in a frenzy of warning. Yes, this was what she feared, this was what she was afraid to face, that somehow she had failed to teach Lindsay something intrinsic to her future happiness. She thought back to when the girls were young, and she would overhear them swearing or discover one picking on the other. "What are you doing?" she would scold, astonished anew to discover that her angelic little girls could be vulgar or spiteful. "You didn't learn that in this house. In this house, people are kind to each other."

She longed to take Lindsay in her arms and ask her why she let her fiancé determine when she could visit her family and for how long, why she let him intimidate her into covering up his lie, why she hung up on her sister rather than let Brandon know they were speaking. *You didn't learn that in this house*—but Lindsay had learned it somewhere, and Donna was at a loss, uncertain what to do about it, how to teach her daughter at this late date something she should have been learning all her life.

Suddenly grief welled up in her throat. She wished she had the words to reassure Becca, but she couldn't even reassure herself. For months the Cross-Country Quilters had been encouraging her to trust her instincts, but her feelings were so muddled that she hadn't known what to say. Now she realized she couldn't let another day pass without speaking frankly to Lindsay. She knew she risked offending and possibly alienating her daughter by voicing doubts about the man she loved, but surely Lindsay would understand. Surely when Donna asked her if this is what was she truly wanted and reminded her that it was not too late to back out, Lindsay would know that she was speaking from the heart, as a mother who wanted only what was best for her child.

She picked up the phone beside the computer. "Are you calling her?" Becca asked.

Donna nodded and listened to the phone ringing, once, twice, a third time—and then, finally, her daughter's voice. "Hello?"

"Lindsay, it's Mom."

"Oh." Lindsay's voice lowered to a whisper. "What is it?"

"Why are you whispering?"

"I'm not," Lindsay said, and her voice returned to a normal volume, almost. "Is something wrong?"

That's what Donna wanted to know. "Sweetheart, I need to ask you something and I want you to give me an honest answer." She steeled herself.

"Are you sure you want to go through with this marriage? Are you sure you and Brandon will be happy together?"

On the other end of the line, there was only silence.

Donna quickly added, "Because if you want to call it off, it's not too late. We would all support you."

Donna waited for Lindsay's indignant reply: *How could you ask such a thing?* she might say, or *Why in the world wouldn't I want to marry Brandon? I love him.* But Lindsay said nothing. Donna heard her breathing; if not for that, she would have thought the line had gone dead.

When Lindsay finally spoke, she said, "I can't. I couldn't do that to him."

"What about you? What about what this is doing to you?"

"Mom, I can't talk right now."

"When can you talk about it? Let's go out to lunch tomorrow, honey, okay? We can—"

"I have to go," Lindsay whispered. "I'm sorry." And with that, she hung up.

Slowly Donna replaced the receiver and met Becca's hopeful gaze. She shook her head. Becca sighed and lay her head in her mother's lap again. Donna stroked her hair in silence, wondering what to do.

Eventually Becca said, "Since Lindsay doesn't seem even close to changing her mind, I guess I ought to tell you what she asked me today."

"What's that?"

"She wanted to know if you've started her wedding quilt yet."

Donna's breath caught in her throat. "Oh, dear." Her own daughter's wedding was a mere six months away, and Donna hadn't sewn a stitch of her bridal quilt. Not only that, although she had made many others for her nieces and nephews, it had never occurred to her to make one for Lindsay and Brandon.

"I didn't think you'd started it yet, so I thought I ought to warn you she's hoping for one."

"Thank you, honey."

In response, Becca hugged her, rose, and told Donna she'd be in her room. Donna nodded absently and watched her leave. Lindsay wanted a wedding quilt made by her mother's hands. Lindsay knew what a wedding quilt symbolized—enduring love, patience, commitment—and she would not ask for one lightly. She would not hope for one if she had any uncertainties about marrying Brandon.

Alone in her quilt room, Donna put away the pieces to the Hen and Chicks block, which now seemed inappropriately whimsical. She went to the bookshelf and took down one of her best-loved pattern books and began paging through it, searching for inspiration for the wedding quilt that she had somehow forgotten to begin, that she had not allowed herself to remember would be expected. She tried to find a pattern that would celebrate a lasting union between Lindsay and Brandon, but every block reminded her of her daughter, of Lindsay alone, the way she used to be—joyful and confident and self-assured, and not the apologetic, silent ghost of herself who had come home that Christmas day. She searched through one book, and then another, until all the books were scattered about her on the floor like wind-blown leaves, but she could find no way to stitch together the lives of her daughter and the man she had agreed to marry, no pattern beautiful, harmonious, and whole that had Brandon in it.

❦

For weeks, Adam had been following the grim story of Lindsor's department store in the newspaper, wondering what its gloomy prospects meant for Natalie. He knew she would be feeling threatened, angry, and frustrated—so he was not surprised when she called him a few days after Christmas and asked if he were free New Year's Eve, and if he wanted to get together.

He wasn't free; as much as he sympathized with her plight, he didn't intend to cancel his plans with Megan to spend the evening consoling Natalie. She persisted, and since he did care about her and wanted to reassure her that whatever happened at Lindsor's she would find a way to land on her feet, he agreed to meet her for dinner the first Friday evening after New Year's Day.

She picked their favorite French restaurant downtown, which pained him, as he had asked her to marry him there and hadn't returned since she broke off their engagement. He was waiting at their table when she arrived twenty minutes late, apologizing for a crisis at work that had delayed her. He rose to pull back her chair and breathed in her perfume as she seated herself. The fragrance, exotic and yet so subtle that he had almost forgotten it, flooded him with memories, none of them particularly pleasant. As he returned to his own seat, wishing he had never come, he reminded himself that he was the one who had suggested they remain friends and that right then Natalie needed a friend.

"You would not believe what a fiery pit of hell work has become," she said, shaking her head in disgust and opening the menu. Her eyes snapped with anger, which somehow enhanced her beauty. He suddenly realized she was wearing her red silk dress. It had always been one of his favorites, off the shoulder and clinging to her curves in a way that was undeniably alluring. It wasn't the sort of dress she wore to work, so she must have changed before meeting him.

"I've read about the takeover," he said, refusing to second-guess Natalie's intentions. She enjoyed the challenge of charming people; naturally she would choose a dress she knew he liked. "Do you think it's a possibility?"

"It's not only a possibility, it's happening." She paused as the waiter arrived to take their order, then added, "Whatever you see in the news is at least a week out of date. Lindsor's has already accepted their offer."

"I'm sorry," Adam said, with genuine regret. "How will this affect you?"

She shook her head and took a drink of wine. "I don't know. It's too soon to say." Suddenly she looked tearful. "They're going to close stores and cut jobs, and not just on the lower end. They're consolidating upper management, but they haven't told us yet who goes and who stays. The office has been a nightmare—everyone scrambling to prove how essential they are to the corporation and accusing everyone else of being dead weight. People I trusted, people I thought were my friends—they're just like everyone else, backstabbing and conniving."

Adam thought Natalie more than capable of holding her own in such a situation and told her so, but she shook her head. "It's different there now. I can't make alliances and can't make compromises, not when everyone knows the person you help today could be the one who has your job tomorrow."

"You'll be fine," Adam assured her. "Think of all you've accomplished there. They can't afford to lose you."

"That's what I keep telling myself, but in the meantime, I've been working on my résumé." She smiled and reached across the table for his hand. "All that socializing you always made fun of might finally pay off. The CEO and CFO like me, and that might just give me an edge."

"It couldn't hurt." Out of habit, he ran his thumb over her knuckles as he held her hand.

"I could have used your help New Year's Eve," she scolded him gently. "I attended a function and ran into the presidents of two other chains. It would have been wonderful if you had been there to charm their wives in case I'll be asking them for a job in a few weeks."

"I had other plans," Adam said, and didn't elaborate. Megan had invited him to her house, where they and Robby had some kind of delicious beef wrapped in a pastry crust for supper. Afterward they watched videos, and when Robby fell asleep on the floor in his sleeping bag, Megan snuggled up beside Adam on the sofa and they held each other. At midnight, they kissed, and it was the most gentle, warm, and loving kiss he could remember ever receiving. Then they woke Robby to wish him a happy new year, and Megan put him to bed. Adam hoped she would ask him to stay the night, but he didn't expect it, not so soon and not with her son in the house. She didn't, but she did kiss him in a way that made him hope that the night they could stay together wouldn't be too far off.

Suddenly Adam realized Natalie's hand was still in his, and abruptly, he released it. The waiter arrived then with their entrees, and as they began eating, Natalie asked him how school was going. He reminded her he was still on break and told her how the semester had gone, keeping it brief, because he knew lengthy narratives about his students bored her. To his surprise, she listened as if she were interested, and even prompted him for more details about a student she remembered from the previous year.

"You seem to be doing well," she said when he had finished, and gave him a wan smile. "I think you're doing better than I am."

"Our careers are too different to compare—"

"I wasn't talking about work. I was talking, you know, just in general."

Adam wasn't sure what she meant, but something in her expression made him uncomfortable. "You're going to be fine."

"I hope you're right." She drained the last of her wine and set down the glass, her slender fingers grasping the stem, her gaze lowered. "Adam, I've been thinking. I've had a lot of time to think about my future, and about us, and about how it ended."

In a flash of insight, he realized where she was going, and he urgently wanted her to say no more. "Natalie—"

"No, please, let me finish. I've been thinking that I made the biggest mistake of my life in letting you go. I had a good thing, and I threw it away." She hesitated. "You don't have to answer now, but please think about it. I know I hurt you, but I also know you're the kind of man who forgives. I was wondering if you thought you could ever forgive me, and if maybe we could try again."

Adam couldn't believe what he was hearing. Once he would have rejoiced to hear Natalie speak those words, but that was months ago. "Of course I forgive you," he said. "And I hope you forgive me. But you were right to break it off. It wouldn't have worked. You were just the first of us to realize it."

"But I think I was wrong." She smiled at him. Her eyes were warm with encouragement and wistful hope. "What do you say? Shall we start over?"

"Natalie, are you sure . . ." He chose his words carefully. "Are you sure you'd be saying this if not for the troubles at work?"

She sat back in her chair, stung. "How could you say such a thing?" Her eyes were bright with tears.

He felt horrible. "I'm sorry. It's just that you're upset and anxious—and maybe that's why you think we ought to try again. In hindsight, especially compared to how awful things are at Lindsor's these days, maybe our relationship seems better than it really was."

"I know how good it was," she said stubbornly. "I know you loved me once, and I think you still do. Why can't we try again? Is it because you think I'll break up with you? I promise you, I swear to you I won't."

"I can't."

"Why not? There isn't someone else, is there?" She stared at him in disbelief. "Oh, my God. There is, isn't there?"

He took a deep breath. "Yes, I'm seeing someone."

"Oh my God." Natalie raised her wineglass to her lips, forgetting it was empty. "Is she the one who answered the phone at your house?"

"What?"

"Who is she?"

"You've never met."

"Is it serious?"

He hated hurting her, but he had to be honest. "I think it might be."

Natalie was incredulous, close to tears. "Do you love her?"

He had not yet asked himself that question, but now, confronted with it, he found he knew the answer. "Yes, I think I do."

"I can't believe this." A tear slipped down her cheek, and angrily, she whisked it away with a fingertip, careful not to smudge her mascara. "Well, you must not have loved me very much if you could fall for someone else so soon."

Her words stung. "That was an ugly thing to say. You know I loved you."

"Apparently not as much as I thought," she said with a brittle laugh. "Is she prettier than me? Wait, don't answer that. I don't want to know."

"Natalie—"

"Just tell me one thing, though, would you? How long have you two been seeing each other? Were you seeing her while we were still engaged? Did it start before or after we broke up?"

"After." Adam fought to keep his irritation under control. As difficult as Natalie had been sometimes, he never would have considered betraying her. "Months after."

"Then you couldn't have been with her for very long, a few months at most. What's that compared to the years we've shared?"

"This isn't something we can negotiate." Adam kept his voice low in an attempt to prevent hers from rising even higher.

Her tears were falling freely now, and she made no attempt to conceal them. "You love her," she said. "Tell me something else. Why her? Why her, and not me?"

"Let's not do this, please."

"No, really, I want to know." She folded her hands on the table and regarded him with cool, businesslike interest, but her tears betrayed her. "Maybe this will help me in the future."

Adam didn't see how, but he was willing to do anything to help her stop crying. "She's a good person. I think you'd like her—"

"Oh, *please*. Give me some specifics."

"What do you want me to say? She's smart, she's kind, she's a wonderful mother—"

"So that's what this is all about. It's always kids with you, isn't it?" Suddenly she softened. "Look, I'm willing to consider it, okay? Maybe having kids wouldn't be so bad. I might be willing to compromise on that."

"You shouldn't compromise on having kids," Adam said, incredulous. "I never wanted you to have them for me. If you don't want them for yourself, you shouldn't have them." Suddenly he felt exhausted, drained by her anger and the effort it took to try to avoid hurting her when hurt was inevitable. "I don't know what else to tell you. I'm sorry. I hate hurting you, but I can't try again, knowing how it will turn out."

"You don't know how it will turn out."

"I do know."

"You can't. I'm different now. Things won't end the same."

But Adam was different, too, and he realized then that Natalie would never see that. "I'm sorry," he said, at a loss, knowing nothing he said would comfort her or convince her he was right.

Natalie took a deep breath, and then another, staring at the table. "All right." Her voice was hollow. "I can accept this. You're punishing me. I suppose I deserve that, after breaking off the engagement."

"That's not it." Frustration gave his voice an edge. "I care about you, I really do, but it just won't work."

"Because of her."

"Not only because of her."

Natalie sniffed scornfully, then fell silent, one graceful hand toying listlessly with her wineglass.

"I'm sorry," Adam said again, helpless.

"You can stop saying that." She took another deep breath, and then, much calmer, she met his gaze and said, "Can we at least still be friends, or will that upset your girlfriend?"

"Of course we can be friends," he said, ignoring the snide emphasis she had given the last word, unwilling to start a new argument. "I hope we'll always be friends."

She nodded and looked away. "Well." She gathered her purse and coat and cleared her throat. "If you don't mind, I think I'll be going. I'm not very hungry, and I have a lot of work to do this weekend."

Adam rose with her, but she hurried away from the table before he could say good-bye.

He sank heavily into his chair, wondering if he could have possibly made a worse mess of things. He pictured Natalie's tears and silently berated himself for causing them.

Disgusted with himself, he signaled the waiter for the check, eager to be away from there.

Ten

TO: Donna Jorgenson ‹quiltmom@USAonline.com›
FROM: Megan.Donohue@rocketec.com
DATE: 11:34 AM 1/4
SUBJECT: Re: Happy New Year!

I haven't been avoiding your questions! Yes, I did have a date for New Year's Eve, and yes, you guessed right, but I wish you would stop calling him the Apple Pie Guy.

TO: Grace Daniels ‹danielsg@deyoung.org›
FROM: Donna Jorgenson ‹quiltmom@USAonline.com›
DATE: 4 Jan 12:35 PM CDT
SUBJECT: We were right. . . .

It's true, Megan and Adam are dating!

TO: Donna Jorgenson ‹quiltmom@USAonline.com›
FROM: Grace Daniels ‹danielsg@deyoung.org›
DATE: 1:26 PM PT 4 Jan
SUBJECT: Re: We were right . . .

I can see Vinnie celebrating already. She's going to finish her Challenge Quilt block first. I wonder if I'll ever be allowed to start mine.

TO: Donna Jorgenson ‹quiltmom@USAonline.com›
FROM: Megan.Donohue@rocketec.com
DATE: 4:57 PM 1/4
SUBJECT: Re: Happy New Year!

About my earlier message . . . Don't tell Vinnie, all right? Adam and

I have been seeing each other, but Robby is almost always with us so I'm not sure how serious this is. You know how I've been disappointed before, and I refuse to set myself up for another fall.

Megan stopped, read over her message, and hit the Delete key until most of the words had been erased, leaving only:

About my earlier message … Don't tell Vinnie, all right?

She added, "Thanks" and sent the message off through cyberspace.

When Donna received it, she bit her lip and thanked heaven Vinnie didn't have email and that the mail carrier had not yet arrived to pick up the letter waiting in Donna's mailbox. Donna hurried outside to retrieve it, then returned to the computer, wondering if she should confess. There was no need, she decided. Megan had said not to tell Vinnie, not that she couldn't tell *anyone*. And it wouldn't be fair to tell Grace without also telling Julia.

January 8th

Dear Vinnie,

Just a quick note for now—I promise I'll send you a longer letter soon. Thank you for the pumpkin bread but please don't send me any more sweets or I'll burst the seams on my Sadie costumes. A pox on whoever invented the corset!

I have delightful news. I have it on very good authority (Donna) that Megan and Adam are seeing each other. Now, you have to promise me you'll keep this to yourself. Donna told me not to tell you, but I remembered what you said about a grandmother's right to know, and I couldn't bear to keep you out of the loop. I hate it when people keep secrets from me. It makes me feel so unpopular.

I'm sending some California sunshine your way.

Your quilting buddy,
Julia

PS: Remember, not a word to Donna! She'll never forgive me, and you wouldn't deprive me of my quilt tutor, would you?

Vinnie whooped with delight and danced around her living room, waving the letter over her head and cheering with such sustained enthusiasm that her next-door neighbor grew alarmed and called the Meadowbrook Village emergency line. Thus was Vinnie forced to spend a good hour of her afternoon having her vital signs checked and explaining to a concerned nursing staff that she had not lost her marbles, and if they didn't mind terribly much, she had important quilting to get back to.

Donna was in her quilt room when the phone call came that changed her life.

"May I speak with Lindsay Jorgenson, please?" the woman asked.

Her voice was pleasant and professional, but Donna didn't recognize it. A telemarketer, she decided. Everyone else knew to call Lindsay at school. "No, I'm sorry, she's not here."

"Is this her mother?"

"Yes. May I help you with something?"

"Oh, dear. I hope I didn't get you out of bed."

"I beg your pardon?" Donna asked, confused. "Who is this, please?"

"I'm Alicia Solomon, one of Lindsay's professors. Last night Lindsay left a message on my answering machine about your illness."

"My illness?"

"I hope it's nothing serious. Lindsay sounded so upset on the phone that I was worried. Is there anything I can do?"

"N-no," Donna stammered. "Actually I'm . . . feeling much better, thank you."

"I'm relieved to hear that. When Lindsay said she had to go home to take care of you—well, the entire department was concerned. She's quite a favorite around here."

"Yes . . . well, thank you."

"Please let her know she can make up the exam in my class whenever she comes back to campus. I'm sure her other professors will be willing to make arrangements for anything else she's missed."

"Oh, of course. I'll let her know."

"Thank you. Do you know when she might be returning? I'm also the faculty advisor of the drama society, and I'm wondering about the play. We just started this semester's production. We should be able to manage without our director for a few days, but if she'll be away longer—"

"She won't," Donna broke in, eager to get off the phone. "I'll have her contact you, okay?"

"I'd appreciate that. Thanks very much," the professor said. "It was nice chatting with you. I hope you're feeling better soon."

"Thank you. Me, too," Donna said, and hung up. Her heart racing, she hurried downstairs where Becca was lying in front of the television doing her homework. "Becca, do you know if Lindsay cuts classes? Would she tell you if she did?"

Becca looked up from her Spanish textbook, eyebrows raised. "You're kidding, right? Lindsay, cutting classes? Teacher's pet Lindsay?" Then she must have detected the alarm in her mother's expression, for suddenly her manner changed. "What's wrong? Who was that on the phone?"

"One of her professors."

Becca looked uneasy, but she said, "College isn't like high school. Everyone skips a class now and then. Lindsay told me so."

"But Lindsay skipped an exam." Sick at heart, Donna went to the kitchen to phone her. Becca jumped up from the floor and followed. "I think she's also skipped rehearsals. She told her professor she had to come home because I'm ill."

"Lindsay wouldn't miss a test unless she was sick," Becca said. "And that's a perfectly good excuse, so she wouldn't lie about it."

That was exactly what Donna thought. Her hands trembling, she dialed Lindsay's number. The phone rang four times before the answering machine picked up. They had changed the outgoing message; instead of Lindsay's voice, Brandon spoke in her ear, cordial yet somehow cool. "Honey, this is Mom," Donna said after the beep. "Please call me back as soon as you get this message." She hung up and glanced at the clock. Five minutes after four.

"Mom?" Becca asked in a small voice. "Is something wrong?"

"I don't know, sweetheart." She picked up the phone again and dialed Paul's cell phone number. He had told her that morning he planned to be out of the office all day, inspecting a site for an insurance claim. The phone rang only once before a recorded message announced that he was out of range. "I'm sure everything's okay," Donna assured her visibly stricken younger daughter, wishing she felt as confident as she sounded. "Lindsay must have decided to play hooky today."

"Lindsay doesn't play hooky."

Donna checked the clock, hesitated, and dialed Lindsay's number a second time, only to reach the answering machine again. Donna left another message, then hung up the phone. She wished she could talk to Paul; she wished she knew what to do. She wished the university wasn't so far away.

Donna grabbed her purse off the counter. "I'm driving down there to check on her."

"Don't go by yourself. Wait for Dad."

"He won't be home for two hours."

"Then let me come with you."

Donna was about to refuse, but when she saw the urgency in her daughter's eyes, she nodded. Donna scribbled a hasty note to Paul as Becca grabbed their coats; within five minutes, they were on the road to the Twin Cities.

The mid-January afternoon was overcast and bitterly cold, but the freeways had been cleared since the last snowfall, and only a few icy flurries blew in the wind. Never had Donna traveled from Silver Pines to the university so quickly, nor with such fear and trepidation. When they pulled into the parking lot of Lindsay's apartment building nearly an hour later, Becca pointed and said, "There's her car. I don't see Brandon's."

Nodding, Donna parked nearby. They hurried up the sidewalk, where Donna looked up at the third floor and saw a light on in one of Lindsay's windows. Becca reached the front entrance first and pressed the buzzer for her sister's apartment. A moment later, the speaker beside the door crackled with Lindsay's voice, barely audible as she asked who was there.

"It's us, honey," Donna said into the intercom. "Mom and Becca." She glanced up and saw a shadow move toward the living room curtains, then away.

"What are you doing here?"

"Professor Solomon called for you at home. You weren't answering your phone, so we came to see if anything was the matter."

Silence.

Donna buzzed again. "Honey, are you still there? Will you let us in?"

"You shouldn't have come."

Before Donna could reply, Becca put her face close to the intercom and said, "Lindsay, would you let us in, please?"

There was another silence, and then, like a sob, came Lindsay's voice. "All right." The door buzzed and clicked. Becca seized the handle and yanked it open, then raced ahead of her mother upstairs, taking the steps two at a time.

Donna reached Lindsay's front door just as Becca finished knocking. Donna heard a bolt slide back, and then the door opened a crack, enough to glimpse part of Lindsay's face but nothing of the room within.

"Please," Lindsay said, her voice oddly muffled. "Please go away before Brandon gets back."

At those words, a surge of rage filled Donna and she shoved the door open. Lindsay quickly turned her back and began to walk away, but Donna took her by the shoulders and spun her around. Behind her, Becca gasped.

Lindsay's lower lip was split and swollen, her right eye a mass of fresh bruises.

"Dear God," Donna breathed.

"I'm okay." Lindsay tried to turn away, and her hand trembled as she lifted it to brush her bangs over her face. "I'm okay."

"You most certainly are not," Donna snapped with pain and angry grief. "Did Brandon do this to you?"

Lindsay froze, then suddenly she dropped her guard. She nodded and sank into a chair, burying her swollen face in her hands.

"Becca, lock the door," Donna ordered. She marched into the bedroom and searched until she found Lindsay's steamer trunk and suitcases. Flinging open the closet, she put Lindsay's clothing, hangers and all, into the first bag, then started with the chest of drawers. Anger, blinding and white-hot, propelled her through the room. *This is not happening,* she thought as she snatched up Lindsay's belongings. *Not to my daughter.*

"I have her books," Becca said, clutching Lindsay's backpack. She was crying.

Donna snapped the first suitcase shut and gave Becca her car keys. "Put this in the car," she said. "Hurry back." Becca did as she was told, wearing the backpack and lugging the suitcase with both hands.

"Mom, don't," Lindsay begged. "Please."

"If there's anything you want from the other room, you'd better get it," Donna said, fighting to choke back her sobs. "I don't know what's yours and what's his."

"I can't leave."

"You can and you will. Today. Now."

"I can't do this to him."

"You can't do this to *him*?" Donna whirled to face her. "Did I raise you to be a punching bag? It won't get any better, Lindsay. If it's like this now, it won't get any better once you're married."

Lindsay's voice broke. "He loves me."

"This is not love," Donna said. "You know that." She had to. "You know this is not love. Where did you learn that Brandon—that *anyone* can hit you? Did your father ever lay a hand on me? Did we ever hit you?"

Lindsay shook her head, tears streaming down her lovely face, made ugly by Brandon's fists. "I don't . . ." She gulped air. "I don't . . . know what he'll do . . . if he comes home and finds me gone—"

"He won't do anything. He'll never get close enough to you to do anything." Donna went to her and held her tightly. "You have to get out of this now. It will never be any easier."

Lindsay clung to her, weeping. Donna sat down on the bed and held her, murmuring to her and rocking her back and forth—but her heart leaped into her throat when the front door slammed. Lindsay stiffened. "It's only me," Becca called, and Lindsay went limp in her mother's arms again.

"Come on." Donna pulled Lindsay to her feet and gestured toward the trunk, which Lindsay began to fill with her possessions, first dazedly, and then with gradually increasing haste. Lindsay carried the second suitcase out to the car, then returned to help her mother with the trunk. As they were maneuvering it down the staircase, Becca remembered the computer. While Donna started the car, shivering with cold and apprehension, her daughters raced back upstairs. It seemed forever until they hurried back out to the car again, Lindsay carrying the computer, Becca, the monitor.

"We had to leave the printer," Becca gasped, breathless from exertion as she climbed into the back seat.

"Forget it," Donna said. Urgency had stolen over her as the afternoon sky turned to dusk, and she expected to see the headlights of Brandon's car as he tore around the corner, at any moment. As frightened as she was, she knew Brandon was fortunate she had not seen him that night. She wanted to leave before he returned; she wanted to stay and tear his heart out as he had torn hers. She was no hen pecking haplessly after her chicks; she was a mother bear, her blood raging hot with fierce love, her overwhelming instinct to lay her teeth and claws into anything that dared hurt her cubs.

She reached over and squeezed Lindsay's hand, then raced toward home with her most precious cargo.

⚜

"Did she call the police?" Adam asked. Robby had long since gone to bed, and Megan and Adam were sitting in front of the fire Adam had built to ward off the cold from a spell of frigid temperatures that had descended that last week of January.

"I don't think so." Megan stretched and settled back against him, enjoying the comfort of his arms and the warmth of his breath on her cheek. "She says Lindsay refuses to say anything against him. Donna probably thinks it's enough that she was able to convince Lindsay not to accept his phone calls."

"While Lindsay's at home that might be fine, but what about when she goes back to school?"

"She's on special leave, so that won't be until August." Megan remembered how relieved and happy Donna had been when Lindsay agreed to return to school. Now, only a semester later, Lindsay had been compelled to withdraw, and for reasons none of them ever could have predicted. "Maybe they think it will all blow over by then."

"I hope they're right," Adam said, but he sounded doubtful. He kissed Megan and added, "I'd better go."

"Already?"

He stroked her arm. "Unless you want me to stay."

Megan knew he meant stay the entire night, but she couldn't agree to it, not with Robby there. Robby might not mind finding Adam at the breakfast table the next morning—in fact, he would probably be pleased—but Megan wasn't comfortable with such casual overnight arrangements. She didn't want to make an implicit promise to either of them, and for her, allowing Adam to stay the night implied an understanding, a commitment. Although Megan was confident and hopeful that they were headed in that direction, she was content to wait. They had all been through too much heartache not to proceed carefully now, and they were happy, so she felt no urgency to hasten into anything before she and Adam were both certain the time was right.

So she shook her head and said, "I'm sorry."

"Don't apologize," he said, and kissed her. "I understand."

He did understand, and he accepted her feelings and her right to them without judgment or complaint, which was one of the reasons she loved him.

She went with him to the door, and as he was putting on his coat, she said, "Oh, I've been meaning to give you your key back. I accidentally left it in my purse that day you were sick."

"Keep it."

"Are you sure?"

"Of course." Adam smiled and touched her face. "I'll see you next week."

After one last embrace, Adam went outside into the cold. He waved before getting into the car; Megan waved back before shutting the door against the bitter night air. She shook her head and smiled at herself for being so pleased that he wanted her to have his key. He lived far enough away that she would never be in the neighborhood and able to drop by unannounced, so she would probably never use the key unless Adam locked himself out. But somehow it touched her, as if in giving her his key he meant to show how much he trusted her, and how he expected them to be together for the long term.

The next morning when Megan checked her email, she found a message that Adam had sent the night before:

TO: Megan.Donohue@rocketec.com
FROM: wagnera@rogerbacon.k12.oh.edu
DATE: 12:43 AM 23 January
SUBJECT: Missing you

When I came home I thought of how much nicer it would be if we were together. Now that you have the key, every morning when I wake up, I'll open my eyes hoping to find you here.

I love you, Megan.

Megan wanted to write back that she loved him, too, but she had never told him so before, and the first time she said those words to him, she wanted it to be in person.

⚜

January passed with bitter cold and heavy snows and no end to Brandon's phone calls. Lindsay flinched whenever the phone rang, and refused to read her email unless Donna or Becca downloaded it first and deleted Brandon's messages. Or so she said—twice Donna had entered Lindsay's room only to find her seated at the computer, her face wet with tears. She would jump in her seat at her mother's approach and quickly shut down the computer before Donna could see what she was doing. It made Donna sick at heart to think that Lindsay was still in contact with the man who had treated her so brutally, and it troubled her even more when Lindsay would not say for certain whether she had broken off the engagement.

This infuriated Paul, and he implored Lindsay to press charges against Brandon for striking her. "If he had been a stranger on the street," he stormed when he and Donna were alone, "there wouldn't be any question of protecting him like this."

Donna tried to soothe him by emphasizing that at least they had separated the couple and Lindsay was safe in their home. Privately she thought that Lindsay's refusal to go to the police was only in part to protect Brandon, and partially to protect herself. For weeks Lindsay had drifted about the house gingerly, as if she thought she might shatter from the impact of a stray thought or harsh word. The young woman who had been so willing to forgo her education the previous summer now seemed to consider her decision to withdraw from the semester as evidence that she had failed her parents and herself. It didn't matter that Paul and Donna supported her choice. Lindsay had retreated into a world of her own, and Donna feared the old Lindsay might be lost to them forever.

But as the days passed, Lindsay gradually lost the haunted look in her eyes, and by the end of February she had resumed some of her usual interests. She went out with old high school friends who had remained in town; she visited the public library often to check out books on stagecraft and filmmaking. She rented videos of stage plays, which she and Donna would watch together and discuss. Each day brought a new, positive change in Lindsay's behavior, and only infrequently did Donna hear her crying in her room.

Then one gray morning, when Donna and Lindsay were alone in the house, Donna heard a car pull into the driveway. There was no mistaking the car, or the young man who jumped out of it and strode purposefully toward the house.

Donna hurried to the door, glancing up the stairs to Lindsay's bedroom and praying that she had been too engrossed in her reading to have heard the car. The doorbell rang, and before she could respond, a fist pounded on the door. "Lindsay," she heard Brandon shout. "Lindsay, it's me. Let me in."

"She doesn't want to see you," Donna shouted back.

A pause, and then, louder, "Lindsay, it's Brandon."

Donna checked to be sure the chain was fastened before opening the door a crack. "I said, she doesn't want to see you."

Brandon glared at her, his face pale with outrage. "Then let me hear it from her."

Donna heard Lindsay's door open and the faint creak of her footfall on the stairs. "I'm going to shut this door," Donna said, "and you're going to get in your car and drive away. If you don't, I'll call the police."

To her shock, instead of backing off, Brandon shoved the door, straining at the chain. "I know she's in there. Lindsay," he shouted. "We're supposed to get married in a few months. Talk to me."

"If you have something to say to my daughter, you can say it to me." Donna glanced over her shoulder to find that Lindsay had not descended past the top step.

"I need to talk to her alone."

"That," Donna said fiercely, "is one thing I will never allow."

Brandon swore and gave the door another hard shove before stepping back and raking his fingers through his hair. "You can't keep me away from her. We love each other. We won't let you come between us."

"She isn't coming back to you, Brandon."

"That's her choice, not yours," he shot back. "And she'll choose me."

"Stay away from Lindsay," Donna's voice was clear and emphatic and trembling with anger. She closed the door. "Stay away from my family."

"She'll choose me, and do you know why?" Brandon shouted through the door. "Because she doesn't have anything else, and she knows it. You hear me? She knows it!"

Donna carefully locked the door and forced herself to walk away, back to the kitchen, where she watched through the curtains as Brandon paced around the front porch for a while, until he threw up his hands in frustration, stormed back to his car, and sped off.

☙

Valentine's Day fell on a Sunday that year, but Adam invited Megan out for the preceding Saturday night instead. After spending the afternoon ice skating with Robby, Adam hurried home for a quick shower and a change of clothes, then returned with roses and a box of chocolates for Megan. She laughed but seemed pleased, and Adam saw as if for the first time how beautiful she was, not just because she had dressed up for the occasion, but because when she was happy, she glowed with an inner light. He was drawn to her anew each time he glimpsed it, and it made him never want to leave her side.

When they took Robby to her parents' house, Megan invited him in to meet them. They were down-to-earth, pleasant people, and Adam saw in them the source of Megan's common sense and good humor. He liked them, and to his relief, they seemed to like him.

The evening went as perfectly as Adam could have wished. The restaurant was romantic, the food delicious, and Megan such lovely company that for long moments he could do nothing more than marvel at how lucky he was and how blessed by the circumstances that had brought them together. Afterward Megan invited him home, as he had hoped she would; when he kissed her and told her he loved her and she returned the sentiment, he was so overcome with happiness that he held her close and wished he never had to let her go.

He longed to spend the night rather than return to the loneliness of his empty house, but Megan gently reminded him that her parents were expecting them to pick up Robby. "He could have stayed overnight," she said, chiding herself. "But I didn't plan . . . this."

He kissed her and said, "Some of the best things in life don't happen according to plan." She smiled at him then in a way that left him overcome with desire, but her family was waiting. After retrieving Robby and seeing the two safely to the door, Adam kissed Megan one last time, then drove home alone.

In the morning he woke from dreams of Megan to early sunlight spilling in through the windows. Something had roused him, and as the sleepy cloudiness left him, he heard it again: a rapping on the front door. Groggy, he padded to the door wearing only his pajama bottoms. Fumbling with the lock, he opened the door—and found Natalie standing on the front porch, smiling at him.

"Natalie," he said, suddenly conscious of the cold. "What are you doing here?"

She held up a paper bag from a coffee shop they used to frequent together. "I brought breakfast. Bagels and cappuccino." Then she brought out a hand from behind her back and held out a single red rose. "Happy Valentine's Day."

He didn't take it. "Natalie—"

"Those pajamas have a top, you know," she said, eyeing his attire. "I should know. I bought them for you." She tossed her hair over her shoulder. "So are you going to let me in or what?"

"Sure." He held the door open for her, and she entered. Yawning, he indicated the kitchen and said, "I'll get dressed and be there in a minute."

Natalie laughed. "Don't bother if you're comfortable. I've seen you in far less than that."

Instead of answering, Adam went to his bedroom and threw on a pair of jeans and a sweatshirt. By the time he returned to the kitchen, Natalie had set the table for two and had placed the rose in a bud vase she had once bought him. She smiled when she saw him and began unpacking the bag. "Hungry?" she asked.

Adam nodded and sat down. "You should have called."

"Why? Do you have company?"

"No, but I might have." He didn't intend for the words to come out so sharply, but Natalie took no offense. Instead she served him his cappuccino, and he wasn't surprised to find that she had remembered exactly how he liked it. Resigned, he helped himself to a bagel. "You should have called."

She just laughed at him and changed the subject. She looked bright and fresh and pretty, not at all as she had the last time they were together. If she remembered how angry and hurt she had been that night, she gave no sign as she asked about his family and updated him on the ever-worsening situation at Lindsor's.

She was well into a description of the most recent layoff scare when the doorbell rang. "Aren't you popular," she said, irritated by the interruption.

With a sudden surge of anxiety, Adam went to answer the door.

It was Megan, smiling and carrying a paper bag.

"Happy Valentine's Day," she said, kissing him. "I was going to use my key, but I saw the car in the driveway and figured you had company. . . ." Her gaze traveled past him and her voice trailed off.

He didn't need to look to know Natalie had joined them in the foyer.

"Hi, I'm Natalie," Natalie said, stepping forward to shake her hand. "And you are?"

"Megan." As she shifted the bag to shake Natalie's hand, Megan met Adam's gaze with pained confusion. "Megan Donohue."

"What's in the bag?"

"Oh." Megan looked down distractedly. "Groceries. I thought I would make breakfast."

Natalie smiled indulgently. "How sweet of you, but we've already eaten."

"Natalie came over just this morning," Adam broke in. "I wasn't expecting her. She surprised me." He heard how his babbling was making the truth seem false. "Do you want to come in?"

"No—no, thanks. I'd better get home." She wouldn't look at him. Abruptly she turned and headed for her car.

Adam followed her outside. "Megan, she just showed up about a half hour before you did. Uninvited."

"Uh-huh." She fumbled the key in the lock.

"It's true."

"Fine, it's true." She opened the door and placed the bag inside.

"If you believe me, why are you acting like this?"

"Acting like what? I'm not acting like anything."

Adam put his hands on her shoulders and turned her to face him. "Megan, I wasn't with her last night. I was with you."

"I know." Finally she looked at him, and her gaze was cool and steady. "It's this morning I'm concerned about."

He couldn't believe the coldness in her expression. He remembered then how Keith had betrayed her and felt a tremor of something close to fear, fear of losing her. "I wouldn't lie to you. You know that."

She nodded, but said, "I have to go."

"Megan . . ."

But she climbed into the car and shut the door. He stood shivering in the driveway and watched her drive off.

He walked back to the house. Natalie was waiting in the foyer. "Isn't she going to stay for breakfast?"

"Stop it, Natalie."

"I didn't know she was coming over," she protested. "But what's the problem? It's just a misunderstanding. You'll sort it out."

Adam wasn't so sure. "You should leave now."

"Don't take this out on me—"

"Just go." He returned to the kitchen without looking back and called Megan's house.

He waited all day, but she didn't return the message he left on her answering machine, nor did she respond to his email notes. After school the following afternoon, he hurried home to check his answering machine, but if Megan had phoned, she had not left a message.

He tried her number again and hung up as soon as the machine picked up. Later that evening he phoned again, and this time, Robby answered.

"Hi," Robby greeted him happily. "Guess what? I got an A on my spelling test today."

"That's great. Congratulations." Adam was about to ask for Megan when he heard her voice in the background.

"It's Adam," Robby told her, then paused. "Oh. Okay. Adam, my mom wants to talk to you."

"Megan?" Adam waited, eager to hear her voice. "Are you there?"

Her voice was soft, nearly a whisper. "Yes."

"Are you still angry?"

"No."

Relief washed over him. "Can I come over tonight so we can talk?"

There was a long pause. "I don't think that would be a good idea."

"But Megan . . ."

"I also don't think you should see Robby anymore."

"Megan, please don't do this."

"Good-bye, Adam." He heard a gentle click, then the line went dead.

⚓

Days later, Megan reflected on what Vinnie had said at quilt camp, that there were no coincidences, that in life you meet the people you need to meet. Perhaps that was true, but as Donna had added, perhaps the reason one needed to meet someone wasn't what one thought. Perhaps she and Adam had been destined to meet, but not because they were meant to spend the rest of their lives together. Adam might have come into her life to prove to her that she could find love again—although not with him.

She accepted the situation sadly, because she had no other choice. She only wished she could explain things in a way Robby could accept and understand. She couldn't tell him what had really happened that morning at Adam's house, but although it would have been simple to say that Adam was too busy to be Robby's friend anymore, somehow she couldn't bear to say something so untrue. So she simply told Robby Adam couldn't come over anymore, and when Robby asked why, she fell back on the phrase she had promised herself never to utter as a parent: "Because I said so."

⚓

Julia couldn't think of any place she would less rather be than Kansas in late February, except for the more specific hell of the *Prairie Vengeance* location shoot in Kansas in late February.

A knock sounded on her trailer door. "Five minutes, Miss Merchaud," someone called. With a sigh, Julia rose, checked her hair and makeup, and drew on her parka. They must have finished shoveling off the cabin, a task that wouldn't be necessary if the weather would cooperate, or if production hadn't been delayed so long. The scene scheduled to shoot that day was supposed to take place in September. Since even in this part of the country a six-inch-thick blanket of snow didn't suit September, the cabin and grounds standing in as the Hendersons' homestead had to be cleared off. Ellen grumbled that if they had used her original script, they would have been able to film these scenes on schedule, which would have meant last October at the latest. Privately Julia agreed with her, but she worried that the young woman was growing careless. At first she had had enough sense to keep her complaints to herself when Deneford was around, but as the script changes accumulated, she had abandoned her sense of discretion. Julia had warned her to be cautious, since Deneford could ruin her movie career, but Ellen had said, "I almost don't care anymore."

"Wait until you're sure you don't care anymore, and then you can gripe to your heart's content," Julia had retorted, and Ellen contritely pledged to try.

Someone had shoveled a narrow path from the door of Julia's trailer to the cabin, where the crew was busily preparing for the shoot. The cast, barely recognizable in their thick coats, sipped coffee from foam cups or paged through their scripts. Julia spotted Noah McCleod, the actor playing her elder son—and the only member of the cast she was in any mood to speak to that morning—sitting in a chair reading a book.

He smiled as she approached. "Do you know much about geometry?"

"Not much," Julia admitted. "Although a friend of mine has a grandson who teaches it. Unfortunately, he's in Ohio, so he won't be much help. Where's your tutor?"

"In the trailer with the flu."

"Delightful." No doubt they would all catch it soon. Suddenly she had a hopeful thought: If she fell ill, she might have to go to the hospital. "Where's Cameron?"

Noah shrugged. "In the wardrobe trailer, last time I saw him."

"Again?" The actor who played her youngest son seemed to grow half an inch every day, much to the chagrin of the wardrobe mistress.

Deneford joined them. "Are you two ready?" Without waiting for an answer, he said, "Julia, you'll be at the quilt frame with your friends. Noah, when you and Cam run up to tell her about the rattlesnake, I want to see real fear. Okay? Can you do that?"

"Sure, I'll just think about my geometry homework," Noah said good-naturedly, and set his book aside. "See you soon, Ma."

Julia smiled. "Very well, son." The extras had already removed their coats and sat shivering around the quilt frame in front of the cabin. Julia kept her parka on until the last minute, taking her place just before the shot.

She sat down, greeted the extras cordially, and slipped her thimble on the first finger of her right hand. Closing her eyes, she summoned up her character and called up memories of warm autumn days. When she opened her eyes again, she could almost forget the cold.

"Action," Deneford ordered, and the scene began. Sadie and her fellow settler women worked on the quilt, discussing the ominous news that cattle ranchers planned to buy up their town.

Out of the corner of her eye, Julia spotted a grimace from the cinematographer, who made a gesture of disgust as he spoke to Deneford. "Cut," Deneford called out. "Take a break. A short break." Shivering, the extras scrambled into their coats.

"A break, already?" Ellen groused, arriving to hand Julia her coat.

Julia thanked her and was about to suggest they get some coffee when Deneford called her over. "Don't let them change the lines," Ellen hissed. Julia gave her a look that said, *As if I have a choice.*

She joined the two men, who had withdrawn somewhat from the others. "Yes?" she asked.

"We have a small problem," Deneford said. "It seems that your hands . . ." He looked to the cinematographer. "How did you put it?"

"They're too old."

Stung, Julia fought off the instinct to hide her hands behind her back. "I beg your pardon?"

"They look too old," the cinematographer said. "When I move in close enough to follow your quilting, the camera picks up every wrinkle and vein. When I pull back far enough for your hands to look Sadie's age, I can't tell what you're doing."

"Well, what do you suggest I do about it?" she asked crisply.

Deneford and the cinematographer exchanged a look. "Is there anything you can do to make your hands seem younger?" Deneford asked. "Could you wear gloves? Not those winter gloves. You know the type I mean. Kid gloves, I think they're called."

"I can't quilt with gloves on."

The cinematographer shook his head and said to Deneford, "We aren't going to find a local hand model who knows how to quilt."

"We don't need a hand model," Julia snapped. "My hands are perfectly appropriate for my character. Sadie was a frontier farm wife. She worked with her hands from dawn until dusk in every season. She would have had weathered hands."

"There's weathered, and there's aged," the cinematographer remarked. Julia glared at him.

Deneford intervened. "All right. We'll go ahead and film it as is. If I don't like the dailies, we'll think of an alternative."

Julia gave them a sharp nod, not trusting herself to speak. She stormed back to her place and practiced her relaxation breathing. Silently she cursed the cinematographer. Her ability to quilt had won her that role, and in another moment Deneford might decide to put Samantha Key and her Young Sadie hands in Julia's place.

She calmed herself in time for the second take, which went perfectly. Always the dictatorial perfectionist, Deneford called for a third and fourth without giving the women around the quilt frame time to slip into their coats and warm themselves. Julia contented herself with dreaming up horrible accidents that might befall him this far from civilization.

Finally Deneford was ready to move on. "Okay, kids, rattlesnake time," he said to Noah, then looked around and asked, "Where's Cameron?"

Noah shrugged. "Try the wardrobe trailer."

"Again?" He raised his voice. "Everyone be back here in fifteen." With murmurs of relief, the cast and most of the crew headed for their trailers. Deneford strode off toward the wardrobe trailer, the assistant director at his heels.

Julia waited until they were out of sight before hurrying off to her trailer, unwilling to let them see how they had alarmed her. So her hands looked too old for close-ups. Very well. She'd find a new pair of hands, and not those of Samantha Key, who had already taken over too many of Julia's scenes. And she didn't want some hand model with fantasies of becoming an actress, either. She needed someone who would be content with this small, uncredited role and wouldn't dream of stealing Julia's part, someone who would stand by her and believe in her despite her flaws, despite her aged hands and her mediocre quilting and her failures of the past.

She needed a friend.

✦

Julia's cell phone transmitted her voice with perfect clarity, but Donna still wasn't sure she understood what her friend had said. "You want me to be a what?"

"A stunt quilter," Julia repeated. "You'll sit in for me during all my close-up quilting shots, although I'm afraid only your hands will be on film."

"That's fine," Donna said, with a tremor of excitement mixed with stage fright. "I don't think I'd want any more of me to show. I won't have to speak any lines, will I?"

"No, just quilt."

"Well, I can certainly do that."

"Please, Donna, say yes. You'll be paid the standard rate, and I'll cover your travel and housing expenses personally. I'm afraid the accommodations aren't exactly luxurious out here on location, but when we return to California—"

"You mean I'll get to go to Hollywood?"

Julia laughed. "Sure, we can visit Hollywood if you'd like. When we're done with the location filming, we'll have more scenes at the studio to shoot. I'd love it if you'd stay with me in my home in Malibu until the movie's finished." Her voice turned wistful. "It would almost be like quilt camp again. Except for the climate, at least while we're on location. I'm a bit embarrassed asking you to come to Kansas at this time of year."

"Oh, that's no problem. I wouldn't mind some milder weather for a change." Donna's thoughts were racing with the possibilities. "I'll do it under one condition. Let me bring Lindsay. Give her a job, too."

"Your daughter?" Julia asked. "But I only need one stunt quilter."

"That's all right. She doesn't quilt. But she is a drama major at the University of Minnesota, and she's performed in and directed many plays. I know that's not the same as movies, but she's very bright and she's a hard worker, and there must be something she can do."

Julia paused. "And this would get her away from Brandon."

"Exactly." Distance would provide Lindsay with safety and perspective, and working on a movie would remind her of her talents, her interests. *I'm all she has, and she knows it,* Brandon had said, and those words had haunted Donna ever since. If there were any chance Lindsay truly believed that, Donna needed to prove him wrong.

"I'm sure we can find something for her," Julia said. "We always need gofers and assistants. I'll look into it. In the meantime, may I take the liberty of making your airline reservations?"

"As long as you reserve two seats."

"I'll do that," Julia promised. "And Donna—it'll be so good to see you again."

After they hung up, Donna stood lost in thought for a moment. She probably should have discussed this with Paul and Becca first, but Paul would understand the urgency of seizing this opportunity, and he and Becca would get along fine without her for a while. They would be glad to if it meant helping Lindsay.

She went upstairs to Lindsay's room, hopeful and yet anxious. Lindsay might refuse to go. Since Brandon's visit she had lost the ground she had gained earlier in the month and spent most of her time alone in her room. Once she told them Brandon had written to her, suggesting they attend couples' counseling. "We could sort out our problems now, so we won't have to postpone the wedding," she had said wistfully. Paul had overheard and had become outraged, more angry than Donna had ever seen him. She, too, could not understand how Lindsay could even consider marrying Brandon after all that had happened, and the way Lindsay clung to the hope that he would change bewildered Donna. She and Paul had begged her to break off the engagement, and Paul had even declared that he forbade her to marry him, but Lindsay still wore the engagement ring Brandon had given her the previous summer.

But now Donna had a chance to change all that. She took a deep breath, knocked on Lindsay's door, and softly called her name. She received a muted, "Come in," in response, and entered the room. Lindsay was lying on the bed, holding a pillow to her chest and gazing at the ceiling.

"Honey?" Donna said. "There's something I'd like to discuss with you."

She told her daughter about Julia's phone call and the troubles she had been facing with the movie ever since accepting the role. At first Donna wasn't sure her daughter was paying attention, but as she narrated the twists and turns of Julia's misery on the set, she detected a flicker of interest in Lindsay's eyes. Eventually Lindsay sat up and began to react to Donna's story, by turns laughing and shaking her head in disbelief.

"What is she going to do?" Lindsay asked when Donna concluded. "Do you think she'll lose the part?"

"That's where we come in. Julia offered me a job. She wants me to be her stunt quilter."

"A stunt quilter?" Lindsay laughed. "That's wonderful! You're going to be a star."

"Well, I don't know about that. Only my hands are going to be on film." Donna bit her lip, feigning the uncertainty that was so close to the nervousness she already felt. "That's if I take the job."

"If? Why wouldn't you want to? It sounds like so much fun."

"I don't know." Donna shrugged. "It would be hard to be away from the family for so long."

"I think we can manage, Mom."

"It's not that. I'll get lonely. So I told Julia I'd only take the part if you came with me."

Lindsay started. "Why did you tell her that?"

"Because I want you to be there." Donna sat down on the edge of Lindsay's bed and took her hand. "When I told her you were available, she asked if you would come work on the set, too. You'd be an intern, or an assistant, something like that. You'd get to work behind the scenes of a real movie. Just think of what a great experience this would be."

Lindsay looked tired. "I don't think I can do it."

"Why not?"

"I just don't think I can." She lay down again and closed her eyes.

"A year ago you would have done it."

"A year ago." Lindsay's voice was faint. "A year ago I was a different person."

Watching her, a spark of resolve kindled in Donna's heart. "Come here." She stood up and, still holding Lindsay's hand, pulled her to her feet. "I want to show you something."

She led Lindsay to the quilt room, where she opened her closet and brought out a pile of quilt blocks, all different patterns, some traditional, some of her own invention. Each had spoken to her heart as she assembled it, whispering messages of hope and faith and encouragement she alone understood.

"I tried to make you a wedding quilt," Donna said as she spread out the blocks on the table. "I couldn't do it. When I thought of you and Brandon together, not a single pattern came to my mind. But when I thought of you, Lindsay, just you, the ideas kept coming, one after another. The quilt blocks just spilled out of me." She picked up one, an appliqué block of the traditional symbol of the theater, the masks of comedy and tragedy. "I made this one first, and then this"—she picked up a second block—"to accompany it. The names of all the plays you've ever worked on are embroidered on it."

She handed the blocks to her daughter, who traced the outline of the masks with a finger. "This one I made from your high school basketball uniform," she continued, holding up a Weathervane block. "Do you remember? You were a guard, and in your senior year your teammates chose you as captain."

"I was only second string."

"Yes, and they chose you anyway, even though you weren't the best player, because of who you are. Because of your character and your kindness. Because of what you contributed to that team when you encouraged the other girls to do their best."

Donna passed her another block, a photo transfer made of a snapshot from Lindsay's first day of kindergarten. "Remember this?"

Lindsay let out a small laugh and bit her lip.

"I was so proud of you that day," Donna said. "I hated to see my baby grow up, but I loved your confidence. Remember when that other little girl at the bus stop wouldn't stop crying because she was scared to go to school? You held her hand and promised you would be her friend, and you would sit with her on the bus and play with her every day."

"Her name was Molly."

"That's right. I had forgotten." Donna held up a blue-and-white LeMoyne Star block. "Do you recognize these fabrics?"

Lindsay touched it. "The blue—it's from my prom dress."

"And the white is from the hem of your graduation gown. This one—I call it the Golden Gopher block. Remember that T-shirt you wore constantly your freshman year?"

Lindsay smiled and nodded, tears shining in her eyes. "I washed it so much that it shrank to half its size. I thought you threw it out."

"I saved it." She had saved it, and two years later cut out the emblem and appliquéd it onto a quilt block so Lindsay could keep it forever. Donna waved her hand over the table and watched as Lindsay took in all the blocks, all the patchwork memories Donna had created to celebrate her life. "Look at all you've accomplished," she implored. "Think of all the people who care about you and have always cared about you. You are a wonderful, talented, beautiful, and loving young woman, Lindsay. You deserve to be happy. You deserve to be cherished." She reached out and brushed away her daughter's tears, then cupped Lindsay's cheek in her hand. "Please don't ever let anyone convince you otherwise."

Lindsay threw her arms around her mother and wept. Donna patted her on the back and murmured to her soothingly. Lindsay cried until she cried herself out, then she pulled away, brushed the tears from her eyes with the back of her hand—and then, slowly but with resolve, she removed the engagement ring.

She placed it on the table with the quilt blocks. The she turned to her mother, who embraced her and held her tightly, as if she could pass strength from her arms to her daughter's heart, so that Lindsay would forever be protected by her love.

Eleven

Winter gave way to the first signs of spring, and on the Kansas set of *Prairie Vengeance,* Lindsay blossomed. She started out as the assistant to an assistant, but before long she had proven herself to be capable and smart. She was promoted once, and then again, until she was named a production assistant. Even Deneford took notice of her, after some subtle hints from Julia, and he told Lindsay if she wanted work during the summer, he could get her an internship at the studio.

For her part, Donna didn't see herself becoming a professional stunt quilter anytime soon, but she enjoyed working with the other extras and seeing what went on behind the scenes. Deneford's behavior quickly confirmed that Julia had not exaggerated in her stories about him. It heartened Donna to see Lindsay stand up to his blustering and moving confidently about the set as if she had been the production assistant for dozens of films.

Before leaving for Kansas, Lindsay had phoned Brandon to break off the engagement. Paul later reported that Brandon showed up as scheduled to pick up the ring, but when he learned Lindsay wasn't there, he refused to take it. "Why should I," he told Paul, "when I'll be giving it back when she changes her mind?" Back then Lindsay had been distressed by his refusal to accept her decision, but by the time the cast and crew were closing down the Kansas set, her determination had strengthened. While Donna and Julia flew to California, Lindsay went home to Minnesota. She arranged to meet Brandon at a restaurant adjacent to campus, one popular with professors and students from the medical school. There she handed him the ring and told him in no uncertain terms that they were finished. Since they were in a public place, and Brandon was intelligent enough to realize what losing his temper in front of his colleagues could mean to his career, he contented himself with shoving the ring in his pocket and snapping, "Fine. You were never good enough for me, anyway." Lindsay merely stood up, went to her car, and drove home to visit her father and sister before catching a plane to LAX.

Julia, Donna, and Lindsay spent the days working on the set; in the evening they relaxed by the pool or saw the sights of southern California. Some nights Julia and Donna would work on their blocks for the Challenge Quilt. They spoke fondly of their friends from camp and looked forward to the day they would meet again at Elm Creek Manor.

Then Donna was struck by a delightful idea: Why wait until August? Why not meet at the American Quilter's Society show in April?

Megan was the first to promise she would be there, and each evening when she left work, she crossed off a day on her calendar with relief. The passage of one more day brought her one day closer to seeing her friends, to getting over Adam, to helping Robby accept the loss of Adam's friendship. Robby still saw his counselor every week, but lately he had been making no progress, and in some ways was worse off than before. The low point came when he had to serve an in-school suspension for tearing up the poster another student had made for science class. Megan tried to talk to him, both alone and with the counselor, but only succeeded in making Robby feel miserable. "I'm sorry I'm so bad, Mom," he said one night as she tucked him in, breaking her heart. She hugged him and told him she loved him and always would, no matter what. He drifted off to sleep, and she went into the other room and cried.

Megan needed a break, and the trip to Paducah, Kentucky, to see her friends would be a balm for her wounded spirit. She only hoped they wouldn't talk about the blocks they were supposed to make for the Challenge Quilt. She had chosen her pattern, inspired by the gentle snowfall outside Adam's house, and selected the fabrics, but as Robby's newfound happiness faded, so did her eagerness to complete the block. Now the pieces sat on her sewing machine, and she did not know when she might take them up again.

Vinnie might have found herself in a similar situation, except that she had finished her block the day Julia's letter arrived, revealing the secret romance between Adam and Megan. She wondered grumpily if she ought to remove the stitches now that everything had ended so badly. Not that Adam had bothered to tell her it was over; instead he merely showed up at his mother's birthday party hand in hand with Natalie. "We're not getting married," he assured Vinnie privately, when he finally stopped ignoring the glares she had been shooting him all afternoon. "We're just seeing how things go." Vinnie thought he ought to see how things would go with Megan instead and told him so. A shadow of sadness crossed his face, and he replied, "That's not up to me." Vinnie didn't know what to make of that, but since she suspected Adam wasn't happy with this turn of events, she was willing to travel much farther than Paducah to get the opportunity to talk some sense into Megan.

When Grace learned that the others planned to be there, she abandoned her hopes that the plans would fall through and forced herself to decide whether she would join them. Throughout February she had been plagued by exacerbations, and only by the last week of March had she recovered enough to walk unsteadily about the loft Gabriel had renovated for her, instead of relying on the wheelchair. She had no idea whether her symptoms would improve or worsen by mid-April, but she knew she couldn't bear to have her friends see her in her current condition.

But since it was her practice to attend the AQS show every year, eventually she agreed to meet the others in the lobby of the convention center on Friday afternoon of the quilt show. If she were still symptomatic, the quilt show would be large enough that she could avoid the Cross-Country Quilters. But by then she might be feeling fine, and, she hoped, she might have a new quilt started. By then she might have something more than false starts and abandoned sketches to show for the months she had struggled to keep the promises she had made at Elm Creek Manor.

❦

On a Wednesday afternoon in mid-April, Vinnie rode a chartered tour bus from Dayton to Paducah with a few quilters from Meadowbrook Village and many others from throughout the city. She wore her favorite quilted vest and a red hat studded with pins from all the quilting events she had attended throughout the years. The Elm Creek Quilts pin was displayed proudly in front, and she missed no opportunity to tell the other passengers how she had won it.

Some of the women slept on the drive, but not Vinnie. She introduced herself to all the quilters in the nearby seats and chatted happily, thrilled to be attending another American Quilter's Society show. The best of the best entered their quilts in this competition, and although Vinnie considered herself an above-average quilter, the masterpieces displayed at this show humbled her—and humbling Vinnie was not easy. In addition to the more than four hundred quilts entered in the competition at the Executive Inn Convention Center, there were classes taught by renowned master quilters from around the world, lectures, award banquets, fashion shows, and the nearby Museum of the American Quilter's Society, where the Best of Show quilts from previous years were displayed. Then there was perhaps Vinnie's favorite venue aside from the quilts themselves: a merchants' mall where hundreds of vendors set up booths selling every sort of fabric, pattern, and quilt notion imaginable. Each time she attended the show, Vinnie resolved to stick to a budget, but within a day the dazzling display of wares would prove to be too much for her willpower, and she would invariably exceed her allotment for the entire weekend. The only solution, of course, was to expand her budget, which she cheerfully did.

The tour bus reached their hotel, which was already packed with some of the thirty-five thousand other quilters who would double Paducah's population that weekend. Vinnie was sharing a room with another member of the tour, but she didn't mind, knowing she was lucky to have a place at all. Every hotel room within fifty miles was booked up; those in the Executive Inn itself had been given out by lottery a year before. Megan and Donna had taken advantage of the city's Bed and Breakfast program, in which local residents provided the visiting quilters with a room and a meal for about the same rate as a hotel. Vinnie wasn't sure what Julia's plans were, but she wouldn't be surprised if Julia had used her star power to finagle a room in one of Paducah's finest hotels.

On Thursday she rose early, eager to see as much of the show as possible before the crowds descended in full force. She rode the hotel's shuttle to the convention center in downtown Paducah, on the shore where the Tennessee River fed into the Ohio, and was among the first hundred viewers to enter the show. She was not disappointed. The quilts were breathtaking, inspiring; she saw examples of every style from watercolor to Baltimore Album to others so innovative she wasn't sure their styles had a particular name. There were quilts from every state and around the world, some made by professional quilters, others by amateurs, although Vinnie was puzzled by that distinction because she detected no difference in the quality of artistic expression or craftsmanship. She took snapshots of her favorites and wrinkled her nose at others, wondering what on earth that particular quilter had been thinking. But she figured one person's art was another person's drop cloth, and just because a quilt didn't suit her tastes didn't mean it wasn't a good quilt. She, for example, thought she might keel over dead if she had to look at another Sunbonnet Sue quilt, but she had friends who thought little Sue was the most adorable creature on the face of the earth. Vinnie figured there was room enough in the quilting community for all manner of tastes and styles. She wasn't as opinionated as some of the other viewers, who evaluated each quilt in loud, obnoxious voices, as if anyone listening gave a fig what they thought. Once, after an irritating old biddy had made a particularly thoughtless remark about a Mariner's Compass quilt, Vinnie said, "I'm sorry you didn't like it. I worked very hard on it and tried to do my best." The old biddy's jaw dropped in horror, and Vinnie turned her back and walked away with a satisfied smile. That would teach her to be a little more sensitive. Honestly. They were fellow quilters, after all; if they were going to offer criticism, it should be constructive, and it should never be unkind.

By lunchtime Vinnie was fatigued from being on her feet all morning, so she met up with a group of ladies from the tour and strolled downtown for lunch. Spring was much further along in Paducah than in Dayton, and the skies were clear and sunny above the blooming dogwood trees. The downtown streets were charming, as all the shops—from the hardware store to the women's clothing boutique—displayed quilts in their front windows. Vinnie considered it a thoughtful, friendly gesture, the way the entire city welcomed the visiting quilters.

After lunch Vinnie toured the Museum of the American Quilter's Society, then returned to the convention center to attend a lecture by one of her favorite quilters. She waited until later that afternoon, when most of the other visitors were at supper, before visiting the merchants' mall, so she could shop without too much jostling from the crowd. She quickly snapped up several yards of fabric and a pattern for a quilted pullover, then added a box of notecards and a few books to her purchases. She might have gone on until all her money was spent and her charge card melted from so much use, except her tote bag was getting too heavy to carry. She decided, reluctantly, to call it a day, because she wanted to be in top form when she met the Cross-Country Quilters the next afternoon.

Vinnie tried to sleep in Friday morning to make the afternoon come sooner, but she was up at dawn, bursting with energy and impatient to see her friends. She distracted herself pleasantly enough by seeing the rest of the quilts and continuing her shopping, but it was a miracle she made it to lunch. An afternoon class kept her busy for a few hours, and then, at last, it was time.

She arrived at their designated meeting place in the lobby of the Executive Inn a half hour early, but there were so many other visitors milling about, she worried that she might not see her friends. She managed to find one of the last empty chairs in the place and gingerly climbed on top of it, the better to scan the crowds, but before long, a security guard asked her to get down. She did, but only because he asked nicely and seemed genuinely concerned for her safety.

Four o'clock arrived, and at last Vinnie spotted two familiar faces. "Megan," she shouted, waving her arm in the air. "Donna! Over here!"

They worked their way toward her, and a moment later they were embracing. "It's so good to see you," Donna said, hugging her. "You look wonderful."

"Well, naturally. You look lovely yourself." She did, indeed; she had slimmed down some, and her skin had a healthy glow. "That California sunshine suits you."

"Oh, don't tell me that," Donna said, laughing. "I'm already tempted to move in with Julia permanently."

"And where is our Julia?" Vinnie asked, searching the crowd behind her friends. "Didn't she come with you?"

"No, she had to cancel. She was afraid of what might happen if she left the studio for too long."

"From what she writes about that Deneford character, that was probably a sensible decision." Vinnie smiled at Megan. "Megan, honey, how are you?"

"Fine." She hesitated. "I've been better."

Vinnie sensed her apprehension. She knew she shouldn't mention Adam, but she couldn't help herself. "I suppose you're upset about my grandson? I know you two had a falling out."

"You weren't even supposed to know about us."

"Grandmothers have their ways. Now, surely you know how disappointed I am. Can't you at least tell me what went wrong?"

"It's hard to explain." Megan studied her for a moment, then sighed. "It's true we never actually agreed not to see other people, but I thought we were seeing each other exclusively." Then her expression hardened. "I fail to understand how you can tell someone you love them and, at the same time, be involved with someone else. Keith did it, but I never expected Adam to."

Shocked, Vinnie said, "You think Adam cheated on you?"

"I didn't say he cheated on me. We never specifically said we wouldn't see other people. Is that still cheating?"

"Yes," Donna said.

"Megan, honey, I know my grandson. He's not perfect, but he isn't cruel. I know he wouldn't betray you like this."

Megan fixed her with a penetrating look. "Can you honestly tell me he isn't seeing Natalie?"

Oh. Vinnie glanced at Donna, but Donna's expression told her to expect no defense of Adam from her. "He is seeing her now," she admitted, "but I'm sure he only took up with her afterward."

Still Megan watched her, as if sifting her words to find the truth in them, or to find hope. Then she softened. "I wish I could be that certain, but I can't deny what I saw. I can't ignore evidence when it's right before my eyes. I did that with Keith for too many years, and I won't do it again."

Vinnie knew there had been a terrible misunderstanding, but she could not see how to resolve it. "I'm sorry it didn't work out." She took Megan's hand and gave her a sad smile. "But I hope that whatever happened between you and my grandson, you and I will always be friends."

"Of course we will," Megan said, without hesitation and so warmly that Vinnie felt her throat tightening with emotion.

"Okay, now," Donna said. "Let's not start weeping in the middle of the quilt show."

Vinnie and Megan laughed, and before they could become sentimental again, Donna launched into a narrative of her adventures on the set of *Prairie Vengeance.* Her story was so lively and full of fun Hollywood gossip that before they knew it, forty minutes had passed.

"I wonder what happened to Grace," Megan said. "Did she know where and when to meet?"

"I sent her the same email I sent you," Donna said, scanning the crowd.

Vinnie shrugged and said, "There are always delays at that airport. She might be late, but she'll be here."

Their conversation broke off as they watched the quilters passing their way to and from the main entrance to the quilt show. Suddenly Donna pointed and cried, "Look who's here!"

Vinnie expected to see Grace, but instead discovered none other than Sylvia Compson. She was exiting the quilt show with a kind-looking man carrying a shopping bag in each hand. "Sylvia," Vinnie cried out. "Yoo hoo! Come say hello!"

She had to shout a second time before Sylvia turned their way, but when her eyes met Vinnie's, she smiled and waved. She and the man made their way across the busy lobby to the Cross-Country Quilters. "My goodness," Sylvia said, giving Vinnie a warm hug. "Vinnie Burkholder. Of all the people to run into."

"I should have known I'd see you here." Vinnie laughed, then indicated her companions. "I don't know if you remember these two from quilt camp. They were first-timers."

Vinnie reintroduced Megan and Donna, and in turn, Sylvia introduced them to the man, a friend from Waterford named Andrew. Then she gave them a quizzical frown and said, "Why are you three standing around in the lobby? Are you bored with the quilt show already, or are you waiting for a bus?"

"We're waiting for a friend of ours," Donna said. "Grace Daniels. She was at camp with us."

"Oh, yes, I know Grace," Sylvia said. "I haven't seen her yet today, but she should be around here someplace. She was at the banquet last night."

The Cross-Country Quilters exchanged a look. "She was here last night?" Megan asked. "We thought she wasn't coming in until today."

Sylvia shook her head, puzzled. "No, she's here. We sat together at supper." Suddenly her expression brightened. "There she is now. Grace!"

Vinnie saw her then, too, and she added her voice to Sylvia's. When Grace looked around to see who was shouting her name, Sylvia and the

Cross-Country Quilters waved wildly. She spotted them through the crowd, and then, to Vinnie's astonishment, she froze. An indecipherable expression came over her face, and a heartbeat later, she had spun around and disappeared into the crowd.

Vinnie was too astounded to do anything but stare. "What on earth?" she finally managed to say.

Her friends seemed equally dumbstruck. "That was Grace, wasn't it?" Megan said. "I mean, there were a lot of people walking between us, and she was on the other side of the room—"

"No, that was Grace, all right," Sylvia said.

"Maybe she didn't recognize us," Donna said.

"I don't believe that for a minute," Vinnie declared. "She looked right at us."

"And even if she didn't remember you three, she would certainly remember me," Sylvia said. "We've been friends for fifteen years."

Vinnie didn't know what to think. One glance at Megan and Donna told her they were equally at a loss.

"Well," Vinnie eventually said, "I guess it's just us three, then."

Megan and Donna only nodded in reply.

They bid Sylvia and Andrew good-bye and went inside the conference center to enjoy the quilt show, as much as they could enjoy anything knowing that one of their friends hadn't shown up lest she jeopardize her career and the other had fled the building rather than speak to them.

⚜

Shaking, Grace walked as rapidly as she could away from the convention center, which was slow indeed, encumbered as she was by the two metal crutches she now needed to walk more than a few steps. She had no idea where she was headed, but the urgency to get away compelled her forward. She had waited an hour. That should have been long enough. They should have given up on her and left the lobby, allowing her to sneak upstairs to her room undetected. Now what was she going to do?

She tired too easily to go far, so she went to the Museum of the American Quilter's Society, which to her relief retained its air of contemplative serenity despite the excitement surrounding the quilt show. She found an unoccupied bench in front of one of the older exhibits and sat down, pretending to study the work in front of her, but in truth, resting and trying to sort out her thoughts. Had they seen her crutches? Then she had a more disturbing thought: Had they pursued her, but stopped when they saw her crutches? That was exactly what she had feared—and exactly what Justine insisted would never happen, not with true friends. "You shouldn't be ashamed of the tools that help you to live your life," Justine had admonished her, but Grace had been too exhausted by similar arguments to explain. She wasn't ashamed of the crutches, nor was she ashamed of strangers' seeing her use them. As an African-American woman in a white world, she was used to sidelong glances from ignorant people; it mattered little whether they came because she was black or because she looked disabled. What she could not bear was the uncomfortable reactions of friends and acquaintances. At first even her own family had pretended to ignore the wheelchair, and the crutches in their turn until they got used to them, but at least her family soon resumed treating her as they always had. She could not say the same for her colleagues at the museum. Some ignored the crutches and spoke to her loudly, with false cheer in their voices; others looked askance at the crutches and avoided talking to her at all; most humiliating were those who assumed her mind was as weakened as her body, and either no longer entrusted important tasks to her or explained the obvious in slow voices as if she were a child.

And then there was Gabriel, who phoned at least twice a week, offering to pick up her groceries or run her errands or stop by to see if anything around the loft needed to be fixed. For her part, Justine seemed to have forgotten that Grace was the mother and she the child; she checked in every day to see what Grace was doing, where she was going that day, what she was eating, and how often she rested.

How would the Cross-Country Quilters have reacted? Grace couldn't say for certain, but judging by the reactions of her other friends, they would respond with nervousness, the sort of transparent phony encouragement one saw in cheerleaders for the losing team, or pity. Of the three, Grace despised pity the most.

She stayed in the museum for another hour, long enough for the Cross-Country Quilters to have given up waiting for her to return, enough for them to be well into their tour of the quilt show. Only then did she return to the Executive Inn, and she made sure her friends were nowhere in sight before she rode the elevator to her room.

She had planned to attend a dinner lecture that evening, but instead she ordered room service and read a book until it was time for bed. Saturday morning she had breakfast delivered, and then she hung the Do Not Disturb sign on the door and spent the entire day alone, watching a local cable station's continuous broadcast of quilt show highlights and wishing she had never left home.

Sunday morning she ventured out of her room, hoping the Cross-Country Quilters had not changed their travel plans. According to their last emails,

Vinnie's tour bus had departed the previous evening, Megan intended to drive home right after breakfast, and Donna's flight was due to take off at any moment. Since she didn't have to be at the airport until the afternoon, she could enjoy a few hours of the last day of the quilt show without worrying about running into them.

The crowds had dramatically diminished compared to Friday and Saturday, and Grace found that she was now able to get around the convention center rather easily. She viewed half of the quilts before having a quiet brunch of muffins and grapefruit in the convention center restaurant. She then browsed through the merchants' mall, which still displayed an impressive array of wares despite having had most of their stock depleted over the previous three days. Grace saw several items she would have liked to purchase, but she did not want to attempt maneuvering with the crutches while toting a shopping bag. Next time she would plan for that, but then again, next year her condition might necessitate using the chair instead of the crutches, or she might not be able to come at all.

At the thought, she abruptly left the merchants' mall with its reminders of her limitations and returned to the quilt show, where she tried to lose herself in the beauty of the quilts. She found her own, a quilt she had completed three years before, the last full-size project she had made and perhaps would ever make. With machine appliqué and silk ribbon embroidery she had created a portrait of Harriet Tubman encircled by folk-art motifs symbolizing events from her life. A second-place ribbon hung beside the quilt, and for a moment it brought her a small thrill of joy, which quickly faded when a voice in the back of her mind whispered that it could be the last award of her career.

"Well, my goodness," came a voice from behind her. "Second place. I would have given it first, myself, but no one asked me."

Grace recognized the voice, and didn't turn around. "Hello, Sylvia."

"Hello yourself." Sylvia walked around her, studying the crutches, looking at Grace from beneath raised brows. "Is this some type of fashion statement, or do you actually need those contraptions?"

Grace's grip tightened on the handles. "I need them."

"I see." Sylvia nodded thoughtfully. "I suppose this is why you took off so suddenly the other day?"

Grace could only manage a nod.

"I must say you can move along quite quickly on them. I don't think I could have caught up with you at my sprinting pace. Granted, my sprinting pace isn't what it used to be."

Grace took a deep breath and slowly let it out. "Aren't you going to ask me why I need them?"

"I assumed you need them to walk."

"Well, yes, but . . ." Sylvia's dry matter-of-factness flustered her. "But don't you wonder why?"

"Of course I do. I imagine it must be something serious if you'd go to so much trouble to conceal it from your friends. I also assume it must have been afflicting you for some time, including when you visited Elm Creek Manor, which would account for your odd behavior there. On the other hand, I also realize it's none of my business, and if you wanted me to know, you'd tell me."

"I have MS," Grace heard herself say.

Sylvia's expression became grave. "Oh, dear. Grace, I'm so sorry."

Grace felt tears spring into her eyes. "Don't pity me. I hate pity."

"Grace, dear, it's not pity I feel." Sylvia's voice was warm with compassion, and she placed a hand on Grace's shoulder. "Let's find somewhere to sit down, shall we?"

Sylvia nodded toward a bench several yards away, and as they made their way to it, Grace composed herself. Grace marveled at how easily the truth had slipped from her when she had tried so hard for so long to conceal it. "Are you angry that I didn't tell you in August?" she asked as they sat down.

"Of course not. You're under no obligation to share your secrets with the world, or even with your friends." Sylvia looked at her appraisingly. "I do wonder how it's been for you, though, keeping this particular secret, having no one to talk to about it."

"It's been awful," Grace blurted out. "It's bad enough knowing I have this disease, knowing its prognosis, but seeing how other people react to me, how they change—sometimes I think that's worse."

"People deal with illness and disability in odd ways sometimes," Sylvia remarked. "After I had my stroke, Sarah—she's the young woman who runs Elm Creek Quilts—she's like a daughter to me, but she was so shaken up that she couldn't even visit me in the hospital. She avoided me after I returned home to recuperate, too."

"I don't want people to treat me any differently than they did before."

"Are you different?"

Grace's instinct was to say no, but Sylvia's bluntness forced her to think before responding. "Yes," she said, realizing that truth for the first time. "I have a sense of my own mortality. I have limitations I didn't have before. I see the world differently; I see other people differently. I'd be lying if I said my MS has left me unchanged."

"People probably see those changes in you, and they need time to get to know you as you are now."

"No, that's not it," Grace shot back. "They see the crutches; they see the wheelchair. They see the tremors and the clumsiness. Then don't see Grace adjusting to a disease; they see the disease."

"I'm sure some of them do exactly that," Sylvia admitted. "But others would not. It seems unfair not to let them show you. It seems wrong to deny yourself the comfort their friendship could bring you." Sylvia paused. "Especially since, as I'm guessing, your quilting brings you little comfort these days. Your MS is the root of your quilter's block, isn't it?"

"It *is* my quilter's block," Grace said bitterly. "It's stolen my creativity along with everything else."

"A disease can't take your art from you unless you let it."

"You don't understand. If you could see my studio, you'd find it littered with dozens of sketches, as shaky as if my grandson had drawn them. You'd see appliqués cut awkwardly and sewn with haphazard stitches." She held out her hands, the hands that had once created so much beauty and now betrayed her every time she held pen or needle. "My mind knows what to do—how to draw, how to cut, how to sew—but my hands can't do it."

Grace struggled to hold back the tears, but one slipped down her cheek, and she brushed it away angrily. The blood was rushing in her head, all the anger and helplessness that had plagued her for months, fighting to be let out. "I would give up walking forever," she choked out, "if I could just have my art back."

"It never left you," Sylvia said gently. "You tell me you can't do what you used to do. Very well; so be it. Accept that and move on."

"Move on to what?"

"Move on to what you can do now. Grace, you think your creativity is in your hands. It isn't. It's in your heart, your mind, your soul, and until you lose those three, you can never lose your art." Sylvia placed a hand on her shoulder. "You must find some other way to create."

"What other way?"

"I don't know. Only you can discover that for yourself."

"I don't know how. I don't know where to start."

"I know where. You admitted you're not the same person you were before this disease afflicted you, so stop trying to create the quilts that quilter would have created. Art is supposed to tell the truth. Don't use your quilts to hide your MS; use your quilts to expose it. Let us see your pain and frustration in every stitch. Let us see how you struggle to make beauty out of your grief. Tell the truth."

Tell the truth. The words rang in Grace's ears and resonated in her heart. She had been lying for too long, to herself, to her friends, and she knew suddenly that it was time to stop. It was time to tell the truth and accept the consequences both certain and unpredictable, to let come whatever pain, rejection, or unhappiness must, and as an artist would, embrace it, and find the meaning in it.

☙

It was Sunday morning, and Adam had been listening to Natalie gripe about work for nearly fifteen minutes when his call-waiting clicked. "Hold on a minute. I have another call," he said, grateful for the momentary escape. He was trying to be a concerned friend, but Natalie taxed his patience. He hadn't seen her for weeks, not since his mother's birthday party and their argument in the car afterward, but every so often she would phone him to vent about the latest Lindsor's upheaval or indignity. He wondered if Natalie realized she knew nothing of what was going on in his life, both because she never asked and because she never gave him an opportunity to volunteer the information.

"Wait—" Natalie said, but he quickly switched to the other line before she could complain.

"Hello?" he asked.

"Before you say it's none of my business, just listen. I've had days to think about this, and I need to get something off my chest."

"Nana?"

"I know you care about Megan, and I know you aren't a scoundrel," Nana said. "But somehow you've done something to convince her otherwise. I don't know what you did, I don't know what happened, and frankly, I don't want to know. All I want is for you to talk to her and get this nonsense straightened out."

"Megan doesn't want to talk to me. She's made that perfectly clear."

"And you're going to leave it at that? She doesn't want to talk to you because she thinks you deceived her. Now, unless you did—"

"Of course I didn't."

"Then nothing's stopping you from patching things up."

Nothing except Megan's refusal to return his phone calls, her unwillingness to answer his email, and her suspicions, which he understood but in another sense resented, because he had done nothing to earn her mistrust. He had never lied to her, but the first time she doubted his word, instead of giving him an opportunity to explain, she shut him out of her life—and Robby's life—forever. He loved her and he missed her, but he was angry, too, angry and hurt.

But he didn't think he could explain this to his grandmother. "It's not that simple," he said instead.

"I never claimed it would be simple. Nothing worthwhile usually is. But because it's worthwhile, you owe it to yourself to try."

"Nana—"

"I don't want to argue. I just wanted to speak my piece," Nana said. "And now I've done that, so the rest is up to you. I love you, Adam, but you can be a stubborn fool sometimes."

"I'm not stubborn," Adam protested, but he was talking to a dial tone. He sighed and switched back to Natalie.

"What was all that about?" Natalie asked, irritated.

"It was my grandmother."

"Still pestering you about coming to that Mother's Day thing?"

Suddenly he pictured Valentine's Day, and the way Natalie had acted the gracious hostess in his home when Megan came over. "No, she's not pestering me," he said, unable to keep the annoyance out of his voice. "She doesn't need to. I already said I'm going."

"She isn't your mother."

"I know she isn't, but my mother will be there, too. The Mother's Day brunch is a family tradition."

"I swear to God, you and your family have a tradition for everything," Natalie groused. "What about the luncheon?"

"What about it?"

"I asked you a week ago if you'd come with me."

"And I told you then I couldn't."

"But I need you there," she protested. "I can't show up without an escort."

"Why not?"

"It just isn't done. Forget the brunch. Your family won't disown you."

"That's not the point."

"Then what is the point? The CEO of the corporation that's buying Lindsor's is going to be there. This might be my only chance to impress him, and you want me to go alone?"

He struggled to maintain his patience. "Natalie, I'm sorry, but I can't take you to the luncheon."

"This is your last chance, Adam." Her voice was like ice. "If you don't come with me, I'll find someone else who will, someone unselfish, someone who is willing to support my career."

"I'm sure you won't have any trouble finding him," Adam said. "You've always been able to get what you want."

In response, she slammed down the phone. For the first time in the history of their relationship, she had let Adam have the last word.

It was late afternoon by the time Megan reached her parents' house to pick up Robby, so she gratefully accepted her mother's invitation to stay for supper. To her relief, Robby seemed glad to see her; lately his behavior toward her ranged in a wearying, unpredictable arc from loving to resentful. She had feared her trip to Paducah would set off a bad phase, or worse yet, frighten him as her trip to Elm Creek Quilt Camp had, but he was cheerful as he told her about his visit with his grandparents, and even remembered to ask her how her weekend had gone.

They drove home, stopping across the street to pick up the mail and newspapers their neighbor had collected for them in their absence. Most of the mail was advertisements and bills, but there was also something for Robby, a small card with his father's return address.

Robby sat down at the table as Megan sorted the rest of the mail on the counter. She watched him out of the corner of her eye as he opened the envelope, took out a card, and read it. His expression changed from the hopeful gladness any communication from his father elicited to confusion, and he sat, brow furrowed, studying the card in silence.

She didn't want to pry; she knew he was entitled to privacy in his relationship with Keith, as much as she might long to monitor every detail. Just as she thought she couldn't hold out another moment, Robby said, "I don't get it."

"What don't you get, honey?"

"Is this a birthday card?" he asked, still studying it. "My birthday isn't March twenty-second. Must be from Gina. She got my middle name wrong, too."

"Mind if I take a look?" With a shrug Robby held out the card, so she sat beside him and took it. "Oh. It's a birth announcement," she said, noting the baby bunnies and chicks pictured on the front. "Gina must have had her baby."

Then she opened the card, and disbelief flooded her with the numbing force of cold water.

"It's a boy!" the card declared, a boy seven pounds four ounces in weight and twenty inches long, a boy born March twenty-second to proud parents Gina and Keith Donohue. A boy named Robert Keith Donohue.

Megan couldn't believe it. She prayed she had read the card wrong; she desperately wanted to have read the card wrong. She felt ill. She looked from the card to Robby, speechless, and tried too late to disguise her expression.

"They named the baby Robert?" Robby asked, his voice disbelieving, but his expression oddly blank.

Megan glanced at the card. "It seems so."

Robby looked away, silent. She had never seen him so stunned before, and his stillness frightened her. "Maybe it's a mistake," she said, groping foolishly for something, anything, to reassure him. "Maybe Gina was thinking of you when she filled out the card, and—"

"It's not a mistake." He slid off his chair and left the kitchen. A moment later, she heard the door to his bedroom close.

Megan's heart pounded as she reached for the phone and dialed Keith's number. She couldn't believe he would do such a thing, not even after everything else he had done and had neglected to do. It had to be a mistake.

The phone rang twice before a woman answered, her voice weary and young. "Hello?"

"This is Megan Donohue," she said, stiff with formality. "May I speak with Keith, please?"

"Oh, Megan. Hi." Gina sounded startled. "Hi. Um, well, yes, Keith is here, but he's taking a nap. Can he call you back?"

Megan's anger became too much for her. "I suppose he can, but he probably won't. Would you put him on the line, please?"

A baby began crying in the background. "I really hate to wake him. He's been so tired lately—"

"Gina, I remember what it's like to have a new baby in the house, and if anyone should be taking a nap, it's you. I need to speak to Keith, and if he doesn't talk to me now, I'm going to keep calling back until he does."

Gina hesitated, and the baby's wails grew louder. "Okay, I'll get him." The phone clattered as if she had dropped it.

Megan waited, and heard the baby's cries subside. Long after she began to suspect Keith wouldn't answer, he did. "What is it?"

"Keith, this is Megan."

"I know. What do you want?"

"Robby just received the birth announcement." Megan took a deep breath. "I'm hoping there's been a mistake. Robby's card says you named the child Robert."

"Yeah, that's right. Robert Keith."

Anger made her words distinct and hard. "You already have a son named Robert."

"I know that."

"Isn't there enough danger that an older child will feel replaced by a younger sibling without giving that sibling the older child's name?"

"Not that it's any of your business, but I didn't give the baby Robby's name. Robby's Robert Michael, not Robert Keith. So we won't call the baby Robby. We'll call him—I don't know, Bob or Rob or something."

"Why?" Megan managed to ask. "Why would you do this?"

"Ask Gina. Robert is her father's name, and her grandfather's, and so on and so on. Do you think this was my idea? I wanted to name him Keith, but I had to settle for the middle name."

"Robby is very hurt."

"It can't be that bad."

"It is."

"Well, he's a tough kid. He'll get over it."

"He isn't as tough as you think, and if he were, it would be because of the calluses he's had to develop because of how you treat him."

"Oh, don't start—"

"You're going to have to explain this to him, because I don't think I can when I don't understand it myself."

"Thanks, Megan," Keith snapped. "This is just what I need. I have a baby crying day and night, Gina moaning over every little thing, and now I have to listen to you. I don't have time for this." He hung up.

Slowly Megan replaced the receiver, wondering what she should do, how she would comfort her son. She went down the hallway to Robby's bedroom and knocked softly on the door. "Robby?" she called. "May I come in?"

"No."

Megan touched the door with her fingertips. "Honey, none of this is your fault."

Suddenly the door flew open. "I know it isn't," Robby shouted. His face was streaked with angry tears. "It's your fault. You made Dad go away and marry *her,* just like you made Adam go away. You won't even let him be my friend anymore. You ruin everything. Just leave me alone. I hate you!" He slammed the door shut with all his strength.

Tears sprang into Megan's eyes. *He doesn't mean it,* she told herself. Robby didn't really hate her; he was angry at his father and Gina—and, she admitted, at her, too, because of Adam—but she was the only one of the three he could confront. Her heart ached with the knowledge, but she decided to leave him alone. Tomorrow his rage would be mostly spent, and she could try again.

But in the morning, he averted his eyes and shoveled down his breakfast without even the smallest response to her attempts at normal conversation. He went out to the car without waiting to be reminded of the time, as if he couldn't get away from her quickly enough. When she dropped him off in front of his school, he pulled away when she tried to kiss him good-bye and jumped out of the car without a backward glance.

At work, she tried to lose herself in her research, but Robby's bitterness and accusations were always there, nagging at the back of her thoughts. She told herself not to take Robby's anger personally, because that would only interfere with helping him. Her resolution changed nothing, but somehow she felt a bit better. She was engrossed in the analysis of the burning rates of a new synthetic rocket fuel when her phone rang.

"Megan, honey?" her mother said.

"Mom?" Megan glanced at the clock. It was nearly four. "What's going on?"

"I don't want to alarm you, but did you make some other arrangements for Robby today?"

Fingers of cold dread crept around her heart. "What do you mean?"

"When your father went to pick Robby up from school, he wasn't there. We hoped . . . we thought maybe he stayed home sick, and you forgot to tell us."

"No, I dropped him off at school this morning." Megan's throat was dry; she tried to swallow. "Did Dad talk to his teacher?"

"She said he left with the other kids as always. Your dad didn't want to worry her, so he told her he'd check the playground."

"Oh my God."

"It's probably nothing," her mother hastened to say. "He probably went home with a friend. There's probably a message waiting on the answering machine."

Megan nodded numbly, as if her mother could see her. "I'm going home."

"We'll meet you there," her mother said, and hung up.

Megan snatched up her bag and left the building, pausing only to tell a coworker that she had to rush home for an emergency. Twenty minutes later she pulled into her driveway beside her father's truck, not remembering a single mile of the drive. Her parents were waiting in the kitchen. She knew from their expressions that no message waited for her, and that Robby wasn't anywhere in the house.

Her mother embraced her, her face drawn with concern. "Are you certain he didn't tell you he was going anywhere after school?"

"I know he didn't," Megan said. Her legs felt too weak to support her, so she sank into a chair. "He hardly spoke to me at all this morning. We had a fight last night—well, not exactly a fight. He was angry, and he shouted."

"Angry about what?" her father asked.

Wordlessly, Megan gestured toward the birth announcement, which she had left beside the phone after calling Keith. Her father read it and scowled, then passed it to his wife. She sighed and shook her head. "No wonder he's upset," she said.

"He probably just ran off to be by himself for a while," her father said. "It's his way of punishing all the grown-ups who have let him down."

As hard as that would be to accept, Megan prayed it was true. Considering the alternatives, the horrible, nightmare alternatives . . .

In an instant her mother was at her side. "Megan, honey." She held her daughter tightly. "Everything's going to be okay."

Megan nodded and gulped air, squeezing her eyes shut and clutching desperately at her mother. She couldn't fall apart. It was too soon to fall apart. She had to stay in control to find Robby. He would be found; he would be home within the hour.

She reached for the phone. "Are you calling the police?" her father asked.

"Not yet," Megan said, hoping that wasn't a mistake. "I thought I'd call some of his classmates first."

Her father slipped on the jacket he had draped over the counter. "I'll walk around the neighborhood and look for him."

"I'll drive up to the school," her mother said, picking up her purse and glancing at Megan. "Unless you want me here?"

Megan preferred for them to be out searching, so her parents left. Megan tried to calm herself as she dialed Jason's number. His mother answered cheerfully enough, but her voice grew troubled when Megan asked if Robby was there.

"No, he isn't," she said.

"Would you mind asking your son if he saw Robby leave school?"

The other woman's voice telegraphed alarm. "Is Robby missing?"

"He isn't home," Megan managed to say, unable to get her mind around the darker possibilities. "Would you ask Jason, please?"

"Of course." There was a scramble on the other end of the line, and muffled voices. "Jason says he saw Robby on the soccer field after school playing football with some other kids."

"Does he know who these other kids were?"

There was another pause while she inquired, then she returned with a list of five names. Megan thanked her and hung up, already paging through the phone book for the first number. Her brief stirring of hope wavered and then flickered out when one by one, each of the children's parents told her that their children had come home long ago, and Robby had not accompanied them.

"I have the phone tree for the PTA," one mother said. "I'll call around and ask if anyone has seen him."

"You should call the police," the last father said. Megan decided to take his advice.

The officer who took her call tried to reassure her, saying that Robby hadn't been missing very long, and he would probably come home before the squad car arrived. Megan was not comforted. She paced around the kitchen looking out the windows and praying she would see her son walking down the sidewalk. Her mother returned just as the police arrived. Megan watched as the two officers spoke to her briefly in the driveway, then all three came into the house.

The two men introduced themselves as Officers Hasselbach and DiMarco. They began with a series of what Megan assumed were routine questions—Robby's age, height, weight, hair and eye color. Megan's mother hurried into the living room for a photograph, which Hasselbach studied and passed to DiMarco. "May we keep this?" Hasselbach asked.

Megan nodded.

"Is Mr. Donohue home?"

"Robby's father and I are divorced."

The two officers exchanged a look. "Have you tried to reach him?"

"No," Megan said, surprised by the question, surprised that calling Keith had not occurred to her. "But he's in Oregon. I don't think he'll be much help, and I'd hate to alarm him."

DiMarco picked up the receiver and handed it to her. "Let's just make sure he's still in Oregon."

Suddenly Megan understood. "It's not like that," she said, but she dialed the number. "Keith wouldn't take Robby. Not even for a visit."

The officers exchanged another significant look. "So the divorce was unfriendly?" Hasselbach asked.

"What divorce isn't?" Megan replied, then broke off as the phone was answered. It was Gina, and when she said Keith wasn't home yet, Megan remembered the time difference. "Could I have his number at work, please?"

"I really don't think you should be calling him at work."

"Please, Gina, it's an emergency."

"Like yesterday was an emergency?"

Megan closed her eyes and willed the churning in her stomach to subside. "Not like yesterday. Robby's missing."

There was a pause, and then Gina said, "I'll call him and have him call you back. You should keep your line open in case Robby tries to reach you."

Megan stammered her thanks and hung up the phone. "Keith's wife is going to call him at work."

DiMarco was watching her quizzically. "What did you mean when you said, 'Not like yesterday?'"

Megan sat down at the kitchen table and buried her head in her hands. "I phoned them yesterday to discuss another matter."

"Child support?"

"No. It's complicated." Suddenly Megan grew exasperated. "Why are you wasting time asking me about my ex-husband on the other side of the country when my son is missing?"

"We're just trying to cover everything, ma'am," Hasselbach said.

DiMarco said, "I'd like to look around the house, if you wouldn't mind showing me around."

"I'll take you," Megan's mother said crisply. She brought Megan a glass of water and hugged her before leading the officer out of the room.

Hasselbach eyed her thoughtfully before saying, "The call yesterday—was Robby angry at his father?"

"Yes." Megan forced herself to say the rest. "And at me."

"Why?" When Megan showed him the birth announcement and pointed out the baby's name, Hasselbach nodded and said, "Is it possible Robby might try to go see his father?"

"In Oregon?" Megan said, incredulous. "Robby's only nine, but he knows how far it is to Oregon."

"If he has an allowance, he might have raided his piggy bank for a bus ticket. I've seen it before."

"Not Robby."

"You said he was angry at you, too?"

Megan nodded, gulping the water and glancing out the window in time to see her father walking up the drive, alone. "He blamed me for sending away his father and for not letting him see Adam."

"Who's Adam, a classmate?"

"No." She glanced at the clock. It was approaching six; Robby had been missing for nearly three hours. "He's a friend of mine. Robby's fond of him."

"A boyfriend?"

Megan heard the front door open and shut. "Yes. He was. Not anymore." She rose as her father entered the room. Megan quickly made introductions, then asked, "Anything?"

Her father looked grim. "Not a sign of him. I talked to a few kids and some neighbors who were outside. No one saw him walk home."

Hasselbach asked Megan, "Any chance your former boyfriend might know where Robby is?"

"I don't think so."

Hasselbach nodded thoughtfully, then asked for Adam's name and phone number, as well as Keith's. After Megan provided them, he indicated the phone. "Mind if I call the precinct?"

Megan nodded just as her mother returned with DiMarco. "Nothing," he told Hasselbach. Hasselbach nodded and dialed the phone.

"Nothing what?" Megan's father asked.

"No signs of a struggle, no signs of forced entry." DiMarco nodded to Megan's mother. "Mrs. Levine found Robby's suitcase in his closet and said none of his clothes seem to be missing."

"I couldn't be certain, though," she said, giving Megan an apologetic look.

Megan nodded slowly, feeling panic rising in her chest. "You think he ran away?" The thought should have comforted her. If he had run away, he might come back on his own, but if he had been kidnapped . . .

"That seems the most plausible explanation," Hasselbach said. "He was angry at you and his father. He might be trying to get back at you. We'll have officers checking the bus stations just in case."

The phone rang. Megan jumped, heart pounding, and glanced at Hasselbach. He nodded, so she picked up. "Hello?"

"Megan?" It was Gina. "I'm so sorry. I called Keith at work, but they said he left early for a dentist's appointment. I didn't know he had one, so I called the dentist, but they said he wasn't scheduled for any work. So I called the doctor, thinking maybe I had heard wrong, but he wasn't there either. I'm sorry, Megan, but I don't know where he is."

"I understand." More than anyone else in the world, Megan understood. "Will you have him call me when you hear from him?"

"Of course. The police have phoned here already asking to speak to him. Megan . . ." Gina sounded as if she were crying. "Robby sounds like such a sweet boy. I hope . . . I mean, I'm sure—"

"Thank you," Megan said quietly, and hung up the phone. The officers were watching her. "That was Gina. My ex-husband's wife."

"Still no sign of him?" DiMarco asked.

Megan shook her head, and nearly gasped aloud as the phone shrilled again. Without waiting for Hasselbach's signal, she answered. "Hello?"

"Megan?"

It was a man's voice, so altered by emotion that it took her a moment to recognize it. "Adam?"

"Megan, what's going on? The police just called, asking if I've seen Robby."

The warmth and concern in his voice dissolved her shaky courage into tears. "He's missing."

"Missing? What do you mean?"

"He wasn't waiting when his grandfather went to pick him up after school." She struggled in vain to regain her composure. "I don't know where he could be. He's angry at me. I think he ran away, but where would he go? Where would he go? He's only nine."

"Where was he last seen?"

"On the soccer field, at school. Another boy saw him playing football with some classmates."

"Are you alone? Is anyone with you?"

"My parents are here. And the police."

A pause. "I'm coming over."

"Adam—"

"I'll be there as soon as I can." Before she could protest, he hung up the phone. He was coming. The control she had fought so hard to maintain crumbled, and she began to sob, shaking, until her mother came and wrapped her arms around her.

Another hour crept past. Around her, the officers talked quietly, making arrangements, checking in with other officers. Hasselbach agreed that Megan's father could help by going door to door in the neighborhood, asking if anyone had seen Robby. Megan's mother remained with her, saying little, but comforting Megan with her presence.

A neighbor called; she had been contacted by the PTA phone tree and wanted to know if there was anything she could do to help. Another woman Megan didn't know, but whose name she recognized from the phone list, phoned to pepper Megan with questions until she began to feel dizzy and nauseated. After that, DiMarco began taking the calls. Still no one had heard from Keith.

As darkness fell, Megan felt herself becoming still and numb. Robby was out there somewhere, lost or hiding, hungry and cold. The police had searched everything within a child's walking distance of Robby's school, to no avail. She could not believe Keith had taken him, and yet if Robby had run away, surely he would have been found by now, unless something far more malevolent had befallen him.

Then, suddenly, headlights shone through the kitchen window as a car pulled into the driveway. As Megan watched, a figure exited the driver's side and came around to open the front passenger door to let out a much smaller figure.

"Robby," she breathed, and bolted to the door. In a heartbeat she was outside embracing him, tears running down her face. "Robby. Thank God."

"I'm sorry, Mom," he said, his voice muffled against her shoulder.

She loosened her desperate grip to get a better look at him. "Are you all right? Are you hurt?"

Behind her Hasselbach asked, "Was he with you?"

"No," came the answer, and only then did Megan look up to see who had brought Robby home. Adam gave her a reassuring look before returning his attention to the officer. "I found him at the middle school, practicing his kicking."

"And you are?"

"Adam Wagner. A friend of the family."

Megan rose, clutching one of Robby's hands. She placed her other hand on his shoulder and steered him inside. Robby was home, home and safe, and nothing else mattered.

The rest of the evening passed in a blur. The officers remained while she fixed Robby some supper and phoned in their report to the station as she took him upstairs to get him ready for bed. She lingered in Robby's room for a while, stroking his hair as he drifted off to sleep. When she returned to the kitchen, she thanked the officers for everything they had done, and saw them, along with her parents, to the door.

In the sudden quiet, Megan realized that she had not said a word to Adam the entire evening. "Thank you for finding him," she said, and felt her emotions welling up until it was almost impossible to say any more. "I don't know what I would have done if he hadn't come home tonight."

"He's safe. That's all that matters," Adam said, his voice an echo of her own thoughts.

"How did you know where to look?"

"When I was driving here, I remembered that you said he was last seen playing football. We had a lot of fun that day we practiced kicking at the middle school. He talked a little about his dad while we were there, and about you. Somehow it seemed right to check."

"I'm very grateful," Megan said, and she meant it with all her heart.

Adam shrugged and gave her a smile that was encouraging and yet sad. They stood for a moment in awkward silence. Megan didn't know what to do or say, but Adam told her good-bye and left.

⚜

Julia was sorry when shooting ended and Donna and Lindsay went home. Except for her maid, Julia had lived alone since her second divorce, and she had forgotten how pleasant it was to have company around the house. She consoled herself by thinking of Elm Creek Quilt Camp, where she would be reunited with her friends. By then *Prairie Vengeance* would be out of post-production, and Ares might even have a new project lined up for her.

To reward herself for surviving Deneford, she spent a week at Aurora Borealis. When she returned home, pampered and refreshed, she found two new scripts Ares had sent for her review—and a note from Deneford summoning her to a meeting.

She met Ares outside the studio, and together they entered Deneford's conference room just as they had so many months ago for the first script meeting. Deneford wasted no time in small talk. "I have bad news," he said when the principal actors, their agents, and the assorted assistants were seated. "We played some scenes for a test audience, and it didn't go well."

A collective mutter of frustration went up from the table. "You have a first cut already?" Julia asked, surprised.

"Not a complete cut. Like I said, just a few scenes."

Julia sensed the people around her relaxing. "What's a few scenes?" Rowen's agent asked. "That doesn't sound like any cause for concern."

Deneford fixed him with a piercing look. "You of all people should be concerned, for your client's sake. Our test audience was our target demographic."

"Men eighteen to thirty-five?"

"Exactly. They hated it."

Rowen paled. "Even the cattle-rustling scene?"

Deneford hesitated. "No. Actually, they liked that."

Rowen smiled and sank back into his chair, relieved.

"Hold on," Ellen said. "Since when is our intended audience eighteen- to thirty-five-year-old men?"

Deneford ignored her. "The numbers are low, but I have hopes that the project is still salvageable. Sorry, people, but that means we reshoot."

Above the groans, Samantha's agent said, "What's your timetable? Samantha is the guest VJ on MTV all next month."

"We'll work around her. We might need that much time for the rewrites anyway." Deneford looked at Ellen, slouching unhappily in her chair at the far end of the table. "Is your calendar clear?"

"Clear enough," she said. "I'm almost afraid to ask, but what sort of changes did you have in mind?"

"I've decided to ax all the quilting stuff."

Julia started. "I beg your pardon?"

"We're going to lose the quilting." Deneford regarded her, puzzled. "Surely you don't have a problem with that. Now you won't have to admit to the world you hired a stunt quilter for your scenes."

"I could live with that," Julia retorted. "Whatever would compel you to get rid of the quilting? It's the heart of the story."

"Rick Rowen is the heart of the story," his agent said.

"Give me a break," Samantha's agent muttered.

Julia was in no mood for their bickering. "Stephen, do you really think such a drastic change is necessary?" she asked in her most reasonable tone. "Quilting is the metaphor that binds the entire story together."

"Not to mention that it's how Sadie supports her family and saves her farm," Ellen added.

"I had some thoughts about that, too," Deneford said. "Our test audience thought earning money from quilting was, well, a little tame. I decided she'll run a bordello instead."

Deneford's assistant held up his hands as if framing a sign. "Think *Little House on the Prairie* meets *Die Hard* meets *Pretty Woman*."

Julia gaped at them. "Sadie is going to be a hooker?"

"At least at first," Deneford said. "Later, when the money starts rolling in, she'll become the madam."

"I don't believe this," Julia said, disgusted.

"It might not be so bad," Ares said in her ear. "You're still sexy. With the right lighting and costumes, you could still carry it off."

Julia wanted to slug him, but she kept her attention on Deneford. "I don't think this is a good idea. Maybe you're not choosing the right test audience for this picture. Why don't you show those scenes to women? I'm sure you'll get much better numbers in all age groups."

Deneford shrugged. "We might, but that's not the audience we're going for."

"That's not the Rick Rowen audience," Rick's agent chimed in, and Rick nodded.

Julia felt her anger rising. "Women do attend movies, you know."

"Come on, Julia," Deneford said. "Don't go all feminist on me. We both know women will go see a man's picture, but men won't go see a chick flick unless they're dragged there kicking and screaming."

"As long as they buy their tickets, does it matter how they go?" Ares countered.

Julia glared at him. "Thanks for that brilliant contribution."

Deneford raised his hands. "All right, all right. Everyone take a deep breath. We all want to do what's best for the movie, right? We all want to salvage the hard work we've already put into it. This is the way to go. I'm staking my career on it."

Not only his career, Julia thought, but hers as well. She knew she could balk and complain all she wanted, but ultimately Deneford would have his way. Her only choices were to cooperate or to quit, and she couldn't afford to quit.

"I quit."

Julia spun to face the back of the room.

Ellen, her expression weary, had risen from her chair. "I can't do this anymore."

"Ellen," Deneford said quietly, "sit down."

But Ellen remained standing. "I can't do this. Sadie Henderson was my great-grandmother. I can't let you make my great-grandmother into a prostitute. That's not the way it happened. I won't do that to her memory. I won't do that to my family."

All eyes were upon her as she walked around the table toward the door.

"Think carefully before you do this," Deneford warned.

Ellen removed from her bag a battered, dog-eared script marked with dozens of bright sticky notes and threw it into the wastebasket beside the door. "Think *This Script* meets *The Trash Can.*"

"Think *Another Dime-a-Dozen Nobody Writer* meets *Unemployment,*" Deneford shot back icily. "Don't forget, Miss Henderson, I was giving you a break based upon a student film and the minuscule talent you displayed in that abominable first script despite the fact that you've never done anything and no one's ever heard of you. If you think you'll ever get another chance like this again, you're gravely mistaken."

Ellen blanched and swallowed, but reached for the doorknob.

"You're not that important," Deneford said, his voice rising. "I bought your script. I own it. This movie will be made with you or without you. There are four people essential to this project—me, Rick, Samantha, and Julia. I need them, but you need us much more than we need you."

Ellen's hand trembled—and she released the doorknob. Her gaze went from Deneford, around the table, and came to rest on Julia. She said nothing, but her gaze pleaded with Julia as loudly and as clearly as if she had shouted.

Julia remembered how she had loved that young woman's original story, how she had longed to know Sadie, to be her, and she thought of how drastically her history had been altered since then. She thought of Donna, and how thrilled she had been to work as a stunt quilter; she thought of the extras around the quilt frame in Kansas and the quilters at Elm Creek Manor, and how much they would have loved a movie about their passion and their art. Most of all, she thought about the Cross-Country Quilters, and how they stood by each other and supported each other in their times of greatest need.

"I'm out, too," she said softly.

Deneford stared at her. "What did you say?"

"I'm out." Julia pushed back her chair and rose.

Ares seized her arm. "Are you out of your mind?"

She freed herself and gathered her things. "Sorry, Ares." She looked around the table. "My apologies to all of you. But I'm ashamed of what we've done to Ellen's story, and I can't be a part of it anymore."

She thought she heard Ellen let out a glad sob, but Ares held her attention. "If you do this, it will mean the end of your career."

"I know that."

His eyes narrowed with fury. "It also means that you and I are through."

Julia smiled. "Why, Ares, you just made my decision that much easier."

She turned, went to the door, linked her arm through Ellen's, and led the dumbfounded young woman from the room.

Deneford pursued them as far as the doorway. "Your leaving will only improve the project," he snapped at Ellen. "But you, Julia, you'll be hearing from my lawyer."

Julia felt a tremor of queasiness, but she disguised it by waving her hand and saying airily, "Oh, very well, Stephen, if you must litigate, litigate. As if you don't have more important things to do with your time. As if you don't have Samantha ready and waiting to take over my role, as she has already done to some extent. You took a few liberties with our contract, too, did you not?"

She glimpsed the speechless consternation on Deneford's face as she spun around and strode away, half propelling Ellen along, half leaning upon her for support.

She kept smiling as they walked down the hallway to the exit, and nodded as Ellen thanked her over and over, but her thoughts were of the career she had thrown away, the resurgence in fame she would never see, the Academy Award she would never hold, gleaming in all its golden beauty.

Then she thought of the Cross-Country Quilters. She imagined them cheering her on, proud of her, assuring her she had done the right thing.

She and Ellen left the building together, and as Julia stepped into the bright California sunshine, a flicker of joy rose in her heart, growing until it burned away her remorse and misgivings, until her smile transformed the mask of an actress into the face of a true friend.

Twelve

Donna's flight arrived in time for her to catch the first shuttle from the airport to Elm Creek Manor. She settled into her seat with a happy sigh as the van full of excited quilters left for Waterford. When Donna's status as a veteran camper came up in the course of conversation, the first-timers peppered her with questions, which she tried her best to answer. But when they asked her what Elm Creek Quilt Camp was really like, she could only tell them, "You'll have to discover that for yourself."

She indulged in a contemplative mood and spent much of the trip gazing out the window at the rolling, forested hills of central Pennsylvania, daydreaming about the week to come. For more than an hour they drove, past farms and small towns, past historical markers and a sign for Waterford College, until at last the van turned onto a gravel road that wound its way through a forest. This Donna remembered; she looked for the bridge over the crystal waters of Elm Creek, and when they reached it, she knew they were almost there.

Not far across the bridge, the forest opened suddenly into a broad clearing from which a lawn sloped gently upward toward the gray stone manor. Donna felt a pang at the sight of it, a sense of homecoming and nostalgia she couldn't quite explain.

"There it is," the driver announced. "Elm Creek Manor."

The travelers who had not yet broken off their conversations did so then, peering through the windows expectantly. Donna heard murmurs of delight, and she smiled to herself, remembering how she had first reacted at the sight of the gray stone walls and tall white columns. Now the scene was colored by memories of picnics in the gardens, quilting with friends on the broad verandah, and passing through the tall double doors to and from her morning walks.

As the van approached the manor, Donna searched in vain for a familiar face among the women unloading cars parked in the circular driveway. She waited on the sidewalk as the driver unloaded their suitcases, hoping the other Cross-Country Quilters would arrive soon.

Suddenly from behind her a voice cried out, "Donna!"

Donna whirled around. "Vinnie," she exclaimed with delight. "It's so good to see you."

"You, too, honey. My goodness, you're looking sharp."

"Thanks," Donna said, pleased. In the past twelve months, she had lost twenty pounds, and she now felt years younger. She had hoped her friends would notice. "You look great, too."

"Tell me something I don't know," Vinnie said, primping her hair. The two friends laughed and embraced.

Megan arrived not long after Donna had checked in and settled into her room. Two hours later, Julia's limousine pulled up in front of the manor, creating a stir just as it had the year before. As the four friends welcomed each other with laughter, hugs, and tears of gladness, Donna was struck by how everything felt so comfortably familiar and yet so new and full of promise.

Only Grace's absence cast a shadow on their reunion. After months of silence following Grace's inexplicable behavior at AQS, each had written asking her to meet them again at Elm Creek Manor as they had planned. No one reproached her for her actions or even asked her to explain; all they wanted was her company, and each had tried in her own way to show her how eager they were to see her again. She had never responded.

When they had finished unpacking, they gathered in Vinnie's room for show-and-tell before supper. Donna was the first to unveil her block for the Challenge Quilt. She had abandoned the Hen and Chicks block and made a Bear's Paw instead, with the autumn leaf print as the four feet, and a rich purple for the claws and the small square in the center. Julia and Megan admired her piecing, but Vinnie said, "What does a Bear's Paw have to do with your challenge? You should have chosen a block with 'Daughter' or 'Mother' in the name."

Donna was quiet for a moment, thinking of the fierce mother-bear rage that had filled her as she brought Lindsay from the apartment where Brandon had beaten her, and the protectiveness that had compelled her to spirit her daughter away to California, where at last Lindsay remembered who she truly was. "To me, Bear's Paw symbolizes how I overcame my obstacle. Wasn't that how we were supposed to choose?"

"If that's what this block means to you, then it's perfect," Megan reassured her.

Julia agreed, too, so Vinnie accepted her explanation grudgingly, but added, "I would have settled for a block with 'University' or 'Student' in the title. You could have made a Schoolhouse block, only in the University of

Minnesota's colors." Vinnie's eyebrows rose. "Lindsay *is* returning to school this semester, isn't she?"

"She is, but not at Minnesota. She's transferring to the University of Southern California's film school."

Her friends burst into exclamations of delight, and Julia's was the most joyful of all. "You'll have to come visit her," she said, "and whenever you do, you and Paul can stay with me. Becca, too."

Donna agreed, and immediately Megan and Vinnie pretended to pout over their exclusion. Julia teased them at first, but soon expanded the invitation to include them all. "Come in winter," she suggested. "Get away from that awful cold."

To the others, Donna said, "She thinks anything below fifty degrees is arctic."

"I do not," Julia protested, but joined in the laughter.

Next Megan showed her block, a beautiful Snow Crystals pattern with diamonds cut from the autumn leaf print and a lovely blue floral. In the center, eight diamonds formed a LeMoyne Star; in each corner, six diamonds fanned into a partial star, so that the design seemed to radiate from the center. Julia gasped at the perfect precision of Megan's sewing. "How did you make all these points so sharp?" she asked, tracing the tip of a diamond with her finger.

"Sharp points or not, she should have chosen something else," Vinnie protested. "Snow Crystals. What on earth does that have to do with helping your son?"

Megan's smile faded, and a wistful look came into her eyes. "It's hard to explain," she said. "I suppose my situation is like Donna's. Maybe there isn't a literal connection between this block and my challenge, but this is what I was inspired to make." She paused, gazing at her block, and quietly added, "The pattern just came to me on a night when I finally realized that I could be happy again."

Donna reached over and squeezed her hand, wondering what secret Megan kept, and wishing she could do something to remove the sorrow from her friend's voice.

Vinnie sighed in exasperation. "I don't think you two followed the rules very well."

"At least I met my challenge," Megan said. "Robby's counselor says he's making great progress."

"Has Keith helped?" Donna asked.

Megan hesitated. "A little. He invited Robby for a visit in June, and Robby said they had a good time. He's crazy about his little brother, and he said Gina's not so bad, either."

"That's good news," Julia said.

"It's a start, anyway. A lot depends on Keith, but I'm hopeful. Robby's disappearance shook him up. I think . . ." Megan paused, thoughtful. "I think he'll be a better father from now on, despite the geographic distance between them. I think he'll be a better father to little Bob, too, and maybe even a better husband."

Donna was glad to hear it, but she wished that Megan had added something about her own happiness. Megan had never mentioned Adam since the day he had found Robby at the middle school, but Donna remembered how his affection had transformed her, and hoped she would know as great a happiness soon.

"My turn," Vinnie said, and reached into her red canvas tote bag. Before bringing out her block, she pursed her lips and glared around the circle of friends. "Now, no laughing," she scolded them. "I finished my block in January, when circumstances were quite different." Donna caught the quick glance she gave Megan as she unfolded her block, sighed, and held it up for them to see.

It was a Wedding Ring block.

Donna, Julia, and even Megan burst into laughter. "All right," Vinnie said, with just the barest hint of a smile. "You're all very amused, I'm sure. But you have to agree this burgundy complements the autumn leaf fabric well."

"It's a lovely block," Donna assured her.

"I know that, and that's why I wasn't about to throw it away just because I didn't meet my challenge." Then she frowned, thoughtful. "Although in a way I did meet at least part of it."

Donna and Julia exchanged a look of surprise, but Megan's gaze was fixed on Vinnie. "What do you mean?"

"I wanted my grandson to get over his broken engagement and find someone new. Well, perhaps he hasn't found someone new, but he must have gotten over his former fiancée, and if he hasn't, I'm sure he will soon."

Megan's voice was a study in nonchalance. "What makes you think so?"

"Because she's marrying someone else," Vinnie said. "He's a big shot, too, and almost twice her age. He's the owner of the company that bought the store where she works."

"You're kidding," Donna exclaimed.

"That's one way to insure your job security," Julia remarked.

"Now, I'm not saying that's why she did it," Vinnie said. "She might truly love him. On the other hand . . ." She shrugged. "Well, she's stopped pestering Adam, and that's what counts."

"Pestering him?" Megan said.

"Oh, my, yes. She was always showing up unannounced, making a nuisance of herself. Once she even came to his school because she was upset about one thing or another that had happened at work. Would you believe she didn't understand why he wouldn't interrupt his class to console her?" Vinnie shook her head, exasperated. "He can be too kind for his own good. If I were him, I would have told her to buzz off a long time ago."

"That doesn't seem like Adam's style," Donna said, giving Megan a side-long glance. Megan didn't notice, as she was staring at Vinnie's block, her expression reflecting her conflicting emotions.

"Then I suppose I'm the only one who failed to meet her challenge," Julia said with a sigh. She held up her Friendship Star block for inspection, and smiled as the others admired it.

"I'm glad you didn't meet your challenge," Vinnie said. "It was a far better thing you did, sticking up for that poor girl."

"I am disappointed about the movie, though," Donna remarked. "I was looking forward to seeing it."

"I was looking forward to starring in it," Julia said. "But that's show biz."

"Show biz sounds like a lot of malarkey to me," Vinnie said. "When's *Prairie Vengeance* coming out? I want to know so I can be sure to boycott it."

They laughed, and Megan put a comforting arm around Julia's shoulders. They all knew how disappointed she was, how much she had counted on this movie to revitalize her career. After watching Julia on the set and seeing how devoted she was to her craft, Donna knew perhaps better than anyone how bravely she had persevered in the face of disappointment and humiliation. Deneford and his cronies had treated her shabbily, and Donna considered Julia well rid of them. She hoped Julia was wrong, and that Deneford didn't have the power to blacklist her, as Julia was certain he had done. Her sacrifice for Ellen merited a reward, and Donna believed wholeheartedly that good deeds eventually brought rewards, especially when the doer wasn't expecting them.

"May I still include my block in the quilt, even though I didn't accomplish my goal?" Julia asked.

"Of course," Vinnie declared. "You earned your place. Besides, we're going to need all the blocks we can get, now. . . ."

She left the thought unfinished, but Donna suspected they all understood her meaning: They would need every block to complete their quilt, now that Grace would not be contributing hers.

Just then, there was a knock on the door.

"Come in," Vinnie called out, but the door remained shut. She brightened. "Maybe someone was passing by to call us to dinner."

"She would have said so," Megan said, and called out in a louder voice, "Come on in. It's not locked."

After a pause, someone on the other side of the door said, "It would be much easier if you would open it, please."

Donna looked to Vinnie for permission, since it was her room. When Vinnie shrugged and waved her toward the door, she rose and opened it.

Grace stood in the hallway, supporting herself upon two metal crutches.

✣

"Grace," Donna exclaimed. "What happened? Were you in an accident?"

"Not exactly." In the room beyond, Grace saw the others rising and coming to the door, then hesitating as they spotted the crutches. She fought the urge to run away—not that she could run. "May I come in?"

"Of course," Vinnie said, pushing the door open wider and assisting her into the room.

"My bag—"

"I have it," Megan said. She brought it into the room and shut the door.

Vinnie led Grace to the bed and helped her sit down as the others settled into chairs or on the floor. Nervously, Grace waited for them to ask her about Paducah, about the crutches she unfastened from her arms and leaned against the bed, but they sat watching her expectantly, waiting for her to speak. Grace intended to tell them everything, but now, facing them, she didn't know where to begin.

Vinnie broke the silence. "It's good to see you, dear."

"I guess you weren't expecting me."

"No," Donna said, "but it's a wonderful surprise."

The others nodded, and suddenly Grace couldn't bear their polite caution, their tentative attempts to draw her out when they had always been so open with her. "I'm sorry about Paducah," she said.

Vinnie waved it off. "Don't worry about it. We probably got the time mixed up or something."

The others nodded, but Grace wasn't about to let herself off so easily, not when she had come to make amends. "No, I saw you, and you know it. I saw you and I ran away." She glanced at her crutches and let out a small laugh. "Or tried to run."

Megan's voice was gentle. "What happened, Grace?"

"I didn't want you to see me. I didn't want you to see me with these." She indicated the crutches. "I didn't want you to know I needed them."

"But why?" Donna said. "We're your friends. You don't need to hide from us."

That was precisely what she had been doing for far too long: hiding from her friends, from everyone who cared about her, from herself. "I have MS."

She watched their faces as this sank in. "It's gotten worse since last year, when I could hide it, and it will probably continue to worsen."

"Why didn't you tell us?" Vinnie said. "Honestly, dear, to go through something like this alone . . ." She shook her head.

"I didn't want anyone's pity."

"We wouldn't have given you pity," Megan said. "We would have given you friendship. A shoulder to cry on, if you wanted it."

"I know that now," Grace said. "But I'm not used to needing people. Whatever problems life has sent my way, I've always handled them alone. My ex-husband tells me I'm the most stubborn and fiercely independent woman he's ever met. If I am, he's partly responsible, but I can't ignore the fact that sometimes even fiercely independent people need to share their burdens."

Vinnie reached out and patted her knee. "That's not an easy lesson to learn."

"No, but it's easier than lying." She looked around the circle of friends and felt herself warmed by their compassion. "And I've lied to you from the beginning. I knew what caused my quilter's block, and it wasn't my daughter's supposed romance. It was my MS and my refusal to admit that it had become a part of my life." She quickly bent over her bag until she could blink back tears. "All this time I've been trying to live in spite of MS, to quilt in spite of MS. It wasn't working, because living a lie never works for long. It took a good friend to show me I need to live and quilt *with* my MS, not in spite of it."

She reached into her bag and brought out the quilt she had begun the day she returned home from AQS, Sylvia's words still resonant in her heart. Her friends reached forward to grasp the edges, unfolding the quilt so all could see.

It was a wild, chaotic work, a whirlwind of angry reds and oranges and yellows, blazing on a black background. Sharp, jagged lines conflicted with uncontrolled spirals over the barely recognizable outline of a woman crouched beneath a burden of grief. Into every uneven, undisciplined piece and crooked stitch Grace had poured all her rage, her anguish, her loss. She felt the emotions nearly overpowering in their intensity, but as she gazed upon her handiwork, she reminded herself that creating this quilt had freed her from pain, and that if she permitted it, she could sustain the peace that had come from completing the final stitch, filling up the empty spaces in her heart, until the grief subsided beneath a blanket of calm.

Her friends held the quilt tenderly, as if they were cradling a piece of Grace's soul in their arms.

"This is the quilt that helped me get through my quilter's block," Grace said. She meant that this monument to her pain was the only quilt powerful enough to smash through the barriers she had erected around herself. Looking into her friends' eyes, she knew they understood.

She set the quilt aside lovingly, as if it had been a joy to make, although she had often succumbed to tears of rage and anguish as she worked upon it. "Since I faced my challenge, even though I wasn't completely honest with you about the true nature of that challenge, I decided I was allowed to complete my Challenge Quilt block." She smiled, reached into the bag, and brought out a Carpenter's Wheel block made in burgundy and green and the autumn leaf fabric Vinnie had given her.

"Not you, too," Vinnie said. "Why Carpenter's Wheel?"

"Because she discovered she's the architect of her own fate," Megan said.

Grace laughed, delighted at the hidden meaning she herself had not considered. "I like that answer, but I admit I didn't think of that at the time. I chose this pattern because a carpenter taught me it's possible to transform your life even when all manner of obstacles are placed before you."

Vinnie nodded in approval, and as Grace's friends admired her block and showed her their own, she knew the quilt they would make together would be as strong as its creators and as enduring as their friendship, which had been tested by time, distance, and misunderstanding, yet on that day shone brightly, untarnished, as if newly minted.

⚓

All that week the Cross-Country Quilters worked on their quilt, attending only a few seminars and spending most of their time in a vacant classroom Sylvia had set aside for them. First they arranged the blocks in a three-by-three grid, separating their pieced blocks with solid setting squares of background fabric. Donna's Bear's Paw block was in the upper left corner, and a solid setting square separated it from Megan's Snow Crystals block in the upper right. Julia's Friendship Star occupied the center position, with setting squares on either side. The Carpenter's Wheel block Grace had made took the lower left corner; Vinnie's Wedding Ring, the lower right.

They united the sampler blocks and setting squares, then encircled the finished unit with a narrow border of background fabric. Together they scrutinized the quilt and decided that it needed something more. They considered prairie points, or solid fabric borders, and several other ideas before Donna had a brainstorm. One of her infamous unfinished projects was a quilt made of Autumn Leaf blocks in autumn colors. She had brought those blocks with her for a seminar entitled "Finishing Your UFOs," a class she suspected Sylvia Compson had added to the program with her in mind.

Since Donna had completed eight blocks already, they would only need to make sixteen more to create a pieced Autumn Leaf border to surround their sampler blocks.

"*Only* sixteen?" Julia said, alarmed.

"With all of us working together, we'll finish in no time," Megan reassured her. "We can use some quick-piecing techniques, too."

Julia shuddered. "Please, no quick piecing." They all laughed, remembering Julia's disastrous first class the previous year.

Grace shook her head, smiling. "It's a wonder you stuck with quilting after that introduction."

"It is a wonder," Julia agreed, "but I'm glad I did."

Their laughter rang through the halls of Elm Creek Manor, as it had so often that week. Other campers, made curious by the noise and their feverish excitement, stopped by to see what they were doing. The Cross-Country Quilters took turns telling onlookers the story of how their project had come to be, how each had faced a challenge in her life and had commemorated her success with a quilt block. Some campers asked what those challenges were, but by unspoken agreement, the Cross-Country Quilters refused to divulge the confidences of their friends. Grace had the final word that put an end to the persistent inquiries: "Think of the challenges you face as a woman, as a wife, as a mother. The problems we faced were no different than those any woman faces."

They completed the pieced top on Wednesday just before lunch, and interrupted the meal with a special unveiling. When the other campers burst into cheers and applause, the Cross-Country Quilters exchanged smiles and knowing looks. The other campers celebrated them for their hard work that week, little realizing that the real work had taken place over the course of an entire year.

❧

After lunch, Sylvia invited the Cross-Country Quilters to a far corner of the ballroom, a place that had not been converted to classroom space. There she showed them a wooden quilt frame that had been polished both with a craftsman's care and with usage over time. The rectangular frame was the height of an ordinary table, with slender rods running along the longer sides, and knobs and gears at the corners. As the others placed chairs around it, Megan returned to her room for the batting and backing fabric she had brought from home. They placed the layers in the frame: backing fabric on the bottom, batting in the middle, and the colorful pieced quilt top last of all.

They took their places around the frame, but not long after they had begun to quilt, Sylvia returned to tell Julia she had a phone call. Julia followed her to the formal parlor and discovered that Ellen was on the line.

"Ellen," she exclaimed, astonished. They had spoken only once since walking out of Deneford's meeting in April. "It's good to hear from you."

"It's good to hear your voice again, too. I hope you don't mind my interrupting your vacation. Your assistant gave me the number."

"That's fine," Julia assured her, and she meant it, surprised by how pleased she was that Ellen had tracked her down. "How are you? Are you working on anything new?"

"As a matter of fact, I am. How about you? Is your schedule full?"

"Hardly," Julia said. "I guess you could say I'm semiretired. I've looked at a few scripts—all of them awful—but without an agent soliciting work for me, I don't expect to be working again anytime soon." She smiled, thinking how a year ago she would have trembled in fear at the very thought.

"If a good project came your way, would you consider it?"

"Oh, certainly. But I'm not as hungry as I used to be. I won't settle for another *Prairie Vengeance* to make a quick buck, that's for sure. There's been some talk about doing a *Home Sweet Home* anniversary reunion, and if it comes together, I'd do that for a lark. Otherwise I only want serious, high-quality work, something worth the time and effort I'll put into it."

"Would you consider playing Sadie Henderson in *A Patchwork Life*?"

Julia laughed. "In a heartbeat, but that's not an option, is it?"

"Actually, it is."

Julia almost dropped the phone. "What do you mean?"

"PBS wants to produce it. I'm going to direct, and I'd like you to star."

"But how is this possible?" Julia stammered. "Deneford bought the rights to Sadie's story."

"Ah. But he didn't. He bought the rights to my original script. I own the rights to Sadie's diaries, and therefore, her story. I'll have to rewrite the script to make it all nice and legal, but it will be legal. My father's an attorney, and I had heard enough nightmare stories about Hollywood to be very careful when I signed over my script."

Julia was impressed. "Ellen, my dear, I underestimated you."

"So did Deneford."

His name reminded Julia of a new worry. "Deneford might object to your releasing a film so similar to his. He might even sue."

Ellen laughed. "First of all, *Prairie Vengeance* barely resembles *A Patchwork Life*. Second, I don't think Deneford will want to remind anyone of *Prairie Vengeance*. It's caused him enough damage without him airing his failures in the media again."

"I don't understand. Wouldn't the publicity help the release of *Prairie Vengeance*?"

"Didn't you hear?"

"Hear what? I've been somewhat out of the loop."

"*Prairie Vengeance* went so far over budget in the reshooting that Deneford had to promise the studio he'd take no salary and cover the extra expenses himself. He thought he'd end up making a profit, but the test audience response was so negative that the studio sent the movie straight to video."

"No," Julia said, with only the smallest wicked surge of glee.

"Yes. There are even rumors that he's going to be, shall we say, encouraged to void his contract with the studio." Ellen paused. "So what do you think? It won't be the feature film you wanted, and it certainly won't pay what you were getting from Deneford, but are you interested? Do you want to think it over and call me back in a few weeks?"

Julia didn't need a few weeks. "I'm interested. Send a contract to my home."

"You mean it?"

"Of course."

"You won't be sorry."

Julia laughed. "That's what you said last time."

"This time will be different," Ellen promised, and Julia knew in her heart it would be.

Julia returned to the quilt frame with a heart so light she wanted to skip across the marble floor of the grand foyer singing the Hallelujah Chorus. A new project, something she could be proud of. Whatever Ellen's terms were, she would accept them, although she might ask Maury to come out of retirement to read over the contract first, for old times' sake.

She couldn't wait to tell her friends.

⚜

Each morning, the Cross-Country Quilters met for an early breakfast before gathering around the quilt frame. As the hours passed, their stitches added dimension and texture to their sampler, and their progress urged them on despite sore fingers and tired eyes. They talked as they worked, baring their hearts and unburdening their souls as they felt they could with no other friends, even ones they had known all their lives. There was a sanctity about the quilt frame that promised that secrets could be shared there, and no confidence would be broken or judgment passed.

On Friday afternoon, they finished the last quilting stitch and removed their masterpiece from the frame. Megan made a long strip of bias binding; Donna machine-sewed one of the long sides a quarter inch away from the edge, all around the front of the quilt. They decided a change of scene would invigorate them, so they carried the quilt outside to the verandah, where they arranged chairs in a circle, the quilt in the center. Each woman took one section of the edge, and together they folded the binding around the raw edges of the quilt and blind-stitched it in place on the back.

By late afternoon, they were so close to finishing their project that they decided to skip dinner and work all through the night if necessary. A half hour into the dinner period, Sylvia came looking for them.

"Aren't you ladies going to take a break?" she asked.

They shook their heads, and Grace said, "Not when we're so close to the end."

"Some rest might give you more energy to finish."

"Or it might make it all the more difficult to continue afterward," Julia said.

Sylvia sighed. "Very well. You're forcing me to pull rank. As the founder of Elm Creek Quilts, I'm ordering you to put down those needles and join me in the banquet hall. Now."

The Cross-Country Quilters exchanged looks of surprise and dismay. "We'll grab a snack later," Megan said, but Sylvia would have none of that. Ignoring their protests, she ushered them inside. Resigned, they allowed themselves to be herded along, realizing that they were a bit hungry after all, and that maybe a minute or two of rest wouldn't hurt.

When they walked into the banquet hall, they were greeted by dozens of women of all ages shouting, "Surprise!"

Vinnie nearly reeled from astonishment.

One by one, the Cross-Country Quilters began to laugh as other campers surrounded their friend, hugging her and wishing her a happy birthday. Sylvia led them in singing "Happy Birthday" as she led Vinnie to a place of honor, a seat at a table with a birthday cake in the middle.

"I can't believe we forgot," Donna whispered to Megan in dismay as Vinnie made a short speech thanking everyone for their good wishes.

"Don't feel bad," Megan said with a shrug. "Vinnie forgot, too."

And it was true. This year, Vinnie's Elm Creek Quilt Camp surprise birthday party was indeed a surprise.

⁜

Sylvia's prediction came true; after the birthday party, the Cross-Country Quilters were in such good spirits that they finished the quilt in no time.

Each signed the back with her name, her city and state, and the name of the block she had made. All that remained was to admire their handiwork and praise themselves for the hard work, quilting and otherwise, they had put into their masterpiece.

But then Vinnie frowned. "Who gets the quilt now?"

All they could do was look at each other. Somehow, the thought of what would become of the quilt after its completion had never occurred to them. They could hardly divide it into equal shares, as they had the autumn leaf fabric the year before.

"Maybe we should ask Sylvia to display it here," Donna suggested. "To inspire other campers."

"Not on your life," Vinnie retorted. "If that's our best option, I'm taking it home."

"Why you?" Julia protested, nudging her.

"I have seniority," Vinnie said in a lofty voice, and they all laughed.

"We could draw straws," Megan said, but she didn't look satisfied with that solution.

"We should take turns," Grace said, and soon it was decided that Vinnie would be allowed to take the quilt home first, since it was, after all, her birthday. Next year, and every year after that, they would meet at Elm Creek Quilt Camp to renew their friendship and pass on the quilt to the next in line.

Vinnie was pleased that she got to be first, but she still looked doubtful. "A year is an awfully long time to wait."

Donna smiled. "Not if we keep busy with a new project."

She reached for her bag and brought out two yards of fabric she had been saving for exactly this occasion.

⚜

Good-byes were even more difficult and tearful than they had been the year before, even though each knew she would be seeing her friends again the next summer. Megan reflected that if their friendship had survived that first, most difficult year, it would surely endure as long as they nurtured it.

Julia left first, waving her fat quarter of Donna's fabric out the window at her friends as her limousine pulled away. Donna and Grace rode the shuttle to the airport together, able to postpone their farewells for another two hours. Then only Megan and Vinnie remained in the parking lot behind Elm Creek Manor, waiting for Vinnie's ride and watching other campers load their cars.

Megan's heart began to pound with nervousness as a familiar car crossed the bridge over Elm Creek, slowing as it approached them.

"Well, there's my ride," Vinnie said, sighing. She hugged Megan and added, "Take care of yourself, dear."

"You, too," Megan said. "I'll see you next year."

Vinnie nodded, and they both fell silent as Adam got out of the car. "Hi, Nana," he said, bending over to kiss her cheek. His eyes went to Megan. "Hi."

"Hi."

"My goodness, my legs are so tired," Vinnie said, hurrying toward the car with a speed that belied her words. "I'd better sit down." She let herself in the passenger side and shut the door.

Megan and Adam watched her, then looked at each other. "She's still at it, I see," Megan said.

"She doesn't give up easily."

Megan nodded, unable to think of anything more to say.

"How's Robby?" Adam asked.

"Good. He's good."

"Good."

Megan nodded again, pained by the deep loss she felt seeing him again, and wishing that things had turned out differently. "Well," she said, when she could no longer bear the awkwardness between them. "I'd better get going."

"Me, too," he said, indicating his car with a tilt of his head. Suddenly he extended his hand. "Have a safe trip."

She shook it. "You, too."

"Say hello to Robby for me."

"I will."

He nodded, and gave her a smile that was both wistful and understanding, then placed Vinnie's suitcase in the trunk, got into his car, and drove away.

Megan watched him go, then sighed and carried her bag across the parking lot to her own car. It had been difficult seeing him again, as she had imagined it would be, but her heart ached only a little, and she would get over it. Next year, she promised herself, she would be able to face him without the slightest hint of regret.

Or maybe she would spare them both another awkward scene. Someone else could wait with Vinnie next time.

⚓

"Well?" Nana asked as they drove through the forest toward the main road.

"Well what?"

"Did you apologize?"

Adam glanced at her. "I apologized months ago. It didn't do any good."

"So you're just going to give up? Don't you sit there and tell me you don't care about her. I know you still love her."

At first Adam said nothing, reluctant to discuss the deepest feelings of his heart with his grandmother, who, it had to be said, didn't always recognize the importance of keeping a secret. Then, suddenly, he didn't care whom she told. She could tell all her quilting friends if she liked—she could even tell Megan if she was determined to do so. It was the truth, and he was tired of pretending otherwise.

"I never stopped loving her," he said quietly.

Out of the corner of his eye, he could see Nana glaring at him. "You should have told her."

"She doesn't want to hear it. She doesn't want me in her life, Nana. She's made that perfectly clear."

"You should have told her anyway."

Frustrated by the suspicion that maybe she was right, Adam shot back, "Maybe I'm tired of humiliating myself."

"I'm ashamed of you," Nana retorted. She folded her arms and turned her head firmly toward the window, as if she would have turned her back on him if the seat belt permitted. "My only comfort is that your grandfather isn't here to witness this appalling display of cowardice. You are a prideful, ignorant young man, and because of it, you're going to lose that lovely young woman."

Adam was about to protest when suddenly, with a flash of insight, he realized that if he let Megan drive away without attempting to talk to her, he would deserve every word of his grandmother's criticism.

He turned the car around.

Nana started. "What are you doing?"

Adam said nothing. Determined now, he sped along the highway back the way they had come and turned onto the road through the forest. He passed the fork that led to the front entrance of Elm Creek Manor and continued along the narrow road that wound through the trees toward the back of the building. Megan would have taken the same road he had traveled on, and since he hadn't seen her, she must still be back here—

"You're driving like a madman," Nana shrieked. "Do you want to crash us into a tree? If another car comes—"

But just then the forest gave way to a clearing. Ahead of them on the right was a two-story red barn built into the side of a hill, and coming around it at that moment was Megan's car.

Adam honked his horn and flashed his lights, slowing his car and pulling off the narrow road onto the bordering grassy meadow. He parked and kept honking, knowing she would recognize his car, but watched with a sinking heart as she drove toward him without slowing, and then passed.

She didn't even stop, he thought, bitter with disappointment. She had kept driving as if he were invisible. He reached for the keys and was about to start the engine when a glance in the rearview mirror told him he was mistaken.

Megan had pulled her car off the road.

Quickly he left his car and went to meet her. By the time he crossed the distance that separated them, Megan had exited her car and stood, arms folded, beside it.

He waited until he reached her before saying, "I'm glad you stopped."

"I thought it might be an emergency."

"It is." He searched for the words, but before he could think of something gentle and romantic to say, the truth spilled out. "Megan, you haven't been fair to me. I never gave you any reason to doubt me, or to doubt how I feel about you. I know you've been lied to in the past, but not by me. Never by me."

She watched him, her green eyes wide and calm. "I know that."

"Then how could you have assumed the worst instead of believing me when I told you what happened? You know what Natalie's like; I *told* you what she was like. Couldn't you see she was baiting you?"

"Not at the time, I couldn't."

"What about now?"

"Now . . ." She hesitated and looked away. "Now I think I gave Natalie exactly what she wanted."

"Not everything she wanted."

"You went back to her."

"No, I didn't," he said firmly. How he regretted every minute he had tried to soothe his loneliness for Megan by giving in to Natalie's requests to try again. "Not in the way you think."

She fixed him with an inscrutable look. "And how is that?"

"You think I love her, but I don't. I couldn't. How could I love her, when I'm still in love with you?"

She was silent. "Are you?" she asked softly.

"Yes, I am. And you'd better get used to it, because you can doubt me as much as you like, but I'm not Keith and never will be. And I'm not going to stop loving you no matter how much you want me to. And if you don't want to see me again, you'd better forget about ever coming to back quilt camp, because I'm going to be here every year to drop off Nana and pick her up again, and every time I see you here, I'm going to ask for another chance."

He had to pause to take a breath, but her expression would have cut him short anyway.

She was smiling.

⚓

Two sisters pulled out of the parking lot behind the manor and drove across the bridge over Elm Creek, discussing whether they should stop at the charming quilt shop in downtown Waterford on their way home, or if the delay would cause their husbands to worry. They had just decided to drop by for a moment when they rounded the bend beside the barn and spotted two cars parked at the bottom of the hill where the road disappeared into the trees. A man and a woman stood beside the car closest to the forest.

"What's this?" said the elder sister, who was driving.

"I have no idea," said the younger, who looked more carefully and added, "Isn't that Vinnie in the first car?"

Sure enough, Vinnie's familiar cloud of white hair was visible above the front passenger seat headrest.

"Has there been an accident?" the elder sister wondered aloud. Vinnie smiled brightly through the window and waved as they passed.

They waved back, puzzled. "Should we stop and offer to help?" the younger sister asked.

The elder sister, her eyes on the young couple by the second car, suddenly broke into laughter. "They must be all right," she said. "She's kissing him."

The younger sister let out a wry chuckle. "Maybe we should ask *them* to help *us*."

Laughing, the two sisters drove past the couple in their warm embrace and into the shade of the forest, while behind them, within gray stone walls just down the road and across the creek, Sylvia Compson and the Elm Creek Quilters were congratulating themselves on another week of camp success-fully concluded and preparing to welcome the next group of quilters, friends, and friends-to-be.

About the Author

Jennifer Chiaverini lives with her husband and two sons in Madison, Wisconsin. In addition to the six volumes in the Elm Creek Quilts series, she is the author of *Elm Creek Quilts: Quilt Projects Inspired by the Elm Creek Quilts Novels* and the designer of the Elm Creek Quilts fabric line from Red Rooster Fabrics.